To Jo[illegible]

with f[illegible]
regards

[illegible]

CW00862934

The Outrider

By

Lindsay Douglas

1663 Liberty Drive, Suite 200
Bloomington, Indiana 47403
(800) 839-8640
www.AuthorHouse.com

This book is a work of fiction. People, places, events, and situations are the product of the author's imagination. Any resemblance to actual persons, living or dead, or historical events, is purely coincidental.

© 2005 Lindsay Douglas. All Rights Reserved.

No part of this book may be reproduced, stored in a retrieval system, or transmitted by any means without the written permission of the author.

First published by AuthorHouse 07/28/05

ISBN: 1-4208-3029-5 (sc)

Printed in the United States of America
Bloomington, Indiana

This book is printed on acid-free paper.

Acknowledgements

To Sally

I am indebted to my wife for her encouragement, editing and advice and suggestions on reading the initial drafts.

I would also like to thank Doug, Helen, Bob and Liz reading and offering suggestions after reading the early manuscript, and in particular Stevie for his expertise on SAS tactics and Albert's knowledge on how to effect entry on locked doors

Chapter 1

Venezuela

It had all began three years previously when Niles had fled from the UK in order to preserve his own life. He'd managed to fake his death but in doing so had lost his Passport. This meant that he was now an illegal immigrant in whichever country he attempted to live in.

To get out of the UK Niles had bribed a deck hand of a Container ship to stow him on board. The guy managed to smuggle food to him and he'd remained hidden until the Ship docked at Port of Spain, the capital of Trinidad and Tobago.

There were too many British ex-pats on the Island for his liking and there was a danger of one of them seeing and recognising him. So he'd stolen a small launch and motored up the River Orinoco into Venezuela. After some hair raising escapades and some brushes with local police he eventually managed to make his way to Caracas the capital.

During the past three years times had been difficult for him; occasionally he'd taken to petty crime in order to feed himself. Altercations had to be reconciled without the police, usually with his fists and being quick witted. On several occasions he'd been involved in serious brawls to save his life, one involving a serious knife fight - he'd won. But there was an upside to his new lifestyle. His sharp wits had now been honed to a razors edge. And although he'd tried to avoid physical confrontations he'd discovered a dark side to his character. When push came to shove he had no compunctions about fighting dirty. It was now acknowledged in the back streets of Caracas that he was a mean, lean street fighter and not a man to be crossed. With his physical attributes and his quick wits he'd now become a master at getting out of tight situations. His Spanish although not fluent was passable and improving daily - he could now make himself understood with no problem and providing the locals didn't speak too quickly he was able to understand most of what was said. It was his ability to think and act quickly in tight situations that had got him his present job

For the past month Niles had been employed as a chauffeur and general 'dogsbody', to a Mr Chase. Who was an American business man with a rather shady background? It was Niles command of English rather than his ability to speak Spanish that got him the job. The few local thugs willing to drive Chase into the interior couldn't speak English whilst the more educated ones were not prepared to. This had given Niles steady employment for the past month – something that didn't occur too often in his present circumstances. Chase conducted most of his business in the hinterland with some South Americans of a most dubious character. He suspected that Chase was involved in the sale of illegal weapons but he was not certain of this as he was kept well clear when Chase discussed business with his colleagues. For the past month he'd been getting steady meals; somewhere decent to sleep at night and was reasonably well paid, so he kept his mouth shut .Further more, without a passport or

I.D. if he'd reported Chase to the police there was a chance of his own position being jeopardised; ending up with him being thrown in jail or out the country.

Chase had anticipated staying a further three days in the southern part of Venezuela conducting business when they received the warning concerning 'JUDY'. They were warned to leave the area straight away. Chase had insisted on remaining another day.

'JUDY' was a hurricane and apparently one of the strongest ever recorded since records had been kept. The cyclonic winds were estimated to be in excess of a hundred and twenty knots. It was causing tremendous damage. Cities, towns and villages in the path of 'JUDY' were all being evacuated in order to get the population to safety.

Hurricanes usually passed much further to the north of Venezuela but for some unknown reason (the meteorologists were still working on this) this one had swung much further south and had hit the eastern seaboard of the country. Because hurricanes were unusual in Venezuela the authorities had no evacuation plans ready to implement and the situation had quickly become chaotic. It was speeding rapidly across the country creating massive flooding and extensive damage. This, not unnaturally had caught a lot of people unprepared. The death toll had already reached double figures.

It was at this stage that Chase panicked and decided it was time to get out of the country.

'Niles', he shouted. 'Get down to the local airstrip and see if you can get something to fly us out of this shit hole. If there are any arguments tell them I'm prepared to pay big bucks to get out of this midden - pronto'.

Chase was one of those nondescript men of average height and build and capable of wandering into a room completely unnoticed. He usually wore a light weight-expensive grey suit and beige desert boots. His hair was loose and limp and his bland face seemed almost characterless.

However he was no fool, his deep sunk grey eyes were alert and always on the move, they were never still. He was very quick at sizing up new situations and quite immoral, a prerequisite for a man of his occupation. But he had that unfortunate characteristic so many of the 'self made men' have of treating his employees with contempt.

Niles gave him a stony look.

'You'll be bloody lucky Mr Chase. By now anything that can move let alone fly will be long gone. The last scheduled prop' flew out yesterday. I warned you to leave straight away but No! You insisted on remaining another day and now you expect me to work a fucking miracle'.

His boss returned his stony look and continued, 'Well there's no way I want to be hanging around here when the hurricane arrives, so get down to that airstrip and see if there's anything capable of flying us out of this dump'.

Niles shrugged his shoulders; the last statement was too stupid to bother answering. He'd no idea how they were going to get clear at this late stage.

However, he was reasonably well paid but at times Chase could be a real pain in the arse. He turned about and decided to drive out to the strip and see what was available. You never know your luck. There was always a slight chance of a light aircraft being available for hire. More to the point, it was his arse that was on the line as well as Chase's.

He stepped out of the hotel and looked up the street. It was a typical small town often found in the interior of Venezuela with a single row of houses sited on either side of the main street with virtually nothing behind them. It was reminiscent of the old Hollywood Wild West towns portrayed in films. The buildings were mainly of wooden construction with galvanised tin roofs most of which were badly rusted. Without air-conditioning they must have been stifling to live in. A few of the more affluent owners had managed to roof their houses with clay brick tiles and he could see that most of these buildings were fitted with air-conditioning units. As the electric supply had already been disrupted none of them were now functioning. Not that it mattered - most of the locals had shown more horse sense than Chase, they'd high- tailed it to the hills or further south to escape the impending floods. The high cirrus cloud was already giving way to nimbus stratus. He decided that they had about an hour or possibly an hour and a half before the heavy rain started. He was dressed in his only clothing, denim slacks and shirt, a light weight weatherproof anorak and a stout pair of desert boots. The latter, the only item that cost real money (getting packed and ready to move at short notice was a fact he'd lived with for the past three years).

He clambered in to the four-wheel drive Jeep; cranked the engine over, shoved it in gear and started to motor off to the town's small airstrip. He'd never seen it but he'd heard that the main grass runway was only 3500 feet long so there was not going to be any Commercial Jet available — the last Turbo Prop' (A Skyvan) had left yesterday – in fact, at this late stage he doubted that there would be anything flyable.

It took him approximately twenty minute driving down an old rutted track to get to there. He drove at forty mile an hour; the maximum speed one could manage without being thrown out the vehicle. The rutted surface of the track was still dry and hard but he had no doubts that when exposed to heavy rain it would quickly become boggy and almost impassable. The countryside he was driving through must have been some of the most scenic in the world but with the approaching hurricane the beauty of it was lost to him. He noted that to the north of the track there was a coconut plantation which was surprising so far inland.

He and Chase had driven from Caracas to this location so this part of the countryside was new to him - (It had taken them four days to get here conducting business with various shady characters en-route).

When he arrived at the strip it was much as he expected, it was very basic – he was not impressed. The only runway was orientated on an East and West direction with a grassed/laterite surface which meant that it was not weatherproof. Once exposed to heavy rain it would become too boggy and dangerous. The approaches to the runway were good; they'd been well cleared of all vegetation so there were no immediate obstacles to takeoff and landing. The northern side of the runway had obviously been part of the old coconut plantation; this had also been well cleared so as not to compromise aircraft using the strip. Beyond the cleared section there were plenty of palm trees but the whole area was overgrown and unkempt evidently no longer of commercial use. To the south of the runway stood an old corrugated iron building, it was no more than sixty by forty feet in dimension and appeared to serve the purpose of a small terminal building. The side facing the strip had a double door with a ramp to facilitate the movement of baggage trolleys to and from the aircraft dispersal. A small glass faced hut adjoined the main building, built on four wooden stilts, which set it higher than any other buildings indicating that it was the local Air Traffic Control Tower. As far as he could see it was not manned at the moment. The whole building complex had been painted in a glare reflecting white. To the south of the building there was a small car park where two four wheeled drive vehicles were already parked – presumably the owners had taken to the air to expedite their departure. Apart from a corrugated iron building and a clapped out rusting hanger at the far end of the strip there were no other buildings – although there was a small lean – to, which covered a refuelling pump at the far end of the dispersal apron. The only aircraft visible was a beat up old Dakota adjacent the fuel pump. Although the aircraft was obviously ancient it did look serviceable and capable of flying; in fact, he wasn't sure, but he thought could see someone moving around in the cockpit.

He drove into the compound and parked alongside the two vehicles behind the corrugated iron shack. He was surprised to see that the two vehicles standing there were unattended and not even locked, suggesting that their owners had left in a hurry. Bright lads! There was also stairs leading to the Airstrip control tower. Prior to arriving he'd expected to see the place heaving with activity. But there was not a soul in sight! Reinforcing the point he'd made to Chase that they had left it too late. The place seemed to be deserted. *'Christ'*, he thought. *'I've seen more activity in an oyster bed during a feeding frenzy'*. It did however, suggests that the locals had more horse sense than Chase and had evacuated the area well before disaster was due to strike.

As he entered the Terminal he shouted. 'Any one at home?' He wasn't expecting a reply and was somewhat surprised when a voice answered him.

'Ola', the voice came from behind the counter, which Niles assumed passed as the booking kiosk. He leaned over the counter. Behind it, laid out on an old army surplus camp bed, was this sweaty tubby individual. He was below average height, wearing a chequered cowboy shirt, a pair of ubiquitous blue Jeans, and a pair of off white Reebok trainers and a ready smile. His dark hair was thinning and flopped over his brown eyes. He looked your typical friendly Latino.

Niles gave him a bemused look.' What the hell are you doing down there? Don't you know there's a hurricane due in the next hour or so'?

'Se Senor', replied the grinning sweaty individual, 'I am waiting for the film crew who are due here in the next forty minutes'.

'You mean they are actually going to fly in that beat up Goony bird out there?' Niles nodded towards the Dakota.

'Se Senor. They have some very important people and

they have radioed ahead to book the Dakota. They are members of an American film company that had been filming an adventure film about the American Peace Corps'.

Jose (the sweaty controller)then went on to explain that the majority of the film crew flew out of the jungle location as soon as they had received a warning of the approaching hurricane. However the film director had insisted on remaining a further day with sixteen of the cast and crew to finish a sequence involving an eleven year old American girl. Then they were too late to catch a scheduled flight'.

Niles nodded his head in sympathy. 'I've had a similar problem. Is the old Dakota there serviceable to fly'?

'Se Senor, although it hasn't flown for two weeks it is fully serviceable and it's the only aircraft left. The crew are already aboard checking the aircraft over'.

Niles suddenly had an inspired brainwave based on the fact that in many organisations the left hand never knows what the right hand is up to.

'Why the hell did they radio ahead when they knew I was coming by jeep to make the bookings personally?' He lied.

The sweaty controller looked slightly nonplus

'I'm not sure senor I think they just wanted to make sure that the aircraft would be available for you when you got here'.

'Did they tell you how many passengers there would be?' He asked. 'And oh; by the way; what's your name?'

'Please call me Jose and I think they said about sixteen', he replied.

'Typical' Niles snarled. 'They couldn't even get that right; there will be eighteen of us. Do you think the Dakota will get off with that number of passengers?'

'Se Senor, we have flown out of this strip with up to twenty passengers on board'.

Not flying within the, 'Group 'A' requirements' Niles

thought, shuddering to think what would have happened if an engine failed at this height and temperature whilst taking off with twenty passengers.

However, beggars can't be choosers; his main worry at this stage was to keep this guy believing that he and Chase were members of the film crew.

'Right!' Niles said, 'I'm off to pick up the film producer in town and I should be back here in about thirty minutes', With that he turned, and left before Jose could ask any searching questions. He realised that their only chance of his bluff working was to get back to the airstrip in time to 'organise' the loading of the aircraft. The time scale should just about get them back here before the arrival of the film crew. He had no time to lose.

He leaped into the Jeep, cranked the engine over and started back to town to inform Chase of the situation. He made it in fifteen minutes practically shaking the fillings out of his teeth doing so. Knocked on the door of Chase's hotel room and walked in before being bid to enter. Chase looked up annoyed at Niles unauthorised entry but before he could say anything Niles started to explained to him that the only remaining aircraft available to get them out of the country before the Hurricane hit was the beat up old Dakota. Chase was not exactly enamoured.

'You mean' he snarled,' we have to risk life and limb on some bloody clapped out, piston engined, aircraft that was built some sixty years ago?'

'That's about the size of it', replied Niles. 'It's that or shank's pony which I don't think you're in the right physical shape to attempt. There are no further roads to the south and west of here so our four wheeled vehicle is going to be about as much use to us as tits on a bull. And there's no way we will be able to get back to Caracas in it. All the roads are going to be flooded in the next hour or so. And; by the way, when we get back to the strip, we're going to have to bluff our way onto the aircraft by pretending to be associated with a filming crew and are responsible for the organisation their departure. If we play this right the silly bastards will actually be grateful to us for getting them out the country'.

'What the hell are you babbling about?' Chase shouted, 'what film crew? I'm not associated with any film people so what are you on about?'

He decided he was going to have to level with his boss and give him a blow by blow description on how they were going to con' their way onto the aircraft.

'Look', he said. 'When I got to the airstrip this Dakota was the only thing flyable. The guy in charge, Jose, said that the aircraft had been booked over the radio for some film company. I've managed to convince him that we are part of the film company's organisation, that you are actually one of the producers. We've been sent ahead to organise the readiness of the aircraft, if we keep it a bit vague but act with plenty of confidence and bullshit'. 'We should be able to pull it off with no problems. These guys are so used to having someone wipe their arses for them that they will think its only natural that the company has organised their departure. Further more, if we don't get a move on the dirt track to the Air strip is going to get washed out in the next hour or so'

'You're not expecting me to start humping their baggage' growled Chase.

Niles gave him a cynical look. 'No way boss; with eighteen passengers plus the pilots and the guy who runs the strip on board, the aircraft going to have a problem getting off that short strip without the additional weight of baggage. And I hate to hassle you, but if we don't make tracks back to the strip immediately, apart from the track getting washed out, there's a danger of the celluloid crew arriving before we do which will make our scam almost impossible to carry off'.

Chase started to throw a few items into a suitcase,

Niles quickly interrupted him. 'You won't be able to take those. Just grab your brief case and any essentials you might need, and I'm not kidding about the weight problem'

'Look here', he snarled, 'If you think I am going to leave here taking nothing but what I stand in your sorely mistaken'.

'And you look here Mr Chase' Niles said.' You've employed me as your chauffeur and your general bloody run around; I'm not a miracle maker. How the hell do you expect all these film star prima donnas to leave their kit behind whilst you appear humping a bloody great hold all?' Further more, had we left yesterday as I suggested we would be clear of this sink hole and out of danger.

'Okay' he replied, 'Have it your way but if and when we ever get out of this fucking mess you're going to be looking for another job.

'That's your prerogative, but in the mean time just dump those bloody clothes and let's get down to the strip.

He did. Niles felt quite relieved he was severing ties with Chase. Although he paid well, he liked his employees to jump through hoops whenever he wanted. He'd just about had a bellyful of being screwed around by Chase from arsehole to breakfast time.

Niles slammed the Cherokee into four wheel drive and drove down the rutted track at breakneck speed determined to get back to the strip before the other passengers arrived. Chase was hanging on for dear life.

'For Christ sake! Niles, slow up - you'll kill us both before we ever get there!'

He was ignored. Niles drove on at an unabated reckless speed. He looked at Niles in astonishment: he used to be so biddable and polite'. Now the bastard wasn't even bothering to answer him.

As luck would have it, they arrived at the strip a good ten minutes before the film party.

Jose had mentioned that the Film Company was called, 'Global Home Movies', (GHM) quite a well-known company who made films mostly for TV but occasionally for the big screen as well. Niles was quick to note this otherwise they were going to look complete mugs trying to arrange an aircraft for a Company they didn't know the name of.

'Right Chase' Niles growled. 'Are you with me on this scam or not, because I have no wish to be lumbered in this sink hole when the hurricane comes even if you are'

'If it is going to get us out I'm with you' said Chase, 'and its Mr Chase to you Niles'.

'Not any longer, you've sacked me; remember? '

Chase looked a little crestfallen; although he had plenty of animal cunning in the boardroom this was an entirely different environment he now found himself in. He began to regret having dispensed with Sandy Niles's services so quickly, especially as the bastard looked so completely at home in what was obviously a very fluid and potentially dangerous situation

Niles took a careful look around the strip just to get familiar with the layout. His main concern was whether the Dakota would be able to get off the strip with twenty passengers on board. There were certain aspects of his former life that he didn't wish to disclose. And one of them was that until three years ago, he'd been a professional pilot.

'What's the latest time for the arrival of the film crew?' Niles asked Jose.

'They've had problems getting across the small bridge two miles to the east but they should be with us in two or three minutes Senor'.

'Where are the pilots?' Said Niles somewhat perturbed.

'No problem' replied Jose. 'They're already in the cockpit ready to start when you and your passengers are on board'

'What sort of a Flight Plan have they filed - or is that not possible from here? '

'Normally yes' said Jose 'But at the moment, all the land lines are down and my short wave band radio doesn't have the range to contact any Air traffic control Centres. But once you get airborne, Senor Niles, the Captain will pass an airborne flight plan'. Their intention is to fly to Bogotá, the only international airport within range that's not going to be affected by the hurricane. There the passengers will change to a schedule Jet to take them on to the States. All airfields to the north are going to be affected by the hurricane in the next hour or so'.

Niles pondered this last statement about Bogotá. He'd no Passport or I.D. papers therefore he was going to have to box clever when they landed in Colombia. However he'd cross that bridge when he had to.

Their conversation was interrupted by the arrival of a ramshackle wheezing old bus with the awaited film crew on board. Niles's heart sank as he watched them debus. He'd never had much time for the thespian fraternity considering that many of them were overly fond of themselves with egos which surpassed their talent. This lot looked typical examples of his worst suspicions. Not true Stars in the normal sense of the word. These were your up and coming character actors who were often described by the modern media as stars. They generally like to throw their weight around to massage their egos. Niles considered he'd be lucky to get through the day without planting one of the nerds between the eyes.

Niles strode towards the passengers in a bold and positive manner and shouted in an authoritative voice.

'Right everybody, can I have your attention please. We have approximately twenty minutes to get our selves airborne before the Hurricane is arrives, I'm afraid we haven't got any weight to spare for excess baggage so it's hand luggage only'.

'Just who the hell are you', snarled a short dumpy guy with a pronounced paunch who appeared in front of Niles as if by magic. His remaining hair formed a halo around his bald head and his eyes were so deep sunk into his podgy faced that they reminded Niles of 'piss holes in the snow'. He drew himself up to his full five feet six inches. He just oozed self importance. Three years prior to his 'conditioning' in Caracas Niles would have been too embarrassed to carry off the scam he was now executing. Now a days, he didn't give a shit!

'I'm the guy sent by the company to ensure you and your minions get to hell out here,' snarled Niles in a confident manner. 'And further more,' he continued, 'just who the hell are you?'

'I'm Nathan Costello the director of this film' said the short dumpy guy with his feet splayed out to the nine and three o'clock positions

'Well Mr Director unless you get your self and your friends aboard this aircraft bloody pronto you are going to be filming one of the biggest natural disasters of the century.

And while you're at it you might like to consider your future with the Company. They are not amused at you ignoring their warning to get out the country yesterday'. Niles had no idea what the Company thought but was dammed sure that Costello didn't either. But it would give the little fat bastard something to worry about whilst Niles got things moving.

Nathan Costello was initially inclined to argue with him but decided against it. Although Niles had made no threatening moves towards him there was an air of confidence and a touch of menace about man that he found faintly un-nerving. Plus which, his last remark about the Company Directors anger was cause for concern. More to the point, he stood at least seven or eight inches taller than Costello with a definite athletic build that emphasised his pear shaped. So he held his council.

The wind, which up to about ten minutes ago had been just a gentle zephyr, was now gradually increasing in strength, causing swirling dust clouds and gusts up to thirty knots. Overhead, the flying mare cirrus cloud had given way to thickening cumulus cloud that threatened rain at any minute. The usual brassy blue sky was now turning a to dull leaden colour.

Even to the inexperienced eye it was obvious that there was some very nasty weather brewing. All the shouting had raised the two Dakota pilots.

The Captain, a short swarthy man with a suspicion of a paunch and good natured features with plenty of good white teeth which he now exposed to Niles, walked up to him and said,

'Senor, I'm Dino the captain of the aircraft - we must get airborne as quickly as possible the wind is already about thirty degrees across the strip and there is no alternative runway. If it gets much stronger I will not be able to keep her straight during take off. Can I leave you to organise the loading of the passengers as quickly as possible?'

'My name is Sandy Niles', he replied. 'No sweat - I'll get the passenger loaded straight away', as he shook the extended hand.

He was probable the only other person present that realised that the flight conditions were already getting hazardous.

'If you agree Dino I'll arrange for the heaviest passengers to sit at the front for take off which should enable you to get your tail up quickly and expedite the take off'.

'That's a good idea Sandy but please be quick. I will leave the arrangements to you while my co-pilot and I get the aircraft checks completed as quickly as possible'.

Niles nodded his head in agreement. 'Right', he roared. 'Let's move arse, every one aboard the aircraft as quickly as possible - I want the heaviest people in the front seats for the take off. Once safely airborne you can then move to sit along side your friends'

His commands were issued in such a confident manner that the film director and his crew started enplaning without further ado. As Mr Chase passed him getting aboard he gave Nile a puzzled look and said,

'For a bloody chauffeur you seemed to know a lot about flying'.

'Enough to know that if we don't get a blasted move on we are going to be in serious trouble', he snapped. 'Chop, chop, you buggers' he shouted at the film crew, 'we haven't got all day '.

Inside the aircraft, Johnny the Co-pilot; a man about thirty years old with dark wavy hair and a broad handsome face, He was medium height, and sleeves rolled up displaying powerful hairy forearms was endeavouring to get the passengers sorted out with the heaviest to front. In the cockpit, the Captain was going through his start up checks

Niles had just got himself strapped in when he heard the groan of an exhausted battery trying to crank the port engine over. The propeller blades never completed more than a quarter of a turn before coming to a halt. The significance was lost on most of the passengers who were still busy getting strapped in – but not Niles. He dashed down the fuselage to the cockpit, 'why is the battery fucked!' He shouted at the pilot, still acting the part of an irate Company official.

'Senor Niles', explained the exasperated Dino patiently. 'This aircraft has not flown for over two weeks and further more, it was not due to fly for another week so it has not been properly serviced'.

'Have we got any Trolley ack's for external power?' Niles enquired.

The captain shrugged his shoulders and shook his head. 'No - and with all the power lines down there is no way we can charge the batteries – even if we did have time, which we haven't'!

The tension in the cockpit quickly filtered back to the passenger's who suddenly realised that there was a serious problem and they might be stuck on the airstrip which was almost certainly going to flood once the hurricane arrived.

Costello came bustling importantly up the cabin and shouted at Niles.

'I'm going to hold you responsible for this fuck up. You were sent by the Company to ensure we got out of this shit hole safely. Why didn't you ascertain that this aircraft was fully serviceable before booking it for us?'

Costello suddenly realised that he had overstepped the mark. Sandy Niles's blood had drained from his face – He'd gone into the, 'Fight or Flight', mode and he was certainly not about to run. Costello was in serious trouble his gut began to tremble and he had problems holding his water – he thought he was about to be hit.

Niles stood his full six feet two inches and glared. 'Because it was the only fucking aircraft available you dim witted cretin – how many other aircraft did you see on the strip when you arrived? If you'd responded to the Hurricane warning yesterday as you were supposed to all of us would be safely out of this midden by now. So shut the fuck up and get back to your seat while I see how we can get this bloody machine started'.

Costello blanched. Niles seemed to have grown to a height of seven feet and his fierce reaction had wrong footed him completely; he was so used to getting his own way that he was not sure how to respond. He huffed and puffed but finally turned round and scuttled back to his seat muttering. 'I'll be reporting you to the directors as soon as we get State side'.

Niles thought to himself for a moment. *How the hell were they going to get out of this crock of shit?* In another ten minutes the rain would be upon them and shortly after that the strip would be unusable. Then he remembered a story and old Argentinean pilot had recounted. He decided to give it a go.

'Okay Dino', he said, 'I have only ever heard of this being attempted once before, we are going to tow start the aircraft'.

'Are you crazy!', shouted the Captain, 'you can't tow start an aircraft'.

'Lets have the crew and the strip controller out side and I'll explain what we are going to attempt'.

They all gathered at the front of the aircraft and Niles commenced his briefing.

'We've got about five minutes to get this all together, after that it's all academic, he said pointing to the east where a dark ominous curtain of rain was approaching. 'So I'm going to be brief. You are all familiar with the toggle rope that we used to start out board engines on launches?'

They all nodded their heads in agreement.

'We are going to wind a rope around the propeller boss which houses the constant speed unit and attach the other end of it to the bus which will drive off and spin up the engine. And if we do it correctly the engine will start. This will bring the generator on line and we will have electrical power to crank the starboard engine over'.

For a moment the other three just stood looking at him gob smacked.

'You', he pointed to the co-pilot. 'What's your name?'

'Johnny'.

'Well Johnny I need you to drive the bus when I give you the thumbs up and keep going until you are clear of the aircraft'.

'And you', continued Niles, indicating the strip controller. 'I want 15 metres of stout rope. Can you do that?'

'Se senor, I'm on my way'.

Dino, the aircraft's Captain rubbed his chin thoughtfully, 'I have heard of some crazy things in my life time but this one takes the cake. What happens if the rope gets wrapped up in the propeller?

'It won't; provided Johnny keeps driving the bus away towards the wing tip the rope will get thrown off the propeller boss as soon as the engine speed exceeds the towing speed. Further more, I will give you the thumbs up to switch the magnetos ON just as the rope is about to come off. If you are too late there's a danger of flooding the engine. Too early and there is a small chance of the rope getting tangled in the propeller - Okay let's get moving - I figure that we have about five minutes to go before the weather makes all this academic'.

'Sounds a bit dicey to me' replied Dino. 'But to be quite frank, I can't think of an alternative'.

As Dino went past his co-pilot he gave him an old fashioned look and murmured. 'Have you ever heard of this before?'

'No way boss – but lets face it, we don't really have the time to discuss the pro's and con's – if we don't get clear of this strip in the next five minutes or so we're going to be stuck here, Ok, I'd better get this bus ready – see you in a couple of minutes – fingers crossed!'

'You're right there Johnny I am afraid if we don't get off in the next ten minutes we've had it!'

Jose had worked the oracle; he reappeared in under a minute with an Aluminium Step ladder and forty feet of stout hemp rope.

'Exactly what we need' Niles growled, as he shinned up the ladder with one end of the rope.

He finished wrapping the rope around the propeller boss, of the port engine that housed the 'Constant Speed Unit' climbed down the stepladder and kicked it clear. He then took the other end of the rope and secured it to the bumper on the back of the old bus. The bus was parked in front of and parallel to the leading edge of the wing facing towards the wing tip. Niles's idea was quite simple; as the bus drove away towards the wing tip the rope which was wound around the propeller boss would spin the prop like an outboard engine.

He checked that they were all in position and ready. Dino, the captain gave him the thumbs up.

He then gave the thumbs up to the bus driver, the co-pilot, who let the clutch out gently, took up the slack in the rope, and pulled away. The rope turned the prop' slowly at first but quicker as the bus gained speed,. The weight of the spinning propeller blades gave the engine plenty of momentum, and just as the rope was coming off the propeller boss Niles gave the thumbs up to Dino in the cockpit and shouted, 'Contact'. The Captain switched ON the magnetos and the engine coughed, faltered, and then finally caught, initially running ragged but as the engine warmed up it settled down to a steady beat. A muted cheer from within the aircraft's cabin greeted their success.

The co-pilot and Jose stood there with their mouths open mesmerised by the engine that was now running smoothly unable to credit what they had just achieved. The first spatters of heavy rain and a warning shout from Niles broke their reverie and he motioned to them to get aboard at once. They quickly climbed into the aircraft whilst Dino cranked over the starboard engine as they were still getting strapped in. With the DC power available from the port engine's generator, now running smoothly the starboard engine was quickly started. The Captain had the aircraft taxiing before his co-pilot had even got himself seated. Luckily in this climate the engine's temperatures and pressures were quickly within limits for take off.

Dino lined the aircraft up the strip into the gusting wind. Locked the tail wheel and holding the aircraft with the toe brakes opened the throttles to take off power. As soon as the thrust exceeded the brakes pressure holding the aircraft he released them and accelerated down the strip. The passenger's, now fully aware of the hazardous conditions and the gusting wind that was rocking the aircraft, were in the main, staring fixedly ahead and gripping their seats with white knuckles gleaming. Some of the women passengers were beginning to sob and others were praying softly as the crosswind tried to weather cock the aircraft off the runway, although Niles noticed that the eleven year old girl who was grimly hanging onto her attractive mother's arm managed to keep a brave face. As their speed approached seventy knots a very strong gust of cross wind caused the aircraft to yaw violently to starboard. Passengers sobbing started to scream as the aircraft careered towards the edge of the runway.

'Jesus' cried Dino slamming a bootful of left rudder to compensate – No effect! They were now close to catastrophe – he savagely reduced power on the port engine. Niles in the back of the cabin braced for the coming crash. The more emotional passengers now screamed and panicked. Then!..... quite suddenly, the combined effect of full left rudder and the differential power setting took effect and the aircraft gradually realigned with the runway. The increasing forward speed was now giving the rudder more aerodynamic authority making it easier for the Dino to overcome the gusting crosswind. Quickly and smoothly Dino reapplied the port engine power to take off setting as the end of the runway was now rapidly approaching. Johnny; swearing like some drunken trooper held the throttles fully open leaving Dino the use of both hands to wrestled with the flying controls keeping the bucking aircraft lined up with the runway. Niles grinned with relief appreciating that the crew had now got the situation well under control. Other, less well informed passengers continued to scream not realising that the worst of the danger was over. As the speed approached ninety knots Dino deliberately held the aircraft down to ensure full flying speed before lifting it off. At one hundred knots he lifted the Dakota cleanly off the runway and kicked it twenty degrees to starboard to maintain track and immediately called to his co-pilot. 'Gear up Johnny and then flaps as soon as you can'.

'Gear coming up and flaps retracting', Johnny sang out.

Dino now appreciated the reasons why Niles had suggested that the heaviest passengers were seated to the front of the aircraft, he'd been able to get his tail up that much quicker, and this had put the aircraft into a more efficient aerodynamic profile which had enabled them to reach full flying speed that much sooner.

As wheels left the ground all the passengers visibly heaved a mighty sigh of relief. As is the want of Americans, they voiced their appreciation to the crew with a round of cheering and clapping.

'Jesus!' Johnny said. 'I don't want to have another thirty seconds of flying like that again. I thought we were going to veer off the runway on at least two occasions. I think I need a change of underwear'.

Dino gave a wry grin in agreement. 'Me too; I must say that putting the heaviest passengers in the front seats was a big help in getting us airborne quickly. It's not something one normally associates with civil airline flying. That joker Niles seems to have an intimate knowledge of flying that you don't pick up on some computer game – He's a strange man and to be quite frank I think he's been exposed to military flying at some time in his past'.

Johnny concurred. 'You can say that again I've never come across that trick of his of turning our port engine over like some bloody out size outboard motor. Having said that, without it I figure we'd still be on that blasted airstrip, I can't think of any other way of starting that engine'.

Dino nodded his head in agreement as he settled

down to flying by reference to instruments on entering the thickening dark clouds.

The passengers sensing that they were now safely airborne and out of a danger continued to applaud the crew for their safe take off. And then, as the rush of adrenalin subsided, fatigue kicked in and they gradually began to settle down and doze off to sleep.

Niles who had appreciated just how difficult the take off had been murmured to himself, 'well done Dino that was some take off'.

As they entered the dark clouds the aircraft began to buck and weave as the turbulence increased. However the turbulence did not worry Niles and he gradually dozed off in company with his colleagues.

Hurricane, 'Judy' was beginning to make her presence felt.

Suddenly, Sandy Niles awoke with a start. Groaned and stretched his cramped legs, rubbed the sleep from his eyes and stretched his arms above his head. It took him several seconds to orientate where the hell he was. He craned his head forward and looked up the cabin Twisted his neck and looked down the cabin of the Dakota. All the other passengers appeared to be asleep so what had woken him? He could see nothing untoward. Shrugged his shoulders and muttered to himself that he must be getting senile in his old age. He checked his watch but couldn't remember exactly when they'd got airborne – must have been about an hour ago. He was worried. His 'gut instinct' warned him that something was amiss. Over the past three years he'd learnt to trust this feeling. To ignore it was to court trouble. However, the monotonous drone of the Dakota's two engines and the surge of adrenaline he'd had in the last hour soon caused him to doze off'.

Again - he awoke with a start! What the hell was it that kept causing him to wake up? A further check of the other passengers confirmed nothing unusual. They were all asleep after their nerve racking bus ride to the airstrip followed by their hair raising take off. He decided it wasn't the turbulence so what in God's name was causing him to wake up so startled?

He looked out the window of the Dakota. Through the gaps in the low cloud he was surprised to see how low they were flying. Without oxygen supply for the passengers the aircraft was limited to a maximum height of thirteen thousand feet but the tops of the trees couldn't have been more than five hundred feet below. The terrain must be bloody high to be this close to the ground. And they were obviously still over flying the rain forest, amongst the most inhospitable terrain in the world. The turbulence of the approaching hurricane was getting more physically evident, but he was convinced that this was not the reason he kept waking up. The synchronised noise of the two engines gently lulled him back to sleep again.

Again he awoke with a start. He had no idea how long he'd been asleep. He checked his watch. He still wasn't sure what time they got airborne. He looked up and down the cabin, could see nothing unusual. But he still had this strange feeling in his guts that something wasn't quite right. However, fatigue took over and five minutes later he was back asleep.

Chapter 2

Barranquilla

It was rather an old Hacienda probably been built in the mid twenties and despite a considerable amount of modification it still managed to project the era in which it had originally been constructed. The walls were of stone quarried locally and painted a brilliant white to reflect the harsh heat of the sun. It was situated on the north coast of Colombia close to the town of Barranquilla. Out to the East stood the Sierra Nevada Santa Marta Mountains with the highest peak in the entire country, the Pico Cristobal with its gleaming hat of snow. Normally the cap of snow glistened like the icing on a wedding cake but not today. The lowering cloud from the approaching hurricane to the north was beginning to creep across the mountains and was already throwing a deep shadow across the snowy caps making it difficult to distinguish the line between the top of the mountain and the base of the lowering cloud. Although the centre of the hurricane was due to pass a hundred miles north into the Gulf of Mexico the outer edge of the storm was going to make its presents felt many miles into Colombia

The front of the building reflected its original Spanish style with the green shutters giving some relief to the glare of the white walls. A large veranda which faced out to a considerable expanse of open lawn that ran down to a golden sandy beach and the beautiful azure sea. Normally the sea was unruffled and smooth but today it was beginning to get choppy. The increasing winds unimpeded further off shore was already causing 'white horses' to form. The remaining yachts and pleasure craft that normally frequent this area were already making haste back to their Marinas. The lawns of the house were immaculate with half a dozen golf putting holes set out at varying distances. The whole set up reflected grace and affluence. To the rear of the house there were spacious gardens that ran back to the edge of the tree line where once the rain forest grew. Although the area was laid out with numerous flower beds there were no shrubs to interrupt the line of sight. Beyond the cultivated garden the vegetation had been further hacked away to provide an uninterrupted field of view out to about eight hundred metres or so. This was not done just to improve the beauty of the vista. There were more sinister reasons for the good field of view. The gardens had been planned by an expert landscape gardener and it showed, never-the-less, it was impossible to get to within four hundred metres of the house without being observed. Two hundred metres to the north of the house was a helicopter pad on which stood two Jet Ranger helicopters with their rotors tied down. They were due to depart after lunch in order to avoid the approaching storm. Closer to the building but still on the landward side, was a large car park on which were parked half a dozen cars. Four of which were of the four wheel drive variety. The remaining two cars were both expensive BMWs. However, the panoramic beauty outside the Hacienda was not echoed by the men within.

Inside the conference room the owner of the hacienda,

Francesco Domingo, a big man with hard flat features that reflected his upbringing from the slums of Medellin was standing at the head of a large mahogany table and addressing his seated colleagues. The colour of his eyes was difficult to discern as they were set well back in his head. His once sturdy physique was beginning to run to fat. And although he was attired in an expensive light weight grey suit all his trousers now had elasticised waist to accommodate his ever increasing paunch. He'd fought his way up from a drugs runner to dealer and in due course to take over one of the largest drug gangs in Colombia. He was now one of the richest men in the world. He stood looking down at his fellow accomplices, his thin lips so compressed that they looked like a dark red razor slash - five of the most influential drug suppliers in Columbia. They sat round the large mahogany table which was all of twenty feet long by ten wide. The wall opposite the large patio window was hung with three expensive Picasso original paintings and on the large scatter tables were many artefacts of the early Mayan culture. The whole room reflected affluence and surprisingly, good taste, which was more than could be said for the men seated around the table. Although they were all expensively attired they were thugs to a man and looked it. Individually they had been taking a hammering from a newly formed arm of the police, the Field Force Police (FFP). Normally they were competitors and six months ago would have considered one another if not enemies, then certainly bitter competitors. But recently that situation had changed. They'd been forced to form a loose coalition to counter the latest threat to their cocaine production.

Domingo (the richest and most powerful of them) looked around at his peers: drumming his powerful stubby fingers on the table: A habit he's acquired as a teenager and been never able to get rid of. Satisfied he'd their undivided attention and began.

'This is the third time one of our processing laboratories that has been put out of action by the new Field Force Police in the last two months. As we've seen these guys are too bloody good for our liking. They're being trained by Western Special Forces and so far they have resisted all bribes made to them; therefore, we've no idea of when or where they are going to strike next or even how much knowledge of our operations they have. As we all appreciate it's not just the cost of material lost in these raids but more to the point it's the loss of production that is hurting our organisations. Further more, we are loosing face to our younger and hungrier competitors who might consider us weak enough to usurp us'.

'I am therefore going to propose three points to discuss', he continued.

'One; we must build our new laboratories further into the rainforest making them much more difficult to detect.

Two; I suggest we increase the bribe money to a suitable candidate in this newly formed Field Force. Every body has a price. So it's up to us to find someone who can inform us, of all likely strikes and more importantly, keep our intelligence up to date.

And last but not least, we must put pressure on our three Senator friends in America to see if we can get these dammed advisors out of our country'.

Pablo Ferreira was the first to respond. Like many of his colleagues he was now eating at the top of the food chain and his figure reflected it. He was badly over weight. His high sloping forehead denoted intelligence but the effect was spoilt by his eyes being too close together. His black eyes seemed to emit no emotion and his history was one of violence with little or no regard for human life. Like all his peers seated around the table, he was used to running his own cartel and therefore making his own decisions. He found it rankled to have to act subservient to Domingo but never-the-less the bastard was the most powerful and richest member of their newly formed group so as there had to be one man overall in charge, he was the man.

'Christ we pay them enough money to keep us informed' he growled.

'Your dammed right and I intend to find out why the bastards didn't inform us about these latest Special forces that have been brought in'. Francesco' replied.

Francesco turned and faced Pedro DeGannes. 'I think Pedro is the man to organise the new Laboratories. We have already discussed it informally and provided the rest of you agree he's prepared to take on the task. Al! – would you be prepared to help Pedro in this operation?' asked Francesco.

Al Menzies was one of the quieter members of the Cartel but never the less a very tough, cruel character who'd a reputation for getting the job done. Above average height with a twisted nose that had been broken in his late teens. His features were almost Neanderthal with a dark jowl. If he shaved before breakfast by the time he'd finished it he looked as though he needed another.

'Consider it done' he said nodding his head. 'I'll liaise with Pedro and get to it straight away. I've some areas to the south of here in the rain forest which should be secure from any prying eyes, They would be ideal. Further more, the areas are so isolated that should any arsehole discover them we can get rid of them easily and no one will be any the wiser'.

Francesco stared at him for a couple of seconds. Scratch his balls and continued, 'good - now we are getting somewhere. Teddy: I want you to infiltrate this bloody Field Force and I don't care how you do it, break their god dammed legs if you have to or increase the bribes up to 100,000 dollars. We must know what these bastards are up to so we can plan accordingly,'

Teddy Garcia was the only skinny member present;

about six feet two inches tall with a long beaky nose and a badly pox marked face. Although Garcia did not look particularly bright and was barely literate he made up for this with plenty of pure animal cunning. There were at least half a dozen bodies in unidentified graves around the country that had tried and failed to get the better of Garcia in drug related scams.

'I have two informants in the police at the HQ in Bogotá. They will be able to finger the most susceptible characters in the Field Force likely to accept bribes. Failing that, I am sure we can bring pressure to bear on their families or break their legs or maybe even both'.

'Now we are getting there' said Francesco beaming like an indulgent parent. 'I think Franco you would be the best man to co-ordinate the three tasks we have just outlined. You have your offices in Bogotá and will be in a best position to keep in touch with all of us'.

Franco De Nero was the only member of the Cartel who had anything like a decent education. He was much darker than any of the others and at one time must have been a very handsome man. However the past ten years of debauchery had dissipated that and now his face was florid which bespoke of high blood pressure. And where he had once had a tough athletic figure he was now, as were all the others, except Garcia, badly overweight. But like his associates, he was a nasty piece of work who had attained his position as a drug baron not because of his education but by his ruthless and violent ambition to get to the top.

Franco shuffled in his chair trying to get a more comfortable position and stared at the hard face of Domingo stood before him. 'No problem', he snarled, 'It's about time this shit was sorted out. I have lost a god dam lot of money over these last three busts. It's time these Field Force Police were given a good kicking and the sooner the better. And further more, these bastard American Senators that we are paying have got to start earning their keep. Why haven't we been informed of the Special Forces training the police, Jesus, they have been here for at least three months – that's the sort of information we are paying them for'.

Muttered cursed rumbled from his colleagues in accord.

Domingo nodded his head in agreement. 'I think we've covered all pertinent points so if no one has any thing further to discuss we can adjourn for lunch – any other points' he continued looking at the others expectantly.

His colleagues all shook their heads.

'Good!' Francesco rang a bell and a swarthy giant appeared at the end of the Room. 'Reynaldo' he commanded (The man stood at least six feet eight inches tall and weighed in at two hundred and eighty pounds). 'Tell Marie to serve lunch now and tell the women we will see them on the veranda'.

He looked around at the assembled thugs. 'Anyone got any further points?' he repeated as they rose to leave the room. 'Good I think we should have an early lunch so we can depart to our homes before this blasted storm hits us'.

'When are you going to contact our American friend', asked Pablo as they were walking through the door.

'I'll do so whilst we're having lunch' replied Francesco 'In fact, if you guys go on and I'll phone them now and join you as soon as I have an answer to this Special Forces problem'.

'It can't be too soon as far as I'm concerned', said Franco.

'Ok I'll see you as soon as I have some answers from our Gringo friends,' growled Francesco as he made his way to his study. The study was at the back of the house and from the outside its appearance resembled a blockhouse. There were no windows and the room was completely sound proof. It was only about twelve by twelve feet with a large mahogany writing bureau sat against the wall opposite the only door. There were three short band radio sets which had been built into the bureau, on top sat three head sets and three phones one of which was red coloured. Apart from a large scale map of Colombia and a calendar on the wall above the bureau the walls were bare. This was the room where Domingo conducted all his business – no one, including his giant body guard was allowed in here. The red phone was fitted with the latest American scrambler system. This was the one he picked up. The Cartel had learnt in their earlier days the danger of making unscrambled calls to the United States.

Francesco dialled a number and a woman's voice answered almost immediately. 'Is Senator Jackson there?' He asked.

'One moment', she replied, 'I'll get him'.

'Is that you Francesco?' growled a gravely voice.

'Of course it's me' snarled Francesco. 'Who the hell did you suppose it would be on a secure one to one telephone line?'

'Hey, hey!' snarled Senator Jackson. 'I'm not one of your god dam Peons, so just wind your scaly neck in Domingo'.

'Don't give me that shit', ranted Domingo, 'part of our deal was that you would warn us of any American Special Forces sent here to train the Police, and yet we find that Gringo Special Forces have been training a new Field Force. They have already attacked three of our drug processing plants over the past two months and put them out of action'

'What the hell are you talking about', growled the Senator, 'I'm the chairman of the Special Select Committee to combat drugs and I'd have been informed about any Special Training Groups being sent to Colombia. Even the CIA would've had to clear it with our committee before sending any agents or training groups to your necks of the woods'.

'Well someone has sent them here and from all accounts they're bloody good, too good to be locally trained and our informants say they are definitely gringos. So you will find out where they have come from and let me know'.

'Okay! Okay!' replied Jackson. 'But I'm dam sure they are not American, so it may take a little time before you get your answer. Will you be in this evening?

'Yes, I'll be here for the rest of the day but I will be leaving this evening to avoid the approaching hurricane. As soon as you have any information call me immediately' answered Francesco.

'I'll get back to you as soon as I can'. And Jackson ended the conversation by slamming down the phone.

'Bastard', muttered Francesco as he sauntered onto the patio to have some lunch. 'Hey hey' look what the ladies have prepared for us,' he roared. 'Come on every one tuck in. Business is over, now we eat before the hurricane blows it all to hell'

The ladies had excelled themselves, albeit with the help of their many domestic staff, the table was groaning under the weight of the food. All of the people present had come from dirt poor backgrounds and now they could afford it never finished eating until they were completely sated. Despite the cold meats weighing the table down there was also a piglet being barbequed on the spit at the end of the veranda. All the wives and even some of their children were now beginning to reflect this excess of eating and most of them were overweight, some seriously so.

None of his colleagues had needed any prompting they were already shovelling food down their throats at as fast as they could. All of them stood there grinning, with grease running down their chins from wolfing the hot juicy pork with their bare hands. They were not known for their cuisine etiquette.

Pedro handed him a plate. 'What did our gringo friend

say?' he snorted as he continued to shovel food down his throat as if there was no tomorrow'.

'He said he would get back to me today as soon as he had anything definite. He's definite that they're not American otherwise he would have been informed', replied Francesco.

Chapter 3

United States

Senator Jackson stared at the portrait of Abraham Lincoln that hung on the wall opposite his desk, alarmed at the phone call he'd just received from Colombia. He was a tall man and a snappy dresser. His hair was dyed a deep auburn. Eyes were grey and showed little emotion. He was also a keen advocated of the Sun Bed. His tan was just too perfect to be natural. He was a typical politician i.e. he was not averse to using his political appointment as a means of lining his own pockets and had no qualms about dumping on people less fortunate than himself. His Gods were power and money. He drummed his well manicured fingers on the table whilst he thought over the content Domingo's last call. He and two other Senator colleagues were being paid a great deal of money by the Colombian Drug Barons to lobby in the Senate and try and ensure that hard drugs never became legalised.

This might sound counter productive to the sale of drugs but whilst drugs remained illegal there were huge profits to be made and although the American Drugs Enforcement

Agency were working overtime to try and kill off the illegal trade they were fighting a losing battle. There was just too much money sloshing around to prevent the drugs from entering the country.

Senator Jackson and his two accomplices, Senators' Thornton and Beck, were being paid big bucks to ensure that the illegal trade remain so and thus maintain the massive profit margins enjoyed by members of the Drug Cartels. This was not as easy as first supposed. There was an increasing number of Senators who thought the only way to beat the drug trade was to legalise it. This they surmised would remove the huge sums of money available to the Drug Barons. Also this would bring the drug problem out in the open and those who could not or would not give up drugs would be able to purchase them at a reasonable price and at the same time be to get medical help as required. At the moment for every kilo of drugs intercepted by law enforcers another ten were getting in onto the streets. The western World was fighting a losing battle against the illegal trade.

Since most drugs related crimes were committed by people who stole or mugged to get the money to pay the inflated prices demanded by the drug dealers. It was thought that if they could afford to pay for their stupid habit out of their own salaries then the number of drug related crimes would rapidly reduce. This in turn would reduce the massive profits available to the drug dealers. Crime is always associated with easy money; gambling prostitution etc. once the easy money had disappeared it was thought that the crime rate would also drop. True, this may result in more drug addicts but some people are always looking for an emotional prop to see them through life. The halt to prohibition did not turn America into a nation of drunks as prophesied by many, 'know alls', in the 1930's. Therefore, there's no reason to suppose that if drugs were legalised that the nation would all become drug addicts.

During the American Prohibition in the 1930's it was quite evident that if people were determined to drink then they would find ways of doing so. But the American Government failed to recognise this until many hoodlums and the Mafia in particular, had made sufficient money to diverse into legal operations, which in many cases enable them to launder their own illegally money. By the time that the American Government had taken cognisance of this problem many of the hoodlums were some of the richest men in the States.

One of the main problems of trying to legalise drugs was getting all countries to agree to do so in unison. Doing it unilaterally would simple be a waste of time. All the drug misfits from the neighbouring countries would inundate it and swamp the medical and re-habilitate system.

Although some drug shipments were being intercepted by drug enforcement agencies many more were getting through. Furthermore, with the massive profits now available to the Drug Barons they were able to devise extremely sophisticated means of smuggling shipments into the country. As one DEA agent was heard to remark. 'The bastards will soon have enough money to hire or buy Nuclear Submarines to smuggle the shit in'. The truth of the matter is that in Western Society, it is not the supply of drugs that's the problem but the demand. If the demand for drugs could be stifled through social education where people are taught that taking drugs was stupid and childish rather than dangerous, then the supply problem would simple wither and die away. At the moment too much emphasis is placed on the dangers of taking drugs. Unfortunately this appeals to the younger generation who are always inclined to experiment with anything if it is considered to be dangerous.

Thus the three Senators were on the Cartel's payroll to ensure that the drug trade was not legalised and so make sure that the price of Cocaine remained sky high. Part of the deal was that the three Senators were to keep the Cartel informed of any American involvement with the Colombian Police/ Security Forces which so far they had managed well.

Jackson decided that Thornton was the most likely candidate to know what was happening on the Special Forces front so he phoned him first on the secure phone line.

'Al Thornton here. What can I do for you?'

'Sam Jackson Al, we appear to have a problem with our friends down in Colombia. It would seem that there are some Special Forces training a new Field Force for anti-drug operations and our friends down there are going apeshit because we haven't warned them. I have no knowledge of who these guys are and wondered if you could throw some light on the situation'.

'News to me buddy' replied Thornton. 'But General Hacker owes me one so I'll get onto him and see if we can rustle up some answers. Give me thirty minutes and I'll get back to you Sam'.

'That's fine' said Jackson,' In the meantime I'll get hold of Carl Beck and see if he has any information that might indicate where these guys hail from'.

Jackson dialled up his other colleague Carl Beck. 'Beck here', said the squeaky voice. The high pitch voice always came as a surprise to people meeting Beck for the first time. He stood well over six foot and with his powerful build he gave the impression of having a deep gravely baritone.

'Carl I've already spoken to Al Thornton' Jackson eased the phone into a more comfortable position'. 'We've had a gripe from our Colombian friends about some Special Forces training their Police force in anti drug operations. Apparently they've already taken out three of their processing camps and they're somewhat annoyed that we've not warned them about this new training team. Neither Al nor I have any knowledge who these Special Forces are and we were hoping you might know something.

'I afraid not', squeaked Beck. 'As you must know Sam any information of that sort gets passed to you, like yesterday. I know of no US forces down there at the moment but Al has some good military connections so he should be able to throw some light on the subject. I figure the Brits' to be the most likely contenders. They've been using the SAS as a means of earning foreign exchange for the past twenty years or so and they don't charge cheap for their expertise either. Other than that I can't help Sam'.

'I've got Al talking to some of his hard nosed Army friends at this very moment and he will ring me back whenever he has any thing positive to report. In the meantime Carl, keep your ears peeled and let me know if any thing turns up. Cheers for now and give my love to Karen'. With that salutation Jackson put the phone down. We're going to have to be careful thought Jackson or their little deal with the Colombians could well blow up in their faces. If their financial deal with the Domingo and his friends ever did come to light their political careers would be finished and they would be very lucky to escape a jail sentence.

Within the American Government there was still very mixes feelings as to whether they should legalise drugs. There appeared to be good cases for both sides of the argument.

But at the moment, the consensus of opinion was that drugs should be banned until social education could be seen to be strong enough to discourage teenagers and some of the elite members of society from using them. And that was certainly not the case at present.

Senator Jackson made several phone calls to other colleagues to try and establish who the Special Forces were now operating in Colombia. Came four o'clock in the afternoon and Jackson had had enough. 'Sod it' he murmured as he stood up from his chair. 'I've had enough for today'.

He'd got to the door when the secure phone rang. He turned and picked it up. 'Yes' he barked as he cradled it to his ear.

'Sam its Al here - I have just finished talking to General Hacker, who has been in touch with some friends in the UK and it transpires that there's been a SAS team of eight men training the Colombian Police for the past four months'.

'Shit', exploded Jackson. 'So that's why we've heard nothing about this training team. And if they have been training this Field Force for the past four months one can only assume that they are now a force to be reckoned with'.

'No wonder our friends in the south are going apeshit' murmured Al. 'They'd better get their act together before they loose any more camps. Is there anything else I can help with in the meantime?' queried Al.

'Not for the moment', said Sam Jackson with a grimace. 'I'll let you know if any thing else comes to mind Al. I suppose I'd better get on to Francesco and give him the bad news. He's not going to like it but there is nothing we can do at this stage to help him'. And with that

Senator Jackson rang off.

Chapter 4

Bogotá

Captain Bryant was the officer in charge of the SAS detachment. A shade less than six foot with a close knit well balanced physique that just radiated energy. His brown hair was just starting to recede and his eyes were a deep blue. He had a small scar on his left cheek of his rugged face – a relict from days when he played rugby to quite a high standard. He projected an air of quiet self confidence and self reliance. Women found him very attractive.

Tony Bryant came to the SAS from the 3rd Battalion of the Parachute Regiment having been encouraged to do so by his Commanding Officer. Normally CO's do everything in their power to persuade their best young officers to remain with their units. However, Bryant's CO was an ex' SAS Troop Commander and appreciated that once Bryant had completed his two year tour with the SAS he would return to his Battalion considerably more skilled and experienced than when he left. He was delighted when Bryant applied to join the SAS and had complete confidence that Bryant could pass 'selection' and that he would be accepted. Before he left his battalion his CO briefed him on what to expect. He explained that in SAS Sabre Squadrons the relationship between officer and 'other ranks' was 'unorthodox'; which took some getting used to. In many situations on operations, it was the senior NCOs that made most of the tactical decisions. He had also been warned by his Battalion CO, that as a new officer on operations he would have little, if anything to contribute to his 'new command' and that he would have to rely on members of the Troop to get him through his difficult and potentially dangerous indoctrination during his first few weeks. Clever officers, that recognised and acknowledged this limitation, were in no hurry to assume command or control. They listen, watched and learnt. Taking over control of the Troop was a steady transition throughout their first year as they learnt and gained experience. Capt Tony Bryant was a very clever officer and had watched and learnt. He'd been blessed with a very good and experienced Troop sergeant who'd nursed Bryant through his initial period with the Regiment but as Bryant gained experience his sergeant had gradually and insidiously passed the command of the Troop to Bryant without him becoming aware of it. He had been with the SAS for almost two years and was now fully accepted by his Troopers as a first class Troop Commander.

He headed the team that had been training the Colombian Field Force for the pass four months. And so far he was rather pleased with the results that they had achieved in such a short time. Their Colombian trainees had successfully wiped out three Drug Processing camps twenty miles to the east of Bogotá during the last two months and that was good going by any yardstick. As head of the SAS team Bryant was attending the weekly debrief with the commanding officer of the Field Force police.

The Colonel in charge of the police Field Force, Colonel DeSuza, was a large swarthy man with a broad humorous face with deep brown eyes and a ready smile. He was a man of considerable integrity. He'd resisted many bribes during his tenure of office and could now have been a rich man had he accepted even just half of them. He was now a 'marked man' as far as the Drug Barons were concerned which necessitated a two man body guard to accompany him at all times, on and off duty. He was wearing the smart American disruptive pattern combat clothing and a light beige pair of desert boots. He was seated in a swivel chair behind his desk looking at the British officer sat the other side.

'You will be pleased to know' he smiled at the British Officer, 'that the Government is extremely pleased with the results we've achieved in the last two months and have suggested that you and your men are entitled to a weekend in Bogotá. The Government will pick up the tab'. I hope this is to your liking Rupert'. Colonel DeSuza smiled as he referred to the British Officer by the nickname his troopers used rather than his first name, Tony'.

'I don't think you will have any complaints from the lads on that score', grinned Tony Bryant. 'They've worked pretty hard over the last two months and I'm sure they would love to visit the bright lights of Bogotá and I'll make sure they are hot to trot on Monday morning'.

'Hot to trot' murmured the Colombian Colonel. 'That's a new expression. I presume it means they will all be ready and fit to start work on Monday morning?'

'You got it right first time', laughed Tony. 'Your English is improving faster than my Spanish'.

'Maybe', said the Colonel. 'But English is now the International language of the World so if you want to get on in life you have to learn to speak it. Okay Tony, I'll see you and your trooper's first thing Monday morning at eight o'clock'. Here is your hotel and I have arranged for two Range Rovers to be available with drivers so if necessary your men can drink themselves into oblivion without having to worry about driving under the influence. I have also provided a short list of some of the better night clubs to visit bearing in mind that there are some parts of Bogotá that are best avoided. Is there anything else you need Tony?'

'No - I think you have covered all bases Colonel and I'm sure the boys will appreciate all the trouble you have gone to on their account'.

'Please think nothing of it Tony it's the least we can do to show our appreciation for all the work you and your men have put into the training since arriving here – please ensure the lads have a good time and we will see you all on Monday'. The Colonel reflected for a moment about the SAS men. Most of them were of average size but no where as large as the American Special Forces soldiers he had seen but what had impressed him most about the SAS troopers was their stamina, mental toughness, ability to improvise and respond to fluid situations. His country had paid big bucks to get this training team but never-the-less, DeSuza felt the government was getting good value for money. The SAS team had been in the country for the past three months and this was the first official time off they had been granted

Colonel DeSuza stood up and shook Bryant's hand. 'Pass my congratulations onto your men Tony and I look forward to seeing you all on Monday'.

'Consider it done Colonel'. Bryant threw the Colonel a smart salute, turned and went down the corridor to the Briefing room to inform his troopers of the good news. He couldn't help but reflect on how well the training had gone over the past two months. His troopers had not only done a good job of training the Colombians but had taken part in all three of the operational sorties (although they had been strictly told in the UK not to take part in any operational sorties). But what the hell! Continuous training can become bloody boring and allowing his troopers to go out on the operational sorties had kept them sharp and up to speed, further more it helped to bleed off some of the excess testosterone his Troopers seemed to manufacture all too readily . They had also gone out of their way to make friends with Colombians consequently the whole operation was proceeding very smoothly. At the moment, so long as none of his troopers went apeshit and got themselves shot they would come out of this exercise earning plenty of, 'Brownie Points'.

'I've got some good news and some bad news,' quipped Bryant as he entered the briefing room.

'Don't give us that shit', Sergeant (Rusty) Irons grinned. 'You wouldn't know good news if you trod in the bloody stuff'.

Sgt Irons was the senior NCO of the team. A man of medium height with a square rugged faces which displayed plenty of character. His deep sunk grey eyes always seemed to be amused at something. His blond hair always appeared unruly and when he walked he seemed to roll like a sailor on the balls of his feet

Rusty Irons was an Ex- Army Boy Apprentice who had joined 22 SAS as a corporal from 9 Parachute Squadron, Royal Engineers, more than ten years previously. This unit had a reputation possibly only second to that of the SAS. On passing selection he, like all successful NCO candidates, had to revert to the rank of Trooper. Rusty had had to work hard at maintaining his stamina as he was one of those men blessed with plenty of, 'Fast twitch muscles', which gave him plenty of explosive power. But by the same token he did not have so many, 'Slow Twitch Muscles', which was required for stamina. He was one of the few men in the Regiment who could climb up a rope by the use of his hands only

Bryant was fortunate to have inherited Rusty Irons as his Troop Sergeant. He'd liked Rusty from the start, finding him extremely tough both physically and mentally but at the same time, he had a ready and quick sense of humour.

He quickly recognised that the one thing that stood out more than any other of Rusty's many qualities was that of leadership. He was particularly skilful at man management and was one of the most popular Troop Sergeants in the Regiment.

Bryant was extremely grateful to Rusty for the manner in which he had integrated him into the troop without trying to make him feel foolish or inadequate. It wasn't until some months later that Bryant realised that Rusty had begun transferring responsibility to him from day one. The handover had been almost imperceptible. About four months after joining the Troop he suddenly realised he was in control.

Bryant eyed his troopers and realised just how close they had grown together over the last two years. The respect between him and his Troopers was mutual. When he left the SAS he was going to miss these bastards.

'Aha' Bryant smirked. 'Well pin back your ear holes and get a load of this', he continued. 'Apparently the Colombian Government is so pleased with the result that we have achieved over the last two month that they have 'lost their heads' and decided to give us a free weekend in Bogotá and, wait for it! - They are going to pick up the tab. Further more, Colonel DeSuza has asked me to pass on his congratulations for a well done'.

'What's the catch', said Cpl Finnegan, (Fingers to his mates) a long steak of a man with a hooked nose, extremely wiry and a fantastic long distance runner i.e. plenty of slow twitch muscles. (His mates kept threatening to enter him for the Grand National but felt they wouldn't get reasonable odds on him) 'That's obviously the good news, so what's the bad?'

Bryant eyed his seven troopers. 'The only bad news is that we have to be back here sober and ready for work at eight o'clock Monday morning, so go easy on the booze

Sunday evening. You are all big boys so I'm not going to labour the point, but I don't want anybody earning black marks by turning up here Monday morning pissed as a 'pack rat'. So far we have done extremely well and I want to keep it that way'.

'No problem boss' Said Rusty Irons. 'Will you be joining us or have you other arrangements?' In the SAS it was not unusual for the Officers to join the NCOs and troopers when overseas and partying for the evening.

'Not for Saturday'. Bryant laughed. 'I've to attend a function at the British Embassy. But I'll probable join up with you later on Sunday morning Rusty when we can plan something for the rest of the day including an evening's jaunt, if that's okay with you shower?'

'Sounds fine boss, I figure your Embassy do will be the shitty end of the stick so we'll try and organise something more exciting for Sunday evening' Rusty replied.

'That's great', said Bryant, 'There are two Range Rovers to take you to the hotel and they're yours for the weekend. We've also been provided with drivers so our drinking need not be inhibited – within reason I might add. See you Sunday morning. Try not to get into too much trouble'. Then he ducked out the door before having to listen to the insults being hurled at him from his motley crew.

Chapter 5

Rain Forrest

Suddenly; Sandy Niles, yet again, was fully awake. He was not sure what had woken him but it was the third time in as many minutes. He looked at his watch realised that they had only been flying for about an hour and a quarter. The turbulence was getting worse but he was pretty sure that this was not what had woken him.

He glanced out of the window of the Dakota and realised that they were still much lower than they should have been. Suddenly; he realised what had woken him – the piston engines of the old Dakota were no longer synchronised. A good pilot always tried to ensure that both engines turning at the same speed. I.e. they were in synchronised harmony. Niles had seen enough of Dino to know he was a first class pilot. Something was definitely wrong; in fact, one of the engines was beginning to run rough.

He got quietly to his feet. Most of the other passengers were still asleep after their rush to get to the Airstrip and the adrenalin surging take off. He walked quietly down to the cockpit taking care not to wake any of the passengers.

An atmosphere of tension and worry pervaded the cockpit. Dino, the Captain was sweating and there was a distinctly worried look on his face. The Co-pilot, Johnny, was also worried, looking out to the front and either side of the cockpit windows and trying desperately to fit the ground to the chart he had spread over his knees. Normally Civil Airliners navigated by reference to Radio Aides – not topographical maps, so something was seriously wrong if Johnny, the co-pilot, was trying to orientate their position by reference to a map.

Niles had seen the same expression many times before whilst training young sprogg pilots – he knew that the co-pilot was lost and hadn't a bloody clue where they were and Dino, who had his hands full trying to nurse a sick motor was in no position to help.

'Problems', he said nodding to the obviously lost co-pilot.

'You can say that again', said Dino as he tried to manipulate mixture control to resolve the port engine's rough running. We've also been blown so far south of our intended track by the hurricane that we are not even sure we're on the fucking chart that Johnny's consulting. All we really know is that we are now somewhere over Colombia and there is some very high ground in this neck of the woods'

'What sort of heights are we talking about', enquired Niles whose knowledge of Colombia was pretty sketchy.

'Well the highest peak is at Sierra Nevada de Santa Marta, its called the Pico Cristobal Colon and that goes up to just under 19,000 ft but we are definitely too far south of track for that to worry us. Unfortunately that's the good news. Some where in front of us and running perpendicular to our track, are three fingers of the Andes mountain range, which run north to south throughout the length of Colombia. They are called the Cordilleras, The Occidental on the west coast, then the Central one and the eastern and nearest one called the Oriental. Bogotá; our destination is located on the Oriental at a height of approximately eight thousand feet and it's this high ground I'm beginning to worry about. Unfortunately we have no idea how far it is to our front. We should be flying over the Llanos which is a rolling pampas type of countryside. As you can see, Senor Niles we are flying over dense rain forest so I suspect we are well south of our intended track.

'Jesus' murmured Niles. 'With that sick motor there's no way you are going to be able to climb over those mountains. You're only at six thousand feet now and your engines are already running out of grunt. Have you any idea how long before we approach them?'

Before Dino could answer, the port engine began to misfire badly. Dino slammed in a boot-full of right rudder to checks the yaw and quickly trimmed the rudder to reduce the asymmetric load on the rudder pedals.

'I don't think we are going to have to worry about those mountains' croaked Dino. 'We have definitely got fuel contamination of one sort or another. We are already too low and far away from any VORs or other Navigation aides to be of any help and I don't know how long our starboard motor is likely to run. It was playing up about ten minute ago so I'm pretty certain that the fuel on that side is contaminated as well'.

Just then the port engine quit and he noticed that Dino and Johnny completed the shut down drills quickly and competently. Niles was impressed.

'Shit' exploded Dino. 'Keep your eyes peeled for some reasonable real estate senor Niles, we're going to have to make an emergency landing within the next few minutes or so before that fucking starboard motor quits'.

Niles and Johnny both started to scan the rain forest below looking for any break amongst the trees, which would reduce the chances of a hazardous landing. There's nothing like an imminent crash in the rain forest to focus one's attention. The ground they were flying over was now mostly undulating rain forest - forbidding at the best of times, but now the low cloud was also reducing their visibility and scanning range to about two miles their situation appeared even more precarious.

'Dino!' cried Johnny, 'Over there - at two o'clock - there's a logging track with just about enough clearance to get in and we'll almost be able to land into wind'.

Luckily the logging track ran almost straight into the gale force wind and the vegetation to the sides of the track had at some time, been cut back probably to form a firebreak. Although there were some small bushes in the centre of the track there seemed nothing substantial enough to hinder a landing attempt.

'Senor Niles - you have obviously flown before, and although you have denied it one has only to listen to you holding forth on aviation matters to know this is not true. I would appreciate any constructive input you might like to make about our attempted landing'.

Niles could see no point in trying to deny this. Further more, he was impressed that Dino had the sense to canvas any knowledge that might be helpful'.

You are obviously a very competent pilot Dino and I am sure you and Johnny here will make as good a landing as is possible under the circumstances. My only comment is that the surface of that track looks pretty rough and suspect to me. If we land with the undercarriage lowered there's a strong possibility one of our wheels sinking into a pothole or soft ground causing us to be slewed into some pretty hard timber at the side of the track. Therefore, I think a wheels up landing might be the safest option. Lets face it Dino; landing into this wind you are going to have plenty of rudder control right up to the moment we come to rest, further more, with this wind speed we are only going to have a ground speed of about forty to fifty knots maximum'.

'I agree', said Dino. 'That confirms my thoughts exactly. Could you go into the passenger's cabin senor Niles and warn the others and organise them for an 'Emergency Landing'. We shall be landing in about two minutes I want to get this heap on the ground before that starboard motor packs up'.

'On my way', he said and made his way into the passengers cabin convinced that although the situation was serious the aircraft was in good hands. He'd been very impressed with the way Dino and Johnny had coped with the difficult take off and the subsequent engine failure and they had remained cool under very trying conditions. Most of the passengers had been woken by the sudden shut down of the port engine and a few were beginning to panic. Niles knew that he would have act in a bloody positive manner in order to prevent panic from spreading.

'Can I have every ones attention' roared Niles above the sound of the overworked remaining engine. 'I'm afraid that we have lost one engine due to fuel contamination and the remaining one is also giving trouble. The Captain has decided to make a powered emergency landing whilst he still has power on his remaining engine. We will be making a wheels up landing on a track in the jungle. Now don't panic! We'll be landing into a strong wind associated with the hurricane so our ground speed will be very slow. I'll now demonstrate the position I want you to adopt until the aircraft comes to a halt'.

'What the fucks going on here', roared Nathan Costello the films director racing up the passenger cabin before Niles could demonstrate the emergency position.

'Shut up and listen', shouted Niles. 'This is an emergency. We are going to have to land along a logging track in the middle of the rain forest whilst we still have power available or crash without power in ten minutes time. So, shut the fuck up and get sat down and do as you're told. We'll be landing in another minute so I haven't got time to have a Chinese Parliament with you. Now get sat down or I'm going to plant you right between the eyes – NOW move it!'The tone of Niles Instruction brooked no argument. Costello turned muttering to himself and sat down. Niles glowered at him and continued. 'The captain is going to land up a logging track into wind so it should be reasonably safe. Now this is the position I want you to adopt'.

Luckily most of the passengers although near to panic, were still recovering from a fitful sleep and weren't exactly compos mentis but they quickly adopted the position that Niles had demonstrated. Some of the women again, began to panic but Niles quickly strode down the cabin and made them adopt the crash position speaking to them softly but firmly which had the desired effect.

However, one of the young women began to panic and started to scream.'My god we are all going to be killed.These old airliners always burst into flames when they crash- we are going to be burnt alive'. She started to undue her safety harness but Niles was on top of her in a flash.

'What in god's name are you trying to do – adopt the crash position you were shown and keep your harness buckled up – and we are not crashing - we are making a powered emergency landing okay'.

Niles pressed his large left hand against her forehead forcing her back into her seat and held her motionless whilst he tightened her harness with his right.

'You do realise that this landing we are attempting is far safer than the take off we had back in Venezuela and you never panicked then – so why now? Further more if that young girl back there', said Niles pointing to the eleven year old with her mother, 'can control her feeling so should you'.

Niles could see the panic in her eyes beginning to subside and he gentle released the pressure of his left hand.

'Thank you - I'm sorry for causing such a fuss – I'll be alright now', she murmured.

Niles nodded and turned and made his way back to rear of the aircraft.

As Niles was getting seated a very attractive woman in her late thirties with the young girl of about eleven or twelve years of age spoke to Niles and said'. 'Please tell me, are we in much danger?'

Niles decided not to bullshit her and played it straight. 'I'm not going to lie' he said. 'It will be quite rough on touch down but in this case the hurricane is helping us. We are landing into a very strong wind so our touch down speed will be very slow and although it will be very rough it should not be dangerous providing you maintain the crash position I showed you'.

'Thank you' she said quietly. 'What's the best way of protecting my daughter?'

'One moment' said Niles and he grabbed a blanket from the overhead bin lockers and wrapped around the young girl. 'That should give her some protection just in case the landing is worse than I imagined'. In fact I have a better idea', he said, 'The landing is going to be pretty rough so I'll hold on to your daughter until the aircraft comes to a rest'

Mrs Fields looked at Sandy Niles and liked what she saw. He was a tall rangy man of about thirty years' of age with sandy hair and grey or green eyes, difficult to distinguish in the subdued lighting in the aircraft. Regular features that were slightly freckled with plenty of crow's at the corner of his eyes – a man used to living out doors. He had extremely large and powerful looking hands but it was the self reliant and confident manner in which he conducted himself that finally decided her to release her daughter into the care, of what was to all intents and purposes, a complete stranger.

'Okay' she said. 'I guess you have more physical strength than me so she should be safer with you than me'

'I promise I won't run off with her laughed Niles.

'Your right there, if you try, you'll find yourself trying to run with my teeth fastened to your ankle'.

Niles replied by just giving a grin and thumbs up and motioned to her to take up the crash position.

He turned to the young girl and said. 'Okay pet when I tell you I want you to hold onto me as firmly as you can and I'll wrap my arms around you very tightly – understand?'

She looked at him and just nodded, obviously very scared but trying to look brave.

Niles turned round and made sure that every one of the passengers was adopting the correct crash position. He felt the landing flap lowered and knew they were on the final approach to land.

Dino and Johnny had their hands full and although the gale force winds had reduced the approach speed to less than fifty knots they had to cope with the strong turbulence generated by the wind passing over the tops of the trees.

As Dino started to flare the aircraft just prior to touch down he said to Johnny. 'Right Johnny after touch down cut the starboard engine and operate the fire bottle and with luck we wont have to worry about an engine fire if things get too rough'.

As the Dakota's tail touched down, Dino eased the control column hard back to achieve maximum aerodynamic braking whilst Johnny cut the engine and initiated the fire bottle.

The aircraft slithered along the old logging track bouncing and bucking but the strong wind kept the aircraft weather-cocked into wind up the line of the logging track. As there were no wheels lowered the aircraft quickly decelerated but even so Dino still found himself subconsciously trying to use the wheel brakes until he realised how foolish his efforts were. However with the howling wind on the nose Dino found he still had plenty of aerodynamic control with the rudder which enabled him to keep the aircraft lined up with the logging track right up to the point of the aircraft just coming to rest.

The aircraft ground to a halt. Apart from some items of loose luggage that had cascaded into the aisle no damage seemed to have been done. Outside the edge of the hurricane finally caught up with them and it started to rain. The falling rain made the hot engines sizzle and give off steam. This caused a moment of panic as some passengers thought the engines were about to catch fire. Niles quickly put their minds to rest when he roared. 'That's not smoke coming off the engines you bloody fools, that's steam – so stop panicking'.

The passengers looked around wide eyed at one another scarcely believing that they were down on the ground and uninjured.

For the moment they were safe.

Chapter 6

Barranquilla

Francesco put the phone down and stood and pondered for a moment. Senator Jackson had phoned him and told him who the Special Forces were who had been training the Colombian Field Force. He thought over the ramifications on what he had just been told. This could cause the Cartel serious problems. Although he'd never come up against them, the reputation of the British SAS was well documented and he had no wish to tangle with them.

He sauntered back to the party that was now in full swing but he decided to get their new plans into action as quickly as possible. He nodded to his five colleagues and motioned them towards his study.

Domingo closed the door and waited until his colleagues were seated and he had their full attention.

'I've just had Senator Jackson on the phone and it appears that the Special Forces unit we have been getting a hard time from are British SAS. This statement immediately grabbed the attention of all sat round the table. Although none of them had knowledge or experience of the SAS they were all aware of the Unit's reputation. '

Therefore it means'. Continued Francesco, 'that getting our new processing plants up and running way out in the rain forest away from any prying eyes as soon as possible - like yesterday!. Pedro - I want you to set the first two camps up near the old logging sites on the banks of the river Meta. You will have to use our Super Puma chopper to get the initial stores and weapons out there. Do you think you can manage it starting tomorrow Pedro?'

The Cartel had decided to moved their plants much further from habitation towards the east which meant that they would have to use helicopters and fixed wing aircraft to transport the coca leaves to the processing plants and then fly the paste back out again.

'I think so, apart from this shitty weather caused by the hurricane. The two sites we discussed have got some old buildings still standing so we can use them for temporary shelter until we can chopper the rest of the stuff out' said Pedro. 'I also think we may have to hire or buy some more choppers as we are going to be using more aircraft than we've ever needed before'.

'Well, we have two Super Pumas as well as a couple of old Hue's. At the moment the Hue's are unserviceable but should be back on line in the next three days or so and that should get things started. We have got to get our Lab's out of the way of these new Patrols or we will go out of business' added Francesco'.

'Jesus! Franco DeNero said. 'With all these choppers going up and down like a brides fucking panties aren't they going to attract a lot of attention'.

'No way', said Francesco.' That part of the country is practically uninhabited, there will be next to no one there and the choppers have been briefed to make their approach low level to disguise the landing areas'.

'Al, will you make sure that there are plenty of weapons

available to the guards and I don't want anyone poking their noses in to our fucking affairs. Any bastard not known to us gets wasted. Okay!

Al just nodded; he was a man of few words but never short on action.

'Right hombres!', Francesco addressed the remainder. 'Let's get things under way, the weather is going to get pretty grotty during the next few days and we need to get this operation up and running before the weather closes us down'.

'What about the logging companies that work in the area?'. Teddy Garcia said.

'No problem', shrugged Franco DeNero. 'They have closed down their operations over a year ago in response to pressure from UN to prevent any further depletion of the rain forest. Mind you' he continued. 'They are being paid millions of dollars for not logging – not bad pay for sitting on your arse and doing nothing. Further more most of the area down there is unexplored and uninhabited'.

'Okay then. I guess that is all I have for the moment other than to emphasise that we get our arses in gear and start this thing moving. It goes without saying that we keep all this information to ourselves. None of our families need to know of what we have just discussed. All agree?' The five nodded in unison.

'Back to the party' hombres and lets have a good time', he concluded.

Chapter 7

Logging Track

Initially, nobody moved in the aircraft, and all that could be heard was the hissing and spitting of the rain as it poured onto the hot engines. Some of the women were still close to panic. But Niles rapidly asserted his positive personality

He quickly unfastened his seat belt. Unwrapped the blanket folded around the young girl. 'What's your name?' He asked

'Karen.'

'And I'm her mother, Mrs Fields', she said, 'But please call me Jackie'.

Now that she was stood up Niles could see that Jackie Fields was a very attractive woman indeed. She was very tall and willowy with first class legs. She had beautiful dark auburn hair a longish face with very wide set blue eyes. She had a generous mouth and a ready smile. Even in the middle of the rain forest she managed to project an air of class and haughtiness and at the same time be approachable, a rare combination.

'Okay, please follow me quickly we must get off this

aircraft as soon as we can', said Niles followed by a roar of, 'every one out in case of fire'.

He quickly guided people down to the passenger door of the aircraft whilst keeping an eye open for anyone who appeared to be injured. Luckily, due to the aircraft's slow speed at touch down, all the passengers appeared to be just shook up and no one had sustained a serious injury. However, it did not stop some of them complaining that it was raining and they didn't want to get wet.

He ignored them and jumped out the main door first. Due to the aircraft's retracted undercarriage it was only about three feet from the doorsill to the ground so he helped Karen down first followed by her mother.

Jackie Fields was very impressed with the ease in which she was lifted clear of the door by Niles. Not so much by his show of strength but with the lack of effort he displayed. It seemed to cost him no effort at all. She also noticed that he helped all the women passengers down from the door with the same apparent lack of effort and some of the women were no lightweights either.

Niles gathered the passengers together, 'Right!' Every one up wind of the aircraft until we are sure it's not going to brew up', shouted Niles trying to make himself heard above the noise of the pouring rain and the hissing steam as the water ran off the hot aircraft's engines.

Again, a few of the women started to complain about getting their hair wet but they all reluctantly moved up the logging track into wind away from the aircraft.

Niles noticed that his first impression of the film cast was not far off the mark. Many of them were already beginning to act like spoilt kids and others were already acting as though they were going into shock.

'I'm going back to see if the crew needs any assistance', said Niles. 'Once the danger of fire has died down we can all get back into the aircraft and decide on a course of action'.

'Well get a fucking move on', snapped Nathan Costello. 'We are getting fucking soaked out here'.

'I thought I could rely on you to engage your mouth before switching on your brain'. Snarled Niles, he turned before Costello could reply and cautiously approached the cockpit of the aircraft.

'Dino, Johnny, are you guys okay?' enquired Niles. The crew, being at the front of the aircraft often take the brunt of any crash landings. In fact many crews remark that they were part of the 'designed crumple' zone in all aircraft.

'With you in a moment', called Dino. 'I'm just getting Johnny free, He's taken a bang on the head but he's okay now'.

Johnny had a bruise the size of a pigeon's egg sprouting out of his forehead and had been slightly concussed but was already beginning to recover. He was quite a tough hombre.

Niles gave Dino a hand to get the still dazed Johnny out the aircraft and upwind.

'I don't think she will catch fire now', said Dino. 'But we better give it another ten minutes before using the aircraft as a shelter'.

'What about the Emergency Crash Locator Beacon, do you think it is activated?' asked Niles.

'Well it was armed before take off and with the 'G' Forces during the crash landing it should have switched ON. But with this bag of shit', said Johnny. 'I wouldn't bank on it'.

The rain continued to lash down with increased fury, which made life unpleasant, but it at least decreased the chances of the engine catching fire. The film crew were now really beginning to bitch in earnest.

'How much longer to we have to stay out here in this pissing rain' snarled Peter Milo the middle aged singer of some repute. 'Surely the aircraft is not going to burn now?'

Niles shot him a 'drop dead' look and started to survey the area around the downed Dakota. Unfortunately the torrential rain reduced visibility to twenty to thirty yards. But it was possible to make out that apart from the logging track they had landed on they were surrounded by Rain Forest. Their situation did not look good.

After about five minutes he went back to the aircraft, climbed in through the door and found a wooden crate in the baggage hold. He dumped it below the door sill where it could be used as a step to help the passengers up into the aircraft. He got the nod from Dino and motion for the passengers to re-emplane.

Once every one was back in the aircraft and had finished bitching Dino, as the captain of the aircraft took control of the proceedings and decided to hold a conference and discuss what their next move should be.

'Can I have every ones attention please, its normal procedure,' began Dino, 'to remain with the aircraft for two days before deciding on any other action. This is based on the supposition that it easier to spot a grounded aircraft from the air rather than people. As you heard us discussing outside we are not sure whether the Emergency Crash Locator Beacon is working or not. Further more, with this low cloud and heavy rain no aircraft or even helicopter is going to be able to get to us until this weather improves'

'So what's the point in remaining here if no one knows where we are?' Nathan Costello snarled.

'Well for a start', said Niles, 'If we remain with the aircraft for the moment we will be reasonably dry and further more if the Crash Locator is transmitting then the signal will be picked up by an orbiting satellite that's programmed to listen out on 121.5mhz or 243.0mhz. This will relay a position to the nearest Search and Rescue (SAR) station so that rescue arrangements can be made'

'Are you sure about that?' said Dino giving Niles a puzzled look.

'About the satellite; yes I'm positive', said Niles. 'They

orbit this area at least once a day and they can pinpoint a distress beacon to within about one hundred meters. When and whether the report will be acted on depends on the authority that the information is passed to. By the way Dino do you have any idea where we are in Colombia?'

'Not really', said Dino. 'We were IMC for some time trying to get over the mountains and then when we broke cloud the static electricity screwed our ADF up and we were too low to raise the VOR at Bogotá airport. When we broke cloud I had expected to see the Llanos, the grasslands to the east of Bogotá. I figure we must be much further south as this area is typical rain forest'.

'What about this logging track we landed on?' queried Peter Milo. Who in fact, was quite a famous singer in his time but was now definitely getting towards the end of his career, 'It should lead us back to civilisation, although I must admit, it does not look as though it has been used for some time'.

'It probably hasn't', replied Johnny. 'Brazil, Venezuela and Colombia are being paid millions of dollars by the G7 countries to cease logging for ten years in an effort to try and preserve the rain forests. So the chances are that this track has not been used for more than a year'.

'How's your head Johnny?' Niles enquired

'Not too bad - though it is still aching'

Niles looked around the cabin. 'Do we have any survival provisions on the aircraft Dino?

Dino pointed to two bin lockers adjacent the main door. 'There will be an inflatable life raft in each locker and there should be some survival rations in each'

'Right, let's get our selves organised and see what provisions we can muster up in case we do have to trek out of here', declared Niles.

'You sure have a big mouth', snarled Costello. 'Mister Chase here has already told me of your spoof to get on this aircraft and that you are nothing to do with 'Global Home Movies'. All you are is a god dam chauffeur so when we want your advice Mister we'll ask for it'.

Costello was a typical self-made little bumptious American arsehole but Sandy Niles had to be careful. The last thing he wanted at this stage was too many questions about his personal history. However, he wasn't going to take any such crap from a little cretin like Costello. Further more for the last three years he had been living off his wits and felt that these arseholes needed his support more than he needed theirs.

'Listen you little bag of shit', as he jammed two of his fingers up Costello's nostrils forcing him upwards until he was standing on his tiptoes. 'As of now you and your little band of arseholes are on your own; I'll make my own arrangements from now on and you can make yours'.

Chapter 8

Washington USA

The Secretary to the US Defence Secretary rapped the door of his office. 'Come in', said George Fields as he continued to write a memo.

'What is it Grace?' he enquired as his secretary came into the room. 'And before you say anything may I say how gorgeous you are looking this morning, as you do every morning'. He gave her a boyish grin, which took any rancour out of his remarks. He always went out of his way to compliment his staff and Mrs Dalton was worth her weight in gold to him. She was calm, efficient and had a 60 gigabyte memory and more to the point she was immune to his flattery.

'I am afraid we have just received some bad news about your wife and daughter. Apparently they and the rest of the Global Home Movie Company boarded an old Dakota to fly clear of the hurricane that hit Venezuela and they have just disappeared over the hinterland of Colombia.' Grace Dalton looked very white and shaken as she delivered the bad news to George Fields.

'Jesus' he gasped. 'Has there been any news of their where abouts. How long have they been missing?'

'We had a message from Venezuela not long after they took off but the weather conditions were atrocious and it seems about half an hour after they got airborne Air Traffic lost radio contact with them. Is there any one I can contact for you sir?' She added.

'Yes, get me Chris Brooker on the phone. He's our Head Security guy In the Embassy down in Bogotá and I'll lean on him to make sure a rescue team is jacked up straight away. And after that, get me the Director of the DEA, he has interests in that neck of the woods and further more he owes me some favours. He should be able to pull some strings down there and get things moving'.

'I'm on my way', replied Grace as she moved to the door. 'Do you want me to phone any of your family whilst waiting to get through to Bogotá?'

'Not for the moment. I'd like to have a little more information about the accident and their well being before phoning her Mother and Father'.

George Fields sat there thinking and regretting at ever agreeing to his wife and daughter flying off to the wilds of South America to make a film in which his daughter had quite a large part. He'd had some misgivings when his wife had first broached the subject of Karen being involved with the film being made down in Venezuela. But they had both been so keen on the venture that he'd not the heart to turn them down. Anyway, once the two of them had ganged up on him there was no way he could have changed their minds.

However, things had definitely turned out for the worse. At the moment George Fields did not know whether either of them had been hurt or killed. The original plan had been that once they had finished the film they were going to visit Angel Falls in Venezuela. Then fly to Caracas by a feeder airline and get the Scheduled Jet to the States. Obviously the Hurricane 'Judy' had changed all that and it now transpires they and the Film Company were wrecked in the rain forest somewhere in Colombia.

Grace buzzed from the outer office. 'I have Chris Brooker on the secure line from Bogotá'.

'Thanks Grace put me through please'. Fields drummed his fingers impatiently whilst waiting.

'Brooker here', the tinny voice came over the secure line. 'What can I do for you Mr Secretary?'

'It's George Fields here and I have a major problem. I'm not sure if you are aware of it but apparently an aircraft has come down somewhere Southeast of Bogotá with about sixteen American Citizens on board including my wife and daughter and not unnaturally I'm extremely concerned as to their where about and what their condition is. Do you know of the accident and if so can you give me any details?'

'As matter of fact the SAR people have informed us that a distress signal has been detected in that area from an Orbiting Satellite', said Brooker. 'Unfortunately the weather there is so bad that we can't get any air search in there until tomorrow or the day after. I don't wish to add to your worries', continued Brooker. 'But the natives in that area are almost exclusively involved with the Drug trade and they are not particularly fond of American Citizens. In fact they have a nasty habit of making hostages of any outsiders and demanding money for their release'.

'Okay, so that's the good news', growled Fields sardonically. 'Now give me the bad news, how the hell do we get assistance to our people and get them out without them falling into the hands of the unfriendlies'.

'As a matter of fact I have just had Senator Sam Jackson on the phone going apeshit about some Brit' SAS detachment that are down here training the Field Police Force.' added Brooker. 'He claims that as the Chairman of the Special Select Committee on Drugs he should have been informed of their presence down here. Anyway, I told him that we don't control the deployment of the British SAS. But as speed is of the essence then our best option is for me to contact my counterpart in the British Embassy and see if we can get them to the crash site as soon as possible. I figure it would take two or three days just to get clearance to get American Forces to be involved.

'Do you think the Brit's will agree? After all, there could be shooting and someone could be hurt or even killed', said Fields.

'I'm sure they'll agree, apparently the British Embassy here have had more problems trying to keep the SAS guys out of fights than anything else. They are not supposed to go out with the Field Force Police on operations. But according to my Informant there have been three or four SAS on every operational sortie conducted by the Field Force Police since their arrival. And this type of operation is right up their street'.

'Leave it with me for the moment', continued Brooker. 'I'm sure we can get these guys out to the crash location as soon as the weather permits. And as soon as I've any news I'll get back to you straight away'.

'You've taken a hell of a weight of my shoulders Chris. I won't forget this buddy. Be sure to call me when you have any news what so ever'.

'No problem'. And with that Chris Brooker rang off.

Fields buzz his secretary and said, 'cancel the call to the Director of the DEA for the moment Grace. I think we have things in hand with Brooker down in Colombia. If I need DEA assistance I'll come back to them later'.

'Consider it done boss'.

Chapter 9

Bogotá

The SAS Troopers had cruised around the capital trying to find the club that had been recommended by the Colonel. After much misdirection and being driven by (would you believe it) a driver who came from Cali finally found the nightclub they sought. With the noses of a highly .trained 'Blood hound' they had found it. They'd already visited three that Saturday evening and they had been garbage. At last they'd found the one they were looking for. It looked like the real McCoy. Inside it was absolutely 'heaving' - It was called the Penguin club, apparently two decades ago one could only get into the club if dressed in Tuxedos. Further more, this was the club that the Chief of Police had booked them a table. Otherwise they wouldn't have got in. The dress code had been relaxed over the past twenty years. This was just as well because Rusty Irons and his cohorts couldn't have rustled up a Dinner Jacket between them let alone a Tuxedo.

The entrance to the club was small, enabling a small number of people trying to get in to create an illusion of popularity. Inside the hall rapidly expanded in a circular manner with entrances to the two lifts on the left and a marbled staircase on the right, both giving access the hotel accommodation situated on the two upper floors. The entrance to the club itself was located opposite the main street entrance via another smaller marbled staircase. In the centre of the circular hall was the reception area for both the club and hotel accommodation. This was manned by two receptionist - both very attractive girls - one in particular was an absolute stunner.

After showing the tickets supplied by Col DeSuza to the club receptionist Rusty and his SAS Troopers tried to chat the two girls up but the pressure of more guest arriving curtailed any further progress. They were escorted from the foyer and directed to a large table which had been pre-booked for them and proceeded to get themselves organised. The interior of the nightclub had been constructed like a small semi circular amphitheatre with rows of tables set up in increments from the centre of the club so that the people at the back still had an excellent view of the Cabaret floor and the small dancing area immediately to its front. The club appeared to have sufficient tables to accommodate around 150 patrons.The dimmed lighting was supplied from six crystal chandeliers which bathed the club with a warm intimate glow. The inside walls were covered in old faked Inca and Mayan tapestries and artefacts. The whole effect was quite stunning if rather garish by Western European standards The cabaret had been going for a good half an hour before the SAS team arrived Once they had sat down there was not a vacant table to be had. Although the team had been given one of the tables at the back they were about six feet higher than those at the front giving them an excellent view of all that was happening.

There must have been over a hundred patrons in the club smoking. Apparently, the phobia about smoking in public buildings had not been registered in Colombia yet. If you didn't smoke before you entered the club you sure as hell did for the duration of your stay, at least passively so.

Rusty (Sgt Irons) organised the seating so that they all had a good view of the floorshow, which was now in full swing. Although the Spanish dialogue of the performing Colombian Magician was a little fast for the team they were able to follow his act quite clearly.

The local Colombians had all been there for some time and were now well into the party spirit. Almost all were well liquored up and giving vent to their exuberate nature, shouting and whistling at the floorshow and enjoying themselves.

The cost of their evening was being borne by the Colombian Police so the SAS guys decided to stick to the local beer to keep the costs down and they were also mindful of the fact that they had another night to go and needed to be 'switched on' first thing Monday morning.

After their second round of beers the guys had really settled down and were entering into the spirit of the party, shouting, whistling and singing with the best of the locals. Not to be out done Cpl (smudge) Grimes called on the management to,' Roll back the carpet so everyone could see the floor show'.

It was not long before their boisterous behaviour began to attract the attention of some of the locals at the adjoining tables. People began by lifting their drinks and toasting, 'Manchester United are a dam good team'. Liverpool was also getting some acclaim and the party looked to go on and become a real swinger.

Trooper Lance, who was sitting at the extreme left hand end of the SAS party's with nobody behind him minding his own business. When he suddenly noticed this gorgeous creature had sidle up along side of him ostensible to get a better view of the floor show, He realised she was the 'stunner' receptionist they'd seen on entering the club. In her late teens or very early twenties, she was about five feet six inches tall, with that beautiful honey toned skin that so many of the Latino women are blessed with and legs that went on for ever! Her long jet-black hair was complimented by her almond shaped dark brown eyes with quite the longest eyelashes Lance had ever seen – she could have swept the floor with them. Her figure was slightly too voluptuous to make any fashion magazine but she portrayed sensuality not normally associated with models. Knowing that the country was predominantly Catholic and most young girls were strictly chaperoned, he took little notice at first. But after a few minutes, she edge even closer towards him until her right thigh was gently resting against his shoulder.

Rusty Irons gave Cpl Finnegan (Fingers) his mate, sitting next to him, a dig in the ribs with his elbow.

'It looks as though Sir Lancelot is about to strike again', he grinned. 'Get a gander at the look on her face. Talk about take me I'm all yours – she couldn't make it any clearer if she sent him a 'telegram'.

Lancelot (Tpr Lance - he'd achieved this nickname through his ability to bed just about every woman that laid eyes on him). Was beginning to get excited but at this stage was not quite sure what to do. He was certain that she was not a hooker and although skimpily dressed her clothes looked extremely expensive.

She was now rubbing her right hip gently against his left shoulder and it was far too blatant a movement to be accidental. Lance gentle slipped his hand down onto her right calf and trailed his fingers gently up and down, making the caress look almost accidental (just in case he had misread her signals). Her only response was to move against him even closer.

Lancelot was now becoming extremely excited, he had always been able to pull women and in fact, some had even knocked on his hotel door on previous occasions for the sole reason of climbing into his pants. He stood six feet three with the classical 'V' shaped physique, lean and muscular with dark hair wavy hair and craggy good looks. But his most remarkable feature was his startling blue eyes. Whenever he gazed at women it seemed they automatically wanted to start taking their clothes off. But this girl was something else - she was knock down bloody gorgeous and obviously, (by the look of her coiffure, clothes and shoes) from a well off family.

Lance could hardly credit his luck but there was no doubt about it, she was definitely making overtures to him. He now began to stroke her leg in a more positive but still slow and gentle manner. His caresses were rewarded as she started to gently tremble. Lance looked over his left shoulder and could see no one was behind them, and those to the front, were too busy watching the floorshow. His caresses now became much bolder. The girl's trembling increased even more and her thighs began to involuntary twitch and as Lance's hand advanced above her knee her teeth started to chatter with either excitement or fright. Lance was not sure which, all he did know was that it was getting him bloody excited. The most remarkable thing was that the girl's eyes never left the floorshow and to all intent and purposes Lance did not exist. By now he had the biggest and most painful erections he had ever experienced. He was also getting the full attention of his comrades who were all digging one another in the ribs and trying to hide their grins while swigging their drinks.

Suddenly the she gripped his shoulder, and gasped. 'Come Hombre'.

He rose unsteadily to his feet as though he had been hypnotised. His brain had definitely left his cranium and was now firmly ensconced in his penis. It was quite obvious that at this stage Lance was no longer able to make rational decisions. His only desire at this moment was to bed the gorgeous creature that was now towing him towards the exit.

Rusty Irons was immediately aware there could be some problems if no one kept an eye on Lance in his present excited state.

'Pedro', he said. 'Follow them and see that Lance gets into no trouble. You speak the lingo better than any of us and you could pass as a local'.

'Piss off! He's big enough to look after himself', declared Pedro Gonzales. 'Why the hell should I miss the floor show just to wet nurse Lance while he gets his end away?'

'Normally I would agree', said Rusty. 'But you saw the look on his face, the poor bastard pussy smitten he doesn't even know which end is up. Once you have established where they are shacking up let me know and we'll take turns at keeping an eye on him'.

By now the gorgeous Colombian bird was leading a dazed Lance by the hand out the door to an elevator in the foyer just outside the clubs entrance which led to the accommodation upstairs. Pedro slipped into the same elevator as Lance and his bird. They weren't even aware of his presence. Both pairs of eyes were burning holes in one another. As Lance caressed the girl's derriere with one hand and he nibbled her neck with his well-manicured teeth.

They all debussed at the second floor and Pedro noted the number of the room – 9B and returned to the lift and back to the floorshow. He was fucked if he was going to miss any more of the floor show just to keep watch outside while inside Lance screwed the arse of his latest conquest.

Lance kicked the door to as he entered the room and the girl simple threw her arms around him and wrapped her long legs around his waist making it obvious that this was not going to be just a platonic evening's entertainment.

Up to this point neither had spoken a word to each other than to moan or groan.

'What's your name?' gasped Lance.

'Maria and what's your Senor?'

'Edward' grunted Lance as he shuffled them towards the bed. 'I think you're the most beautiful women I have ever seen'. Even as he said it he felt what a hammy chat up line but was surprised to realise that he really meant it.

'Oh Eduardo, I thought you were so beautiful when I saw you sat there with your friends. I had to get to know you. Please understand that I have never done anything like this before'. Strangely enough Lance believed her.

She stood before Lance still trembling with a complete look of acquiescence and looked so vulnerable but at the same time desirable,

'Don't be too gentle with me' she hissed and slid her hand down the front of his slacks and grasped his raging penis that was clamouring for entry.

Lance decided to take charge in no uncertain manner; although Maria had behaved in a very wanton manner something about her manner convinced him that she'd little or no experience at such encounters.

He began slowly to remove her skimpy light clothing with his large bony hands relishing in the vision of her gradually exposed body as he peeled off each layer of clothing calmly and gently and reduced her to her underwear. She was breath taking! Lance already excited, felt a further surge of excitement; his penis already engorged grew even further until it was literally painful; at the sight of this incredible creature before him; Maria simple stood there trembling with excitement and then suddenly; she began to rip Lance's shirt off over his shoulders whilst he took off her bra' followed by her brief silken panties.

Maria finally got Lance's slacks off and ran her hands over his deep chest and powerful shoulder noting how the muscles in his chest felt almost like warm marble. She realised that with all the caressing she had felt in the

Night-club that her excitement was already at fever pitch and she wanted Eduardo in her NOW and to hell with the consequences.

But Edward was an extremely experienced lover and knew dam fine that if he entered her now he would not be able to control himself and it would all be over in a matter of minutes. He gentle manoeuvred her to the bed and stretched her out so he could take a long lingering look at her perfectly proportioned body. He could still not credit how beautiful she was and how the hell he had been so lucky.

'Please! Please!' she whimpered and tried to mount his rampant penis. But he slid his hips to one side so to avoid entrance. He wanted to explore the marvels of this gorgeous body and take his time over it. He started to kiss her with long lingering kisses at the same time easing his finger into her secret domain and gentle caressing the magic button.

Her response was instantaneous, she levered her hips off the bed desperately seeking to engulf his enormous cock. But Lance continued to evade and brought her to a shattering climax with his finger causing her to scream. 'No no, I want you inside me!

He neither knew nor cared as to whether she had taken any precaution against getting pregnant and frankly he didn't care. All he knew was that he had to have this woman now come hell or high water.

However, he was now definitely in control. She was now so sensitive down there that he could pleasure her as she had never been pleasured before. He gentle eased himself into her knowing that she was now ready to respond without any clitoral stimulation. He felt her gasp as his penis probed for entry and then she gave a little cry followed by a gasp as he affected entry. He slowly eased himself in until he could feel her cervix resisting further progress. It felt as though his cock was being immersed in warm honey. It was only a matter of seconds before she began to heave her hips up towards him and was soon experiencing a further violent climax. It was now that Lance began to thrust in earnest. They were soon covered in sweat and slithering around together like two mating eels. And when she reached her third violent climax he didn't even pause but continued to ride her to a fourth and fifth one, after which, she appeared to have one long continuous orgasmic climax before he finally exploding into her.

Maria threw her arms around him and was sobbing quite loudly with the emotional strain. Lance cradled the girl in his arms making soft crooning noises to try and comfort her.

'Edward Lance', he thought, 'you're in deep shit. There's no way you are going to be able to get up in the morning and walk away from this relationship'. He was experiencing emotions that he had never felt before and realised that if he had never been in love before then it he sure as hell was now. Prior to this he had been a life member of the,' Wham, Bang, thank you Mam' and then of into the night. They finally fell into an exhausted sleep cuddled up like two spoons in a drawer.

The floorshow was just beginning to wind up and there were now three girls in tow at the SAS table. A member of the team had gone up at half hourly intervals to check that Lance wasn't about to be bounced by some jealous husband/ boy friend. The general consensus of opinion was that they would be lucky to see Lance before they were due back to camp on Monday morning.

It was almost midnight when who should appear at their table but their 'Rupert', Captain, all singing, all dancing, all weather Tony Bryant,

'Jesus', looked what the bloody cat has just dragged in' smirked Cpl (Hatch) Hezeltine.

'Don't worry, I haven't come here to slum with you bloody shower' laughed Bryant. 'I'm afraid I come with bad news. We have to report back to camp straight away. I'll brief you on the way back once we are clear of the local ears'.

'We are all here except Eddy Lance and to get him we will need a bloody crow bar to separate him from his latest bit of crumpet', said Rusty Irons as he got to his feet.

Don't tell me he has scored again', laughed Bryant. 'Christ! No wonder you call him Lancelot, I've never come across anyone who could bed women so quickly'

'Yea, well this one is no ordinary pick up Boss she is absolutely gorgeous and she would even have you with your tongue hanging out. If you had stood between them they would have melted you down, I don't think they had spoken more than two words before she took him off to her room', said Rusty Irons.

'I checked the hotel register boss and her name is Maria Mendoza' interrupted Pedro Gonzales. 'And from what the clerk said her father is a very rich man, so Lance may have to box a bit clever on this one'.

'Right! - Lets get him out of his pit and be on our way', and Bryant turned and led the team up to the second floor.

It took four or five good thumps on the door before Lance appeared with a towel wrapped round the lower half of his body. To say he looked knackered was to put it mildly.

Before Captain Bryant could utter a word Hatch Hezeltine chirped in. 'Trooper Lance, you have just appeared on Candid Camera and your performance for the past hour has been viewed on video in the Nightclub. You will be please to know that the jury assessed your performance; nine point three out of ten'.

'Fuck off', snarled Lance and attempted to throw a punch at Hezeltine but as he swung his fist the towel fell off his waist and he ended up in having to make an undignified grab for it.

'You might also like to know Trooper Lance, that you

scored very high marks for execution but the consensus of opinion was that you could have even higher marks for style if you had stuck a Union Jack up your jacksee during the vinegar strokes', added Cpl Smudge Grimes who was determined to get his two cents worth in.

'Enough! Enough!' snarled Captain Bryant. 'I'm not here to conduct a fucking circus. There's been a flap on. We have to return to camp and be ready to move into the interior sometime tomorrow depending on the weather. You! Lance, have got ten minutes to say farewell to your bird and get your arse in gear. Meet us in the foyer. Okay.

'Right boss - ten minutes and I'll be there'.

Eleven minute later the whole section was crowded into one Range Rover and on they're way back to Base.

'I'll just give you a brief rundown on what's happened and then we can have a more detailed briefing before we deploy into the ulu', shouted Bryant over the vehicle's noise.

'It appears that an American Film Company which was making a movie about the American Peace Corps and Rain Forest Conservation in Venezuela was fleeing from the Hurricane 'Judy'. Apparently the only aircraft available at the film location was an old Dakota that was planned to fly them as far as Bogotá where they would then changed to a schedule jet to take them back to the States. It seems that the aircraft was forced well south of its intended track and ended up having to make an emergency landing somewhere south east of our base.

The Crash Locator Beacon is only – or was only, working intermittently so we do have a fairly good idea where they went down. As soon as the weather lifts we are going to be 'choppered' into the crash location or as near to as the pilot can get. Our main worry is that the only other people out in that neck of the woods are likely to be unfriendly and we will therefore be going in fully armed and must be prepared to do some shooting if necessary'.

'How many in the film party boss and trust the bastards to screw up the only weekend we have had off for two months?' Queried Cpl Grimes.

'We are not sure of the numbers but if my knowledge of the old Dak's correct it couldn't have carried more that fifteen to twenty at these heights and temperatures. However, I'm sure that by the time we are ready to go in we'll have more information'.

Chapter 10

Southeast of Bogotá

The weather was now improving. Domingo and his colleagues started their helicopter operations from a forward fixed wing strip located to the east of Bogotá. By the morning of the following day the sun was beginning to make its presence felt. Most of the heavy rain clouds had now disappeared apart from odd patches of mist rising from the tops of the trees like steam off a boiler. The Rain Forest was coming alive again as the insects crawling from cover in anticipation of catching the warmth of the early morning sun making their presence known. Rain drops glistening like diamonds on the green foliage acted like miniature prisms scattering the light in all directions causing small rainbows to quickly form and then suddenly to collapse. This was the Rain Forest at its most beautiful.

Their operation was now in full swing. They'd started flying the prefabricated parts of their Processing Lab's as under slung loads on the helicopter's cargo hook out to a destination which was located only five miles from the downed Dakota. This was not far from an old disused

Emerald mine. The rationale for building the Laboratories here was that it was deep inside the Rain Forest, far from any inhabitation. At the same time, any activity observed by over flying American Satellites would be mistaken for work being carried on new mining operations.

Pablo Ferreira had expected to have the place up and running within the week of the airlift commencing.

The operation was going well. They now had two Super Pumas, each capable of lifting 4000lbs and with the improving weather they had both made three trips. The initial one consisted of the workers and six guards, with a small arsenal of weapons to fight off any Police or Guerrillas who might be stumble on the area.

'How long before we can start operating the Laboratories?' Pablo asked the Construction Foreman. Most of the cartel's foremen or boss men as they were referred to, were hulking great brutes inclined to use their fist to establish authority and get thing done; this one was no exception. Well over six feet tall and broad with it. He was built like the preverbal brick built outhouse. Although he was now running to seed his cauliflower ears and broken nose reflected his brutal past – none of his work force dare question his instructions or commands. He was a great believer in the old Axiom, 'Might is right'.

'Give me two days and I'll have two buildings erected and then the Lab' technicians can start operating while I get the roof covered with turf and soil for camouflage and to cut out any Infra Red signature.

'Good', said Pablo nodding his head in satisfaction. 'And don't forget that we don't want any one nosing around here. If you see or catch anyone we want them to disappear – permanently!

'You've got it boss; any fucker we catch here will disappear for good. You could bury an army out here and no one would be any the wiser'.

'Good! You got it right in one Carlos - Right, I'm going back to the base to turn the wick up under their arses and get things moving quicker. By the way, I don't want any of your Peons wandering off at night and getting lost. Anyone that does so is on their own; we are not sending any search parties out to look for them. They will just have to get their TST punched', as Pablo turned towards the Puma helicopter.

'What's TST boss?'

'It's a gringo expression and means get your," Tough Shit Ticket punched"', laughed Ferreira as he climbed into the cabin of the helicopter.

Pablo Ferreira was quite please with the speed at which new Processing Laboratories were being constructed. The last of the cloud associated with the hurricane was disappearing to the north and the sun was now shining and the visibility was unlimited. If construction work continued at the present rate he was going to have one Processing Lab' up and running before the week was out and the second one well on its way to completion. Good progress despite the terrible weather that had delayed the initial deployment of the working parties for 24hours. Things were now progressing nicely.

Carlos Barseos, the big burly foreman of the site was a man of mixed racial descent. His mother was a Colombian national but his father was an American miner who had worked in the Emerald Mines about fifty miles south of their present location. His father had done a runner and never returned when he was about ten years old and as a consequence, he had harboured a grudge against Americans ever since. However the one good characteristic he'd inherited from his long gone father was his 'get up and go'. Members of the Cartel had quickly appreciated this and he was their automatic choice to get things moving in the field.

'Right you guys, lets have those sections of the Portakabin over here and the first thing I want constructed is a dry and safe place for all our weapons', roared the foreman.

He indicated to the workers exactly where the cabin was to be built – clear of the helicopter pad and into the edge of the jungle hidden from view of any one over flying the location.

Although there were a few logging tracks and fire breaks cut into this area of the rain forest it was now almost completely uninhabited. Never the less the foreman was determined to get the Processing Lab' and all its associated buildings well out of sight from any prying eyes. He was also determined to post pickets during the night to ensure that no strangers inadvertently or otherwise wandered into the complex.

The fixed wing landing strip associated with the construction of the new labs was about eighty miles North West of the jungle location. It was here that Al Menzies was supervising the unloading of the Fixed Wing aircraft - the Short Skyvan. It was transporting the men and material for the Laboratories from Bogotá Airport to this strip on the Llanos.

The Cartel had decided to buy the aircraft instead of hiring them and thus hopefully keep the area of the new Laboratories a secret. The cost of purchasing the two Super Pumas alone came to sixteen million dollars and a further two million dollars for the Short Skyvan. This was the amount that the Cartel was prepared to pay in an endeavour to keep the locations secret.

The Super Puma landed adjacent to the fixed wing strip and Pablo Ferreira jumped clear of the chopper before the Rotors had even run down. The strip was a 'heaving' scene of intense activity. Scores of workers were running around unloading stores from the Skyvan, stacking them prior to being loaded onto the helicopters for transit to the Jungle location. There were also two huge fuel bladders waiting to be lifted out to the jungle site to facilitate the refuelling of the choppers out there, this would enable them to carry a bigger payload of stores outbound with a reduced amount of fuel, and then refuel before returning to the strip.

'How's it going at this end Al', Pablo raise his hand and waved to Al as he approached.

'Great, now the fucking weather has improved it's going like clockwork' he indicated the Skyvan which had finished unloading and was now departing to pick up another load from Bogotá. 'I figure three more loads by the Skyvan will see all our equipment clear of Bogotá and I estimate that by tomorrow evening we will have all our equipment necessary for completion'.

'That's great; I'll fly back on the next return trip to Bogotá and let Francesco know how things are progressing. I think he will be pleased. If he isn't then he fucking well ought to be!'

Pablo studied the scene of activity as he boarded. If all goes well he mused we should be able to reconcile our financial loses in the next three months or so.

Francesco Domingo sat in his temporary office looking please with himself. Forming a coalition with his hitherto competitors could turn out to be one of the best decisions he'd made in the last year. If they continued to work as a team they should easily be able to frustrate the actions of the new Police Field Force. He sat at the desk looking at the computer terminal in front of him. On the desk were two normal phones and the red one fitted with the scrambler devise for talking to their Senator colleagues in the states. It had only been install the previous day. The office was sparsely furnished and apart from his desk and chair there were only another four chairs and two filing cabinets in the room. He had had a large scale map of the area that the new laboratories were located other wise the walls were bare. At the moment there were no soft furnishings. That would have to come later. He had just been informed that they had managed to bribe a member of the newly trained Field Force. Things were looking up. However he'd also heard some rather startling news. The phone rang. He picked it up.

'Hallo Domingo here: Ha! - Pablo; all goes well, that's good news. Now that the weather has improved we should really make good progress. We must have the plants up and running by Friday. We've had to outlay a lot of money on this operation and we want to see some return in the near future. Once the construction is completed I figure we keep one Puma and then sell the other and the Skyvan which will restore most of our financial outlay'.

Francesco eased the phone over to his left ear and continued. 'Bye the way I have just received some disturbing news. Apparently an old Dakota with some American passengers has made a forced landing in your area. They're not too sure of its location but the general area looks too close to ours for comfort. Tell Carlos Barseos, the foreman to keep an eye open for them and whatever he does make sure they don't see or find out where our Plants are located. If he finds them I want him to hold them prisoners and he and his crew to pose as bandits holding them for ransom. Hopefully this will disguise our reason for being out there, and then he is to let us know as soon as possible.'

'I think Al or I should remain at the Plant location until this matter is resolved. Whilst Carlos is a good field man he is not exactly blessed with grey matter,' replied Pablo. 'Further more, Carlos could continue with the construction whilst Al or I lead scouting parties and prevented the gringos from discovering our plants'.

'An excellent idea Pablo, why didn't I think of it, however, if we capture these gringos we will have to consider most carefully what action we are to take. If it can be seen that they all died in the aircraft crash then there is no problem but if it's been established that they've survived, then we'll have to think most carefully before wasting them.'

'I agree and I think the others will agree with your comments but who would you rather return to the Plant location, me or Al?' Pablo Replied.

'I'd rather have you back here' said Francesco'. You're a much better organiser than Al and I think his talents would be better served out there in the Jungle. Al has a God given talent for persuading people to do as they are told. If he catches any of the gringos he must wait until we have decided what to do with them. Impress on Al I don't want him practicing any of his knife skills on the Gringos'.

'Okay, I'll return on the next aircraft to the plant location and brief Al and Carlos personally. I take it you don't want any of the foot soldiers to be included in the brief?'.

'You're bloody right there Pablo', and Francesco rang off.

Francesco sat down and considered the options the Cartel would have if any of the downed Dakota survivors fell into their hands.

The bogus Bandits at the moment would definitely be the safest and most plausible excuse for having armed men out there in that location. Although most Bandits and Guerrillas usually operated much closer to civilisation where their main source of income is from plunder and kidnapping, that is, apart from what they could squeeze out of the dirt poor villagers located close to the Jungle.

'I think its time I gave our friend Senator Jackson a call and see if he has heard of any information about the down aircraft' mused Francesco and dialled the Senators number on the secure phone.

'Sam Jackson here, what can I do for you?'

'Francesco here, afternoon Senator, I'm phoning to enquire about a Dakota aircraft that has crash landed in Colombia about a hundred and fifty miles or so south east of Bogotá. Do you have any idea who the passengers are or the number onboard?'

'As a matter of fact I've only just learnt about it because the Secretary of Defence's Wife and Daughter were onboard and all hells broken out here on Capital Hill and Francesco get this. The British Embassy in Bogotá has been asked to help. And they have responded by sending in the same SAS team that's been causing you problems into the Jungle. There're to try and locate the aircraft and bring out any survivors'

'Shit', snarled Francesco. 'There the last people we need scouting around in that location. Do you know how many they are?'

'Not really - but they normally operate in four man patrols but on this sort of operation, considering the VIPs that were on board I imagine they'll send all their troopers. However, on training missions such as instructing your Field Force Police I would estimate that no more than eight men would be involved'

'Thank you Senator I have twenty men in that area already and can get another dozen out before night fall, so if they do run into any of my men they will get a nasty surprise'.

'For fucks sake', exploded Jackson. 'Your not thinking of having a shooting match with the British SAS are you? These guys are trained in just about every type of warfare you can think of and some forms we haven't thought of, Plus which, the Diplomatic fall out will bury you'.

Francesco held his breath moment. He was dam sure he did not want the Senator to know why the area concern was so sensitive, the less people that new the location of the processing Laboratories the better chance of them remaining secret. 'No, no, senator, it's just that I have been training some our foot soldiers in that area and I don't want the SAS stumbling across their training camps'.

'Okay, if I have any further details I'll pass them onto you, but for fuck sake, keep clear of that SAS team', and with that Senator Jackson rang off.

Francesco sat there reflecting on the conversation he had just had with the Senator. And although he had heard of the SAS he had never come into contact with them or seen how they operate. He decided that they had ploughed too much money into their new operation to allow it to be buggered up by a bloody bunch of interfering Gringos.

Domingo sat for a while considering his options. His thought process (and that of his colleagues) was constrained by his parochial upbringing. When he was young he was too poor to travel abroad from Colombia. After he became rich, his notoriety left him viable to extradition outside its borders. The Cartel's criteria of well trained troops were that of their own thugs they'd recruited to resolve their gang wars. He was convinced that if they could establish a superiority of two or three to one against the SAS, then their thugs would prevail.

It was obviously time to hold another Cartel conference and decide what action to take. However, Francesco had already decided that if push came to shove then they would blow the gringos away and bury them deep in the rain forest where their bodies would never be discovered.

He pondered the various options open to them. If they managed to capture the wife and daughter of the Defence Secretary alive they may well have a very powerful bargaining tool in their hands. It was certainly worth considering and he would discuss with the other members of the Cartel during the next meeting.

Francesco picked up the phone and arranged further meeting of the Cartel, they should all be available except possible Al Menzies, who at this stage, might well be in the bush.

Chapter 11

Rain Forest

After his argument with Costello Sandy Niles decide to hold his council and go his own way. The man was a bloody cretin. The abomination was that he seemed to exert considerable influence over the remainder of the film party and would probably lead them into trouble. It appeared that the film cast were so used to him having the last word as the Film's Director that they were now condition to follow his wishes. Niles also suspected that he suffered from, 'delusions of grandeur'.

He was not sure if the Crash Locator Beacon had activated but it was normal policy to remain with the crash aircraft, the rationale being, that it was easier to spot a crashed aircraft from the air than people. Being spotted by an aircraft was their most likely chance of discovery. Unfortunately, Costello had already convinced the others that walking down the overgrown logging track; would lead them to civilisation. Niles having looked at the logging track considered that it hadn't been used for at least six months – any longer than that and the jungle would have completely encroached and the track would have been almost impassable. Secondary growth within the jungle is harder to transit than primary jungle. The canopy of the giant trees often kept the ground below in deep shadow thus stunting the undergrowth. Although the track was still navigable it was obvious that the passengers were going to have to cut their way through it in some areas. Niles shook his head in frustration and decided that Costello hadn't bloody clue on what he was about to undertake. Further more, although he might be a film director it was quickly becoming obvious that the man couldn't organise a, 'piss up in a brewery'.

'I say we have wasted enough time sitting on our arses and doing nothing', Costello stood in front of the other passengers oozing self importance and demanding their attention.

'But Sandy Niles is quite correct when he said we should remain with the aircraft, it's our best way of being discovered. And further more I insist you listen to me as the Captain of the aircraft I'm still responsible for your safe keeping and I say we stay for at least two days'. Interrupted Dino, the aircraft's Captain.

'Horseshit!' Snarled Costello pointing his finger at Dino, 'it was your incompetence that got us into this situation in the first place so you've had it as far as I'm concerned, we're not going to listen to you any longer. I'm certain that if we walk down this logging track we'll soon reach some form of civilisation.

The logging track in question had been widened to form a firebreak. Even so, it must have been a long time ago as the secondary jungle was already quite well established and in certain parts, anyone using the track was going to have to cut their way through. The weather had now improved and apart from the steam raising from the top of the trees it was a beautiful day. The bright sun had stimulated the birds into a vocal chorus and the various types of humming birds were making their iridescence presence known. This was the rain forest at its most beautiful. The heavy torrential rain had cooled the forest down. The skies were now a crystal clear blue with unlimited visibility. Unfortunately the beauty and tranquillity of the moment belied the hazards of the forthcoming trek down the logging track. Once the effect of the tropical sun got to work on the saturated surface it was not only going to get extremely hot but stifling with the high humidity. Costello and his colleagues had no idea what they were letting themselves in for.

Although the logging track was still wet it seemed firm underfoot and to the uninitiated appeared to offer little problem in walking down it; particularly as the landing Dakota had flattened all the undergrowth for two hundred yards during its emergency landing. However, beyond the touch down point it was going to be hard going. There were in fact two machetes in the aircraft survival pack, but Sandy Niles doubted that any of the film crew had even felt one before let alone used it.

Costello now started to organise his rather nervous colleagues into some form of walking party. Issuing orders and counter orders. Whilst he was doing so, Mrs Fields and her daughter, Karen, approached Niles and looking somewhat nervous said to Niles. 'Sandy, I would feel much safer if you would agree to come along. I don't think Nathan has any idea what he is up to. I really believe he thinks he is still directing a movie'

'I'm sure of it', scoffed Niles. 'The man's a bloody menace, he's living in cloud cuckoo land - he has absolutely no idea what he is up against. And further more, I hate to point this out Mrs Fields but even if you do meet some people down the track I'm not sure that they would be friendly. I appreciate I don't know much about Colombia. But I do know for a fact that the main occupation in the interior is the production of cocaine, so anybody you meet out here is likely to be hostile.'

Niles looked over his shoulder to make sure others where not in ear shot. 'Look Mrs Fields'.

'Please!' She interrupted him. 'Call me Jackie'.

'Okay Jackie, this is what I'll do. I'll follow your party at a distance, keeping well away but maintaining contact. That way should you fall into the wrong hands hopefully, I'll still be in the clear and maybe help to arrange an escape', he grinned to try and ease her worry. 'Look, just think of me as an, "outrider", you know, like the President being driven around in his limousine - he has motorcycle outriders' ready to descend on anyone that tries to attack him'.

'Thanks Sandy, I'll feel much safer if you are around'. But she still looked worried.

Jackie Fields had not really had a chance to study Sandy Niles before, as she had been too worried about getting her daughter clear of the film location before the arrival of the hurricane. But whilst they had all been waiting for the rain to ease off she had had a chance to study him. What she saw she liked. He appeared a shade over six feet and was quite spare in build with long arms with large hands and feet. His forearms were extremely muscular with rather pronounced vein covered with sandy freckles. He'd sandy hair (which presumable, accounted for his first name and she even wondered whether it was his real name or nickname). The colour of his eyes was difficult to discern as they were very deep sunk but as far as she could make out were green with hazel flecks and when he smiled she noticed how the corners of his eyes crinkled. Something one normally associated with people who had an out door occupation. And, he was one of those people who seemed to radiate energy. But the most impressive feature about him was he seemed completely at home in what was to all intents and purposes a strange and hostile environment. Even Dino the aircraft's captain appeared happy to seek Niles's advice.

Her apprehension about Costello was heighten by the fact that she was not a member of the film crew and therefore not conditioned to him having the last word. Even now she was in two minds whether to throw her lot in with Niles or continue with the rest of the crew. But the apparent safety in numbers prevailed so she decided to remain with the rest of the crew.

Their attention was drawn to another outburst from Nathan Costello as he tried once more to make himself heard over the bickering herd. Whilst Nathan was haranguing the film company Dino the aircraft's Captain walked over to Niles and said. 'Are you sure you wont come with us Senor Niles? As the Captain of the aircraft the survivors should really come under my control but Senor Costello wont listen to me, and seems to be able to influence the others as he feels fit'.

'I think he is a walking disaster area and could well lead this crowd into serious trouble' Niles nodded his head in the direction of Costello.

'I can only think', he continued. 'That they are so use to him issuing orders as the as the Film's Director they've been brain washed into thinking that what he says is gospel and frankly I don't want anything to do with him'.

'That's okay for you Senor Niles you have no formal responsibility to the passengers but I have, so I guess I'll just have to tag along and try to keep things in order'.

'I wont be far away', said Niles. 'I've told Mrs Fields that I will be following you at a distance. So if you do bump into the wrong people hopefully, I will elude capture and might be able to help later on. Keep this to your self Dino, I've only told you and Mrs Fields my plans, but the less people that knows of it, the better'.

'Thanks Niles, you have proved to be a man of some resourcefulness and I will feel much easier knowing you are out there if help should be needed. I think I will leave you one of the machetes but I'll take the flare pistol, which is the only thing we can use to scare off any wild animals'.

'The only wild animals you are likely to have problems with are humane ones' smiled Niles. 'Your biggest problem will come from the smallest creatures, Mosquitoes, Leeches and Ticks. You'll find the big animals trying to avoid you, even the Jaguar is supposed to be shy of people'

'I'd better go', Dino nodded towards Costello who had at last got his followers into some form of order. 'I think our Napoleon is ready to trek – do you think you will have any problems following us Niles?'

'You have got to be joking', he laughed. 'You could follow the bloody noise this lot will make from two miles and still know exactly where they are. It's probably the nearest thing to a travelling circus that's ever been seen in the Rain Forest'. He gave Dino a wry grin and a wave of the hand as he bid him goodbye. 'Cheers for now Dino'.

Picking up the machete that Dino had left for him, he waved to the departing passengers and climbed back into the aircraft to search for anything that might be of use whilst trekking in the jungle. The layout in the fuselage was typical Dakota; two seat either side of the central isle, with bin lockers which were all now empty.

The two life raft stowage's had mostly been cleaned out of water and provisions by the departing passengers.

He did manage to salvage some first aid packs from the Dinghies and a small crow bar which he then used to lever the Aircraft's small stand-by compass from its mount overhead the instrument panel in the cockpit. He also grabbed a couple of aviation charts, which might be of some help although the scale would be too small to be of any practical use – however, if he ever found out where he was, they could be used to give him the correct direction in which to go.

Initially the line of the logging track was quite clear and easy to follow due to the undergrowth being swept aside when the Dakota had landed, and initially, moral was high among the passengers. With all the bushes and small trees being brushed aside by the emergency landing they made good progress but beyond the aircraft's touchdown point, they encountered nature where it had begun to reclaim her own. Small trees some over ten feet tall with creepers and tangled undergrowth had sprung up through the track surface. Large leafy ferns had crept in from the sides further hindering their passage. With only one machete available their progress was reduced to a crawl. In fact the party were reduce to having to look sky wards to establish the direction of the logging track which was indicated by the large gap in the overhead foliage.

Nathan Costello had only progressed about four hundred yards with his fellow passengers when he began to realize the size of the task he'd taken on. Although they had no problem keeping to the logging track with the help of the huge trees delineating the edge of it thus giving them a direction in which to travel, having to stop and keep looking upwards to confirm their direction exacerbated their slow progress. Parts of the logging track were overgrown where the jungle had crowded in making their passage difficult. In the last hundred yards they were forced to use their machete on six occasions to hack the undergrowth aside in order to make progress.

The truth of the matter was that Nathan Costello was the oldest person in the group with the possible exception of Dino and he was already feeling the heat and humidity and started to sweat profusely.

He turned his head and looked at the crocodile following behind. Jose, or whatever the fuck they called him, was immediately behind him (the guy that controlled the airstrip) he was also fairly long in the tooth but he was acclimatised to the area and used to walking so he was having no problems as yet,

The rest of the party comprised of seven women - all young, with the exception of Mrs Fields who appeared to be in her late thirties or early forties with her young daughter. Of the nine men in the party, only the singer Peter Milo, Jose and Dino were in their thirties. The Camera man and his Assistant didn't look very fit, and he knew from earlier experience that his own Assistant was a boozer and a typical couch potato so he was not going to be of much use either. The two male actors were young and obviously good looking and Dale the older of the two had quite a strong build but the younger one, Mark, looked a right bloody wimp.

Luckily all of the women were wearing sensible shoes. (Mostly trainers) and although not ideal for trekking through the jungle they were certainly better than the standard footwear most women teeter around on. Unfortunately two of the girls were wearing shorts and were beginning to complain about their legs getting scratched.

'Hey, Nathan!' yelled Olivia the younger of the two in shorts. 'Can't you get your guys to cut the undergrowth lower – Cathy and I are getting our legs scratched'.

'You don't know when you're lucky' shouted Dale the older actor, who was swinging the machete to try and clear a path through thick undergrowth. 'Up front here you would be getting your pussy scratched let alone your legs'.

'With your mouth I thought you could have talked your way out of this situation' replied Cathy the older of the two in shorts.

'Yeh! - Well if you girls think you can do better your welcome to come up front and try because I have just had about enough and could do with a spell'.

'Okay Mark you take over the machete and give Dale a rest. We'll have to take it in turns as each one tires', said Nathan.

'How long do you figure we are going to be doing this' snarled Mark. 'For Christ sake we don't even know where we are going'.

'Shut your bloody winging Mark, this god dam track has got to lead somewhere, so get hacking', Nathan stopped for a moment to wipe the sweat out of his eyes.

'It may have led somewhere years ago but the fucking thing has obviously not been used for sometime', continued Mark.

Nathan was beginning to appreciate the size of the task they were committed to, however he wasn't about to give up yet and be made a fool in front of his film crew.

Niles who was following the noise of the bickering about a hundred yards behind smiled grimly to himself. It was like following a travelling Pantomime. There was no chance of losing contact with them with that racket going on. He was in fact, trekking about twenty yard to the left of and parallel to the logging track. This part of the forest had not been lumbered yet so the canopy of the giant trees kept most of the undergrowth stunted and easier to transit.

They'd been trekking for about two hours when Niles suddenly heard a noise he was familiar with, it was the characteristic chopping noise of an approaching helicopter, from the 'Doppler effect' he new it was approaching his location. He just managed to catch a glimpse of it as it thundered overhead. He was surprised to note that it had a large under-slung load dangling from its cargo hook – it appeared to be following the line of the logging track.

He recognised it straight away as a Super Puma and wondered what it was doing out here in this neck of the wood. He stopped just beside the track while he considered the possible reasons for a Super Puma being in this location. He discounted the fact that it might be a rescue helicopter looking for the Dakota's survivors. There's no way it would be over flying the jungle looking for survivors with a load under-slung on its cargo hook.

This left only two rational reasons for the chopper to be out here. Logging had been banned for the next ten years to his knowledge so it couldn't be that. Therefore, it had to be either something to do with a mining operation or more likely, associated with the illegal drug trade. If the latter was the case, then survivors were in serious danger. It could be a case of out of the frying pan and into the fire!

As the noise of the helicopter receded he could hear the cheering of all the passengers in front and could imagine them waving their arms and desperately trying to attract the attention of the helicopter crew. He knew from his own experience that if the chopper was directly overhead that it was most unlikely that the crew would have seen them especially if they were not specifically looking for them.

The passengers heard the chopper about the same time as Niles and they all stopped and started to scream and shout to try and attract the attention of the crew – some even took their shirts of in an attempt to wave to the helicopter but by the time they had stripped the chopper was gone. There was a loud groan of disappointment from the passengers as it disappeared to the south.

'I don't think they saw us', groaned Peter Milo the aged singer. Even Costello couldn't hide his look of despondency as the chopper roared over the horizon. Some of the women began to weep. Just as they thought they were about to be saved, their expectation had been dashed by the receding chopper. Suddenly there was a change in the engine note of the chopper.

'Hey you guys I think that chopper is landing up ahead' yelled Dale excitedly. 'Listen! You can hear the engine running down; they only do that after they have landed'

'Yes but how far ahead did it land I can't go much further, I'm absolutely knackered', moaned Susan one of the Film's leading ladies.

'For Christ sake stop winging', snarled Costello. (It appeared to be one of his favourite expressions). 'If little Karen can keep up so can you. How far ahead do you think it is Dale?

'Well I guess the chopper was travelling at about one hundred miles an hour and it was less than a minute before we heard it closing down so it can't be much more than a mile if that'.

'Right', shouted Nathan to the rest of the party.' Listen out, we think the chopper has landed about a mile up ahead and as it was travelling up the line of the logging track we should have no trouble finding it'

Just then Sandy Niles came crashing through the undergrowth drenched in sweat and covered in scratches where he had made desperate progress to catch up with the main party.

'Costello' he shouted. 'You're not thinking of barging into that chopper's location without checking who or what they are – are you?'

'Look, what we do has nothing to do with you. You decided to stay with the aircraft because you said we couldn't walk out of this shit hole. Well we've proved you wrong Mr smart arse. If you want to tag along that's fine –Just keep your mouth shut'

Niles realised that there was no point in trying to reason with the man. He'd convinced himself that he led the survivors to safety and he was not going to allow anything or anybody to spoil his moment of triumph.

'Right you guys', shouted Nathan Costello excitedly. 'Lets push on and we will be clear of this shit hole before nightfall. Right Phil! '. He said to the assistant Cameraman. 'Take over as machete man and let's turn the wick up and get out of here pronto'.

Sandy Niles sidled over to Jackie Fields and nodded in the direction that the chopper had landed.'I don't think those people up ahead are necessarily going to be very friendly. I suggest you keep a close watch on Karen and when you meet up with the new guys try and keep yourselves well in the background. Meanwhile I'm going to slide out and I'll try to approach the chopper location from a reciprocal direction'.

'Don't you think it might be a rescue helicopter that has been sent to look for us?' She murmured fearfully.

'Not with an under-slung load on the cargo hook I don't' and Niles disappeared into the jungle.

Niles managed to keep abreast of the main party mainly due to the noise they made as they slashed and fought their way along the disused logging track. He had chosen the left hand side of the track as this was higher ground and had not been logged and therefore it was still primary jungle, which made progress fairly easy. It would also give him better visibility should the jungle ever allow it.

He stopped to break off a willowy twig of about three feet in length, it was nice and light and very springy. He ran his hand down it stripping all the leaves and twigs off of it until he was left with nothing but a light springy wand. He now began to move extremely cautiously. The way Niles figured it; if the location ahead was drug related then it would almost certainly have a defence perimeter with possible booby traps and roving armed guards. He made use of the small stand by compass that he had taken from the aircraft to keep himself parallel to the logging track.

He could now hear quite clearly the noise of the Puma helicopter still running at Ground Idle and realised that he must now be quite close to the landing pad. He had to be careful, at this stage he did not know how far the camp site extended from the Helicopter Landing Site (HLS) Niles now decided it was time to start using the twitch. He held it out in front; about a foot off the ground waving up and down in such a manner that should he come up against any trip wires then the twitch would bend without setting off any booby traps. Niles had only gone another twenty yards when suddenly the willowy twitch bent. In the poor light under the jungle canopy he had trouble seeing the trip wire at first. It was about four feet above the ground and stretched around three trees for about fifteen yards. Niles looked around carefully and finally saw a modified M18A1 Claymore Mine strapped to a tree with heavy duty masking tape. The people who had set the mine up had not been very conscientious about camouflaging – not only that, but they had left the safety pin that could be inserted to make the mine safe dangling from the mine itself. Thank you very much he thought as he inserted the pin, disarmed the mine and rolled the wire up. These mines were usually initiated with a 'clacker' which when squeezed sent and electrical charge down a wire to the mine causing it to explode; this blasted 700 ball bearings out in a 60 degree arc mangling or killing anyone out to a range of two hundred and fifty yards. He decided that the mine could probable be replaced to his advantage if later push came to shove. There was no doubt about the location he was approaching, it was definitely most unfriendly. In circumventing the landing pad Niles had come across a further two trip wires to modified American Claymore mines. There had been no warning notices. Had Niles not taken the precaution of using his twitch he would have been dead three times over.

'Bastards', he growled to himself. 'I'll give them something to worry about'. After he had careful disarmed the mines he changed their location and rearmed them so that when they were initiated the blast would be towards the chopper location. These mines were absolutely lethal. These had been modified to be initiated by trip wires. He'd just completed relocating the third Claymore when he heard the sound of automatic fire quickly followed by people screaming.

The helicopter crewman, who had been leaning out the

main cabin door looking for the HLS, happened to catch a fleeting view of the passengers, as they roared overhead. He told the pilot who in turn warned Al Menzies over the radio about the approaching survivors. Menzies, who'd in fact, been organising a search party to hunt down the survivors when he heard the noise of them approaching the clearing. Al quickly positioned his gunmen one side of the track just prior to location of the processing Laboratory.

Unfortunately, at this stage, Al Menzies was not privy to the knowledge that the survivors contained some American VIPs. What he did know, was that the Cartel did not want the new locations to be compromised and this is what he was about to ensure.

As soon as the first of the survivors appeared Al Menzies raised his AK 47, which was his favourite weapon. It was one of the most popular automatic rifles in the world. Millions of these guns had been made and many had found there way into the hands of criminals and terrorist. It fired a 7.62mm round at about 2350ft/sec and in the automatic role had a cyclic rate of 600RPM. They were also known for their ruggedness and there ability to function under dusty and dirty conditions that caused some of the more sophisticated weapons to jam.

Al had set his gun in the semi-automatic role. He shot the leading two men. Fortunately for the remainder of the survivors Al Menzies had fired too soon and the remainder of the survivors managed to rush into the jungle as Menzies gunmen opened fire.

Costello and his colleagues knew they were closed to the helicopter pad as they could hear people talking and the sounds of construction. Fortunately in their haste to get to the site of the landing helicopter the survivors had become strung out. However, they never knew what hit them. Suddenly; the camera man wielding the machete and his assistant who was close behind were cut down by rapid rifle fire followed by burst of automatic fire from all-round them. The fact that the crocodile of survivors had become badly strung out during their last ten minutes of trekking saved them from sustaining greater casualties. Those not cut down by the initial burst of gun fire panicked and tried to rush off into the woods only to run into the arms of the grinning gunmen. It was only the fact that the gunmen caught sight of the women that saved the party. Not for humanitarian reasons but for lustful games to be played out back at the camp.

Al Menzies jumped to his feet and was about to roar his men on when he felt someone tapping his shoulder; it was the helicopter pilot. 'Senor Menzies, Senor Domingo asked me to pass on a message. He said there was an important American women and her daughter with this group and we were to take them prisoners if possible'.

'Why the fuck have you waited till now to tell me'.

'Senor Menzies I was waiting to complete the unloading of the helicopter, but before it was finished all hell broke loose I came to inform you as soon as I realised what was happening'.

Jackie Fields had kept to the rear of the column as advised by Niles and she and Karen immediately hit the ground when the firing started. After the initial bursts of fire there was confusion all around them and much shouting and the firing stopped.

'Quick Karen', whispered Jackie. 'Follow me'. She quietly got to her feet and holding on tightly to Karen's hand gentle started to creep back down the track fearfully looking over her shoulder to make sure they weren't followed. She suddenly felt Karen stiffen. She turned round to be confronted by a huge bearded ruffian pointing his Armalite automatic rifle at her and grinning lasciviously. She did not understand his Spanish but he made his instructions plenty clear enough.

She tried to knee him in the groin but only managed

to catch him in the thigh. He rammed the butt of his rifle into her gut and she doubled up with pain, all the breath knocked out of her. By the time she had made any sort of recovery she was tucked under his right arm with Karen tucked under his left. He dragged them back to the camp site taking every opportunity to squeeze Jackie's breast grunting with pleasure.

'Hold your fire you fucking arseholes – try and capture as many of the bastards as you can', roared Menzies.

Chapter 12

Rescue Party

The forest canopy stirred into life as the screeching birds alarmed at the thudding signature of the approaching twin engined Hue 212 helicopter with the SAS team on board, rose out of the trees and attempted to get out of the path of the low flying chopper. It roared over the jungle at tree top level the height where it achieved its best flying speed trying to reach the estimated position of the stricken Dakota as quickly as possible. As they flew further to the west the weather rapidly improved. Initially they were flying over the Llanos the rolling grass plains with the occasional scrub trees intersperse with large pools of water on the saturated surface. As they flew further east the scene gradually changed from rolling grass lands to a areas with more trees.. The clouds, associated with the hurricane had completely disappeared, and apart from pools of fog in low lying ground, visibility was unlimited.

As it was a weekend it had taken up most of the day trying to hire a helicopter. Colonel DeSuza had advised the team to hire a chopper privately as there was less chance of the Cartel being forewarned. Although the new Field Force Police were very reliable they had no helicopters. Unfortunately the Colombian Armed Forces who had plenty of choppers were riddled with informants eager to supplement their meagre pay by passing on information to the Drug Cartel.

Now at last, they were on their way. Tony Bryant had given his men an abbreviated ball park briefing prior to take off but was now giving them a more detail one as the flew to their objective.

'It appears that this party of Americans were making a film about the work of the Peace Corps among South American Indians when they got the warning about the approaching hurricane 'Judy'. The majority of the Film Company screwed the nut and left the area straight away. They flew to Caracas and were on the next schedule flight to the States. But apparently, the Director; some bloody nutter called Costello, decided he knew better than the Meteorology man and decided to stay on for a further twenty four hours and shoot an important scene to complete the film. By the time they were finished it was too late to get out on a schedule flight and they ended up making a dash for safety in some bloody clapped out pre World War Two Dakota'

'Christ I didn't think they had any of those still in commercial service', grunted Cpl (Fingers) Finnegan.

'Well there are some but they're mostly used for Feeder Airlines in out of the way locations such as this film crew found themselves in. At the moment we have a position that was picked up by satellite but apparently the Crash Locator Beacon has only been working intermittently and no one knows whether there are any survivors or not'.

'Do we know how many there were on the aircraft Boss?' said Sgt Irons.

'Well there were sixteen in the filming party possible plus two crew – I doubt they had any Air Hostesses, although by Airlaw they should have and I can't imagine there were any more people on board or the bloody thing would've never got off the ground.'

'Hey! Did you hear that Lance – no Air Hostesses. Looks as though you are going to have to keep your mutton dagger zipped up', quipped Trooper Miles one of the normally quieter members of the group.

Trooper Lance failed to respond, he just sat there with a slow bemused smile on his face. In fact Lance had failed to field any of the sarcastic comments thrown his way about his latest conquest. The consensus of opinion was that the famous Lancelot had become broody and gone into the nest-building mode and he was now running around with, 'twigs in his beak'.

Tony Bryant was well aware of Trooper Lances reputation with women and he had to concede that he had never seen him react in such a manner before. His normal modus operandi was, "Wham. Bang Thank You Mam".

'Lance – are you feeling okay?' enquired Bryant.

'Never felt better Boss', he murmured softly.

'Well at the moment I have to admit you don't look fully compos mentis – are you sure you feel up to this mission'.

'No problem Boss at the moment – whilst I have the time; I'm just reflecting on what happened earlier this evening'

'He's bloody pussy smitten', snarled Rusty Irons.' Just make sure your "with it", when we hit the deck Eddy. I don't want to be running around in the jungle with you with your brains still buttoned up in the end of your dick'

'It's now firmly back in my head where it belongs' and still Eddy Lance refused to be fazed by all the insults being levelled at him.

'Oh Eduardo, you are so big and strong, please don't

leave me', mimicked Hezeltine in a high pitched girlish voice.

'Hold it you guys'; interrupted Bryant. 'The pilot says we are now approaching the probable location of the downed aircraft. Right, eyeballs to the, "search mode", and let's start looking for this aircraft'

The landscape had been gradually changing over the last five minutes and the grass land (Llanos) had now given way to thick Rain Forest. It was also noticeable that the further east they flew the denser the jungle canopy was becoming. The visibility was impeded slightly by steam coming off the trees' canopy. Indicating just how wet the terrain was after the torrential downpour over the past two days. It was also getting hillier. Although the hills were not steep the SAS team knew from experience that the terrain they were now flying over would not be easy transit on foot.

The banter ceased as all eyes searched the terrain for any clues leading to the where the downed Dakota might be.

The pilot started to climb the chopper in order to increase the field of view. As they were passing through fifteen hundred feet the co-pilot sang out.' Got it! Just there! Along that logging track running up to the north, and the aircraft it still seems to be in one piece and reasonable intact. And the coordinates we got from the satellite are spot on!'

Leaning out the chopper as far as his safety harness would allow him Bryant spotted the Dakota.

'From the looks of it there's a good chance that people survived the landing. Can you land beside it?' He asked the pilot.

'I'm not sure about my tail rotor clearance but in any event I will certainly be able to come to a very low hover and you should all be able to jump out or repel, which ever you wish'.

'Make it a six foot hover and we'll jump it', commanded Bryant.

The Huey came to a six-foot hover aft of the crashed Dakota and the SAS team bailed out one at a time with all their weapons and kit. Trooper Hezeltine, the first to deplane, rushed over to the Dakota. Had a quick search, and confirmed that there was no one there.

Tony Bryant turned to the pilot still wearing the headset on an extended lead and said.

'It appears the passengers have moved out. It may take us some time to locate them. You return to base and await our call to pick us up at this location. Failing that, return here in five days, same time, and same place – okay'.

The pilot nodded his head indicating he fully understood. Bryant slung the headset back in the helicopter slammed the cabin door closed and gave the pilot the 'thumbs up'.

The pilot acknowledged Bryant's instructions. Pulled pitch and the chopper rose to the hover and quickly transitioned away.

Rusty Irons quickly scouted around whilst Trooper (Butch) Hezeltine took up a defensive stance whilst the remainder of the team got all the weapons and kit organised.

'Over here Boss, It looks as though they are trying to follow the logging path, you can see where they have been slashing the undergrowth away', roared Rusty

'Why the fuck didn't they stay with the aircraft as there're supposed to?' Bryant cursed. 'Just what we needed; the bloody passengers going for walk about -Great! – Fingers, (Finnegan) make a quick circuit of the area and see if there are any other tracks in case the survivors have split up and gone their separate ways'.

A quick circuit of the crashed Dakota established that the only tracks leading away were those going down the logging path to the south.

Bryant gave the Dakota a rapid survey and turned to Irons and said

'It looks as though they had a fairly successful emergency landing Rusty. The aircraft doesn't appear to have sustained any substantial damage. I can't imagine that they had many injuries?'

'I agree Boss - I've had a good look around and can see so signs of blood. I think we can assume that apart from being shook up they escaped without serious injury or they would never have left this location. Why the fuck they buggered off I don't know? If they'd remained with the aircraft as they're supposed to we would all be on our way back to base by now'.

Bryant nodded his head in agreement. 'Silly buggers must have panicked and thought they could trek down this logging track to civilisation. Boy! Are they in for a shock? Right! Rusty lets get ourselves organised and chase after them'.

The SAS team set off at a fairly quick pace and was making good time due to the previous path clearance by the Dakota and then the survivors. The lead man (point) was Trooper Lance – still with a bemused smile on his face carrying a Remington 870 Wing master Pump Action Shot gun, much favoured by troops operating in the reduced visibility of the jungle. Fired at close quarters it had a wide and devastating effect.

They had only moved about two hundred meters down the track when they heard the sound of distant firing. It was too far away to pose an immediate problem to the team but they stopped and immediately took up defensive positions on either side of the track. At the same time Tony and Rusty discussed what looked like becoming a potentially dangerous situation.

'As it's most unlikely that the passengers of the Dakota had any weapons I can only surmise that they have run into serious trouble. That means Bandits/ Guerrillas or probably Druggies', said Bryant. 'Not that it makes much difference to our action because it looks as though we are going to get ourselves some real action. Any you guys have an input?'

Most of the team deferred to Sgt Rusty Irons as he had by far the most combat experience and it was normal for good officers; and Captain Bryant was a very good officer, to check with their senior NCOs before making a decision.

'I figure that the problem lies about two or three miles straight up this logging track and I suspect that our passengers may have run into some serious trouble. I'll take the lead. Give me about a hundred meters – then follow. We'll liaise as soon as I have scouted the, 'contact point', then we have another 'O' group to consider to our options- how does that sound Boss?' Sgt Irons looked to Bryant for official confirmation of his plan.

Bryant nodded in agreement. 'OK guys you know the drill – as we get closer to the, 'contact point', lets keep our eyes peeled and get the twigs out for any booby traps that are almost certain to have been set out and be prepared to outflank them'.

The team checked their weapons and equipment and set off towards their destination giving Rusty Irons about a hundred meters to scout ahead.

Niles made his way cautiously through the undergrowth towards the perimeter of the camp – luckily all the commotion was coming from the other side of the camp so there was little danger of him being spotted. He worked his way around the perimeter to the south of the camp location until he had a good view of it from a well-concealed position. The camp site appeared to have been located at the confluence of four tracks. The tracks were roughly orientated on north, south and east, west directions. Vegetation that had been cut down had just been dragged to the edge of the clearing making it easier for Niles to remain unobserved. There were various pieces of constructions materials stacked around the site and a giant fuel bladder had been dumped on the eastern leg of the track but as yet there appeared to be no fuel in it.

He arrived just in time to see Al Menzies and his six gunmen herding the remaining passengers into the camp clearing. He could only see about four men, he was unable to see exactly who they were but he counted what looked like seven women –he could make out young Karen being cuddled by her mother followed by a huge thug with a beard.

A further series of single shot rang out and Niles suspected that one of the gunmen was dispatching the wounded passengers. He realised that six of the male passengers were missing and presumably, had been murdered. He later found out that most of the men who'd been killed or wounded were at the front of the column and were caught in the first fusillade of bullets which struck down all six of them before Menzies could restore order.

He felt completely helpless. The only weapon he had was a machete and although it was a fearsome weapon at close quarters, he realised that to try and use it to mount a rescue bid against armed men was suicidal. He would have been cut down in a hail of bullets before he'd gone ten yards.

Niles considered his options, it was now half past five and in the next half an hour it would be dark. There was virtually no twilight at these Latitudes so he made the best use of the remaining light to recce' the camps layout. There were three Portakabins, two of which were being constructed to house the Laboratory equipment located under the forest canopy on the southern end of the track junction. The third one, located on the eastern leg of the track junction, appeared to be used as a store and possibly the camps armoury. It was obviously going to be used as a refuelling area once the fuel bladder had been filled. He noticed gunmen going to the cabin and stowing their weapons within. He paid particular attention to this cabin.

'Get all the prisoners over here', snarled Al Menzies waving his AK47 in the air. 'Make sure their hands are secured behind their backs and search the bastards for weapons'.

Only four of the men remained alive, the others had been killed or wounded in the initial outburst of firing. The two who had only been wounded had been dispatched with a single bullet to the back of the head.

'Which one of you bitches in the wife of the American Defence Secretary Mrs Fields', Menzies glared at all the women prisoners balefully. Initially no one made a move to reply. Menzies strode over and grabbed young Karen by the front of her Denim Jacket and pulled a Beretta Pistol out of his belt and forced it between the young girl's teeth.

'You have got three seconds Mrs Fields to come forward and identify yourself or I blow the little girls head off'.

Jackie Fields had no option.

'I'm Mrs Fields and that is my daughter you have there, if anything happens to that child you are going to attract an awful lot of grief from the US Defence Secretary', Jackie Fields dashed forward and snatched Karen from his arms before Menzies appreciated what he'd just learnt. He had been made aware of the Senator's wife but no one had mentioned that his daughter was also amongst the survivors.

'Keep these two apart from the others and see no harm comes to them. I think we have just acquired two good bargaining tools. In the meantime, we'll have some chow and then I'll radio the Cartel and find out what we are going to do with the prisoners' and Menzies strode off to the chow tent.

As it quickly got dark Niles noticed that only one man was guarding the cabin where all the weapons appeared to be kept. Not only that, but every so often the guard would creep round the back of the hut to have a crafty smoke. There was obviously some form of discipline within the camp or he wouldn't have bothered at keeping his smoking a secret. He also noticed with considerable interest that as it got dark all the guards were now stashing their weapons in the Armoury. The only exception appeared to be the boss man, a Senor Al Menzies as he was often referred to and the two guards. One stationed outside the Armoury and a further roving piquet who wandered haphazardly around the camp site

A portable generator sprang into life and a series of light bulbs strung around the camp in a haphazard manner lit up and illuminated the camp area. However the lights had not been positioned with any real thought, consequently, many parts of the camp were in deep shadows.

About an hour after dark the cookhouse began to serve the evening meal and apart from the guard at the stores cabin all the camp workers and guards made there way to the cook-tent. Niles noticed that there was a definite demarcation between the guards and the peons who had been recruited to do the construction work. They made no attempt to mix. With their food, both groups began to break out the alcohol. They were obviously quite confident there was no one else within a hundred miles of this location. They quickly began to relax and became more and more boisterous as the liquor took its effect.

As the guard went round one side of the cabin to grab another crafty smoke Niles came to a decision. He would have to get some form of fire weapon. With a pounding heart he crept cautiously round the opposite side to where the guard was having his crafty drag, taking great pains to avoid making any noise. He knew if he was caught he was dead meat. He got to the front door which was locked. He inserted the broad blade of the machete and gentle levered it to one side until he had sprung the doorpost far enough for the lock to disengage. He entered and quietly pulled the door to behind him and locked it in the same manner as he had used to effect entry. Using one of the torches he'd taken from the aircraft's dinghy he carefully examined the cabin's contents. There must have been about thirty to forty weapons of all sorts and calibre's.

He noticed a leather rifle case and checked inside. It was a beauty! And it must have cost the owner a small fortune. It was a Holland & Holland 0.264 with Zeiss telescopic sight complete with attachment. This gun fired 0.458inch cartridge necked down to 0.264 which gave it some impressive ballistics. It threw a 100-grain bullet at approximately 3700ft/sec. This resulted in very a flat trajectory with little gravity drop over any thing other than extreme ranges. Further more; within the leather case was a leather bandoleer that held approximately one hundred rounds. Niles realised that he could probably steal the gun and leave the leather case buckled up and the chances were that it absence wouldn't be noticed for some time.

He also helped himself to a Beretta US Army M9 (Model 92SB/92F) 9mm handgun of which there appeared to be about a dozen or so. Most of the remaining weapons appeared to be of American origin, Even the Beretta, although of Italian design, was the standard handgun issued to the American Military. 'It would seem that the American Military was missing quite a few weapons. I wonder if our friend Chase is involved? He mused.

Now came the tricky part. He'd have to wait until the guard disappeared around the back of the cabin for another crafty smoke. Niles considered his options. If the present guard was relieved by a non smoker he was going to have problems getting out the armoury unnoticed. After a further ten minutes he was getting really worried. He'd considered killing the guard before breaking into the weapon storeroom but there was always a danger of some one finding his body or missing his presence before he could get clear.

Then, just as Niles thought his luck had run out. He

heard someone approaching and calling the guard to open up the Armoury so he could deposit his weapon. Niles looked around frantically for some where to hide. He desperately cranked his brain over trying to decide what to do next. He had about twenty seconds to go before being discovered. There was absolutely no where to hide. He would have to make one. There were several crates at the back of the Armoury – if he could stack some of those and the six boxes containing ammunition adjacent to them it might provide him with sufficient cover. He could hear the Armoury guard berating the other guy for being so late on returning his weapon. He thanked god for small mercies and rapidly started to stack the crates and boxes. He could hear the key grating in the lock. He dived behind the wall of boxes he'd erected carrying the last two boxes with him and was still placing the last box in position when the two Colombian guards entered and switched on the light. He lay there with his heart beating trying to control his breath. He realised he could if necessary kill the two guards with the Berretta should they discover him and probably make a get away. However, his chances of rescuing the remainder of the passengers would be well and truly scuppered. But the two guards were fully occupied bickering about the late return of the weapon. The weapon was stacked (none were secured by chains or any other means) against the side wall of the building and both guards departed still arguing heatedly. He found himself sweating and his heart still beating like a run away diesel after the near discovery.

His next problem was getting out the Armoury without being discovered. He knew the guard had been on duty since he had arrived and that was over an hour ago. He might soon be relieved by another, possibly a non smoker. If that was the case then he was going to be up shit creek without a paddle.

Ten minutes had elapsed since the guards had left and

Niles was now really beginning to feel the strain. He would have to get out soon if he was going to make a positive move on behalf of the passengers.

The guards craving for another fag prevailed and ten minutes after entering the Armoury he wandered around the back for another drag. As soon as Niles heard the match flare he crept quickly to the door, levered it open with the machete blade and then gentle closed it again before disappearing into the shadows with his newly acquired weapons

The SAS team had made good progress and was only about a mile short of the camp location when night fell. Capt Bryant and his team discussed their options. Normally it was too difficult to navigate in the jungle at night unless able to follow a well-defined track. This they had with the logging track. Unfortunately there was a strong chance of the track being booby trapped as they got closer to the campsite.

Sgt Irons had volunteered to go ahead and recce', the campsite and then report back to the Troop and then they would decide what their plan of action would be.

Al Menzies was on the radio to Francesco Domingo. 'I have the Gringos Francesco but unfortunately some were shot whilst we were trying to capture them – but we have definitely got the Defence Secretary's wife and her daughter alive and well'

'What the fuck do you mean? Some were shot! We had decided to keep them hostages and try and get some money for their release. Didn't you get the message that they were not to be shot', raged Domingo.

'No I didn't, not until we had sprung the ambush on them, then that fucking arse hole of a helicopter pilot informs me right in the middle of the firing that you wanted them taken prisoners. And! Don't forget that at our last meeting, it was decided that any one approaching the camp location was to be wasted. If you guys change your minds and don't tell me how the fuck am I supposed to know – I'm not a bloody clairvoyant'.

'Okay! Okay! Al point taken - you were not aware of our change in plan. But if we eventually release these people we have to make sure that they think you are bandits and not involved with the processing of Cocaine'.

'Well that's not much of a problem; but we had unfortunately killed six guys before I could stop the shooting and three of them were American so I suggest you get your Senator friends, what's their names; Jackson, Thornton and their sidekick, to try and forestall any inquiries down here. I have already question some of the prisoners and they have no idea where they are in Colombia so provided we keep it that way they will never be able to disclose our camp location'.

'That's good Al, keep it that way, and have your men behave badly towards the prisoners to enhance this charade. Not that your bastards will need any encouragement to act badly I think their ultimate wish in life is to screw a blonde gringo'.

'That's fine by me' replied Menzies'. 'But don't come complaining to me at a later date about soiled goods. Okay – see you soon'. Menzies released the transmit button and left the radio shack.

Menzies wandered over to the large lean-to that served as a temporary cookhouse and social centre during the construction of the camp. His guards were all ready well on the way to getting liquored up. The rest of the construction workers tried to keep well clear of the guards who tended to give them a hard time given half a chance. They'd all wandered away from the guard's side of the camp to form their own social circle on the other side of the clearing.

'Where's the rum?' Menzies swaggered into the lean-to

as his cut –throats diffidently made room for him on one of the fallen logs they used as a bench. 'Later on tonight when those peons get drunk and piss off to bed,' he waved his arms contemptuously at the workers. 'I think we have some fun with the women eh!

His cut-throats all grinned lasciviously. It was quite obvious that this was all they had thought about since the women had been captured. Menzies main problem would be keeping things from getting too badly out of hand.

'I think two guards will be enough and we will arrange a schedule of two hours guard duty for each man, one man to guard the weapons store and the other as a roving piquet. Manuel; you arrange the roster and let me have a list in ten minutes. And I want no arguments about who's on duty and when Okay' ordered Menzies.

'I think I'll go and have a look at some of the women and make my selection for later on', smirked one of the guards nicknamed 'Donkey' because of his large appendage.

'You can look but not touch until I say so', growled Menzies.

'You're the boss' leered the 'Donkey' as he swaggered over to where the prisoner had been tied and roped to stakes driven into the ground. As he wandered towards the women prisoners he was followed by a series of cat calls from his comrades. Mostly to the fact that he would have to wait until they'd finished with the women before he performed otherwise they would be no use to man or beast.

Two of the women prisoners understood enough Spanish to get the gist of the conversation and were able to interpret for the others. In any event the general tone of the drinking guards and the lewd body language was enough to let the women know what was in store for them. They shrank back as the 'Donkey' stood over them leering and smacking his lips and making obscene thrusting motions with his right arm while slapping his right biceps with his left hand. The crude gesture universally made by yobos to make their intentions painfully clear.

'Bugger off and leave the women alone you fucking animal', raged the helpless Dale.

The 'Donkey' kicked Dale in the stomach and said, 'you shut up hombre, when I finish with the women I give you a taste of my sword'. He followed this up with a further kick to Dale's unprotected stomach.

Niles was watching from the cover at the edge of the clearing and was trying to work out what he could do to prevent the women from being raped. Although Niles Spanish was not fluent he'd a good working knowledge after living in South America for the past three years, so he understood enough to know what was going to happen. The body language was also sufficiently clear as to what was to transpire. Only a blind man could fail to see what was about to happen.

However, one thing appeared to be in Niles's favour. The only people carrying a weapon were those on actual guard duty. The guy he heard referred to as Senor Menzies was quite clearly the boss and he and his cut-throats obviously thought the area was secure. As far as Niles could make out in the poor light, only Menzies had a side arm, which made the odds slightly better in his favour than he first thought.

Most of the construction workers were now making their way down to the further end of the clearing and Niles could sense that this was what the guards and Menzies had been waiting for.

'Right, lets draw cards – Ace high, to see who has first screw with the Gringo bitches', smirked Menzies. 'But I'm telling you guys here and now that the little girl is mine. They're six other women and twelve of you, so some of you are going to have to take seconds'.

Menzies predilection for both young boys as well as girls was a well-known fact amongst permanent thugs employed by the Cartel. None present dared to argue with him.

Carlos, the camp construction boss, organised the draw amid raucous shouts of glee punctuated with the occasional groan as some one drew a low card.

Nile knew that the situation was about to become critical. Behind him he'd have the guy guarding the weapons store and he was definitely armed. So if he was going to try and prevent the women getting raped he would have to take him out first.

He crept quietly around to the back of the weapons hut and waited for the guard to appear for one of his clandestine smokes. He drew the machete and waited behind a large tree.

The draw for the women had been finalised. Menzies and the six winners approached the women. The women began to shriek for help and twisted and turned against their bonds to no avail. All they succeeded in doing was to titillate and excite the approaching thugs.

Menzies reached for and grabbed young Karen whilst her mother Jackie screamed and beg him to leave her alone.

Karen started to cry hysterically. 'Please don't hurt me please! Please!

Her pleading only seemed to excite Menzies even further. He just grinned and dragged her to her feet.

Jackie Fields was already struggling with the ruffian who had won her in the draw screamed at Menzies. 'Leave the girl alone. She's only eleven years old for Christ sake. If you need a woman so badly have me'.

'You're about to be had and you've been had plenty of times before. Now this one here', snorted the excited Menzies. 'Has never been had before and it will be my pleasure to be her first'.

Niles knew that if he was going to intervene then he would have to act now. The fucking guard of the Armoury had become so wrapped up in the impending orgy he had forgotten about his ten-minute smoke. Although he had never killed a man before, since his arrival in Caracas he had been involved in some very vicious brawls but if he didn't intervene now it would be too late. He could feel the adrenaline coursing through his veins and his body responding into the flight or fight mode. He suddenly felt quite calm. He knew the moment of truth was upon him.

He crept behind the hut and rapped the side of it with the butt of the Beretta then, threw it on the ground where it was clearly visible and stepped behind the adjacent tree.

The guard crept cautiously round the corner looking to see what had caused the noise. He saw the Beretta pistol on the ground, looked around, could see no one and bent down to pick it up. As he was picking it up he heard a swishing noise, which was the last thing he was ever conscious of.

Niles machete blade bit so deeply into back of the guard's neck it almost decapitated him. He was so hyped up and anxious to prevent any harm coming to young Karen Niles found he was completely devoid of any remorse for what he had done. He looked at the body in a detached manner expecting to feel nauseous and was surprised to find that he experienced no horror at all.

He checked that there was a round up the breech of the Holland & Holland then Niles with his heart thumping, steadily strode round the hut into the clearing over towards where the women were being molested. The only name of the thugs he knew was that of their leader – the one manhandling the young girl

'Menzies! Release the girl or I'll blow your fucking head off ', said Niles in his crude Spanish

Menzies and his thugs look up in shock to find a gringo standing twenty yards behind them with Francesco's sporting rifle aimed at his guts. He seemed to have appeared as if by magic.

'Where the fuck did you come from? And if that is

Domingo's rifle you have there Senor you are a dead man. No one is allowed to touch that gun on the penalty of death'.

'Under the present circumstances I think this gun poses a bigger threat to you than me. Now release the girl or you are dead'!

It was probable the booze that had unhinged his sanity but Carlos, the construction boss, decided to get aggressive. 'Heh! Senor you a big man eh! You think your little pip squeak rifle can kill us all … he never finished his sentence. Niles bullet took the back of his head off before he had even got chance to finish. Niles had decided not to dither about – he'd have to stamp his authority over the gang or he would be overwhelmed.

It was not the accuracy of the shot that impressed the onlookers or the fact that Niles had fired from the hip – it was the fluent speed at which he manipulated the Mauser turn bolt action and chambered a fresh round into the breech. Most of the guards had had military training but were all used to semi or fully automatic weapons but to a man they were visible shaken by what they had just witnessed

Quick though he'd been, Menzies had drawn his Beretta and was holding the gun to Karen's head. Niles cursed himself for not taking Menzies out first. He was the only man with a gun.

'Drop the gun Senor or I'll kill the girl'. Menzies threatened Karen ramming the muzzle in the terrified girl's ear. He turned to his henchmen and said, 'quick get his rifle'. Unfortunately, Menzies had that typical Latino characteristic of using his arms and hands to emphasise his speech and he wave the Beretta to urge his men on. It was the last conscious move that he was ever to make.

Niles struck with speed of a striking Cobra. In one fluid motion he raised the Holland & Holland to his shoulder and squeezed the trigger.

Niles second shot of the evening entered the bridge of

Menzies nose, tore out the back of his head and pierced the brain of a man standing all of ten feet behind him. This time he had fired from the shoulder to ensure he didn't hit the girl but his reload was again, so fluid and quick, he had another round up the breech before the echo of the shot had died away.

'Right you bastards – on the floor face down and your hands out in front of you'. Niles decided to press his luck while the guards were in a subdued mood. He also needed to charge the rifle's magazine. The Holland & Holland only held four in the magazine and he had fired two already. And if they saw him reloading they might try rushing and overpowering him.

The guards lowered themselves down and turned face down and stretched their arms out to their front. In less than ten seconds they had seen their boss and two of their comrades eliminated by the strange gringo and they were in no mood to argue.

Niles had just handed the machete over to Jackie Fields and asked her to cut the remainder of the prisoners loose when a voice from over the other side of the clearing said. 'Hold it right there Senor I have you covered. Drop the gun! I think my boss, Senor Domingo would like to meet you and watch you die in some pain. Not for killing his friend Senor Menzies but for using his beautiful rifle.

'Shit'! Exploded Niles. He'd forgotten the second guard, the roving piquet. Who not unnaturally, had been attracted to the scene of all the commotion.

It had taken Sgt Rusty Irons about two hours to negotiate the remaining distance to the clearing since nightfall. He had arrived just in time to see Sandy Niles performance. And he was very impressed. He had not made any move initially as he wasn't sure whose side Niles was on. However once he had killed the chap they called Menzies

Rusty realise that Niles was a friendly.

Rusty's main weapon was the American ubiquitous Colt M16A2 a US Marine version of the famous Armalite AR –15 (M16) Rifle modified to fire three round burst of 5.56mm rounds at a muzzle velocity of 3250ft/sec. It was three of these rounds that stitched the roving piquet's shirt to his chest, killing him instantly.

'Stay down you bastards', roared Irons as he strode into the clearing and just to give his command an added emphasise he fired two three round burst over the heads of the prostrated guards.

Irons nodded to Niles and said. 'I don't know who you are but that was a pretty impressive performance you just put on. It takes years of practice to work one of those old bolt-loading rifles as slickly as you did.

'I have used this type of rifle before but I must admit that tonight is the first time I've ever fired it at anyone let alone kill them'.

'Well all I can say is you're a fucking quick learner – by the way, my name is Irons – Rusty to my friends for pretty obvious reasons'.

'Niles – Sandy to my friends – also for obvious reasons' said Niles pointing to his sandy coloured hair.

'My next question might sound a little strange', continued Niles. 'But what the fuck are you doing in the middle of the Colombian Rain Forest pulling my arse out of a fire. You aren't walking your dog by any chance?'

'No', Irons grinned. 'But I think I've found the people we were sent to locate'. He nodded towards the bemused passengers who'd watched their fortunes fluctuate from one extreme to the other over the past ten minutes with bated breath.

'How many are there of you?', inquired Niles. 'They sure as hell didn't send you out here all on your own to find us'

'There are another seven of us leaguered further down

the track. I was supposed to recce' the area and then report back to discuss a plan of action. Mind you, after all that shooting they'll be on their way here now.

By now Jackie Fields had finished cutting all the remaining prisoners free. They all hobbled over to thank their rescuers. Irons made sure than no one came between his weapon and the guards on the floor.

Just then one of the passengers, Dale came over to Niles and said, 'I think I can hear someone in that cabin over there talking on a radio'.

Niles looked at Irons who gave a quick nod of his head. They both realised what this meant. One of the Cartel's men was radioing their base and informing them on what had just taken place.

Niles rushed over to the cabin burst open the door. There was a man sat at the table using a short wave band radio gabbling away in excited Spanish. Niles slammed the butt of his rifle into the operator's skull. He never bothered to check whether or not he had killed the man. He was out for the count and was going to take no further part in events for the next day or so. But it was obvious that the operator had been transmitting for some time. He was now certain that the Cartel knew of what had transpired at the camp site.

They discussed their next plan of action. Rusty Irons figured it would be at least another half an hour before the rest of his team appeared so he ordered the male passengers to raid the cook-lean-to and rustle up some food. As luck would have it, they discovered plenty of Americans Military MREs (Meals Ready to Eat) or as the American military wags were prone to remark, 'Meals Rejected by Ethiopians'. However whilst they might not be particularly appetising they were nourishing, light and easy to carry. And this was by far the most important fact.

'What about the weapons in the hut - do you reckon we

should give some to the passengers? Enquired Niles as he indicated to Rusty where the hut was.

'No fucking way! Rusty murmured. 'I'm not sure about you but I don't fancy running around the jungle with any of this crowd armed with an automatic weapon. They'd be a more of danger to themselves and to us than any enemy. I tell you what Niles, I'll get this shower ready to march and I would appreciate it if you could find any grease in their hut/armoury and push some with plenty of bits of earth and grit down the barrels of any of the more lethal weapons. When you have done that toss in these two grenades – any problems' he looked at Niles enquiringly. Not sure whether Niles was clued up on grenades.

'No problem', Niles grinned appreciating what Rusty had in mind. If any of the Cartel's men attempted to fire the guns before cleaning out the grease and grit there was a strong chance of the gun blowing back into their face.

Ten minutes later and the party were ready to move out. 'Rusty' whispered Niles. 'Can I suggest you lead the party out of the clearing to the south, opposite to where your guys and the Dakota are located. But for Gods sake don't go more than twenty yards before circumventing the clearing and then marching north up the track.

'Why's that?'

'Well, I came in from the south and found and relocated some Claymore mines. If you disappear in that direction this crowd are bound to see which direction we leave and will eventually try to follow and I am hoping they will get an unpleasant surprise'.

'You evil bastard' grinned Rusty. 'I'm fucking glad you are on our side. You sure we will be safe at twenty yards'.

'Definitely – and I'll keep these bastards on the ground until you and the others are well clear and then I'll leave in the same direction to reinforce the spoof.

Tony Bryant and his team were very worried. Sgt Irons had been gone for two hours. Their Anxiety was compounded by the sound of a high velocity shot - a very distinctive flat crack. This was followed shortly by another of the same type.

'That's not a gunshot I am familiar with Boss, any one else identify it?' whispered Cpl Finnegan.

The remainder of the team all shook their heads. The SAS like to claim that they were able to identify almost any weapons by their signature.

A couple of minutes after the unidentified shots there was a short burst of automatic fire followed by two further short bursts.

All the SAS team immediately identified the shots as coming from a M16A2.

'I guess we had better push on to the campsite and find out exactly what's happened. I think Rusty is too canny a soldier to have got himself into to trouble but at the moment I can't think of any other reason for the shooting', murmured Capt Bryant thoughtfully. 'Trooper Lance take point, and we will have to press on even though its dark just in case Rusty got his knickers in a twist'.

Although the night was as black as pitch the team were able to follow the line of the logging track even though it was still badly overgrown despite the earlier efforts of the passengers who had passed the same way.

The team had been, 'tabbing' for about half an hour when they could distinctly hear the sounds of voices some distance to their front. As they got closer to the sound of the noise Bryant quickly motioned the team to take up ambush positions. The team fanned out to one side of the track and waited for the mysterious voices to materialise.

Sgt Irons had been trying to keep the noise of the American survivors down. Although they were now well clear of the campsite if any of the Cartels guards had escaped Niles attention then they could still cause trouble. All he or they would have to do was follow the bloody din the Americans were making.

Rusty Irons lost his temper for the third time since they had made good their escape. 'Will you bastards stop fucking yakking. You're making more bloody noise than a travelling circus, don't you realise that the unfriendlies could home in on the bloody noise you guys are making'. He hissed angrily.

Just then an enormous explosion interrupted his chastisement. Cries of alarm went up from the passengers and some looked close to panic. 'Calm down, calm down', soothed Irons', I think one of Mr Niles tricks has just reduced the odds in our favour. Hardly had the sound of the explosion died away when the night was punctuated by two flat cracks of a high velocity rifle.

Rusty Iron instantly recognised the sound of the Holland & Holland and knew that Niles was making the most of the confusion that had followed the explosion of the Claymore mine. He figured that with those two shots Sandy had probably accounted for another two guards. If he keeps this up there isn't going to be any left for us he thought to himself.

Rusty and the passengers turned to continue up the track, when from the dark shadows menacing figures just materialised. This again caused panic in the ranks of the rescued passengers who felt they were staggering from one crisis to another. It took a full two minutes to convince the passengers that Capt Bryant and his team was friendlies.

'What the fuck has been going on?' demanded Bryant.

'Let's get the passengers back to the aircraft and radio for the chopper and I'll brief you on the way back boss. From the look of all the clouds that are building up I imagine that we are going to get rain later tonight', replied Irons.

The stars in the clear bright night sky was now beginning

to be blanked out by shrouds of clouds drifting in from the east. Flashes of lighting and the distant roll of thunder in the distance indicated more rain on the way

'What are the chances of us being followed by unfriendlies back to the aircraft', asked Bryant.

'Not much. There's a character back there that is following us called Sandy Niles and He's a bloody natural Boss. Apparently he escaped capture when the rest were taken. He then sneaked into their camp. Killed a guard, stole a rifle, and killed their leader and two others. Oh! - And another thing. He worked his way round to the south of their camp, found and relocated three of their Claymore mines. One of which we have just heard go off and those two flat cracks you heard was Sandy's Holland & Holland. Having seen him use it I will be most surprised if he didn't kill another two. I tell you what boss; he'll make a welcome addition to our team'.

'Are you saying he is ex-SAS Rusty?'

'No.... but I have the impression that I have seen him somewhere before but I'm not sure where, though I'm fairly certain he's not ex – Regiment'.

'We'll give him five minute and then we will have to push on with or without him. I'd like to get this crown under cover before the rain starts and then put some sort of a defence plan into effect before some of the Cartel's morons come after us'.

'There's not much chance of that happening tonight Boss. That guy Niles killed five and I shot another for certain and I figure the Claymore mine and Sandy's shooting probable took out another two or three. I believe there were only about a dozen guards to start with so until they get reinforcements I can't see them coming after us'.

Just then their conversation was interrupted as Niles strode in view cradling his newly acquired Holland & Holland.

Chapter 13

Bogotá

Domingo was going ballistic. He'd gone to bed early only to be woken by one of his servants at half ten and told of an incoming radio signal from the first of the Cartel's new processing plants. He'd got to the radio just in time to hear the call for help and learn that his colleague Al Menzies and half his guard's had been wiped out before the radio went off the air.

'Try to raise then again', snarled Domingo.

The radio operator tried again and after no success tried to raise the camp on the pre - arranged alternate frequency to no avail.

'Their set is definitely not responding – it is either switched off or it is broken. I'm not even getting a carrier wave', complained the operator.

'Never mind – there's not much we can do for the moment. I'll have to get some more of our foot soldiers over from Cali in the morning and have them transferred to the site'.

Most of Domingo and his colleagues' former operations

had revolved around the Cali area over on the West Coast. They now had the logistic problem of flying men by fixed wing from Cali to their forward airstrip to the South East of Bogotá, after that, having to chopper them to the new processing site. It took time to do this and at the moment, time was not on their side.

Domingo made several phone calls to Bogotá airport and ordered the Short Skyvan into operation immediately. With luck, they might be able to start transferring some of their soldiers from Cali to the forward airstrip by first light. But on Sunday night most of them would be as drunk as, 'pack rats', and no good to either man nor beast.

Domingo wrestled with the problem for two hours then decided it was time to update his colleagues. Despite the early hours he rang them and brought them up to date at what had transpired.

They all agreed that the situation was dangerous and as they were all in Bogotá decided to hold a conference at five in the morning. After speaking with his colleagues, Domingo decided to have another go at trying to raise the camp site by radio – to no avail.

They assembled at five in the morning. The Cartel's mood was sombre and tempers were short. They'd poured a lot of money into this new operation and were not prepared to see their money channelled down some sink hole without doing something about it.

Domingo opened the meeting in his usual aggressive manner.

'As you know, I was woken last night to be told that problems had occurred at the new site. Prior to that, Al Menzies had called me earlier to report that all the passengers had been captured including the wife and daughter of the American Defence secretary and everything was under control. Apparently he spoke too soon. One of the passengers managed to avoid capture, killed a guard and stole my Sporting Rifle. Before the radio went silent, it was reported that this passenger: Niles I think his name was, managed to kill Al and three others and release the passengers. Since then we have heard nothing from the site'.

'Are you saying that this man Niles was one of the passengers on the Dakota' snarled Pedro Degannes in disbelief. 'And not only that - but he managed to outwit and get away from our twelve armed guards'.

'We don't know the full story yet', continued Domingo. 'But bear in mind that the usual procedure is to lock the weapons up at night unless we are expecting trouble. The only people that were actually armed would probably have been Al and two or three guards on piquet duty. The remainder would have been made to stash their arms in the Armoury. If you remember three years ago, when it was customary for my guards to carry their weapons all night the numbskulls got stinking drunk and ended up shooting holes in one another. By the following morning I'd lost five of my best gunmen. Even so it's hard to believe that this one man has managed to overcome twelve guards and get away with all the prisoners'.

'If he has how long is it going to take to get additional guards transferred from Cali, and get them on the ground at the new site?' Franco DeNero asked.

'Pablo – you have the most intimate knowledge of the area. How long do you reckon it will take to get about twenty men on the ground out there?' Domingo nodded to Ferreira.

Ferreira thought for a moment. 'The most awkward part is getting the men together in Cali. None of them were warned for duty so they will be spread all over the bordellos in town – most of them as pissed as, 'pack rats'. However, out of the sixty or so on our payroll we should be able to rustle up twenty by six this morning. It will then take another hour to get them to the airstrip, plus another forty minutes to the campsite. Say two hours at the outside – mind you, it will take plenty of arse kicking to achieve that but we've got the right men to do it'.

'Good, then let's start kicking arse and get them out there as soon as we can', growled Domingo. 'We must eliminate these people – I'd hoped to use the wife and daughter of the Defence Secretary as hostages but I think events have moved on too far for that now. And this fucker Niles or what ever they call him – I want his balls for stealing my rifle and then using it to kill one of our friends. If it's at all possible, I want him taken alive so we can take our time in extracting our revenge. Pablo - make sure our men are made aware of this fact'.

'Consider it done, Francesco. I would like to leave now unless any of you've anything further to add – it's going to take a lot of arse kicking to get things moving, so if you guys have nothing more I'm on my way. If you do need to contact me I'll be at the forward airstrip where I can chase up both the fixed wing and the chopper flights', and Ferreira stood up. Turned and strode out the room.

'Do you think it is wise to murder the wife and daughter of the US Defence Secretary Francesco? This could cause a lot of grief to be unloaded on us', Teddy Garcia queried.

Domingo shrugged his shoulders and raised his open hands. 'But it's not us that murdered them. The crime would've been committed by bandits who lurk in the rain forest to the South East of Bogotá. At this point there is no one to associate us with dastardly deed. Our most important consideration is that our processing sites to the Southeast remain a secret. And if ever any of these passengers get out alive they will be interrogated by American Intelligence as to what they saw and heard and their location will be cross referred to the crashed Dakota's from which they will be able to pin point out site location. No! - these bastards have definitely seen too much to leave the area alive'

'If any one can offer another safe solution to the problem I would like to hear it'. I don't want to be accused at a later date of making the wrong decision – we are all in this together', concluded Domingo.

His query was greeted with a stony silence – initially no one had another solution to offer.'

'Yes – I have a suggestion', ventured Teddy Garcia

'I think we should capture and kill all these fucking passengers. Put them in the fuselage of the crashed aircraft, soak them and the aircraft with aviation fuel, set light to it and claim that they were all killed when it crashed and brewed up. It would also be a handy way of disposing of the bodies of those killed in the ambush. Obviously we would have to remove all bullets in their bodies but if we make the fire intense enough all that will be left of their bodies to check is their dentures'.

'What a splendid idea. That's the sort of input I'm looking for', declared Domingo admiringly. 'Any dissenters?' he continued looking at his four colleagues. There were none.

'I agree, it's the best idea we've had all morning. This way they can have as many suspicions as they want but won't be able to prove a bloody thing. I vote we go for this idea'. Frank DeNero raised his hand to emphasis his belief.

Domingo noted the other three raised hands. 'Great! Then that's what we will brief the guys to do going out to the site this morning'.

The meeting ended. They retired for an early and somewhat solemn breakfast. However, the decision on what to do with the passengers had lifted some of the gloom that pervaded the start of the meeting

Domingo had finished his breakfast and was tying up details for the movement of his soldiers to the new site when the phone rang.

'Get to a secure phone', the voice said on the other end of the line and the person rang off. The nearest secure phone the Cartel owned in Bogotá was at Pablo's Offices. Domingo made his way there in about five minutes flat. It could only be one of three people who wanted to converse over a secure line and they were all in the States.

He picked up the secure phone and dialled the number to raise Senator Sam Jackson.

'What's the problem Senator?'

'I'll tell you what the problem is', snarled Jackson. 'Some arseholes of yours have been using our names on an unsecured radio net and it's been picked up by the American Intelligence Listening Service. They are attuned to specific words – like, Drugs, Bombs, and American Senators etc. that triggers an alarm system which sets off fucking bells, whistles and hooters across the whole of the United States. I've had the CIA and the DEA all asking fucking questions as to why my name and Senator Al Thornton's are being bandied around by recognised members of the Colombian Cartel. I thought it was made quite clear during our initial meeting that we would only converse by secure means'.

'Yes that was our agreement and the person responsible for the lapse in security is no longer with us. He was unfortunately shot yesterday but in the meantime, I've told the only other members who know of your involvement on no account to discuss the fact over the phone or by radio – it wont happen again'.

'Well let's keep it that way Francesco. I've actually managed to turn what was an embarrassing situation to our advantage. I've told our people that the Cartel is anti Thornton and me because we are so adamant that drugs must never become legal. So far they have bought our explanation, but if our names keep getting mentioned in association with yours someone is going to rumble our arrangement'

'Did your Intelligence Service pick up on the fact that

we had some American survivors in our hands?'.

'I don't think so – the part about American senators was not in the same transmission. So long as your goons don't mention American passengers or the word 'hostages' it's unlikely that the transmission will be recorded and the authorities alerted'.

'I'll make sure that is implemented Senator. If you have nothing further I'll ring off we have plenty to keep us busy out at the new sites at the moment'.

'Not at the moment – the only other point I would like to make is that you keep a tight lid on what you do with the American survivors. If it ever gets out that you murder them you will be in deep shit and there is nothing that any of us State side can do to help you'.

'We have discussed this within the Cartel and we have decided that the only option we have left is to put the bodies in the crashed Dakota and set fire to it. Making it look as though the aircraft crashed on landing, caught fire, and all the passengers and crew died in the ensuing inferno'.

'Sounds all right in theory, but with the wife and daughter of the defence Secretary involved I don't wish to be a party to your plans', replied Jackson callously. 'But are you sure you can prevent the real story from ever surfacing?'

'I'm sure', and Domingo put the phone down and decided then and there that he would fly out to the forward airstrip and keep a personal eye on what was happening. They could not afford any more mistakes.

Pablo Ferreira was pleasantly surprised to see the number of men they had managed to raise in Cali and transfer to the Forward Airstrip. It was just coming up to half seven and the first batch of ten men plus a 300gal fuel bladder that was to be used for refuelling the Super Pumas at the Camp site was already on its way there. The second Puma was refuelling and would soon be leaving with a similar load.

Ferreira had figured that if he could get twenty fighting

men on the ground at the Camp site then the two Pumas could both make an additional trip with fuel drums to fill the bladders previously positioned at the processing site. This would enable the Helicopters to refuel there without having to return to the Airstrip. Allowing the choppers to spend more time in the air helping to search for the missing passengers.

Whilst the Puma was still refuelling the Skyvan, a twin engine turbo prop' fixed wing aircraft landed and rolled up to the Dispersal where Pablo was standing. The aircraft had barely stopped when out jumped Francesco full of his own self-importance.

'Pablo, I've spoken to our friends in the States and they're doing their nut about the use of their names over insecure radio nets. Their names have apparently been picked up by the US Intelligence Listening Service. Naturally they are not amused and as you and I are the only ones here who know of their involvement we must ensure that no mention is made of their names –okay'.

'That's fine by me and as you do all the phoning to them, I'll leave any liaison necessary to you'.

'Good! Now who is in charge of our men going to the Camp site?'

Rudy Goodge, He's an ex- South African mercenary. A bloody good man, if any one can catch the survivors he's your man'.

'Call him over please'.

Pablo called Goodge over and introduced him to Domingo.

Goodge was an impressive looking man standing well over six-foot and build like a Springbok second row forward. He had that hard look that reflected his profession. His nose had obviously been broken (probably on several occasions) and his square flat face was badly pitted with old pox scars. His light blue eyes had a strange vacant look about them until he turn his full gaze on you. Then they were very unnerving. His whole ambience projected menace. And after giving him a good once over, Domingo decided that he was the ideal man for the unpleasant task to be undertaken.

'Look Rudy', began Domingo. 'At the moment, out at our new Processing Laboratory Camp Site we have a grade, 'A' fuck up going on and you are the man we have chosen to try and rectify it. This is what you are going to have to do'.

'There are some passengers from a crashed Dakota out near our processing site who were capture by Al Menzies but have managed to escape. They have seen and heard too much. Plus which, several of their colleagues were mistakenly killed in an ambush that should never have happened. However that's water under the bridge and there is nothing we can do to rectify it. So we're going to have to remove all the witnesses. This is what you are going to have to do. Are you clear so far?'

'It doesn't take a brain surgeon to understand what you have said so far', grunted Goodge with a shrug of his massive shoulders'

'Well believe it or not, that's what we all thought before this present fuck up. That's why I want to make sure you are completely certain of what is required before you get out there. Okay'

'No problem'. Goodge shrugged his shoulders again.

'These survivors from the air crash have to be caught and eliminated in such a way that if the bodies are ever discovered they cannot be traced back to us. To do this we want you to kill them and place them in the fuselage of the Dakota, soaked it and them with fuel and then set the whole lot on fire. The fire must be intense enough to completely incinerate all bodies to hide any physical injuries that they may have incurred during their capture. You can use some of the Avtur fuel from the fuel bladders to ensure a really intense fire. This will of course, mean that any bullets in their bodies must be removed before they are incinerated. Are you quite clear on this?

'No problem boss'. If Goodge felt any nausea about carrying out such a gruesome task he failed to show it.

'Are there any women involved and if there are, do you mind if we amuse ourselves before they meet their maker'.

'That's up to you - but I don't want any fuck-ups. When you have finished with them, and I mean all of them. I want them incinerated to such an extent that their remains can only be recognised by dental checks. - Okay!'

'Yep! - And what I'll do if you don't mind I'll keep the execution squad down to just four of us, that way it will be easier to keep the matter quiet'.

'Good thinking Goodge, the fewer the better'. Domingo had a quiet smile to himself and admired the way that Goodge was covering his arse. Goodge knew that if he reduced the execution squad to less than four there was a strong chance that they could be wasted in turn to remove all evidence of linking the massacre to the Cartel.

'Okay I won't keep you any longer Goodge but remember the most important thing is that there is no evidence left that can link the deaths of these Americans to us'.

Goodge just grunted, gave a wave of his hand, turned and boarded the chopper that had just completed its re-fuelling.

'Do you think we will get away with this?' Pablo asked. 'It's a lot of bodies to dispose of".

Domingo shrugged his shoulders.' I figure that out there we could murder a whole fucking village and nobody would be any the wiser for months after the event. For Christ sake - there are areas in that neck of the woods that haven't' even been explored. Let's go get some coffee - I presume you have some Pablo?

Chapter 14

Rain Forest

Captain Tony Bryant gave Niles a pretty intense scrutiny and was very impressed with what he saw. Niles was obviously completely at home in the jungle and appeared quite calm after what must have been an intense hour or so.

'Rusty tells me you acquitted your self extremely well back there. But how come you weren't taken when the others were captured Mr Niles?' Bryant asked.

'The name is Sandy. Well it's quite a long story but I'll be as brief as I can. I disagreed about leaving the aircraft and trying to walkout but the Film Director, that arse hole over there'. Niles nodded in the direction of cress fallen Costello. 'He insisted that if the passengers trekked down the logging track they would eventually reach civilisation. Against the advice of the aircraft's captain I might add. Not only that, but when they saw the Puma helicopter; with an under slung load on, he rushed off headlong into the clearing without checking to see who or what they were, this, despite me advising him to the contrary. Anyway, I separated from the main group before they set off for the camp and followed at a safe distance to the rear well apart from the main party. When they were ambushed I was well to the east of the track and evaded capture. I circled around and approached the camp site from the south - the opposite direction to where the ambush was mounted. Whilst the guards were having their supper and getting pissed I managed to break into their armoury and steal some weapons. The rest you probably know from Rusty.'

'Just about – what are the chances of us being followed tonight? – You were the last to leave'

'No chance, there were actually only twelve guards - the remainder were workmen and Lab' technicians building what I think, is a Drug Processing Laboratories. I suspect this is why they are so sensitive about strangers. Rusty shot one guard. I killed four initially. Then two or three were killed or maimed when the Claymore mine detonated and I shot another two during the subsequent confusion. They were both hit but in the dark it was impossible to say how badly. At the moment I would say that there is only about three or four at the most who are not injured. I don't know if Rusty told you but unknown to us there was a guard in the radio shack talking to his base. So I've no doubt that by tomorrow morning we're going to see further reinforcements being choppered in'.

'Right I think our immediate priority is to get these people under cover before the rain starts, In fact we'll be lucky to get under cover before it commences. Lance! - take point. Finnegan and Gonzales right flank. Grimes and Miles left flank. Sandy could you pair up with Rusty and watch our six o'clock just in case some of those Cartel idiots have a rush of blood to the head, go ape shit, and decide to try and follow us. Hezeltine and I will remain with the main party and help with stragglers'. Bryant waved his arm forward and they set of at a fairly brisk pace.

Although the night was still pitch black they were moving along the track with the knowledge that there were no booby traps to worry about, consequently they made good progress.

Niles and Rusty Irons took up the rearguard of the party, stopping in turn to listen for any follow up by members of the cartel's foot soldiers but never loosing sight of one another in the dark night. Apart from using hand signals to communicate their intentions to one another Niles and Irons had not spoken once during the trek back to the crashed Dakota.

As they approached their destination it became increasingly obvious that they were not being followed.

Suddenly Rusty said.'You know Sandy, there's something about you that leads me to believe we've met somewhere before – were you ever a member of the SAS?

'No. I'm afraid not'.

'Well you sure as hell have certainly served in the British Army Sandy'.

'What makes you think that?' Sandy Niles queried.

'Because for the last hour you and I have been using hand signals for tactical movement that are specific to British Army and not once did you have to ask me what I was indicating'.

Niles realised that he had been hoisted by his own petard. There was no point in trying to avoid the obvious. He had responded to Rusty's signals without question and he initiated his own without thought.

'As a matter of fact I did serve with the British Army but it is not a subject that I am happy to talk about Rusty and I would be most grateful if you would let the matter drop'.

'No problem Sandy all I can say is you must have been one hell of a soldier from what I've witness this evening'.

Their conversation was drawn to a close as they reached the Dakota's fuselage.

'Okay – let's have all the passengers inside the aircraft', said Bryant. 'Rusty are we sure there was no follow up by Cartel thugs?'

'Definitely not boss. We alternated waiting behind at various intervals and checked for follow up. There was none'.

The rain was now upon them so they delayed making an evening meal and decided to get under cover in the aircraft and have a briefing. As with all SAS briefings, every member of the patrol was involved and Bryant made a point of including Sandy Niles. As Capt Bryant was about to start the briefing, Nathan Costello approached the team and said, 'as the senior civilian here and the Director of the Film Company I should be privy to your briefing'.

Niles was about to give Nathan a roasting when Bryant held up his hand.

'All of you will be apprised on what action we intend to take but at the moment, I only want members of my team whilst we discuss the tactical situation'.

'But I must insist that I be included', stated Costello pompously.

Niles nodded to Bryant indicating he would like to say something.

'Look Nathan - it was you who insisted on filming for another twenty four hours after receiving the hurricane warning, which prevented you and your friends from getting clear of the area. I would also like to point out, that it was you who decided to try and walkout of here after both Capt Dino and myself told you our best chance of rescue was to remain with the aircraft. You do realise don't you, that if we had remained here with the aircraft as Dino and I suggested, all of us would have been flown out in relays on the same helicopter that brought the SAS team in'.

'Well any one can be wise after the event' replied mollified Costello.

'I'm afraid you suffer from, 'Delusions of Grandeur'. You live in; 'Cloud Cuckoo Land' and apparently you have problems separating reality from your celluloid world. Therefore my advice to Captain Bryant and his men would be to completely disregard anything you have to say'.

Bryant asserted his authority and said with voice that brooked no argument. 'Mr Costello, this is a military briefing - you are excluded – however once we have decided on our plan of action you and all the passengers will be told what we have in mind. Now please leave us'.

Capt Bryant set the briefing going. 'Right lets get the maps out and see what options are available. We have established to within ten meters the position of the Dakota with our Magellan GPI's (Global position Indicators). Cpl Finnegan can you radio our position to the Helicopter Company and ask them to lift us out of here first light tomorrow '.

'I've already tried twice during our march back here – no joy. I don't think they are likely to open shop until they come into work tomorrow morning, and that being Monday I wouldn't bank on them being in before oh nine hundred hours'.

'Shit!' Bryant murmured. 'This is going to be awkward. I can see this developing into a race as to who gets to us first – the Huey or the Cartels reinforcements. Get Capt Dino over here and let's ask him what the chances are of any choppers getting out here tonight'.

'I think I can answer that for you', said Niles. 'For a pilot to fly out in this part of the world where there is no artificial light to give him a horizon he would have to be instrument rated. I have lived in Venezuela for the past three years and I can tell you that Instrument Rated Helicopter Pilots in this part of the world are about as rare as 'Rocking Horse Shit'.

Bryant gave him a long hard look. 'Sandy I like what I have seen of you so far but you are beginning to unnerve me. As I understand it you were just a chauffeur. Yet you display all the characteristics of a fucking good soldier. Now you are talking in a most positive and knowledgeable manner about flying helicopters. Just what the fuck is your background. If we are to accept your input into this briefing we must be sure you know what you're talking about, otherwise you can join your friend Nathan and the others over there'.

Niles realised that the team was too intelligent to be fed any more bullshit.

'As a matter of fact I was a professional pilot and flew helicopters in the North Sea out to the Off Shore Oil Platforms. In fact I was a Training Captain and an Instrument Rating Examiner so I know a bit about helicopters. However I had to leave the UK for health reasons and would be most grateful if you kept this information within this group'.

Suddenly Rusty Irons exploded. 'Got you! Got you! I knew I'd seen you somewhere before. You were the Flight Commander of the SAS Augusta 109 Helicopters at Sterling lines (The 22 SAS Regiments Base Camp in the UK). I remember you now. You spent all your spare time on the bloody ranges shooting as much as any man in the regiment. If I remember correctly you established a hell of a reputation with the Accuracy International L96A1 7.62mm. The snipers rifle – that's why you're so bloody good at manipulating the Mauser bolt action'.

There was a stunned silence for few seconds whilst the rest of the team absorbed Rusty's outburst. The rest of the team was considerably younger than Niles and Rusty so the events under discussion happened some time before they joined the Regiment.

Bryant gave Niles an even further hard look. 'I think I can speak for all of us about keeping your background private. But the most important thing for the moment is that we have established your pedigree and you are definitely qualified to take part in this briefing. Which brings us back to the original question Niles – you believe that it's most unlikely that any one will fly out into the hinterland in the middle of the night'.

'Correct; with the present cloud cover there's going to be no horizon; however, I do fore see a problem looming tomorrow. I heard Menzies, their boss, the man I shot, mention a forward airstrip forty minutes flying time away to the East of Bogotá where their Super Pumas are based. As I understand it, your Huey is based in Bogotá Airport which is to the west of Bogotá and a Huey only cruises at about 120kts maximum. Now the Super Puma clods along at about 145kts, so if both aircraft took off at the same time I figure the Puma is going to arrive at least thirty minute before your Huey'.

Bryant looked thoughtful for a moment. 'That is going to cause us some problems so I figure we'll have to keep the guards at the campsite occupied in order to delay their search for us. Okay you guys let's hear some ideas'. He looked round his team expectantly.

Trooper Lance was the first to comment. 'If there's a danger of the Cartel's men getting here first I think we should have an alternative plan in case they come North up the logging track. I think we should check the map and see what our options are at walking out to the Northwest'.

Bryant nodded in agreement and spread out a large-scale map of the local area. This was the first time that Niles had been able to orientate himself since the crash. The aerial chart he'd obtained from the Dakota was much too small a scale to be used for ground map reading.

The Logging track that they were positioned on at the moment continued further north for about another five miles where, according to the map, it finally petered out. However, there appeared to be a fairly steep ravine about two miles northwest of their present location, which had a footbridge, marked as crossing it. Although the ravine did not appear to be very wide the map contours were so closely knitted they were almost touching one another indicating that the sides of the ravine were extremely steep.

'Any one noticed this ravine as we flew over it yesterday'. Bryant looked around his team expectantly.

Cpl (Fingers) Finnegan was the first to respond. 'Yeah I noticed it. It was not long after we cleared the Llanos (open grassy plains) say about ten minutes or so and then we were over the rain forest prior to spotting the downed Dakota'.

Niles was the quickest to interpret the time scale. '120kts that's two miles a minute say twenty five miles plus two miles this side of the ravine. We're looking at about thirty miles in ballpark figures to walk out of here. With the passengers in tow it might just as well be three hundred miles. We would never make it with them'.

'Let's shoot all the bastards – that'll ease the problem', laughed (Hatch) Hezeltine grimly.

Rusty nodded his head in agreement. 'True Hatch but I don't think we would win many "Brownie Points"'.

'Enough of that crap. Our sole reason for coming here was to extract them not annihilate them', said Bryant grinning in amusement. 'But I have to agree with Sandy - the chance of walking out with this lot is not feasible. However, if we could get this crowd to the other side of the footbridge we could avoid being outflanked and hold the Cartel's men off until the chopper lifted us out. Any one else has anything to add?'

Irons nodded to Bryant and said. 'How about Sandy and I setting off about an hour before dawn, we would arrive at the campsite just as dawn is breaking and make, 'real bastards', of ourselves. That would give you and the passengers a better chance of getting across the footbridge safely and await the arrival of the Huey.'

Bryant thought for a couple of seconds. He was surprised to hear Rusty suggesting the use of Niles rather than another SAS Trooper.

'Sounds good but that could leave you and Sandy trapped on the wrong side of the ravine'.

'No problem - we will have a tactical radio and a Sarbe beacon and can be lifted out at a later date'

'It sounds great to me', said Nile. 'Both Rusty and I know the camp location so it figures that we're the best pair to create a diversion'.

Bryant got to his feet, folded the map and said. 'Normally Sandy I wouldn't agree to using you as a civilian but with your military background and your performance so far I think you are going to prove a valuable asset - therefore I agree. Right lets join the passengers and brief them of our intentions'.

Niles nudged Rusty's arm and asked. 'That big chap – the one you all call Lancelot. He's had nothing but a bloody great grin on his face ever since I've seen him – what's his secret?'

'If you had screwed what he had screwed Saturday night I reckon you would also have a bloody great grin on your face. She was drop dead gorgeous. Mind you, Lance beds more crumpet than the rest of us put together, including the boss and he's no slouch when it comes to corralling women'.

'I can see where he gets the nickname Lancelot'.

'You might find this hard to believe', continued Rusty. 'But we have been on some detachments in quite civilised parts of the world and women who have seen him but never been introduced or met him have actually bribed the hotel receptionist to get his room number. They then knocked his door. Lance has taken them into his room, bedded them and then they have left, and he has never even asked them their name. Mind you, he has all the right equipment and the women seem to sense it'.

'However', continued the grinning Rusty. 'The consensus of opinion amongst the lads is that this time he has been smitten by this last lass and he has now definitely gone into the nest building mode'.

Niles just grinned, 'Some people get all the luck'

The rain had ceased as quickly as it had started. The clouds had now rolled away leaving a beautiful starlight sky. But there was further lighting out to the east indicating that more rain might be on its way. It was decided to have the meals outside the aircraft.

The SAS team quickly organised some hot meals using the American MREs that they had stolen from the Cartel's camp. Most of the passengers were now very hungry. They had not had a proper meal since leaving the crashed aircraft the previous day.

It was quite noticeable how the passengers relaxed as the SAS team mingled with them and before long were laughing and chatting, despite the potential problems of the coming day. Although Sandy Niles had been accepted by the SAS as an operational colleague he was still reluctant to talk about his background and kept very much to himself and avoided company and making small talk.

Jackie Fields noticed how he tended to isolate himself and wonder why. Being a woman she was a natural 'sticky beak' so she thought she would try and find out why. She decided to go over and thank Sandy hoping that this would lead to him opening up and inveigle some information about his background.

'You don't seem to be mixing much Sandy so I thought now might be a good time to thank you for all you did back there at that dreadful camp. I shudder to think what would have happened if you hadn't intervened'.

'Well we were very lucky that Rusty turned up when he did otherwise I think I would be six foot under by now'

'Yes, but you didn't know Rusty was there when you

prevented that animal from molesting young Karen. And I've heard from some of the SAS guys that you and Rusty are going back to the camp again in the morning in order to delay the search for us. Wouldn't it be more sensible for two SAS soldiers to go rather than you – a civilian?'

'Not really, I was a former paratrooper with experience in the jungle warfare - but more importantly, Rusty and I know the camp layout and on this type of a sortie that's a big bonus'.

Just then young Karen crept over to Niles, slid onto his knees for comfort. She was shivering and obviously suffering a bit from delayed shock so Sandy put his arm round the young girl and gave her a comforting hug. His body heat warmed Karen helping her to relax.

'Hello little girl what's your name?' He teased.

'My god you're honoured', said the startled Jackie Fields. 'The only two other people I've seen her do that to are her Father and Grandfather'.

'Well I don't know about that', murmured Niles. 'But I think our little girl has been through a lot in the last twenty four hours so I think she's due some TLC'

Karen looked up at Niles and said. 'What's TLC Sandy?'

'Well in my country it stands for Tender Loving Care but I'm not sure if the initials have the same meaning in the States', answered Sandy.

'I think it means the same in the States but if it doesn't then we are going to make dam sure it soon does – aren't we Karen', replied Jackie.

The sky was now pitch black but studded with brilliant stars making it a balmy night. And now the rain had stopped the rain forest came alive with insect and animal noises. Several of the young women were now gently flirting with the SAS soldiers somewhat to the annoyance of Peter Milo the middle aged singer. A rich man, and normally used to getting all the attention from the attended ladies but out here in the jungle he was out of his normal environment and his nervousness showed. His lack of assurance was sensed by the women.

However they quickly recognised the self-assurance displayed by the SAS Troopers who were completely at home in the jungle and so relaxed that the women just naturally gravitated to them.

Jackie looked at Sandy Niles and noticed him smiling. 'What the joke Sandy?'

'I'm just looking at the big 'White Hunter Syndrome' kicking in'. He laughed

Jackie laughed also. 'Okay - what's that supposed to mean'.

'Oh it's a situation that used to develop in the African bush in the days of the Big Game Hunting Safaris. Rich, powerful men with their beautiful wives who were used to being the Alfa male in the civilised world found themselves in a totally new and strange environment, suddenly, they are no longer sure of themselves and their wives/girl friends sense their uncertainty. However, the big white hunter is totally at home in the bush and the women quickly sense this and it is not unknown for the women to transfer their affection to them. In fact there have been several recorded cases of very glamorous film stars having affairs with white hunters during a film or Safari'.

'My god you make us sound so shallow and conniving', said Jackie accusingly.

'Don't knock it', laughed Niles. 'It's been going on for thousands of years and I figure it will go on for thousands more. It's natural for the dominant male to spread his genes as much as possible and at the same time for the female to select the best male to protect and provide for their offspring. Mind you, in the more sophisticated parts of the world the roles between male and female are becoming more indistinct. Physical strength is no longer a requirement in most occupations. And in some cases the woman has become the major provider. However out here we are back to old world values'.

Jackie Fields noticed that although she was getting Sandy Niles to talk it was like trying to get blood out of a stone to discuss his background. It was like trying to observe his personality through a Venetian blind. They had been chatting for about an hour and Jackie realised that she knew no more about his background than she did when they first met back at the airstrip.

Apart from the two soldiers on guard somewhere outside the aircraft most of the SAS team were chatting up the four younger women. As usual, Trooper Lance was attracting a lot of attention from the opposite sex but for once in his life he politely ignoring it, much to their chagrin.

By ten o'clock the exciting events of the day began to take their toll and the passengers rapidly tired and one by one started to fall out looking for some where to sleep

Niles nodded to Jackie Fields and said. 'I think there's a nice spot in the tail section where you and Karen can bed down for the night. I think our little girl is getting tired and she has walked a long way today. I'm sure once we have made her comfortable she'll be able to get some sleep'.

"Are you staying in the aircraft tonight Sandy?'

'No I'm the outrider, remember'.

She laughed. 'Oh yes I do remember'.

'No - I'll be bedding down outside in the bush with the rest of the SAS team. That way, if any one tries to approach the aircraft they will have to get past us first. See you two lovely ladies in the morning after we get back from the campsite'

Niles gave them a wink and marched out of the aircraft

Chapter 15

Camp Site

The Monday morning transfer of men from the forward strip to the camp site had started well but was now being hampered by some ground mist, which had been stirred up by the early morning sun. It was swirling off the tops of the trees and forming a layer of cloud about a hundred feet above the jungle canopy. This made it impossible for the second helicopter pilot to identify the helicopter Landing Site (HLS). As the sun climbed higher over the horizon it would gradually burn off but in the mean time it was causing a slight hiatus in the transferring of the Cartel's men.

Domingo had managed to get Rudy Goodge and twenty men plus two refuelling bladders out to the campsite but now the mist was delaying the transfer. Although he now thought he outnumbered the SAS team by almost three to one he wouldn't feel really confident until he could get thirty, or better still, forty men on the ground.

Once they'd got the refuelling bladders up and working it would mean that the choppers could refuel at both ends and thus increase their outbound payload to the campsite.

And more important, use the choppers to search from the air for the missing passengers.

The first Puma had found the campsite without difficulty before the sun had stirred the mist up. The second one that had been flying Rudy Goodge had to circle around for about ten minutes above the decaying mist, before finally locating the HLS.

The first thing Goodge did after landing was to set up a re- fuelling point for the incoming helicopters. Goodge had encountered the Rhodesian SAS during his years in the South African Army years ago and knew how capable they could be. He wasn't going to take any chances. The forward refuelling point would give them much greater flexibility later in the day when they could, if necessary, use the Pumas for aerial recce' and inserting the Cartel's men to cut off and catch the survivors.

After landing Goodge quickly started to get patrols organised. The men had been grabbed so quickly at Cali that many of them had no weapons. These were ordered by Goodge to grab a weapon from the camp armoury. Although two grenades had blown up the camp armoury they'd done more damage to the building than the weapons themselves, most were still serviceable.

Goodge was organising his men into four man patrols and was doing it too efficiently for the two pairs of eyes that were watching him with considerable alarm and interest.

Rusty and Sandy had set off from the aircraft site about an hour before daybreak aiming to get to the campsite just before dawn. Rusty had the small tactical radio but it was switched off and would only be switched on when they wanted to transmit. They'd decided to keep just clear of the track to reduce any obvious signs of it being used.

Once they were within about eight hundred metres of the camp site they broke off some thin wands to use for locating any booby trap trip wires. In the jungle they were normal set at chest height to prevent jungle animals from inadvertently setting them off. Holding their wand gentle in front of them they managed to locate only two Claymore mines and these were two that Niles had relocated the previous day.

They reached the campsite about twenty minutes prior to the first of the helicopters arriving with the reinforcements. As they approached the camp site they could hear the early morning activity as the workers and guards set to with their morning ablutions and started cooking their breakfast. By the time they had reached it they were both absolutely soaked to the skin. The rain fall from the previous night had left the vegetation absolutely saturated and Niles remembered how lucky he'd been to qualify as a pilot and leave this type of soldering to the hard nuts like Rusty and his colleagues. Rusty and Niles carefully circulated the area and as they had noted earlier, the site was in fact, located on the confluence of two tracks. One, which ran from north to south with the crashed Dakota, located five miles to the north of the camp. The other track ran east to west with the camp located where the tracks crossed over. This gave the Cartel's men an easier area to clear and four natural approach lanes regardless of wind for the helicopters to land and take off from. The Portakabins (Prefabricated cabins) had been sited well into the sides of the tracks making them impossible to see from the air. The roof of one had already been camouflaged with sods of earth to mask the infra red signature.

During their recce around the campsite they had discovered a further two Claymore mines which Rusty had disarmed and lifted. They decided to take the mines with them so they could be used if necessary, against the Cartel's men. The previous camp boss had moved all the cut down vegetation to the edge of the clearing. Rusty and Niles used this as a screen whilst circumnavigating the camp site.

They finally found a good position to the south of the campsite from where to observe the camp's activity.

The first Super puma landed about thirty minutes after dawn and off loaded 400gal fuel Bladder and eight men. Shortly afterwards the early morning sun has stirred and increased the mist masking the HLS and they could hear the second Puma circling overhead trying to get a clear view of it. After a short delay the strengthening sun burnt the mist off sufficiently for the pilot to approach and land. This time, ten men deplaned and six forty-gallon drums of Avtur fuel were also off-loaded.

Rudy Goodge immediately started getting the new arrivals organised.

'I want that re-fuelling site set up in the next half hour or somebody is going to get my boot so far up his arse he'll be cleaning boot polish off his teeth for the next week', he snarled.

Rusty and Sandy looked at one another. 'I wouldn't like to meet that bastard down a dark alley' whispered Rusty.

'You're right there I figure he rules with his fists as much as anything else. Further more he's got too much, "get up and go", for my liking', replied Niles 'And more worrying, he seems to know what he's about. From the way and speed in which he's organising things this bastard is going to be a real problem'.

'Right! - Let's have you bastards organised into four men groups', roared Rudy Goodge 'I want you four men to circle the camp and try and find any trace of the survivors. When you have done so let me know, and we'll get a chase party organised. Now move your arses'.

One of the original guards approached Goodge and said. 'Boss, when the survivors left they went down the southern track but it was too dark to follow especially after we ran into the mines they'd set'.

'What fucking mines? Where the hell did the passengers

of a crashed aircraft get mines from?'

'I don't know', replied the cowed guard. 'But it was too dark and dangerous to follow them there were only four of us uninjured'.

'Yeah well we will look into that later on – but setting off to the south could well have been a bluff so I want you guys to circle the camp and try and pick up their trail. Now listen out loud and clear. All survivors and their rescuers are to be taken to the crashed aircraft five miles to the north of this location and I mean dead bodies as well as live ones – is that quite clear!'

His men gave a series of nods and grunts to illustrate that they had understood his instructions. Goodge then waves three groups of men off to start their patrol.

Rusty looked at Niles as the ramifications of what Goodge said gradually sunk in.

'Can you think of any reasons as to why they want all the survivors taken to the location of the crashed aircraft?' Rusty queried.

'I can only think of one reason they would bother to do that and it's not a very pleasant one. I think they're are going to try and set light to the aircraft with all the passengers inside, making it appear as though we were all incinerated during the crash. Mind you, they'll have to come up with a different solution for you and your team', Niles replied.

'Maybe they're not bright enough to work that one out. It would sure look queer if they did dump the team in the aircraft, especially as we didn't get out here until two days after the crash'.

Rusty scratched his chin thoughtfully and mused.'At the moment we are playing straight into their hands by having all the passengers located at the aircraft site. However, I think that big bastard has got to go. He's just a bit too smart for my liking. I figure with him out of the way that our chances of getting out of here will increase by 100%'.

'I agree and I think our best plan is for us to withdraw as far as possible whilst still keeping our friend Goodge visible. I'll take him out with my trusty Holland & Holland and you ensure our line of retreat is clear. After the shot, I should imagine that for twenty seconds or so, there's going to be pandemonium in the camp before they get themselves organised. What do think?'

Rusty nodded his head in assent. Niles Holland & Holland had a much higher muzzle velocity than his weapon and he'd seen enough of Niles shooting skill to know he wouldn't miss.

'With their boss man dead I fancy they'll be running around like headless chickens for some minutes'.

They both edged their way carefully backwards careful not to tread on dead branches for fear of giving their position away. They needn't have bothered. The racket going on within the camp site drowned any noise they might make.. They continued edging backwards as far as they could but ensuring that they could still see Goodge organising his men. They found a nice position about forty metres from where Goodge was still kicking arse.

'Do you think you can hit him from here?' Rusty smirked

'Are you kidding - I could piss on him from here, if I miss him from this distance I promise you, I will personally go over there and club him to death with my rifle'.

'You'll need a fucking step ladder to get high enough to hit that bastard over the head', smiled Rusty grimly.

With that final remark Rusty gently withdrew to ensure that their immediate escape route was clear.

Sandy Niles got himself comfortable and rested the edge of the gun's muzzle against a tree and took careful aim at Goodge's head. He nestled the wooden stock into his right cheek. The gun was made for him. It was already beginning to feel like an old friend. He had a momentary qualm about killing some one who didn't even know that he was being observed. Then he remembered the fate that was going to be young Karen's until he'd intervened.

'This should add a little lead to you pencil. As the Actress said to the Bishop', muttered Niles as he gentle squeezed the trigger. The 6.2mm 100grain bullet left the barrel of the rifle at 3700ft/sec. That's approximately three times the speed of sound. The bullet struck Goodge just above the right ear, went straight through his head and took a large part of his skull as exited just above his left ear. It looked to an observer as though he had just run into a shut door. Goodge dropped to his knees when a second round hit him about half an inch to the left of the first hit. Goodge had died before the sound of the shot had even reached him.

Pandemonium broke out in the camp just as Rusty and Sandy had anticipated. Niles never stopped to observe what happen next but used the ensuing confusion to extricate himself. He withdrew quietly into the bush until he was well out of sight from the camp and then made his way towards Rusty. About ten yards or so Rusty called, 'psst – over here. Why the two shots Sandy?'

'Because I wanted to make sure that I didn't have to go over there and club him to death'.

They departed the campsite area to the south in the hope that the pursuing party would take off in that direction. They then circled to the North intending to join the logging track about a mile or so north of the camp. They were well pleased with the results they'd achieved. Getting rid of Goodge was a good move. The man was obviously an experienced mercenary and looked a good tactician - too good for the SAS team who were lumbered with the Film Company survivors.

After half an hours trekking they turned due east to intercept the northern logging track. Once on the northern logging track they would be able to expedite their progress back to the site of the crashed Dakota.

Just as Rusty and Niles came up to the logging track about a mile north of the camp. Niles wiped the sweat off his brow and said, 'Christ I think I've walked this bloody track more times than I've driven round the M25'. Just then, they were stopped in their tracks by a voice from behind.

'Turn round nice and slowly hombres and don't make any sudden moves'.

Rusty and Niles were caught completely flat footed. They had no option to do other than they were bid, so they did as they were told and found themselves facing one of the four men patrols that Goodge had sent off directly after he had landed. Rusty was absolutely livid with himself for being caught out in such a foolish manner. Had they moved forward covering one other in turn as they should have, they would never have been caught in such a manner.

The four Colombian gunmen were not trained soldiers but they knew how to handle weapons – further more, they had their weapons up to the shoulder in the firing position. Any sudden movement by Rusty or Niles would result in instant death. There was no way they could bring their weapons to bear without being shot first.

'Aha it looks as though we have caught the hombre who stole Senor Domingo's rifle. You!' The leader of the four gunmen said pointing his American M16A1 at Sandy, 'Are going to suffer pain for a long time at Senor Domingo's pleasure. But you', he indicated Rusty.'Are going to die here and now and not very quickly I might add'. Having said that, the gunman took aim at Rust's stomach and squeezed the trigger.

Tony Bryant was beginning to get worried. For the past hour they had tried on numerous occasions to radio the 'Blades Company' that had hired them the Huey 212 helicopter. They were getting no response and Bryant was beginning to smell a rat. Their instructions to the Company had been quite clear. They could radio the Company any time during daylight hours and the Huey would be with them within the hour. If all else failed, the Huey would return in five days time to the same point where they had been dropped off to lift them out.

But the most disturbing suspicion was that someone had informed the Cartel which company had hired the chopper to the SAS team. Albeit there weren't that many companies that hired large Huey helicopters in Bogotá. This inferred that someone at the Police Field Force had been bought and had talked. Therefore, giving their position to and asking for assistance from the Police Field Force could be counter productive. If the informer was to get this information then it would be relayed to the Cartel within minutes.

Bryant called all his team together after the last abortive radio call.

'I think we have a problem with the helicopter lift out. I can't believe that the Company who hired the chopper to us isn't hearing our transmissions. This leads one to believe, that they may have been bought out or pressured not to cooperate by the Cartel. If this is the case, then we have a serious problem on our hands. Whilst it would be no great problem for us to walk out of this situation, I'm afraid that it would be an impossible task with all the survivors'.

Glum looks on his Troopers' faces confirm his appreciation.

'I think we are going to have to take up defensive positions and be prepared for an assault on this location. Fingers and I will come round to co-ordinate arcs of fire. If Rusty and Sandy have not returned in the next two hours we'll have to leave this location and march out to the ravine we talked about last night. We can then get the passengers across the bridge and possibly hold it for another six hours just in case Rusty and Sandy make it. After that I'm afraid we'll have to destroy the bridge in order to give ourselves sufficient lead to get the passengers clear of this area'

Bryant asked if anyone had any questions or suggestions. There were no takers..

The team had not considered it necessary to have their Satellite Communication Set with them which would have enabled them to contact their base back in the UK. They had been briefed that they were going on a rescue mission, not to war!

'Yeah boss, but what's the plan if Rusty and Sandy do get here, that will still only add another two guns to our defence perimeter' asked Pedro Gonzales.

'We have a quick heads of sheds meeting and all being well get over that bloody ravine as soon as possible. This location is going to be too easy to out - flank and we would be quickly surrounded. They wouldn't even have to bother attacking us. They could just sit there and eventually starve us out'.

Lance held up his hand. 'Boss I have a confession to make'.

'He's only managed to screw four of the women passengers so far', joshed Butch Hezeltine.

Lance looked very embarrassed. 'I know it's strictly against the rules boss but I thought this was going to be a straightforward Search and Rescue Mission. So before I left the hotel, Maria - that's the bird I met at the Night-club, gave me her Mobile phone so I could contact her as soon as we had finished the Op'.

'For Christ sake Lance – that bloody dick of yours is going to get you skinned one of these days. You do realise that if you were captured or the Cartel people acquired the phone that poor girl would be in serious trouble,

'That's true boss but at the moment, it does give us communications back to Bogotá that are reasonable secure'.

'But how is that going to help us out of our present

situation. How much power and influence does she have bearing in mind the Cartel has dug a bloody great hole for itself and the only way they can fill it in is by burying us in it. If they find out your girl friend is involved with our rescue she's as good as dead'.

'I obviously don't know an awful lot about her, but I do know that her father is a very rich and powerful man in Colombia. He has several Emerald Mines and is involved with oil exploration to the south of the country. So he's not short of a bob or two and apparently he dotes on Maria, not only that but she has asked me to meet her folk as soon as we get back'.

The look on the faces of the rest of the team after that last statement was something to behold. To say that they were gob smacked was to put it mildly. Normally such remark would have elicited howls of derision and laughter from them but at the moment they were so stunned they were struck dumb at what they'd just heard from the biggest Ram in the Regiment.

Tony Bryant tried hard not to smile but look thoughtful at Lance's revelation. 'I take it that if you're agreeing to meet the parents then you must be quite serious about her'.

'Yes I am boss, I have never felt like this before and, I might add – this was well before I knew how rich her parents were'.

'Be that as it may Lance. Her parents might have something to say about you getting seriously attached to their daughter. As you know they're strict Roman Catholics in this part of the world and many parents here still believe in arranged marriages. So I shouldn't get too excited about any permanent arrangements just yet'.

'Look boss this girl and I only talked for about a total of one hour but we discussed more in that hour than I have ever discussed with any other woman. We are going to get married to one another come hell or high water'.

'Okay Lance you're a big boy now. You have our permission to talk to your girl friend and see what help she can offer but for god's sake tell her to be careful'.

Lance nodded to Bryant and wandered away to phone his girl friend.

It was quite obvious to the rest of the team how serious Lance was about his new romance in that there was no attempt to take the piss out of him as was usual on such occasions.

In the meantime the rest of the team started to set about planning the best defensive position for the next hour or so to await the arrival of Rusty and Sandy.

While they were setting up their positions there were two very faint but distinctive cracks of a high velocity rifle. The team recognised the signature of Niles's Holland & Holland. They all listened for any additional gun fire but heard nothing.

The leader of the four-man patrol grinned as he continued to squeeze the trigger. Rusty braced himself for the shock and as the gun went off, he dived to the left away from Niles. The blast of the shot was followed by a horrendous scream from the man who'd fired it. He was reeling backward with his hands covering his face and blood pouring out between his fingers. He had just suffered a, 'Blowback' caused by the grease and grit that Niles had rammed down the barrels of some of the guns in the camp's armoury.

The excessive build up of pressure within the gun's muzzle had caused the rear part of the breech block and the cartridge case to blow out backwards into his face. His colleagues, for a full second stood rooted to the spot, trying to come to terms on what had just happened to their patrol leader.

That was approximately half a second more than Rusty and Sandy needed to react. Quickly rolling onto his feet

Rusty fired a three round burst into the man on the extreme left followed by another burst into the man stood along side him. Niles shot the other man to the right of the leader who was still staggering around with blood pouring from his face. He thought about letting the wounded guy go. He was obviously blind so he'd not be a problem to them. However Rusty had other ideas.

'Just a moment' he snarled. 'That bastard was going to shoot me in the stomach and watch me die in agony. But no hard feelings sport, I'll demonstrate to you the difference between a gentleman and a thug'. And with that Rusty lifted his M161A and shot him between the eyes with another three round burst.

'Please note gentlemen how I eased that poor souls suffering in a quick and clinical manner' said Rusty as though he was addressing an imaginary audience.

After that lapse in vigilance which nearly cost them their lives they continued up the logging track with more care. They were a much chasten pair but for Rusty's contingency plan of ramming dirt and grease down the barrels of the guns in the Armoury the previous night they would now be both dead. Now each man moved in turn whilst the other covered him.

The rest of the team at the Dakota heard the shooting which was much nearer than the previous shots identified as coming from Nile's rifle. One more shot sounded as though it had come from the Holland & Holland plus a two, three round burst. Followed at a short interval by another three round burst. The burst of fire sounded as though they were from an M161A, but as some of the unfriendlies had theses weapon it was impossible to grasp what was happening. Bryant warned his team to stand by, and expect the worse but hope for the best.

The best it was. Rusty and Niles arrived within the half-hour after some pretty impressive tabbing and explained to Bryant exactly what they had seen and done.

Bryant started to unfold the map and said. 'You think that killing that big chap will slow things up enough for us to get clear over the ravine Rusty?'

'I'm certain', said Rusty. 'He was the motivating force. He was kicking arse left, right and dead centre. When we left the rest of them were running around like headless chickens. They will obviously replace him but I figure it will take time, they may even have to fly some one out from Cali for all we know'.

'Sounds a good move', continued Bryant. 'But it's only a matter of time before they discover where we are. The trouble is that time is not on our side. Since you've been gone we've managed to establish, with the help, I might add of Lance's new girl friend, Maria, that the Helicopter Company has been nobbled by the Cartel. It looks as though we are going to be marooned out here until Maria's father can organise another chopper without the Cartel knowing'.

The team looked at Rusty, the guy with the most experience. 'I figure we must get to the other side of that ravine as soon as possible. It's our only chance of preventing them from outflanking and surrounding us'.

Niles indicated that he had something to say. 'I obviously agree with what Rusty suggests but I do have another idea that might expedite us getting out this mess'.

'Okay I'm open to any suggestions which might help', said Bryant.

'As you know I am a qualified Helicopter pilot and I was a rated Training Captain on the Super Puma. Whilst Rusty and I were doing a recce' of the Camp we noticed that they were doing what is called, 'Rotors Running Turn Round', in other words they were not closing the engines down whilst refuelling it. I think we could jump the pilot, steal the Puma and fly ourselves out'.

Every one looked at Niles as though he had gone stark raving mad.'What do you figure the Cartel's soldiers are going to be doing when you are stealing their chopper? Just sit there wiping their arses?' Butch Hezeltine asked sarcastically.

Bryant nodded his head in agreement with Butch's remark. 'He's right you know - we would suffer a lot of casualties trying to get every one aboard the chopper. Plus which, with the amount of firepower they can muster they would blow us out the sky before we could even get clear of the HLS'.

Niles nodded his head in agreement 'That's where we need a diversion plan', he continued. 'I suggest that we go ahead with the original plan and get all of the passengers over the other side of the ravine. Now we know that that big bastard Goodge, before we wasted him, ordered his four man patrols to search all points of the compass to try and pick up our trail. They have already got some idea of where we are from that brief fire fight with a four-man patrol thirty minutes ago. So let's pretend that some of their patrols have found us and we are all engaged in a major fire fight much further to the east by setting off explosions etc. That should attract the attention of most of their foot patrols.

Rusty interrupted.'Sound good to me boss two of could cause a diversionary foray whilst the remainder get the passengers over the ravine'.

Niles continued.'In the mean time, Pedro Gonzales and I will make our way back to the camp site ready to grab a Puma towards last light'. Niles could see that Rusty was a little put out that he had not chosen him, especially as they had work so well together over the past twenty four hours.'I think Pedro would be the best choice because he can speak fluent Spanish and has a Mediterranean complexion. So if we are challenged at any time Pedro's linguist skills and Latin looks might just save our bacon and give us time to get clear. We must get Pedro into some civilian clothes and as we both now have beards, we look as villainous as any of the Cartel's men'.

'That's the broad outline of what I am suggesting', continued Niles. 'If no one else can suggest an alternative I think we ought to get down to the details now. I reckon that we can expect company within the next hour or so, therefore we don't have long before it's time to move'.

'First question', said Bryant. 'Why are you going to wait until last light to try and grab a chopper?'

'Its almost mid day now –Pedro and I are going to have to walk quite wide of the logging track to avoid their men who will probable make as much use of the track as we did. We may have to lay low as their patrols pass by us so it will take time to get there. Plus which, I am hoping that if we steal one just before last light the other chopper will be at their forward airstrip and will not be making another trip into the interior that evening. Hopefully they will not be able to chase us in the other chopper'.

'Next question', said Rusty. 'You said earlier on that choppers couldn't fly out here at night. If it's dark how are you going to fly and find us Sandy?'

'This is where our planning must get quite detailed. First of all I am or was, a fully Instrument Rated Pilot and I foresee no problems with me flying you all back to Bogotá at night, even in cloud if needs be. But two of you guys have got to recce a clearing on the other side of the Ravine this afternoon so the sooner that two set off the better. Remember it is not necessary that I land. I can come to a low hover and provided you all enplane one at a time there's no problem. But I must know my tail rotor is clear of any obstruction. Once the clearing has been located you will have to give the co-ordinates to the main party and as soon as I am airborne pass them to me using the speech facility on the Sabre Beacon. If it is completely dark as soon as I get close enough I'll switch on my landing light and you can take a compass bearing on me I'll use the reciprocal to fly towards you. I will NOT land unless you flash V in Morse to me. (All SAS troopers know the Morse code) – is that quite clear?'

'I think that covers most of the points', said Bryant. 'But do you really think you can get away with snatching the chopper Niles? The whole plan hinges on you and Pedro getting away without being killed',

'The way I see it', Niles replied. 'Is that if we approach the chopper from the far side where they refuel, and we walk out of the jungle with plenty of confidence, no one will pay much attention to us. In any event, most of their foot soldiers are going to be up here trying to get you guys. A further point in our favour is that they've imported so many men during the past day it's unlikely that they're going to personally know one another. We'll be just another two foot soldiers going about our business. We must also remember that they have a second Puma, which during daylight hours they might use to insert their men into the jungle. But they won't want to do that at night. This is why we must steal the chopper at last light. Thereafter we're going to have to play it by ear. My last point is, as you have already mentioned, we ***have*** to get these passengers on the other side of the ravine to prevent us getting surrounded by the unfriendlies. So if my plans to steal the chopper come to nothing we'll be no better or worse off than we are now'.

Bryant looked at all the others and nodded his head in agreement. 'How many Magellan sets do we have Fingers (Cpl Finnegan)?'

'We have three Magellan Global Positioning Sets with us. We could give one to Pedro who can update Sandy as he flies', suggest Fingers.

'That should be enough. As the Bishop said to the Actress', smirked (Kilo) Miles

'Enough of that crap,' ordered Bryant. 'Right, if we have

no further questions, lets brief the passengers on what's about to happen and get Pedro clothed like a local. Bye the way Sandy, I think you should change that bloody Holland & Holland with Rusty's M16A2. By now half of Colombia's population must know you are running around with that bloody canon. It could be a right give away'.

Rusty and Niles just grinned. 'Anyone got a crow bar', shouted Rusty. 'We've got to try and prise this cannon off Sandy and that's not going to be easy'.

This lightened the mood as the team wandered back to the aircraft.

Dino the Captain of the Dakota was the nearest in size to Pedro so they changed their clothes. It had to be said that now he was in civilian clothes and with his natural dark complexion that Pedro could easily pass as a local.

Bryant briefed all the passengers on what the plan involved. He thought it wise not to enlighten them about the Cartel's plan to have all their bodies interned and incinerated in the fuselage. At the conclusion when asked if they had any questions most of them looked too stunned to reply.

Niles as an Ex- SAS support pilot knew that all the Troopers were familiar with helicopter marshalling signals. So he was quite happy at being marshalled into a confines area at night by any of the Troopers.

Chapter 16

Bogotá

Maria switched off her mobile phone and sat on her bed for a moment to contemplate her next move. Her heart wouldn't stop hammering. The thought of losing Lance after only just finding him was devastating. Her mind was in a complete turmoil. She was not sure what to do next. She'd already told her parents of her passionate night with Tpr' Lance. Although she knew he was in some form of service unit this was the first she heard that he was a member of the elite British SAS. Although the initial attraction to Lance had been purely physical she now realised that she was completely besotted with him. The longer she pondered the problem the more determined she was to do something positive about it. The thought that he was now in danger caused her protective instincts to come to the fore. She now felt like some Tigress whose cub was about to be threatened. She was determined to do something to help him and his friends.

Her parents had not been too pleased about her liaison with Lance but she was over twenty-one years of age and was a rich woman in her own right. They'd hope she would find and settle down with one of the local Colombians or at least some one who they considered to be of equal social status. Her grandfather had left her a lot of money in trust so all her parents could do was to help and advise her. She was rich enough to be completely independent if she so wished.

However Maria loved her parents and they in turn had always done their best to protect her from the harsher realities of life. Although she had a short fling previously with a local Colombian man it was nothing like the intensity of feeling she had experienced sleeping with Lance. The thought of losing him now was too dreadful to contemplate.

Maria knocked on her parent's sitting door and she was bid enter. It was a large room opulently furnished. The highly polished parquet floor was partially covered by three very expensive Chinese carpets. The large bay windows looked out onto a Japanese landscaped garden beset with delicate water features in which Alfred Mendoza kept his prize winning Japanese Koi Carp. The walls of the room were hung with expensive Chinese silk tapestry. The Mendoza's were keen collectors of far eastern artefacts. In the two corners of the room adjacent to the large window sat two large Ming jars of considerable antiquity. Further far eastern antiquities were scattered around the room in a tasteful manner. The room reeked of opulence and affluence.

Alfred Mendoza was a very tall and distinguished looking man. He was fifty five years old with his dark full head of hair just beginning to go grey, which if anything enhanced his already good looks. His eyes were grey as opposed to the usual dark brown associated with Latin men and his slightly hooked nose had been broken when he was a young man playing soccer. He was stood alongside the magnificent fire place opposite her mother and Aunt Jenny.

Her mother, Helen, was just approaching forty four

years of age and it wasn't difficult to see where Maria got her ravishing good looks. She was about the same height as Maria, about five foot six with beautiful dark hair swept high up on her head. Her eyes were much the same as Marie's, almond shaped with enormous long eye lashes and the colour was a deep dark brown, almost black in certain light conditions. She also had the same figure with flowing lines but not quite so athletic. She was wearing a beautiful simple white dress that emphasised her high bust and her dark Latino good looks. With her mother was her Aunt Jenny, who was nine years younger than her mother. And although it was obvious that she was also a very beautiful woman she was dressed completely in black with no make up. Her sombre mien tended to disguise her vivacity and good looks. She had been widowed for about eight months but was still in mourning for her late husband

Maria stood before them with tears running down her face. Her farther strode across the room realising that his daughter was sorely troubled and took her in his arms. It could only be about her new found boy friend. She gasped the story that she had learnt from Lance via the mobile to her parents and Aunt Jenny.

'Papa – there must be something we can do to help. They are trapped in the Jungle with these survivors and the Drug Cartel's gun men are hunting them down. Surely with all our connections we could do something to help?'

'Maria', her Father said. 'Although we hate the drug Cartel it is a fact of life that we have to live in the same country with them. And whilst I leave them alone they will leave me alone. If we were seen to oppose them then I would have to guard against them taking revenge on you or your mother. That is a risk I'm not prepared to take. Whilst I am quite happy to take the risk personally I can't possibly endanger the lives of you or your mother'.

'But we must do something Papa. Lance said that they

may be able to get to Bogotá but they will need to get the survivors out the country as soon as possible without the Cartel being aware of it. We can't let all these people die there'.

'This is basically an American problem so our best course of action is to contact Chris Brooker who is their Head Security Officer at the American Embassy in Bogotá. I have met Chris at the Embassy functions and know him quite well. He is a very resourceful man. I'll phone him and arrange a meeting, ostensibly, to talk about the import of Emeralds to the States. I'm afraid I don't trust our phone system. The Cartels have too many informers on the phone staff. I'll try and arrange it immediately!'

Alfred went to the writing bureau and picked up the phone and dialled the US Embassy. 'Hi could I speak to Chris Brooker please, this is Alfred Mendoza of the Mendoza Quality Stone s Company. Yes! Yes! Chris is a personal friend of mine'. Mendoza was determined to ensure that he got Chris to the phone.

After waiting a few minutes Chris Brooker was on the line. 'Hi Alfred long time no see, how's that soccer team of yours doing?'

'There doing well Chris. Look - something important has come up about the last shipment of Emeralds we sent to the States and I could do with some of your excellent advice. Could we meet in 'Terry's Bar' on The Avenida Boyaca in thirty minutes?'

Because of the drug related problems associated with Colombia the US Government had selected one of their top men to head their security team in Bogotá, Chris Brooker.

had been selected as the Head of Security because of his qualifications and outstanding record in Beirut and Afghanistan. He stood a lean mean six feet one inch tall with a lean craggy face, a rather aquiline nose and dark jowls that despite shaving daily before breakfast left him looking as though he still needed one immediately after it. His grey eyes reflected his calling being flat and emotionless. However when he smiled his whole persona changed – then, women found him devilishly attractive.

Chris Brooker was quick on the up take and knew that the meeting had nothing to do with Emeralds so he was somewhat intrigued.

'I might be a little late but I should be able to make it within the next forty minutes. See you there'.

They decided that it would be more appropriate if only Alfred and Maria went. The sky was now crystal clear and the temperature was just a pleasant twenty three degrees. Bogotá whilst being close to the equator was eight and a half thousand feet above MSL. They parked Alfred's Mercedes Coupe in the private car park and proceeded to the second floor terrace which at that time of the day had very few customers. Alfred had a quiet word with the waiter to make sure that Brooker would know exactly where they were when he arrived

In fact Brooker made Terry's bar in exactly thirty five minutes. Alfred and Maria were already seated out on the terrace overlooking the Avenida Boyaca ostensibly enjoying the view of the distant park. It also meant that they were rather isolated and their conversation would be difficult to overhear. And hopefully not many people could even see them. The view from the Terrace was magnificent but as soon as Brooker caught sight of them he knew something was wrong

'What's the panic?' Brooker asked taking a seat opposite the lovely Maria. 'My god Maria you look lovelier every time I see you'.

Maria just nodded her head glumly.

'I think you should tell Chris the story', said Alfred.

'Okay papa. It's like this Mr Brooker - My boy friend is with a SAS patrol that went to rescue some Americans who crashed into the jungle South East of Bogotá. Apparently they found the survivors but are involved in a running battle with Drug Cartel gunmen. The company that hired them a helicopter appears to have been compromised by the Cartel and will not send a chopper out to pick them up as agreed. Eduardo, that's my boy friend, phoned me and said that they hoping to get to Bogotá Airport by some means that he would not disclose. But they will need transport to get the passengers out the country before Cartel's gunmen catch up with them. He also stated that he thought the passengers had seen and heard too much for the Cartel to allow them to live. Papa says we can't be seen to help these people without incurring the wrath of the Cartel. Can you help?'

'Jesus Christ'! Brooker exploded. 'We knew the aircraft crashed but we weren't sure how many passengers survived. And I'd arranged with the British Embassy for the SAS patrol to be inserted to look for the survivors. I thought a helicopter had been organised to pick them and the survivors up. What the hell has happened? Did you know that the wife and daughter of the American Defence Secretary were aboard that aircraft?'

'No', replied Maria. 'But Lance – my boyfriend out there – said that the only casualties so far were four American men and two Venezuelan men but no women. Apparently they were all killed when the gunmen ambushed them. But he also said that they had overheard the gunmen's plan which, was to have all the passengers killed and incinerated in the aircraft fuselage making it look as though they were all killed by fire on impact'.

'Only an idiot like the drug barons here in Colombia would think up a scheme like that and imagine they could get away with it. But the most important thing is to save their lives before it's too late. It could take me two or three days to jack up another helicopter. So how in God's name are these guys going to get themselves out of the jungle to

Bogotá Airport?' Brooker asked.

'Lance said he would let me know later on when they considered it safe to do so. But if they do get out can you arrange for them to be picked up and flown to the States'.

'I'm dam sure I can but what time scale are we looking at'.

'Lance said that if all goes well they can be at the Airport by twenty hundred hours, I think that's eight o'clock in the evening'.

'Christ! That doesn't give us much time – lets see its fourteen hundred hours now, that's two o'clock in your time', he smiled at Maria. 'It's going to be a close run thing so I had better get onto it straight away. I have a secure line to George Fields – he's the Defence Secretary - so with his wife and daughter in the line of fire we won't have any problems jacking up an aircraft. I'll phone you later and confirm the time with you Alfred. We will talk in veiled speech on the phone that way we wont compromise you with the Cartel, I can't thank you enough and given the chance, I'm sure that George Fields will also like to thank you. I realise the risk you and your family are exposed to Alfred so I'll make dam sure that your name is not mentioned in any way'.

With that, Brooker was to his feet and off down the road in a flash.

'I don't think we can do much more for the moment Maria until your boy friend calls you. Brooker is one of the best men in his line of work. If any one can work the oracle he's your man. And I must say, for that young man to have had such a strong effect on you, he must be some man. You mother and I look forward to meeting him.

On his arrival back at the Embassy Chris Brooker lost no time getting to the security room and phoning George Fields.

Grace Dalton rang through to George Fields and said. 'Chris Brooker on the secure line from Colombia Sir, can you take the call now?' George Fields knew the call could only mean one thing and snatch the phone up quickly.

'Chris – what's the news? Are Jackie and Karen safe?'

'It would appear so for the moment Mr Secretary but there is a problem. They are in the Jungle with a British SAS team but are being harried by Drug Cartel gunmen. Now the information I have is that the SAS claim they can get all the survivors to Bogotá Airport by twenty hundred hours local time. Don't ask me how because I don't know. What they're requesting is jet transport to get them out the country to State side as soon as possible. It would appear that the passengers have seen and heard too much for the Cartels liking. I know it doesn't give us much time but do you think you could arrange an executive jet to get to Bogotá Airport by that time'.

'It's going to be fucking tight but I'll get my contacts in the DEA onto it straight away. They have aircraft based at Miami international, which is about 1500nm north of Bogotá. Provided they can get the aircraft jacked up in the next hour it should be able to get there in time. They have a couple of large executive jets, the Canadair Challenger that can cruise at around five hundred knots. They should fit the bill nicely. How many guys are we trying to lift out Chris?'

'Well, the only figures I have for the survivor's state that there are seven women including your wife and daughter, and only four men. Plus which of course, we have the SAS team of eight men, who have been compromised and the Brit's will want them lifting out. Theoretically of course they're not our problem but seeing how they were sent in at our bequest I think we are honour bound to extract them with the survivors'.

'I agree Chris but the only problem is that I think that's too many for one aircraft. However I'll off load that problem to the DEA but it sure complicates the situation. In the meantime, do you think you could arrange an alternative plan to get these people to the American Embassy clandestinely without the Cartel's knowledge?'

'If they arrive at Bogotá Airport I suspect the Cartel will know within the hour. The bloody airport is crawling with their informants. But if we can get them located somewhere close to the city then there's every chance of getting them to the Embassy without the Cartel's knowledge'.

'That would sure help Chris. Once we had them in the Embassy we can make sure that we have the means to get them all back to the States. Do you envisage any problems of getting the survivors from the Embassy to the Airport without the Cartel knowing?

'I think we could jack that up easily enough. We could use our official Diplomatic Baggage Vans to transport them to the Airport. It would mean breaking some rules on Customs and Emigration but at least we would get them out alive. Presumably the President could square this up once they're all back in the States with the Colombian Government. The fact that three of the passengers that were killed are American should give the President some weight to lean on the Colombians Government'.

'Well the Colombians are keen to be re-selected for American foreign aid so I think they'll be glad to co-operate. I'm going to try and get out there on one of the jets if I can arrange it. Trouble is I've to get from Washington to Miami so it's going to be a close run thing. I'll have to get things rolling at this end. Speak to you later'.

Fields thumbed the intercom.

'Grace, would you get me the DEA in Miami straight away and when you have done that please book one of the executive jets to get me down to Miami immediately'. The Defence Secretary's mind was now moving into top gear. He went to the bathroom where he kept a few toilet accessories and packed them in a hold-all. The speed that events were unfolding precluded him going home to pack.

His last action was to phone the President's secretary and inform him of what was taking place. 'Please tell the President that I'll phone him as soon as all the details have been confirmed'.

Because of all the uncertainty in Bogotá the American Embassy kept a number of different types of vehicles that they could use without attracting attention.

Chris Brooker decided to drive a laundry van to Alfred Mendoza's Villa and then, if they agreed, bring them back to the Embassy where they could all keep up to date as the events unfolded out there in the jungle. On arrival at the trades' men entrance Chris was ushered into the study where Maria and her parents waited anxiously for any further news from Lance.

'Afternoon, Helen, Maria, Alfred. I've been in touch with the States and they are arranging one or possibly two aircraft to pick up the passengers and take them back to the States. The biggest problem is going to be getting them there by eight o'clock. There aren't that many executive jets that can carry twenty odd people, so we are considering having to use two or having to hire a small airliner. Unfortunately, this all takes time'.

'I think it would be best', continued Chris, 'if you and Maria came to the Embassy so we could liaise with your friend, Lance, and make alternative arrangements should the jets not get here on time. I have a bogus laundry van outside to get us to the Embassy so nobody will know you are there. This would reduce the risk of someone eavesdropping on the phones and informing the Cartel of what we are up to. How does that sound to you?'

Alfred looked at the three women and they all nodded in agreement. 'I think my wife and her sister will also want to come along. You know what Latino women are like Chris, they are determined to give this Lance character who has stolen my daughter's heart the once over. In some ways I feel quite sorry for him'.

'You hush yourself', said Helen Mendoza. 'This is our only daughter. She is beautiful enough to have practically any man of her choosing. My sister and I want to make sure she is not getting involved with just some gigolo'.

Chris had to laugh', I wonder if the poor devil knows what's awaiting him once he gets here. However, there are five seats in the van, one in the front, four in the back, which are not very comfortable. I'll leave it to you and your ladies to decide who sits where'.

Chapter 17

Rain Forest

Capt Bryant quickly organised his team into their separate duties. 'Okay Rusty, you take Smudger (Grimes) and Butch (Hezeltine) and set up the diversion and blocking team. Without wishing to teach you how to suck eggs Rusty, your priority is to ensure that the hostiles don't get between you and the bridge. Easier said than done but Rusty, if the unfriendlies do rush the bridge we will probably have to blow the bloody thing up whether you three are still on the other side or not'.

'No problem boss. I'll make sure our escape route is kept clear'. Rusty replied.

However both knew that with the restricted visibility within the jungle this was easier said than done.

'Finnegan, continued Bryant. 'You and kilo (Miles) go ahead and establish a HLS not too far from the ravine, a mile at the most – We're not too sure just how far or fast the passengers can march. I don't want to be stumbling through the ulu with this crowd at night.

'Lance and I will escort the passengers across the bridge and then hold it till Rusty's team gets across. Lance, make sure you don't lose that bloody mobile of yours. That and Niles's chopper are the keys to our success'.

He looked around the team for any further questions or comments. There were.

Rusty was the first. 'I think we had better get a little closer to the bridge before we start the fireworks otherwise there's a danger of us being outflanked before we get to the bridge. You agree boss?'

'A good point Rusty, any one else?'

'Who gets the third GPS set?' Finnegan asked. 'Pedro and Sandy have one. Miles and I have the second who gets the third?'

Bryant thought for a moment. 'Give it to Rusty – Once we are over the ravine you and Kilo (Miles) will be coming back to lead us to the HLS. If – God forbid, that Rusty and his team get stuck on the wrong side of the ravine there's a chance that after we've delivered the passengers we can return and pick them up'.

Bryant immediately got the passengers sorted out. 'Try and carry a blanket or a warm coat just in case we have to sleep another night in the jungle. During the march to the ravine and then onto the HLS you must insure that you are always in visual contact with the person in front of you. If you start to drop behind please sing out. I will lead and Trooper Lance will bring up the rear. Try not to talk and be as quiet as possible. Remember, if anyone hears you; bear in mind that they are most likely to be hostiles, so if you're talking they can home in onto the noise No questions! Then good lets go'.

The passengers were aware of what they were up against and most had tried to cooperate with the SAS team. There were some however who still continued to bitch.

Nathan Costello and the American singer, Peter Milo

were beginning to cause some unrest by demanding that they have more say in what is happening. Finally Bryant, who had been listening to their bickering whilst leading the march lost his cool and rounded on them. 'Listen gentlemen'. He spoke in a very calm exaggerated upper class English manner. 'My men and I were having the first weekend off in over two months when we were called out in the middle of the night to pull your arses out of the fire. Now if you had stayed with the aircraft as Capt Dino told you, all of us would now be back in Bogotá or on our way to the States. It wouldn't surprise me Costello, if on returning to the States, that some of your colleagues don't sue you for the trauma you have caused them by insisting that they leave the aircraft's location against the express instructions of the Aircraft's captain. That, plus you're your insistence on remaining behind a further twenty four hours after receiving the hurricane warning must rate as one of the stupidest decisions I've ever heard of. Further more, if you continue to bitch and try and undermine my authority or that of my team, then I'm going to turn you loose once we have crossed the ravine and you can make your own way home. Is that clear?'

'We're not used to being spoken to like this', huffed Nathan Costello. 'We are men used to making decisions and as such, I think we should be consulted before a plan of action is put in motion'.

'That's great, so once we've crossed the bridge you and Milo are on your own. In the meantime you were briefed not to talk during the march, so keep quite!'

Further response was curtailed by the sound of gunfire that was extremely close behind them. This shut Costello and Milo up immediately. Bryant never bothered to enlighten them that it was Rusty and his team trying to attract the attention of the Cartel's men to lead them away from the bridge and the direction that the survivors were going. However it had the added bonus of keeping the passengers quiet. Something that Bryant and Lance's continual reprimands had singularly failed to do.

Passengers were now walking quicker in an effort to put as much distance between them and the gunfire that was still going on at random intervals. The going was tough but Lance was a dab hand with the machete which he used as sparingly as possible to try and disguise the direction in which they were going. The game trail they were following was already partially cleared so they made better than expected progress.

A further hour brought the party to the small bridge that crossed the ravine.

It was not a reassuring sight.

It was only about thirty meters long but the drop to the bottom of the ravine was all of four hundred feet. Further more, the Bridge construction looked extremely flimsy. There were four main heavy-duty ropes connected to stout poles at each side of the ravine. Two parallel at chest height and two parallel at foot level. The upper ropes were about a meter apart. From each of these smaller ropes were suspended, which were then attached to the lower heavy-duty ones. These in turn, were joined together by a series of wooden planks located athwart ship that formed the walkway. The planks were a foot apart which was safe enough but gave a very alarming view to any uninitiated person looking downwards.

'Right' Bryant grinned. 'Who's going to be first? Mr Costello or Mr Milo, I believe you two gentlemen were asking to be given a more demanding role. Which one of you would like to cross first?'

Neither was prepared to be the first across. Nathan Costello never short on excuses said. 'I think you or Trooper Lance should go first – you are the professionals'.

'Of course we are going first but to save time we are

going to escort one of you across at a time. Now listen out every body, these bridges are quite safe provide you walk with confidence and don't look down through the planks at the river below. Right Mr Chase you and Dale first with Lance and I and then we will return for each of you in turn. And please note; just one pair to cross the bridge at a time. Ok Lance I'll take Mr Chase you follow with Dale'.

Bryant stepped softly but firmly on to the bridge with Chase. 'Don't look down and try not to sway and we'll have no problems'.

Chase could feel his legs shaking but with the women looking on he gulped and tentatively followed holding desperately onto the harness of Bryant's Bergen. He suddenly realised he was crossing with his eyes tightly shut!

They made the other side with no problems although the bridge did sway it was quite tough if a little unstable.

It was noticeable how the woman jostled one another to have Lance escort them over. Jackie Fields and Karen went together with Bryant. Jackie had a horror of heights but was determined to hide her unease in case it infected Karen. She needn't have bothered, as is often the case with the young, Karen seemed to actually enjoy the crossing. Dale was also beginning to prove an asset and took a turn at escorting Susan across.

'My God'! Olivia said one of the young actresses. 'I wouldn't like to do that too often'.

'Actually', said Lance. 'If you lived in this part of the world you would quickly get used to this sort of bridge and think nothing of crossing it daily. In other parts of the interior we have actually seen small children playing on similar bridges'.

'Christ they must be hard up for entertainment', gulped Olivia hanging onto Lance at the same time rubbing her boobs against him and fluttering her eyelids.

Lance with the thought of Maria ever present in his

mind pretended not to notice. Never-the-less the precarious nature of the crossing and the continual erotic massage he was getting from Olivia had the desired effect as far as she was concerned. By the time they got to the far side he was rampant. However he was determined to be a good boy and behave, so he just quipped.

'Normally Olivia, I'd give you twenty fours hours to stop doing that but I'm afraid there are more mundane matters to attend to - Boss! I think this might be an excellent place to set up one of the Claymore Mines'.

'We only have the one with us - Rusty has kept one on the other side for possible use when the Cartel's yobos approach. Let's set it up so that the blast is funnelled across the bridge. With luck we might take out a couple of men at the same time as destroying the bridge. I'll leave you to rig it up Lance while I get the passengers sorted out. I hope Fingers gets that fucking HLS sorted out and gets back here before nightfall. I don't fancy trekking through the jungle at night with this crowd',

Lance set the Claymore Mine up. He used the sight on the top of the mine to ensure that the mine's sixty degree arc of lethality completely covered the bridge. On both sides the ravine the approaches to the bridge had been cleared back to about twenty to thirty yards. This gave a clear field of view to the bridge on both sides. Lance selected a large tree stump behind which to hide. From here he had a clear view of the approach to the bridge on the far side. Behind the stump there was some dead ground which should enable lance to retire without being shot. He looked out to either of his flanks to make sure his position was secure form both directions. It was. As they had no "Clacker devise" he was going to have to use a trip wire to initiate the mine. The 'clacker' device which was normally used with the mine was squeezed which generated a small electrical charge. This charge then initiated the mine. He looked at his watch.

'If I remember correctly boss the trees were considerably thinner about a mile this side of the ravine so it should not be difficult to find a HLS'.

'Yes but don't forget Lance that works both ways. It means that tomorrow they could use the second chopper to airlift guys across the ravine'.

'True boss, but if Sandy and Pedro manages to snaffle that chopper this evening we should be long gone by then'.

'Amen to that', grunted Bryant.

Niles had struck a good rapport with Pedro. His movement through the jungle was as good as Rusty's and much better than his. They had made good progress initially but now as they approached the campsite they had to slowdown and move more cautiously. They'd already had to go to ground and hide as two four-man patrols slipped past them on the way to the sound of the gunfire coming from Rusty, Grimes and Hezeltine.

Niles missed having the Holland & Holland but had to concede that the M16A2 was shorter and easier to handle in the dense undergrowth.

If their plan was to work, the Cartel's men must think that all the survivors and their rescuers were well to the north of their campsite. To ensure this Niles and Pedro kept to the thick bush to avoid any possible contact. Pedro had a military prismatic compass so they had no problems keeping parallel to the logging track and the GPS gave them an accurate position at all times. Rusty and his team were now making quite a lot of noise to simulate a running battle to the north. So far it seemed to be working.

'How much further,' hissed Niles. Pedro checked the GPS.

'According to the GPS we have about another eight hundred metres to go. Which side of the clearing is the chopper located?'

'They had the Fuel Bladders located in the Eastern arm of the cross tracks. So if we swing a bit further east, then south, we will hit the track that run perpendicular to the way we are going then carefully make our way westward adjacent to the track until we hit the campsite'.

'How many guards do you reckon will be at the campsite Sandy?'

'Difficult to say but from the numbers we've seen and heard going north I'll be surprised if there are more than half a dozen at the most. There will be a dozen or so workers who are actually constructing the site, but they are unlikely to cause a problem. When Rusty and I left with the passengers previously, the workers kept out of the way and never tried to hinder us'.

Pedro and Sandy were making their way along the East, West track towards the camp when suddenly; a man stepped out in front of Pedro. After the initial shock Pedro's brain went into overdrive. He knew that Niles was keeping him covered as he moved forward. They had been leapfrogging one another for the past ten minutes as they'd got closer to the camp site and therefore it was most unlikely that the man had seen Niles.

Niles, who was covering Pedro as he moved forward kept behind cover out of view. To use a fire arm this close to the camp could jeopardised the whole plan. Pedro took it all in his stride and behaved as though he had every right to be there. Their earlier supposition that there were now so many gunmen imported from Cali and Medellin that the chances were that many were strangers to one another was proving correct.

'Hey Hombre, come and see what I have found here'. Pedro gestured to the guard to follow him pointing to imaginary footprints in the ground. 'Somebody has been walking down this track I think we must inform the boss'.

The guard was having problems trying to make out

the non-existent footprints. 'Look, look, just here, No! Not there - here!', Pedro was encouraging the guard to examine the ground closer.

As the guard walked adjacent to Niles's position behind a large tree he swung his machete viciously, catching the guard on the nape of the neck, almost completely taking his head off and killing him instantly.

Pedro looked at the body dispassionately for a moment and said. 'This is the sort of job where one could easily loose their head'.

'We'll have to drag him well clear of the track to ensure that his body is not discovered', grunted Niles as he started to drag the body clear of the track. 'If you make sure all signs of blood are covered I'll try digging a shallow grave to hide the body'.

Burying the body had hindered their progress but they still had to move carefully as they were now getting much closer to the camp site. However it was now almost five o'clock. They had just about another hour before it got dark so Niles and Pedro had to move quickly but with caution or they'd miss the last chopper. They arrived about forty minutes before the last light and were worried that they may have missed the last chopper. They were in luck - one was just off loading men and stores before moving to the refuelling point. Apart from the construction workers there appeared to be only three guards within the camp site. There could be others possible on the perimeter but with luck they would not pose a problem if all went as planned.

Pedro and Niles managed to get well-hidden in the undergrowth about twenty yards from where they anticipated the chopper refuelling. Again, the cut undergrowth which had been dragged and dumped to the sides of the clearing was an added bonus for concealment.

Niles noted that it was the AS 332L which was the long-range version. This was the type that Niles had flown in the North Sea so he was reasonably confident that he could quickly orientate himself within the cockpit.

Niles nodded to the refuelling Bladders. 'We wait until they are well into their refuelling before we make a move. I want you to go in the aircraft and asked the pilot if he can take a wounded passenger back to the airstrip. Without being disrespectful Pedro you look more like one of their cut throats than I do – plus which, you speak the lingo like a native. There are normally two pilots with choppers of this size but we noticed when we were here before that they were only using one, probably to save weight'.

'Are you sure you know how to fly this bloody thing Sandy? It looks a bloody complicated beast to me. We could always force the pilot to fly us out'.

'Yeah, but we're already going to be at maximum all up weight after we pick up the others. I would rather dump him here or down the track somewhere but in any case, I have to be sat in that right hand seat to fly the beast by myself. I would prefer to get him out of it and me into it with the chopper on the ground, not in the air'.

The Puma came to the low hover and gently hover taxied to the refuelling point. As it got nearer Niles and Pedro could see that they were still operating it with just the one pilot.

'The Gods appear to be with us for the moment', whispered Niles nodding to the single pilot.

Niles was beginning feel the tension building up within him. It was some years since he had last flown but at least this had all been on the Super Puma. He noted that Pedro was as steady as a rock and shown no strain on what they were about to attempt. An ideal man in a tight spot he thought.

They noticed that it was two workers and not guards that came to refuel the chopper. Niles was quite impressed to note that the re-fuellers actually carried out a water test on the fuel before replenishing the chopper.

Niles gave Pedro the nod whilst the re-fuellers were busy coupling the hose to the chopper.

Pedro stepped out into the open and confidently and without an apparent care in the world strode round the chopper and climbed in the passengers' door. Niles waited with bated breath. His weapon was cocked with a round up the breach. If their ruse was tumbled he was determined to sell his life dearly. This was probably the most important and risky part of the whole plan.

It was only about two minutes later when Pedro reappeared and said to Sandy. 'Welcome aboard. He's says it's no problem'.

Pedro hesitated for a moment. 'I've just had an idea Sandy - your straw coloured hair is a right give away'. With that, Pedro whipped out a Shell Dressing and wrapped it around Sandy's head and chin disguising the compromising coloured hair.

'Actually Sandy, you should do this more often. It 'Aint arf' improved your looks', he joked.

'Yours would improve if you put a bloody bin liner over it. Hold it! They have finished refuelling now we have to make our move'.

They moved round to the passengers' door with Pedro pretending to help Niles who was dragging his feet and acting in a dazed manner. Pedro helped Niles up the steps who kept his head low and groaned as though experiencing great pain. Pedro swung main passenger door closed and they made their way forward to the cockpit.

The chopper was still running at Ground Idle. The pilot was just about to open the throttles to Flight Idle when his attention was attracted by Niles yelling at the top of his voice and pointing to a point on the reverse side of the forward bulkhead directly behind where the pilot was sitting indicating that something was seriously wrong.

The pilot muttered a curse undid his harness, trimmed the rotor disc level and clambered into the passengers' compartment.

'What the fuck s a matter back here?' He snarled. He sounded like an American, probably a mercenary. He turned to look at the bulkhead that Niles kept pointing to.

Niles didn't hesitate - he crashed the butt of his Beretta into the Pilot's skull and knocked him senseless.

Niles rapidly donned the Pilot's Baseball cap and headphones while Pedro quickly wrapped the Shell Dressing around the pilot's head. Niles quickly opened the throttle to Flight Idle and engaged the Auto Stabilisation equipment, (On the Puma it was almost as good as a full Auto Pilot System). He adjusted the collective pitch gave Pedro the thumbs up when there was a knock on the passenger cabin door and the door was opened from outside and a guard put his head through the door and said.

'You are to take six wounded passengers back with you tonight Senor'.

Rusty Irons and his two men where having a hard time trying to ensure a running battle at the same time making sure that they weren't' out flanked. If any of the Cartel's men managed to get between them and the bridge over the ravine they'd be cut off and would either have to walk out of the jungle or wait for a chopper lift at some later date. The trouble was that in the jungle, visibility was as often as not, no more than five or ten metres.

The only way they could keep ahead of the cartel's men was by listening to the noise they made. Rusty made sure that they were well ahead but from the noise the enemy were making it sounded as though there were at least twenty to thirty of them.

Bryant had been established at the far side of the bridge for about an hour when Cpl Finnegan, (Fingers) and Tpr

Miles (Kilo) turned up saying that they had earmarked a good HLS and had left a blazed trail to help with navigation back, should it get too dark.

'Okay, let's have all the passengers. Now listen out - I want you to follow Cpl Finnegan to the Helicopter landing Site. Dale, could you act as "Rear End Charlie", and make sure that no one gets lost?' Bryant looked at Dale expectantly.

'No problems boss', he grinned using the SAS parlance for addressing an officer and immediately set about helping Finnegan to organise the passengers.

'Before you go Fingers I would like all your M203 grenades. Lance and I have only got four each and we need as much firepower as we can get to cover Rusty and the other two when crossing the bridge'.

Finnegan gave his four grenades to Kilo and with the four that he had, it gave the team a total of sixteen that could be used to extradite Rusty, and his team. Hopefully they wouldn't need all of them but they could produce a devastating effect out to a maximum range of just over a hundred meters.

Ten minutes after the departure of the passengers all the firing from the other side of the ravine had ceased. This probably meant that Rusty and his merry band had broken contact with the Cartel's men and were now making a beeline for the bridge.

Suddenly, Grimes appeared at the other end of the bridge and he started to cross immediately. He made it in quick time and was panting heavily.

'Boss - Hezeltine has taken a hit in the calf and can barely walk. Rusty is staying on the far side to help him and evade the enemy, He suggest you blow the bridge and carry on as planned and then try and return a day or so later to extract them. He has the GPS and we have given him the Tactical Radio. He'll call you tomorrow mid day exactly'.

Grimes report was interrupted by the appearance of the Cartel's men on the other side of the bridge. This was too good an opportunity to miss and the four SAS started to fire their M203 grenades to a devastating effect.

'Don't forget that every one we kill now reduces the number available to hunt Rusty and Hezeltine', snarled Bryant.

The cartel's gunmen were trying to return fire but they were taking a mauling from the exploding grenades. They were forced to withdraw out of range of the grenades which mean they could no longer see the SAS team through the dense undergrowth.

After about thirty seconds Bryant and his men could see no further signs of the enemy as they withdrew into the trees on the far bank. They had inflicted a number of casualties but with the restricted visibility in the undergrowth it was difficult to assess how many. Bryant waited a further five minutes to see if another attack developed. He checked his watch. He wanted to ensure that the passengers to the HLS preferably before dark. He would have to follow them now.

Bryant gave Lance the third GPS and said.

'We're off now Lance - don't take any chances, if they haven't tried to cross within the next ten minutes just blow the bridge and follow us'.

Lance nodded his head and took hold of the pull wired he had attached to the Claymore Mine facing across the bridge. He laid down behind his tree stump for cover as the other three set off for the HLS. As he lay there he started to think of Maria and immediately had an erection. He was very angry with himself and quickly got his mind back to the problem in hand. However, it was the first time in his amorous career that thoughts of a woman had come to mind whilst on active service. If nothing else, it reinforced the fact that this liaison was very different to all the others he'd been involved in.

It was not long before the Cartel's men began to gather cautiously on the far bank. After considerable bickering and much shouting three of the Cartel's gunmen were harangued into attempting to cross the bridge. Lance lay as quiet as a shadow, hidden in the lush undergrowth behind the tree stump hoping they would think that his side of the bridge was no longer manned.

At last, they decided to cross and three of them were crossing at five metre intervals as apposed to the manner in which the passengers had crossed. Lance waited whilst the adrenaline heightened his senses. The leading man was only ten metres from his side when Lance pulled the wire and ducked his head. The sound of the mine exploding reverberated around the hills. The blast and seven hundred ball bearings swept the three men clear off the bridge as though they had been chaff. At the same time the force of the explosion completed wrecked the bridge. It tumbled, a mass of tangle rope and broken wood into the ravine following the bodies of the three men the blast had decimated. The shrapnel, which flew across the ravine in a deadly hail killed or maimed at least half a dozen of the enemy on the far bank.

The morale of the gunmen men was now completely crushed. With the grenades and the mine blast they had suffered over fourteen casualties. It was now approaching night. The bridge was completely destroyed. There was nothing further they could do until next day. They knew that when they returned to the campsite their arses were going to get a good kicking.

It took almost an hour for Bryant and the other two SAS to get to the HLS. Cpl Finnegan had used a couple of the male passengers to clear some of the taller undergrowth and he had briefed them on how to approach the helicopter if and when it arrived.

At the same time Lance used the mobile to get an update

on what was happening at Bogotá. He spoke for about five minutes, and then he approached Bryant.

'Boss I have just spoken to Maria and she put me on to this guy called Chris Brooker. He's the Head of Security at the American Embassy and he reckons that the Yanks can't get the fixed wing aircraft to Bogotá until nine this evening at the earliest. They want to know how this affects our plans and to keep them posted'.

'Well the flying side of the operation is Sandy's problem so until he gets back here we can't give them a definite answer. I know Chris Brooker. I met him at the Embassy party the night you and the lads went to town- he's a good man. Tell him we will get back to him as soon as Sandy and the chopper arrive. Mind you, if Sandy doesn't get the chopper Christ knows what we are going to do'.

The Puma was now at Flight Idle and the Autopilot engaged and ready to go. For a second, Niles was tempted to lift the chopper straight off and accept the gunfire, which was almost certain to follow. However, he realised that they would be lucky to get clear without sustaining damage to the aircraft or injury to Pedro and himself. He broke into a sweat as he considered his options. Work brain! Fucking work! If he didn't come with an answer in the next ten seconds their goose was cooked. He suddenly had an idea.

'Pedro tell the boss man that we are too heavy to take that many with all the fuel we have just taken on board. Tell him we are going to take off and do two circuits around the base to burn off excess fuel. That will be quicker than trying to de-fuel. Then we'll return, land and pick up the other wounded and fly them back to base'.

Pedro grinned with relief and rattled away in Spanish to the guy in charge and with much gesticulating and curses the wounded withdrew to the perimeter of the landing site.

Niles; with the baseball cap pulled well down over his

forehead, gave the ubiquitous, 'thumb s up', signal to confirm he was about to lift off. He increased pitch smoothly at the same time feeding in more right boot to compensate for the increase in torque. Brought the Puma to the right wheel low hover, (French Helicopter Rotors turn in the opposite direction to American) then transition smoothly away and disappeared over the horizon.

It took the stranded wounded and their boss a good ten minutes to realise that the chopper wasn't returning. They had no alternative but to inform the new Camp boss who had only been in situ' for two hours. He'd not found the passengers, had suffered numerous casualties and lost a helicopter all in the space of two hours. His bosses in Bogotá were not going to be pleased. He was about to become as popular as a 'Pork Chop in a Synagogue'.

Niles quickly felt at home in the Super Puma in which he'd accumulated two thousand hours flying in the North Sea. A fuel check showed over two thousand lbs of fuel, enough for two hours at economical cruise. He started to calculate the weight of the passengers, it worked out at 25 times the standard weight of 170lbs about 4250lbs. Max' all up weight of aircraft used to be 18410lbs minus the role weight, say 12000lbs giving a total disposable of 6410lbs. Minus the fuel weight of 2000lbs left him with approx.' 4410lbs to play with.

'We are laughing kit bags ', mused Niles. But we will have to dump the American pilot as soon as we can. There is no point in lugging dead weight around plus the fact that the fewer people he could identify and a later date the better. Niles diverted down the southern track away from the crashed Dakota. Came to the hover over the track and Pedro unceremoniously dumped the semi -conscious pilot. Took off, and circled round to the north keeping well clear of the camp site.

Niles showed Pedro how to work the UHF set and said,

'Try giving the team a call when we are only five minutes away from them. We should be close enough to raise them on the Sarbe Beacon and get the Grid reference of the HLS'. It was already completely dark so Niles was going to have to rely on the radio aides to get them to the HLS.

Pedro gave the team a call and was answered straight away and was given the grid, which he entered in the GPS. This gave Niles a heading and distance to steer.

'We should be there in four minutes Pedro and they should flash us a 'V' in Morse as we come over the HLS. You look out to port and I'll look starboard'.

'Christ is that all it will take – four minutes! No wonder you gave up foot slogging as a soldier and took up flying'.

'Yes, but having tramped through the jungle as a foot soldier I never forgot how hard it was which helps when you're flying in support of soldiers on the ground. Especially when they ask you for a grid reference, you always ensured that it is was as accurate as possible knowing that a wrong one could cost the blokes another day's march'.

'I think I've got them', said Pedro. 'Some one is flashing a light......yes! We have three dots followed by a dash. That's the 'V', we were looking for. Are we going to land Sandy?'

'Yep, nothing to be gained burning fuel up here might as well land'. Niles lowered the landing gear and checked he had three greens. Though they may not be actually landing it was safer to have the wheels down now rather than to forget them whilst in the hover.

He turned the chopper into wind and switch his landing lamp ON then began his approach to the clearing trading off speed for power as he got slower. As they descended into the clearing he said, 'Pedro could you stick your head out the window just to ensure my tail rotor's clear'.

'No problem', Pedro pulled the window back and craned his neck out the window. Although it was dark he could clearly se that the tail rotor was clear.

Sandy Niles could now clearly make out Lance giving landing hand signals in the glare of the landing lamp. The signals indicated it was safe to land. Niles gentle landed and brought the speed levers back to Ground Idle to conserve fuel.

Bryant clambered into the aircraft plugged in the spare headset and gave Niles a grin of relief that nearly split his face in half. 'Thank Christ you made it', he whooped. He then informed Sandy of the latest developments.

'We've been in touch with Chris Brooker at the American Embassy and he says the Fixed Wing Aircraft will not be available until 2130hrs at the earliest. It's basically your call Sandy but I don't fancy having all these passengers sculling about the airport for two hours. I figure the Cartel would be made aware of our arrival at the Airport within half an hour.

Niles thought for a minute, 'It's about a hundred and fifty miles to Bogotá from here and it's only just coming up to half six. If we set off now we would be there by eight o'clock. I don't want to close down here in case we having trouble trying to start the engines on internal batteries. Our best bet would be to fly to somewhere just outside Bogotá close down and wait till the right moment. If we can't start the engines your Embassy friend will have to arrange road transport. How does that sound?'

'That sounds good but we also have a added complication. Rusty and Hezeltine were trapped the wrong side of the bridge. Hezeltine took a hit in the leg and is barely mobile. Although the team has been compromised and the Brit' Government will want us out as soon as possible, there's no way we are leaving this country without Irons or Hezeltine'.

'Then you can count me in as well Tony there is no way I'm leaving without doing my best to get those two out"

'This is not your problem Sandy; you have done more

for this rescue operation than anyone. More over, I suspect that you are numero uno on the Cartel's hit list. I think you should get out the country with all the others whilst you're still in your own skin'.

'Unfortunately Tony that's not going to be easy. I have no passport. So I will have to extract my self from this mess as I've had to do for the past three years. But we do have one thing going for us which may not have been appreciated by the Cartel'.

Bryant looked puzzled. 'What the hell are you on about Sandy?'

'We have this Puma and if we can get it refuelled we can use it to extract Rusty and Hezeltine from the bush and I will fly you any where that the fuel will allow. How does that sound'!

'But where will we get refuelled' asked Bryant.

'Well if all else fails, why don't we pay the Cartel's forward Airstrip that is this side of Bogotá an early morning visit. Like just before first light. If six highly trained SAS men were to hit them first thing in the morning while they are still in bed playing with themselves. I don't think we would get much resistance'.

'You know Sandy you have a real talent for creating mayhem. You have the making of a first rate bastard. As Rusty said to me, I'm bloody glad you are on our side. However, there is a chance that we could take further casualties refuelling that way. Let's discuss our options during the flight back'.

'Sounds like a good idea Tony. Could you get every one aboard and we'll set heading for Bogotá and talk to your friend Brooker on the way in and see what options he can come up with'.

Tony Bryant gave Niles the thumbs up, disconnected the headset and set about organising the seating of the passengers. There were in fact only twelve seats, so Dale and the SAS team anchored them selves to the floor with harness straps to the cargo ring bolts.

Niles eased the throttles to Flight Idle. Engaged the Autopilot and they were off. Once clear of the trees he doused his landing light and set heading for Bogotá. The As332L has seven fuel tanks that need to be managed in flight so he elected Dino the Dakota Captain to fly as co-pilot. Although he was not Helicopter qualified he was a professional aviator who knew his way around the cockpit. He was also clued up on the local Air Traffic frequencies. Not that Niles intended to speak to Bogotá control - unless he had to.

'I must say you handle this helicopter very well for a car chauffeur', murmured Dino smiling at Niles. 'And it not the sort of beast you can learn to fly by playing around with a computer simulator'.

'I'm afraid it's a long story', said Niles. 'Too long to discuss now but if we ever get the time I'll tell you all about it'. He then showed Dino how to manipulate the fuel controls during the flight. Before they could continue with any further conversation Bryant appeared at the cockpit door and plugged the spare headset in.

'I've spoken to Chris Brooker. Here's the plan subject to your approval, as you are the 'bus driver. Brooker has given us an old farm to land at eleven miles south east of Bogotá. Here is the grid reference. They will have two Embassy Vans ready to transfer us to the American Embassy where we wait until the fixed wing jets have been refuelled and are ready to leave. The same vans, which are normally used to transport diplomatic mail and baggage, then transport us to the aircraft. We board the aircraft and 'hey presto', we are out the country before the Cartel even get a sniff of us – how does that sound to you Sandy?'

'That sounds bloody excellent. But have they any suggestions about refuelling the chopper. By the time we land we will only have about half an hour's fuel remaining, that's not enough to search for Rusty and Butch'.

'Brooker reckons he can organise a truck with some forty-gallon drums to be taken to the warehouse first thing in the morning. He has also organised small petrol driven pump to take the hard work out of the refuelling. His only request is that you make your landing as unobtrusive as possible'. He said he has also spoken to Col DeSuza and has established that one of the guys you trained has been bought by the Cartel but at this stage he's not sure who it is'.

'Well I can land without using the landing lamp provided they get the vans to put on their headlights. But I can't disguise the noise of 3400 SHP pouring out my exhaust. However if the place is only sparsely populated we should be able to get away with it. Bye the way Tony, could you phone ahead and get them to have the cars arranged so their headlights are converging into an arrowhead pointing into wind. That will assist with the landing.'

'Consider it done'. Bryant unplugged the spare headset and went aft to grab Lance's mobile phone.

Chapter 18

Bogotá

The sun had sunk below the horizon an hour previously and the headlights of the vehicles driving along the Autopista del sur seem to accentuated the height of the 14th floor and isolate the solitary occupant seated at a large rectangular mahogany table.

Francesco Domingo pondered his problems whilst he awaited the arrival of his colleagues. Despite the cool of the evening and the fact that he was dressed in thin cotton shirt and an expensive lightweight suit he was sweating profusely. A suit that had cost him more than he'd earned in an entire year prior to becoming a drug baron. This had not been a day to relish. In the space of twelve hours they had lost a senior member of the cartel, two of their best crew chiefs, approximately sixteen men dead – god knows how many injured. One of their new Super Puma helicopters (costing approx.' twelve million dollars US). His beloved Holland & Holland rifle and their new Drug Processing Plant compromised.

It seemed that whatever move they had made to safe

guard their new plants location had been stymied by bad luck or those bloody SAS bastards who were sent to rescue the downed survivors. There were thousands of square miles of rain forest in Colombia much of it unexplored. Why in God's name had the blasted aircraft come down alongside their new processing plant?

They could have still stabilised the problem had that cretin Al Menzies not lost the head and killed six of the men four of whom had been American citizens. After that, they were in the shit and their only option was to try and wipe out the remainder before they got back to civilisation. His friends in the Colombian Government were now going to have to work overtime to cover their arses.

His silent thoughts were interrupted by the arrival of his colleagues. Most of them had delayed their arrival in the hope that Domingo would have calmed down by now. His temper was well known. And although they were all bosses of their own organisations since the coalition they had agreed that Domingo was the man to make things work. Even his secretary had fled the office when the news of the stolen Helicopter and the escape of the survivors had come through. Domingo had gone absolutely ballistic; and no one dare go near him for an hour.

They had left a space to honour the memory of their lost comrade, Al Menzies. Once they were all seated there was a long silence. It was the blackest day in the memory of all members. None could remember when so many of their plans had turned belly up. To a man, they were angry and upset with the events that had just taken place. However, no one seemed prepared to speak until Domingo, now generally accepted as the leader in this uneasy alliance had spoken first.

He gave a sigh and started the meeting by picking on Pablo.

'Pablo, you were the one tasked with arranging the

field element of this operation. What in Gods name has happened? As far as I can make out every thing that could go wrong went wrong, the operations are nothing but a fucking shambles. What have you got to say?'

'Things started to go wrong just after Rudy Goodge landed. He was getting patrols organised when he was executed. He was shot twice in the head. We think with your Holland Rifle Francesco'.

'Jesus Christ', exploded Domingo. 'Didn't they have any piquet's out guarding the campsite – how in Gods name did these people gets so close as to shoot Rudy in our own bloody camp?'

'We think they must have approached the camp during the hours of darkness early in the morning. Laid up and waited to take out the boss man'.

'But you can't march around in the jungle at night', said Domingo sarcastically.

'These bastards can. That same evening they apparently sucked our men into an ambush at a bridge over that steep ravine to the north west of the camp. They used one of the Claymore mines that we had positioned outside our camp to blow the bridge. That mine killed six of our own men. Another two were injured when their guns suffered a blowback'.

'What blowback? – What the hell are you talking about?'

'I'd never heard of it until today. We discovered that during the initial rescue of the survivors one of the rescuers went into the camp armoury and forced some grit with grease down the muzzles of about six of our Armalites. Later on, two of our men were badly injured when they tried to fire their weapons'.

'Did nobody think to check their weapons before using them? I thought we had trained these guys better than this'.

'True Francesco but they are still not trained soldiers they have only had the basic weapon training. Most of them have never actually fired their weapon at anything other than some forty gallon drums we used to practice on'.

'Okay, Okay. Do we know where the survivors are now? Domingo looked around the table. However he got no answers.

Pedro DeGannes eventually said. 'If they've used the helicopter then I suppose they could be anywhere, even out the country by now'.

Frank DeNero rubbed his chin thoughtfully and said, 'To get out the country from that location would mean having to refuel at least once or even twice. Panama and Ecuador are both about five hundred miles away. Although the nearest part of Venezuela border is only about two hundred miles it's all rain forest and the nearest civilisation must be another two hundred beyond that. I think they must be still in this country – but where..... That's any ones guess'.

'But what's the point in trying to stop them now', said Teddy Garcia. 'The bloody horse has bolted the stable so what's the point in trying to close the door. The only member of the Cartel they have seen is Al Menzies. And he's dead! We can claim it was a solo operation being run by him – nothing to do with us'.

But Domingo was not happy with that. 'How is our street credibility going to look if these guys get away Scot free after causing all this grief? And we are seen to do nothing. There is always some bastard somewhere waiting to take over our operation. We must be seen to take revenge or risk being usurped. Now I want some positive ideas on how to get back at these bastards. In the mean time I propose we put a bounty of two hundred thousand dollars US, for any persons capturing or killing anyone involved with the rescue of these passengers. Do we all agree?'

All nodded their heads. Domingo continued. 'That's it then, done - we'll put two hundred thousand on their heads and see what materialises'.

'The next thing we must do', said Domingo wagging his finger at his colleagues. 'Is to alert all our informants and instruct them to let us know immediately any of the survivors or the British SAS team is seen. Then take it from there'.

Pablo Ferreira raised his hand for attention. 'We are not certain but we think one or two of the Rescue team did not get across the ravine. Unfortunately it was too dark to confirm it but tomorrow morning we must get out there early and see if we can pick up their trail'.

'What the fuck do you mean they may not? Did they or did they not get across?' Teddy Garcia snarled.

Pablo who had been responsible for the field operations was getting pissed off with every one trying to lay the blame at his door.

'It's all very well for you guys to sit here and tell me what we should have done in hindsight. During the time our men were trying to storm the Ravine Bridge they were under heavy rifle fire plus having grenades fired at them. We definitely saw one guy cross but no others - however they may have got across before we got to the bridge'.

'Okay.., let's cool it', said Domingo trying to pour oil on the proceedings before it got totally out of hand. 'First thing tomorrow we go back to the bridge and try and establish whether they all got over or not. Senator Jackson warned us that the SAS men were extremely well trained, unfortunately we did not heed his advice'.

'Our biggest mistake', suggested Frank DeNero.' Was in trying to take the passengers as hostages instead of just airlifting them out, they hadn't a bloody clue where they were at that stage so it's doubtful that they could have compromised the Processing plant'.

'In retrospect I agree but it's too late now. Any other business? - Domingo looked around expectantly. 'Good'. He sighed.

Domingo thumbed the table.' Let's get to it! However, I would sure like to get my hands on the bastard that stole my Rifle and the two guys that hijacked our Helicopter. They are to be wasted even if it takes years to do it. Okay let's go - and we meet here in another six hours to get an update'.

Just as Domingo was about to leave the room Pablo Ferreira put his head round the door and said.

'Our friend from the States is on the secure line and he sound very agitated. He wants to talk to you pronto'.

Domingo strode into the office and picked up the secure phone. 'Sam - I hope this is fucking important because we have had nothing but grief down here without you unloading more shit on us'.

'Yeah, well your shit down there is ricocheting all the way up here. Those unsecured radio transmissions your cretins made yesterday and the reference to me and Al Thornton has now been linked together and we are being threatened with an investigation by a Special Select Committee which our friend the Defence Secretary has organised'.

'Well what do you want me to do about it', exploded Domingo. 'You have all been well paid for your help – your Government is your problem not ours'. At the moment we have plenty of problems of our own, I can't see how we can assist you from down here'.

'If you could kidnap Field's wife and daughter it might give us enough time to cover our tracks and forestall the investigation'.

'For Christ sake!' Domingo yelled. 'What the fuck do you think I've been trying to do for the past twenty-four hours? In attempting to capture them and the other survivors I've had sixteen men killed and Christ knows how many wounded; Two of our best Crew bosses killed; A Super

Puma Helicopter stolen, and My Holland & Holland Rifle stolen. And now you want me to help you by capturing the people I have been chasing all day. That's a laugh'!

'Jesus Domingo what the hell have you been doing down there – trying to start World War Three, I think you've suffered more casualties in twenty-four hours than America did in the duration of Desert Storm'.

'It's this bloody SAS team; it's like trying to put your finger on mercury. Just when you think you have them they disappear and then reappear somewhere completely unexpected. They have disappeared again this evening in one of our Super pumas and no one knows where the fuck they are. I have even checked my own arsehole just in case they were hiding up there, we are guarding all avenues out the country but they have outguessed us each time'.

Sam Jackson resisted the urge to point out to Domingo that his arsehole was just about big enough to accommodate the passengers and the Puma. Instead he said. 'How the hell did they steal a Puma helicopter. That's one hell of a big machine to steal and you would normally need a professional pilot to fly it. Did they hijack your pilot as well?'

'They did initially but then they dumped him after clearing the campsite. So as far as we know, one of the team must be flying it'.

'I find that difficult to believe but at the moment I can't think of any other solution Francesco'.

'Never mind that Senator, if the passengers do get back State side, can we count on you to give us some support if we try and kidnap the wife or daughter? Obviously we have no men in the States who could be relied upon to carry out such a mission'.

'We will give you any information we can but you must realise that there is no way we can be physically involved or associated with any kidnapping or assassination'.

Domingo thought on that for a bit. 'You know it might

be easier up there than here. At the moment every one here has their guard up, once the passengers get back to the States they will all relax and feel much safer. This would make the wife or daughter much easier to get to. Tell you what Sam let me think on this one for a while and I'll get back to you when we have something positive to say, Cheers for now'.

Domingo sat down and considered the possibilities. The kidnap itself would not be too difficult but trying to keep the hostage hidden in America was fraught with problems. Francesco had no allusions about how good the FBI was. They were without doubt the most technically advanced police force in the World. Trying to keep one step ahead of them in the States would be almost impossible.

If he could get one of them back to Colombia the problem would be much easier. The difficult part was getting them out of the States. All things considered, he thought the daughter would be the easiest to abduct at the same time the mother would then put the husband under more pressure to have her restored. He decided the crux of the matter was to try and kidnap the daughter and get her to Colombia before her absence was noted. This would alleviate the problems with the transport.

If they could get the hostage on a Light Jet Aircraft and have her out of America before she was missed they would not have to worry about being tracked by radar. The best plan would be to fly first to Cuba, land at one of the Cartel's clandestine airfields used for Drug flights. Refuel, and then fly on to Colombia. The details could be all worked out later. He would run his idea pass the other members of the Cartel when they met in five hours time.

Chapter 19

Back to Bogotá

Exactly two miles away from the Cartel's meeting another was in progress. In the American Embassy, Chris Brooker had finally got a VHF Am radio hooked up that covered the civilian aircraft frequencies from 116.0 to 136.0.

He dialled up Maria's other Mobile and got an answer straight away from Lance on the inbound helicopter.

'Hi Lance, could you get hold of Sandy and tell him to listen out on frequency 119.0 MHz. Tell him to call himself Zero One and we will be Zero Two. Have you got that? Oh! And tell him we don't know if anyone else is listening out on this frequency so use veiled speech'.

'No problem'. Answered Lance and went forward and gave the message to Niles.

He acknowledged the information and said to Dino. 'Could you dial up 119.0 on the number one box Dino? We'll only be using veiled speech in case any of, "our friends", are listening out on the same frequency'.

Niles decided to use some of the Off Shore parlance as

though he was flying in from a Rig off shore.

'Hello Zero Two this is Zero One inbound to your location with sixteen souls on board and estimating you at zero eight request refuel and details of out bound load over'.

Brooker was on the net in a flash. 'Roger that Zero One, refuelling is available and we're just working out the details of your out bound load. Call five minutes prior to landing, over'.

'Roger Out'. Niles was speaking with an affected American accent to compliment that of Bookers. A lot of the helicopter pilots working on oil exploration in the area were American. So with luck, their radio transmissions should avoid raising anyone's suspicions.

'Dino could you tune in the TVOR on the number two VHF and get the weather and QNH there's not going to be much difference between the Airports QNH and the point where we are landing? I figure we have ten minutes to run'.

Captain Tony Bryant was now dividing the passengers and SAS team into two equal vanloads. He'd decided to put three SAS in each van so if they were attacked each vehicle had some firepower. He was not sure what Brooker wanted to do about the chopper overnight but they'd have to work that one out after landing.

The night was calm and barmy, stars shone bright in the sky with no artificial light to defuse them. The GPS gave then a heading and distance to fly. Visibility must have been in access of twenty miles. Apart from the occasional small group of artificial lights the night was pitch black and Niles realised he was now flying mainly by reference to the aircraft's instruments. The area they were flying over seemed to be devoid of habitation. However with the good visibility, Niles expected to see the landing site lights with at least ten miles to run in the present Met' conditions.

Niles gave his five minutes to landing call and got an

acknowledgement from Brooker. 'Ground party waiting to refuel you and you are clear to land. Runway lights are on, over'.

Niles set the QNH and started to look for the landing site. 'We're looking for two sets of head lights that form a 'V'. It should be about eight miles in front'. Dino nodded that he understood and Niles completed the Landing checks making sure he had three greens denoting the gear was down and locked.

'I have the lights', Dino pointing out to the eleven o'clock position, where the illuminate 'V' was now clearly visible.

Niles nodded his head. 'Thanks Dino contact'. Niles set the helicopter up for landing and noticed that they were at eight and half thousand feet. Bogotá was somewhat higher above sea level than he had appreciated he therefore made his approach a nice steady one at a conservative rate of decent - touching down exactly in the apex of the 'V' form by the two sets of headlights.

The situation on the landing ground was extremely well organised. Brooker had even provided a marshaller with two torch wands to ground taxi him into a large warehouse. A building previously used to house large agricultural machinery some time in the past. As soon as the chopper was inside, the doors were closed keep out prying eyes. Niles quickly closed the engines down and applied the rotor brake then gave the, 'thumbs up', for people to deplane.

The warehouse was about a hundred and fifty feet long and at least another eighty wide. With the doors closed no one would know that there was a helicopter housed inside. The floor was reasonable clean so there was no real problem of picking up FOD in to the turbines. There was even enough room within the warehouse to manoeuvre the helicopter under its own power. There would be no problem refuelling in the warehouse.

The passengers couldn't stop talking and laughing, this

was the first time in three days that they had felt any thing like safe or secure.

Jackie Fields and Karen came over and thanked Niles and the SAS team for all they had done. Karen took a running jump into Nile' arms and gave him a big hugs. 'Oh thank you Sandy I thought you were absolutely brilliant - don't you mummy?'

Jackie Field face was creased with a brilliant smile. 'You're a man of many talents Sandy Niles and I'm not sure which one I admire the most. I'm sure my husband would like to meet you and thank you for all you have done'.

'Let's face it Jackie it was a team effort. I don't think we would have made it without the help of Tony Bryant and his merry men', he said.

At the very moment, the other three women came over to express their thanks to Niles.

'My hero', cooed Susan giving him a big hug and a kiss.

'Please! Please! - No applause; just throw money', he joked.

The other two girls quickly replaced her in turn, first Olivia and then Cathy. As Cathy kissed him she whispered in his ear.

'If you ever get to the West Coast of the States be sure to look me up. I can promise you a good time'.

'I'll take you up on that if you are not careful', Niles grinned.

Jackie Fields noted that where as Niles had been completely spontaneous and relaxed with Karen he seemed slightly uneasy by the attention of the older women and wondered if he was in fact gay.

A man who called himself Rex interrupted Niles and said, 'I understand you are the guy that piloted this beast. My name is Rex Heaton and Brooker has sent me down here to get all you guy's back to the Embassy. There are three of us, all guys from the States I might add, the fewer locals that know what's happened here the higher the security. We'll remain in the warehouse to guard the chopper until you take off tomorrow'.

'That's great', said Niles. 'There are some loose ends I would like to tie up with Brooker before we depart tomorrow prior to first light. By the way are you cleared to refuel choppers?'

'I'm not, but the two guys coming here with the fuel truck are. They've also been instructed to have some extra heavy duty batteries available to start the chopper. They won't be coming until about two in the morning when the roads are almost deserted. We are trying to ensure that the owner, Mr Mendoza, is not compromised'.

'Good thinking Rex. I see Tony Bryant has all the guys on the transport so I had better be off. We will see you about five-tomorrow morning all being well'.

'Look forward to it,' grinned Rex, giving Niles a firm handshake.

The journey back to the Embassy was quiet and uneventful. Most of the passengers were deep in thought and still worried at being in Colombia. Their euphoria at being safe on the ground was now tempered by the fact that they still had to get out the country safely.

They arrived at the Embassy gates and were checked by the American Marines on guard. The two vans were guided around to the back of the Embassy where they could be unloaded out of sight.

All the lights at the back of the Embassy were extinguished. Even the hall lights were not illuminated until every one was indoors and the outer door was closed and locked. The passengers and team were then guided into the inner sanctum of the Embassy to a room with no external windows.

The room was about sixty feet long and thirty wide with

plenty of sofas and armchairs. One of the adjoining doors led to a smaller room where occasionally they could hear radio transmissions being made.

Brooker burst out the smaller room with an immense grin on his face. 'Hi you guys - great to see you. The name's Brooker and I'm head of security here at the Embassy. I must admit there were times when you had me worried. I've heard of some crazy stunts in my time but hijacking that helicopter and flying you guys out the jungle takes the cake, however, more of that later. I've got the Embassy catering staff to rustle up some hot food and coffee. I expect you are starving. Once you have had something hot to eat and drink I'll fill you in with the departure details'.

Four Embassy staff appeared with trays of steaming hot dogs and huge thermos flasks of boiling coffee and started to serve the starving survivors. Being mostly Americans they fell on the hot dogs as though there was no better food to be found. Even the SAS team joined in. The consensus of opinion was that nobody but Americans could make hot-dogs that tasted as good.

Brooker strolled over to Bryant and Niles who were each wolfing a hot-dog down at the same time trying to drink their coffee. 'After the snack and the passenger briefing I think we should all go into the operations room and discuss how you want to organise the rescue of the two guys you still have out there'.

Bryant swallowed a piece of hot-dog and cleared his throat. 'There's no way we are leaving this country without attempting to get our two guys out'.

'I'll give you all the assistance I can but at the moment we don't have much hardware out here. Give us a couple of days and I could get you anything you want but I'm afraid time is not on our side at the moment. The American Defence Secretary is inbound on the first aircraft and I know he wants to meet you all personally. As you, know his wife and daughter were amongst the passengers you rescued so he has taken a keen interest in their safe recovery'.

The hot food and drink was having the desired effect and they were all beginning to relax. It was noticeable that now they were reasonably safe how Costello and Milo voices' became more strident and bossy and attempting to attract attention.

'Can I have every ones attention please'; Brooker stood in the middle of the room so all could see him.

'The State side aircraft are due in about an hour's time but in order to camouflage your departure we are going to delay it until Two o'clock in the morning when the Diplomatic aircraft normally leave for the US. This should allay any suspicions the Cartel might have about there being two aircraft instead of the usual one. In the meantime, the Ambassador is going to make an official complaint to the Colombian Government about the missing passengers who were reported to be alive this afternoon in the Hinterland. Obviously the intention is to make it look as though we have no idea of your whereabouts and thus add to the Cartel's confusion. I would therefore ask you all, please co-operate in this delusion by remaining in this room and having to suffer another uncomfortable ride in the Embassy baggage vans to the airport. Your co-operation is appreciated'.

Costello was determined to have his say. 'I think all this subterfuge is entirely unnecessary. God dam it, were are on American soil here and the Cartel wouldn't dare try anything. As the Director and man in charge of this group I demand that we be shown more respect. Surely you can provide us with an air-conditioned bus to the airport'.

Before Brooker could reply Niles interrupted him and said. 'Chris - if you want to know the wrong way to do anything you can guarantee that Costello will come up with the answer'.

Brooker was not head of security because he had a pretty

face. ' Mr Costello when you get off the Embassy's aircraft in the States you do just what the fuck you like - but until then, you will do exactly as I say or I'll have you bound and gagged until you are out of this country – Do I make my self clear'!

Costello was about to object but the look on Brooker's face made him change his mind and hold his tongue.

Brooker continued. 'I'm sorry about the inconvenience but I'm sure you will agree that the first priority is to get you safely out the country. We have cable TV and magazines to read and I would be most grateful if you could keep yourselves amused until departure'.

Jackie Field approached Brooker and said. 'What time do you anticipate the arrival of my husband Chris? Will he be coming here or staying at the airport?'

'About nine o'clock this evening and he will be most definitely coming to the Embassy Mrs Fields. He has expressed a desire to meet all the SAS team and you too Sandy', Brooker nodded to Niles. 'He's also keen to see what can be done to extradite the two men still out there. Without wishing to over state the obvious, your husband, as the Defence Secretary, has a hell of a lot of political muscle to throw around. If any one can help in this situation he's the man to do it'.

'Please call me Jackie. My next question; how are the SAS team and Sandy going to get out of the country. If the aircraft are leaving tonight it means that they are going to be stranded here?'

'That's something we are going to discuss when your husband gets here Jackie. Technically, they are not citizens of the United States and therefore not our responsibility but in view of the service they have provided to you guys I'm sure as hell we're going to do my utmost to get them out of the country. At the moment, we have liased with the British Embassy and the consensus of opinion is that we get every one out to the States then sort out the details'.

'My God I should hope so - if it wasn't for Sandy's intervention young Karen and the rest of us women were about to get raped. Plus which, two of the SAS team are still in the jungle and at the moment - we don't know whether they are alive or not'.

'Not to worry Jackie we'll get a plan of action sorted out when your husband gets here. In the meantime I suggest you and young Karen get as much rest as possible while you can - bear in mind that you will be flying out at two in the morning'.

At the other end of the room Lance was getting a hard time being interrogated by his possible future in-laws.

When Maria had introduced Lance to her Mother, Father and Aunt they were all impressed by Lance's physical presence. Alfred Mendoza was quite amused at the way his wife and her sister preened themselves as they were introduced. However whilst admitting that Lance was a fine looking man Alfred wanted to make sure that his potential son-in-law had more than just beefcake to offer.

Alfred Mendoza waved to Chris Brooker, 'Chris is there anywhere that Edward and my family could go to talk in private?'

'No problem, there's a small room just here. I'll make sure refreshments are sent in and then I must make arrangements for all the survivors to have a shower and freshen up. So give me a shout Lance when you are ready to shower'.

Although the survivors had only been in the jungle for a couple of days they were all beginning to smell a little high and they all welcomed the chance to freshen up.

After they'd showered the adrenaline flow began to ease off and the passengers started feeling extremely drowsy. Most of them were beginning to curl up in the various armchairs and sofas and catch up on some much needed sleep.

Jackie Fields turned round to look for Karen and got

the shock of her life to see her curled up on Niles's lap and already fast asleep.

Niles smiled, raised his eyebrows, looked at Jackie and put his finger up to his lips and went; 'Shush'.

Jackie Fields was again struck by how natural and relaxed Sandy Niles was with Karen. She had noted that whenever any of the older women approached Sandy he seemed to erect a mental barrier. He was never rude and always answered when spoken to but made no effort to engage in small talk. In fact she noticed that even when talking to the men unless it was planning some mayhem with the SAS he kept very much to himself.

His insular attitude had intrigued Jackie from the first time he spoke to her in the Dakota. Tony Bryant and the SAS team knew some of his history but refused to disclose it, but to the rest of them he kept insisting that he was just a chauffeur. This was obviously nonsense – how the hell does a chauffeur get to fly a complicated helicopter like the Super Puma.

Jackie Fields was determined to root the truth out one way or another. But that would have to wait for the time being she was beginning to feel absolutely shattered and retired to the sofa next to Niles and Karen and was soon fast asleep.

It seemed to Jackie that she had hardly closed her eyes when she felt a gentle but insistent tap on her shoulder. Opening her eyes she saw Chris Brooker standing over her. 'I thought you would like to know that your husband has just arrived and will be here in seconds'.

'My God what time is it Chris?'

'Almost ten o'clock. I'm not going to wake the others. The aircraft will be refuelled by now. But we won't be leaving here until about one thirty in the morning'.

Just then George fields strode through the door accompanied by three hard faced men whose occupation was clearly etched on their faces.

Jackie Fields got to her feet and just flew into her husband's arms. She wrapped her arms so tightly around his neck she almost throttled him.

'That's the last time you and young Karen go on any jaunt without me', he growled into her neck. 'And where is that young scallywag?'

'There'! She said pointing to Karen curled up in Nile's lap. 'And before you lose your rag about your daughter consorting with older men, he's the one that saved us from being raped and flew us out of this terrible mess'.

'Did he by God, then I'm certainly in his debt'.

As Jackie was about to shake Niles, Chris Brooker came across and introduced Tony Bryant to George Fields.

'Evening Mr Secretary, I would like to introduce Captain Tony Bryant the leader of the Brit' SAS team who were mainly responsible for rescuing all the passengers'.

'Please call me George. My wife says this guy here is the one that flew you out and saved my wife and daughter from being raped,' said Fields pointing to the still sleeping Niles.

'That's true', said Bryant. 'But actually he's not one of our team he was one of the Dakota passengers.

'I think he said he was a chauffeur', added Bryant with a twinkle in his eye.

'No way', snapped Jackie Fields. 'If Niles was just a chauffeur then I'm a two humped camel'.

'Actually', said Bryant. 'We managed to screw it out of him that at one time he was a British Army pilot in charge of the SAS flight in the UK. And that later, he also flew in the North Sea for some years as a civilian pilot which of course, is where he learnt to fly the Super Puma. Apart from that he would tell us nothing more'.

George fields raised his eyebrows. 'I understand that you are going to try and get your two lads out tomorrow. Is there anything we can do to help?'

'Actually, we are about to start planning the options we have for getting those two out in five minutes time. Would you like to attend Sir?' Brooker indicated the small Op's room where he had laid out some large-scale maps of the area concerned.

Chris Brooker had decided to invite Alfred Mendoza with the SAS team and Niles. Mendoza had more detailed knowledge of Colombia than the rest of them put together. They assembled in the briefing room and Brooker ensured the door was closed and locked. He started the briefing by introducing every one.

'Okay you guys most of you know one another but I thought it a good idea to have Alfred here to give some advice on the local terrain. I've known Alfred well for the past two years and am prepared to vouch for his integrity. This gentleman on my right is the Defence Secretary of the United States; Mr George Fields who would like to thank you all personally for the rescue of his wife and daughter as well as the other passengers. After I have finished the introductions I will hand over to your boss, Tony Bryant to conduct the detailed brief for the pending operation. Mr Secretary would you like to add anything before we get down to the actual operation details?'

'I certainly would! Let me start by thanking you for the splendid and efficient manner, in which you and your team, plus I believe, with a little help from a certain chauffeur, snatched all the passengers from the Cartel's gunmen. The whole operation has been conducted with all the élan and expertise that one has come to associate with your marvellous unit and my thanks and admiration will be passed on to your Government. At the moment, we do not have much hardware down here but if necessary, I can get you practically any thing you need in the next two days. I believe you still have two of your team trapped out there in the jungle so I wont delay the briefing, other than to thank you with all my heart for returning my wife and daughter safe and sound'.

Brooker indicated to Tony Bryant that the floor was now his.

Bryant positioned the large-scale map on the table so that all could see. 'As you know we have two of our team trapped on the other side of the ravine'. Bryant pointed the position on the map.

'Now the intention is to use the Puma we acquired from the Cartel. It has been refuelled at the warehouse ready for our use. Sandy Niles, our chauffeur, insists that he can fly out to the location where Rusty and Hezeltine are holed up. We will have six SAS on board so we can put down quite a weight of firepower. Mr Brooker has some light weapons and more importantly, some M203 grenades. So we will have our full complement of ammunition. As you know Hezeltine has been wounded in the calf which has reduced his mobility. Although Rusty will have cleaned the wound we all know that in the jungle it can quickly become sceptic so time is not on our side'

Bryant looked around his team for the expected questions.

Cpl Finnegan indicated he had a question. 'What time do we anticipate leaving tomorrow morning boss? And assuming we get Rusty and Hezeltine out fairly quickly where do we go from there. We can hardly fly straight into Bogotá Airport and thumb a lift to the UK'.

'Sandy will cover the details of the flight out and timings. As far as the return trip is concerned this is about to be discussed with the Defence Secretary, Chris Brooker, Mr Mendoza and us. But first I'm going to hand over to Sandy to discuss the flight out and the rescue plan. Sandy!'

'Thanks Tony. Okay, let's take things in a chronological order. We aim to take off an hour before dawn in order to be over the rescue location before first light. Hopefully at this time in the morning the hostiles will still be in their beds. The Cartel doesn't appear to have an instrument rated pilot and our last information on the other Puma was that it's still at the forward airstrip. Now that's an hours-flying time from the rescue location. Further more; their ground troops will have to trek up the logging track to get anywhere near to Rusty and Hezeltine's location. That's about an hour trekking too. Therefore, we could have thirty or forty minutes in which to locate and lift out our two guys. However there is another scam I would like to jack up after this briefing which might confuse the Cartel's men, however more about that later. Now is the time to discuss the return to Bogotá. Over to you Tony'.

'Thanks Sandy', said Bryant. 'Basically', he continued. 'We have got a possible ten hours of daylight to waste before we can fly anywhere near Bogotá without tipping our hand to the Cartel. Sandy and I have considered flying out the country with the Puma but Sandy assures me we would have to refuel at least once and possibly twice to get clear of Colombia. Now this is where our American friends may be able to help'.

Chris Brooker took over the floor. 'Sandy and I have discussed a possible plan but it will need the sanction of a very senior official of the American Government'. He looked expectantly at George Fields who said.

'You've got it'!

'We think that if Mr Fields and his wife and daughter could be persuaded to remain over night as guest of the Embassy one aircraft would be all that is needed to fly the remaining survivors out this evening. If the rescue goes according to plan and we get the two SAS out, we then have eight SAS, three of the Secretary's party plus Niles. That's a total of twelve who could be flown out the following night in the second Executive Jet we have on the ground already.

George Fields rubbed his chin thoughtfully. 'My wife and daughter have had a pretty traumatic time and they may want out the country as soon as possible. Give me five minutes while I have a word with them'. George Fields got to his feet and went to the adjoining room.

'Sandy', said Bryant looking at Niles, 'Could we fly part of the way back, land, close down and then wait for night fall before flying into Bogotá. We could then land and board the jet before the Cartel had time to react'.

We are obviously going to have to do something like that. I won't have enough fuel to stooge around all day. We could do as you suggested or if Mr Mendoza is agreeable, we could do something similar to what we did tonight. That way we would probably be out the country before they were aware of it. The only problem with the second proposal is that I don't want to compromise Mr Mendoza and his family'.

'I have an idea', said Mr Mendoza. 'My wife's sister's late husband had a farm that she has been trying to sell and it is away out in the bush – very isolated – but there is a dirt track that is driveable. It's about thirty kilometres to the east of Bogotá. You're on a tarmac road for at least ten kilometres so you could use the same means of getting to the airport as you used tonight. How does that sound?'

'That sounds ideal', said Niles. 'It means I don't have to worry about having to restart the Puma engines. Further more landing at a different location reduces the chances of compromising you and your family'.

'The actual position of the farm house is very secluded', said Mr Mendoza. 'And there is a ravine about four hundred metres away which is about ten meters deep. It would be an ideal place to hide the helicopter. It's so secluded there it might be months before someone discovered it'.

'It gets better by the minute', Niles laughed. 'I could drop you guys off at the Farmhouse door and then hover-taxi over to the ravine. If I can crash the aircraft into the ravine and destroy it - so much the better. Any thing we can do to upset the cartel I'm all for it'.

'Any thing else that we can help you with?' Chris Brooker asked

'Do you think you could let us have a small recorder set to make some recordings on?' said Niles. 'I want to try something out with the SAS team which may help us get the other two guys stranded out there back home. It will need to have a fairly loud output and be reasonably Hi Fidelity'.

Brooker gave Niles a puzzled look. 'I guess so. I'll check around and see what we can come up with. What mayhem are you planning this time Sandy?'

'Could I leave that until we have had a dry run to see if it works? If it does we will give you a demonstration'.

'Okay I've been able to get you some additional FM tactical radios and they cover the same band as the one that Rusty has out there. So with the Sarbe on UHF and the Tactical VHF we should have good communications all round'.

'Any further questions before we wrap the meeting up', Brooker looked round the table but no one had any thing else to add. 'Right – that's it then. I'll leave the various groups to get on with their detailed planning and the rest of us; I suggest, should try and get some much needed rest'.

George Fields had been speaking to his wife and discussing whether or not she would remain with him until the second night.

'I feel I owe it to the Brit's to remain here until we have cleared up the out standing problem of the two guys stranded out there in the bush,' said Fields. 'Whilst I accept that Chris Brooker is a first class man I can lend an awful amount of political muscle should it be needed'.

'I think you should remain darling', said Jackie fields. 'But I am not going to be separated from you or Karen until we get home so we'll stay here in the Embassy until the problem is resolved. We will be quite safe here in the

Embassy and I would like to see the safe recovery of Rusty and Butch Hezeltine'.

'Right, it's agreed then, we are staying here until tomorrow night and fly out with the SAS team – I'll let Chris Brooker know now so that the arrangements can be made'. And he made his way to the small room where the planning was going on.

The door to the small OP's room had been closed ever since Brooker had re-appeared with a Hi fidelity recorder. The passengers could hear some loud talking and the occasional sound of laughter but could not make out what was going on.

Eventually the door was opened and the SAS team all piled out grinning and laughing.

Jackie Fields flew across to her husband who was also grinning and said, 'what the hell was all that laughter about, what's going on?'

'What's going on; I'll tell you what's going on, the SAS and your chauffeur friend in there are planning more mayhem, that's what's going on. There're not content to just fly out to the jungle location and pick up the two survivors. There're determined to over- fly an Airstrip that the Cartel has out there to the East of the city and bomb any helicopters on the strip with M203 grenades. I just hope they know what they are up to. Then they are proceeding to the rescue location to drop a recorder about four hundred metres away from the extraction point. There it will be playing the sounds of a wounded soldier crying for help. Hopefully this will draw any of the gunmen away from the pick up point and give the SAS the necessary time to make the extraction'.

'Do you think it will work?' She queried.

'From the way Tony Bryant and your friend Niles puts it over, it should. As Tony Bryant said, Niles has a positive talent for creating mayhem. At the moment I'm almost beginning to feel sorry for the Cartel leaders. I bet they rue the day they rattled their cage'.

'Don't you dare'! Jackie flared. 'Those bastards were all set to rape your daughter and me and if it hadn't been for Sandy and Rusty they would have succeeded'.

'Okay sweetheart I'm only joking'. Fields was some what taken aback by his wife's language. She was obviously very upset because it was seldom he heard her resort to strong language.

Trooper Edward Lance had also been getting a form of interrogation from the Mendoza family. Lance had just had a shower and shaved and was looking far more presentable than at their first meeting.

Although still dressed in the disruptive pattern military combat kit Trooper Lance was an impressive looking man. He stood at least six foot three inches tall with broad shoulders and lean hips. He had a good looking craggy face with firm regular features but his most arresting feature was his startling vivid blue eyes. Alfred Mendoza could see how attractive he was to women. Even his own wife and her sister stood tall and preened themselves as soon as Lance approached. But the Mendoza's were a very rich family and Alfred was determined to find out just what the young trooper was made of.

'You know young man; my daughter could probably marry any young bachelor in Colombia of her own choosing'. This was Alfred's opening probe. 'However, she appears to have chosen you, some one I might add, who we know nothing about. Therefore I am not going to apologise for asking you some searching questions'.

'My first one is of course rather old fashioned but I want to know if your intentions to my daughter are honourable?'

'They are and were before I knew how wealthy Maria was', answered Lance with a hard glint in his eye. Maria and Lance had already decided to get married with or without her parents blessing.

'After your marriage do you intend to live in Colombia or elsewhere?'

'We have not decided yet but it will be here or maybe in the States but not the UK'.

'Why not the UK?'

'There is still a lot of class snobbery in the UK and it's more difficult to start a business there than in the States. Look Mr Mendoza there is not much more I can say at this stage, as I will be leaving very early in the morning. But once this coming operation is over I'm going to see about getting out of the service. I'm not trying to avoid the issue but I have to get some sleep before tomorrow's operation after which I will give my complete and undivided attention. I can only repeat that I'm besotted with your daughter and will ensure that no harm ever comes to her. That's all I can predict at the moment'.

'I understand Eduardo, come – let's have drink and discuss what options we as a family can offer'. Alfred Mendoza had been pleased by the way the young man had conducted himself; there was more to this young man than just good looks.

Chapter 20

Rain forest

Once young Butch Hezeltine had taken the hit in his right calf Rusty Irons knew that there was no way they could get across the ravine ahead of the Cartel's men. Although Butch could hobble with a certain amount of pain it would only be a matter of time before they were completely outflanked and cut off from the bridge. The situation was now becoming critical – do they leave Butch to fend for himself until they could extract him later or, should he and Smudge remain with him. The latter option would leave Tony Bryant and the remainder of the team on the other side of the ravine short on manpower for getting the passengers out to safety. Rusty made up his mind.

'Smudge', ordered Rusty. 'Make a bolt for the bridge and let the boss know what's happened. I'll stay with Hezeltine and we'll find some where to lay low overnight and try and contact you tomorrow'.

'We would stand a better chance Rusty if I stayed with you,' countered Smudge.

'No way, Smudge I want you to be seen, or at least heard,

getting over the bridge and then blowing it. That way they may not be aware that Butch and I are still this side of the ravine. Further more if Sandy's plan to steal the chopper all turns to, "ratshit", he's going to need all the help he can get to extract the passengers - Now go man! Before it's too late. If I have to give you covering fire from this side of the bridge it will disclose our predicament'.

Grimes could see the logic of Rusty's reasoning and waited no longer. He took to his heels like a scalded cat making no effort to hide the noise of his progress. The commotion made by Grimes running through the undergrowth had the desired effect and dragged the Cartel's men further to the west of Hezeltine and Iron's location.

Grimes arrived panting at the bridge saw Lance, waved and made his way as rapidly as possible over the swaying bridge.

Butch Hezeltine was all of six feet and an extremely powerful man. He weighed at least fifteen stone and was not an easy man to assist in hobbling through the jungle. Their progress was slow but silent with just the occasional grunt of pain from Butch. However shortly after Grimes departure they heard a lot of firing and explosions from the direction of the bridge. They assumed that their colleagues were giving the gunmen a hard time. The noise also helped to disguise their progress away from the gunmen's presence.

Ten minutes after Smudge's departure they heard the powerful roar of the Claymore mine exploding when the bridge was blown and calculated that they must now be about four hundred metres north of its location.

They eventually found a suitable spot to camp for the night. There was plenty of ground cover and sufficient ferns to cut and lay for a bed foundation. The thick bamboo clumps made it almost impossible for anyone to approach their location without making a noise. Rusty decided to dig a small hole to light some solid fuel tablet for heating soup and making tea. Using the fuel tablet in a hole reduced the chances of anyone seeing the light and kept the smell of burning to a minimum. He carefully place the soil he'd removed into a heap which would be replaced when they had finished with the fire thus hopefully, disguising their presence. The weather was kind to them, the sky was clear of clouds and the gentle wind prior to night fall had decreased to an absolute calm. Apart from all the insect noise which always erupted in the rain forest at night they appeared to be completely on their own

'You'd better let me have another look at your leg Butch. We don't want the bloody thing getting septic'. Rusty gently unwound the shell dressing whilst Butch sucked in his breath trying to suppress the pain.

'I'm afraid I am a liability at the moment Rusty. If you leave the Sarbe with me you could leg it out and fetch help'.

'No way Butch, the boss and the others know where we are and I'll try and contact them on the radio after I have done a quick sweep around our immediate area to make sure no one is within earshot of us. Further more, in case you have forgotten the bridge is no more so there's no where to run to otherwise, you might well be talking to yourself by now', laughed Rusty; as he finished wrapping the clean shell dressing on and secured it.

Rusty ensured Butch was comfortable and he had his weapon to hand and whispered.

'When I return Butch I'll make the noise of a croaky frog just to confirm its me – Okay1'

Butch just grunted to confirm he understood and Rusty gave him the thumbs up sign and departed to circle their location making sure they had no immediate neighbours close to their location. He dare not go more than twenty or so yards from Butch's position for fear of losing it in the dark. They'd chosen their lay up location because it was hard to spot. The last thing he needed was to end up losing their location at night. During his sweep Rusty noted two game trails leading off in the direction that Butch and he hoped to trek the next morning He made a note of them.

When he was approximately due south of their location Rusty detected the smell of wood fire. As there was no wind he realised that the source of it must be fairly close. There could only be one reason for the smell of fire way out here in the jungle. It had to be some of the Cartel's gunmen. This part of Colombia was virtually uninhabited. He decided not to investigate otherwise he might have difficulty in relocating Butch's location. Further more if he stumbled onto their camp in the dark there was a chance of stirring up a Hornets nest. Rusty was a great believer in the old saying, "Never trouble trouble until trouble toubles you". He continued his sweep, avoiding the area that the smell of fire was coming from. There were no other problems.

On his return Rusty broke the disturbing news. 'It looks as though we have company tonight Butch. I caught the smell of wood fire to the south. I figure some of our, 'friends' have left it too late to get back to their camp site and have decided to sleep out rather than try to get back'.

'Either that or they suspect that not all of us got across the bridge', sighed Butch.

'Whatever the reasons we're going to have to get some rest, then try and put some distance between them and us, that's for sure. I can't operate the radio so close to them in case they hear the transmissions '.

'Give me a couple of hours rest just to make sure the bleeding has stop', said Butch. 'And then we can move off towards the ravine. At the moment my leg is still bleeding and there is a danger of me leaving a trail. Before we move off I'll stuff all the bloody foliage down the cook hole and bury it before we leave. Hopefully it will hide all our evidence that's unless of course, the bastards have brought some dogs out with them. They'll soon ferret the debris out'.

Rusty nodded his head in agreement and opened his map, made a note of a grid reference about two miles north of the blown bridge. He then entered its co-ordinates into the GPS it showed that they had about one and a half miles to trek along one of the game trails to get to the ravine.

'I figure that if we set off at midnight along this game trail', indicated Rusty on the map. I figure we should be able to average about four hundred metres an hour. With your gammy leg we can't bank on travelling any quicker even along the game trail.'

'I agree but with a couple of hours rest I will be much stronger. When do you figure on giving the Boss a call?'

'I'd like to put at least four hundred metres between us before risking a call, you know how sound carries at night. At the moment, the Cartel's men can't be sure that any of us are still this side of the ravine and I would like to keep it that way. I'll give you another small shot of morphine to help you sleep and keep the pain level down'.

They both lay down on the bed of cut ferns to rest and Butch dropped off into an uneasy sleep. There was no way Rusty was going to remain awake for five hours so he decided to grab some sleep as well. Their location was so well hidden in the centre of a Bamboo clump that someone would have to literally stumble on them to discover it. Further more, anyone approaching their location in the dark was bound to tread on some of the dead Bamboo fronds which littered the jungle floor. These would go off as loud as fire crackers; the noise would be enough to wake the dead. He knew from previous experience that in such uncomfortable conditions that four or five hours sleep was all he could manage before he woke up. He often used to envy some of his colleagues who could sleep all night in the most outlandish and uncomfortable conditions. Rusty on the other hand, could only sleep for a couple of hours at the most, to slake his deep tiredness and once that was sated he'd wake up. He would then just lie there desperately trying to get back to sleep. He could never make it.

And so it proved, at one o'clock in the morning, Rusty woke up and carefully stretched himself. Pulled his face veil away from his face, (Used to keep the mosquitoes and other insects from biting his face). He checked his watch, Time to move. He then rolled over, stretched again and gently shook Butch until he awoke. Whilst Butch was gathering his senses Rusty searched for the game trail he had noted earlier that evening. Having orientated himself he then returned to Butch

'How do you feel Butch?'

'Much as I expected', groaned Butch. 'The pain level is down and the bleeding has definitely stopped but I fancy I am going to find it bloody stiff to try and move'.

'That's for sure. Once we get moving and the blood starts to circulate it should get easier. Keep your eyes peeled for a stick that we can use as a crutch. If I cut one and the Cartel's men see the evidence it will confirm our presence this side of the ravine, so we are going to have to find an old piece of wood to use'.

'We'll manage - just give me a shoulder to cry on', Butch smiled grimly.

Rusty lined up the compass until he got the bearing that he had read off the GPS and with that, Butch using his shoulder for support, they set off hobbling down the game trail towards the ravine.

It was slow and painful initially but as Butch's stiffness wore off they made better progress. Rusty stopped every hundred metres or so and checked to ensure that Butch's wound was not bleeding and leaving a trail. Occasionally the trail was overgrown which slowed their progress. Rusty was reluctant to use the machete for fear of leaving evidence of their presence so they push their way through as gently as possible without leaving any broken foliage giving evidence of their presence. This was not easier. After they'd trekked for about a half mile Rusty considered it was safe to use the radio and called the base on the agreed frequency. His call was initially answered by an American voice but it was quickly replaced with Bryant's.

'How are you and your passenger making out? We all arrived at our destination tired but safe, over', said Bryant using veiled speech just in case any one was listening out on the same frequency.

'Okay at the moment but we need to get her to hospital fairly soon the baby is due in the next two days or so. Can you tell us when an Ambulance will be available over?'

'Yes we have one leaving with your favourite chauffeur driving first thing tomorrow morning. He will give you a call ten minutes prior to picking you up and then you can give him all your personal details. Have you anything else for me over'.

'Not for the moment - things here are as well as can be expected but we are looking forward to the arrival of the ambulance, out'.

'It sounds as though that crazy bastard Sandy is flying the stolen Puma out to pick us up', grinned Butch.

'It certainly sounds that way. I would sure like to know what he's been up to over the past four years or so and how in Gods name he ended up in a dump like this'.

'Just as well for us he did', said Butch. 'Without his help this operation would have turned pear shaped long ago'.

'True, that's true but in the meantime I think we had better get moving again. I would like to be at the intended pick up point before first light and we've another mile to trek yet – how do you feel Butch?'

'Fine - just lend me your shoulder to lean on – oops! Butch stumbled, looked down and could just make out the outline of a stout branch that he had just tripped over. 'I do believe we have a stick here that could be used as a crutch'.

Butch bent down and picked up a sturdy stick with a "Y" yoke that fitted neatly under his arm. This increased their mobility considerably.

Chapter 21

Embassy Bogotá

There was great excitement in the American Embassy. Captain Bryant had just informed every one that Rusty and Butch were both alive and free.

Bryant kept all the details of the impending rescue for the following day to those who were actually involved one way or another. Most of the passengers were too excited about their return to the States to worry about the fate of the two SAS men. However Niles noted that his old boss Chase was trying to pump members of the team on what they intended to do about extracting the two left behind.

Niles approached Bryant and whispered in his ear. 'I should be very careful what we tell Chase. I drove him around this neck of the woods for about three weeks prior to the hurricane and I'm telling you, he met up with some very dodgy characters. I'm not sure, but I think he was involved in gun running. If he is, then there's a strong chance he may know the Cartel characters that we have been having a running battle with. Rusty and I noted that a lot of the weapons at their camp site were of American military origin.

The chances are that they were channelled from the States through Chase to the Cartel. In any event, I wouldn't trust that bastard further than I could throw him'.

'Thanks for the warning Sandy but he will get nothing out of the lads but I had better brief the Mendoza's to keep well clear of him for the moment, we don't want them being compromised at this late stage. At the moment he thinks their association with the team is purely due to Maria's involvement with Lance, we had better keep it that way. I'd be grateful if you could do the same to the Fields'.

Niles warned The Defence Secretary and his wife about nefarious dealings of Chase. And in particular not to mention to Chase the fact that the Mendoza's had been of assistance in the extraction of the passengers. However; although Niles comments were noted George Fields seemed more anxious to try and find out more about the enigmatic Niles.

'Sandy, how on earth did an obviously well educated and resourceful man like you end up in South American bumming around as a hired chauffeur? Jackie has been telling me of your exploits and it seems to me that without your help the SAS team would have been too late to save the survivors and even then, it was your plan to hijack the helicopter and fly the passengers back here'.

'It's a long story Mr Fields, too long to start now. I really must get some sleep, as I have to be up at four o'clock to get airborne by five. If you like we can discuss when I get back tomorrow evening'.

'But surely it's not your problem. The SAS could well get a Huey from the Defence Force later on tomorrow. Let's face it Sandy you could easily get killed and or not get back'.

'Actually Mr Fields it's not really necessary that I get back; but to wait for the Defence Forces to find a helicopter would take too long. We suspect that the local Helicopter Companies have already been intimidated. Further more, if we tried to get a helicopter from local sources the news would quickly be relayed to the Cartel confirming that we still had two of our team out there in the jungle. They would almost certainly find a way of delaying our departure. With Butch Hezeltine wounded he and Rusty are going to be hard put to stay ahead of the Cartel's gunmen. If their extraction is to be successful, we have to get out there at first light or it will be too late. Would you please excuse me sir - I think it is time I got my head down. Good night Jackie'.

With that, Niles made his way to the small room that had been set aside for the team members.

'Did you notice, the way he carefully avoided answering your questions about his former life. He has this characteristic of erecting a mental wall as soon as you inquire about his past life', said Jackie Fields.

'Yes, I most certainly did. I've also observed that the more you see of him the more dangerous he seems. When you first meet him he projects this attitude of almost subservience in order to ovoid being noticed, a most enigmatic character. However as Tony Bryant has said to me on several occasions tonight, I'm glad he's on our side'.

'He seems very standoffish with the women George, I even wondered if he was gay. What do you think?'

'I don't think so, he gives me the impression of some one who is very leery and has some dark secrets to hide. Any way, that can wait for the moment, it's time we got you and Karen upstairs to a proper bed – Chris has arranged sleeping accommodation for us as we're staying overnight'.

Chase had tried on several occasions to find out what the SAS team had planned for the morning. He'd attempted to so without arousing suspicion but all he'd got was some stony looks plus a couple of, "Go forth and multiply', from the SAS members.

Niles assumption that Chase was acquainted with the Cartel was correct. Although he'd nothing to do with the drug trade Chase was responsible for most of the American arms sold to them. He knew that if he could contact them and pass on any intelligence he might be able to call the favour in at a later date.

The trouble was that all those that had attended the rescue briefing were not talking. However, Chase figured that if he could let the Cartel know of the impending rescue missions they might be able to fore stall it.

Chase opened his briefcase, (the only baggage that bastard Niles had let him take aboard the aircraft) and pulled out a small filofax. He thumbed through the telephone numbers until he came up with the number he wanted.

It was almost midnight before Chase felt it was safe enough to wander from the room where all the other passengers were gathered to look for an outside phone. The Embassy was very quiet. Chase eventually found a phone in the Embassy's main corridor and said to one of the US Marine guards patrolling the Embassy.

'Say buddy can I get an outside line on this phone to talk to my family?'

The Marine, who had not been privy to the briefings that had been going on, saw nothing untoward in one of the survivors phoning his family replied.

'No problems sir – just dial one nine followed by the number you want and that will put you straight through'.

'Many thanks', said Chase dialling the required number.

'Franco DeNero here', a voice said at the other end.

'Hi there, I'm a friend of Francesco Domingo and he asked me to ring this number whenever I was in Bogotá. I provided you guys with a big shipment of hard ware last April. You may recall it'.

'Yes if you are who I think you are, then I do, what can I do for you?'

'Actually it's more a case of what I can do for you. I

thought Francesco might like to know that there is a rescue mission planned for tomorrow to lift two SAS guys out of the jungle. These are members of the team that having been giving you and your colleagues a hard time. I can't get any further details other than to say it's planned for first light'.

'Thanks a lot; I'll pass that information onto Francesco straight away. Do you know where any of the other survivors are?'

Chase was prepared for that one. There was no way he was going to put his life on the line by having the aircraft that was due to take them home being shot or blown up at Bogotá Airport. 'I'm afraid not, I can't help you there. Please pass my regards onto Domingo'.

'No problem', and Franco rang off.

Chase made his way cautiously back to the large room hoping that no one had noticed his absence. The rest of the survivors were still asleep or dozing and Chase thought he had got away with it.

Unfortunately for Chase, the Marine sentry had reported the incident to the Gunny Sergeant who in turn reported it to Chris Brooker.

The ringing phone woke Brooker who was trying to get a bit of shuteye prior to the early morning sortie.

'Brooker here', he murmured.

The Gunny Sergeant then described what had happened and asked if any further action was required.

'First thing tomorrow get onto the exchange and try and find out where that call was routed to and let me know ASP'.

'You got it sir', replied the Sergeant.

'Shit', thought Brooker. From the description he had been given the caller had to be Chase. Sandy Niles had expressed misgivings about him and it looks as though he was right.

Brooker considered his options. Chase was an American

citizen who'd just been rescued from a hazardous situation. If they stopped him going home with the other survivors and his phone call was proved to be completely innocuous then Brooker was in deep shit. If they confronted him about the call he could tell them anything. They would not be able to confirm the destination of the call until tomorrow morning by which time, Chase would be long gone.

Bryant felt the gentle shake and came awake immediately to find Brooker standing over him looking slightly worried.

'Sorry to wake you at this time of the night Tony but I have just had some disturbing news that our friend Chase has been phoning some one on the outside. I'm afraid we won't know who he has been phoning until about nine o'clock in the morning by which time it might have compromised your sortie'.

It took Bryant a couple of seconds to get his thoughts together. He sat there for about thirty seconds rubbing his eyes and trying to hold his temper. He then said, 'so long as Chase doesn't know we're on to him we might be able to turn this to our advantage. But first, I think we had better speak to Sandy as he is going to have to fly us out there'.

Niles was asleep on the next bed. They gentle shook him awake and gave him the news. He just gave a wry grin. 'I just knew that bastard was up to no good from the first day I met him. The chances are that he's the bastard who has been selling the American guns to the Cartel. I agree with Tony, lets use him to spread false information rather than confront him with our suspicions. Have you got any suggestions Tony?'

Bryant thought for a while and then said thoughtfully. 'Let's pretend that we have liased with Rusty and agreed to extract them along side the crashed Dakota. That's at least an hour's march from the real extraction point. It also means that we must take out their other helicopters on our way out in the morning. We have got to reduce their mobility'.

'I agree with Tony' said Niles. 'We have definitely got to clobber their choppers to give us time to get Irons and Hezeltine out'.

'I must say it's a pleasure to work with you guys', laughed Brooker grimily. I'll make sure that Chase gets to hear of our deception in the next ten minutes. Otherwise he is not going to have enough time to contact his friends. Further more, if we see him making another phone call we can be sure that he's up to no good. Mind you we still won't be able to prove anything until he has gone but I will advise the FBI in the States of our suspicions. I'll get onto that now'. Brooker strode off to inform the States of their suspicions

'Looks as though we are going to be up earlier than we originally thought', said Bryant to Niles.

'I reckon so; I wonder if our friend Chris can rustle up some PNG goggles. It would make life much easier trying to find that strip before it gets light',

'I'll check with him but in the mean time I think you should try and get some sleep Sandy. You're the one that's going to be working the hardest first thing in the morning. We'll give you a shake at about Four o'clock. Okay!'

'That's fine - look forward to seeing you in the morning Tony, once again goodnight'.

Franco DeNero lost no time in informing Francesco Domingo about the two phone calls that he had received.

Domingo sat at the table, contemplating their next move. Should he convene another meeting with his colleagues? Did he have time to arrange the meeting? No. He'd have to make his own decisions.

Five minutes thinking over what Franco had said was enough. Domingo went to the radio room and contacted the site boss at the new processing Laboratory location about the intended extraction that was to be attempted at the crashed Dakota site.

The camp boss, a new one who had replaced the previous

guy who had been sacked for incompetence, a thug named Mark said. 'We have six men camped near the Dakota overnight. It was too late for them to return to base last night. I will instruct them to foil the extraction'.

'You do that and make sure there are no fuck-ups this time. Further more try not to damage the helicopter too much. That fucking machine cost us a lot of money'.

'That's going to be difficult boss. If we fire on the chopper it is going to get damaged and if we kill the pilot and the chopper crashes it is going to be a 'right off''.

'Okay I see your point but try and shoot it up when it has landed. In fact I will motor to the Airstrip tonight and then be aboard the first chopper to arrive in the morning'.

'Roger that boss'.

Domingo put the phone down and re – dialled. 'Franco here', growled the voice at the other end of the line.

'Look Franco, I've decided to go out to the Airstrip tonight and catch the first chopper to the campsite in the morning and personally organised the attack on the SAS team when they try to lift out their guys'.

'Why for Christ sake! We pay these soldiers good money to do the shit work. Why risk your life in this manner'.

'That's true but they've fucked up ever thing we've given them in the past three days. You know the old saying – if you want something doing properly do it yourself'.

Without further ado Domingo ordered up a four- wheel drive Toyota Land Cruiser to pick him and Franco DeNero up with two of their bodyguards and drive them out to the forward landing strip

Niles was woken at three forty five in the morning. Initially he didn't know where the hell he was as he flounder between consciousness and sleep for all of thirty seconds. It took all of five minute before he became fully composed.

Tony Bryant who'd woken Niles said. 'You might be

interested to know Sandy that Brooker has played a blinder and come up with a pair of PNG NVG/PVS – 7 Night Vision Goggles'.

'That's bloody great, even with the GPS co-ordinates it would still be difficult to locate the forward strip at night without them if they're not displaying any lights'.

'Have you used them before Sandy?'

'Of course, and guess where?'

'Northern Ireland', grinned Tony.

'You got it in one as the Actress said to the Bishop. Give me five minutes to re- acquaint my brain with my body and we're ready to go'.

'You'll also be pleased to know that our friend Chase appeared to pass on the duff info' we fed him last night just before he and the other passengers departed for the airport. With luck our hostile friends could end up chasing their own shadows at the wrong location - cutting us a bit of slack to get Rusty and Butch out'.

'That's good news Tony – we need all the help we can get on this enterprise'.

Niles completed his ablutions gave Tony Bryant an engaging grin and said. 'Okay Tony we're hot to trot, let's go kick arse'.

Tony Bryant returned the grin at the cavalier nature of Niles about flying out to what was after all, potentially a very dangerous mission. He gave the impression that he had no worries about the success of the sortie. He wondered if Sandy suffered from a, "Death wish". He certainly gave the impression that he didn't give a toss whether he lived or died. Tony on the other hand, was acutely aware that he was responsible for the men under his command and if they suffered casualties he might be asked to qualify his actions by higher authority.

However, there was no doubt that their proposal to put the Cartel's other helicopters out of commission was the most sensible tactical move.

The more Alfred and Helen Mendoza saw of Edward Lance the more they were impressed with him. There could be no doubting the affection that he had for their daughter, which she clearly reciprocated. They had had a long talk with him discussing the various options open to him in Colombia before allowing him to sleep and rest prior to the early morning sortie.

Lance had another two years service before he was due for discharge but there were ways and means of buying yourself out that Lance was going to investigate on his return to the UK.

Earlier in the evening Tony Bryant had suggested that Lance apply to do an exchange tour for six months with the American Special Forces in the States. Although it was too early to be definite, the boss had promised to give him a strong recommendation for the exchange. If successful this would at least put him on the same side of the Atlantic Ocean as Maria.

The team boarded the laundry van that had transferred them from the warehouse the previous evening. As well as a full complement of arms and ammunition they had a tape recorder and a PRC –320 tactical radio for communications to Rusty and back to the American Embassy.

Lance, not unnaturally was the last to board. Maria wrapped her arms around him like, 'Cling Foil', and was reluctant to let him go. Lance didn't seem in any rush to disentangle her either. That's when Fingers Finnegan called for a crow bar to separate them. The Fields family were still in bed asleep, after Jackie and Karen's harrowing experience over the past three days it didn't seem fair to wake them just to did goodbye

The journey to the warehouse was straightforward but very cold. Bogotá was eight thousand feet above sea level and at that time in the morning the temperature was often below freezing. They arrived at the warehouse cold but spot on time.

On arrival Niles immediately set about giving the Puma a cursory pre –flight inspection whilst the SAS team got their weapons and equipment organised. Then Bryant called them all together for the final detailed briefing.

'Okay men listen in. Whilst we've been kipping, Brooker has been doing some investigation on our behalf concerning the two airstrips one of which, the Cartel have been using. Apparently, after some phoning around he managed to establish that Short Skyvans have been seen landing on this airstrip here'. Bryant pointed to the grid reference on the large scale map he had laid out on the top of a forty gallon fuel drum. 'He's also managed to establish that helicopters have also been seen landing and taking off from the same strip. This being the case I think we have located the Strip that the Cartel has been using. As mentioned earlier, to frustrate any attempt to hamper our rescue mission we've decided to fly past the Strip and fire M203 grenades at any helicopters we can see. Now Sandy and I have discussed this and we reckon that we can only do one fly past, otherwise there is a strong chance of us taking casualties. For the actual approach to the strip I'm going to hand over to our 'Outrider'.

Every one grinned at the Boss's last remark. Like it or lump it, as far as the SAS team was concerned Sandy would probably always be referred to as the 'outrider'. Once you had acquired a nickname in the British Forces you were stuck with it. Trying to get rid of it was like pissing into the wind – it always came back to you.

Niles just grinned having served in the Forces he knew he was stuck with the name.

'At this time in the morning there will be no wind so we will aim to approach from the west up this small re-entrant. I'll be wearing NVG Goggles and with the existing clear skies we have at the moment I will have plenty of ambient light so I'll have no trouble in seeing any obstacles. At this time in the morning the Cartel's men will be in bed - hopefully still sleeping. The guards will not be able to see us but they will probably be able to hear us. To neutralise them I want three of you to fire at any guards visible to neutralise them, the remaining three of you to fire your M203 grenades at any choppers on the ground. The initial approach will be at about a hundred and twenty knots but as I come adjacent the Strip I will flare to about thirty knots, this is when you guys fire your weapons, any problems so far?'

'How will we see the helicopters in the dark?' asked Grimes.

'I'm just coming to the execution now', he answered. 'The first thing we have to do is make sure you guys can open and close the sliding cabin door in flight. We can fly at 150kts with the door open but we must not exceed 70Kts when physically opening or closing it. Please note that all the windows are jettisonable, which we will do to the Port side ones prior to take off. That way you won't get in one another's way whilst shooting. Niles looked around the group to canvas any queries.

'Okay! During the initial run in, the Boss, who will be sat alongside me in the front of the aircraft; will fire a Very cartridge to illuminate the strip. As Tony does this I'll have to bank the aircraft to the right so the cartridge clears the rotor disc. On no account must you fire until the aircraft is straight and level or there's a danger of you shooting our rotor blades off! And be advised, we need all of them! We have three headsets, one each for me and the Boss and the third for you Fingers. You will be controlling the firing party at the back of the aircraft. Are we all clear so far?'

'My last point, without wishing to teach you guys on how to suck eggs is; that when firing laterally from a moving aircraft at a static target there is a factor called 'Velocity jump'. I'm not going into the physics of it now but when you shoot at the choppers on the ground make sure you aim towards the back end of the target. Hopefully we will be only flying at thirty knots so the velocity jump will be quite small. Are we all clear on this?'

'Could you just enlarge on that last point Sandy?' asked Pedro Gonzales

'Okay Pedro let me give you an example. Imagine the chopper is side onto you and pointed in the same direction as we are flying and you want to hit the cockpit. You aim just behind the cockpit and the forward momentum imparted to the round by the helicopter's forward speed as it leaves the rifle will carry it into the cockpit. So what I want you guys to do is aim at the aft end of the fuselage. The "velocity Jump" will walk the rounds into the vulnerable part of the chopper. A helicopter is a pretty vulnerable piece of machinery and if your M203 grenades hit it you will almost certainly put it out of action for a long time. Okay are we all clear on the points just covered?'

'Now my last point is that your boss is the tactical commander whilst I command the aircraft. We've both agreed that the only, "aim" of this sortie is to extract Rusty and Butch out of the jungle. The only reason we are attacking this strip is to prevent the Cartel from using their choppers to frustrate our mission. However, if we get fired upon whilst trying to destroy their choppers we will abort straight away. So be advised that we are only going to take one bite at the cherry. Therefore, it will be straight in; bank, fire Very cartridge, straighten wings, fire weapons and then straight out, Hopefully, the bastards will still be in bed playing with themselves after we've been and gone'.

'Do you think they will hear us approaching Sandy?' This time it was Lance who queried.

'Yes - I think their piquet will probably hear us as we get close but I'm hoping the noise of the generator there're using for their electrical supply will drown the noise of our approach until the last moment. This is why we must get in fast and get out even faster'.

'If you have no further questions lets get aboard and get these windows taken in and let's make sure you know how to open and close the main door in flight.

The whole team set to preparing the Puma for its forthcoming sortie. The aircraft had already been refuelled so all that remained to be done was to jettison the windows on the port side and prepare the safety harnesses.

After they had pushed the chopper outside Bryant suggested that they stay out in the dark to build up their night vision, ("Visual Purple", is produced within the eyes which aides night vision, it takes about twenty minutes to build up to full effectiveness. Unfortunately, this effectiveness can be destroyed within seconds when exposed to bright white light).

At a quarter past five local time, the warehouse lights were extinguished and the doors were opened. Niles cranked up the Puma's engines and in no time the turbines were running nice and smoothly and all the instruments and systems came on line.

Niles gave the thumbs up sign to Tony Bryant and the remainder of the team to board. Tony Bryant climbed into the port pilot's seat and plugged in his headset. The remainder of the team boarded through the main cabin door and took up their firing positions. Cpl Finnegan plugged in his headset and acknowledged the intercom check call from Sandy. Niles opened the throttles to Flight Idle, He gently increased the power eased the cyclic stick slightly forward to get the aircraft moving and taxied clear of the warehouse. Once clear of the buildings he and took off in an easterly direction - there was no wind worth considering.

It had taken Domingo and Frank DeNero two hours of hard driving over a pot holed track to reach their Forward Airstrip. The weather was good and the track was reasonable dry so despite the poor surface of the track they made fairly good time. It had been decided that if both of them went to the Airstrip, Domingo could then be choppered to the Camp site at first light, while Frank DeNero remained at the Airstrip to ensure that the transfer of men from Cali continued smoothly.

On arrival Domingo immediately set about making the camp more secure. The bloody place looked like a refugee camp; there was equipment and stores lying around all over the place, all of it awaiting transit to the camp site. Because it was all in transit no one had taken the trouble to stack it tidily and securely. The main security problem at the Strip in such a rural area was petty thieving by the locals. Even such mundane articles as tentage and corrugated galvanised tin sheets were attractive items to the poor peons of the area.

To negate this petty purloining Domingo ordered more arc lights to be erected and switched on, illuminating all the accommodation, Trucks, Helicopters and the refuelling point. There was going to be no petty thieving whilst Domingo was on site. After the extra lighting was erected the chances of some urban scrounger stealing stores was reduced to zero.

Domingo called the American mercenary pilot over and said, 'look here Chester, what time can we get airborne tomorrow? I have information that requires me to be north of the Camp site first thing.

'Well let's see', murmured Chester. 'It gets light by about six o'clock so we can get airborne smack on six and we should be in the Camp site area by six forty five – how does that grab you?'

'Cant we get there earlier?'

'No way - I'm not flying over this country without being able to see the horizon. There's no habitation to speak of once we get east of here. That means there will be no artificial lighting to give us a visible horizon, so there's no way you can discern when you are flying straight and level'.

'How come I pay you guys so much money and you say you can't fly in the dark', snarled Domingo in exasperation.

'We've had this argument before Francesco and I explained it to you then, if there's a town or village lighting or there is a moon we can - if there isn't, then we can't. You need to be instrument trained to be able to fly with no visible horizon'.

'How long would it take you guys to become instrument rated – the cost is no problem'.

'I'm not sure but I guess about three weeks or so should be sufficient. They run courses in the States which are mostly for Off Shore pilots who are required to fly at night or in Instrument Met' Conditions; usually for casualty or medical evacuation. But it's pretty costly'.

'Right, next week book a course for you and Max and we will cover the costs'.

'That's fine by me boss but you have also got to appreciate that once qualified we have to maintain practice in order to retain the skill'.

'Okay Chester you get yourself and Max booked up and I'll see you first thing in the morning'.

Chester gave a wave of his hand and disappeared for his nights sleep. Domingo and the other bosses of the Cartel had never had the need to fly Choppers at night over the hinterland so they'd never bothered to insist that their pilots were instrument rated. This was something they'd have to consider more carefully in the near future.

Frank DeNero approached Francesco after the departure of Chester and said, 'Francesco we have fourteen men here tonight waiting to be transferred to the Camp site and as usual, they have been drinking themselves bloody stupid prior to us arriving. Do you think they should keep their guns with them or do we stack them as we have been doing for the past two years?'

'We're more likely to get shot by those drunken bastards than any hostiles if we allow them keep their guns tonight. I think we should have two armed roving piquet's and we'll get the remainder of those piss heads to stack their weapons before we have another episode of the, 'OKAY CORRAL' similar to the one we had several years ago.

Domingo was referring to an episode that had happened several years previously when their soldiers had kept their guns throughout the night. They'd all got drunk one night and quarrelled and it finished up with a gun fight in which many of their men killed one another.

Franco nodded in agreement and said. 'Right! I'll get the piquet organised and get the Strip boss to have all the other weapons handed in before they shoot us full of holes. After that, I suggest we both try and get some sleep and I'll see you first thing in the morning'.

Domingo grunted goodnight and made his way to his own camp bed.

Niles was flying at two thousand feet above the ground. At this stage he was still flying by reference to his instruments and maintaining the heading that they'd got from the GPS. It now showed only fifteen miles to run to the Strip. Although he had not flown on instruments for three years he had accumulated over a thousand hour's instrument flying. Therefore, although his flying had been rough initially he'd soon settled down and was now flying smoothly and confidently. Rather like having learnt to ride a bike and not ridden for some years. The skill never disappears but your initial efforts are not very smooth until you have been back in the saddle for a while.

Tony Bryant sat up front with Niles in the co-pilots seat began to see what Sandy meant about the ability to fly by reference to instruments. Looking out the front of the helicopter was akin to looking into a black velvet curtain; he good see nothing and there were times when he couldn't make out whether the chopper was climbing, descending or even banking.

'I think I can see what you have been banging on about being instrument qualified Sandy. This is the first time I have sat up the front in an aircraft at night and at times I don't know whether I'm on my arse or my elbow.

'Actually it's not bad tonight because we have starlight which helps with orientation but when you have cloud cover it can be very dangerous if you don't fly by reference to the aircraft's instruments – how much further Tony?'

'Not long', said Tony Bryant sat next to Niles in the left-hand seat. 'I figure we'll be at the strip in seven minutes'.

'I agree', said Niles and started to descend. He checked to make sure his NGV were switch ON. He would need them once they got below two or three hundred feet AGL (Above Ground Level).

'I tell you what' said Tony, 'There's a bloody great illumination just where I figure the Strip ought to be Sandy'.

Sandy looked up from the aircraft's instruments. 'Jesus', he said. 'It's like fucking Blackpool illuminations – I don't think you're going to need the Very pistol Tony. A pair of sunglasses might be more appropriate'.

Tony laughed. 'I suppose from their point of view it would seem sensible to have their strip fully illuminated. I doubt an over flying aircraft has ever attacked them before. Out here their only problem would be from people pilfering. I suppose it makes sense to have the Strip brightly illuminated'.

Niles nodded in agreement and was now descending through five hundred feet and pulled the NVG Goggles down. He was now looking at a pale green landscape with a port- hole effect. There was plenty of ambient star light to be amplified so he was able to see all obstacles straight ahead quite clearly. However with the goggles on there was no peripheral vision.

Tony called to Finnegan in the back. 'Standby Fingers we have three minutes to run and the target is well illuminated so there will be no Very cartridge fired or banking of the aircraft'.

'Okay boss!'

Niles slowed down to below seventy knots and called, 'open main passengers door and secure. Tony will you call when abeam I'm going to have to concentrate on taking my Goggles up as the bright light will cause then to 'white out". (Looking at any bright source of light saturates the sensitive optics of the goggles and renders them useless)

The team in the back of the aircraft were now getting keyed up and apprehensive. They say that the grass is always greener on the other side of the fence except in the armed services. This is quite simply due to training to work in a certain environment. Submariners didn't like to fly and flyers don't like going down in submarines. The SAS team had never been involved with firing and fighting from a helicopter and felt extremely exposed – however their basic training still enable them to put that to the back of their minds and concentrate on their task.

As they got closer Tony could clearly make out two Hue's and one Puma helicopters tethered down for the night. They were lined up adjacent to the Strip making them easy targets.

Tony called out. 'Standby to fire and remember it's the helicopters we are after. We're slowing down to thirty knots so don't forget what Sandy said about aiming towards the rear of the cabins'.

Niles had reduces their height down to one hundred feet AGL. He whipped the NGV Goggles up clear of his eyes. There was so much illumination in the target area that no artificial sight aides were necessary.

He had positioned the aircraft about fifty metres to the right of the Strip and was now flying at only thirty knots and feeling very exposed.

Lance and Miles both sang out at the same time. 'I have armed men visual and am engaging'.

Both of them then poured short bursts of accurate fire down on the two armed piquet's who still had their rifles slung over their shoulders. At that close range they couldn't miss. The noise of the diesel generator for the camp lighting had masked the noise of the approaching helicopter right up to the last minute. It wasn't until the Guards had sustained several hits that they realised that anything untoward was taking place. By then it was too late - from there-on they were non-players.

At the same time, Finnegan Grimes and Gonzales managed to get three grenades off at each of the helicopters. Gonzales, who fired on the Super Puma, managed to score two hits out of three, the last one exploding in the cockpit of the Puma. The amount of the damage was impossible to see but it must have been extensive.

Finnegan had hit one of the Huey helicopters with two but the damage was masked when, the third Huey blew up with a tremendous flash and roar, Miles had managed to hit it with all three of his grenades. Debris scattered all over the Strip starting many minor fires. Parts of the flaming Huey landed amongst the accommodation tents stating fires and creating panic amongst the rudely awakened occupants.

Tony Bryant Called. 'Guns tight'. And Niles applied full pitch and accelerated away as fast as possible. No one had managed to get a single shot off against them.

The Cartel's men had been caught completely by surprise. The noise of the approaching Puma had been masked right up to the last minute by the noise of the Diesel Generator, supplying their electricity. Domingo and DeNero, who had been sharing a tent, were not aware that anything was wrong until the actual shooting started. Domingo had just got to the door of his tent when the Huey exploded. Part of the debris hit Domingo in two places, a piece of the Huey's engine cowling gouged a lump out of his right calf and part of the pitch change mechanism glanced off his head knocking him unconscious.

Frank DeNero was unlucky. A sheared engine mounting bolt slammed into his throat and crushed his neck vertebra. He died choking in his own blood.

When Domingo returned to consciousness he discovered that a tourniquet had been applied to his right leg and his head was swathed in bandages.

'What the fuck happened', he murmured painfully to the camp boss who was bending anxiously over him.

'Some one in a helicopter has attacked us. They shot up the guards and bombed our three choppers. One was blown up and the other two are badly damaged. None are flyable'.

'Jesus fucking Christ get me the two men who were supposed to be on guard. I'm going to shoot their fucking balls off '.

'I'm afraid it's too late for that. Whoever attacked us has beaten you to it - they are both dead. We have also lost another two men killed by flying debris and worst of all Frank DeNero has been killed'.

At this last piece of news the camp boss thought that Domingo was going to have an epileptic fit. For a good five minutes he ranted and raved even to the extent of foaming at the mouth. The camp boss ended up having to physically restrain Domingo to prevent himself from opening his wounds. After another five minutes Domingo quietened down and became coherent.

'Did any one see who they were or what type of helicopter it was?'

'No boss – the only people awake when it arrived were

the two guards and they are both dead. Most of us were just getting out our tents when one of the choppers exploded and we all hit the dust. By the time we had got our feet the chopper had gone'.

'It must have been those fucking British SAS. No locals would dare to take us on up front like this. Our informants within the Armed Services would have got word of any such attempt long before the choppers could even have got airborne. No; it has to be that SAS team'.

'But where would they get a helicopter boss? Do you think the Americans have arrived with a Special Forces chopper?

'That is a thought', murmured Domingo. 'If the Americans have got a Carrier off shore they could have carried out the attack. But they are great believers in Diplomatic protocol and I can't see them operating clandestinely in another country's airspace. No - the more I think of it, the more I'm convinced it was those fucking SAS bastards using that chopper they hi-jacked yesterday evening.'

'What now boss?'

'Get onto our offices in Bogotá and tell them to arrange one of the Sky vans to get out here bloody pronto. There is nothing left here for me to do. Tell them we need some kind of body bags to evacuate the dead'.

'Aye, Aye boss' and the camp boss left for the radio shack or what was left of it!

Niles had climbed to and levelled off at two thousand feet and set course for the extraction point. Tony Bryant called on the intercom to Finnegan. 'What's the sitrep Fingers?'

'One Huey completely destroyed another badly damaged and we think the Puma is also badly damaged. We didn't see any incoming fire and there is no visible damage to our aircraft as far as we can see.'

Niles chimed in. 'How badly damaged was the Puma, that's the one I'm more worried about?'

'Gonzales claims that one of the two grenades that hit the Puma exploded in the cockpit so we think it's immobile,' replied Fingers.

'That's great,' Niles whooped. 'If the grenade exploded in the cockpit it's going to take a dockyard job to repair it. That bird won't be flying for at least six months or longer'

'Okay every one lets have a bit of hush for the moment whilst I try and contact Rusty and Co'. Tony Bryant switched headsets and transmitted on the PRC –320 tactical set to contact Rusty.

Rusty responded after Tony's second call.

'Hello Tony this is Rusty we are at the arranged pick up point and my patient is well but eager to get to hospital over'. They had decided to use veiled speech when on the radio rather than use correct military procedures.

'Hi Rusty with you in about fifteen minutes. As we get closer we will contact you on other means when we're five minutes out from your location over'.

'Rusty roger, out'.

Tony switched his headset on and updated everyone on Rusty's condition.

They continued flying with little or no conversation for the next ten minutes. At this time of the morning meteorology conditions were absolutely stable. It was completely dark with no horizon and just the occasional glimpse of the ground below. It was like flying in a smooth black void.

Bryant called Rusty on the tactical set and they both changed over to the UHF set. The aircraft carried a UHF set as part of its radio fit so Sandy could switch all three headsets into the radio net.

Rusty was now using the speech facility of the Sarbe beacon, which was good, for about a maximum of ten miles or so but it had to be use sparingly to conserve the life of the battery.

'Hi boss this is Rusty be aware that there are some unfriendlies two miles south of out present location'.

'Roger that Rusty we have a scam, which might give us enough time to get you and Butch on board. Sandy wants you to get as close to the edge of the ravine as you can. He claims he only needs enough space to get his main rotor in and put one set of wheels on the ground and we can get you both aboard'.

'That's no problem we are already at the ravine and the GPS co-ordinates are as follows 522631. Be advised we have heard our unfriendlies crashing about earlier on but at the moment we have no idea how near or far they are'.

'Sandy is going to make some dummy approaches further to the east of your location to try and draw them away from you – so don't get worried if you see us making what appears to be approaches to the wrong location okay?'

'Roger out'.

'Okay Sandy I guess it's up to you now', said Tony.

'Right I'm turning to the east of Rusty's location so we might attract some gunfire any moment now. Fingers warn the lads to expect shooting any second now. Return fire as you will but for Christ sake not while I'm banking the aircraft I don't want my rotor blades shot off'.

Fingers acknowledged. Just then Gonzales shouted. 'Bandits below and there're shooting at us. Sandy took the Puma down so that it was literally skimming through the tops of the jungle canopy. He carried on for another four hundred metres and then set the chopper up as though to make an approach to land.

Niles brought the puma to a high hover and said to Fingers in the back of the chopper. 'Switch the recorder 'ON' and lower it into the Canopy until it's on the ground and then dump the rope'.

After a couple of minutes Fingers called. 'Recorder is on the ground and running'.

Niles continued to hover taxi around the area as though looking for a clearing to land.

That previous evening the Cartel's men had discovered no evidence of Rusty and Butch's presence. But the patrol leader was pretty sure that all the SAS did not get across that ravine the previous evening. Now that the Puma had turned up he was even more certain of it. It had been light enough for the past fifteen minutes and they'd searched for all of that time but found nothing.

As the Puma flew overhead several of his men had managed to get off a quick burst of automatic fire but the pilot was flying very low over the tops of the trees so their arc of fire was very small. Never the less they could hear the chopper and occasionally see it making approaches to the hover, evidently looking for some where to land.

The leader of the patrol had two men with him. He shouted out to try and attract their attention but to no avail. The other three men were further to the west and out of ear shot. If he delayed until they joined him there was a chance that the chopper would complete the extraction before they could get there. He decided to go straight away. If they timed their actions correctly and caught the helicopter in the hover with their automatic weapons it would be a sitting duck.

Niles gently flew round the false location for another five minutes to try and consolidate the spoof. Although the gunfire was only four hundred metres away it would take at least fifteen minutes for the Cartel patrol to reach the false location.

As the patrol got nearer to the hovering helicopter they could hear a voice this voice calling out in agony.' For god sake don't leave me I'm wounded please don't leave me. There's a clearing here for Christ sake land and pick me up, for Gods sake don't leave me'.

One of the gunmen turned to the leader and said, 'It looks as thought we wounded one of them last night and they have sent the chopper to extract him'.

His leader nodded in agreement waved his hand forward and said. 'Quick we may catch the bastard in the hover. If we can they will make an easy target'.

They set off making rapid haste in the direction of the landing helicopter.

Niles continued flying around the location for another five minutes and then orbited well to the north so that there was no possible chance of the enemy patrol seeing where he went. He decided that the spoof had gone on long enough. Although the enemy had not reached the false location yet they were now so far away from the real extraction point that they could not interfere with its operation.

Tony Bryant called Rusty up and told him to prepare to be lifted out. Rusty confirmed that he and Butch were at the edge of the ravine and there was sufficient room for Sandy to touch down.

Niles circled round to the north and then flew up the ravine gradually reducing speed as they approached the intended pick up point.

'I have them', called Bryant pointing out to the ten o'clock position.

'Seen!' Niles said and quickly lowered the landing gear and began to flare off speed. 'Right Fingers, get the door open and standby to give Butch a hand getting on board. I'll put the nose wheel on the ground and hold my hover with the tail rotor out into the ravine. I want two guys to keep a good lookout for any enemy who might be in the area'.

'You've got it' called Fingers. 'Lance cover port, I'll cover starboard, Miles and Gonzales help with the enplaning'.

Niles gingerly placed his front wheels on the ground whilst the rear end of the helicopter stuck out into the ravine. Checking that his rotor disc was clear of any trees he gradually eased the Puma until the main cabin door was opposite Rusty and Butch. He was surprised to note that his main emotion was not of fear but mostly of excitement as the adrenaline coursed through his body. Everything seemed to be happening in slow time his whole body tingled with suppressed awareness.

Miles and Gonzales grabbed an arm each of Butch whilst Rusty heaved from below until they had him on the doorsill. There he was gently dragged into the cabin. Rusty threw all their personal equipment aboard and then leaped onto the doorsill and scrambled aboard.

At that same instant there was a cry from Fingers. 'Bandits at ten o'clock'. He immediately laid down rapid fire which was quickly reinforced by fire from Lance.

'Jesus' cried Lance. 'One of those guys has got a rocket launcher it looks like a RPG 7!'

Niles had also seen the problem at the same time and was reacting to it before Fingers called out on the intercom. It was the combined withering fire from Fingers and Lance that initially saved the day.

Niles quickly lifted the Puma clear of the ground and hovered backwards, at the same time yawing it until it was lined up parallel within the ravine. He then lowered the pitch and dived into the ravine and accelerated away using the ravine as a trench to shield them from the enemy's fire .All appreciated that if they were hit by a RPG projectile it would be the end of them.

It was the three members of the Cartel's patrol who had lost contact with their leader when he'd set off to attack the helicopter. They'd been much further to the west than the leader – only about a hundred metres from the ravine when the noise of the Puma flying up it and then coming to the hover had attracted their attention.

They had quickly homed in on the noise the Puma was

making and they had arrived at the location just it time to see Rusty climbing aboard. This was too good an opportunity to miss. The guy with the rocket launcher quickly loaded it and had raised it to his shoulder when the withering fire from Fingers and Lance forced them to duck for cover. The 5.26 rounds cut through the surrounding foliage, one guy had his Ak47 shot out of his hands. Suddenly the firing stopped and they heard the Puma accelerate away and looked up expecting to see it climbing in the distance. They could see nothing! But they could still distinctly hear it.

It took a good four seconds for the Cartel's men to appreciate what had happened. They rushed to the edge of the ravine to see the Puma all of two hundred feet below the lip of the ravine and now a hundred metres away.

The man with the launcher quickly raised it. Aimed and fired.

Niles was almost bending the collective lever and pulling seventeen degrees of pitch, way above the normal limit. Suddenly Fingers called. 'There're about to launch a fucking missile'.

Niles had two options. They were approaching a bend in the ravine that if he could negotiate it would screen them from the missile or he could zoom up and hope the missile would pass beneath them. A RPG7 missile is unguided so the aim was to turn as quickly as possible; Sandy chose the former - they were just around the corner when an enormous explosion blasted the Puma.

Initially they all thought that the Puma had been hit and this was the end of the line. As Lance was heard to say later, he was just bending over to kiss his arse goodbye when he realised they were still flying. But for the bend in the ravine the rocket would have completely destroyed them. The blast they felt was the concussion of the missile hitting the outside of the curve of the ravine.

Niles checked the aircraft instruments but could detect

nothing wrong, 'any damage back there?' He asked Fingers.

'We have a couple of nice size holes in the cabin but other than that nothing that we can see'.

'Every thing at this end looks Ok for the moment but I'll continue flying up the ravine for another mile or so just in case our friends down there have any more nasty surprises'.

'I'm not sure how we got out of that', breathed Tony Bryant.

'Neither am I', said Niles. 'Those bastards don't seem to lack for hardware do they? I think that was an Anti Tank missile. What do they need them for in this neck of the woods? Surely they weren't expecting to come up against tanks out here'.

'I'm just glad it was a RPG 7 and not some Light SAM missile. Let's face it Sandy they have enough money to purchase SA7 or Stingers'

'Why do you think I'm still flying down here along the ravine Tony? At the moment the bends in the ravine are sheltering us from any fire. Another mile and we will be well out of range of any thing that can be man packed. Then we will set heading for home'.

'Tony could you ask Fingers to have a good look to check for any damage we may have sustained', said Sandy.

'Roger, stand by Sandy. Fingers, have a good check back there and see if we have sustained any damage other than those air conditioning vents you mentioned earlier'.

'One moment boss and we'll have a good look round once Sandy gets us out of this fucking chicane. At the moment we're being thrown around in here like hamsters in a biscuit tin'!

Niles just laughed. 'Okay pulling up now but I will still be flying low level to disguise the direction we are going. Slowing up to sixty knots and you can now close the cabin door'.

'Door closed and locked', Fingers reply.

'Standby Sandy I'm going to call the Embassy and let them know that the extraction has been completed'. Tony swapped headsets and called the Embassy on the tactical FM set.

Chris Brooker turned to the small crowd who was anxiously waiting to hear how the team had made out.

'They have made it', he grinned giving them the thumbs up sign to confirm it. 'Apparently they had a close call when a rocket was fired at them but apart from aerating the chopper they are all fit and well, no injuries other than those of Butch which we know of'.

'Is Lance safe?' Asked Maria Mendoza clearly showing where her loyalties lay.

Alfred Mendoza gave his wife a nudge and a grin. He'd got the impression that as long as her lovely Eduardo was unhurt the rest could have gone to hell for all she was worried. That was probably a little unfair to think that of his daughter but her remark did emphasise just how besotted she was.

Chris was still listening on the tactical radio. 'Tony wants to know if we can pick them up in the daylight as they are keen to get Butch proper treatment. We can cope with that Alfred but is it likely to compromise your sister-in-law with the use of the farm?'

Alfred shook his head, 'the farm lies quite some way to the north of the metalled road and is completely screened by small hills. The other road is never used other than people going to the farm and that has been out of commission for a couple of years'.

'That's great', exclaimed Brooker, and then turning to one of his sidekicks he said. 'James, ask Paul our resident medic whether he would be prepared to ride a motor bike out to the farm and render some medical aid to young Hezeltine as soon as they have landed'.

'On my way boss; Paul is always moaning about not

having enough to do – now's his chance'. James practically ran to inform Paul of his mercy mission.

'In the meantime I'll arrange for the van to get out there and transfer them back here. I'm afraid the chopper will arrive before the van but they will just have to wait'. This is the life thought Brooker getting things jacked up and feeling the surge of adrenaline in his veins. He was on the phone in a flash.

'Is that you toothpick? (Toothpick was the nickname for one of their local agents who was so thin if he swallowed an apple he'd have look pregnant) Get the Laundry van jacked up. And then get your arse up here for your instruction, and bring a large-scale map for the area to the east of Bogotá with you'.

Bryant was now back on the intercom and really enjoying life. 'It looks as though they have responded to our alteration in plan and Brooker is sending a medic out on a motor bike post haste to meet us. He should get there about the same time as us. The van will arrive later'.

Niles nodded his head and said. 'Good - Butch will need hospital care as soon as possible but I'm not sure that he should be interned in Colombia.'

'I agree' said Bryant. 'The Embassy will have access to the best hospital here in Bogotá but there is a danger of the Cartel men getting to him especially as they now know we've a wounded man. They'll have informants posted at every blasted hospital this side of the equator'.

'I agree', said Niles, 'By the way, we have only ten minutes to run. Fingers! Warn the rest of your guys we will be landing in about ten minutes. Keep your eyes peeled for any sign of people on the ground and I am now descending to very low level. Hang onto your goolies'.

He now descended to what used to be called tactical low flying. At times he was as low as ten feet above the ground and at a 130kts it was exhilarating.

The SAS lads in the back were lapping it up. They had now been acquainted with Niles for almost three days and had come to trust him as one of their own.

'If he gets any lower', crowed Gonzales, 'we'll be wiping our arses on the ground. Any one got any bog paper?'

'I tell you what Pedro, I'll pass you a broom', laughed Miles. 'You can shove it up your arse and sweep the road as we fly along it'.

'Fine just so long as you sit in front of me so we have the shit before the broom'.

Tony Bryant had a final word on the tactical net to Chris Brooker to inform him of their landing time. He replaced the aircraft headset and he turned round to look in the passenger's cabin.

'Hey! Sandy, get a load of those silly buggers back there'.

Niles eased the Puma up a shade and turned round to look at what was going on in the cabin. The SAS team were sat on the floor with their backs to the forward bulkhead pretending to row the aircraft along with Cpl Finnegan stood at the back shouting 'In' 'Out' 'In' Out', and 'layback' like some demented coxswain.

'It's nice to see that humour is still abounds in the British Army. I swear to Christ that without it we would never have been so effective', laughed Niles.

They had cleared the rain forest a good ten minutes ago and were now flying over the Llanos, the rolling grass plains with small bushy shrubs even so there was still no indication of habitation. The countryside seemed entirely deserted. Niles enjoyed the low flying which had always been exhilarating but in Northwest Europe the whole continent appeared to be held together with high-tension cables. Out here he'd been low flying now for ten minutes and not seen one high tension cable or a telephone wire – this was the life!

They both saw the farm complex at the same time and

Sandy immediately did his landing checks whilst Bryant warned the 'rowers' in the back to get strapped in.

The complex consisted of an 'L' shaped main building with two smaller building about thirty yards away from the maim building; Further south were some barns and stables with fenced paddocks adjoining. Although the area was completely deserted the whole complex appeared to be well maintained obviously to keep the market price as high as possible.

He landed between the farmhouse and the out buildings on scrubby grass which kept the dust down. The farmhouse shielded them from prying eyes although there appeared to be no body within miles of the place. Niles wound the Puma down to Ground Idle and used the rotor brake to bring the blades to a halt.

As soon as the blades came to a halt a man came from the out building and introduced himself as Paul the Resident Doctor at the American Embassy. They all helped to off load Hezeltine gently and took him into the farmhouse.

Paul undressed the wound and examined it carefully. 'With what you had out there in the field I couldn't have done a much better job myself', he said. 'I'll just clean it up and put on a fresh dressing and give you an antibiotic shot. How is the pain? Do you require a morphine shot?' He enquired of Butch who was lying there quite stoically.

'No thanks', murmured Butch. 'The pain has subsided now - it only hurts when I look at those arseholes over there'. He said indicating the other team members.

Tony Bryant realised that Sandy Niles was still sitting in the Puma with the engines running. He got the thumb up sign and wandered over to the cockpit and asked him why he'd not closed the aircraft down.

He shouted down to Tony. 'I'm worried about leaving the Puma here in case the Cartel links it to Alfred Mendoza's Sister-in-Law. If we could run that motor bike up into the cabin I could fly the Puma back to that small gully we saw about five miles further back. Land in the gully and ride the bike back here to disassociate the helicopter from the farm. What do think?'

'Its sounds a bloody good idea to me Sandy. Let me see if we can find some planks to use as a ramp. If you like I could send one of the lads with you to help to unload the bike at the other end', suggested Bryant.

'Sounds good to me Tony, whom do you have in mind?'

'I'll send Smudger Grimes; the bastard is as strong as an ox. He could probably lift the fucking bike off manually if needs be'.

It took another five minutes to find a suitable plank that was used as a ramp to run the bike up into the Puma. The bike was a Honda 500cc trial bike with plenty of ground clearance. Without further ado, Grimes started the bike, put in first gear, gave it plenty of throttle and rode it straight up into the cabin with all the panache and élan of a rodeo rider. In fact he came in so fast Niles half expected to see him come out the other side of the aircraft. Grimes closed the bike down and lashed it securely in the upright position. He then came forward and sat in the co-pilot's seat and gave Sandy a big grin.

Niles just laughed. Without saying a word Grimes had told Sandy that he was not the only one who could fly/drive with élan. He opened the engines to flight idle, completed his pre take off checks, applied pitch and set off for the gully. The trip there took only three minutes but it was remote to the farm and that was all that mattered.

The banks of the gully were a little too steep so he landed on the bank and Grimes rode the bike off and waited while Niles took off again and landed the Puma in the gully from where it was completely screened from prying eyes.

He scrambled up the bank and jumped on the pillion seat. Smudger then set off for the farmhouse at a speed which scared Sandy Niles shitless. He was still being paid back for his low flying stunt! Niles was sure that Smudger got them back to the farmhouse quicker that he had flown the outbound journey.

It took another ten minutes before the van arrived. It was a big Ford Transit without any seats but plenty of cushions available. They cleared a space for Butch to lie in and it was decided that the Doctor should accompany him. Sandy Niles was the only other person dressed in civilian clothes so it was considered prudent for Niles to ride the bike. The team's British disruptive pattern uniform was rather unique in this part of the world and likely to attract attention.

'I suppose it's a waste of time asking you if you can ride the fucking thing', said Tony nodding at the bike.

'I'll have you know', sniffed Niles with a pretentious air. 'That for three months in Caracas I was a motor cyclist delivery man'.

'Why in Gods name were you doing such a menial job as that', enquired Tony.

'Because it negated me doing what I am doing now'.

'And what's that?' Tony asked in a puzzled manner.

'Having to answer dam fool questions such as you are asking now', grinned Sandy.

'Okay so how do you want to play this? If you were one of my Troopers you would be detailed to ride ahead and scout for any likely trouble'.

'You took the words right out of my mouth, but before doing so I would like my Holland & Holland back please. And then I'm going to look for some canvas or sacking to wrap it in to disguise it. I still have the Beretta if I need anything rapidly'.

'Lance ', roared Bryant. 'Give this ornery bastard his rifle back; he's suffering from withdrawal symptoms.

Chapter 22

American Embassy

Chris Brooker took off the headset and turned. 'They've arrived at the farmhouse safely and have transferred Hezeltine to the van. They're just about to depart for here. It appears that the doctor will travel with the patient and Sandy, who is the only one in civilian clothes, will ride the bike back and act as an outrider'.

'What time do you reckon they'll get here Chris? George Fields asked.

'Well providing there's no hold ups they should be here within the hour. Mind you, once they get in the Bogotá's traffic that could cause a delay. Say an hour and a half at the outside.'

'What's the plan once they get here Chris?'

'I figure we'll play it similar to yesterday, we keep every one inside the Embassy building until we move out at one thirty in the morning. Aiming for the Diplomatic Aircraft to get airborne at its usually time at two o'clock in the morning, the nearer we stick to our normal schedule the less chance there is of tipping our hand'.

George Fields grunted, 'Hmm - there's not much chance of getting out and visiting the down town side of Bogotá city then. I hear there are parts that are quite beautiful'.

'That's true Mr Secretary but at the moment I would be much happier if you stayed within the Embassy. Further more Sir with a man of your political status we would normally have to clear your visit with the Colombian government. Not advisable at the moment. These Cartel people wield tremendous power within Colombia. At times it's difficult to know who runs the country – the Drug Barons or the Government. Oh! And another point that Tony Bryant mentioned on the radio. It appears that Sandy Niles has no passport and still refuses to render any information about his background. This could cause all sorts of problems trying to back load him to the States'.

Before George Fields could answer his wife interrupted him. 'Look George it's true that we know very little of his history but that man was instrumental in saving all our lives and it behoves us do try and do something in return. The Cartel would dearly love to get their hands on Sandy. If we leave him here in Colombia we are sentencing him to death'.

'True enough', added Brooker, 'after the way he has rubbed their faces in the dirt the Cartel would splash out big bucks to get their hands on Sandy. Could we not get him into the Witness Protection programme?'

George Fields thought for a bit before replying. 'Yes - we do it for plenty of criminals so I figure I could make a strong case for Sandy. The main problem is, he is not a US citizen and if he has committed a major crime in the UK and his true identity ever gets out at a later date, there'll be all hell to pay. In any event, when they get back, Sandy and I had better have a long discussion. We sure as hell have plenty of time to play with'.

'If you don't get him out I might be able to forgive

you but I'm not sure that your daughter would', said Jackie Fields.

'I think your probably right there Jackie – they seemed to have cemented quite a bond in the short time they've known one another'.

George Fields looked at Brooker and said. 'Chris, when they get back, have rested and cleaned up, is there an office that I could use to have a private chat with Sandy. If it's kept quiet and confidential there's more chance of him opening up?'

'No problem Sir there is plenty of offices that we could make available to you –I'll show you some and you can take your pick'.

Jackie Fields gave her husband an old fashion look and said, 'just what do you want to ask him?' She enquired.

'Well if I am going to sponsor him getting into the States I need to know rather more than just his name, which incidentally, I believe may not his real name anyway. My other thought is that Gary our Company S76 Pilot is I think, approaching retirement. If this is the case, then providing Sandy can get his licences we could offer him genuine employment. If he has flown in the North Sea as a commercial pilot then he has to be pretty good. Further more, Tony Bryant who has flown many times with different pilots was extremely impressed with him.'

Jackie Fields nodded her head in agreement. 'I must say I was very impressed with the way he conducted himself during the last three days, though obviously I am not in a position to comment on his technical ability as a pilot. But your idea sounds pretty good to me. He's far too clever to have just been a chauffeur'.

'Right that's settled it then. I'll have a chat with Sandy as soon as he gets back and has had a rest. Actually – you could also sit in providing Sandy has no objection. How does that grab you?'

'Yes that sounds great but we must check with Sandy that he has no objections', his wife replied.

Alfred Mendoza who had been sitting opposite George and Jackie Fields had heard much of the conversation made a polite cough to attract their attention.

'Excuse me Mr Fields, but I couldn't help but hear what you were discussing and I can think of another very good reason for you taking Sandy Niles back to the States with you'.

'I'd be interested to hear your reasons', said Fields with a warm smile put Alfred at his ease.

'The Drug Cartels that we have been involved with for the past three days involve some very vicious men. One in particular who has been heading the Cartel coalition is a man called Francesco Domingo. He is a particularly nasty and vindictive man. He is quite capable of carrying his vendetta against you all the way to the States. I don't know what safety arrangements you have at home but without wishing to alarm you or your wife I would certainly take precautions to have you and your family protected'.

'Do you really think they would pursue their revenge to the States? I have secret service men looking after me but I will probably have to make private arrangements for guarding my family'.

'Exactly! Mendoza said, 'and that's where it might be wise to have that man Niles around. We were speaking to Edward Lance; the Trooper our daughter hopes to marry. All the SAS team appear to be extremely impressed with this Niles chap. Lance said he was bloody glad Niles was on their side and not the Cartels'.

'I think you have a good point there Alfred. My wife and daughter are both very keen on the man so that should make the job that much easier to offer to him. But surely this man Domingo hasn't got the clout to attack us in the States?'

'How much to you know about the Colombian scene Mr Fields?'

'Not a lot Alfred and please, call me George'.

'Thank you George .Well it's a sad fact of life that Colombia is one of the most violent societies in the world today – in fact I believe that Nigeria is the only country that suffers more murders per head of population than us. And it is particularly bad in the urban areas of Medellin and Cali. We lost over 200,000.0people in the last civil war, which did not end until 1964. Even now there are close on 140 paramilitary groups operating in the country. Francesco' Domingo was hoping to blame the death of your wife and friends on one or other of these groups and had they succeeded, it would have been very difficult to prove otherwise'.

'But surely the Government can jail these thugs', growled George Fields.

'That's easier said than done', continued Mendoza. 'The Drug Barons have become major employers in this country and they often hire professional assassins to remove any one that hinders their operations. They've used their vast sums of money to buy politicians and prevent any extradition. They have already killed a Minister of justice, Rodrigo Lara Bonlli and an Attorney General plus over 200 Judges. One has to appreciate the vast sums of money that is being generated in the processing of cocaine. Although the best leaves are grown in Bolivia most of the processing is done here in Colombia. I believe the last figures I had, stated that Colombia earns roughly $5 billion a year from the sale of cocaine. Two Colombians; Pablo Escobar Gaviria and Forge Ochoa were amongst the 20 richest men in the world and as far as I know, Francesco' Domingo is not far behind them. So as you can see George, you have incurred the wrath of a very powerful enemy'.

'But do you really think that Domingo will continue

this vendetta all the way to the States', Fields reiterated.

'The trouble with men like Domingo', continued Mendoza. 'Is that they are extremely cunning but not well educated, unfortunately they wield massive amounts of power in this country and sometimes they can't separate their delusions of grandeur from reality. Remember that many of these Drug Barons have never left Colombia for fear of being extradited. All they can visualise is the power that they can wield here and see no reason why it can't be transferred to another country. And with the money they can throw at a problem there's much truth in that as well.'

'Why doesn't the government crack down on the growing of coca?'

'They have tried but coca plants are so easy to grow and offer such good financial return. For example, coca plants produce three to six crops per year for up to forty years. It will also grow in areas where the soil is too poor to support other crops. A peasant farmer can earn over US$500.0 per hectare. The return he'd get from other crops is less than one tenth of this. Plus which, the Cartel will give the farmers fertilisers and protection, which is something the Government, has failed to do so far'.

'I can see you have your problems down here', added Fields. 'It seems I'll have to make arrangements to have my family protected until this threat is resolved'.

Their conversation was interrupted as Chris Brooker came in from the control room.

'I've just had word from Bryant and his team and they are on their way back. Niles is riding ahead on the motor bike and has Maria's mobile to contact Bryant or us if he sees any problems'.

'Are they likely to encounter any?' asked Jackie Fields.

'The nearer they get to Bogotá the less chance there is of being ambushed. So if they keep clear of trouble for the next thirty minutes they should be home and dry', explained Brooker

Chapter 23

Road Block

Bryant gave the thumbs up to Niles who started the bike up and sped away. He'd figured to keep about one mile ahead of the van. This hopefully would give the van's occupant's time to react if things started to go wrong. The weather was beautiful, a balmy blue sky, unlimited visibility. The temperature was a nice twenty one degrees although the sun was already almost overhead. He'd noted on landing that the altitude was just over eight thousand feet which accounted for the relatively low temperature for these latitudes. The terrain was still mainly grassy scrub dotted with the occasional trees and bushes. Habitation was still pretty sparse apart from the odd farm complex they had passed, no villages so far. As they got closer to Bogotá the road started to get busier and so far every thing was proceeding peacefully.

As he came to the brow of a small hill about ten miles from Bogotá, the road curved gentle to the right, and climbed another small hill, he noticed in the distance that there was a queue of vehicles up ahead. But at this stage because of the crest of the smaller hill he couldn't see the reason for the hold up.

He decided to flag down one of the vehicles coming in the opposite direction and asked the driver in his improving Spanish what the hold up was.

'Se Senor there is a roadblock up the road, which is manned by Para' militaries. They seem to be looking for some one. They're only interested in vehicles going towards Bogotá'.

'Many thanks' said Niles and continued for another half mile until he came to the rise of the small hill. From here he could see the roadblock - it was about another half mile down the road. They'd placed some forty-gallon oil drums in the middle of the road to form a chicane. The road block was manned by six men, four were stopping and searching the vehicles and the other two were manning a machine gun sited on a small mound which gave a good field of fire in both directions.

He noticed that the men manning the roadblock had not bothered to conceal the machine gun so he assumed it was so positioned to intimidate all the drivers passing through. At this distance he couldn't make out what model the gun was, in any case it was a fairly academic point. From its present position the gun could completely destroy the transit van and its occupants.

It was time to warn the lads in the van. He dialled up the doctor with Bryant and got an answer straight away.

'Look Tony - you have a problem about a mile ahead. Some one has put up a roadblock and they are searching all vehicles. I'm about 800 metres away and I can smell the stench of fish from here. What I propose to do is leave the road and motor in dead ground until I get close enough to get a clear shot at a machine gun that is mounted on a small hillock. I aim to fire at the breech of the machine gun which will neutralise it and then pin the other guys down while you drive through the chicane as fast as possible. Do you foresee any problems with this?'

'How many are there?' Bryant asked.

'I've counted only six, two manning the machine gun and four others searching the vehicles, mind you there are all armed. But once I've sorted the machine gun out I reckon I can keep them pinned down. The problem is that if you guys start shooting you will have blown your cover and they might have a radio. In which case, the Cartel might well mount further road blocks nearer to Bogotá and be specifically looking for a white Ford Transit van'.

'Not so fast Sandy, you can't lay down sufficient fire power by your self to completely neutralise six armed men, hang on a minute while I discuss this with Rusty and Co'.

Twenty seconds later Tony was back on the phone. 'Sandy come and collect Rusty he can ride pillion. With his M16A2 you should have the necessary fire power to keep their heads down. Don't forget that we're all cooped up in this bloody transit van like fish in a barrel unable to return fire. If they get that machine gun firing at the van they'll massacre the lot of us'.

'Point taken Tony – I'm on my way'. Niles turned the bike round and roared back to the transit van and skidded to a halt alongside it. The back door of van flew open and Rusty was astride the pillion in a flash. And then they were away.

Tony was quickly on the mobile.

'Okay Sandy if you can keep them pinned down we will drive through with the normal haste of people caught in cross fire. I can't imagine the other vehicles hanging around once the firing starts. I reckon it will be a case of the devil takes the hindmost. Once we are clear of the road block we can meet up again further down the road and Rusty can re-embark'.

'That sounds fine to me Tony we should be in a position

to start brewing them up in five minutes. As far as I can see you will be number five in the queue by the time you get here'.

'Roger that'.

Niles turned off the road and ensured that they had high ground between them and the men manning the road block. When he was some four hundred metres south of the road he paralleled it and rode the bike as gently as possible to reduce the sound signature. As they got closer Rusty pointed to a small hill that was significantly higher that the mound on which the machine gun was located. It was only about fifty metres from the machine gun's position. They parked the bike at the bottom of the hill on its back stand with the engine still running. When they left it could be in a hurry and he didn't want to hang about trying to start it.

Rusty and Niles crept forward another thirty or so metres until he was just on the crest of a small hill overlooking the road block. Although the temperature was not too high Niles was sweating profusely by the time they reached the top, he noticed that the temperature failed to have any effect on Rusty. He seemed completely cool and unfazed. Niles unsheathed the Holland and Holland rifle checked the magazine had four shells loaded and placed another dozen on the canvas next to where he was going to be lying. They gently moved some small boulders to provide some screening and support for their weapons. At this close range and with the aid of the telescopic sight Niles anticipated he'd have no problems in wrecking the machine gun. It was decided that the Holland Rifle had the greatest hitting power and therefore Niles would wreck the machine gun. Rusty, meantime would take out those men manning the actual road block. Niles took a couple of deep breaths to steady himself. He was again surprised to note that he had no qualms about possible killing another couple of men. He looked across at Rusty who turned to him and gave a quiet confident grin to reassure him. With his long service with the SAS he'd been in many similar situations before and this was reflected in Rusty's cool attitude now. He was the ideal man to have as company in the present situation.

Niles knew he could get two shots off before the gunmen knew what had happened. After Rusty had also fired they wouldn't know what had hit them. Then it would depend on their reactions. Well trained soldiers would immediately hit the deck after the first shot and then all things being equal would start laying speculative fire onto the nearest highest ground – His and Rusty's position.

They were banking on the fact that these guys had probably never actually been under fire before. In which case, they reckoned to immobilise another two of them before they got their act together.

Rusty nudged Niles. 'They've made no effort to defend their position. This is going to be easy meat. Once the firing has started, other than the forty gallon drums, (and these looked empty), there's nowhere for them to hide'.

The gunmen had obviously picked this location because it gave them a good uninterrupted view of the road. However, if it came to a fire fight, they were going to stand out like the balls on a, "Bull Terrier". Rusty gave Bryant a call on the mobile.

'Boss we're in position and ready to start battle. Are you ready?'

'We have just reached the end of the queue, there're another three vehicles in front, after that we are ready to Rumba. You had better make this good Rusty because we are cooped up here like pigs in a slaughter pen'.

Niles took careful aim at the machine gun. Looking through his Zeiss Diatal- C 4 X 32 telescopic sight, he could now recognise the gun for what it was. A World War Two German MG 42 developed from an earlier version called the MG34. It was an extremely efficient gun with a cyclic rate of fires of 1200RPM and a muzzle velocity of 2480 ft/second. Many arm chair critics during World War 2 pontificated that the rate of fire was too high for good accuracy. However this was not the opinion shared by those soldiers who'd had to face it in battle – it was rightly feared and respected by all Allied troops who'd faced it in combat.

There were two men manning the gun and they'd toyed with the idea of taking them out first. However Niles changed his mind. If he fired at the breechblock he could render the gun unusable. The four men manning the road block were wheeling the drums back and forth as they let each vehicle through so the drums were definitely empty and if necessary Rusty could shoot straight through them at any gunman attempting to use them as cover

The Ford Transit van was the third vehicle waiting to be searched when Niles suddenly had a 'brain wave'. He quickly dialled the mobile. 'Tony - don't drive off until I give you the all clear I have an idea which might get you a safe passage to Bogotá'.

'It had better be a good one', said Bryant. 'Those guys are carrying some pretty impressive fire power and at the moment we are cooped up here like fish in a barrel – the lads and I are getting pretty edgy'.

'If we get this right those same guys are going to lead you back to Bogotá'. Niles was relying on the fact that the gunmen had been recruited from the Medellin or Cali district and therefore were unfamiliar with the immediate country side. He then gave Bryant a brief resume of what he intended.

'Okay Sandy but if it all turns to rat shit we will drive away and the rear doors of the van are going to open and the lads will be baling out at nifty intervals and coming to their feet shooting – so keep your fucking heads down'.

'Roger that Tony. We won't start firing until you are the vehicle about to be searched – okay'

'No problem Sandy'. Tony briefed his team on what was about to take place and they made themselves ready. They unlocked the rear door and lined up in the back van ready to execute a rapid exit should it be necessary. The team were getting psyched up; theirs was not a pleasant situation to be in. Just one burst of automatic fire into the van could be catastrophic. They were now ready to spring into action should Niles spoof fail.

Rusty hearing what had just transpired over the mobile gave a big grin and said.

'You know what Niles; you're a really cunning underhanded little bastard'.

As the vehicle in front of the Transit drove off Niles rested the barrel of the rifle against the edge of a boulder and took careful aim at the breechblock of the MG 42. (At this range he couldn't miss), he aim to hit the breechblock where the ammunition belt fed the rounds into the gun and squeezed off a shot. It hit the breech block exactly where the ammunition fed into the breech and the gun was rendered useless. The M42 was smashed sideways out of the arms of the dumb founded gunner

Rusty's two single shots fired in quick succession took out the knee caps of two of the men searching the vehicles who were desperately trying to find out where the shooting was coming from. He fired again hitting a third man in the foot before the vehicle searches knew what the hell had hit them.

'Drop your weapons', Niles shouted in his colloquial Spanish. 'You are completely surrounded. You have three seconds to comply or you'll all be shot dead'.

The three remaining unwounded men were still trying to ascertain exactly where the shots had come from. One of the men that had been manning the machine gun had guessed where the shots had come from and quickly raised his gun but before he could get it to his shoulder a Holland

and Holland 6.2mm round had crashed into his shoulder. He fell to the ground. His screams adding to those with the shatter knee cap and broken foot. This last shot took all the fight out of the Cartels gunmen. As suspected, they were not highly trained troops who would have hit the ground after the opening shots and returned fire to the highest ground.

'Throw your weapons away and lay face down with your hands behind your heads and I promise you there will be no further injury to you', shouted Niles.

The gunmen complied. Niles broke cover and ensured his rifle was loaded and with Rusty giving him cover, turned and shouted to imaginary accomplices, 'Keep me covered if any one makes a move shoot them dead'.

Rusty, just to emphasise the point, fired a short burst over the heads of the stunned gunmen whilst Niles approached the gunmen. 'Who's the boss man among you?' he asked.

They all pointed to the guy who had attempted to get a shot off at Niles.

'Okay Mr Boss man you have just fallen foul of the Colombian Liberation Army and you can go back to Bogotá and tell your Bosses that this area is now under the control of the CAL. No one operates in this area without our permission. You tell your bosses that. However, we are not vindictive men so we are going to let you go back to the hospital at Bogotá and get yourselves fixed up. Do you know where the hospital is?'

The boss man shook his head and said. 'No Senor - we are from Cali and we have only been in this area for the past two days'.

'Right – I'll see if the driver of this White Transit Van knows and if he does, he will show you where it is. Just in case your leaders have put any further roadblocks up ahead you will lead until you get to the outskirts of Bogotá and then the transit Van will take over the lead and show you the hospital. Are my instructions clear?'

'Se Senor, we understand'.

'Good - remain there and don't move whilst I check your Nissan Trooper for further weapons'. A quick check revealed no further weapons. Further more it gave Niles a chance for his nerves to settle – he couldn't believe their luck. Audacity appeared to be working; so far these guys really believed that there were further gunmen out there surrounding them ready to shoot if they made a wrong move. Having Rusty out there was worth three normal men giving him cover. He gave a sigh and kept a poker face and returned to the gunmen.

'Right', he called to them. 'Before you get aboard the Nissan throw your mobile phones on the ground. They only had two amongst them. But Niles insisted that they stayed face down whilst he checked for weapons and phones. They were clean.

'Right keep flat on your faces and I'll put temporary bandages your wounds. It will reduce the bleeding until you get to the hospital.

Once the gunmen were face down he gave a wave to Rusty who then high tailed it round the small hill and into the Transit van whilst Niles attended to their wounds.

'Get aboard your Nissan and I will instruct the van driver to lead you to the hospital'. Niles had relied on the fact that there were many guerrilla and political groups throughout Colombia who seemed to sprout like mushrooms, so much so that nobody seemed to be able to keep track of them.

Niles approached the Transit van and put his head in the window.

'Tony I think I've convinced these goons that I am a member of a dissident political party who have taken over this area. And to show good faith we're not going to kill them. But they're to keep their arses out of our territory. Further more, we're allowing them to take their wounded to the hospital. They will lead you into Bogotá just in case there are any further roadblocks – which I doubt. I've taken all their phones which appear to be their only means of communication. Once you get to Bogotá I presume that our driver knows where the hospital is?' The driver nodded in assent. 'If you show them the hospital there is no reason for them to suspect this vehicle or its occupants. How does that sound to you?'

The whole bloody van was shaking with the laughter of the occupants. 'Sandy', snorted Bryant. 'Where in the fuck do you dig up these schemes? Are you sure you couldn't arrange for the Cartels men to have a guard of honour to greet us in Bogotá'

'Sorry I charge extra for miracles', laughed Niles. 'In the meantime I'm going to try and stash these weapons just in case I ever need them again'.

'What the hell are you talking about'; said Tony Bryant'. By this time tomorrow you'll be in the States'.

'Maybe and maybe not, for one thing I don't have a passport and you know how prickly the Americans are about having no passport, especially as I'm trying to get out via the US Embassy. Imagine the shit hitting the fan if I got to the States and they found out I'd no passport. They'd go Ape shit'.

'Jesus – we can get that sorted out. Lets face it Sandy they owe you some big favours'.

'It was politicians and their favours that put me in this position in the first place so I don't place much faith in them. So in the meantime I'll just hide these weapons and catch up with you later'.

The big Nissan was already moving so Niles withdrew and waved farewell to Bryant and his team as they set off.

Niles examined the hard ware left by the departing gunmen. There were some pretty impressive looking weapons. They included three modern Heckler & Koch HK 33 Rifles and a Heckler & Koch PSG – 1 7.62 Sniper

Rifle and an AK-74-SU Assault rifle. Niles looked around to see where he could hide the weapons – there were far too many to carry on the bike. And even in Bogotá, riding a motor bike and carrying six automatic weapons was likely to attract attention.

He noticed a dilapidated shed which stood about 400 hundred metres off the highway. He gathered the weapons in the canvas wrapping that he had used to conceal the Holland & Holland rifle, placed them on the petrol tank of the bike and gentle rode over to the broken down hut.

The hut had not been used for years and the floorboards and roof were quite badly damaged. Niles used the barrel of the damaged MG 42 to lever up some of the floorboards and found a suitable place to hide the guns. However his next problem was how to stop the guns from going rusty and being rendered useless.

Niles decided that he could not possible preserve all the weapons. The MG 42 would require workshop repair to become functional so there was no point in trying to preserve it. He decided to use some oil from the motor bike's oil tank to preserve the Holland & Holland, the PSG Snipers rifle and one of the HK 33 rifles. It would not last as long as grease and would eventually evaporate but it would keep the guns in working order for at least two or three months. Before which time, he would have retrieved them or no longer have need of them.

He use his handkerchief and dipped it into the motor bike's oil tank and then smoother the working parts of the weapons with oil and then squeeze a liberal amount down each of the barrels. This left him with just his Beretta handgun for protection until he got to the American Embassy but he was not anticipating trouble from here on. At the first sign of trouble he could take to riding cross-country if necessary until he reached the city.

As the Nissan Trooper entered the outskirts of Bogotá it eased over and waved the Transit van to take the lead. It took a further ten minutes for the Van driver who knew the city intimately, to show the gunmen to the hospital and then it set off for the Embassy. Bryant had no idea how the gunmen were going to explain to the doctors how they received their bullet wounds but with the money the Cartel had sloshing about he had no doubts that they would end up getting the best of treatment. He just hoped that Butch Hezeltine was going to get likewise.

They arrived at the gate of the Embassy and were waved in once the US Marine sentry had established their identity. They had still not seen any sign of Sandy Niles since the roadblock. However, Tony Bryant was beginning to appreciate just how streetwise he was. He couldn't think of many people who could think so quickly on his feet as Niles.

As the transit drew up at the back of the Embassy there was a full medical crew complete with stretcher to hustle Butch into the building. Brooker had arranged for a further two Doctors to be in attendance to ensure that Butch got the very best of treatment. The rest of the team went to the same large reception room they had used the previous night.

Brooker came forward to greet the team but was almost knocked off his feet as Maria pushed him to one side and flew into the arms of Trooper Lance. She was almost hysterical with relief to see her lover back and unharmed. This immediately switched the rest of the SAS team into the piss taking mode.

'You wouldn't wrap your arms around him like that if you knew what he has been up to today', scoffed Smudger Grimes.

'There's no way you should contemplate breeding from that trooper', added Fingers Finnegan.

'I bet your wife would like to see what you are up to now Lance', shouted Pedro Gonzales.

This last remark struck home; and Maria stood back and looked at Lance with tears beginning to swell up in her eyes. 'You never said you were married Lance is this man speaking the truth?'

Gonzales realised that he had gone too far and apologised in rapid Spanish, too fast for most of the team to follow. However, Maria's reply was even faster and although they couldn't make out what she was saying the meaning was amply clear. 'Don't ever come between me and my Lance or I'll have your eyes out'.

Rusty claimed later than the tone of her scolding just about scorched the Middle Eastern tan off Gonzales's face!

Brooker was looking around and suddenly said, 'Tony, where's Sandy?'

'I'm not sure where he is at the moment we got held up at the road block as I explained over the radio and he stayed behind to hide the weapons he had taken of the Cartel's gunmen'.

'Why in God's name did he bother to do that, he'll be in the States by this time tomorrow'.

'Sandy said that is not a fore gone conclusion – apparently he has no passport and can't leave this country by normal legal means and seems prepared to live here by his wits if necessary'.

'He must be fucking crazy', said Brooker. 'The Cartel's men will most certainly be on the lookout for a Sandy Haired Gringo. Knowing Domingo, the bastard will have every Sandy Haired Gringo hauled in off the streets and put through the wringer until he gets the right one. I think Domingo considers the stealing of his Holland & Holland the most heinous crime that Sandy has committed'.

'I think you are right', said Bryant. 'Unfortunately the bastard has got so used to living by his wits I honestly think he doesn't give a dam one way or the other whether he goes or stays put'.

'Well the Defence Secretary has a proposition to put to Sandy which may help, provided he agrees. He certainly seems to have a talent for getting in and out of scrapes. I think George Fields would like to make use of Sandy's talents to forestall any revenge plans that Domingo might come up with'.

George Fields hearing his name mention came over. 'What's this you are saying about Sandy?'

'I spoke to Sandy earlier on about his lack of passport and he doesn't seem in the least perturbed that he may not be able to leave the country', answered Bryant.

'Have you any idea why he was in Venezuela in the first place?' said Fields.

Bryant looked thoughtful for a minute. He did not want to compromise Niles in any way so he considered what he had to say very carefully.

'We know he was the Flight Commander of the SAS Helicopter Squadron at Sterling lines about ten years ago. That's where he established quite a reputation as a red-hot shot. Rusty claims he was at the shooting range every chance he had. He then left the service and was flying in the North Sea for three years and then had to leave the country in a hurry for some reason or other. He wouldn't tell us when we queried why he was in this neck of the woods'.

'Well I'm going to have to establish why he left the UK before I can get him States side. Provided he is not wanted for murder or some serious crime I'm determined to get him into the States. And I might add this is not just in gratitude for what he did for my wife and daughter. If this Domingo problem follows us to the States I can't think of any one I would rather have to look after my wife and daughter'.

By now Jackie and Karen Fields had noticed the absence of Niles and came across to the three men.

'What's happened to Sandy', Jackie asked in an anxious manner.

Bryant repeated what he had just told Brooker and added. 'He should be here any minute now. He stayed behind to hide some weapons he hi-jacked from some of the Cartel's gunmen. However he was riding the motor bike that the doctor rode out to attend Butch so he should not be much longer'.

'Right in the meantime, I guess you guys would like to wash and tidy up and then have some well earned rest before flying out tonight', said Brooker waving the Team to follow him.

Another hour had past since the arrival of the Transit Van and people in the Embassy were beginning to get worried. Every ones thoughts were on the where about of Niles. Even allowing for half an hour to bury or hide the weapons he should have arrived by now.

Alfred Mendoza had given up trying to contact Niles on the mobile phone. He had either lost it or had it switched off. The batteries could have even been flat as they had not been charged for a couple of days. Maria was notorious for letting her Mobile get flat before remembering to get it charged.

Another hour had passed and still no news of Niles

Chapter 24

US Embassy

Niles had a problem. He'd found and entered Bogotá with ease but realised that he was now lost within the city. He wasn't sure what action to take. Normally getting lost was no big deal – one simply stopped and asked a local the way to the American Embassy. Although the streets were busy, with the motor bike he was able to negotiate the traffic with no difficulty. The trouble was that Niles didn't have a bloody clue where he was in relation to the American Embassy. And he was not sure whether the Cartel had got word out onto the street to be on the lookout for a 'Sandy Haired Gringo'. If he did stop and ask directions to the Embassy and was recognised he was up a well known creek without a paddle. Further more, he'd have undone all the good work in trying to keep the location of the SAS team secret.

He now realised that he should have quizzed the van driver for directions to the Embassy before allowing them to drive off whilst he hid the weapons. He was extremely angry with himself. He'd been so pleased with his scam at getting the gunmen to accompany the team back to Bogotá that finding the Embassy location had completely slipped his mind. To make matters worse, his sandy coloured hair was not even covered – whilst he was moving this would not prove to be too much of a problem. Once he stopped and asked directions he'd be bringing attention to himself, however, he decided that by using his 'Street wise nous' he'd developed over the past three years he could still turn this situation to his advantage.

As he could negotiate the traffic easily enough he decided to use the time looking for the Embassy as a means of reconnoitre for getting familiar with the city. If he couldn't get out of Colombia because he'd no passport he could end up isolated on the streets of Bogotá. It therefore followed that the more he knew of the locality the better his chances of survival. He realised that if he protracted his recce' for too long he'd be pushing his luck and there was always a chance of some one seeing and recognising him - then he was really in trouble.

After about an hour and a half of riding around the city Niles was beginning to get his bearing. He'd tried on several occasions to raise the Embassy with Maria's mobile phone to no avail. He was getting the audio warning telling him the batteries needed recharging so he gave up trying.

Eventually, he found the Embassy and rode past it several times to check whether or not it was under surveillance, could see no one following him so did a 'U' turn and rode up to the Guard at the Embassy gates.

Niles dismounted and walked up to the guard and said, 'Could you contact your head of security, Mr Chris Brooker and tell him that Sandy Niles is requesting admittance?'

'One moment sir' and the guard picked up the phone giving Niles unkempt look a suspicious once over, he spoke to some one inside the building for a while – obviously making sure that Niles was who he claimed to be.

'Yeh, Yeh, okay that seems to fit his description – I'll let him in'. The guard terminated the phone call and turned to Niles.

'Could you ride the bike round to the back of the Embassy and some one will escort you into the building via the back door sir', said the smart Marine.

'The bastards just arrived at the gate', yelled Brooker. 'I've a good mind to keep him waiting after the worry he's caused us'.

'Keep him waiting', yelled Grimes. 'I'm still cleaning my underpants after that low flying stint of his'.

Tony Bryant shook his head. 'No let's get him in here and find out what the delay was and why he never contacted us with the mobile. Besides which Mr Fields is anxious to talk with him and time is getting short'.

'Yes, It would help if I could have a talk with Niles as soon as possible', said George Fields. 'I may have to contact the States to get things in motion if we are to get Niles back with us. There maybe several State Departments I have to notify and it's already two in the afternoon'.

'That's Ok' sir, I've had the guard send him straight up – we will give him something to eat and then he's all yours Mr Secretary', said Brooker pointing to the spare room that had been set aside for them.

Just then Niles crept into the room almost un-noticed except for Lance and his new family to be. Who drew Tony Bryant's attention to his entrance.

'Hey boss! Look what's just crawled in'.

Bryant gave Sandy Niles a puzzled look. 'What happened Sandy? We were expecting you an hour and a half ago?'

'The local driver who was driving you guys obviously knew the way to the Embassy. Have you forgotten that this is the first time I have ever visited Bogotá? The situation wasn't helped by the fact that the mobile phone battery has gone kaput. It took me forty minutes to find the Embassy so I decided to use some time to familiarise my self with the street layout of Bagota. Just in case you have forgotten Tony I've no passport so there is no way I can legally leave this country. In fact I'm illegally in this country as well. When you guys jet out of Colombia I'm going to be slung out on my ear and have to fend for my self'.

'Actually Sandy I think the Defence Secretary is going to have something to say on that matter. And further more', continued Brooker. 'There is no way we're going to toss you to the dogs after what you have done for our guys. Christ! Sandy, I'd hire you as a local spook before I'd waste your talents'.

'Thanks Chris, it's nice to know you're appreciated. But you must be aware that I'm ostensibly a British subject and not an American'.

George Fields came over with his wife and Karen. Little Karen took a running leap straight into Niles arms and said, 'we thought something terrible had happened Sandy when you didn't turn up with the others'.

'You should know Sandy by now Karen he's not that easy to get rid of,' he replied and swept her up into his arms and gave her a hug before lowering her to her feet.

George Fields grinned at the show of affection displayed by his daughter. 'Look Sandy I have a proposition I'd like you to consider. Could we go to the room over there that Chris has set aside so we can talk in private?

Niles was now feeling a little apprehensive – he'd a pretty good idea that he was about to be quizzed about his background. Niles thought it over for a couple of seconds and decided that he could always listen to what Fields had to say and if he didn't like the way the conversation was going he could just back out and take his chances outside in the city. He'd lived that way for the past three years without anyones assistance. So he was not particularly worried about having to do so again. The beauty at being at the bottom of a social pyramid meant that there was not much anyone could do to him to make matters worse. At the moment he was completely on his own and self-sufficient and owed no one favours. He had no intentions of becoming obligated to anyone either.

They entered a small room and Sandy noticed that Chris Brooker and Tony Bryant were also present.

'Sandy', began George Fields. 'I'm led to believe that you've lost your passport, which makes life very difficult for you. I've a proposition I'd like to put to you and I've asked Chris and Tony to be present to bear witness to what's said. I hope you have no objections to their presence?'

Niles thought this over for a moment but for the life of him he couldn't think of any reason to object. What little he knew of them had impressed him so far and he knew he could count on their integrity. 'No that's fine by me'.

'We're considering getting you into the States on a Witness Protection Programme. From what Chris is saying you are just about, 'numero uno' on the Cartels hit list. Chris and Tony also estimate that so many of the Cartel's gunmen have now seen you, that if you remain here, it's only a matter of time before you get recognised and wasted'.

Niles looked at the other two and nodded his head. 'True enough, but I'm not easily wasted, I've survived for the past three years by my wits and I figure I could get out of this country one way or another without getting shot'.

'Maybe – but it's a big maybe', continued Fields. 'However, we now come to the sticky bit. We've all noticed – including my wife - that you are reluctant to talk of how you lost your passport and your nationality. Before I can arrange to get you State side I must have some idea of your history – for example, are you wanted in the UK for murder or some other serious offence? If you don't wish to answer the question I'll understand, in which case, there's no way I can help you get into the States'.

'It could take a long time to answer that question', said Niles.

'We have at least 12 hours to waste before we fly so shoot away'.

'Well, it all started about five years ago when I was a Squadron commander in the Army Air Corps serving in Northern Ireland. Every month there was a meeting for all Commanders at place called Lisburn to discuss tactics and Standard Operational Procedures etc. One of the problems the Royal Ulster Constabulary, the (RUC) had was getting convictions for known terrorists committing crimes because witnesses were terrified to testify due to threats made against their families. It was during one of these meetings at Lisburn that I suggested that we just make these terrorists disappear. Dump their bodies in the Rockall Trench, a very deep stretch of water to the west of Ireland. Nobody would know what had happened to them. I even suggested that the Government could start a rumour that the terrorist had absconded with some of the IRA's funds'.

'But surely the higher echelon of the IRA would know that the funds hadn't been touched', interrupted Fields.

'True, but the rank and file would not necessarily believe them. I also suggested that we work our way up the ranks of the IRA. Before wasting a terrorist we'd ensured that the next higher in the chain of command had been identified. Like a lot of terrorist organisations the IRA foot soldiers were trained on the," need to know basis". Normally, this meant they only knew their immediate superiors and juniors so it would be important to establish this link prior to killing anyone. After the body had been smuggled aboard a helicopter and dumped at sea we could start more rumours about IRA funds missing – this was bound to affect their morale.

'So what happened then?' queried Fields. 'Did they take up your idea?'

'Are you kidding? the top brass nearly shit themselves when they heard of it. "It wasn't cricket old man". We couldn't possible be involved in any thing like that. Like a lot of people in high office they were more worried about how history would perceive their actions than they were of getting the job completed. However, not all the seeds had fallen on stony ground as I'll mention in a minute', continued Niles. 'My Squadron and I were only there for a three month tour and then we returned to Germany. I subsequently, "Prematurely voluntary Retired" (PVR'd) my commission to fly as a civilian pilot in the North Sea. I'd been flying there for about eighteen months when I was approached whilst having a beer in a pub one evening. This quiet character approached me and asked me my name and said he had a proposition that I might be interested in. Well to cut a long story short he wanted to know if I was the guy who three years ago had broached the subject of making IRA terrorist disappear, if so, would I be prepared to fly out to the west of Ireland and offload some 'packages' into the sea. The flights were to be made in a helicopter clandestinely acquired by MI5 and were nothing to do with the firm I was employed with. To be quite frank, I was sick to the teeth of seeing these murdering bastards getting away with it because they couldn't be brought to account due to witness intimidation. Initially the Catholics had a genuine beef about being treated like second class citizens but since the early days of the trouble both the Loyalists and the Republicans had degenerated into gangsters running drugs and protection rackets for their own benefit and not that of the community So I agreed'.

'Jesus', said Brooker, 'I remember now there was an awful lot of speculation about members of the IRA disappearing and no one knew where they had gone'.

'That's right', continued Niles. My co-pilot, a chap called Harry and I, another ex-service pilot had made five runs to the Rockall Trench, (code named Autumn Leaves) and the scheme was really beginning to have an effect on IRA morale when a halt was called to it. We found out later that the instigator of the scheme was a certain lady who was running MI5 at that time. Apparently the lady responsible was beginning to get cold feet as she developed political aspirations – I think she visualised herself as a second Maggie Thatcher'.

'But how come you lost your passport Sandy?' Fields asked. 'You were doing a job – not a very nice one I might add – which was sponsored by the Government'.

'Ah! Now we come to the tricky bit', smiled Niles. 'After a halt to 'Autumn Leaves', my co-pilot and I continued to operate in the North Sea as before. I would also like to add that we were not getting paid by the Government for any of this, that is, apart from expenses. Nothing untoward happened for six months. Then one day I was reading one of the daily papers in the crew room whilst waiting to fly and I noticed that one of the RUC guys that helped to dump the bodies into the sea had been involved in a fatal car accident. I mentioned this fact to Harry, (my co-pilot during the dumping flights). He then told me that the other two RUC constables involved in 'Autumn Leaves' had also met with fatal accidents. This immediately set the alarm bell ringing. What's the old adage? Once an accident, twice a coincidence, and three times is enemy action'!

'However that was not the end of the matter. Two weeks later Harry's involved in a fatal car accident and was discovered to be over four times the legal alcohol limit. But that's when I really smelt a rat! You see Harry didn't drink – not even wine. Even when we were drinking in a Pub Harry always drank Cokes or tomato juice – or something similar. So I knew that there was a conspiracy afoot to get rid of all people who'd any links to 'Autumn Leaves'.

'So what was your next move?' Fields asked.

'Well it didn't take a brain surgeon to work out that I was probably going to be the next to have an 'accident'. So I began to make arrangements to disappear. I started to withdraw most of my money from my bank accounts. I had no family to worry about. My wife had done a runner four years previously and we were divorced. In retrospect, I think most of us involved in the operation 'Autumn Leaves' had no immediate families which is probably one of the reasons why we were selected'.

'What happened next?' Tony Bryant asked. 'You sure as hell make life interesting Sandy. This is beginning to sound more exciting than what we've experienced during the past two days'.

'Well, at this stage I never realised just how close they were to getting me. I thought I had probably another two or three days before any attempt might be made on me. Not so! I was returning by car from Montrose along the coast road to Aberdeen one night after visiting a friend, when I suddenly caught sight out the corner of my eye, a JCB Tractor driving out of a side road. I realised that he wasn't going to stop, so I accelerated as fast as I could to try and drive clear but he still managed to clip the back of my car, which spun me round. Unfortunately for the tractor driver he'd anticipated hitting me squarely in the beam and then needing full power to bulldoze me over the cliff. However, as he didn't hit me squarely, he had too much inertia in order to stop. So he plunged over the cliff killing himself. Suddenly I realised I'd been given an excellent chance to fake my own death. I then drove my car over the cliff to make it look as though the assassination had been successful. High tide came up to the bottom of the cliff so my body could easily have been washed out to sea. I walked back to Montrose, about ten bloody miles; grabbed a taxi back to Aberdeen and the next morning and decided to get out the country. To cut a long story short I then left my passport at home – let's face it, I couldn't use the bloody thing without disclosing the fact that I was still alive. I then got myself down to Liverpool. I bribed a deck hand of a container ship to hide me on board until the boat reached Trinidad. I figured Port of Spain too small a place to hide with so many ex-pat's about so I stole a small motor launch and sailed up the Orinoco into Venezuela. And then, over a period of three weeks, made my way to Caracas where I have survived for the past three years'.

'Christ that's some story Sandy. But what was the reason for wasting all you guys that were involved in the operation?' Fields asked.

Niles thought for a moment. 'I'm not sure but the lady in question became an MP and was tipped to be the next Government's Foreign Secretary. I suppose any links to operation, 'Autumn Leaves' would have jeopardised her political aspirations. Let's face it; the bloody Army Brass wouldn't touch the sordid scheme with a barge pole so I guess she wanted all links to her involvement severed. Where she managed to get her 'hit man' from God only knows, but he was bloody good - he certainly went through us lot like a dose of salts'.

Tony Bryant gave a loud chuckle 'I don't think you need to worry about the lady in question any longer Sandy. Last year she was struck down with some pretty serious form of cancer she seems to have disappeared from public life and she's not even an MP now. If I remember correctly, according to some of the Daily Tabloids she was only given two years to live. So you could probably claim your passport and regain your old life back without fear of any reprisals'.

'That's a maybe' said Niles thoughtfully. 'But I'm probably the only person who could finger her for all the 'tragic' accidents suffered by the other members of 'Autumn Leaves'. Don't forget, that as the Ex-head of MI5 she will have had plenty of powerful friends and even now could call in some pretty hefty favours'.

'I can see your problem Sandy', said Fields. 'But I think you're probably safe now though I can understand your reluctance in making your whereabouts known. Whilst they think you're dead no one's going to be looking for you. I think we can get you to surface in the States under a new name. Also, if no reference is made to your previous life you should have no worries. My only concern is whether you are entertaining any thoughts of returning to the UK to settle your score with the lady in question'.

'I'm tempted - remember this woman is responsible for the murder of at least four men to my knowledge who thought they were working for the good of the country. But it would seem as though nature has intervened on my behalf, for all we know she might well be dead. But to answer you question. No - there would seem to be no reason to after what Tony's just said'.

George Fields thumbed his chin and said, 'that's great, I'll get things moving straight away and it's agreed Sandy you will definitely be flying out with the rest of us tonight. Mind you; I've another proposition to put to you later but in the meantime, I'd like to get my hands on a secure phone. Chris, I'd like to make use of your secure phone and make some calls to the States – I'll see you guys later'.

Chris Brooker with George Fields in tow left the room.

As George Fields was leaving the room his wife stopped him for a couple of minutes and Niles could see that she was asking what had transpired. What ever George Fields said to his wife brought a smile to her face. She stopped, gave Karen a call, and they both came over to Niles.

'I hear the big boss is happy with your story', she laughed, 'And there's a danger of you flying back to the States with the rest of us'.

'It seems that way', grinned Sandy. 'It will make a

welcome relief to bumming around South America not knowing where my next meal is coming from'.

'Has George said anything about getting you employment in the States yet?'

'No – though he said he'd like to make me a proposition once he'd finished making some calls to the States. Any idea what he has in mind?'

'I'd better leave it to George to tell you but if all goes well we hope to see a lot more of you when we get back to the States'.

This brought a big grin to the face of Karen. 'Oh that's great Sandy I can't wait to show you my horse, I call him 'Fredrick'. Do you ride Sandy?'

'Well I know which is the front because that's where the teeth are and that just about exhausts my knowledge on horses', chuckled Niles.

Tony Bryant couldn't wait to get a dig in at Sandy, 'Christ we've something that Niles can't do', He hooted.

'Well I'll soon put that right', said young Karen archly. 'Once we get home Sandy, I'll soon teach you to ride and I bet you end up one of the best riders in the country'.

Jackie Fields raised an eyebrow at the last remark and said, 'It looks as though your future is already being mapped out for you Sandy'.

Chris Brooker interrupted gently, 'I think Sandy would probably appreciate a shower and then some lunch. After that I'm sure he would like to continue with this conversation. Would you please excuse us Mrs Fields while I get this man fed and watered'.

'Of course Sandy I had completely forgotten, you've had nothing to eat since you left at four o'clock this morning – you must be starving – Karen and I will see you later after you have eaten'.

Tony Bryant and Rusty Irons sidled up to Niles while he was eating his lunch.

'Sandy', said Rusty'. 'Did you know that I was also involved with the operation 'Autumn Leaves?'

'Christ no', he replied. 'How come you're still alive? How come no one try to remove you?'

'No – I think the fact that four of us were still serving in the SAS and were still subject to military discipline and the, 'Official Secrets Act', made the lady in question think we were no threat to her ambitions, where as you and the RUC members, who were being disbanded, were probably considered as, 'loose cannons'.

'What part did you play in the operations?' Niles asked.

'There were four of us who took turns at keeping the guys under death sentence under observation. The idea was that no one was to disappear until the identity of the man in the higher echelon of their command structure had been established. As you know, the plan was to work our way up the IRA's command structure until we'd the top men identified. But then as you stated, the Brit' Government lost its nerve and sold out to the IRA. Actually 'Autumn Leaves' was a brilliant idea and had it been left to fruition we would have completely eradicated their command structure'.

'So who actually did the killings?'

'I'm not sure whether it was the RUC or assassins from MI5. All we had to do was keep them under observation and report all their contacts. This eventually led to their next higher echelon being identified and once that had been established the guy under surveillance just disappeared. Until I heard your story I had no idea what had happened to them. Which could have been the reason why it wasn't considered necessary to have us SAS guys wasted. From what you have just said I figure another six months and their whole movement would have collapsed'.

Niles just grunted and then remarked, 'With that additional six months Rusty, do you realise we could probable have reconciled the Northern Ireland problem'.

'No way', he replied. 'Those bastards would have found something else to fight over. It might have caused a slight hiatus but given another six months and they would have been at it hammer and tongs again. Any way you'd better go and get some grub and we'll see you later'.

Chapter 25

Bogotá

The private Hospital was located on the Avenida 81 just to the north of the Botanical Gardens in Bogotá. From the outside the building gave one the impressions that it was a high tech research establishment rather than the most up to date and expensive hospital in Colombia. The reception hall was quite small but expensively decorated and the receptionists were all young and good looking and presented an image of affluence and efficiency. As with most affluent enterprises in Colombia security was clearly evident in the shape of three heavily armed men within the entrance foyer. All visitors had to have their identity checked before for proceeding beyond the Foyer.

.Francesco Domingo was located on the second floor in what initially looked like a private suite in some upmarket hotel. There were three rooms to each suite. A separate bathroom, a living room/ TV room and the bedroom that was complete with all the latest hospital equipment normally only associated with an Intensive Care Treatment room.

Francesco was seated in the bed looking white and

drawn but never - the - less extremely angry. The remaining members of the Cartel coalition were seated around his bed waiting for Domingo to start the brief. They were all stunned and furious at the death of Franco DeNero killed at the Airstrip the previous day. It was too close to home for comfort. Collectively, they'd all suffered a large financial loss with the destruction of the three helicopters. Although two of the Hues had been insured they were still not sure whether under the circumstances of their destruction if the insurance companies would be prepared to pay out. (Acts of War were not normal considered to be part of the normal cover). They had a team of lawyers working on it.

Francesco started off in a rather more mollified manner than normal.

'Right let's get down to business and sort out where we go from here. Just to summarise what's happened over the last week. We've lost three operating processing plants. And the new one which we were setting up in the hinterland has been compromised plus the fact, we've had two of our own colleagues and about two dozen of our own foot soldiers killed. We have also suffered the lost of two Super Puma and two Hue Helicopters at the cost of Christ knows how many million dollars. The net result as I see it – we've been made to look complete idiots and unless we take action to readdress this situation our street credibility is going to be zero. As you know amigos, this will almost certainly lead to some of our less powerful competitors thinking the time is ripe to usurp us. We've to act strongly and quickly if we're to avoid an attempted take over from some of the crazy crack heads in our own back yard. Has anyone got any suggestions'?

Teddy Garcia gave Domingo a flinty look and said. 'Up to now Francesco you have run things pretty much as you saw fit and so far you have achieved nothing but fuck ups. Whilst we appreciate that you are the most powerful and affluent member of our Cartel you've continued to ignore most of the advice you've been offered. After the initial shoot out with the passengers we could have let them go and blamed local dissidents from the local area. Al Menzies was the only member of our Cartel seen and it's doubtful if any of the passengers or the SAS team could have identified and linked him to us - but no….. You had to get greedy and try and hold them for ransom - since when everything has turned to rat shit'.

Francesco could feel his anger boiling up. His face was red and he knew it. His colleagues had been quite agreeable to have him run the operations when things were going well. Now the situation was turning, "belly up", the bastards were turning on him. He almost blew a gasket but realised that the Cartel was only a fragile coalition. Each member was a boss in his own right and they had only joined forces to try and negate the effect of the new Police Field Force who had been so successful in wrecking their processing plants.

'I never heard much complaining when we had our previous meetings and as I remember it, we were all in agreement with the decisions that were made at the time', snarled Domingo.

'If you recall at the time when you suggested that we hunt these passengers down after Menzies initial cock up I said it was akin to closing the stable door after the horse had bolted and I still think that's the case'.

'Okay, okay, in hindsight we should have let the SAS team chopper the passenger's out and relocated our new processing plant else where but at the time, wiping them out looked to be the cheapest and easiest option. Sam Jackson warned us at the time not to tangle with the SAS team but as there were only eight of them we thought we could get rid of them with no problems – now we know different. That still does not help us in deciding where we go from here'. Domingo finished with a Latino shrug of his shoulders.

Pablo Ferreira interrupted. 'Since you've been in Hospital we've had another telephone call from our friend Chase. He tell us that all the remaining passengers and the SAS team flew into the States last night and have now disappeared to the Four Corners of the country so its pointless in trying to continue this vendetta. And to be quite frank, I've had a gutful of this whole bloody mess'.

'But don't you see', raged Domingo. 'That if we let these gringos get away with this we will have lost so much face that we will end up with a war on our own turf preventing our competitors taking us over'.

Pedro DeGannes who up to this point had remained fairly quiet and calm decided to have his say.

'What you are saying is correct Francesco, never- theless if you are suggesting that we continue this vendetta into the States then I for one do not wish to be associated with it. I'd rather take my chances with local insurrections down here than get involved with what amounts to taking on the US government. For Christ sake - we can kick the locals into shape anytime we like. To take our revenge to the States could be a bloody disaster. We could find ourselves being hunted down by a Regiment of Green Beret Special Forces and for what? Just to get our revenge'.

Teddy Garcia was now getting even more impatient with Domingo. 'Just what are you trying to prove. Are you suggesting we assassinate the American Defence Secretary and his wife? Apart from creating a massive response from the American Government what does it achieve? There would be no financial gain and it would certainly cost us a lot more money. I believe that Pedro is correct - it will cost less in money and men to keep our own house in order than to finance some mad cap scheme in the US'.

Domingo could see that he was going to have a hard time trying to keep the coalition together if he continued to pursue his present line of argument never-the less he was determined to get his revenge on the Americans'

'Okay amigos let us take a vote on it – those who say "yes" to continue our vendetta to the States and those who do not wish to continue with it. Okay those that says "yes"'! Domingo looked at his three other colleagues none of whom raised their hand in agreement.

'Can I take it from your lack of response that you all wish to take no further action against the Americans'?

'You're fucking right there', said Teddy Garcia. 'I've had a gutful of chasing these Americans and throwing good money after bad. I don't know how much money this has cost me personally during the last week but it must run into millions of dollars by now – I'm out - I want nothing further to do with it'.

Pedro nodded in agreement. 'If we had managed to catch up with them whilst they were still in this country I would have agreed to continue. But now that they're out of Colombia it's become too expensive and fraught with danger. As Teddy said, we could find two fucking great American Aircraft carriers parked off our west coast and having to fight a division of American Marines. The risk is too great'.

Domingo made one last appeal. 'Can't you see that the Americans would never do that? That would be tantamount to declaring war on Colombia'.

Pedro DeGannes then interrupted. 'We are not stupid Francesco – the Americans would not take overt action but they would most certainly take covert action which would still involve the Americans deploying thousands of men if necessary. Do you really think that the Americans are going to sit on their arses and do nothing after you have wasted their Defence Secretary. Further more; I can't see the United Nations complaining about four Drug Barons being assassinated in Colombia. If you insist on continuing with this vendetta Francesco then I for one will not be associated with it'.

Pablo and Teddy Garcia nodded their heads in agreement.

Domingo knew he was beaten but he could feel the desire to get revenge burning in his gut and knew from previous experience that the feeling would only get worse the longer it went on. Against his own better judgement he knew he'd have to continue. 'Okay amigos I respect your decision but I will continue this vendetta on my own, no bastard is going to make Domingo look a fool and get away with it. I will endeavour to kidnap the Defence Secretary's daughter and extract a heavy ransom from him, which will help to defray the millions of dollars that I have lost over the past week'.

Teddy Garcia nodded his head. 'That's your prerogative but you just make sure that we are not associated with your mad scheme. I've had a bad gut feeling about this last week and I want nothing further to do with it. I wish you luck in your enterprise Francesco – you're going to need it!'

Domingo watched his former three colleagues get up and troop out. 'Bastards' he thought, 'but I don't need their co-operation. I have the money and the organisation to pull this off without their help. No fucking gringo is going to rub my face in the dirt and get away with it. I must get onto our friend Mr Chase and see what information I can get on this Gringo bastard Niles – that is one hombre it would give me great pleasure in watch die slowly'.

The three remaining Cartel gathered in the hospital corridor and discussed Domingo's obsession.

Teddy Garcia shrugged his shoulders and said. 'I'm afraid despite what we've decided Francesco is going to continue with his vendetta. We must make it clear to all our associates and the American Senators on our pay role that we are not party to any of Domingo's hair brained revenge plots – are we all agreed on this point'?

Ferreira and DeGannes both nodded in agreement.

Pedro DeGannes gestured towards the private ward where Domingo's was bedded.

'I think the strain over the past three days have taken there toll. Francesco is always determined to see that things get done but he has lost all his rational over this last problem and to be quite honest I don't wish to be associated with any more of his hair brained schemes.

'From here on Domingo is on his own', said Ferreira. 'We are going to have to ensure that it is made absolutely clear to all concerned that we are no longer members of the same Cartel otherwise the fall out from his actions could effect us too'.

Chapter 26

US Embassy

Niles awoke from a brief sleep after a meal, rubbed his eyes, stretched, yawned and sauntered off and to have a shower. After which a smart US Marine provided him with a fresh set of clean clothes. He checked his watch and was surprised to see that it was already nine o'clock in the evening. He remembered that George Fields had suggested they have another talk with a view to Niles entering the States.

He wandered down to the main briefing room. No sign of George Fields but Chris Brooker was talking to Tony Bryant. Tony raised his arm and beckoned him over.

'How you feeling ace', he grinned. 'I must say you look quite chirpy considering your lack of sleep over the past twenty-four hours – I believe George Fields has been asking for you. He has some propositions to put to you – I'll give him a bell to let him know you are up and conscious.

Bryant wandered away to get Fields.

Chris gave Sandy a friendly grin. 'You might be interested to know that the big white chief has been on the phone almost continually calling in favours from all sorts of well connected people to help get you State side. Tell me Sandy – I know you are a trained soldier and also a qualified commercial pilot but have you ever done any body guard or close protection training?'

'None at all, I was a British Paratrooper prior to becoming an Army Pilot so I'm pretty well versed in unarmed combat and as you know, and I've always had a passion for shooting. Being posted to the SAS Flight in the UK enabled me to practice more shooting in three years than in my entire service career'.

'The past three days have certainly proved that you are a dammed fine shot Sandy but even more importantly, that you remain cool and calm when under fire. I've had plenty of agents in the American Secret Service who were mighty fine shots on the range but who became wildly erratic when under fire. I think this is an ability that you should cultivate. There are plenty of very powerful men in the States who would pay big bucks to have a man of your proven ability on their payroll'.

'There's no way I'm going to be some ones body guard and end up toting baggage or running messages for their wives. I'm afraid I am too independent to get involved in that sort deal', he replied.

'No no Sandy – times have changed, the type of job I'm talking about is highly qualified – you are made responsible for the safety of your employer. Whenever a potentially dangerous situation arises you call the shots and your boss will normally do as you see fit. The days are long gone when the wife and family used the bodyguard as a general gofer. I think The Defence Secretary is thinking of asking you to ride shotgun for Jackie and Karen. The consensus of opinion is that Domingo is a very vindictive man. Alfred Mendoza knows of the man's reputation and is quite adamant that he will continue to try and avenge the loss of face he has suffered over the past four days'.

Before Niles could reply Bryant appeared with George Fields.

'Sandy! Said George Fields as he came over and gave him a friendly pat on the back. 'You certainly look refreshed. How do you feel about discussing your options State side? I've a couple of angles I would like you to consider. I have a S76 helicopter that is used to transport me around the country and at the moment one of my pilots is coming up for retirement. We could arrange for all your former flying experience to be taken into account without disclosing you previous identity although I understand from one my colleagues in the States you would have to satisfy them that you had the correct technical ability and you may have to sit and pass some technical exams'.

'As a matter of fact I've over a thousand hours of Captain's time on the S76 in the North Sea plus which I was also a Training Captain and an Instrument Rating Examiner. Would it be possible to have these qualifications verified without alerting people to the fact that I am still alive and well?' Niles asked.

'Provided you can give me all your personal details that should be a fairly easy task for the guys running the, Witness Protection Programme – you wouldn't believe some of the subterfuge they have to get up to when establishing a new life for some one. The main problem with most people is they want to be established back into something that they're familiar with. Unfortunately, this can make it easier for people trying to locate them but in your case, you are now dead so that problem will not arise'.

'However, continued Fields. 'I've another reason for offering you employment. You've been instrumental in saving the lives of my wife and daughter as well as the other survivors. But my main reason for asking you is not out of thanks, albeit that goes without saying – but you've demonstrated an ability to act under stress in the most amazing manner. I hope I've not offended you Sandy by discussing your actions over the last few days with both Tony Bryant and Chris Brooker; they both speak extremely highly of you. Tony said you think quicker on your feet in dangerous situations than any man he has ever met. And Chris said he would recommend you for a spook any time'.

'That's kind of them', smiled Niles.

'Alfred Mendoza is also positive that that bastard Domingo will continue with his vendetta all the way to the States. Under the circumstances I'd be most grateful if you would consider acting as body guard to Jackie and Karen until this matter is settled one way or another. It goes without saying that you will be well paid for your services. I also have a son called Douglas but he is away at a boarding School so I'm hoping that Domingo is not aware of his existence. However I will also have to make arrangements to make sure he's protected. I have the American Secret Service looking after me and the family during official occasions, but it would sure give me peace of mind knowing you were hovering in the background keeping an eye on my two girls Sandy'.

'Well I'm most flattered but there are several points that we have to consider – the first is that I have never ever received any training in bodyguard drills. And the second and probable most important one is that if I'm flying your S76 helicopter I can't be looking after Jackie and Karen'.

'I agree Sandy but the first of your two points is that your two SAS friends are leaving the service on their return to the UK and then coming State to set up a Security Company to provide and train Bodyguards. Guess who they've agreed to train for me! Not only that but with all the publicity from the rescue of the American survivors Tony and Rusty are going to be inundated with requests for their services. I'll be giving them all the kudos I can. Why don't you discuss your options with Tony and Rusty I figure if you three were to set up yourselves as a Security Company you'd never be short of clients. All I would ask is that for the first six months or so I would be most grateful if you could act as bodyguard to Jackie and Karen'.

Niles thought for a couple of minutes or so, 'I agree in principle but it's a hell of a responsibility you're giving me. I'd need some assistance but we could discuss this later. For example, when Jackie is at home and Karen is at school, they're in two different locations, so we are definitely going to need a team of men to give you the cover you require'.

'I agree', said Fields. 'I've already discussed this in some detail with both Tony and Chris and they both suggested that I have a formal team of at least four men with you overseeing the situation. Tony said you have this certain, 'feel' for situations. He said it was a talent that you are born with and can only be honed by training but if you didn't have it in the first place there is no way you can develop it'.

'Nice of him to mention it' grunted Niles.

Just at that moment Chris Brooker burst into the room and shouted. 'Heh you guys – we've just received your kit from the Field Force Police. You'll be please to know that Col DeSuza had all your equipment packed and personally supervised its loading into one of our Vans. The driver is one of my guys and took great care to make sure that no one followed him to this location. I figure the Cartel still don't know your where abouts'.

Tony gave the rest of the SAS the good news and they all rushed off to get into some clean civilian clothes.

'Great', Niles growled. 'They will probable think we are still out there in the sticks some where which should make our evacuation much easier. By the time they get news of us flying out we'll be State side.

While Sandy Niles was talking with the American Defence Secretary Tony Bryant and Rusty Irons wandered over. 'I'll leave you for the moment', said George Fields while I check on my family' I expect Tony and Rusty would like to discuss that project I mentioned earlier'.

Tony leaped straight in to the deep end. 'I believe the Defence Secretary has already broached the subject of us leaving the Service and coming State side to set up a Security Company Sandy. Both Rusty and I would like you to consider joining in this venture. We figure that you have a definite talent for this sort of work – something you are probably not even aware of. But we've observed you during the last four days and not to put too mildly you have a rare talent for getting out of scrapes, we are extremely impressed. What do you think?'

'I must admit that I've never considered working for a Security Company until George Fields mentioned it a few moments ago. As you have probably guessed, my first love is flying. If you think my talents as a pilot can be used within the company I would be glad to join you'.

'I think this is the beauty of starting the business within the States Sandy. It is such a bloody great place that people tend to fly where as in the UK they would use a car or train. However we can thrash the details out later. It will take Rusty and I some time to sort things out in the UK. But both Chris Brooker and George Fields reckon that with the publicity of this rescue mission we will have no trouble drumming up some wealthy clients'.

'Sounds good in principal Tony - but how long before you can get over to the States?'

Rusty quickly interrupted, 'Actually I am just running out of time now and if I forego my pre-release courses I could be out within a month'.

'And I have just about finished my time with the Regiment and am due to return to my own unit. As you know Sandy once Officers have completed their three year tour they must return to their own arm. There's no way I want to return to normal soldiering so I'm resigning my commission as soon as I get back. If all goes according to plan I hope to get out here about the same time as Rusty'.

'That's great! Niles said with a big grin. 'With the three of us working as a team what chance to the other poor bastards stand'.

'Another point in our favour', continued Tony. 'Is that we have a very powerful friend and ally in the American Defence Secretary. I can tell you Sandy the man is mightily impressed with what we have achieved and you in particular. Jackie and Karen Fields have left him in no doubt that but for you they would both be dead now. I'm certain we won't even have to ask him for favours. He'll make sure that we get all the assistance he can give'.

'Can I have every ones attention', shouted Chris Brooker. 'Transport to the Airport will be leaving in ten minutes. Please make sure that you have all your kit and documents. Once we get to the Airport there will be no turning back for obvious reasons. Ten minutes after you arrive at the aircraft you will be airborne and on your way to the States. Good luck and I hope to see you guys some time someplace'.

The SAS team grabbed all their kit and was ready to move in thirty seconds. Sandy only had the kit he was standing in so he was ready twenty nine second earlier.

They all bid the American staff and Chris Brooker fare well and made their way to the transport.

Chapter 27

State Side

The flight back to the States was uneventful. Niles spent much of his time during the flight in deep thought. He wondered if he'd made the right decision. For the past three years he'd no body to answer to. He was his own boss. His employment was always of a temporary nature. If he didn't like the job or his employer he simple got up and left. Although life had been tough it was an experience that he had grown to appreciate. No responsibilities. No family worries. However he was mature enough to realise that as he got older he was going to have to face up to facts of life one way or another. Life can be pretty cruel to a fifty year old with no home money or friends and unless Niles changed his present life-style that's where he was headed.

There was a short delay whilst they landed and refuelled at Miami. Niles slipped away from the remainder of the passengers whilst the refuelling took place, still deep in thought. When Jackie Fields attempted to follow him and ask him what was wrong it was George Fields that stopped her seeming to sense the internal struggle that Niles was wrestling with. However, it was young Karen, completely oblivious to his troubled state that rushed over and finally got through to him. Her sheer exuberance and obvious affection for him brought him to his senses. There was no coquettishness about her and her trusting naivety convinced him that he had no option other than protect Karen. He could still remember the black rage that came over him when Al Menzies was about to rape her. Karen and Niles returned the others, his black mood dispelled. George Fields took one look at Niles's face and knew that any one attempting to harm Karen was going to have kill Niles first. He whispered his thoughts to Jackie.

'I think Niles has been having second thoughts about the post we offered him but I think our young daughter has just convinced him that she needs his protection. At the moment I can't think of any one I'd rather have riding shot gun on our little girl'.

Jackie breathed a huge sigh of relief. 'Thank god for that. After seeing him in action over the past three days I think we are making the best choice'.

By the time they re-emplaned Niles was more like his usual self. Now that they were back in the States they all relaxed and to a man, they fell asleep and never woke until they were called upon to fasten their safety belts prior to landing at Washington National Airport.

There was a brief but good-hearted farewell as the Fields, Mendoza's and Niles parted company with the SAS team. The band of brother hood that is often forged in combat between men made the farewell rather poignant for the SAS team and Niles. Never-the–less five minutes after Fields and Niles departed the team set about trying to organise a 'Run ashore' prior to their departure for the UK. They were waiting just twenty-four hours and then they were due to depart for the UK aboard the VC10 on its weekly diplomatic run.

The Mendoza's and Niles were invited to stay with the Fields whilst arrangements were made for Maria to fly to the UK who would eventually return with her, 'Eduardo'.

There were half a dozen men to greet the Defence Secretaries party. Two were members of his staff and the other four were from the Witness Protection Programme Department. George Fields took the four to one side and then introduced them to Sandy Niles.

'This is the guy we've been discussing', said Fields. 'Sandy – Meet, Ed, Frank, Sol and John. They're the guys who have been tasked to get you into the States under the Witness Protection Programme. We've discussed your problem over the phone at some length whilst we were still in Colombia. The consensus of opinion is that you have nothing to worry about from the lady who harassed you. Apparently she died three months ago. Not withstanding that, I've tasked them with getting all your technical qualifications and experience clandestinely from the UK to the States. This will negate you having to repeat exams unnecessarily in this country. If you'll go with them now and let them have your details, I'll get the family organised so as soon as you're ready, we can board the chopper and get to hell out of here. Hopefully once these guys have all your details Sandy, you should never have to see them again – Okay'.

Sandy Niles looked at George Fields with undisguised admiration – the bloody man was a miracle maker - talk about American get up and go. Something like this in the UK would have taken months to finalise.

'I can't thank you enough sir - I still can't believe I'm going o be living legitimately in a country for the first time in three years'.

He grabbed Fields hand and shook it warmly.

'Think nothing of it Sandy it was the least I could do for you. Without your presence of mind and quick thinking both my wife and daughter would now be dead. The interview should not be longer that ten minutes or so, after which, make your way over to the limousines over there`. Fields nodded in the direction two cars stood awaiting his party. 'The family should be aboard by the time you have finished speaking to these gentlemen'.

The interview took exactly seven minutes. It was concise, accurate and most illuminating. Niles couldn't believe that so much information could have been extracted from him in such a short time. There were no unforeseen problems.

Two limousines took the Defence Secretary's party to the other side of the Airport where his S76 helicopter was waiting to fly them on to the Field's estate to the south of Washington.

The two pilots were a waiting to greet the party and as they all debussed from the limousines. George Fields went over to the Captain and grabbed his hand and gave it a vigorous shake.

'Great to see you Gary, and you Rick', Fields had that easy, friendly confident manner (a prerequisite that most top American politicians seem to have) which always seemed to put people at ease 'I can't tell you guys how glad we are to be going home. I'm afraid we have almost a full load – any problems with that?'

'No problems boss', said Gary. 'We have plenty payload available and the journey will only take us the usual fifteen minutes or so depending how they route us out on departure'.

Fields then introduced the Mendoza family and then Niles. 'This is Sandy Niles, the guy who is responsible for saving the lives of Jackie and Karen. I can't wait to tell you guys about what he and his SAS friends did to outwit the Cartel gangsters in Colombia. Sandy is also a qualified helicopter pilot. He's the guy that Hi-jacked a Super Puma from under the noses of the Cartel's gunmen and used it to fly all the survivors out of the jungle'.

Both Gary and Rick gave Niles a searching and diffident look. 'A Super Puma is some Helicopter, it's a professional flying machine Sandy, you must have had some training or experience to handle that beast', said Gary.

Niles gave them both a friendly grin, 'I'll tell you all about it later on but at the moment I'm not too sure how much of my background I can disclose'.

Fields interrupted at this point. 'We've to put Sandy into a Witness Protection Programme. It therefore goes without saying that the fewer people who know of Niles's background the better. But you will obviously get to know of his flying experience, which I am told is very substantial. He is also a British Instrument Rating Examiner and a Training Captain. All this doesn't mean much to me but it will to you guys'.

The two S76 crew appeared to be suitably impressed. 'I take it you were on the North Sea if you were instrument rated Sandy?' queried Rick.

'Yes I became qualified on the S61 and S76, the Super Puma and the Bolkow 105'.

Would you like to have a fly back to the boss's place?' asked Rick, the co-pilot. 'I can always sit in the back and Karen can give me the low down on her adventures'.

'That's very kind of you but I think I'd better ride as a passenger until I've officially renewed my Licences. I also think that young Karen here is keen to point out all the local landmarks and impress me with her local knowledge'.

'That's right Sandy, I can also show you from the air where we can go horse riding', exclaimed Karen.

'You had better take it easy young girl I have never been on a horse in my life but I've heard that it takes some time before your backside gets hardened to the saddle – Is that right Mr Fields?.

'You're right there Sandy, you'll need to take it gently at first or you'll end up so saddle sore you won't be able to walk let alone ride a horse', grinned Fields, who knew his daughter had been riding since she was four years old and was now a very competent horse woman. 'The trouble with young Karen, Sandy is that she's been surrounded by people who have ridden all their lives so you are going to be her first student – you're a lucky man'!

Rick beckoned them all over to the helicopter and they enplaned – Karen making sure that Niles sat adjacent to her so she could point out the local landmarks. It was still quite dark but dawn was slowly breaking. There was no cloud and it looked like the onset of a fine day.

Their flight was cleared to take off and was routed initially to the north with a port turnout not above one thousand feet above ground level (AGL). This enabled Niles to get his first clear view of Washington DC, most of it lying to the north of the Airport. Dawn was now breaking and it was possible to see the various landmarks. Karen had obviously flown this route many times and her knowledge of the locality was impressive.

She pointed out the White House which was just visible to the north and then as the helicopter turned to the south she pointed out Arlington. She kept Sandy occupied with a running commentary as they passed over Alexandra and Huntington. The Potomac River was still shrouded in early morning mist where the River bridge estates were just visible.

'Our house is not far from Riverside Gardens which is just on the nose Sandy', explained Karen.

'There's our house', she shouted excitedly and pointed out the window as the helicopter made a wide descending turn into the northerly wind and set itself up for landing.

Niles was impressed. The house looked like something out of the film, 'Gone with the Wind'. It was massive – huge white building built of stone or granite. From this height it was not possible to determine. When viewed from above the house formed a large square 'U'. The longest part formed by the front of the building. A large tiled porch supported on four large colonnades covered what looked like an impressive entrance to the building. The front of the building extended at thirty yards to either side of the front entrance. At either end of the building the arms of the square U extended back about twenty yards. Niles knew from former experience that when something looked large from the air that when you landed alongside it was going to look positively massive

Within the fenced estate there were about a half dozen out buildings and a further long stable that looked capable of housing dozens of horses. He'd known that the Fields were affluent but he had never realised just how seriously rich they obviously were.

'Are you sure that will be big enough for all four of us ', ventured Niles.

George just nodded his head and laugh.

'I reckon we can just about all squeeze in there, and in fact there will be five of us, Karen's fourteen year old brother, Douglas is away at school at the moment and further more', continued George Fields. 'Jackie and I have decided that you are to be our house guest until we get this witness protection problem sorted. Plus which, we would be grateful to have you close at hand just in case that mad man, Domingo tries anything'.

'That's fine by me, we are obviously going to have to discuss security arrangements with your official body guards and decide which is the best way of giving your family the maximum cover. I never realised that Karen had a brother until you mentioned it earlier on. If the Cartel was to discover that you also have a son then he will also become an obvious target'. Niles deferred from mentioning that Karen was a possible target so as not to alarm her. She was all ears at the moment listening to her father and Niles. But with three possible targets to look after it was going to stretch their resources to the limit.

'I have already given it some considerable thought', said George Fields. But I'm going to have to make alternative arrangements anyway as my son spends most of his time at a boarding school. The school has a pretty effective security system of its own. There are quite a few boys at the school who come from seriously rich families consequently kidnapping is always considered an ongoing possibility; hence the security arrangements'.

Their conversation was interrupted as the helicopter gradually came to the hover in a paddock about thirty yards from the main building. It was gently hovered over to the touch down point, landed and closed the rotors down.

Niles noticed that as they deplaned that there were two shadowy figures amongst the trees in the back ground and realised that there were already some form of security operating.

He nodded to the two shadowy figures. 'I see you've already some muscle working for you Sir'.

'Oh yes - there my official Secret Service agents supplied by the State. The trouble is they are here to keep out any crack pots from having a go at me. We're going to have to discuss how we can use you to get the most efficient results. You may find that initially they'll resent you – but once I have briefed them and relate your actions in Colombia I think they'll change their mind. They'd better! Or they'll be looking for alternative employment. After we deplane Sandy could you go with Jackie and Karen to the drawing room and I'll give you a buzz when I've spoken to my team and I'm ready to introduce you .

Niles nodded in assent.

George Fields assembled all the Secret Service men in his study. He made the briefing short but sharp as he already anticipated some objections to the use of Niles.

'Right you guys I'm going to be brief and to the point.

As you already know both my wife and daughter were captured and held hostage and were about to be raped and then wasted. They were rescued by a guy I'm going to introduce to you and the British SAS. His introduction to my protection team will not alter your duties in the least – you're still officially responsible for my safety and my family when they accompany me. Sandy Niles will have a roving commission and is basically responsible for the safety of Jackie and Karen particularly so when they are not with me. Are we all clear so far?'

Theo Baldwin was the senior of the four men present and felt it was his duty to raise the first point.

'I think the inclusion of this guy is an indication of a lack of confidence in our ability to look after you - Sir!'

'It's nothing of the sort Theo. Your job is to look after me and will continue to be so. This guy has a god given talent for being able to sniff out trouble and I want him guarding my wife and daughter. How many times have you actually fired your gun in anger Theo – any of you? – This guy Niles has wiped out over a dozen Cartel gunmen in three days. And whether you guys like it or not he is going to be protecting my family until we have cleared up this business with the Colombian Cartel. The consensus of opinion in Colombia was that this character called Domingo will continue his vendetta all the way to the States and until this problem is resolved Sandy Niles is going to be riding shotgun over my family with or without your blessing – is that clear. If any of you feel you can't live with that then say so now and we can arrange for your replacement'.

They nodded their heads in reluctant agreement.

Fields gave a look of satisfaction and thumbed the buzzer.

Jackie answered the intercom, turned to Niles and gave him a big smile, 'you have been summoned superman. They're all waiting to get their claws into, but I'm willing to bet that George has already read them the riot act – good luck Sandy'.

Niles approached the study door with a certain amount of trepidation, even with Jackie's assurance, he was still expecting a cool reception from Field's security team. He knocked on the study door.

'Come in Sandy and let me introduce you to my official agents', growled Fields.

Fields immediately noted how the Secret Service men pulled them selves up straight to look impressive whilst Niles seemed perfectly relaxed but some what cautious.

'Ok Sandy let me introduce you to these four guys who have looked after me for the past three years. And, I Might add; have done a dammed good job of it over the past three years. This ugly looking bastard is Theo Baldwin and our head honcho'. Baldwin was rather squat looking man with practically no neck, a shaven head and a pugnacious expression but there lurked a sense of humour behind his grey eyes. He looked tough enough however, to give Mike Tyson a good ten rounds. He was dressed in a light charcoal grey suit. He looked a good man to have on your side in trouble.

Baldwin gave Niles a no nonsense look. 'Hi there – from what we have heard you are almost a one man army - welcome to the tribe'. He offered his hand to Sandy and was surprised at the size of Sandy's hand which was much bigger than he expected.

'Thanks a lot, I'm sure I can learn a lot from you guys', remarked Niles.

'And this is Mike Williams who is Theo's 2i/c'. Williams was about the same height as Niles - about six feet two but a shade slimmer with dark hair, dark coloured eyes and very good looking. However, where Baldwin had had a no nonsense look about him Williams adopted the typical Hollywood, 'tough guy posture' even to the extent of lighting a cigarette with legs astride and rocking backwards and forwards on the balls of his feet

He gave Niles "the hard look" practiced by professional boxers these days when they meet at the weigh in. 'Chris Brooker has given us the low down over the phone Sandy. It appears that you are a red hot shot with the rifle'.

'I'm afraid I am a little rusty at the moment', murmured Niles, then realised that the Americans would probably think this as an un-necessary English understatement as it was already known that he had killed about a dozen men recently.

'Well remind me to keep out of your way when you get back in practice', said Jake Lattice as Fields introduced him to Sandy.

Jake was rather older than the other three but had postured exactly the same way as Williams even to lighting the cigarette. He was about Five feet ten inches tall and what can be described as close nit, with sandy hair similar to Niles's.

Niles was not particularly impressed by the last two men.

'And last but not least we have Brian Johnson known as 'Homer' to most of his friends – something to do with his ability to hit a base ball a hell of a long way I believe', smiled Fields.

Homer was a very big man, at least six feet four inches and well proportioned with it. His hair was probably fair but as it had all been shaved off it was difficult for Niles to figure out. With his light blue eyes and Aryan complexion he reminded Niles of one of the old World One Prussian guards.

'Nice to make your acquaintance Sandy', and he offered a huge mitt to shake Niles's hand and was somewhat surprised to find that Niles's hand was bigger than his.

'Like wise I'm sure', Niles grinned who suspected that

Homer was probably the friendliest of the four and would be easy to make friends with. With his size and build he did not feel it necessary to adopt the tough guy posture. It was painfully obvious that if any one wanted to mess with Homer they were going to come off second best.

'Right lets get down to business', said Fields. 'As I mentioned previously Sandy will not be interfering with your cycle of duties but will be basically looking after Jackie and Karen and Douglas when he's home but I would be grateful if you could acquaint Sandy with the local area and all your procedures, particularly with the electronic surveillance kit and the front door control centre - when you've finished Sandy I'd like to see you and discuss where you're to be accommodated and the details of your flying training which we need to get in hand as soon as possible'.

Niles nodded and then said to Theo, 'Okay, lets get the nitty gritty out the way and then we can all get on with our jobs'.

Fields and the other three left and went about their business whilst Theo gave Niles a complete run down on the security procedures and a brief resume of the local town and immediate area. As the brief progressed Niles warmed to Theo and sensed the feeling was reciprocated. The man was the ultimate professional. By the end of the brief both of them were on amicable terms if not friends. After the brief, Niles set off to rejoin the Defence Secretary and his family.

Niles gently knocked the door of the largest of the living rooms and was invited in.

'Sandy – Jackie and I have discussed your living arrangements and we would like you to live in the west wing and you are to be treated as one of the family. This will enable you to keep a close eye on the family at all times. What to you think?'

'It sounds good but I am not sure that I can offer the best service by being right on top of you, there's a danger of me being too involved with the family and not being able to concentrate on the security aspect. For example, if you have house guests and I'm included my ability to be on the look out is going to be constrained. I'd be far better used prowling around outside and keeping an eye open for trouble. If I'm with you and Karen there's a strong chance of me being involved in small talk which is bound to derogate security'.

'But Sandy', interrupted Jackie. 'We want you to feel as though you are one of the family and not just a hired hand'.

'I'm really flattered and touched', said the embarrassed Niles. 'But the whole point of this exercise is to try and negate any trouble Domingo and his cohorts have cooked up and with all due respect, I can't be 100% on the job if I'm involved with the family and their friends, much as I would love to and I'm flattered and touched at your suggestion'.

Jackie appeared quite hurt at Niles's last statement but George Fields was quick to spot what he was on about.

'I see what you mean Sandy but you will still have to have the run of the house anyway. But from what you are saying you will not be joining us for meals and social occasions, is that right'.

'Much as I'm tempted to join you and your family I'm certain that to do so would invalidate my prime reason for being here'. Niles turned to Jackie. 'I'd still like you to consider me as your friend Jackie but we must face up to the fact that my main purpose for being here is to protect you'.

'I'm not sure what our daughter is going to say about this', murmured Jackie, 'She had her heart set on you becoming one of the family'.

'Just think of me as a distant relative', Niles grinned. 'Is there any accommodation in any of the nearby, "out houses", that I could live in?'

'There's a flat above the forge where the blacksmith used to live but he's passed on years ago and now we have to send to the town when we need any of the horses shod, there're a dying breed these days – you could take that over Sandy'. George Fields pointed out the window to a fairly substantial building about fifty yards from the mansion.

'That looks absolutely ideal', said Niles. 'Is the forge still serviceable?'

'Sure thing', said George.' The blacksmith uses it every time he comes up to re-shoe the horses'.

'That's great then', said Niles. 'If it's okay with you guys I'll move what little I have into the flat and then take a walk around your hacienda and get myself acquainted with the lie of the land'.

'I think our daughter has reserved the right to show you around the estate – I hope this won't distract you from your surveillance duties Sandy', murmured Jackie dryly.

'I figure it will take our friend Domingo at least a week to get himself organised but thereafter we will have to be on our guard. In the meantime this will give Karen plenty of time for her to acquaint me with the immediate district'.

'Okay Sandy in that case we insist you join us for dinner every night for the next week – after that I guess we will have to give you your free rein – see you later'. And with that George Fields left the room.

Niles left the house via the rear entrance of the West wing and strode off towards the Black smithy. He got the impression that the Fields were still not convinced that Domingo was going to bring his vendetta to the states. He'd only walked ten yards when young Karen materialised along side him.

'I hear I'm to show you around the house and grounds Sandy'. She smirked.

'I reckon so – I'll just dump this small travel bag, (which contains Niles total worldly possessions) in the flat and I'm all yours', he grinned.

Niles looked at Karen thoughtfully. It seemed that

she had shaken off all the horrors of her South American ventures. It was amazing just how quick the very young are at absorbing the unusual horrors of life and still surface as though nothing had happened. I hope to Christ no cretin thinks of exposing her to counselling thought Niles – all it will achieve is to reopen the wound that time has all but healed.

Karen took him around the mansion and out houses. The mansion faced south and as he had noted from the air was shaped like a squared 'U' The longest part of the building, the front, facing south, must have been seventy to eighty yards long whilst the two wings were at least twenty yards long and the whole building was three stories high. The whole edifice appeared to have been built from large solid stone blocks and roofed with large red tiles. At the front of the mansion there were three steps going up to the large double mahogany doors. The main entrance was roofed with the same large red tiles as the main building and was supported on four large colonnades. It was impressive. Just inside the main door on the left was the security room where all the sensors and control switches for the entire estate and house were located.

As they walked the estate he noted that initially the security looked good. A six foot high wall with an electronic sensing wire on top which increase the height of the wall to about eight feet surrounded the estate. The sensing wires were apparently wired to the main security room (according to Theo's brief) which was located just inside the main entrance to the mansion. The main security room was manned twenty four hours a day by two armed security guards. At infrequent intervals one of the guards patrolled the perimeter of the estate. These guards were in addition to the four body guards employed to look after Fields.

However as Karen took Niles around the estate he noted that there were plenty of shrubs , trees and bushes located around the mansion which was pleasing to the eye but never-the-less offered good cover to anyone trying to approach the mansion unnoticed.

He also noted that there were eight powerful arc lamps mounted on the corners of the mansion just below the overhangs of the roof. Karen told him that they were switched on every night.

To the rear of the mansion - facing north, there were six other buildings not counting the smithy and the largest building to the north; the stables.

He was pleased to note that the smithy, where he would be living, was slightly isolated from the other buildings but at the same time would give him a good field of view of most of the mansion and the other outbuildings including the stables. The only blind spot was the eastern side of the mansion and the garages which were locate there.

Niles pointed to the stables and said, 'how many horses do you have in the stables Karen?'

'There are ten racing horses and another five which the family use for riding. The racing horses are usually only ridden by the professional staff. Quite often some of the racing horses will be away for four or five days if they're at a race meeting'.

'I'm surprised your father has the time to train horses'.

'Actually, the horses belong to my mother. My mother came from a family in the east who are renowned horse breeders. And although daddy is a good rider mummy is a much better one. I can't wait to get you on a horse Sandy so I can show you the rest of the estate'.

'You mean there is more?' He queried.

'Oh yes, this is only the garden within the wall, our grounds go for a long way to the north. To see it all we would need to be on horse back'.

He realised just how much bigger things were in the States when compared to the UK, 'Karen the sooner you show me the estate the happier I'll be'.

He decided that the best way of getting around such a big area was probably on horse back or riding an Autocross motor cycle. He decided that he was going to make sure he had access to both!

Chapter 28

Bogotá

Domingo gingerly stamped his leg. He winced as he felt the pain stab up through his leg. 'Bastards' he muttered to himself.

It had taken two weeks for Domingo's leg to heal sufficiently enough for him to walk without a stick, Despite the odd twinge of pain it was time to get down to business. Fields and his family were about to get hammered, it was time to continue his vendetta against them.

It had taken Domingo some time to get his own men organised. Had the other members of the Cartel agreed his plans would have been further advanced but as they declined to continue the fight to the States he'd had to wait until he was fit enough to get things organised.

Francesco decided that he would have to call in some favours with the Senators on their payroll in the States. They could help to get the layout of the Fields home which he assumed would be well guarded. He decided to give Sam Jackson a call on the secure line. He knew the bastard would squeal like a stuck pig when Domingo put it to him he'd just have to get his tough shit ticket punched he thought.

His third attempt was successful. 'Jackson here – what can I do for you Francesco?'

'I need some information of the location and layout of the Fields residence and as soon as possible' ranted Domingo

'Look you crazy bastard if you are thinking of making a hit in this country you must be crazier than I thought. Don't you realise that the Defence Secretary is guarded by members of the American Secret Service. And further more this man is a personal friend of the President of the United States. If you did get through and kill Fields or one of his family then you would probable find your self number one on the CIA's hit list'.

'No way', snarled Domingo. 'I'll never leave this country and although they can suspect it's me they won't be able to prove it'.

'If you think that will save you from retribution Francesco your crazy. Be that as it may there's no way I'm going to get involved in such a mad cap scheme. You start fucking about with members of the United States Government and you're going to end up paddling in deep shit Francesco'.

'Now you look here you jumped up gringo arse hole. You've taken our money for the past three years and I've no qualms about making this information available to the American Press and Authorities. I'm not asking you to get involved with the actual hit – you'd probably fuck it up anyway – all I want from you, Thornton or Beck is a drawing of the Fields residence – Jesus Christ! That's not much to ask for considering the money we've put your way'.

'Don't talk so bloody stupid Domingo – if or when one of the Fields gets killed the shit's going to hit the fan. There'll be a regiments worth of FBI agents crawling all over the case. Do you imagine that the American Authorities won't find a link between you and me after they've investigated the killing? It's already common knowledge that your guys tried to rape and murder his wife and daughter down in the Colombian rain forest'.

'Lets get this straight Jackson I'm not asking, I'm telling you - if you don't produce a sketch or drawing showing the layout of the Field's residence then I'm going to blow the whistle on you bastards and leave you up to your necks in shit and you can sort it out State side – they can do fuck all to me down here, so make your mind up'.

'Okay! Okay! Leave it with me and I'll see if we can approach some one who works on the estate and pay them to produce the goods. How do you want the plan delivered, I can hardly fax it to you'.

'I'll give you the telephone number of a certain Mr Chase who arranges goods to be delivered to me. He's due down here next week – so make sure that he has the plan with him. No excuses Jackson – No plan, then the American Press get all the information regarding our deal over the past three years'.

'Okay Domingo you're a bastard but I'll get your plan but make sure the bloody thing can never be traced back to me'.

'That will be a problem for you, not me. Here is the telephone number of Mr Chase. He lives in Philadelphia which I believe is not far from Washington. I'll phone him today to let him know of our arrangement then you can phone this evening and make your own plans'. Domingo passed Chase's number to Jackson and terminated the call.

Sam Jackson was absolutely seething but the truth of the matter was that having accepted money from the Cartel there was nothing he could do about it. He and his two compatriots were caught between a rock and a hard place. If Domingo ever leaked the details of their illegal scheme to the press their political careers were finished, in fact they would be lucky to escape a jail sentence.

Sam Jackson struck pay dirt on his second phone call to Carl Beck who was into horse racing and had actually been to the Field's residence to purchase a race horse. But more to the point; Beck was able to suggest that there was a Motel/Tavern called the 'Ace of Spades'. According to Beck, there were quite a few layabouts and casual workers who were sometimes employed at the Field's residence who often gathered there in the evening to play pool and drink.

Jackson managed to get hold of Chase that same evening.

'Hi there this is Senator Jackson here; it appears that we have a mutual friend who has asked me a favour and he has suggested you as a means of getting this information to him. I would rather not discuss the details over the phone and would like to meet you tomorrow somewhere that's convenient to both of us'.

'I'll need more information than your offering to come a hundred some odd miles. Who the hell is this 'mutual friend for a start?'

'You've been talking to the person concerned during the last week during your adventures in South America – further more, he was supposed to have already phoned you today. That's as much as I'm going to venture over the phone'.

'I think I'm with you now' growled Chase. 'Look I have to go to Baltimore tomorrow so I could continue to Washington and meet you in the evening at a Motel called 'The Herons Keep'. It's on Route 295 adjacent the, Frederick Douglas National History Site. You can't miss it. I often use the Motel when on business in Washington. I could meet you there at nine in the evening – how does that grab you?'

'Yeh, I think I've passed it driving to the Kennedy Memorial Stadium. Okay Chase I look forward to seeing you tomorrow night. Although I will not have the information at that stage we can discuss when and where to meet at a later date.

Chase put the phone down and sat there thinking to himself. He was one of those people who liked to pick his own friends and acquaintances. He was also nervous about letting people know that he was an associate of Drug Barons from Colombia. His Arms business was a most secretive affair, he normally only mixed with people of his own choosing, so he was not keen at having his services being recommended by a third party. He decided to make some discrete enquiries about the good senator before the day was out.

Sam Jackson got back to Domingo that same evening.

'Domingo I have some good news for you. I think I've established a means of getting a plan of the Fields residence and, providing we splash enough money around some possible helpers who hang out in a nearby Tavern. However, it will take a couple of weeks to get it all together so you'll have to be patient'.

'I don't want to wait a couple of weeks and I am not keen on using hombres who hang out so close to the Fields house', snarled Domingo.

'Look Domingo we will have to go gentle with this plan. We can't just rush into the house and start drawing plans especially as they are expecting some sort of revenge action from you'.

'How the hell are they expecting action from me? Nobody has told them of my intentions. You and your friends are the only people who know what I intend. And my amigos down here won't grass - so how will they be expecting trouble?'

'Well the consensus of opinion at this end is that it will take at least two weeks to draw up the plans and get them delivered to you. That's the best we can do without making it patently obvious who's responsible for planning the hit. Take it or leave it'.

'Okay but not a day longer – in the meantime I will

send two of my own men to recce' the area and try and recruit some local s to help out. But rest assured the actual kidnapping or hit will be carried out by my own men'.

'That's your problem and the less I know about it the better but I would point out that your Latino men will stand out like balls on a bull terrier in this area – this is not Miami you know'.

'That's my worry', snarled Domingo. 'You just concentrate on getting the plans of the Field's house and the immediate surrounding area to me on time and leave the rest to me'.

Domingo slammed the phone down but then decided that he would need all of two weeks to get a suitable plan together. He had just the right two guys in mind to send to the States. They were his wife's sister's twins. Their mother had given them movie cowboy names – Grant and Rory a popular fashion these days in South America. However the Cortez twins were both very bright young men and were already moving up the ranks of the Cartel and had been ear marked to take on managerial positions. Another good point in their favour was that they had finished their education at Miami University. They both spoke with a genuine American accent and knew their way around the States – they would be ideal,

Chapter 29

Riverside Gardens

Niles settled down at the Field's residence quickly and smoothly. Karen was proving to be an eager guide and had Niles up on a horse within the first twenty four hours. It was now a week since their arrival and he was just beginning to get some feeling back into his butt. Karen had been an unwitting hard task master, failing to realise just how physically debilitating it was to learn to ride at Niles's age. He now had good background knowledge of the extensive estate. But he was now beginning to feel edgy. They were approaching the time frame when Domingo's hoods were likely to appear.

He'd also taken an interest in the forge located beneath his sleeping quarters. As a young boy of sixteen Niles had initially trained as an Engineer and part of the so called allied Trade Training was a course on Blacksmithing.

During the evening after his flying training which was progressing smoothly (he had passed his technical exams on the Air law and his progress on the S76 was almost complete) he spent two to three hours in the Smithy making his own tools and was attempting to repair a large wrought iron gate that should have hung at the entrance of the estate. The gate had been badly buckled when one of the estate drivers returning from a race meeting failed to stop quickly enough and crashed into and bent the gates. (George Fields was not too happy about the state of the Range Rover either. The gates had rammed the radiator back onto the engine putting the vehicle off the road for two weeks).

Before going to the Smithy Niles had established a routine of riding around the estate and checking for signs of any one laying up to keep the estate under observation. Karen accompanied Niles on these rides but was not aware of what he was looking for. So far so good – he'd found no indications of a lie up position. But he remained convinced that if any one wanted to get at one of the Fields family then they'd have to carry out some form of reconnaissance before attempting it.

Karen insisted on riding with Niles whilst he was conducting these surveys. Therefore he always went armed; it would have been too easy to snatch Karen from an unarmed escort during these rides. She was now spending most of her free time with Niles and despite the age difference their relationship had become more like a brother and sister rather than a bodyguard and his principle. After a while, and before the family realised it, she was in the Smithy assisting him in repairing the estate gates.

Initially Jackie Fields was not amused and George Fields was not particularly happy about it either. They doted on their young daughter and had planned great things for her future and being a blacksmith wasn't one of them. However (after a few tears) they finally relented but insisted that she wore protective clothing. By the time they had finished kitting Karen out she looked more like an alien from out of space rather that a lovely eleven year old girl.

When Karen had all her kit on the only part of her that

Niles could recognise was the end of her cute snub nose. Her parents were dammed sure that her that her complexion was not going to be impaired by any flying sparks. He allowed Karen to stay for about an hour in the evening before she was hustled off to her parents. He suspected that George and Jackie were a little piqued at Karen's attachment to him. However her parents felt that whilst she was with him she was as safe as she could be under the present circumstances.

His introduction to the local social life was orchestrated by three of the other members of the security team. They took him to the nearest tavern to the estate, called the 'Ace of Spades', it was not straight forward. As the name implied, there was a strong Irish clientele. Although there was no doubting that Ace of Spades was the nearest drinking hole, He was certain that he was being trailed down there to get a rough ride. He'd established a good working arrangement with Theo and Homer he sensed that Mike Williams and Jake Lattice still resented his presence. He also suspected that they were jealous of his close relationship with the Fields family.

The tavern was located on the main road towards the small town of Lorton about five miles from the Field's estate. The building was set well back from the road and could have been easily missed by a stranger unless instructed of its whereabouts. The large car park to the front contained about eight vehicles – mostly of the pickup variety, which gave an indication of the type of person that frequented the bar. The main door was a double hinged affair which opened to the middle. With a green shamrock crest nailed to the top of the door lintel to let all who entered to know what to expect. Mike led with Homer and Jake in close attendance followed by Niles to the rear.

If he'd any doubts about the antagonism of the Secret Services agents who guarded Fields it was quickly confirmed the moment they entered the bar.

'Hey you guys meet one of the new addition working up at our estate', Mike Williams had announced as they walked in through the door to the bar. 'He's a Limey just in case you can't make out his accent'.

There was about eight guys in the bar most of whom would have been described as 'red necks' or casual labourers. William's remark had the intended effect – all chat ceased immediately.

The three sat at the bar were already somewhat under the weather and seemed in a belligerent mood. The one in the middle of the three sat at the bar turned round and gave Niles a sneering smirk – he had long black hair, a long crooked nose with an unshaven blue chin. He wore a lumber jack chequered shirt and a dirty pair of corduroy trousers and was shod in a pair of scruffy Hi Tec trainer shoes. He looked about thirty three and obviously considered himself a hard man.

'And where were you when the millions of Irish were dying of famine in Ireland at the turn of the century', snarled blue chin.

'Actually', replied Sandy in a exaggerated upper class English accent that he knew would infuriate 'blue chin' 'I think you must be referring to the period 1845-9. Now even a thick brained arsehole like you must know I wasn't even born then'.

'What the fuck do you mean? Are you trying to start trouble? - Because if you are, I'm just the man to sort you out – you limey bastard'.

'I never start trouble' said Niles. 'But I nearly always finish it. And before you go ranting on about the troubles in Ireland during the middle nineteenth century I suggest you get your facts straight'.

'I know my facts alright,' continued Blue chin. 'I'll have you know that most of the people in this bar support 'The Cause' and the sooner we kick the fucking Brits' out of

Ireland the better'.

'Using your line of argument', laughed Niles. 'You might just as well vacate the States and hand it back to the Indians. Further more I know that most of you idiots in this bar support the IRA – that's why I have been brought here in the first place'. And with that last statement he gave the three who had brought him to the bar a withering look. He could feel the black side of his nature bubbling up and tried to contain it. At least Homer had the grace to look embarrassed and shameful but Mike Williams and Jake Lattice just smirked.

'Put a fucking sock in it Luke,' snarled the man sat on the left of 'Blue chin.

But Blue chin was now spoiling for a fight. Not realising that the worried look flittering across Nile's face was due to the damage he might inflict on 'blue chin'. He really thought Niles was frightened of him.

'Look you Limey bastard I know you weren't alive at the time of the potato famine (overstating the obvious) your fucking limey fore bearers were and they did nothing to help the Irish who were dying at the time in there thousands.

'No you look here you lump of bog shit I'm sick to the teeth of hearing Irish men whining about the potato famine that happened a hundred and fifty years ago. You're talking about a period in England when little girls of eight or nine years of age were pulling coal carts on their hands and knees down the coal mines. You're talking about a period when Girls and Boys of seven and eight years of age were working fifteen hours a day down the coal pits. You're talking of period when young boys who were forced to crawl up and sweep chimneys. You're talking of a period when there was no compulsive schooling. A high percentage couldn't read or write and over ninety percent of the population had never heard of Ireland, and half the remaining ten percent didn't even know where the fuck it was. You're talking of a period when you could be flogged to within an inch of your life for stealing a loaf of bread. Christ! It was not many years previous to that age when the Navy used to keel haul insolent sailors - and not many survived the ordeal. You're talking of days when there was no television; there was no wireless or radios. Most people had never left the village they were born in. How the hell were the normal Brits' supposed to know that there was a famine in Ireland? What do you imagined the workers talked about after working non-stop for fifteen hours every day. They were so tired they had their only hot meal of the day and rolled into bed. Christ almighty - they only bathed once a week. You actually believed that they discussed the problems of Ireland in there free time. They never had any free time you thick headed bastard. Certainly the politicians knew but they have always been duplicitous bastards since the beginning of time. Finally, let me ask you a question. More to the point what were the rich Irish land owners doing about the famine – fuck all! Most moved their families to the UK and lived the life of Riley. Now! If you're really looking to hang the blame on someone the rich landowners are the ones responsible for not doing anything. Further more, if the famine had happened in England what do you think the Irish would have done even supposing they got to hear of it? Fuck all!'

Niles's attacking tirade had taken the whole bar by surprise. The American Irish had become so used to the English being on the defensive when tackled about the potato famine that they'd never considered the realities and lack of communications that existed in the middle of the ninetieth century.

'You bloody Americans', he continued. 'Are fond of applying today's social sensibilities and means of communications of the twentieth century about injustices committed over one hundred years ago by other nations but conveniently forgetting the way your forbearers treated the

American Indian. Don't forget that it was the American settlers that broke just about every treaty drawn up with the Indians. Yet, you stand there and condemn the UK for not handing over part of the UK to the Irish. This; despite the fact that in every referendum carried out in Northern Ireland concerning union with Southern Ireland over ninety percent of the population has stated that they wished to remain part of the UK. If we were to apply the same cockeye logic to the States the United Nations would be insisting that the US be handed back to the American Indians'.

This last outburst from Sandy Niles caused a stunned silence at first and then arguments started all around the bar. Niles had said his bit and was determined not to get involved any further. He was very angry with himself and he had broken one of his own axioms which he had practiced over the past three years, which was, when in a strange environment try and maintain a low profile. However; his main worry was controlling his devil within. A side of his natured he'd never known of until backed into some violent situations during his past three years in Venezuela.

He walked up to the bar and ordered a Budweiser as it was the only American beer that he could think of.

However 'blue chin' (it appears that he answered to the name of Luke) was still looking to make trouble and although Niles had been determined to avoid trouble it looked as though Luke was not finished yet.

'See here you Limey scum bag I don't like the way you called us fucking Americans', Blue chin emphasised his aggressive tone by sticking his chin into Sand's face. 'I find your tone fucking offensive'.

Niles tried to back off but 'Blue chin,' interpreted this as a sign of fear and was determined to make him back down.

Finally Niles lost his temper.

'Look you overblown bag of shit you have done nothing but spoil for a fight since I came into this bar - now if you want a punch up just say the word'.

'Blue chin' was brought up short by Niles's direct invitation to fight. He gave him a 'hard man' look but Niles just responded with a whimsical smile. Finally, Luke the Blue chin backed off and went back to the bar and sat down between his two friends.

Niles sat down at a table by himself and was eventually joined by the other three security agents.

He decided he was not going to mince words.

'Thanks to you three morons my plan to infiltrate the local life and this bar in particular without stirring up a lot of interest has just been blown sky high. You guys are supposed to be some of the best trained agents in the world and yet you stoop to a stupid trick like this. I don't know too much about 'body guards' but it would seem to me that the less obvious you are the easier it should be to do your job'.

'You look here you jumped up Limey bastard we don't need you to tell us how to do our jobs', snarled Mike Williams.

'No but somebody ought to. I met an American agent in Colombia called Chris Brooker and quite frankly he's worth all three of you put together. And further more if you want to keep calling me a Limey bastard you can all fuck off and find yourselves another table to sit at'.

Mike Williams and Jake Lattice both got up and sat at another table. Homer however, remained seated and gave Niles a big warm grin.

'You don't take much shit do you Sandy'.

'It's not that Homer - I meant what I said about being professional. If you wanted to keep the Field's residence under surveillance this bar would be the ideal place to recruit the men to do so'. Niles waved his hand around the bar to emphasise the fact that the number of people in the bar had already increased to about sixteen.

'Do you really think that these Colombian guys would

come all the way up here to attack the Defence Secretary and his wife?' Homer asked

'Personally I'm not sure, but the consensus of opinion of the people that know Domingo in Colombia is that he will pursue his vendetta to the States. I figure it will take a week or so for him to get his forces organised and then we can expect trouble'.

'Jesus you mean any day now Sandy – you have all been back from Colombia for a week today so we could be expecting trouble any day now'.

'Exactly, hence the reason for me being so touchy about that stupid and unnecessary incident just now. I'd hoped to sidle gently into this place and give all the locals the once over without being noticed. I'll be lucky to get out of here tonight without having to flatten that drunken idiot Luke over there or what ever you call him'.

'I think I can sort that out for you Sandy. I'll take care of him for you'.

'Thanks Homer but it will only delay the confrontation until the next time. I'm ready to leave now and providing Luke keeps clear I'll leave peacefully but I'm finished taking any more agro' off him'. And with that Niles finished his drink and got to his feet to leave.

Unfortunately Luke was not prepared to let the matter drop and sidled over blocking his path to the door.

'So our Limey bastard is leaving - what's the matter shit head don't you like our company?'

Niles never said a word. He grabbed Luke by the front of his shirt and gave him a hard push which he quickly reversed into a tremendous pull. The initial reaction to his push had caused Luke to resist it which reinforced the final vigorous pulling motion. The net result caused Luke to fly across the room smashing through three tables, slamming his head against the wall and ending up in a crumbled heap against it.

Niles didn't even bother to turn his head as he left the bar. The people in the bar just stood and gaped at the unconscious body of Luke crumpled against the far wall.

There was a stunned silence in the bar that lasted for about thirty seconds. To the uninitiated it looked as though Niles had demonstrated tremendous physical strength when in fact, Luke had helped matters by his positive resistance to the first push by Niles.

Luke's two drinking partners rushed over to where he lay in a tangle against the wall and dragged him to his feet.

'What the fuck happened?' Luke looked dazedly around the room trying to establish just what had occurred to him.

'I think you were just hit by a tornado – you had better sit down until your senses catch up with you', muttered one of his drinking partners.

Outside in the car park Niles was still seething at having lost his temper and drawn attention to himself.

Mike Williams and Jake Lattice were both looking somewhat cress fallen but all for the wrong reasons. They had still not appreciated why Sandy Niles was so angry at having drawn attention to himself.

As they boarded the Jeep Cherokee Niles turned on Mike and Jake and snarled. 'So much for me trying to mingle with the local population without being noticed, the whole idea of this night's venture was for me to have a quiet reconnaissance of all the local watering holes without drawing attention to myself. Hasn't it occurred to you three arse holes that if some one wants to get local knowledge of the Fields estate that one of the first places they are going visit is the immediate drinking Inns or whatever the hell you call them in the States. All anyone need do to get information about the Field's Estate is pour drinks all night into one of those arse holes in there and he could get a complete run down on the whole estate'.

'Just who the fuck to you think you are speaking to

Niles', snarled Williams.

Before anyone else could say any more Homer Johnson shouted,

'Listen up you guys – Sandy's absolutely correct. We could have seriously compromised the Fields family tonight. We acted like complete arseholes and Sandy is completely right. We knew that most of the guys that hang out in the 'Ace of Spades' were of Irish extraction and all three of us knew that introducing Sandy as English was going to raise the temperature. We got more that we bargained for. And if Theo ever finds out what happened tonight we may well end up looking for employment'.

Niles just grunted. 'That's up to you guys but in future I'll recce' the local watering holes on my own'.

There was an embarrassed silence for most of the ten minute journey back to the estate.

Eventually Mike Williams who was driving the Jeep burst out laughing.

'Christ I bet that's the quickest flying lesson that Luke's ever had. He never touched the first two tables. I bet the poor bastard is still trying to work out how he ended up in a crumpled heap against the far wall'.

Mike's last remark broke the tension. And Jake added.

'It's a good job he landed on his head otherwise he could have done himself a serious injury'.

This last remark finally dispelled all the animosity and Mike said.

'Look Sandy we got off to a bad start but how about coming back to our quarters and having a night cap?'

'Could we make that in an hours time I like to check the high ground around the estate just before last night and first thing in the morning'.

'So that's what you and young Karen get up to when you ride off every morning' grinned Homer.

Niles laughed. 'Actually Karen is teaching me to ride

a horse and I might add, doing extremely well. But what Karen doesn't know is that, when we ride around the estate there are four geographical high spots that I always recce'. I'd rather you didn't tell her why we always ride over these pieces of high ground – I don't wish to worry her'.

'I'm beginning to see why the boss has hired you Sandy' said Jake. 'You are obviously a deep thinker. I must say in all the time we have been guarding the boss we have never considered recce'ing the ground out side the estate'.

'Yeh but your task is somewhat different to mine', he replied. 'Your job is to protect the boss from a possible assassination attempt carried out by some crackpot who'd probably try it on an opportunity basis. We are fairly certain this Drug Baron is going to try and kidnap or kill the boss or possibly Jackie or more likely Karen. At the moment the Drug Cartel doesn't know of the boss's son, Douglas I think you call him. I didn't know of his existence until recently'.

Mike gave Niles a hard look, 'You speak of when rather than if this is going to happen Sandy – are you that certain that these Colombians are going to make an attack?'

He nodded his head thoughtfully. 'Yes! And it's going to take place within the next month at the latest, so now you know why I'm taking this job so seriously. I was hoping for a couple of associates who are coming out from the UK to join me but I'm informed it will be another two weeks at the earliest before they can get here'.

'These associates Sandy, are they a couple of the guys who were with you in Colombia?' Asked Mike

'Yeh they were both members of the SAS and are now retiring from the service and are going to set up a security operation over here'.

They arrived back at the estate and Mike, Homer and Jake sauntered off to their billet whilst Niles went to the stables to saddle his horse knowing that Karen would already be there waiting for their evening ride.

'You're late Sandy' said Karen good naturally.' So I had Josh saddle 'Tee bone' for you'.

'Tee bone' was the name of the horse that had been presented for Niles to ride. It was a bloody great rangy Grey. It must have been all of seventeen hands high. When Niles had first been introduced to the horse he had asked for a set of step ladders to mount it. However 'Tee bone' had a phlegmatic nature and was not easily spooked. Apart from the fact Niles felt he was a long way from the ground he was an ideal horse for learning to ride.

'The usual route Sandy?' as she reined her horse towards the estate gate.

'Yes please Karen I admire the view we can get from the high ground – you lead and I'll follow'.

Karen set of at a gentle canter with Niles following close behind. He liked to keep her in front so he could study the ground for any signs of disturbance caused by some one lying up to observe the estate. This enabled him to do so without arousing Karen's curiosity. As they transited each high point he studied the ground carefully for any signs of human presence, such as cigarette butts food wrappers crushed grass – any thing that indicated that someone had spent some time at the vantage locations.

By the time they got to the third location (to the north of the estate) the light was beginning to fail but Niles thought he could see the faint tyre marks of a motor cycle. However he could see no other evidence but he was determined to give the spot a thorough search the next day when the light was better.

By the time they got to the fourth high point it was too dark to make out any signs on the ground so Niles said to Karen.

'Okay my lovely it's time we made tracks for home or I'm going to get it in the neck for keeping you out after your bed time'.

'Can't I help you in the forge tonight?' Karen asked.

'No, not tonight pet - it's too late and further more, your Mother and Father will accuse me of monopolising all your spare time'.

They arrived at the stables, rubbed and bedded the horses for the night and Niles escorted Karen to the main house. He had decided to have a quiet word with George Fields about the motor cycle signs he had seen to the North of the estate.

After Jackie had departed taking Karen off to bed Niles said. 'Boss could I have a quick word with you before Jackie gets back?'

'Fine Sandy - fire away'.

'Whilst trailing around the estate you know I make a habit of looking over the high ground close to the estate. When we got to the northern high point just to the south of the small copse it looked as though someone had been up there with a motor cycle. Unfortunately the light was failing so it was too dark to make a detailed examination. What I would like to do tomorrow is give this area a miss first thing in the morning when out riding with Karen and then check it out later on - say noon. If I start making detailed examination with Karen there she is bound to ask what I'm up to - so I'll take another look later. If there is some one up there snooping I might be able to catch them. In any event I will be able to examine the ground more closely'.

'That sounds fine to me Sandy. I take it you don't want me to say anything to Jackie at the moment?'.

Niles nodded his head in agreement. 'No - it could be something completely innocent. There's no point in alarming Jackie un-necessarily but we are approaching the time frame when I figure our Colombian friend is likely to make his move, so we can't be too careful'.

'Well I'll leave it all up to you Sandy you seem to have a feel about these situations. By the way, in three days time we are having a Special Select Committee meeting down here for two days. So I'm afraid there will be another dozen guys here but there will also be a significant increase in the number of security men around to keep an eye on things'.

'I take it these will all be people you know and trust Boss'.

'Well let's put it this way Sandy. They are all Senators and people I know but as for trust! I fancy that some of them would skin their own grandmothers if they could make a profit out of it. Having said that - I don't think that any of them are likely to be a hit man'.

'That's true', murmured Sandy. 'But one of them could have been bribed to check the layout of the house and the security system'.

'By Christ Sandy, you sure as hell have got a suspicious mind. However I will instruct Theo and his boys to keep an eye open for anyone acting in a strange manner. What about you Sandy, you will obviously get a security pass but will you be working in unison with Theo and his boys or would you prefer to have a roving commission',.

'I would prefer to act as a free agent coming and going as I feel the situation warrants. And I would be grateful if my role was not disclosed to your Senator friends. Obviously all the security guys will have to know, but the fewer visitors that know what I'm up to the better.'

Okay, oh, Incidentally Sandy; I have still to get you a rifle – I presume you our happy with the Beretta pistol that you brought out of Colombia but try as I can I can't seem to get my hands on a Holland & Holland. But I will keep trying'.

'That's fine by me boss I prefer a bolt action because it gives better accuracy at long ranges but anything will do so long as it's accurate out to six hundred meters or so. I don't anticipate having to fire in access of that'.'

'Okay Sandy I'll see you tomorrow and keep me briefed

about the problem to the north'.

He bid goodnight and went back to his sleeping quarters.

Just as he reached the door of his flat the phone rang.

It was Jackie Fields. 'Sandy we are having a few drinks tomorrow night with the Mendoza's and they have asked if you will be joining us. I said you probably could come but I don't want to interfere with your security arrangements. But we would be grateful if you could come for an hour or so. What do you think?'

I'd love to but I wont want to stay too long – I'm afraid I'm not much use at making small talk or even large talk for that matter', he laughed.

'That's great I'll let them know you will be joining us goodnight for now'.

Jackie turned to her husband and said. 'He's condescended to join us. Getting Sandy to socialise is akin to drawing teeth'.

'There are times', mused George field, 'when I wonder if Sandy is gay, he seems to take very little notice of women'.

'When I mentioned it in Colombia you seemed positive that he wasn't and now I tend to think your original assessment was correct - I have an idea that he's very shy of women despite the fact that he is very attractive to them'.

'Aye Aye, said George Fields. 'Is something going on here that I am missing. Don't tell me my wife has gone overboard for Niles as well as my daughter'.

'Of course not but that doesn't stop me from appreciating that he is a very attractive man – and many of my friends think likewise. I have kept a careful eye on Sandy with our daughter and it's like watching her play with a god dam big guard dog. His only thoughts appear to concern her well being. I'd stake my life on it that he would never harm our girl'.

'I agree with you there. They seem to have formed a

special relationship which at times makes me feel positively jealous – but then I'm only her father'. George ended up laughing.

'Well George, if you want to observe humane behaviour at work, just watch Jenny Valdez when she arrives with the Mendoza's tomorrow night, every time she looks at Sandy when he's not aware of it she practically burns a hole in his back. I get the impression that if she makes a play for Sandy he's going to end up getting hog tied'.

'Jesus! You women', roared George Fields. 'She has only seen the man two or three times at the most and you're telling me she has designs on poor Niles'.

'Think back to our courting day's honey. You chased me until I caught you'.

'True, that's true', grinned George giving Jackie a big hug. 'I was a goner from the moment you decided I was to be your provider. That reminds me, I forgot to tell Sandy that a weapon he had been asking for has just arrived this evening. Never mind I'll tell him in the morning'.

Next morning the weather was absolutely gin clear with unlimited visibility. Whilst out riding with Karen, Niles decided to give the northern high spot a miss. He'd look at it around mid day to see if someone was lying up to survey the estate. He felt sure that something was going to happen within the week. He'd seen nothing to confirm this hunch but was almost willing to bet money on Domingo making a move before the week was out. As they used to say in the Army, "He could feel it in his water"

During their morning equestrian exercises Niles had taken to running along side 'Tee bone' holding on to the bridle – much to Karen's amusement.

'How I am supposed to turn you into one of the best riders in the County Sandy if you insist on running beside your horse instead of riding him'.

'Actually I'm just giving 'Tee bone' a rest while at the

same time it's getting me fit'.

'I honestly think you are losing weight Sandy – your looking very lean and sort of hungry'.

'That's the general idea my little blossom. All this good food you Americans eat was making me put on weight. Any way, it's time we turned for home otherwise you are going to be late for school'.

Although Douglas was boarding out to school Jackie Fields had resisted any attempt to have Karen at boarding School. Even more so after she was selected to star in the film about the American Peace Corps which they had finished filming in South America. She insisted that Karen had as near a normal up-bringing as possible.

When they got back to the stables Niles told Karen to hurry off or she would be late for School. 'I'll rub the horses down Karen you had better move or you're going to be late for school and I'll get it in the neck for holding you back'.

'Mummy always insists that I groom my own horse Sandy – She is quite insistent about it'.

'I know pet but it's my fault entirely so you run along and I'll groom 'Fredrick' and no one will be the wiser'.

Karen dashed off to get ready for school. Two additional security men had been hired to ride shot gun over Karen at school). Niles wandered over to the main house.

He knocked the door of Field's study and was bid to enter.

'Morning boss have you a few minutes?'

'Sure Sandy fire away'.

'Those suspicions I mentioned yesterday about some one laying up to the north of the estate. I gave the location a miss this morning. Karen's an intelligent girl and if she saw me making a detailed examination of the area she would ask what I was up to. I'll check it out later today and see if there has been any further disturbance up there. If I'm careful and there is someone there I might be able to catch a glimpse of who ever it is. When I approach If they have nothing to hide they'll stay put, on the other hand, if they mount their bike and roar off then I think we can assume that we are under surveillance'.

'Thanks Sandy I don't want to alarm the women and I understand from what Theo and the others are saying you think we could have an attack in the very near future'.

'Yes, but to be honest boss the only sign I have seen so far is the one I've just mentioned. It's just a 'gut feeling' I have and the time frame would be about right. By now Domingo has just about got his henchmen ready – and I don't think he is renowned for his patients. It's only a hunch but I think he will try and make a move in the very near future. I'm going to have a look at the northern area at mid day. If some one is using the location to survey the estate then by mid morning I think he will have left visible evidence'.

'I take it the area is too open for you to sneak up on them'.

'Yes I'm afraid so boss. I'll wander up there on horse back. If who ever it is has nothing to hide they will probable hang around and not bug out. As I mentioned however, if he or she gets aboard the motor cycle and roars off before I can recognise them I think we will have to assume that they are up to no good'.

'What do you recommend then Sandy?'

'I think we had better have a council of war this evening and discuss our options'.

'Okay let's have a talk before the Mendoza's get here tonight. Oh! And before I forget, that rifle you were asking for has arrived. Homer has taken it to your billet with about a hundred rounds of ammunition'.

'A hundred rounds! Christ it's a snipers rifle, what do you want me to do? – wipe out the American Senate'. Niles laughed.

'Well, Sandy that's a thought, but seriously, I thought

you might like to get some practice in. I can arrange for you to have some practice at the local National Guards ranges which are only half an hour's drive to the south. There is in fact a pistol range that the Secret Service guys use in the cellars of the main building here but it's only about twenty five metres long- not really long enough for use with a rifle. Ah! - there's my chopper, I'll have to go – see you this evening at six thirty Sandy with Theo and his guys'.

Niles went to his flat to check out the rifle he had ordered. It was sealed in its packing case. He eagerly opened the case.

It was a Heckler & Koch PSG1 7.62mm Snipers rifle. It weighed just less than 18lbs and had two magazines within the case, a 5 round and a 20 round one. The gun came with the standard 6 X 42 telescopic sight with an illuminated graticule, the graticule produced a red dot for thirty seconds which was plenty of time to get off a good shot. It fired a standard NATO round with a muzzle velocity of 2723ft/sec. and in good hands could produce a group of 3" to 4" at a range of 300 metres. The only thing that irked Niles was that it was semi-automatic and therefore lacked the accuracy at long range of a bolt action rifle – such is progress.

Niles had fired the PSG1 at the SAS ranges about six years ago and had been extremely impressed with it.

He quickly made arrangements to get down to the National Guard ranges and zeroed the Heckler & Koch rifle. He was impressed and although he hated to admit it the rifle was probably more accurate than his beloved Holland & Holland over shorter ranges. He shot off about twenty rounds and was finally satisfied with the results he achieved. 'Christ' he thought, 'with this beauty I could shoot the balls off a flea at a hundred metres'.

He returned to the estate just before midday and saddled up 'Tee bone'. He took a detour round to the north to try and disguise his approach. If there was some one up there surveying the estate and they were engrossed in what they were doing there was a chance that Niles might get close enough to see who it was.

He rode well to the east down into a grassy shallow re-entrant which gradually curved round to the north. However from here-on he would be climbing onto the high ground and become visible from the hill he was stalking. Niles tried to keep in the dead ground as long as possible. Anyone looking at the Field's residence would now have to turn round in order to see him, but he was still visible. He turned east. Rode until the small copse to the north of the high ground screened him. He then turned and rode south using the woods to screen his movement. When he'd made his way through the woods he was about four hundred yards from the apex of the hill. He noticed a motor cycle lying on the ground on the reverse side of the hill to the estate. Niles dismounted from 'T Bone. He grabbed the horse's bridle and gentle pulled its head against his own. At the same time cradling the horse's muzzle to prevent it from making any noise He continued towards the bike as stealthy as possible, unfortunately the ground was devoid of any cover. Suddenly; 'T Bone' threw up his head and snorted. A man who'd been kneeling on the top of the high ground turned and saw Niles; He was holding a large pair of binoculars in his right hand. He quickly stowed them and leaped onto the bike, started it up and rode off at break neck speed. There was no point in Niles trying to chase him on the horse. The guy must have accelerated to about fifty miles an hour on the grass. Further more, Niles's riding skill was not good enough to sustain a flat out gallop. He would probably have fallen off had he tried. Karen always maintained that they made quicker progress with him running along side 'Tee bone' than when he was riding him.

He'd managed to get to within two hundred yards before the guy had actually got the bike up and away. He was not sure but there was something familiar about the man but he couldn't quite place him. When he got to the top of the hill it was quite obvious that the guy had been there for some time. Further more, he was not very bright. He'd made no effort to disguise his presence – there were cigarette stubs two sandwich wrappers and the grass was flattened where he'd been lying. He was obviously not a professional.

Although Niles had not been able to collar the man, he'd now established that the estate was definitely under surveillance.

Chapter 30

The Meeting

Sam Jackson crossed the river Potomac south of Virginia on route 495. Turned north onto Route 295 passing through Bellevue then Congress Heights and had driven about another mile and a half before reaching the 'Heron's Keep' motel. He was seething with anger, caught up in a dangerous plan that he'd no wish to be associated with. Once he and his colleagues accepted the money from the Cartel to lobby in the Senate on their behalf they were trapped. Although their initial collusion with them had seemed rather innocuous subsequent events were proving to be more dangerous. He could feel himself being sucked into an opening abyss. At the moment he could see no way out.

The restaurant and bar were to the north of the living accommodation. The Motel was quite large and very popular with tourists. It was only just half eight in the evening the car park was already almost full. The building was well laid back from the main road but this was still not to Jackson's liking. He'd rather have had the meeting in a more secluded area where there was less chance of being seen and recognised.

He parked his car in the short time car park to the front of the building.

Jackson sat in his car for a while ostensibly to ensure that Chase would be there when he entered. However, he was also trying to work out just how the hell he and his compatriots could get out of their present predicament with Domingo without the bastard blowing the whistle on them. He would have to liaise with the other two and see just how the hell they could cut their ties with the Cartel. It was not going to be easy. At the moment they were just being dragged deeper and deeper into the mire. At nine o'clock, he gave a deep sigh, no nearer to a solution. Reluctantly he got out of his car and entered the restaurant carrying his brief case with the flap undone - the recognition signal that he and Chase had agreed on over the phone. The Motel was typically American – facing the main entrance was the reception desk manned by two employees. Immediately to the left was a passage leading off to the accommodation block. The passage to the right led to the dinning area and the licensed bar. Jackson just nodded to the receptionist, turned right and made his way to the large bar room. And entered, looked around cautiously.

Jackson didn't have to wait – no sooner was he through the door when he was tapped on the shoulder. He turned and was confronted by a nondescript looking guy in a well worn but expensive suit. The man was about five foot ten with receding hair who looked about fifty years old and physically was starting to go to seed. However from his bronze complexion he obviously spent much time in hot climates or, he was a sun tan bed addict. Having said that he was the type of man who could pass in a crowd completely unnoticed.

'Dr Jackson I presume', he smiled and offered his hand.

Jackson shook his hand and replied, 'Mr Chase I presume'.

'I have ordered a private room where we can have a meal and any drinks we require served. That way we can converse without being seen or overheard. I hope that's okay with you Jackson?'

'That's fine by me I was getting worried in case any one saw and recognised me. I don't mind telling you Chase I am getting sucked into something that I have no wish to be involved in'.

'Ditto that, I know exactly what you mean. However be that as it may, in my job I'm used to clandestine meetings so it's second nature for me to set things up so one can't be seen or heard'.

Chase led the way to the private room he had booked. It was typical Travel Lodge accommodation. A large double King size bed was set against the wall furthest from the window with a recess cupboard for hanging clothes adjacent to it. There were two comfortable arm chairs and the usual writing table with all the usual lodge brochures. Jackson settled down in the chair nearest to the window.

Chase sat in the remaining chair.

'Would you like a drink or anything to eat before we get down to business?'

It seemed obvious that he was as eager to get their business over and get to hell out of it as Jackson was.

'I see we have some drinks there' Jackson nodded to the drinks cabinet. 'I could murder a bloody big Scotch, I'm not interested in eating so if you agree, we can get on with the business – it shouldn't take more than ten minutes any way'.

Chase poured them both a scotch and handed one to Jackson.

'Well Jackson, have you managed to get a plan of the estate and the house?'

'Yes but it was a close run thing. Some bastard on horse back nearly caught the guy I had surveying the estate. Luckily he'd made a drawing of the house and estate when he arrived first thing in this morning. But whoever the horseman was I suspect his suspicions will have been aroused'.

Chase rubbed his chin thoughtfully, 'Yeah but that does not mean they know what is due to happen. All they know is that some one has been looking at the house and estate'.

'Well lets put it this way Chase - if I was George Fields and in view of what's just happed down in Colombia I would be bloody suspicious of any unannounced person within a mile of my house and I personally think he will take precautions accordingly. But trying to get some sense into that 'numb skull' Domingo is like trying to shove water up a ducks arse'.

'I know what you mean I have had dealings with him before and although he's not had a good education and therefore not considered academically clever he's extremely cunning and vicious to boot. However, in this case I don't think he realises just what he's taken on. The trouble with these South American Drug Barons is that most of them don't leave their own country and sphere of influence for fear of extradition. This gives them a very parochial outlook. Unfortunately, it also causes them to suffer from 'Delusions of Grandeur'. They assume they can wield the same amount of power outside Colombia as they do at home. Domingo has already been fingered by the DEA and knows that if he steps outside of Colombia into a country which has an extradition agreement with the States he'll end up a well known creek without a paddle. So! What information have you for me?'

'Well I have been given this hand sketch of the estate and the immediate surrounding area. But we are still trying to get a plan of the house layout. The layout for the house is not going to be easy. I'm there as a guest in a couple of days time as a member of the Special Select Committee and will be able to give you some idea of the general layout but I can't go trudging around the house without good reason and not arouse suspicion'.

Chase gave Sam Jackson a hard look, 'I'm due to fly to Colombia in three days time and I've no intentions of delaying my departure for you or Domingo. I'm acting as delivery boy only as a favour to Domingo. I've other business down there that has nothing to do with him so come Thursday night I'm on my way with or without your house plan – ok'!

Jackson looked pensive for a moment.

'If I arrange to meet you at the Airport Thursday evening and get you all the up to date information I can gather, will that be ok?'

'Sure - I depart at 2200hrs so you'll have to get the information to me by 2100hrs at the latest – okay - one more drink and then I'm going to hit the road. I don't think we should be seen together so it would make sense if you to left about 15 minutes after me'.

Sam Jackson nodded his head in agreement, 'sounds fine by me – the less time we spend together the less chance there is of us being associated'.

Later, as Sam Jackson drove home that night he was doing some hard thinking. Although he lived in a small town called, 'Burgundy Village' just four miles to the north of the Fields estate he had never visited them before. Under the present circumstances it would be difficult to ask to be shown around the house without raising suspicion. Especially if his visit was quickly followed by an attack on the Field's family, he would immediately become a possible suspect - and to try to snoop round the house without permission was even more fraught. But he had heard from a colleague that the Fields were having an impromptu get together tomorrow evening so he might try to get his friend to have him invited.

That evening, he phoned Al Thornton and was passed a

very interesting piece of information. It appeared that one of the security agents, a Jake Lattice, had got himself into serious debt by betting on the wrong horses. One of Al's estate workers, a man called Ben Hatfield, was a runner of the local betting syndicate who collected bets for the local area had provided this information. If this man Hatfield could pressure Jake Lattice to produce a plan of the house for a substantial sum of money it would negate Jackson from possibly compromising himself. The trick was to get Hatfield to make the approach to the security guy and hopefully keep Jackson name clear of any of the intrigue. Sam decided he was going to have to work on this aspect. The trouble was it was going to take time and he didn't have much of that.

Jackson decided that he would check with Ben Hatfield this evening. From what Hatfield had told Thornton the security guys often used, the 'Ace of Spades' to have the odd drink. Jackson figured that for a reasonable 'kick back' Ben Hatfield could be induced to raise the subject with this security guy; Jake Lattice. Thornton had also said that this guy had two failed marriages and the alimonies were an additional problem to his mounting gambling debt.

Although the Secret Service guys were strictly vetted before being employed by the Secret Service once they had been accepted it was much easier for their morals and integrity to erode without it coming to the service's attention. Subsequent vetting checks on serving members of the Secret Service tended to be taken as read.

Sam Jackson couldn't raise Ben Hatfield until midnight. He had been out drinking at the, 'Ace of Spades'. Sam put the proposition to him.

'Do you know this guy Jake Lattice that works at the Field's estate – he's one of the Secret Service men employed to look after the Defence Secretary'.

'Yep sure do', said Ben Hatfield.

'Right I know it's gone midnight but I want to meet

you tonight. You could earn yourself a substantial amount of money. Can we meet outside Al Thornton's main gate tonight?'

'It had better be a substantial amount to start meeting you at this time of the night', growled Ben Hatfield.

'How do thirty big ones sound?'

'You have just convinced me that it is imperative that we meet straight away', laughed Ben Hatfield.

'Okay but remember no mention of my name or any involvement in what I'm asking you to do'.

'You're on – I can be there in fifteen minutes okay'.

'Great it will only take me twenty minutes'

Although Jackson was splashing money around it was not coming out of his pocket. The Cortez twins were acting as Domingo paymaster and it seemed that money was no object. It would also seem safer if Jackson could arrange for Ben Hatfield to get the security guy to phone or meet with the Cortez twins. To bribe the security guy was going to cost serious money and only the twins could sanction the amount required. And more to the point, if the twins dealt with Lattice personally it kept Jackson's name out of the loop.

Chapter 31

The Party

Niles was not looking forward to the evening drinks. Initially the party was only going to consist of the Fields, The Mendoza's, Jenny Valdez and Niles. Unfortunately, because of their adventures in Colombia many of the Fields' friends had asked to be invited to hear their stories first hand. The party had swollen to thirty or even more. If fact, Jackie was not sure just how many would be coming.

In view of the present security situation he thought it rather foolhardy of them to throw open their house to so many people, particularly as they were now approaching the time frame when he expected Domingo to make his move. The Fields were typical Americans, very open handed and generous to a fault. Unfortunately they had also become very insular and not really believing that they were open to attack. Niles was convinced that Domingo would be trying to get as much information about the layout of the Fields house as he could. The party would be an ideal opportunity to "case the joint". He was also getting worried about his role as guardian to Jackie and Karen Fields. It was hard enough trying to do the job without being asked to socialise at the same time. It also added to the problem of having to scrutinise the additional people invited to the house, although it could be said that they were the responsibility of Theo' team. Even now, after reporting that the house appeared to have been under surveillance he was not convinced that the Fields and their security personnel took the threat of an attack seriously.

He'd warned George Fields that the house could be surveyed during the party but his only remark was not to tell his wife or daughter. Niles held his council but had now taken to wearing his Beretta 9mm automatic which he had acquired in Colombia. He'd cut the right hand pocket out on all his trousers and now walked around with the gun strapped to the inside of his right thigh. To draw it, all he needed to do, was put his hand in his right hand pocket and pull it straight out.

When he arrived the party was already well into its stride. Sandy Niles made his number with the guards who were responsible for the security of house and perimeter. Every thing was in order.

Baldwin and Lattice were both on duty and were circulating and keeping every one under surveillance. It had been agreed that Niles would only be introduced as a friend and there would be no mention of his involvement in the Colombian adventure.

He'd dressed in a suit for the first time in many years, (he'd bought it this very morning) and should have looked very distinguished but in order to avoid drawing attention to himself he settled down to his slightly hunched posture that he'd used in South America to avoid being noticed. It was working; he'd managed to circulate for ten minutes without talking to any one until the Mendoza's and Jenny Valdez accosted him.

Alfred Mendoza gave him a puzzled look. 'What on earth are you doing creeping around like that Sandy; you look as though you should be sweeping the rooms up?'

'I was hoping to avoid having to make small talk to anyone. I'm supposed to be keeping an eye open for Jackie and Karen and at the same time circulate at a cocktail party making bloody small talk. There are times when I don't think George and Jackie realise just what there're up against'.

'But you can't expect Domingo to make a move against the family during a cocktail party – surely'!

'No but I'd like to be able to keep an eye on all the guests just in case one of them is, 'casing the joint', as they say in gangster's parlance. It's kind of difficult to keep my concentration on surveillance whilst listening to some woman banging on about her bloody roses'.

'I have an idea that might help you in this matter Sandy – why don't you escort the beautiful Jenny around. You should be able to avoid having to make small talk. Jenny knows why you are here and could even be of assistance'.

Niles turned round and looked at Jenny and gulped. He had not seen the Mendoza's and Jenny since their arrival from Colombia and at the time Jenny had been wearing black - still in mourning for the death of her late husband. She looked absolutely stunning. Her black raven hair was piled up on top of her head and she was wearing a green creation that seemed to emphasise rather than hide her beautifully formed body. It was almost as though all her female hormones that had been bottled up during the past six months of mourning were now determined to get loose. Her wide set eyes seemed one minute to be green the next hazel depending on the light, which complemented the honeyed complexion that Sandy had come to admire in many of the South American women. Niles realised he could be courting trouble here. He felt an instant attraction to her that he'd never experience in his life before. He could practically feel his male hormones leaping all over her. And it wasn't just the hairs on the nape of his neck which were trying to stand up. His right hand shot into his right pocket to make a physical adjustment. And it wasn't to adjust his Beretta either. Jenny gave Niles an amused smiled – Her secret sex antenna that all women are blest with had quickly registered the positive effect she'd had on him.

'I would consider it an honour to assist the great Sandy in the execution of his duties and I will endeavour to keep any women away from him who might hinder him doing so'. Jenny said all this at the same time arching her eyebrows and giving him a mocking smile. Then to emphasise her propriety rights she slipped her arm round Nile's left arm, pulling it until it nestled against her right breast.

'Christ with you in tow', he said. 'I think I'll just stand with you in the middle of the room, that way I will know where every man is looking'.

Helen laughed, 'Sandy do you realise that since Jenny took your arm you have grown at least two inches'.

He actually blushed at Helen's remark. It was true, he'd sub-consciously stood up straight. He couldn't remember when he had last preened himself for the benefit of a woman. His previous three years in Venezuela had been spent just trying to survive; he'd had no time for women. All his good intentions of creeping around trying to avoid attention had gone out the window.

'What the hell', he grinned. 'With a woman like Jenny on my arm how the devil am I going to be able to creep around the room unnoticed?'

'I promise you Sandy I will do exactly what you want and will not interfere with your duties', Smiled Jenny.

'How the hell am I going to scrutinise the guest – I can't take my eyes off of you?'

'We all have our problems Sandy and mine is to stop any other female from getting their hands on you. Be sure

I will keep these other scheming females at bay', another mocking smile with the arched eyebrow.

Just then Jackie Fields came over.

'My god Jenny! You look positively ravishing and where in god's sake did you pick up that gorgeous hunky man?'

'I found him creeping around the room in a most furtive and obsequious manner; he looked like some hired help. Alfred suggested I put Sandy out of his misery and help him with his surveillance'. Jenny gave Jackie a slow satisfied smile and one of those secret looks that only women can understand.

Jackie laughed and looked at him and said, 'Sandy that's the first time I have seen you dressed in a suite and you look disgustingly fit and hunky. Karen tells me you spend as much time running along side "Tee Bone" as you do in the saddle'.

He laughed, 'I don't think Karen realises how sore my backside gets after half an hours riding, though I must admit it's getting hardened'.

Jackie laughed.

'I won't keep you Sandy I know what you are up to. And if I were you Jenny I would hang onto him real close - there are some positive "man-eaters" here tonight'.

'With Jenny on my arm they don't stand a chance', smirked Niles

Jenny and Niles found it reasonably easy to circulate scrutinising the guests without raising anyone suspicions. It was in fact Jenny that first noticed that a tall, fairly old man who seemed to be taking more than a passing interest in the layout of the house.

'Sandy, have you noticed that tall man over there' she nodded in the direction of Senator Jackson who had in fact been trying to note the layout of the house without causing suspicion.

'I had noticed that he entered the hall but assumed he had just gone to the toilet – has he been in any other rooms?' he asked.

'Yes - I noticed him previously because he was ogling me – then I suddenly noticed that he was missing for at least ten minutes – he came in from the door to the dinning room'.

'That's interesting', Niles mused. 'There is absolutely no reason why he should have gone into the dinning room. There's nobody in there so why go there?'

'Could you wait here a moment Jenny I want to check with the security men in the hall and find out whether our friend has paid them an unscheduled visit'.

'No way! Where ever you go so do I', said Jenny tightening her grip on Sandy's arm. He was also aware of the fact that Jenny had been pulling his elbow into her right breast even tighter for some time now. Needless to say this was having an unsettling effect on him. He'd had to insert his hand into his pocket, (the pocket had been removed to give him access to his Beretta) on several occasions to adjust his rampant member. Although he tried to do it surreptitiously he was sure that Jenny knew the effect she was having on him. He realised the he was being outrageously vamped and he didn't have the wit or will to stop it.

He walked with Jenny still tucked firmly into his arm into the security room just inside the main hall. This was where all the perimeter and main house security systems were controlled from, including the CCTVS and the floodlights mounted on the main building roof. There was also a short wave band radio that was linked to the local police station at Hybla valley.

'Hi Don', said Niles to the elder of the two on duty. 'Have any of the guests visited you this evening?'

'As a matter of fact yes; we had a Senator Jackson in here not more than five minutes ago – said he was going to have a similar system fitted to his house and asked if we could give him a run down on how the system worked. I gave him a general run down on the system but bearing in mind what you said last week about anyone asking questions on the system, we never told him which switches controlled what or where sensors were located'.

'Well done Don you can't tell the guests to bugger off but you can politely tell them that you're not allowed to disclose the specifics of the system'.

'What do you think Sandy?' Jenny whispered.

'Well, it could be quite an innocent inquiry but in view of the present climate I'm going to have a word with George and alert him to our suspicions about our Senator Jackson. Well done my little flower. It was you that noticed his absence'.

'I became aware he was missing because he initially ogled me – every time I looked round there he was practically drooling. Then I suddenly noticed that he was no longer around, until he appeared through the dinning room door. He must have been absent for at least ten minutes He is a most unpleasant man, you can practically feel him undressing you with his eyes'.

'Jenny; the way you look tonight I'd be surprised if there wasn't a man here that hasn't undressed you with his eyes'.

'No no Sandy all women liked to be admired and know that men are often wondering how they would look in the nude but only in a tasteful manner. But this man is most unpleasant. Surely you've not been imagining me in the nude Sandy?'

She gave him an arch look and the eyebrow treatment.

'No of course not Jenny – well, only for about 90% of the time', he grinned.

'You swine', she hissed. 'If you hadn't I would kick you where it hurts most'.

Niles was surprised how quickly the evening passed but

most of all how easy he found it to converse with Jenny. Normally he found it difficult to relax around women but he'd been conversing with her for all of three hours. She'd vamped him mercilessly and he'd enjoyed it. Further more, she'd hung onto his arm and refused firmly but politely to be separated. Every time he mentioned that she might like to circulate and talk to some one else she would look up into his eyes and smile mockingly.

'Sandy you are my assignment tonight, I have been told to help you with your surveillance'. She would then pull his elbow deeper into her breast. This caused his right hand to dive into his pocket to make yet another adjustment.

After the guest had all gone with the exception of the Mendoza's, Jenny and Niles, George Fields looked at both of them and said. 'You two seemed to have become inseparable'.

Jenny looked George Fields straight in the eye and gave a slow secret smile. The meaning of which (being a man) was completely lost to him and said. 'I have been assisting Sandy with his assignment. I was detailed to make sure that no woman kept him from his duties '.

'And she has managed extremely well', said Niles. 'It was Jenny who noticed that a certain gentleman has been wondering around the house and also paid a visit to the security room and tried to quiz Don and his pal on how the security system worked'.

George Fields looked alarmed. 'I hope Don didn't give away any trade secrets – Do we know who this guy was?'

'Don told the guy politely that he was not allowed to discuss the workings of the system and yes! I have established the guy's name. He is a Senator Sam Jackson'.

Fields looked thoughtful for a moment. 'You know this guy is not an acquaintance of ours but he rang the other day and suggested we get together sometime to talk about using units of the National Guard to assist the DEA in combating drug running; yet he never spoke to me all evening'.

Niles looked at George Fields and nodded towards the door. 'Look boss could we have a few words in private'.

'Certainly Sandy – excuse us for a moment '

Once clear of the others Niles said, 'Look boss there is something fishy about this guy Jackson. He spent most of the evening wandering around the house and barely spoke to any one during the entire evening. I think we should have him investigated and see if he has any connections with the Colombian cartels'.

'But dam it Sandy he's the head of the Special Select Committee dealing with drugs and he is well known for his strong opposition to making the drugs legal. He's due to chair the meeting we are having here in two days time. He's hardly likely to be in cahoots with them'!

'Maybe but maybe not – lets put it this way boss – what's the worst thing that could happen to the drug trade if you were a member of the Cartel?'

'All our shipments to the States get intercepted'.

'Yes, but that is almost an impossibility. Whilst there is a demand for drugs, people will find a way of smuggling them into the country. In fact the scarcer the drugs become the higher the street value gets. The last thing the drug cartels want is for drugs to be legalised - if that happened the street value would drop through the floor. So our Senator could be lobbying in Congress to ensure that doesn't happen'.

Fields thought for a moment. 'But legalising drugs is socially unacceptable – why bother having Senators lobbying to prevent them being legalised'.

'I can't answer that boss but don't forget that booze was illegal in this country for many years and the Mafia made millions of dollars importing it illegally. But then it was suddenly legalised and all the big money was gone. I should imagine the Cartel are trying to hedge their bets against that happening – in any event I don't trust that bastard and

I think we should have him checked out for any connection to Colombia'.

'I agree with you Sandy - you have not been wrong so far. I'll get to it first thing in the morning and have him checked out. It will have to be done carefully and quietly after all, he is a Senator and we don't have any real evidence against him. Right! Let's join the others and have a night cap'.

After they had all bid one another good night Niles did his usual check of the Estate and went to his flat above the forge. Read for a while and then dropped off to sleep.

Suddenly Niles was awake, at first he didn't know why but something or someone had made a noise. He looked around the room slowly and carefully. Could see nothing amiss, then he realised that his bedroom door was opening. He slid his hand under his pillow and grabbed his berretta automatic pistol and slipped off the bed onto the floor in one fluid movement. He crouched behind the bed prepared to use it as a shield if necessary.

As the door opened fully he could just make out a shadowy figure. He switched the bedside lamp on and there stood Jenny.

'For Christ sake', snarled Niles. 'You could have had your bloody head blown off creeping into my room like that'.

Niles could see she was trembling quite violently even in the subdued artificial light of the bedside lamp.

'Are you going to love me or send me away and humiliate me?'

Niles was absolutely gob smacked. This was that gorgeous sophisticated young woman who had squired and vamped him all evening who had been so completely in control of the situation that he never knew whether he was on his arse or elbow. Now, here she stood, so completely unsure of her self she was shaking like a leaf in the wind. It was like two completely different women.

Jenny had let her hair down and was dressed (Undressed)

in a short diaphanous nightie. It only just covered her buttocks and was obviously designed to stimulate rather than cover.

Her long and slender legs were incredible – they seemed to go on for ever. Neat shapely ankles which flowed up to beautifully shaped calves surmounted by voluptuous thighs that ran up to her jutting buttocks and a ridiculously slender waist. He could even make out the large erect nipples that were thrusting against her ridiculous nightie. But the most striking aspect of this erotic vision was how vulnerable she looked. All that poise and confidence she had displayed earlier in the evening when she was vamping him had completely disappeared.

He sat there for a few seconds absolutely numb struck, finally got to his feet, crossed the room and swept Jenny up into his arms. This wasn't something he did consciously; He was ordered to by his hormones. He carried her across the room and gently lowered her into his bed. He climbed in beside Jenny who was still trembling like a leaf. He gently stroked her, not to stimulate but rather to calm her down and said. 'How on earth did you get out the main house with all the security arrangements there?'

'I asked Jackie and she made arrangements with the security guards to let me out'.

'Did you say why you wanted out of the main house?'

'But of course'.

'What did she say?'

'She said, good hunting - it's time some woman toppled that macho bastard'.

'You're joking'.

'No I'm not – but she was smiling when she said it'.

'Bloody hell - you women! What chance does a man have when you gang up on him like this?'

Nile noticed that his stroking had now taken on a more intimate nature and Jenny was responding. Her hands were now caressing his chest and stomach and were having the desired effect. He now had an erection that he could have used to pole vault out the bed.

'Why me Jenny? You could have just about any man you please. I'm not rich I have been married unsuccessfully before'.

'I want your children I am thirty five years old so time is not on my side and my late husband couldn't have children. You fascinate me Sandy and although I have only known you a couple of weeks I think I'm in love with you'.

'Bloody hell Jenny I've been married once and I'm not sure I'm ready to try it again even with such a gorgeous woman as you'.

'You will hombre; you will. Did you know Sandy that some of the wives were trying to work out whether you were gay or not'. Jenny gave a loud gasp as her hand closed around his throbbing erection. 'You are a big hombre all over', she gasped.

'I take it you will be telling them that I am completely heterosexual in the morning', he said as he caressed her between the legs.

'I think I will take a photograph of what I have both my hands wrapped round and have it published in the Washington Post. That should clear up any doubts about your preferences', gurgled Jenny.

Niles stopped all Jenny's further conversation by kissing her gently but with ever increasing passion. She quickly responded thrusting her hips up to meet the magic hands that were bringing her to ever increasing heights of ecstasy. Jenny was now moaning between the (ever increasing) passion of his kisses and the knowing way he was caressing her. She could wait no longer - she literally wriggled under him and dug her sharp finger nails into his buttocks when he tried to delay penetration. There was no way he could control himself, he could feel his seed clamouring to get out and in thirty seconds he was reaching his climax and grunting ;B oy! Boy! Boy! If she is determined to have our child I want a boy he thought. She reached her climax shortly after his, attesting to her high state of excitement.

'I'm sorry Jenny I could not make it last longer but you had me so excited I just couldn't control myself – next time I will have better control'

'Sandy that was absolutely beautiful I came just after you but the night is young and I'm staying in this bed until you kick me out'.

He got up and made them some coffee and crawled back into bed with Jenny. She wanted to know about his previous marriage and why it had failed.

'It was my fault', he said reluctantly. 'I was always away in some country or another and she just got fed up being on her own. She liked company and attention which I was never there to give it so eventually she just upped, packed her bag and ran off with some guy or other. I didn't even know his name at the time'.

'Her lost is my gain', said Jenny as she gently stroked his penis. 'Aha hombre! I can feel something stirring in the forest below. Some big creature is coming out of his lair'.

'I'm not surprised. You know what they say about a sleeping dog' if you keep poking him he will come out all aggressive'.

Suddenly Jenny's whole nature changed. She grabbed him and with tears streaming down her face she said.

'Sandy, please make love to me, long and slow, no foreplay I want you in me now'. And with that she climbed on top of Niles and straddled him until she was completely impaled.

Initially Jenny sat astride Niles back on her heels so she could feel the full length of him inside her but as her excitement increased she lowered her body until she was flat on top of him. She was still gently sobbing into his neck.

He'd no idea what had brought on this strange change in mood on but he did realise that she was looking for comfort rather than raw passion. He gently held her close to him and was barely conscious of the erotic nature of their union; this in itself helped him to maintain control of himself plus the fact that his earlier climax enabled him to remain in control with little effort.

Her sobbing was beginning to change to gasps and Niles realised that she was getting highly excited. Now she was just gasping and moaning but he still allowed Jenny to dictate the pace. She suddenly grabbed his face and began kissing him passionately. Their tongues were intertwined like mating eels. Suddenly she shrieked, 'Now! Sandy Now! He complied; who was he to argue - he thrust up with the full length of his body. Jenny began to sob and suddenly she collapsed on his chest. Niles suddenly discovered that he had not climaxed so involved had he been with Jenny's changing moods. This is great he thought I have still got a shell in the gun so if Jenny wants to go another round I'm ready and primed!

It transpired that Jenny was capable of going several further rounds and Niles duly obliged until they both fell asleep sated in one another's arms, Jenny on top of him with his limp penis still trapped inside her.

Niles and Jenny had decided not to flaunt their new relationship and the only other person that was aware of what was going on was Jackie Fields and she thought it was an absolute hoot!.

Unfortunately his nightly liaisons with Jenny were keeping Niles pinned to his bed in the morning something that had not gone unnoticed by Karen.

'You're late again Sandy', said young Karen. 'That's twice this week you have been late – we wont have time to do our usual ride otherwise I'll be late for school'.

'Point taken little one, when we get back I'll rub your

horse down and stable him while you get ready for school'. Niles had checked the high ground to the north but could find no further evidence of anyone surveying the estate. However he still felt that an attack was imminent

He was still working on the wrought iron gates which were now almost completed and Karen still insisted on helping him. However he always finished by eight o'clock and then went down to 'Ace of Spades'.

Niles made it obvious to all that he wanted to be left alone. Several of the regulars tried to involve him in conversation but he politely refused He normally bought a drink then sat at a corner table to ostensible read a newspaper. That way he could keep an eye on all who came and went. He noticed that on several occasions that Jake Lattice was there and seemed friendly with one of the guys that had been sat with Luke, the guy that Niles had had a brawl with on his first visit to the tavern. Although the Secret Service Guys had basically 'buried the hatchet' with Niles he found that although he had established a good cordial working relationship with Theo the only one that he had any real empathy with was Homer.

It was Homer who told Niles that Theo was getting worried about the money that Lattice was betting on the horses. Apparently Lattice had been officially warned a year ago about his gambling habit and his colleagues thought he had stopped. However, Homer thought he had started again.

Homer said that they were worried about Jakes friendship with this friend of Luke's (blue chin – the guy who was involved in the fight with Niles) It appears that he was a tout for a local gambling syndicate. His name was Ben Hatfield and he often rode a bike around all the motels and taverns in the local area collecting bets. Unfortunately Jake Lattice and Ben Hatfield had been observed talking together and money was seen to change hands.

It was now four days since the cocktail party at the Fields residence. Niles was beginning to feel very edgy he was convinced that Domingo was going to strike very soon yet had nothing definite to confirm his hunch.

Karen was still "helping" Niles in the Forge during the evenings. He was having problems explaining to Karen not to bank the forge fire up onto the, 'Chow Iron'. This is the metal vent through which the air is pumped to increase the temperature of the fire. If the fire is allowed to get too close to the 'Chow Iron' there is a danger of it melting.

'If you allow the fire to build up on the 'Chow Iron you are going to melt it and ruin the forge young lady'.

Karen nodded but as often is the case of the young asked Niles if she could make a mini volcano. (He'd shown her how to make one a week ago) She would bank the coke up into a small mound in the centre of the forge then when it was white hot she would turn the electric blower up to maximum speed causing the mound to burst like a small volcano showering sparks all over the forge. Niles was most insistent that she only did this when he was present (in fact she was only allowed in the forge room when he was there) Although she was almost completely covered from head to foot in protective clothing he made sure she kept well away from the actual forge when 'Volcanoing'.

Niles had finished working in the forge at about eight o'clock. (Which was the time that Karen had to go get ready for bed) and he then decided to ride down to the Tavern to eye the locals.

He was sat in the corner of the bar at the 'Ace of Spades'. There were only half a dozen in the room when at nine o'clock a stranger walked into the bar. No body paid much attention to him so Niles assumed he must known to the locals.

The stranger made his way to the bar and sat alongside Ben Hatfield. There was something vaguely familiar about the man. Hatfield and the stranger talked quietly for a few seconds and then got the nod from the barman and both of them made their way to a small adjoining room to the bar.

As they closed the door to the adjoining room Niles suddenly remembered where he had seen the stranger before. It was only four nights ago at the cocktail party (George Fields had heeded Niles advice and moved the Special Select Committee meeting that had been due at the residence to another venue). It was Senator Sam Jackson. At the party he had been dressed in a very smart charcoal black suit where as tonight he was dressed in a casual manner. He was wearing a lumber jack type shirt and faded jean trousers and a base ball cap. Hence the reason that Niles never recognised him when he first appeared.

The fact that Jackson was in disguise indicated that he was up to something and didn't want to broadcast his presence in the bar, otherwise why come dressed as a local labourer. There was also something about Ben Hatfield that kept niggling Niles. He had seen him somewhere before but couldn't think where.

Niles continued to visit the 'Ace of Spades' for the next two nights but saw no further sign of Sam Jackson but he did observe Jake Lattice coming out as he went in. He thought that Lattice looked a bit sheepish at being caught in the tavern without any of the other agents – or at least that's what he surmised. Lattice barely took the time to bid good evening to him and he was convinced that had they not ended up face to face he would not have spoken to him at all.

The following night, Karen and Niles were working at the forge making the final adjustments to the wrought iron gate that was due to be mounted at the entrance of the estate. Niles was working at the anvil when he heard Karen shout a warning but before he could turn felt the end of a gun jammed into the base of his neck.

A professional gun man would not have done that. It is relatively easy to twist the neck or torso quickly enough to deflect the barrel away from the victim. Niles twisted quickly, slammed his left foot down savagely on the gunman's right instep. The gunman shrieked in agony. Niles grabbed the gunman's right hand with his left, forcing the gun up and away, then twisted the gun down, slipped his right hand onto the gun and shot the assailant through the foot with his own weapon. Prior to his three years living on his wits in Venezuela he would never have attempted such a trick. Now he just didn't give a shit. However before Niles could make another move a voice snarled.

'Hold it right there shit head! I have you and the boy covered. Put your hands up and step over there; indicating that Niles was to stand in front of the Forge door thus preventing any one from entering. Niles elation at overcoming the first gunman rapidly took a nose dive. There was no way the second gunman was going to make the same mistake as the first.

Never-the-less they had one thing going for them, he realised that the two gunmen thought that Karen wearing all her protective clothing and goggles was a boy. This was something they'd have to foster.

'I hear that you are the man that looks after the Field's girl. Now I want to know where she is. We can do this the easy way or the hard. Greg!' The guy holding Karen said to the man on the floor with the wounded foot. 'Shove that fucking poker in the fire and get it red hot and we'll tickle this bastards balls. We haven't got enough time for any finesse. We need to be clear of here in the next half hour'.

'Shove the fucking thing in your self'; groaned the wounded man,' Cant' you see that I am in agony. The man called Greg sat on the floor cradling his foot and groaning.

The guy holding Karen shoved her to the opposite wall to Niles; alongside the control panel for the Forge. 'Who is that little arse hole?' He said pointing at Karen.

'He's a local lad that wants to become a blacksmith. He helps me out two or three times a week. I don't even know where he lives,' sighed Niles

The guy with the Browning Hi Power 9mm that kept Niles covered was very young; he could only have been in his early twenties. He had dark wavy hair and was extremely good looking and well dressed and of medium height. Although he acted with plenty of confidence Niles suspected that this was affected and not real. An experienced gun man would surely have searched him and removed his Beretta by now. However Rory shoved the poker into the centre of the fire and then keeping a steady eye on him as he banked the fire up.

'Hey Rory', snarled Greg on the floor still cradling his wounded foot. 'You reckon I can do the honour with the poker after what that bastards done to my foot'.

'If he has two balls I reckon that's one a piece', Rory smirked, waggling the poker about that was now just beginning to sparkle red hot.

Niles managed to catch Karen's eye and whilst the guy with the poker was checking the temperature he nodded to the electric panel alongside Karen and gave a twisting motion with his hands still in the air. He still couldn't believe it that they hadn't disarmed him. His Beretta was still strapped to his inner right thigh.

The sparkles coming off the poker had now changed from red to white indicating that the metal had reached melting point.

'Now we come to the moment of truth', Rory leered as he grabbed the poker which was now showering white hot sparks.

Chapter 32

Kidnap

They'd left their Range Rovers half a mile down the road hidden in bushes at the side of the road. As they approached the outside wall of the Fields estate Grant turned to his twin brother and whispered.

'Once over the wall Rory you and Greg split off to the left and make for the forge. We had better check that the electric wires on top have been switched off'

Rory and Greg nodded their heads in agreement.

They set their Aluminium Extended Ladder against the wall and Rory climbed up it to check the electrified fence with an Avo' metre. The power had been switched off as promised.. Grant passed the second latter up to Rory who then lowered it and set it against the inside of the wall.

Grant cursed the light from the quarter Moon. Its crescent shape was providing just too much light for his liking. He'd argued with his uncle; Domingo's to wait for the Moon to fully wane when they could have approached the house undetected in complete darkness. His uncle was adamant; he would not wait any longer and wanted the job completed straight away

Rory Cortez and one gunman peeled off the main party towards the Forge where they were told Karen was most likely to be. Grant Cortez and the remaining four made their way cautiously to the security room. Their intelligence had been better than they dared hope. Even their course across the lawn had been pre-planned. Lines drawn on a sketch showed which bushes to use to keep them hidden from Field's security guards (the very ones that Niles had expressed misgivings about on his initial arrival). The Fields family and their staff were about to be caught with their, "pants down", despite all their previous planning. Domingo's gang were making a two pronged attack on the Riverside gardens estate. Rory Cortez was attempting to kidnap Karen and the other twin; Grant Cortez, was targeting Jackie Fields. At the same time, a third team had been dispatched to Douglas Field's Boarding School to grab the Defence secretary's son. Domingo's intelligence had been more thorough than the Fields family could have anticipated. They'd managed to get intimate help from within the Field's complex.

The attack was being coordinated so that it took place whilst the Defence Secretary was in Washington. The only agents in the house were Homer and Theo. Mike Williams and Jake Lattice were riding shot gun with the Defence Secretary in Washington.

Grant and his gunmen reached the last bush marked on their sketch about ten yards to the front of the house's main entrance. Grant whispered to his five companions. 'We rush the security room in one fell swoop when I drop my arm. All clear'. They nodded their heads in unison. Grant was looking apprehensive this was his first task with the Cartel that might involve shooting and possibly killing. Trying to keep his nervousness hidden he dropped his hand and they moved as a group rushing the security room just inside the front hall. The security guards who were good operators never stood a chance. Cortez and his thugs had exploded into the security room before they'd a chance to even get out of their chairs. They cut the throat of one guard to emphasise that they meant business and then threatened the other to disclose where Jackie Fields was.

Grant Cortez; grabbed the remaining live guard, twisted his head round to lay his throat bare and snarled, 'were the fuck is this Jackie Fields to be found?'

The guard who was an ex US marine knew he was a dead man. If he told them where Jackie Fields was they would immediately kill him any way so he decided to screw them around for his remaining time on this earth.

'If you look real close up my left nostril you can see her watching the late night TV show'. He followed this up by ramming his right knee up into Grant's balls. Although he didn't connect properly he caused Grant sufficient pain to double up. At this stage one of the other gunmen lost his cool and shot the ex-marine in the head. The sound of the shot reverberated throughout the night. Their cover was blown.

Grant Cortez went ape shit. 'You stupid bastard you have alerted the whole house. Quick get in there and let's grab hold of the Defence Secretary's wife and get the fuck out of here before the shit hits the fan'.

Grant took a quick glance at the plan of the interior of the house which was sketched on a piece of paper, then shoved it back in his pocket.

'Follow me,' he snarled, and dashed out into the main hall. He suspected that Jackie would be in the main reception room at this time of the night the last room off to the right. But speed was now more important than stealth. They would have to move quickly as the alarm was now raised and the Secret Service men would be appearing at any moment.

The luck of the devil seemed to favour the Cartel's gunmen – as they dashed down the hall towards the main reception room Jackie Fields; alerted by the sound of the gunshot should have gone to ground and hid as Instructed by Theo, but worried for Karen's security came running out the dinning room where she had gone to get a book, straight into the path of the approaching gunmen. Had she stayed there, they would have run pass the dining room on their way to the reception room and wasted precious time looking for her.

Grant grabbed Jackie round the neck and rammed the Glock 17 Automatic into her temple and snarled.

'Shut the fuck up or I'll scatter your brains all over this expensive carpet'

The four gunmen, still not sure who they had, started dragging Jackie towards the reception room door when Homer, quickly followed by Theo, came out the main reception room where they had been guarding Jackie prior to her brief visit to the dining room to collect her book.

Homer took cognisance of the situation immediately, drew his Beretta and got off a quick shot. His bullet hit the leading gunman smack in the centre of the chest killing him immediately. His second shot hit another gunman in the left shoulder. The other two, using Jackie as a shield retreated down the hall back into the security room.

'Keep your fucking distance or I'll blow the women's brains out', shouted Grant.

'Don't you worry Mrs Fields', shouted Homer. 'There's no way they can get you out this house. We'll have it and the area completely sealed off in minutes'.

'You fucking stupid ape Homer; you've just confirmed that they have Mrs Fields in their hands', snarled Theo.

'Shit', gasped Homer. 'What have I done?'

'You'd done real well with your gun, it's when you opened your mouth you did the damage', grunted Theo

Theo quickly assumed command of the situation and waved to the back door.'

'Right Homer lets get outside and organise a cordon around the house to make sure that these bastards can't get away with Jackie'. Theo then used his small radio to contact the Riverside Police and arranged for backup from the, Hybla Valley police. They would be at the estate in minutes.

'I'll guard the front of the house until the backup police arrives', said Theo. 'You take control at the back'.

'Right', he continued. 'I'll station myself so I can see both the south and east of the building – you station yourself so you can do the same for the north and west of the building. That way we can keep the complete house under surveillance.

Homer nodded in agreement. 'How in God's name did they get into the Estate let alone the house without tripping the alarm system?

'Christ knows' said Theo as they parted company. 'That's something we'll have to sort out later - our first priority is to save Jackie and Karen'.

Theo arrived at the front of the house just as one of the gunmen was cautiously looking round the front door. Theo loosed off a quick shot at him which thudded into the door just above his head. The gunman quickly withdrew his head and closed the front door.

The situation was now a stalemate. There was no way that Theo was going to let the gunmen go with Jackie Fields without the express permission of George Fields. The boss was due in the next half an hour or so. Not a pleasant home coming.

A voice shouted from the security room window.

'I want to speak to the person in charge'.

'I'm in charge,' roared Theo. 'and you guys are going nowhere'.

'I want a helicopter to fly us out of here or Mrs Fields gets shot'.

'You're going nowhere until the boss gets here then you can do all your negotiating with him.

Rory gave the poker a twirl in the Forge fire and started to pull it out. The poker was white hot literally fizzing as showers of sparks cascaded off of it. Even the wounded gun man on the floor seemed mesmerized by it.

Niles nodded to Karen stood alongside the control panel and he made a twisting motion with his hand and mouthed, 'Now'!

Karen understood immediately and turned the rheostat fully up. The electric fan motor rapidly accelerated to maximum speed forcing the air to surge into the forge and through the Chow iron which was beginning to melt with the excessive heat. The surging air initially met the resistance of the banked up fire and the melting metal. Finally, the mounting air pressure overcame all the resistance and erupted with a tremendous 'Whoom' like a mini volcano.

Thousands of hot sparks from the molten metal and red hot cinders showered Rory Cortez; He went crazy – screaming with pain as he tried shielding his eyes from the particles of molten metal and red hot cinders. His hair was already alight and his suit was smouldering in many places. At this point he was completely incapacitated. The wounded gunman on the floor also got showered but not as severely as he tried to crawl clear.

Niles's hand dove into his right pocket and he withdrew his Beretta and shot the man crawling on the floor who was already raising his gun to shoot Karen. His second and third shot took Rory Valdez in the chest whilst he was still struggling to smother the cinders and molten metal embedded in his scalp. It was all over in a matter of seconds.

Karen stood rooted to the spot in terror with the knuckles of her hands jammed in her mouth trying to suppress a scream. She had just witnessed another two men being killed in front of her. She had only just got over the horrors of the Colombian experience.

'Karen', commanded Niles in a firm but gently voice, 'come to me pet'.

She rushed over to Niles and sobbed.'Why are they still trying to kill me Sandy?'

'I don't think they are trying to kill you pet – I think they were trying to capture and use you to get money from your father'.

Niles was extremely angry with himself. He was lucky to be alive and he knew it. Luck should not come into the equation. Those gunmen should never have been able to get so close to Karen without him being aware of their approach. It must not be allowed to happen again, next time they might not be so lucky.

They both looked up as they heard more firing that appeared to be coming from the main house. Niles realised that his presence was probably required there.

He cuddled Karen until her shaking had subsided.

'Karen I'll have to go to the main house as your mother may be in trouble. I'm going to hide you in the loft above the forge in my flat –okay'

Karen was still too shook up to talk so he gentle took her upstairs and lowered the ladder to his loft and ushered her up.

'Don't you come down from there until I get back Karen – I'll be as quick as I can'.

'Can't I come with you Sandy; I'll do exactly as you tell me?'

'No Karen I can't do my job properly if I have to look after you at the same time – you'll be perfectly safe up there and I won't be long. Jackie may be in danger I must get to the main house as quickly as I can. So be a brave girl and try and remain as quiet as possible'.

'Okay Sandy but please be quick'. She gasped trying to control her fear.

Niles nodded, gave her a reassuring smile, unpacked and made sure that his Heckler & Koch PSG1 Snipers rifle was fully loaded with the magazine that held twenty rounds and departed for the main house.

He made his way stealthy to the main house but by the time that he reached the main house George Fields had arrived and the local Police with a small SWAT team which were already on station.

George Fields rushed over to Niles and gasped. 'Is Karen safe, where is she?'

'She's okay boss – two gunmen arrived in the Forge house and tried to locate her but we fooled them into thinking that Karen dressed in her protective clothing was a local boy from the village'.

'Where are the gunmen now?'

'They're dead on the Forge floor and I've hidden Karen in the loft of my flat until we have everything under control. What's the situation here boss?'

Fields gave a huge sigh of relief and thanked God for small mercies then said. 'There are three gunmen trapped in the security room but they have Jackie in there with them and they're threatening to kill her if we don't provide a chopper to get them out of the country. There were four but Homer killed one and we think he winged another. We are trying to negotiate with them but they are getting very jumpy and I don't want to risk Jackie getting shot'.

Niles noticed that the SWAT team already had four snipers in position. He turned to the Police Captain and said.

'What's the procedure if one of your men gets a chance of a clear shot at the man holding Jackie Fields?'

'He calls me on his radio integral to his helmet and then I decide whether the risk is acceptable or not – under the circumstances I would probably defer to Mr Fields before agreeing to the shot being fired'.

'I see', Niles murmured.

'Boss could I have a quick word with you in private?' Niles guided Fields out of earshot of the others.

'Look boss, if we tell them they are getting their helicopter they are unlikely to do anything desperate until it arrives. Once it's arrived they will have to clear the house, walk down the steps to the lawn here where the chopper is, that's about thirty yards they'll have to cover. During this period there's bound to be a split second when the gunman will become distracted. I can put two bullets between the eyes of the guy holding Jackie before he knows what's hit him. But if we use normal operating modus of the SWAT team by the time they have got permission to fire the split second will have been and gone. Can I have your permission to make the shot at the guy holding Jackie when I think the time is appropriate and use the SWAT team take care of his accomplices?'

Although George Fields had never seen Niles shooting he had heard about it from the SAS team while he was in Colombia. Further more what Sandy was saying made sense, by the time one of the SWAT team had got a clear shot, asked permission to shoot and then waited for the affirmative the chances were it would have been and gone.

They walked back to the Police Captain and George drew him to one side.

'Look Frank the situation is this. We are going to agree to their demands for the chopper which will park here on the lawn. When the gunmen come out with Jackie to board the helicopter Niles here, at the appropriate moment, is going to shoot the man holding the gun to Jackie's head. I want your men to respond immediately without asking permission by shooting his accomplices. Do you fore see any problems with this plan.

'You do realise Mr Defence Secretary that I can accept no responsibility if your man here misses or hits your wife. This is completely contrary to all the text books on this sort of situation'.

'I understand what you are saying Frank and if you like I will give you a written statement to what I have just authorised if that will make you happy'.

'That wont be necessary sir I know you will stand by what you have just said but are you sure this guy knows what he's about. His shooting will only have to be slightly off target and he could hit your wife'.

'I'm certain Sandy wont miss which is one of the reasons I have employed him – just be glad he's on our side'.

The captain of the Police came over to Niles and shook his hand.

'You must be one of a hell of a shot to gain the Secretary's confidence in such a manner Sandy'.

'Thanks a lot Frank and bye the way, there are another two bodies over there in the Forge house. They're the gunmen that tried to snatch the Defence Secretary's daughter'.

'I take it that is some of your handwork?' The Police Captain said eyeing Niles with some respect.

Niles just nodded.

'Okay I'll have the bodies taken care of once we have this situation sorted -is there anything we can do to help you with this tricky shot?' The police captain continued.

'I'll be positioned just outside the circle of light so the gunmen can't see me but you could help by ensuring that no one interrupts my field of fire and making sure that your snipers take out the other two gunmen before they can turn and get a shot off against Jackie Fields'

'Consider it done', Frank turned and went over to brief his snipers on what was about to unfold and what their tasks were when the helicopter arrived.

Niles and George conversed and discussed where the

helicopter should be marshalled to for Niles to get the best shot and the overall situation. Too far from the house and the gunmen would get suspicious and too close reducing the chances of Niles getting off a shot

'I don't want to start a witch hunt boss but we have to consider how these bastards got into the house and the estate without any of the alarms being triggered and the fact that they seemed to have a detailed knowledge of the house and estate. I hate to say this but to disable the alarm set-up without the security guards becoming aware of it takes an intimate knowledge of the system. I think we've a rat in the nest'.

'I agree Sandy. Once we have resolved our immediate problem we're going to get to the bottom of this. I'd have staked my life on all our employees but obviously some big money has been offered and someone has accepted it.'

'I have a sneaking suspicion who that might be, but it can wait for the moment'.

The Police Captain gave a call.

'Helicopter due in two minutes every one standby'.

He then called out to Grant Cortez.

'Ahoy there; your chopper is landing in two minutes are you all ready to leave?'

Grant Cortez acknowledged. 'Yeah we're ready – we'll release Mrs Fields when we get to the airfield where we have a private jet waiting'.

'Do you believe him Sandy?' George Fields asked.

'No I don't', snarled Niles. 'There's no way they have come all this distance and lost some of their gunmen and then leaving empty handed. If we believed that there would be no point in risking a shot. They have every intention of taking Jackie back to Colombia given half the chance. We have to stop them here and now!'

'I agree', sighed Fields.

The S76 chopper approached and was marshalled to the

spot that had been decided on. It was not too far from the house to arouse the gunmen's suspicion but they would have to walk about thirty yards which increased the time and opportunity for Niles getting off the telling shot.

'We are coming out', shouted Grant Cortez. 'Every body keep well clear or Mrs Fields gets a bullet in her head'.

'I have told every one to keep clear I have no wish to endanger my wife's life by any one taking a foolish chance but bear this in mind, if you shoot my wife you will be a dead man – we wont be taking any prisoners - do I make myself clear?'

'Just make sure every one keeps clear and nothing will happen to her', yelled Cortez

The first to appear were the wounded gunmen being supported by his colleague followed immediately by Grant Cortez holding his Glock 17 automatic to Jackie Fields head.

Niles immediately noted the likeness of Grant to the man that he had shot in the Forge house. He was also quite young and this was probably his first experience in such a dangerous mission, and if Niles had anything to do with it; his last.

Their progress across the lawn to the chopper was quite slow mainly due to the man who had been wounded by Homer. He appeared to be in considerable pain and needed to be physically supported by remaining uninjured gunman.

This was making Grant Cortez very nervous and he was beginning to make small gestures with his Glock to speed his wounded colleague on.

This had not gone unnoticed by Niles and he figured as they got nearer to the chopper his impatience would increase.

He was nicely settled into the firing position keeping the illuminated graticule of the 6 X 42 telescope centred on

Grant's fore head. The Heckler & Koch PSG1 was one of the most accurate sniper rifles in the world and from less than forty yards Niles knew he could place a round in each eye with no problem.

They had about ten yards to go and all the watchers were beginning to get anxious. The guy supporting the wounded man suddenly stumbled and Grant lost his cool and snarled.

'For fuck sake get a move on we haven't got all day'.

Grant then swung his boot up the backside of the man who had stumbled but in doing so his gun had come out of alignment with Jacky's head.

Jackie slammed her high heel shoe onto the instep of Cortez who let out a howl of rage.

This was the chance that Niles had been praying for but it had almost been negated by Jackie's action. However Cortez's gun was misaligned. Niles made a quick readjustment with his aim as Cortez threw his head back in pain. It had only occurred for a split second which was all the time it took for him to squeeze off two rapid rounds. The two 7.62 rounds travelling at 2,723 ft/sec hit Grant Cortez between the eyes, there was less than a half a second between the two shots. He died before he'd even heard the shot that killed him. His last conscious thought was how much his foot hurt where that fucking bitch had stamped on it. He slumped to his knees and pitched forward onto his face. At the same time there were two short burst of automatic fire from two members of the SWAT team that instantly killed the remaining gunmen.

George Fields was running to grab his wife before the echoes of the shots had died out.

'Don't tell me', she whispered. 'It was Sandy who fired the shots at the man holding me'.

'Yes' her husband replied. 'We decided that the usual practice of getting permission to make the shot would be too long winded I therefore gave Sandy the option to make the shot when he thought it was safe to do so. Mind you, your stamping on Cortez's foot nearly screwed our plans up but alls well that ends well'.

The Captain of the Police team was having the bodies photographed before the forensic staff arrived.

The SWAT team were all examining Grant's body.

'Jesus' cried one of the team. 'Have you seen those shots, smack between the eyes and I swear to god that a dime could cover both of them'.

Frank, the Police Captain came over to George and Jackie Fields and said.

'You were right about having your man make that shot Mr Fields. That gunman's gun only just wavered off for a split second and he was dead. That man Niles you have is some cool customer'

'That's why I am employing him - you might also like to note that he is the man that saved my wife and daughter down in Colombia and hence the reason I have so much confidence in him.

Just then another police patrol man came over and said to George Fields.

'Excuse me sir but I have just received some disturbing news about your son – apparently he was practicing football on the college pitch when he disappeared and no one knows where he is or even how long he's been missing'.

'Oh my god', whispered Jackie Fields. 'What are we going to do?'

George and Jackie Fields just looked at one another completely stunned. Jackie Fields face crumpled at the significance of the news. They had just this very minute recovered from their own traumatic experience and now this!

'Christ almighty we have just killed all their accomplices here so there's no one left to question', groaned George Fields.

They stood transfixed completely stunned by the new crisis. For ten seconds or so nobody could think or move. George and Jackie Fields were too stricken to think. Jackie just stood there with tears rolling down her face mentally crushed by the latest development.

Niles realised it was up to him to inject some action into the proceedings – it was going to take time for George Fields to start functioning.

Niles looked at Jake Lattice who up to now had remained very quiet in the background.

'I'm not so sure that all is lost. These guys got into the grounds with the help of someone on the inside. You have a very sophisticated alarm system here boss and I am convinced that the gunmen could not have got access without intimate knowledge of the alarm system'.

'I have to agree with Sandy', said Theo. 'You would need to have detailed knowledge of the system to get into the estate let alone the house. Some one has sold us out'.

George Fields slowly recovered and started to look alarmed and very angry.

'Christ I thought I could have trusted all my guys working here. I can't believe they would jeopardise my wife and family'.

Theo nodded his head. 'I'm afraid we are talking big bucks here boss. Someone has been offered a lot of money and they have accepted it'.

Homer who had been stood alongside Niles suddenly said. 'Or some one has got himself into financial difficulties and decided that this was the only way out. Jake how's your gambling debts? You were splashing plenty of money around two nights ago when we were on the town'. With this last remark Homers whole demeanour changed. He gave Jake Lattice a hard challenging look.

Jake Lattice said nothing.

'Boss', continued Homer. 'We could easily check all

our bank accounts and see who has suddenly become very affluent during the last week or so'.

'I don't think that will be necessary', said Niles. I think Jake here can throw some light on how these bastards got into the estate. Further more boss, I think your friend Senator Sam Jackson might be involved'.

'You see here', snarled Lattice. 'Just because I had a lucky win on the horses and threw some money around it doesn't mean I have sold the boss and his family down the river'.

Niles looked exasperated, 'Look all this is academic at the moment because if we don't take action in the next hour it's going to be too late. Young Douglas is going to be on his way out the country in the next hour or so. I think I know where we might get some help albeit reluctantly'. I've seen Sam Jackson speaking to a friend of yours Lattice; Ben Hatfield down at, the 'Ace of Spades'.

George Field immediately took charge, 'Jackie you go to Sandy's flat and you'll find Karen hiding in the loft. Homer I want you to stay with Jackie and Karen whilst the rest of us get down to, 'Ace of Spades' and interview our Mr Ben Hatfield. Any questions...Okay let's move!

There were about a dozen people at the bar when the Defence Secretary and his group arrived – Frank the Captain of police had insisted in coming along. Though for what Niles had in mind his presence was going to be tricky.

As soon as Fields and his group entered the bar Ben Hatfield and Senator Sam Jackson tried to slip quietly into the adjoining room. Niles strode quickly across the room and rammed his foot against the door to prevent it being closed.

Theo Baldwin went over to the Barman, showed his Secret Service Shield and said.

'Listen shit head', he growled politely. 'You've five minutes to close the joint and get rid of all these people except the two that went into the spare room and the party with me. If we have any arguments I'm sure the Captain of the Police here can make your next six months fucking uncomfortable – comprehend?'

'No problem – right! Every one drink up and clear the bar we have a private function about to start'.

A couple of rough necks were prepared to argue about being chucked out so early but when the Police Captain sided up with Theo their combined authority quelled the opposition and they left quietly with the others.

Niles went up to the owner/barman and said. 'I want some masking tape and the use of your spare room and no interruptions until we say so and I suggest you take a long walk; about half an hour should be sufficient before returning to the bar'.

The owner was about to argue but the look on Niles's face and the fact that he was now carrying his Beretta was enough to change his mind.

'Okay I'll visit my friend across the road but if you guys cause any damage here you going to pay through the nose for it'.

George Fields came across and took the owner to one side and briefly told him about the kidnapping of his son and that the two characters that were in the spare room were part for the conspiratory and were about to be questioned – none too gently. Therefore for his own protection it would be better if he was not present to see what took place.

It seemed that by mutual consent that Niles took charge of the situation.

'Right you two bastards sit in those two chairs – Now!. And you'. Niles pointed his Beretta at Jake Lattice. 'Open your jacket nice and gently and drop your hand gun on the floor – make one false move and I will kill you'.

'Who the fuck do you think you are talking to', snarled Lattice. 'There's no way you are having my gun'.

Niles upped with his Beretta and shot Lattice in the foot. The nine millimetre slug crushed Lattice's right big toe. He let out a roar of pain.

'You crazy mother fucker what did you do that for?'

'That's to make sure I have all your attention – including you two bastards', continued Niles nodding at Jackson and Hatfield'.

'Get sat in that chair', he snarled.

'Get stuffed', said Lattice still groaning in agony.

The noise of Nile's huge fist smashing into Lattice's forehead sounded like a butcher's cleaver thudding into a wooden block. Lattice sagged to his knees and Niles grabbed him by the scruff of his neck and rammed him into the chair. Niles could feel the dark side of his nature beginning to kick in. He knew from previous experience over the past three years that when it happened he was capable of anything and to hell with the consequences. He made a desperate attempt to remain cool knowing that if he didn't he could well end up facing a murder charge.

George Fields, Theo Baldwin and the Police Captain were also stunned at Niles savage action. Niles knew that time was not on their side; he was relying on a sharp, brutal approach to get answers quickly.

He quickly bound the three suspects to the chairs with the masking tape that the bar owner had supplied.

'Now you three bastards listen up. I'm going to start with you Mr Ben Hatfield. I've just remembered that it was you who I saw surveying the estate from the north plus which, I have seen you and the good Senator here having parleys in this very room so I am going to assume that you have a good idea of what's going on. This is what I am going to do. I'm going to ask you a question and every time you fail to answer or I think you are lying I am going to shoot you. I'll start by shooting you in the ankle followed by the knee and then the elbows and wrist. By the time I've finished with you you'll resemble a puppet without the string. What I am saying gentlemen, is, that you are going to be crippled for life, you will need a wheel chair'.

'Right', Niles nodded to Ben Hatfield, 'Here is the first question. Young Douglas was kidnapped this evening whilst your other colleagues made an abortive attempt on his mother and sister. What we need to know and fucking quickly, is where and how you intended to get them out the country. It figures that they were all going to meet up somewhere before being transported to Colombia?'

Hatfield looked at the Defence Secretary and the Captain of Police, turned and looked Niles in the eye.

'There's no way you can shoot us in cold blood with the Defence Secretary and the Police chief here to bear witnesses.

'He's right', Sandy', said George Fields. 'I can't stand here and allow you to shoot an unarmed man. We have drugs that can be used to get the information'.

'I know that boss but we don't have the time. It could take hours for the drugs to take effect by which time Douglas will be out the country. I think you and Frank should go next door to discuss the ways and means of arranging transport to get us where they are taking young Douglas. I'm sure one of these gentlemen is going to give me an answer in the next five minutes'.

Fields looked into Niles's eyes and realised that he was looking at one of the most dangerous men he had ever come across. There was a flat implacable look in his face that brooked no argument. Fields realised that no matter what he or the Police Captain said it was not going to alter Nile's course of action by one iota.

'I guess we could go next door Frank and discus how we are going to arrange transport. We can leave Sandy to get on with the interrogation. Remember though Sandy I want to make it perfectly clear there is to be no violence,.

Niles nodded in agreement as George Fields and Frank left the room.

'How are you going to play it now Sandy?' grunted Theo.

'Where I left off prior to George's interruption, I think I'll start with our Senator friend here. He's the most likely to know the overall plan'.

With that Niles made a great play of cocking the Beretta automatic, (which was not necessary as the gun was already cocked from his previous shot).

He walked over to Senator Sam Jackson.

'You lousy bastard, your up to your arm pits in this conspiratory. Chris Brooker mentioned your name in Bogotá. He said it appeared that you were involved with the drug Cartels and it looks as though he was right. You've five seconds to tell us what we want to know or I'll blow your ankle to smithereens and then it's your kneecap next'.

'You wouldn't dare shoot an American Senator. The government would hound you till they had you thrown in jail'.

Niles decided that he was committed to a line of action and there was now no turning back. What the hell, he'd been living outside the law for the past three years; these days authority seems to matter less and less. If after this night's work things got too hot for him in the States he'd just bugger off to some other country. But come what may, he was determined to find out where the kidnappers were taking Douglas. He took aim at the Senator's right ankle and just as he pulled the trigger Theo knocked his hand to one side and the bullet ploughed into the wooden floor six inches to the side of Sam Jackson right foot.

Niles whirled round on Theo and snarled, 'you try a trick like that again Theo and I'll blow your fucking brains out'.

With his back to the three captives he gave Theo a broad wink and said. 'Give me your gun and stand over there out of the way'.

Theo realised that Sandy was getting him off the hook. He could now truthfully deny that he was an accomplice to the torturing of the victims. If there was ever an inquiry then it was Sandy who was going to attract all the flack.

Niles turned back to the Senator and made great play at taking aim at his left ankle.

Jackson took one look at his face and turned ashen white. He realised that Niles was not bluffing, he was about to be crippled.

'For fuck's sake stop I'll tell you what you want to know. For Christ sake Baldwin gets this crazy bastard off me'!

'Sorry Jackson but Sandy's got my gun and there is nothing I can do to help you – even if it were possible I'm not sure I would'.

Niles jammed the gun against Jackson's knee. 'Look you bag of shit you have wasted enough time already you either start talking or you cease walking – it's up to you'.

'Okay okay', whined Jackson. 'A guy called Chase is supposed to make the final arrangements. Each of the two groups were to make their way to a small commercial air strip at a place called Chapman Landing and then the captives were going to enplane on a Cessna 310 – fly to Miami – refuel - then onto Cuba before making it's way to Colombia. Chase claimed that by flying an indirect route they would avoid being intercepted by American aircraft'.

'This bastard Chase; is he the guy that's been running guns to South America?'

'Yeah I think so, I had never met him until the Cartel told me to meet him just over a week ago. He and two men who were twins did the entire organisation I just provided them with a rough sketch of the house. The twins also had the money to bank roll the operation'.

'Okay but who provided the information to by- pass the security system at the Fields house?'

Jackson looked at Lattice and then looked away.

'I'm not sure but Chase said that they had someone on the inside who was confirming the sketch I provided and was going to show them how to by-pass the security system'.

'I think we know who that was don't we Lattice. But that can wait until we get young Douglas back. All I am going to say to you three bastards is that if we don't get young Douglas back unharmed you three are dead meat. Make no mistake about this; I'm one of natures lost souls I have nothing to live for. It will give me something to live for to hunt you down and kill you'.

'Right Theo! Let's get hold of the boss and get down to Chapman Landing before those bastards down there realise that there's been a fuck up at this end. If they get wind of what's happened here they'll cut their losses and fly to Cuba with just Douglas'.

They grabbed Fields and the Police Captain and explained what had transpired and the need for haste to get to the Airstrip before any information on what had transpired got out via the News media.

'I guess we'll have to leave those three in there to your tender mercies Frank. I appreciate that you may or may not have sufficient evidence to hold them in custody but if you could keep them incommunicado for the next twelve hours we would be extremely grateful. After that we'll have either rescued Douglas or we'll have been too late'.

Frank nodded and said to Niles. 'No problem but you just be careful young man, you are sailing pretty close to the wind and you might return to find your self being arrested for physical assault'.

'Point taken but my security is not the problem it's young Douglas that's our immediate concern after we have resolved that problem I am quite willing to come back and face the music. In the meantime boss we need your S76 helicopter to get to Chapman Landing before they get wind of what's happened here and fly the coop'

Fields already had his mobile out and was arranging for the chopper to pick them up at the estate.

'Done', said Fields. 'I've arranged for the chopper to pick us up at the estate. Mike Williams and Brian Johnson (Homer) are there waiting for us and are getting your rifle plus some additional hardware ready. With you, Theo and me that makes five of us. Do you figure that five will be enough to affect the rescue Sandy?'

'More that enough boss, if we play this properly they won't know what hit them until it's too late. I suspect that there will only be two of them – three at the most. A S76 helicopter landing at a commercial airstrip should not alarm the kidnappers. We can hack a plan out whilst we are flying down there. How far is it?'

Theo was the first to answer. 'If my recollection is correct it's only about six miles south of the estate but on the other side of the river. So the chopper would definitely be the quickest means of getting there'.

Fields whipped his mobile out and got onto the crew of the chopper.

'Gary this is the boss – lookup Chapman Landing and make arrangements to land there tonight as soon as possible but don't mention any names of passengers. We have reason to believe that's where young Douglas is being kept prior to flying him out the country. We don't want the kidnappers to realise that this is a rescue mission – see you in ten minutes'.

They all piled into Field's Mercedes and arrived at the estate just as the S76 helicopter was landing on the front lawn. The crew had barely arrived at Washington Airport when Fields request that they return to the house for the flight to Chapman Landing.

There was quite a crowd there to meet them. Homer had rounded up enough hardware to start a small war and Jackie Fields with Karen started pumping George and Niles immediately for any information that they had concerning Douglas

The police Lieutenant was asked to warn the police in the Chapman Landing area to provide back up – details were to be sent later. But the Police were not to make their presence known at the strip until they saw a red Very light fired.

The police Lieutenant nodded and asked where his boss was. Theo explained that Frank was arranging for the custody of three guys down at the Inn. In the meantime the lieutenant was to organise things at the house until Frank returned.

It was decided that the five of them would be enough to handle the rescue and with luck they should get to the airstrip before the kidnappers arrived. It was assumed that they would be going by road. As the journey from Douglas's school was a hundred miles or so there was still a good chance of the rescuing party arriving first.

The chopper lifted off whilst the passengers were still fastening their safety belts. Fields looked at Niles and said.

'What's the plan of action Sandy?'

'We mustn't be too pedantic at this stage. As we approach the strip the first thing is to try and identify their Cessna 310 whilst still airborne and land some distance away from it and cautiously approach their aircraft. Then try and overpower the pilots – I'm assuming that there will be two pilots and possible one or two henchmen – next, we wait for the arrival of the kidnappers. Mike and I will don the pilot's uniforms providing they are wearing them - stand by the aircraft until their car draws up alongside. Homer you're going to have to keep out of sight – your sheer size will give the game away. But if you keep outside the circle of illumination with the Heckler & Koch Snipers Rifle you can keep us all covered and if necessary lay down any needed covering fire'.

'What do you suggest I do Sandy', asked Fields.

'Again, I think if anyone sees you boss they're going to recognize you and it'll give the game away. I suggest you stay close to Homer. When we get there we must establish our arcs of fire otherwise we will end up shooting the shit out of one another. It's pointless at this stage to go into any detailed planning until we have seen the lie of the land and just what we are up against'.

They had now crossed the Potomac River and were just passing adjacent to Fort Washington. Rick came up on the intercom and said.

'Boss we have just spoken to the strip controller at Chapman Landing and have clearance to land. They have also stated that as they have only one departure planned for tonight. We're clear to make as many approaches and landings as we like – this should enable us to get a pretty good idea of the strip layout and we may even be able to spot the Cessna 310'.

'Excellent' said Fields. 'After we've landed please park where it's dark so no one can see how many people are deplaning'.

'Roger that'!

Gary flew the S76 straight over the strip to give them a birds eye view of the set up – Homer, seated on the starboard side of the chopper sang out.

'There's a light twin piston engine on the small dispersal but I can't see any one around it'.

'Can any one see any more light twins?' Fields enquired.

Theo seated on the port side chipped in.

'Affirmative boss there are another four light twins on the other side of the airport all in a line'.

'Seen', grunted Niles. 'But I think they are all piqueted down for the night – I reckon that light twin on the dispersal is the one we want'.

'Right – going in for landing' said Gary. 'I'll park the chopper so the port door is facing away from the lighted area of the dispersal. That way I don't think any one will see you getting out'.

Homer was going to have the most difficult job after landing in trying to hide the baulk of the Heckler & Koch rifle – the rest of the team were going to rely on stealth and hand guns.

Gary touched down on the tarmac runway and got clearance to the small dispersal. As they taxied pass the Cessna 310 Gary said, 'I can't see any one around the Cessna so there either in Flight planning or in the small restaurant'.

Niles thought about this last statement as they were taxing in. And as they were all about to debus when he suddenly had an Idea.

'Gary and Rick could you exchange clothes with Mike and I for about an hour? This will enable us to go to the reception area dressed as aircrew without causing any alarm amongst our Cartel friends. I know enough flying parlance should any one feel inclined to question us and we could move around the whole area without arousing any suspicion?'

'It looks as though you are due to inherit my job once I retire Sandy so I guess you might as well have my uniform now'.

Although Gary was slightly smaller than Niles and had the beginning of a paunch Niles figured that if he kept the jacket open no one would notice.

Rick and Mike were almost the same size so there was no problem there.

'By the way Gary if you get the chance, try and get to that Cessna and let the tyres down. That should be sufficient to prevent them getting away in a hurry', added Niles.

Niles and Mike Williams waited until the others had melted away into the darker side of the dispersal before making their way confidently over to the restaurant/admin area.

They entered the small restaurant. The bar was closed for the night and the only place available for refreshments was the coffee and soft drink dispensers

The only other occupants were three Latino men. Two wore pilot's uniforms and the other wore a light grey suit. The guy in the grey suit was obviously a George Raft fan. He was of medium height with swarthy good looks. He had the ubiquitous cigarette clamped to his lips. Niles suspected he practice his, 'hard man looks' in the mirror whilst shaving every morning. He gave Mike and Niles a hard, 'don't fuck with me look' but they both ignored him. Niles started to make pilot talk to allay the Latino's suspicions.

'That was quite a nice approach you just made Mike. We'll have a coffee and check with the tower and get clearance to carry out some single engine approaches followed by some single engine rejects. If we can keep this rate of progress up we should have you a rated Captain by the end of the week'.

The guy in the grey suit interrupted their conversation.

'The airstrip is not open for training so why don't you guys finish your coffee and beat it'.

Niles paid no attention and continued with getting their coffee out the machine'.

Grey suit obviously thought he was some kind of tough guy. He certainly wasn't over endowed with brains. If Mike and Niles had entertained any doubt as to whether these were the guys they were looking for, "tough guy" couldn't have confirmed it any clearer.

'Look you two just drink your coffee and piss off; comprehend?'

Niles grabbed his coffee and walked over to grey suit

and addressed him in an exaggerated polite manner which he knew would annoy the fellow.

'I say old chap are you addressing me or looking in a mirror?'

This took grey suit back a bit and then he snarled.

'You two shit heads get your coffee down and piss off – AH!!... Jesus Christ!

Niles never gave him time to complete his sentence and had thrown his cup of scolding hot coffee in his face. Niles followed this up by whipping out his Beretta and crashing the butt into the side of grey suit's head. He fell to the floor like a pole axed mule.

'Disarm him Mike while I have a quick word with our two friends here', said Niles waving his Beretta at the two aircrew.

He quickly frisked them but they were not carrying weapons.

'Right gentlemen we can do this the easy way or the hard way – It's all the same to me. I've already killed three of your compatriots tonight so two more and I'll become an Ace. What time are you expecting your passengers to arrive?'

The guy wearing the Captains rings shook his head and said.

'We have no idea senor we are waiting to do as we are told'. He yelped as Niles's Beretta butt crashed into the side of his head.

'Mike cover the co-pilot and make sure grey suit doesn't make a recovery – I'm going to get some answers off our friend here and dammed quickly'.

He motioned to the captain to sit at the table and place his hands on the table.

'You have just about five minutes to give me some positive answers otherwise I'm going to crush your fingers one at a time. By the time I have finished with you will never be able to play with your dick or manipulate any aircraft's controls again'.

'Please senor we don't know'. His scream practically lifted the roof of the building walls.

Niles had not even waited for him to finish his sentence. He'd smashed the butt of his Beretta down on the Captains right forefinger completely smashing the bone

'Look let's get this straight we know why you are here and the attempt by your friends to kidnap the wife and daughter of Mr George Fields has failed. However we know that the half of the kidnap team is already on their way to this location. So I'll ask you one more time. What time are you anticipating take off?'

'Our flight plan is due to be activated at 2300hrs – about half an hour from now', groaned the Captain.

'How many will there be in the party?'

'Just two and the driver – I think the driver is a local man and probably doesn't know exactly what is going on'

Niles sensed that all the fight had gone out the Captain and he was telling the truth.

'Christ Sandy you don't mess about. Where did you learn all this rough house stuff, in the British Airborne?' asked Mike.

'Just the theory', he replied. 'But the practical side was learnt bumming around the back streets of Caracas. Right Mike lets find some rope or flex – get these three bastards roped up and hide them in the boot of Field's chopper. It will be a tight fit but once they are in they will be unable to move'.

They made the co-pilot carry the still unconscious grey suit and together with the still groaning captain made there way to the S76 helicopter. As they got close to the chopper with their captives Fields and Baldwin approached them to get an up to date brief.

'What's the score Sandy?' enquired George Fields.

'We haven't got much time boss their flight plan is due to be activated in half an hour so that means the kidnappers could arrive at any time now. I suggest that Mike and I stand over there by the Cessna and we'll arrange to be on the other side of the aircraft until they've stopped the car alongside it. Mike and I will immediately neutralise the two kidnappers you jump out the aircraft and get Douglas. Theo, if you could look after the driver although I'm not expecting much trouble from him but we can't rely on that. It goes without saying that if Douglas's life looks endangered we don't hesitate to shoot to kill. How does that strike you boss?'

Fields nodded in agreement and said. 'Where do you think Theo and I should be?'

'As I said - inside of the Cessna – as soon as Mike and I take out the two gunmen you leap out and secure your son and Theo neutralises the driver. How does that grab you?'

'Sounds fine to me Sandy – how about you Theo?'

'I think it's a good idea boss it's about as close as we can get to the arriving car without arousing suspicion'.

Theo and Fields clambered into the aircraft while Niles grabbed an Air chart which he opened and spread out on the wing of the Cessna.

'Mike, we can pretend to be studying the chart when these guys arrive. This will keep our faces down right to the last second and further more, we can have our hand guns under the chart available for instant action'.

Mike nodded in agreement and they drew their weapons, cocked them, and took the safety catches off and placed them on the wing under the aeronautical chart.

Niles now had a chance to study the lay out of the airstrip. The pan they were parked on was about hundred yards long and sixty deep. The main airstrip building consisted of a small air traffic tower at the west end with four or five offices alongside. He could only see one guy moving around in the tower. He decided that they did not have enough time to warn him on what was about to happen in the next five minutes or so. Alongside the offices was the restaurant where they'd grabbed their prisoners. This in turn was joined to a further two of three offices at the east end.

Apart from the air traffic controller in the tower the rest of the strip appeared to be completely deserted. There was a further large building to the west of the tower where Niles suspected some of the more expensive private aircraft were hangered overnight. Most of the smaller, less expensive single engine aircraft were piqueted on the grass to the east of the hard standing pan. The whole set up was typical of a small American airport that catered for the large General Aviation of the States.

The main road through the entrance of small perimeter fencing was just about opposite to where the Cessna 310 was now parked. The entrance was only about a hundred yards away so once the car had arrived and turned into the Airstrip it would be upon them in seconds.

Five minutes had passed and they were all beginning to get nervous and fidgety, especially Fields worried about his son. Mike suddenly gave Niles a nudge in the ribs.

'Hey up Sandy, our air traffic friend is coming to see us'.

As the controller got closer he looked at Mike and Niles and said. 'Who are you guys? You're not the guys that flew this bird in'.

Niles whipped his Beretta from beneath the chart. He needed to get the Air Controller's attention quickly and said. 'Look sport, don't be alarmed – we are the good guys. In this aircraft is the American Defence Secretary and we are here to foil a kidnap attempt on his son. The State Police are already throwing a screen around this strip but they won't make their presence known until we have the young boy safely in our hands. Boss, can you quickly show this guy your credentials and convince him we are who we say we are'

It took no more than thirty seconds to convince the controller they were who they said they were.

'Actually I have just come over to tell you that your passengers have phoned through and are expecting to be here within the next five minutes – actually you had better make that three minutes as of now'.

Niles shoved his gun back under the chart.

'Under the circumstances I think you had better get back to your tower and keep your head down until all the shooting is over. We are hoping to avoid any but in these situations you can never tell'.

The controller thanked him, turned and made a rapid retreat to the tower.

In fact the large dark blue Lincoln pulled in through the airstrip gates in less than two minutes. It roared quickly up to the Cessna. Pulled up sharply along side and two hoods jumped out and dashed round to the boot of the car barely looking at Niles and Mike.

'I hope you two are ready to move as soon as the others guys arrive', snarled the leader of the two. 'And give us a fucking hand to get this little bastard out the boot'.

The two gunmen were having a struggle getting what appeared to be a rolled up carpet out of the boot.

As they bent over to get a better purchase on the carpet Mike and Niles just nodded to one another, walked up to behind the two gunmen and smashed the butts of their handguns into their skulls. They both dropped like sacks of cement completely unconscious. Niles booted both of them in the side of their temples to ensure that they were both out for the count. He frankly didn't give a dam whether he had caused them permanent injury or not.

Unfortunately the driver reacted quicker than anticipated. He was out the car in a flash and had drawn his hand gun before Theo could get to him. He was not experienced with guns. His shot was wild it greased Theo's head with sufficient force to spin him round and leave him dazed. Mike and Niles were screened behind the boot of the car so were unable to intervene. The driver was just about to get a shot off at Fields when two 7.62 rounds slammed into his scull in quick succession.

Homer strode over with an immense grin on his face. 'Just thought you would like to know that we can shoot straight too Sandy'.

Fields and Theo recovered in a flash. Fields almost knocked Mike and Niles off their feet in his eagerness to get to his son.

They laid the carpet gently on the aircraft pan and cautiously unrolled it. Young Douglas Fields was very groggy and had obviously been drugged for the duration of his capture.

Niles grabbed the Very pistol from the Cessna 310 and fired a red very light into the night sky.

Homer. Whipped out a pair of handcuffs, cuffed one of the dazed kidnappers, passed the cuff round the car door stanchion and then cuffed the second dazed gunman. 'If they can run away dragging the car behind them they deserve to get free',

Is there anything I can do boss?' he continued.

'Yes Homer, contact the FBI and tell them we have some Government Cleaning up to do. I want this aircraft impounded and all these thugs taken into custody and questioned. You can also tell the local police that this involved a kidnapping and therefore it is now an FBI case'.

'Take it as read boss'. Homer gave Niles the heckler and Koch rifle and made his way off to talk with the local police who had quickly responded to the Very light and were just arriving, sirens wailing and blue lights flashing'.

Niles indicated to the ambulance that had just turned up with the police cavalcade.

'How do you want to play this boss? We can take your son back in the helicopter and have him examined at home or take him to the nearest hospital. I think he's is uninjured and just groggy from the drugs'.

'If there is a doctor in the ambulance we will have Douglas checked here and if he gives us the all clear we'll take him home with us. I can raise our family doctor on the mobile and he'll be at our house within the hour'.

Just then the paramedics plus two doctors turned up and took charge of Douglas. They gave him a thorough examination.

The senior Doctor turned to Fields and said. 'Your son is going to be okay but I think he should be kept under observation in hospital for the night and if all goes well he should be fit enough to go home tomorrow'.

George Fields was looking very apprehensive having nearly just lost his son he was not keen to let him out of his sight.

'I figure Homer and I can mount guard on him whilst he's in hospital' said Niles. 'I think you might need Theo and Mike to organise the security back at the house. Jackie and Karen must be very worried at the moment'

'Which hospital are you thinking of taking him to?' asked Fields.

'The nearest to your residence on this side of the river is at Fort Washington. It is a first class hospital with all the necessary equipment one is likely to need. If your son is fit tomorrow and I can see no reason why he shouldn't be, you could have him airlifted home in five minutes', said the Senior Doctor.

Fields looked relieved. 'Thanks a lot Doc' – Sandy, with you and Homer looking after Doug' I know he will be in safe hands. I can't believe that the Cartel have any more gunmen available but it's better to be safe than sorry'.

He then left Niles for a moment and had a word with

the police patrols. After five minutes Fields returned to Niles.

'Okay the Police will also be mounting a guard but I have informed them that you are responsible for Doug and they will abide with your wishes. Okay Sandy I'm off home, see you tomorrow'.

Niles and Mike had to change their clothes with the helicopter aircrew. Homer and Niles clambered into the Ambulance with the medics and drove off to Fort Washington hospital.

Douglas made a rapid recovery and was fit to return home the following morning. By the time Doug', Mike and Niles arrived back at the house things had returned to normality. There was much fuss made of Douglas and Niles slipped away to get some much needed sleep after being awake all the previous night.

Niles slept all day and was wakened about seven in the evening when he heard a gentle knock on the door.

Niles slid his hand under the pillow and grasped the butt of his Beretta.

'Come in', he growled.

The door open and Jenny glided into the room clasping a thermos of Coffee and a plate of sandwiches. She wore a tight pair of expensive jeans which appeared to have been painted on rather than worn. They emphasised her gorgeous thighs and jutting buttocks to perfection. She wore a thin cotton sweater beneath which she appeared to be wearing a sheep dog bra' (it rounded them up and points them in the right direction). She looked absolutely stunning and she knew it!

'I see our conquering hero is awake and ready to be fed', she smirked, her green eyes mocking him.

She stood with one leg slightly in front of the other to emphasise her curves.

Niles could feel her female hormones jumping all over

him. He'd never met a woman such as Jenny. She could turn him on by just looking at him. Even now after an exhausting night he could feel him self becoming rampant. And the annoying thing was that Jenny knew exactly what effect she had on him.

She sat on the side of the bed and offered Niles a mug of coffee and a sandwich.

Jenny behaved herself while Niles munched a couple of sandwiches and drank some coffee. Jenny kept sliding her eyes up and down the length of Niles body and he knew that she had guessed that under the blanket he was completely stark naked.

'I hear you were in action again last night Sandy. The consensus of opinion is that you are a very dangerous man'. As she talked to him Jenny gently ran her hands up and down his covered body whilst he chomped and drank. Even the blanket cover could no longer disguise the rampant state that he was in. He was now so hard it was physically painful.

'Hmm', murmured Jenny as her fingers brushed over his rampant member. 'I think you are hiding a very dangerous weapon beneath this blanket Sandy'.

Niles mouth was so dry with excitement that he had to gulp some coffee to ease the sandwich down.

However, he noticed that Jenny's eyes were no longer mocking they had taken on a smoky look and her voice had definitely become huskier. She was getting infected by the same excitement she was generating in Niles. She pulled the blanket down to reveal Niles monstrous erection.

'Aye aye! She gasped. 'I see our hero is hiding a highly dangerous weapon under the bed clothes. What on earth can we do with it?'

'Get those bloody clothes off and jump into this bed and I'll soon demonstrate what we can do with it', growled Niles.

Jenny gave a shriek of glee and tore her sweater and jeans off in a matter of seconds. She then stood absolutely naked in front of Niles stretched her arms above her head and said. 'Does the master like what he sees?

It is said that beauty is in the eye of the beholder and women can come in many shapes and forms and still be beautiful. But Niles could not remember seeing a woman that could turn him on like Jenny. One minute she was so cool, haughty and beautiful that Niles was reluctant to approach her for fear of rejection and the next one she appeared wanton and so vulnerable.

Niles whipped the bedclothes back and Jenny leapt into his arms as Niles pulled the covers back.

'We are expected over at the house for an informal party. I said we would be back in ten minutes or so', she murmured huskily.

'The; or so could add another ten minutes to your first ten', gasped Niles as Jenny grabbed his nether regions and guided him into her.

Jenny was not interested in any foreplay and she straddled Niles and sank onto him until she completely engulfed his member. She then rocked her self gentle back and forwards at the same time alternatively contracting and relaxing her virginal muscles giving little lady like grunts of pleasure.

Niles had to close his eyes to control himself – the sight of Jenny riding him with her gorgeous boobs jiggling and the wonton look on her face was just too exciting. Niles cast him mind back to the events of the previous evening in an effort to maintain his self control. Suddenly; Jenny began to gasp and quicken her pace. He opened his eyes as she began to bounce up and down with an increasing frenzy. She grabbed his shoulders with her hands and sunk her nails into him and began to wail. That was it! - Niles could no longer control himself and levered his hips off the bed in order to achieve an even deeper penetration.

They climaxed together and Jenny sank down onto his body and gasped. 'I think I must have Clicked.'

'Clicked? What do you mean you must have clicked?' he queried.

'You know Sandy – it is a gringo expression – I think you must have made me pregnant by now. I think I have clicked'!

Niles had forgotten that when they made love for the first time Jenny had stated that she wanted to bear his child. He was not sure how to respond. His previous experience at marriage had not been very successful and although Jenny was one hell of a woman he was not sure just how far he was prepared to commit. His previous three years as an alien in a foreign country had conditioned him into not making any lasting commitments. He'd had to "leg it" on several occasions in Venezuela when the authorities had discovered that he had no official papers. Niles was still trying to accept the fact that he was now in a country legally and there was no need for contingencies to leave in a hurry.

Jenny; with a typical woman's intuition detected Niles reluctance.

'Don't worry Sandy I have no intentions of trying to corral you. I realise that you are not a domestic animal and don't like to be tied down It's your child I want. If possible I might call on you later for a further two more'.

'For Christ sake Jenny why does it have to be me?'

'Because you and I will produced beautiful offspring, I just know we will - I thought so from the first moment I laid my eyes on you in Colombia'.

'You don't seem to care whether or not I agree Jenny'.

'Sandy, if I tried to force you into marriage you would run a mile. Initially I decided that you would father my children purely for biological reasons. Unfortunately I have also grown to love you ever since we arrived at the Field's residence. Although you might find this declaration of love an embarrassment it just reinforces my determination to have your progeny – so there!

With that mind blowing statement Jenny leaped out of bed and started to dress.

He lay in bed trying to come to terms with what she had just said. He was gob smacked, he simple could not think straight. Normally a woman as beautiful and rich as Jenny moved in completely different social circles to his and yet, here was this beautiful creature saying she was in love with him and insisted on bearing his children. Christ! Thought Niles as soon as you injected a woman into the equation life sure became complicated.

Niles climbed out of bed as though he had just recovered from being pole axed.

Jenny, now dressed picked, up Niles's trousers and was just about to hand them over when she noticed that the right hand pocket lining had been cut away.

'Hey hombre, what's happened to your pocket – it has been cut completely away? I hope this not so you can play with yourself when no one is looking'. She gave Niles another of those mocking looks.

'Trust you to discover that', Niles grabbed his trousers and pulled them on but before fastening the waist band he clipped his Beretta to the inside of his right thigh at the same time looking Jenny in the eyes and returning her mocking looks.

'Aha hombre I see you have two dangerous weapons down there between your thighs'. She then folded up in a fit of giggles.

'It's time we made our way to the big house Jenny – we have been fooling around here for at least half an hour. The Fields will be wondering what has happened to us'.

'Jackie wont, she will know exactly what we have been up to', giggled Jenny.

'You're joking', gasped Niles.

'No way Sandy - Jackie knows exactly how I feel about you and she has given me her blessing and wished me good hunting,.

'Christ in a canoe', murmured Niles. 'Talk about the weaker sex working as a team'.

When they got to the main house all the others were gathered in the main reception room and were obviously waiting for Jenny and Niles to make an appearance.

'You look kind of tired Sandy you should have had a longer sleep', smiled Jackie Fields and she delivered the same mocking look that he had been getting from Jenny.

Niles just grinned. Jackie was perfectly aware of the reason why he and Jenny were late and wondered if the whole god dammed family was aware of what had taken place.

George Fields approach him with young Douglas in tow and said, 'Sandy! You're still looking rather bushed – having said that you have a talent for generating more excitement in one evening than I think I have experience in my entire life. (George Fields was obviously not privy to what had taken place in his flat five minutes ago). Doug; let me introduce you to our body guard but more to the point I would like to think of him as a valuable friend of the family. Karen has already regaled you with some of his exploits'.

Douglas had his father's features and colouring but his mothers eyes. He was quite tall for his age and was already beginning to broaden in the chest and shoulders. His freckled face was already grinning from ear to ear and it was patently obvious that he had totally recovered from his kidnapping.

'Hi Sandy I've heard plenty about you from Karen and the rest of the family so I was not surprised to find that it was largely due to your efforts that I was rescued before they could smuggle me out the country. It appears that I was unconscious most of the time so missed all the excitement.

Dad's a good shot and so are Theo and his team but they reckon you're in a league of your own. I would be grateful for any tips you could give me to improve my shooting. Though I believe I might have to hassle Karen to get some of your spare time'.

Niles grinned and nodded his head in agreement.

'Well that's up to your Mum and Dad son, some parents don't like their offspring getting too interested in fire arms'.

'I'm working on that', Douglas grinned. 'But in any case I would like to thank you for your part in rescuing me. Dad said you are, 'hell on wheels'. Many thanks Sandy'.

'It was a team effort son; I managed to extract the information from some of the unsavoury characters involved in an unconventional manner because I have no officials to answer to other than your father. Luckily it panned out well'

'Mind you boss', said Niles looking at George Fields. 'I think your Senator friend might consider consulting his lawyers with a view to bringing charges of assault over my forceful interview'.

'Not so Sandy. By the time I have finished with him he will be only too lucky to escape a jail sentence. I don't think you need to worry about any of the people we "interviewed last night"'.

George Fields grinned as Karen came over to Niles to thank him before being dispatch off to bed.

'I haven't seen much of you today Sandy – you never turned up for your ride, will you be there tomorrow?'

'I apologise Karen, same time as usual tomorrow morning – goodnight sweetheart'. He looked carefully at Karen without alarming her but could see no ill effects from the trauma she had suffered the previous night. She was going to develop into one hell of a woman – some guy was going to be lucky.

Meanwhile Jackie Fields and Helen Mendoza had

cornered Jenny and were pumping her with questions about her situation with Niles.

'For god sake tell us what happened? Did the question of marriage get mentioned?' asked Jackie.

'No no, I just told Sandy that I realise that he was not a domestic animal and I did not expect him to marry me – however', she continued with a steely look in her eye. 'When I am well and truly pregnant I will put the question to Sandy as to whether he wants his progeny is to bear his name or not'.

Helen looked at her sister aghast in amazement and said, 'surely you must get a commitment out of him now before you find your self pregnant Jenny'.

Jenny turned to Jackie and said, 'Jackie, would you say that Sandy was an honourable man or not?'

'Every thing we have seen of him to date would indicate him being an honourable man with plenty of integrity. Look how conscientiously he has carried out his duties since arriving here'.

'I agree', Jenny murmured. 'I will therefore cut him sufficient rope to hang himself with. If I attempted to force his hand in marriage the bastard will run a mile. However I'm going to let him think he is getting his cake and eating it without any commitment but once I mention the child being born a bastard Sandy will carry me over the stile. He is as good as hog tied', she ended triumphantly.

'And they call us the weaker sex', smirked Helen Mendoza.

Chapter 33

Barranquilla

Hurricane Judy had long gone. The snowy peak of the Pico Cristobal of the Santa Marta Mountains now gleamed like the icing on a wedding cake as it reflected the early morning sun. The cloudless sky shone with a clear blue azure that took ones breath away. The receding hurricane had sucked all the impurities up into the upper atmosphere giving limitless visibility. Not a breath of wind disturbed the lush green vegetation - that would come later as the sun heated the land and the thermals drifted skywards as the cooler air off the sea moved in to replace the ascending air over the heated land. Colourful humming birds, the iridescence of their wings shimmering in the early morning sun were already flitting from flower to flower sipping nature's nectar. The large Hacienda was situated on what must have been one of the most desirable sites in the world. The whole vista was one of beauty and tranquillity.

Unfortunately this glorious tranquillity was not echoed by the owner of the Hacienda Francesco Domingo. Seated in his work study he'd just received a telephone call from

Mr Chase in the States telling him about the shambles of the attempted kidnapping. Further more he was now going to have to tell his wife that her sister's twins had been killed while attempting a kidnap at his request. (Though he suspected that by now her sister would have already told her). Domingo was already "persona none gratis" with the remainder of the Cartel members and now it looked as though he was going to be ostracized by his own family over the death of his nephews.

He moved out the house and sat in his porch looking out to the north overlooking the marvellous coastline view. He could feel the bile building up within him. A more rational man might have cut his losses, put it down to one of life's hard knocks and got on with living his life. Not Domingo. As he studied the beautiful Caribbean shore line with the calm blue sea lapping against the pristine white sand the beauty failed to raise his spirits. He'd worked and schemed hard all his life to lift himself from the gutters of Medellin to his present position as one of the richest men in the world only to find all his plans and aspiration over the past month blow up in his face. Where had he gone wrong? It had all started to go pear shape after the Dakota had crash landed near their new processing Lab's. No - that was not strictly true. It was the inception of the new Field Force Police team trained by those SAS shites who'd made it necessary to move their Lab's into the hinterland. Prior to that they had always been able to bribe the Police and Security Forces and prevent their Lab's of ever being raided.

He studied his hands and then drummed his fingers on the adjacent coffee table and then suddenly made a decision. He picked up the phone and dialled.

A women's voice answered. Good morning, Mr. Chase's secretary here, how can I help'?

'Good morning Madam. This is a Mr. Domingo phoning from Colombia; could you please put me through to your boss'?

'One moment Sir - putting you through'.

Domingo could hear subdued voices but nothing loud enough to be intelligible.

Chase's voice came over the line loud and clear but in a decidedly guarded manner.

'Francesco; what can I do for you'?

'I need some information and I thought you might be just the man to provide it'

'Look Domingo, you are causing a hell of a fuck up here State side. That last stunt you tried has back fired and it's only a matter of time before the FBI find out who initiated the attempted kidnapping. If you think you are going to sit at home and avoid all the flack you have another thought coming. I've heard of this guy Fields and as the American Defence Secretary he can pull plenty of powerful favours. I can assure you that he will already be planning his revenge'.

'Yeh okay I heard you but I would like you to give me the name of some one who can recruit me some gringo mercenaries. You must have contacts in the Arms business that have knowledge of these men. I'd like to recruit some and I'll pay well for your information and their services'.

'Look Domingo I have stuck my neck out enough for helping you. Any further help is going to cost you plenty'.

'Okay Chase if you can give me the names of a guy who can recruit me half a dozen good mercenaries I'll give you a hundred thousand dollars. How does that grab you'?

Chase sucked his breath in. The figure Domingo had just offered was twice the amount he'd had in mind. For that amount he'd sell his mother to Domingo.

'I can give you the names of some good guys but I can tell you now they won't consider the kidnapping of women and children but there's a French man who I can put you in touch with and providing the money is right will attempt anything he thinks he can get away with. His name is John Jack Darcy. I'll put your proposition to him and get his initial response and if it's favourable I'll let him have your home number so he can contact you direct. However; I'll not put him touch with you until my Swiss bank reflects the money you promised me - okay'.

'Fine - I'll have the money sent off straight away. It will be in your bank in the next hour or so but remember this Mr. Chase you renege on this deal and you will never put your foot in South America and live to tell of it'.

'Yeh; I understand what you are saying but I still think you are biting off more than you can chew Domingo. You might be a big gun in Colombia but I don't think you really know what you are up against. The Secretary of Defence of the United States is politically, one of the most powerful men in the world, he is not one of your local Colombian officials that can be bribed or coerced into doing your bidding. This guy has some enormous powerful strings to his bow and frankly I can only see you coming off second best'.

'That's my problem', snarled Domingo. 'You just get hold of this French man and leave the rest to me. This has now become personal, they have killed two of my sister's sons and now I want revenge'.

Chase managed to bite his tongue back before making a reply. The fact that Domingo had caused all the grief in the first place seemed beyond his comprehension.

'Don't say you haven't been warned', continued Chase. 'I'll get Darcy to contact you. I won't tell him your intended target I'll leave that to you and that's as far as I wish to be involved - under the circumstances Domingo I don't think I will be doing any further business with you - its becoming too dangerous. Good day'! And Chase thumped the phone down and gasped with exasperation. The man was a fucking idiot, the less I have to do with him in the future the better he thought.

Domingo was incensed at the way Chase had cut him off. I'll get that bastard the next time he sets foot in Colombia he vowed. Never the less it was becoming apparent that he was rapidly beginning to run out of associates. He'd already lost the collaboration of his former colleagues and he was not sure he liked the feeling of isolation that was creeping over him. He was now going to have to fight the forth coming battle completely on his own.

While he was deep in thought Maria his wife approached.

'Francesco', she murmured softly. 'I've just heard from my sister about the death of her twins. What in Gods name have you got us into?'

'Shut your grizzling woman - I've had enough problems today without you complaining to me. Those two men took their chances as I had to when I was a young man and they fucked up and suffered the consequences. In this game you take big risks and if you are successful you make a lot of money but if you fuck up you are dead - they took their chances and screwed up. I wish to hear no more on the matter woman - now get out!' His wife gave him a stony look of contempt, tossed her head, and went indoors. She knew better than to argue with him in his present mood.

It took two days before Domingo was approached by the French man, John Jack Darcy. In fact he was beginning to think that Chase had reneged on their deal when his swarthy giant body guard, Renaldo, appeared to tell him that there was a phone call from Europe on the secure line..

Domingo grabbed the phone and growled.

'This Domingo speaking - what can I do for you?'

'I think it's more of a case of what I can do for you', said the slightly accented voice.

'I have been asked to contact you by a mutual friend who suggests I might be able to reconcile a problem for you'.

'Did our friend give you any idea what the problem was?' asked Domingo.

'He did in essence after we had managed to establish

a secure link, hence the delay in contacting you. Although this line is supposed to be secure I suggest that the nature of the operation is too sensitive to talk about over the phone and that I fly to Colombia and discuss the details with you personally. I should warn you, from what our friend told me the job you are contemplating is going to cost one hell of a lot of money. Further more I expect to have my travelling expenses reimbursed'.

'That's fine by me - I will wire you the cost of your air fare straight away but I want you out here as soon as possible - can you get here within the next three days or so?'

'For the money that Darcy was thinking of charging he was prepared to be there like yesterday.

'It will take some arranging but I should be out there the day after tomorrow'.

'Did our friend mention the fact that I want a party of about five or six men for the proposed task?' queried Domingo.

'That's affirmative', replied Darcy. 'That's why I'm speaking to you from Brussels. I have four suitable candidates already lined up and I'm waiting for a reply from a fifth. However I'll fly to Colombia myself initially to discuss the financial details and if we can come to an agreement my colleagues can join us within twenty four hours'.

'Okay Darcy I look forward to meeting you and I'm sure that we can come to a financial agreement. However time is pressing - I'd like to get this problem terminated as soon as possible'.

'Look Mr Domingo; you provide the money and I'll provide the necessary expertise and hardware and I'm sure we can have your problem solved in a couple of weeks from you giving us the word GO!'

'I hope so Mr. Darcy this problem has now dragged on for over a month and has cost me plenty of bucks but if you produce the goods I'll produce the money. If you let me know your time of arrival at Bogotá International Aero Porte I will arrange to have you picked up by helicopter and flown to Medellin where we can discuss our plans in detail - Okay?'

'That sounds fine Mr. Domingo. I'll phone you tomorrow on this number and let you have my flight details and I look forward to meeting you in Medellin - Cheers for now - adios'.

Domingo cradled the phone and thought he had a last managed to nail the right man for the job. With the death of his two nephews he'd no one State side that could be relied upon to carry out his plans. Although he had the services of over a hundred men in Colombia none of them were really suited for operating in the United States. Any one approaching the Field's residence with a Latino complexion was immediately going to raise suspicions. His men were going to have to have Nordic features and complexion if the operation stood any chance of succeeding.

Domingo decided that he'd had enough of being silently censured by his family over the death of his nephews and rang for Renaldo his massive body guard.

'Yes boss?'

Renaldo's massive frame stood in the door of the study. He was so tall that he had to stoop to avoid banging the top of his head against the door lintel. He'd now been with Domingo ever since they were small urchins in the slums of Medellin. Even as young boys Renaldo had always been a giant for his age and Domingo was cute enough to realise that although Renaldo was not very bright he was a good friend to have when push came to shove. Domingo had nurtured their friendship as they grew up together and he'd clawed his way to the top of his present powerful Drug Cartel. His friendship was reciprocated by Renaldo ten fold. Although he was not very bright he had enough animal cunning to realise that by remaining loyal to Domingo he would achieve a higher standard of living and accumulate more money than he could ever hope to accomplish on his own.

'Renaldo, arrange for the chopper to pick us up tomorrow after the phone call from Europe and we'll get ourselves down to Medellin and have some fun whilst we await the arrival of this Darcy gringo. Phone Christine up and tell her to be ready to receive us tomorrow evening. I'm getting pissed off listening to my wife and family whining about the death of the twins - lets get to hell out of here'.

A huge grin cracked the giant's face. Domingo had a lover's nest tucked away in the residential part of Medellin that only Renaldo and his other four body guards were aware of.

Unknown to Domingo, Renaldo also had a smart little Senorita down there, who was only too happy to provide the giant with a passionate interlude. He was only too glad to comply.

'No problem boss - how long do you figure us being down there?'

'We'll be meeting this guy from Europe down there so I figure we can stay about a week while we discuss business

'On my way boss', grinned the massive Renaldo as he lumbered away to do his bidding.

. Domingo continued to sit and think. He was not going to apprise his former colleagues of his new venture. Relations between him and the other Cartel members were already at an all time low and although they continued to do business together he's been strictly ostracised from their company. Further more, the less they knew of the intended operation the tighter the security would be

Chapter 34

USA River Side gardens

The phone rang Niles groaned, rolled over and cradled the phone against his ear.

'Sandy could you come over to the main house?' George Fields was obviously still worried. 'I'd like to discuss what methods we could use to counter this maniac Domingo. I agree with what you said yesterday and I believe it is only a matter of time before he has another go at us'.

'Give me five minute to freshen up boss and I'll be straight over'.

He plashed water on his face and after giving himself a vigorous toweling. Jenny had paid him a visit last night and she had only left him an hour ago. He was knackered. He pulled on his jeans, a shirt and his bomber jacket. He made his way to the main house. Knocked the door and was bade enter, walked in and sat down in the chair Fields indicated to him.

'Some good news Sandy; I've just heard from Tony Bryant. He and Rusty are flying to the States the day after tomorrow with a view to starting up and registering the new

Security Company. I've arranged for the S76 to pick them up at the airport and fly them here. They can stay here until they have found their own accommodation. We have plenty of spare rooms – I just wish the rest of the team they had in Colombia could also have come. I can't think of anyone I'd rather have at my disposal than those god dam pirates. It would also make good sense for me to make a formal bid for your services for which I expect you to charge me the going rate. With you three on my side I'll feel much happier. I'm sure with the addition of Tony and Rusty on board we'd have a much better chance of defeating Domingo. Do you foresee any problems with that?'

'I think I can answer for the other two before they arrive and say that we'll be only too glad to take you up as our first employer. I've been mulling a plan over for the past few days which might reconcile your conflict with Domingo. I suggest I run it pass Tony and Rusty first to get their reaction and see if they're in agreement. If they think it's acceptable then we'll liaise with you to get your approval'.

'That sounds fine Sandy are you sure you wouldn't like to discuss the plan with me first?'

'Not really boss; if Tony and Rusty don't agree the plan can't be implemented. If they agree with what I've in mind, I'll get back to you and discuss all the details which we think you should know about. This is not strictly trying to maintain a, 'Need to Know', structure but a case of trying to protect you should there be any unfavourable reactions to our plans. We'll have to consider for example what may happen if you are required to stand up in a court of law. You can deny intimate knowledge of our intended actions without having to commit perjury'.

'You'd be surprised what I'd do to keep my family safe Sandy and that includes committing bloody perjury if necessary', snarled Fields.

'Accepted boss but the point is that if we plan this right

there will be no need for you to know the intimate details of what we're up to. What I'm hoping to achieve will take place outside the United States. Once you have completed the cover story that I have in mind for us, which in fact will be true; you will no longer be involved or in contact with us until we return to this room, hopefully, telling you that your problems are over'.

'Okay Sandy I'll go along with that. How long after their arrival do you anticipate in getting the plan into action?'

'Probably three to four days - some of the delays will be purely administrative which to some extent will depend on how fast your organization can react'.

'This is the U.S. of A, Sandy and I can assure you that my organization will be reacting in a bloody god dam quick time believe you me'.

'That's what I like about you guys', smiled Niles. 'When arse needs kicking there's no one like the Yanks to do the kicking'.

'You're bloody right there Sandy but I've known the Brits' do some mighty fast kicking when required. Ok let's leave things as they are for the moment and get some lunch. If I keep you here any longer I will get hell from Karen not to mention Jenny. As a matter of interest Sandy you and Jenny seem to be making out fine - do I hear the sound of 'twigs being collected?'

'Not by me and I think Jenny appreciates that I'm not really a domesticated person. So I don't think she has any sort of commitment in mind'.

George Fields look at Niles in a thoughtful bemused manner. 'I'm not sure about that Sandy you haven't seen the devastating looks she gives you when you're not looking. I'm telling you boy they could melt an iceberg'.

Niles just shrugged his shoulders but had the uncomfortable feeling that the entire household were into a secret that he knew nothing about.

Next day, apart from his early morning ride with Karen during which he continued to look for any sign of clandestine surveillance, He spent the whole day going over the details of a plan to prevent a further attack at Riverside. It was based on the premise that the best means of defense is attack. To simply wait at Riverside for Domingo to decide when and where to attack was just courting disaster.

Niles decided to stay at Riverside and await the arrival of Tony and Rusty. He wanted to get all his thoughts marshaled on paper before putting his plan to them, rather than flying to the Airport to greet them. Although they would be slightly tired from their cross Atlantic flight he'd no doubt that they would be bright enough to appreciate the plan. Once they had accepted it, they could get some rest whilst George Fields got the necessary admin problems in motion.

The chopper landed on the front lawn just before lunch. The smell from the large patio at the back of the house indicated that a large barbeque was being prepared for their arrival. Once again, Niles was impressed by attitude displayed by the American Defence Secretary towards two soldiers none of whom were of senior officer status. In the UK they would have been politely thanked for their rescue achievement, but it would have been most unlikely that they would have been invited to stay with a Senior Government Minister. Yet here in the States one of the Presidents most Senior Advisors had no compunctions at offering to billet two soldiers. He was impressed.

The two SAS men deplaned looking disgustingly fit as ever. They were both dressed in jeans and polo shirts and carried duffle bags plus some hand baggage but otherwise they appeared to have traveled very light.

Rusty was the first to grab Niles hand.

'Shit you jammy bastard how did you find a shack job like this?' he said nodding to the mansion. 'Typical; all you fly boys seem to land in the cozy billets whilst us poor devils end up sleeping in a ditch full of water – if we're lucky'.

George Fields was somewhat taken aback by the exuberance of Rusty's opening gamut. Although he had met the SAS men briefly whilst waiting for the flight home from Colombia he had little to do with the troopers except to thank them. He found their self reliance completely refreshing. They appeared to have no respect for position, power or money. Whilst this was supposed to be an American trait he noticed it in abundance with the SAS troopers.

'Boss' said Niles Introducing Irons. 'This reprobate is Rusty Irons; you met him briefly in Bogotá. He was one of the two that got themselves isolated on the wrong side of the ravine when we were flying the first extraction. But more to the point he was the guy that dragged our arses out the fire during the initial rescue. Without Rusty's quick intervention Jackie, Karen and I would all be dead by now

'Got you now, Jackie told me all about your rescue – I can't thank you enough. It goes without saying that you will be our guest until you depart,' laughed Fields. 'How's your wounded friend getting on?'

'Oh Hezeltine, the jammy devil is roughing it in a convalescence centre. Give him another three weeks and he will be back in training - he's making a full recovery'.

'Glad to hear it' continued Fields releasing Rusty's hand and grabbing Tony Bryant's. 'Look you guys, we have lain on some lunch for you on the patio and a few drinks and then I think Sandy is going to run a plan he's devised past you. If you both agree, then I'm to be told only that which concerns me. Sandy's playing this one very close to his chest'.

The two SAS men just gave Niles a knowing look and followed Fields through the house to the barbeque.

The lunch was a jovial affair and all three of the Brits' being impressed by the manner in which they were received, wined and dined. It was difficult to appreciate that not only were they being entertained by one of the richest men in the States but that he was also one of the most powerful political figures in the Country and therefore in the world.

At no time was Bryant, Irons or Niles ever made to feel anything but welcome. The class snobbery often associated within the English Social Structure was completely absent. At no time did any of the Fields family and friends attempt to talk down to the three Brits. They were accepted for what they were which was high grade professionals in their chosen careers.

After lunch the three Brits' retired to a study that George Fields had set aside from them. Niles started the meeting off by explaining why at this stage, he did not want to involve George Fields with the planning. Bryant and Irons concurred when he advanced his reasons.

Niles looked at his two colleagues and said.

'During your absence I have been mulling a plan over to prevent out friend Domingo from causing further grief to the Defence Secretary and his family. I thought I'd run it past you two guys, you've had a hell of a lot more experience in this sort of caper than I have. I would like to get your general opinion on whether you think the scheme is feasible. If so, we can then get down to some detailed planning. How does that sound to you guys?'

Bryant and Irons looked at one another and Rusty gave Tony a brief nod.

'That sounds fine to us Sandy, said Bryant. 'If you would like to give us the gist of what you intend we'll make our comments as we go along'.

Niles nodded his head and started to put forward the outline of the plan he had hatched.

'Basically, as I see it, we've got to take the fight to Domingo. To wait here for Domingo to act is to invite disaster. He could plan to strike next week, next month or even decide to wait for an entire year before making a move.

This would throw an unacceptable strain on the whole family. Plus which, if Domingo has the sense to wait a month or so before making an attack, it would be almost impossible for us to remain completely on the ball for such a long period'.

Tony Bryant and Rusty Irons nodded their heads in agreement.

'What I would like to suggest', continued Niles. 'Is that we employ the same policy as we used in northern Ireland during operation, 'Autumn Leaves', Rusty is already familiar with it in principal Tony, we discussed it to a small extent when we were in Colombia. Basically, what I'm suggesting is that we go to Colombia, reconnoiter Domingo's movement and then put a plan into operation to make Domingo disappear without any one knowing what's happened to him. I'm hoping that this will deflect any one of his sons or relatives continuing the vendetta against the Fields family. If they don't know where or how he's disappeared they'll not know who to blame. It might even be possible to start rumours that he has fled the country with some woman – who knows? I think this is the only way we can be certain of protecting the Defence Secretary and his family. What do you think?'

Tony nodded his head in agreement. 'To use the old adage, the best means of defence is attack. I think you are absolutely right Sandy. To simply wait here for Domingo to make his move is courting disaster we would be handing him the initiative on a plate never knowing where and when he was going to strike. However trying to take him out in his own back yard is not going to be easy we'll have to reconnoitre his movements to establish where to strike successfully. What do you think Rusty/'

Rusty had the most combat experience of the three so his input was going to be considered carefully.

Rusty rubbed his chin and said thoughtfully. 'As with all these sort of plans the recce'ing and planning is going to take the longest but I feel that we can't really plan details until we get to Colombia and check the lay of the land'.

'I've already got the provisional recce'ing in hand', continued Niles. 'Our friend Maria's father, Alfred Mendoza has some of his security people keeping Domingo under distant surveillance, nothing too obtrusive but just checking on his movements so it will give us some idea what Domingo's is up to when we arrive. Bear in mind that we don't want Alfred or his family to be compromised in any way. They have to live there after we have flown the coop'.

Tony Bryant gave Niles a searching look and said, 'we're going to need some kind of cover story to justify our arrival in Colombia unless you are suggesting that we make a clandestine parachute entry?'

'What I am going to propose, if you two are in an agreement, is that we arrive in Colombia as a relief helicopter pilot; that's obviously going to be me and you two as geological surveyors, which should give us good reasons for moving around the country without arousing suspicion'.

'The only problem there is', said Rusty. 'I know sweet FA about survey work and I have a sneaking suspicion that Tony here doesn't know much either'.

Niles nodded in agreement. 'We can quickly brush up on a few okay phrases and it will have been noted that I've been allocated as your pilot for the period of the survey so we'll only have to contact with other members of the Company as and when we see fit. We can pretend that we're confirming the location of potential oilfields which for the time being must remain a Company secret for obvious reasons. That way, we'll be almost a law unto ourselves and can move around without generating too many questions from our own company. Let's face it; Oil Companies are always secretive about any new areas of exploration. Bearing in mind that the Fields Exploration Energy Company employs a lot of locals who are bound to express an interest in what the new 'Gringos' are up to. So if we use this cover story it should negate us having to discuss what we're doing to other members of the Company. I'm going to have to dye my hair black and darken my complexion as I've been seen by quite a few of Domingo's henchmen. I figure you two will be safe without resorting to a disguise. Rusty was seen by a few of Domingo's henchmen but most of them are dead, further more, Rusty was using camouflage paint on his face and dressed in combat fatigues so it's unlikely than any one that did see him in the jungle would be able to recognize him – how to you feel on the subject Rusty?'

'I agree Sandy, some of the guys at the road block had a good look at you but the only ones that had a close up of me are now six feet under. However your plan so far shows how we get into the country without arousing suspicion but have you any idea how we make Domingo disappear without compromising the Fields organization?'

Niles consulted a piece of paper on which he had scrawled some notes.

'I'm open to suggestions on this one but basically we have to remove him from society without any one knowing how or where he's gone. At the moment I'd suggest that with the tools we have available; i.e. a S76 helicopter and George Fields organization we smuggle him aboard the chopper and then dump him offshore where hopefully he'll never be found. The most difficult part of the operation will be to ensure that not only do the Cartel know nothing of our involvement but we must also ensure that none of George Fields employees know either'. I figure the most problematical part of the operation will be separating Domingo from his body guards without arousing suspicion. Once we have the bastard aboard the chopper it will be mostly plain sailing, but the first part is going to require some careful planning – what do you think Rusty?'

'I think you are right Sandy but we can't really go into

detailed planning at this stage until we've comprehensive knowledge of Domingo's movements. Once we've established that we can then formulate a plan. What do you think boss?'

'I agree', said Tony. 'And by the way Rusty I think as we are all intending to start a business enterprise together the sooner we get on first names the better. The only problem that I foresee is that Rusty and I are due back in the UK in a months time to get our official discharge from the Service so time is not on our side'.

Niles laughed. 'I figure if we took longer than three weeks to get this out of the way there is a strong possibility of Domingo getting his blow in first and the whole object of this exercise is to pre-empt him before he can mount any attack on Fields. I'm hoping that Mendoza's men will be able to update us on Domingo's movement, this should enable us to save our recce time'.

'Sandy, how much of this information has been discussed with Fields and Alfred Mendoza?' asked Tony.

'All I will be asking of George Fields is to have the Orders made out to transfer us to the Oil operation he has in Colombia and carry out the work we have just discussed –after that I've told him we are not going to disclose our plans to him. That way, he can stand on oath and say he was unaware of any plan to remove Domingo, All Alfred Mendoza knows is that we have requested that Domingo be kept under surveillance in order to fore stall any further attacks on Fields or his family. The only people that know our full intentions are the three of us sat round this table and that's the way I think we should keep it'.

Both Tony and Rusty nodded their heads in agreement.

Niles looked at both of them and suddenly seemed embarrassed.

'Can I ask you guys a personal question?'

Both Rusty and Tony looked somewhat a taken back and Tony said, 'sure Sandy, fire away'.

'Well as you both know I had to rough it in Venezuela for the previous three years and I did some things that I'm not particularly proud of but to my knowledge I had never killed any one until our Colombian episode I've now personally killed over a dozen men and yet feel no remorse. I half expected to have bad dreams or nightmares but the killings seem to have left me with no guilt, yet I feel I should have. Even now I'm sitting down here with you two and planning about the removal of a living person from this God's earth. I'm worried about turning into some amoral killer like our friend Domingo. How does this affect you guys in the SAS? During your service you must have been forced to shoot to kill – do you suffer any form of guilt feeling after the event?'

Rusty who had the most experience within the SAS answered

'The fact that you are worried is answer enough Sandy it's just that you have been forced to shoot to kill from close range which makes it much more personal than it would be if you were firing rockets from your helicopter. Your lack of guilt is not unusual with people called upon to take drastic action – lets face it, you were having to shoot them or be killed yourself There's no doubting that you have a flare for thinking on your feet in very tight situations and I think I can answer for Tony and I by saying that without your natural talent to come up out of the shit like a shiny new pin we would not be so keen to take on this venture'.

'Nice to know I'm appreciated', Niles grinned.

'Rusty is right', said Tony. 'You have not been trained in close quarter fighting as Rusty and I have so this mode of killing is new to you. There's no doubt that you have a flair for survival without which, all three of us would probably not be sitting here. Long may it continue In fact Sandy, when you think of it, your time in Venezuela was rather like some extended survival course where for three years you have been living by your wits. You might even consider it as a blessing in disguise. You'd probably have never made it without your "training" in Venezuela'.

'Thanks a lot I was getting a little worried that I was about to turn into some addicted assassin, and I see what you mean about Venezuela. When I arrived there I couldn't speak a word of Spanish and I was pretty naïve, without that large slice of self survival, I'd now be six foot under', murmured Niles somewhat embarrassingly. 'Well I think that's all we can discuss for the moment – we'll let George know what we need for our cover story but that is all he gets told – he's been warned that he will only be told the details of events if and when they've been brought to a successful conclusion. So if you have no further questions let's retire to the main room and join the drinks party that's been arranged for you two'.

They joined the main party which had now shrunk down to the immediate family, the Mendoza's and Jenny. Karen greeted the two SAS men like long lost uncles; she grabbed them by the hand and immediately insisted that she give them a conducted tour of the house and the estate. Later on she had to leave to attend a birthday party for one of her school colleagues.

With the absence of Karen who was always a little possessive about Niles company Jenny settled on his arm as though they had been an established couple for the last ten years or so. George Fields noted the look of surprise on the two SAS guy's face as Jenny hung onto Niles arm as though her life depended on it. Tony and Rusty walked over to chat with George.

George gave then a big grin.

'I must say it's nice to see you guys again I still can't thank you enough for what you did for my girls in Colombia.

It goes without saying that anything you need whilst you're here, just sing out'.

'All part of the job Mr. Fields' said Bryant. 'I believe that Sandy has already mentioned that we are only going to disclose to you what you need to know. However on the successful conclusion of the exercise we will appraise you with all the detail. By the way what's happened to Sandy? It looks to us as though Jenny has just about got him hog tied'.

George just grinned. 'Well it started of by Jenny saying she wanted a child by Sandy purely for biological reasons mind you – talk about breeding from good stock – anyway, Sandy agreed and I think to be quite honest Jenny was going to be happy with that and no more. But during the past two weeks or so Jackie and I have notice a distinct change in Jenny. When Sandy is not looking she gives him looks that would melt an ice berg and Jackie thinks that Jenny will not settle until she has Sandy up the wedding aisle. I think the only person who hasn't registered the fact so far is Sandy himself'.

Tony gave the pair in question a good look. 'I don't know Mr. Fields Sandy has never struck me as a domesticated animal – she may have trouble getting Sandy to the church'.

George Fields just grinned broader than ever. 'I tell you what Tony, Jackie my wife is giving me odds of ten to one that Jenny will get Sandy to the church on time – always provided you silly buggers don't go and get your heads shot off in Colombia. By the way just how much of this exercise am I going to be acquainted with?'

Tony paused for a moment. 'I think Sandy has already mentioned most of what we need. We are going to discuss things in more detail during the morning but basically we need a cover story from you saying that we are an oil survey party with Sandy as the S76 pilot who has been tasked to survey possible new drilling sites. The locations of the sites are to remain secret for obvious reasons. This will enable us; hopefully, to move about the country without raising any suspicions. And even more importantly, not having to talk to your oil employees and thus disclose our lack of knowledge on oil related matters. By mid day tomorrow we will have finalized our list and hopefully be on our way to Colombia in three days time'.

'Christ you guys don't waste much time do you and, please, call me George'.

Bryant politely nodded his head, smiled and concurred with Fields request. 'Actually George, we don't know how much time we have before Domingo has another attempt- Sandy reckons we have to move against him within the next three weeks to fore stall any further attacks on you or your family'.

'Shit', growled Fields. 'There's nothing like having a proposed attack on you and your family to focus one's attention. It goes without saying Tony that any thing you need you just ask and you will get it like yesterday. If you guys can let me have a list of your requirements I'll make sure you have them before you leave. I'll also contact Chris Brooker and let him know of your arrival. What about weapons? You obviously won't be able to get them through the normal channels but I can have what you require sent through our diplomatic sources'.

'I think Sandy is going to try and retrieve the weapons he hid during the road block episode outside Bogotá. He greased them with oil so provided no one has discovered them we will have plenty of long range fire power but we could certainly do with some hand guns'.

'That's not a problem, Tony, Chris Brooker has hand guns to spare down there already, there's no point in pushing your luck and trying to fly them in with the helicopter. Custom officers down there will go through your belongings with a fine tooth comb. I'll also give you some US Dollars to help pave the way – as you are aware greasing palms is the way of life in South America'.

Tony Bryant stretched his arms above his head. 'That's for bloody sure. It will certainly help us particularly if we have to bribe any locals for information. I hope you don't mind George but I'm going to hit the sack and try and get a decent night's sleep. My body is still working on UK time – so if you'll excuse me I'll see you in the morning, how about you Rusty?'

Rusty gave Fields a big grin. 'Me too George - see you in the morning'.

'Sure thing you guys have a good nights rest and see you in the morning'.

The following three days consisted of getting the cover story for the team as water tight as possible and Alfred Mendoza giving them a talk of local customs. Although Tony and Rusty were well briefed on the country's customs etc, Niles, wasn't. Although he'd lived in Venezuela, he'd never actually done so in Colombia - his time there was confined to living in the jungle and a short period prior to their escape.

Mendoza had been able to establish that Domingo had a habit of leaving his home in Barranquilla and flying to Medellin for extra marital activities. His spies had even managed to establish where he kept his mistress .More to the point, they had established that Domingo's had just recently flown down to Medellin and was visiting his mistress.

Niles found this information very interesting and he remarked to the other two. 'God has given man a brain and a penis but unfortunately not enough blood to use them both at the same time. If Domingo is shagging his arse off in Medellin then the chances are that this is where he'll be most vulnerable. His home at Barranquilla will be guarded like a bloody fortress and so will his places of work. However, if he's busy humping his lover in Medellin he's not going to be overly concerned with security. He will obviously have some body guards but at this early stage I think this location will probably offer the best chances of grabbing and disposing of him'.

Rusty gave a big grin, 'you're bloody right there Sandy and if he's trying to keep the liaison a secret from his wife he won't want too many of his guards aware of what's happening for fear of word getting back to her. Further more, if he's shagging his lover they are bound to be drinking booze or sniffing drugs, maybe both. I think you are right. Medellin probable offers the best chance to lift the bastard and getting away with. What do you think Tony?'

'I agree, although it's early days at the moment, based on the little information we have Medellin looks our best bet. However, at this stage we can't be sure but there is no doubt when you're playing with pussy your mind is only concerned with problems below your belt'.

George Fields had contacted Chris Brooker who had sent his transit van out to the old shed where Niles had hidden the guns taken off the road block gunmen. Apparently all the guns that Niles had greased were fully serviceable and were ready for the team to pick up on their arrival. They could now pick up all their weapons from the US Embassy as soon as they arrived.

Chapter 35

Medellin

Medellin, city in central Colombia is the capital of the Antioquia Department set in the Abburra Valley in the Central Cordilleras at an altitude of approximately 5000ft. It was Colombia's second biggest city but has been overtaken in recent times by Cali and it is now the third biggest in the country and it's an important manufacturing and transport centre.

Medellin sprawls in a lazy anarchic manner of many South American cities kept in check by the verdant Andes. The city has two excellent Airports. The old one Claya Herra Airport is almost in the city centre and it is said than when landing there you think you are about to land in someone's back garden and a new modern Airport called the Jose' Maria Cordoba near Rionegro about 35km to the south of the city.

The city also has an elaborate new Metro (Tren Metropolitano) which runs through the city North to South for 23Kms. It is in fact the only Metro system in the country running from Bello in the north to Envigado and Haguf in the south.

Because of its mild climate and moderate rainfall, (it is some times called the city of Eternal spring) orchids are grown commercially and it has an annual flower show which is extremely popular with both locals and visitors.

In addition to the coffee trade Medellin is also an important producer of textiles, but its main claim to fame is that it used to be the centre of the most powerful Drug Cartel in Colombia. Although the Colombian government likes to claim that the violence within the city is now much reduced but the drug trade still flourishes.

Like every city on the South American continent, Medellin is fringed with shanty towns, however as one moves further away from the centre of the city up the surrounding hills the scene changes and shiny new haciendas appear surrounded by razor wire with well manicured lawns complete with swimming pools but protected by heavily armed guards and high-security cameras. These are the homes of the Cartel drug lieutenants.

One of the largest of these was Domingo's local residence. The Hacienda was situated on the top of a small bare hill which provided good all round vision. The house and estate were surrounded by razor wire neatly camouflaged by careful planted hyacinth bushes. Any one attempting to force his way through the bushes would quickly find himself entangled in the deadly Razor wire. CCT cameras located at every corner covered all approaches to the hacienda. Although the house was contained within four acres this was not one of Domingo's bigger houses but it was still one of his favourites. This was not the house that Domingo entertained his lover in – that was further to the south in the outskirts of the city itself. He never had his mistress to the house he always went to her abode to maintain secrecy.

Domingo had altered his plans and he'd had the Frenchman, John Jack Darcy, flown to his Hacienda in Medellin. This was Domingo's home city and he felt more secure here than any where else. Further more once he had concluded his business with the Frenchman it would take no longer than fifteen minutes to get to his mistress's house. After the initial pleasantries Domingo offered Darcy a drink and they got down to business

When told who the forthcoming target was the Frenchman nearly went apeshit.

'Mon Dieu', cried the Frenchman on being informed that the US Secretary of Defence's family was the target. 'Are you crazy monsieur? Even if we were successful don't you realise the US Government would never cease looking for us until they had us locked up or put us six feet under'.

'But how would they know it was me, us? They might suspect it was me but they would not take action without proof and I'm paying your men enough to keep their mouths shut', snarled Domingo.

'Are you crazy man, if you kidnap the wife and family of course they're going to know who's responsible? If you were to kill them without making it known that you were responsible you might just get away with it but if you insist on all the world knowing that you; Francesco Domingo was responsible the US Government would never rest until they have you behind bars or more likely, terminated. Further more, I'm going to have to offer my team a fucking sight more than the million dollars you've promised to carry out this mission'.

'For Christ sake how much will they do the job for?'

'Well, to start with, we will not touch this job for less than two million dollars and that's for assinsinating the family and or the US Secretary. I could get away with this just using three other men and myself. But to be quite frank, to try and kidnap the wife and two children would involve something in the order of a dozen men. You have cars plus planes even helicopters to arrange and with that number of men it would be suicidal. One or other of them would get pissed one night and start talking and that would be the beginning of the end for all of us. The other problem I foresee is that the US Government is going to be offering possibly a million dollars or so reward leading to the capture of the perpetrators. With a dozen men involved in kidnapping one or another of the bastards is bound to sell out for that kind of money'.

'Okay - but you want two million just to shoot someone – are you fucking crazy',

Darcy gave Domingo a hard insolent look

'You've already tried to do it your way and failed. If it is so easy why have you called on my services? The people I have recruited will not talk and are highly professional but there's no way I can rustle up another twelve men of the same calibre in order to attempt the kidnapping, that would take months - especially as the people concerned have already been alerted to what you have in mind. Any one getting within ten miles of the US Secretary and his family are going to be closely vetted. Our chances of shooting them at their estate are zero. To get close enough to shoot them is going to take a lot of planning and much patience'.

The fact of the matter was that Domingo did appreciated that what he was trying to achieve was almost impossible but the hate and rancour he felt towards the Fields family kept eating into his gut to such an extent that he would not listen to people trying to convince him that he was trying to execute a mission impossible. He knew however that he'd never rest until he'd achieved revenge of one sort or the other.

'I tell you what hombre', he said looking Darcy straight in the eye. 'I'll agree to your two million and a further million if you can ensure that Fields is made aware that it is I! Francesco Domingo, who has arranged for his death'.

'You realise this means to kill the man we are going to have to get within talking distance before killing him.

At the same time we have to ensure that none of his body guards can hear what is said without the whole operation is compromised'.

Domingo howled with rage, 'What is the point in having him killed without him knowing that I was responsible. There is no vengeance there!'

Darcy found it difficult to control his temper, 'what fucking difference does it make – dead is fucking dead, regardless to what you have been told five seconds before you are killed. And if we kill his wife or children and the Secretary is told in no uncertain manner that you are responsible we are back to square one again. We will be hunted out of existence. I tell you what Francesco - if we can let him know that you are his executioner prior to killing him and provided there is no way of any one over hearing it, we will do so. That's the best I can offer. If this is unacceptable I think you're going to have to get another hit squad'.

Domingo nodded his head in agreement and admitted to himself that there was much sense in what Darcy had said. Although Domingo was not impressed with what he had heard of the American Special Forces or their CIA counter part. He realised that they had an awful amount of money and power. Domingo's main worry would be if one of his own guards was bribed to kill him.

Domingo pondered and glowered at his feet for about three minutes.

'Okay Darcy I will agree to your terms but I will still make the additional million available – if – you can let Fields know just before he dies that I am responsible for his death'.

Both men shook and Darcy said,' I will get my men into the States by the end of this week but it will be some weeks and after a lot planning before we can be ready to strike. This is not going to be a suicide mission. We have to be able to make a getaway after the strike. If we're captured, there's no way we can resist interrogation with the use of modern drugs. They'll quickly extract all information of who was involved etc'. He gave Domingo a steely look to emphasis the last point and continued

'As soon as I've some positive information I'll let you know. In the meantime, we'll have to set up secure means of communication between here and the States'.

'That's all in hand and you will have all the details before you leave tomorrow'.

After Darcy had departed Domingo rang the bell for his personal body guard.

The giant appeared as if by magic.

'Yes boss?'

'Renaldo, ring Christine up and tell her I'll be there within the hour or so, I've just about had enough trauma for one day. Tell her to get ready for a night out and then back to her place. Then get the boys and car ready and let's fuck off and have some relaxation. The giant gave a big grin and disappeared to do his bidding.

An hour later as Domingo's Mercedes pulled out of the drive on route to his mistress, they were nearly run off the road by a white laundry van. After various abortive attempts Domingo's driver finally managed to pass the van and hurl verbal abuse at the van driver. The van followed the Mercedes from the Bello area past the Metro Station and stayed with them for a couple of miles. Domingo's body guards were just beginning to get suspicious and thought the van might be following them when it turned up the hill to the east towards the district of Campo Valdez. What the occupants of the Mercedes did not realise was that there was a motor cyclist behind the van that had also been following them ever since the Mercedes overtook the van.

Unknown to Domingo and his body guards the van and motor cyclist were part of a surveillance team that had been organised by Chris Brooker head of the American security at the American Embassy in Bogotá. Chris had been given the address of Domingo's hacienda by Alfred Mendoza's men and to prevent Mendoza becoming involved any further and possibly compromised had decided to take over the surveillance. The motor cyclist had remained hidden behind the van until the van had turned off to the east. It remained tailing the Mercedes for another mile or so when it in turn turned off to the west but was immediately replaced by a dirty blue, high topped jeep which managed to stay with the Mercedes for about another mile when it in turned off to the east. Hidden behind the Jeep was yet another motor cyclist riding a scrambles bike which tailed the Mercedes until it arrived at Christine's apartment in the district of Lorena, about one mile north west of the old city airport. This rapid change of vehicles following the Mercedes negated any chance of the tail being noticed. Domingo's mood had changed over the last hour and he was now looking for a pleasant evening with his Christine – quite a favourite of his.

The rider of the scrambles bike reported back to Chris Brooker

'It looks as though Mendoza's men were right Mr Brooker we have followed the Mercedes to the same address on three different occasions – always the same apartments in the Lorena district. The block appears to have three floors but we are not sure which floor the men you are interested in are going to. However on two of the occasions whilst watching the apartments a Piazza delivery motor cyclist has arrived within ten minutes of the party you are interested in'.

Chris Brooker thought to himself for a while. If he could get the actual apartment floor or better still the number of it then this could speed the whole operation up but if any enquiries got back to Domingo then all surprise would be blown. Chris decided that they had already pushed their luck as far as he dare. There was no point in muddying the water before Sandy and his team arrived. From what little he knew of Sandy it wouldn't take that bastard long to find out which apartment Domingo was going to.

'That's fine Frank you and the boys have done an excellent job. That will be all – you've confirmed our suspicions. But don't forget I want absolute secrecy on this and make sure that none of the local staff get to know what you've been up to. If at a later date, any shit hits the fan at this address I want you and the other three guys to suffer a complete attack of amnesia over this affair – okay'.

'You got it boss'; Frank gave a big grin and departed.

Chris Brooker got on the secure Line to the Defence Secretary.

'One moment Mr Brooker and I'll get him for you', Grace the Secretary's Secretary buzzed Fields.

Fields picked up the phone. 'Hi Chris how's things down in your neck of the woods'.

'Just fine Mr Secretary I just rang to let you know we have most of the information that Niles requested three days ago. I feel rather embarrassed but Sandy was quite explicit and told me not to tell you the information but just to confirm we have what he requested. Does that make sense to you Sir?'

'I'm afraid it does Chris - Sandy is trying to protect me. If anything should go wrong and I was forced to testify in court Sandy claims I can stand there and swear to god that I knew nothing about what was happening. And the way he's operating at the moment that's just about correct; I haven't a clue what he and his mates are up to so I suppose we had better keep it that way'.

'Well Sir if you could just tell him we have the addresses that he requested and we now have all the stores he required stood by in the Embassy ready to be delivered or collected whenever they want, By the way are they leaving today or tomorrow?'

'There're leaving this evening. They were going to fly a S76 Helicopter but it involved too many refuelling stops so they will be flying down on our own Diplomatic Flight and I have already spoken to your Embassy and arranged for them to be picked up at Bogotá Airport. Charles Piermont, my Chief Executive of our oil Exploration Company is arranging for Niles to take over one our S76 for the duration of their stay. I will be arranging for a further S76 to fly down and replace the one that Niles and his mates are using. The way Sandy operates I'll be lucky to get my Helicopter back in one piece'.

'That could be so Sir, but as I've said before, I'm glad he's on our side I wouldn't like to think I was being stalked by Niles'.

'You're right there Chris but keep me in touch bearing in mind my 'Need to know' category'.

'Will do Mr Secretary will do'.

Niles had just about finished packing. They were due to leave in about an hour for the Airport. Fields had briefed Niles on the phone call from Chris Brooker – it was good news Chris had been able to establish where Domingo went for his extra marital nooky – this should cut down the recce requirements that always threaten to be the longest part of the operation. The three of them were only taking a duffle bag each and were carrying nothing that could compromise them if they were searched on entry to Colombia. Although they would be on the Diplomatic Flight they were not on the Embassy staff and therefore not entitled to full diplomatic status. However the consensus of opinion was that they were most unlikely to have to go through Customs. Chris Brooker was able to provide all their handgun requirements and he'd already retrieved the weapons that Niles had snatched during the ambush outside Bogotá so it was pointless trying to smuggle weapons in with them.

He took a quick look around to make sure he'd got everything when there was a knock on the door and Jenny walked in

'I have come to decir adios Sandy. Do you know how long you are going to be?'

'Difficult to say at the moment but I reckon two weeks should see us finished maybe three at the outside'.

Jenny was now certain that she was pregnant. She had tests carried out the day before and they confirmed her suspicions. She had decided that she was going to let Sandy know this week until she'd been made aware of the forth coming expedition to Colombia, but then decided to wait until his return. She'd tried to work out just what it was that made this gringo so attractive to her. He was a big man but she had been courted by bigger. He was an attractive man, but again she'd been chased by more attractive ones. Jenny had only really known her husband prior to meeting Sandy but she found her self so roused in his company that at times she behaved like a complete harlot. As soon as he came into the room she wanted to start taking her clothes off. All she knew was that what had started out as a scheme to produce a child for biological reasons had now grown into something that she no longer had control over. If any thing happened to Sandy she was going to be absolutely devastated.

'I am going to miss you hombre', she murmured as she eased herself into Niles arms.

Niles had an immediate erection but knew that there was not time or the place to start anything carnal.

Jenny slid her hand into Niles right hand pocket (the access to his Berretta)

'Ah Sandy I see your weapon is cocked and ready for action. I hope you are not going to use this on any of those Colombian women down there, they are real man-eaters'.

He laughed, 'so I've discovered', He brought Jenny up as close to his body as he could. As he looked into Jenny's lovely eyes he could see that something was troubling her.

'What's troubling my little Colombian humming bird?' He asked giving her a reassuring hug.

'I just want to make sure that you come back to me. I know you are very attractive to other women and you will be tempted to you use your weapon (she gave Nile's erection another squeeze just to emphasise which weapon she was refereeing to) I don't care just so long as you come back to me'.

He noted that although she had professed not to be bothered about any liaison with other women Jenny had tears in her eyes. He gentle stroked her hair and said.

'Why would I bother with any of those beautiful Colombian birds when I have the most beautiful one of them all waiting for me back here'.

Jenny threw her arms around his neck. 'You bastard you had better believe it'.

Niles disentangled themselves and said, ' For Christ sake Jenny if we don't get out of this room in the next five seconds you are going to get raped - you've already got steam coming out of my ears'.

'Please! Please! She giggled.

He looked to the heavens and said, 'God give me strength', and grabbed hold of Jenny and whisked her out the door before his lust overcame his common sense.

George Fields had arranged for his own helicopter to take the three of them to Washington Airport. As they were boarding the chopper Niles turned and said to George Fields.

'I've been thinking about you and the family boss and to be quite frank, with all three of us down south, I think you and your family might be vulnerable. Is there anywhere you could take the family for a holiday at short notice until we get back? I know you have your body guards but as we have just seen if you throw enough money about, all security arrangements can be circumvented'.

'I have it already in hand Sandy – we're going to visit Jackie's parents who have a lodge in Oregon. I'm taking Douglas as well as the two women and arranging for private protection. The area is very remote so any strangers to the district will be obvious and they will immediately be checked out. I will also have secure means of contacting Chris Brooker in Bogotá so we can communicate through him. By the way, Chris is the only person down there that has any idea what you're up to – Charles Piermont – my Oil Boss, really does think you are checking oil reserves in different parts of the country and you have been ordered to report only to me personally so he will not be surprised at your lack of contact'.

'That's great boss I can think of nothing else at this stage other than to keep your eyes peeled; bear in mind that it is possible that Domingo has already arranged for a second hit team and we could at this very moment be crossing over with them'.

'Point taken Sandy, Theo has been warned and we leave for Oregon tomorrow – best of luck and what is they say in England – Good hunting'.

Niles waved cheerio slammed the chopper's door as it transitioned away.

Four hours later the team landed at Bogotá Aero Puerto and passed through immigrations and customs as diplomatic staff with no interference from the Colombian officials. Chris Brooker was there personally to welcome them and had all three whisked off to his flat. The flat was located in a quiet residential area of Bogotá where most of the residents knew one another. This reduced the chances of Chris ever being followed without him being aware of it. They parked his Jeep Cherokee in the under garage located directly under his flat and made their way to his abode.

'It's great to see you guys again I can't tell you how

fucking boring things have been down here since you went States side. George Fields could not tell me why you guys are here but then I'll bet a month's wages on why you are down here and I have a proposition to make'.

He looked at the three Brits expecting an interruption.

The three Brits just looked at one another but made no comment.

'Look you three bastards I'm dying of boredom down here and I'm certain you have come here to cook Domingo's goose and I want to be part of the action'.

Again - he looked at the three Brits expectantly.

Niles decided it was up to him to comment.

'You're spot on Chris but what we intend to do is highly unlawful. The whole object of us doing the job instead of employing government men is in case anything does wrong then the States can deny involvement. We'd love to have you on our team but if you got caught it would be a tremendous embarrassment to the Embassy'.

'Look Sandy I've taken some long overdue leave for the next two weeks so what I do in my own time is not the problem of the Embassy staff any more than Tony and Rusty here being on leave from the SAS'.

Tony looked at Niles and shrugged his shoulders.

'Chris has a point Sandy our involvement is as much a problem to us as his is. Plus which Chris's Spanish is more fluent than ours and he knows the area a dam sight better than we do'.

Chris looked at Niles knowing that his would be the final decision. 'Come on Sandy what have you got to lose?'

'The only problem I foresee is that our cover story has already been passed on to Charles Piermont; Field's boss man down here, and he is only expecting three guys to turn up for the so called Oil Exploration – how are we going to explain you presence – especially as this exploration is supposed to be a close company secret'.

Chris gave a big smile. 'Look you guys, we have already established where Domingo goes practically every night whilst he's in Medellin - so just how much moving around the country do you have to do. We remove Domingo from the living you three guys can then continue with your charade for another week and I finish my leave and return to work – end of story'!

Niles nodded his head in agreement.

'You've not got the full story Chris – we're going to remove Domingo but we want to achieve it in such a manner that no one knows where or what has happened to him. This way we hope to negate any possible revenge action or a vendetta being carried out by members of Domingo's clan against George or his family. If we pull this off correctly no one will know what's happened to him; he'll have simple disappeared from the face of this earth'.

'Shit', grunted Brooker. 'That's not going to be so easy'.

'Exactly, however Chris you might as well come aboard now you know what we are trying to achieve and you have already made things considerably easier for us. We had already decided that our best chance of success was when Domingo separated his penis from his brain – now you have the address all we have to do is to establish how we isolate him from his body guards and his mistress. Sounds easy if you say it quickly but I figure this is going to call for some careful planning'.

Niles turned to Rusty.

'What are your views on the subject Rusty you have more operational experience than the rest of us put together'.

Rusty took another swig of coffee and paused for a moment.

'Chris has done much of the initial spade work but I think our first move is to visit Domingo's lover's apartments and get a feel for what we are up against. Once we've got the lay of the land we can then start to formulate detailed plans.

I think we're collecting the S76 tomorrow so we could fly to Medellin on some pretext or other and start our Reece's from thereon'.

'That's great', said Brooker. 'The actual area we are concerned with is only about a mile and half north west of the old city airport. I can fly there tonight in my Cessna 180 and we can meet in the airport restaurant at mid day. How does that grab you?' Chris's enthusiasm was contagious he obviously couldn't wait to join and get involved. An added bonus was that as a senior member on the US Embassy Staff Chris had access to many facilities not available to them.

Next morning hailed with a beautiful blue sky very little wind and unlimited visibility, typical of the area. George Field's S76 had been delivered to Bogotá International Airport and had been fuelled and serviced prior to their arrival. So getting to Medellin was going to be no problem.

They arrived at the Airport and were able to get airborne without any delay.

The new Medellin air port, Jose' Maria Cordoba, was situated about 20 miles to the south of the city and the team decided that it was a little too far out for their purposes. So they flew to the old air port, (Olaya Herrera Airport) that was located almost within the city itself. The old airport was originally built outside the city but the burgeoning population and rapid construction to house them had quickly engulfed it. The runways were too short to accept the long haul Jets and these now operated out of the new, Jose' Maria Cordoba Airport. Olaya Herrera Airport was now used by most of the regional flights within Colombia and the traffic density was sufficiently high enough to prevent the arrival and departure of the team's S75 causing any interest. As they approached the main runway which was orientated on a North, South direction, Niles noted that the helicopter dispersal area was to the east of the runway and that the area they were making for was a small collection of huts. There was also a designated hanger just to the north of the main dispersal outside on which stood three helicopters belonging to the Oil Company. Niles requested all instructions in his improving Spanish, which had improved considerably since sleeping with Jenny. (She likes to make dirty talk in Spanish)

They were cleared to make their approach directly to the oil company's dispersal. Niles landed on the hard standing area and ground taxied to the position indicated by the company marshaller.

After landing the team checked the refuelling of the aircraft and made their way to the airport restaurant to contact Chris Brooker.

Chris was already there waiting at the arrival lounge and made a big play at greeting them.

'Ola hombres Buenos Dias, good to see you I have the maps of the area you requested and I have arranged some lunch at my hotel in town'. He then whispered softly to Niles. 'Hey Sandy I like your dark hair and complexion but even with the disguise you still look as ugly as sin'.

'Thanks a lot Chris its just as well I don't fancy you either'.

Chris then started to gesticulate and said loud enough for many of the others diners to overhear.

'It will take several days to get clearance to recce' the areas you wish to see but we can do much preliminary work in my office in the meantime I'll ensure that your helicopter is available for immediate flight. I've also arranged for the experts who you asked to talk with to meet us in my office. We have arranged to have our lunch there – please follow me'.

The ride to the hotel that Chris had booked them was in the Laureles District at the hotel Campus. It was only about a five minutes drive and even of more importance; it was located only a minute to where Domingo's mistress lived.

Once ensconced in his bedroom Chris got down to the up to date briefing.

'As you noticed I've made it known to people at the airport that we cannot fly for a couple of days due to awaiting clearance so no one should be wondering why the chopper is not cruising around the country side. At the moment we've definitely established the apartment block that Domingo's mistress lives in. He's normally accompanied by three body guards. Two hired shooters and his personal body guard, a giant called Renaldo. We have not yet established which room or floor his mistress is located on and this will not be easy to achieve without arousing Domingo's suspicions. This will take some careful planning bearing mind that we are going to try and remove him without any one knowing what has happened to him'.

Tony nodded his head in agreement.

'At this stage we normally try to keep the place under observation for a couple of days to try and see if there is any standard pattern or routine that the targets display'.

'The trouble', continued Chris. 'Is that Domingo does not visit every day so we've not been able to establish any set routine plus which, we've only been certain of the location of his mistress for the last two days. Prior to yesterday, we weren't sure whether he was flitting between various lovers but it seems that whilst he's in Medellin he sticks to this Christine bird'.

'Thank Christ for small mercies', grunted Niles. 'At least that makes things slightly easier but I figure we'll have to move fast, I can't see the bastard remaining down here for long – is there anywhere we can observe the apartment block without being obvious Chris?'

'There's a café about twenty yards away but you can't see what's going on in the apartments or where the apartment elevator stops. But if we keep the place under observation for a couple of days we might be able to establish some sort of routine that could help us. We could do it in pairs; this would make it less obvious. I have also set up a small operation room in Medellin where I've a small staff to help out. They don't know what we are up to but they know it is a god dam secret and have been warned to keep their mouths shut'.

Niles nodded his head in agreement. 'Great we'll start tonight. Rusty and I will take the first night and Chris and Tony can take the next, then, if further Reece's are required we can mix the pairing'.

Chris made the initial reconnaissance of the café from across the road to the apartments where Domingo's mistress resided and reported back to the other three. He had also managed to get four short wave band communication sets with and ear plug for reception and a small transmitter that could be pinned to the collar. Including Chris in their team was now beginning to show dividends.

'The position is this'. Chris continued. 'From the front of the café you can see who comes and goes in the front of the building but not from the back. However up to date Domingo and his goons have always used the front entrance and there is no reason to suppose he'll change. However, there is a room that I have booked from the café owner which can be accessed from the street behind the café and therefore not visible to any one using the apartments. I've told him that we are American consultants hired by the Government to survey roads for repairs. Naturally enough he doesn't believe me and I suspect he thinks we are here to purchase drugs. Not that this matters - he will mind his own business which is the most important part. From the room I've booked you can see both the front and the left hand side of the apartments as you look at the building. I've had a look at the apartments from the room and it would appear that the top floor is a penthouse – I suspect that this is where are friend has his mistress ensconced'.

'That's first class', said Niles. 'Rusty and I will start our vigil at 1900 hours tonight I'll be reading a paper outside the café and Rusty if you could locate yourself upstairs in the cafe we might be able to ascertain which room they are using by checking the lights as they come on in turn. In the meantime, Chris, do you think you could get hold of the plans of the building before tonight – money is no object, George Fields has practically given us an open cheque book till we get this mess sorted'.

'I have some local guys who for the right money would be prepared to get them for me but I'm not sure I could get them by tonight – but I'll give it a good try'.

Rusty and Niles arrived at the café just after half six in the evening. The apartment block they were interested in was only three stories high, quite modern and looked reasonably affluent. The whole building was painted in white masonry paint and at the front to the building was a small foyer at the top of three steps. The foyers had two colonnades, one each side which supported a tiled roof that provided cover from rain and the front revolving door was constructed of a hard wood and opaque glass. On the top of the apartments there was a small parapet which appeared to be accessed through the top of the apartment building. There was a fire escape to the side of the building which had been rigged in such a manner that people from outside the building could nor make use of it. The ladder could only be unlocked from above and then lowered to the pavement below. At the back of the apartments was a very small car park that had room for no more than a dozen cars at the most. Beyond the car park the road went up a quite steep hill the gradient of which increased the further it went. There were only another three houses behind the apartments going up the hill two on the left and one on the right which was the furthest away.

Rusty made the first walk past the building to try and get some idea what the interior of it looked like but the revolving doors, when stationary, prevented any one on the out side looking in.

Niles had a word with Rusty. After half an hour they changed over and Niles took to sauntering past the apartment building.

'Look Rusty I'm going to walk past the apartment entrance with an untied shoelace and see if I can stop to tie up my laces when someone is entering or leaving the building – with luck I might be able to see in the building when the revolving doors turn'.

Niles stood leaning against the wall of the building opposite to the apartments waiting for some one to exit or enter. After ten minutes he thought he had better change with Rusty otherwise his presence was going to cause concern. As luck would have it just as he set off to change with Rusty a car drew up and a very attractive brunette got out. She really was quite stunning, a real head turner. She paid the driver and made her way up the steps to enter the apartment. With out thinking Niles rushed up the steps and gallantly pushed the revolving doors open.

'Please Senorita allow me and I would feel honoured to carry the shopping of such a beautiful lady'. He finished his smarmy request with an exaggerated bow. She gave Niles her hat box with a big smile. She felt a tingle of excitement as their fingers brushed one another but curbed her excitement and thanked him.

'Gracias Senor you are most kind'.

He followed the woman over to the lift and noted that she pressed the button for floor three; the penthouse. This gorgeous woman was obviously Domingo's mistress. (If she wasn't then she ought to be) He gave her an exaggerated bow and waved her into the lift and returned the hat box, had a good look round the foyer before being escorted off the premises by the receptionist who warned him.

'Please beware senor that woman is spoken for by one of

the most powerful men in Colombia you would do well to forget that you ever spoke to her'.

Niles pretended to be aghast, and adopted an obsequious manner.

'Please senor I had no idea the lady was spoken for by such a powerful man - I would be most grateful if you did not mention the episode'.

The receptionist gave Niles a mocking look, 'Just bear in mind what I have said and I'll say no more'.

Niles contrived to look absolutely scared witless and fled the building, down the road and out of sight. He made his way back to the café via the back street and door up to the rented room to liase with Rusty.

'I think we are making progress Rusty I have just escorted a gorgeous brunette into the apartment who is obviously our friend's piece of crumpet and I've managed to confirm that she definitely lives on the third floor and there's a lift and a set of stairs but both are in full view of the receptionist. He also warned me off the young lady concerned as she was spoken for, he said, by one of the most powerful men in Colombia. Thus removing any doubt that she is definitely Domingo's mistress'.

'That's fine Sandy but we are still no clearer on how we are going to extract Domingo from the building without any one knowing that he is being lifted. However after his visit tonight – assuming that he does visit – we may have a clearer idea how to go about it'.

Rusty and Niles took turns at keeping the apartment under scrutiny until about eight in the evening when Domingo's Mercedes drew up and out stepped Domingo and his two body guards plus the formidable Renaldo. The two body guards gave the street a careful look over and then walked on either side of Domingo as they entered the revolving door and out of sight into the apartments.

Niles gave Rusty a nudge.

'Jesus did you see the size of his personal body guard Rusty? I wouldn't like to meet him down a blind alley on a dark night'.

'Christ he's going to take some overpowering if we get into any rough stuff – I reckon it would take all four of us to subdue him alone. This doesn't leave many of us to take on any of the other Indians. I think we are going to have to try and neutralise that bastard Sandy'.

They sat there immersed in their own thoughts whilst watching the building across the road. It was about half an hour after Domingo and his body guards had arrived that a pizza delivery motor cyclist turned up with a snack for some one in the apartments building.

Suddenly Niles had an epiphany.

'Rusty!..... I've just had a thought; whilst I was living in Venezuela there were cases of tourist being drugged and then robbed whilst they slept in their hotel rooms. When they woke up the following morning they had no recollection of what had happed during the night, even to the extent of having their personal jewellery removed from their body without feeling a thing. The drug used was called, 'Burundanga' and originated in Colombia. If we could get our hands on some and contaminate the Pizzas going up to Domingo and his goons we could save our selves a lot of hassle.

'Hang about Sandy we're not even certain that those Pizzas went up to Domingo's apartment'.

'No but I'm pretty sure that's where they went there must have been at least four or five Pizzas that the delivery boy took in. In any case I have an idea on how we can check up on that but we will need Chris's help because it will need some fluent Spanish for it to work'.

There conversation was interrupted as they noticed the Domingo Mercedes appear at the front to of the building. In two minutes Domingo's two body guards appeared to check the street was clear, next came the giant Renaldo who gave his boss the all clear. Domingo came into view accompanied by his mistress. They quickly got into the Mercedes followed by the two body guards. Renaldo was left behind but after five minutes a taxi arrived and the giant got in and the taxi drove off.

'What do you make of that Rusty?'

'I figure that the way Domingo and his broad are all dressed up that they must have gone to take in a show and the big fellow has buggered off to lay some floozy of his own'.

'I think you're right Rusty and we may have a chance to have a quick look at the penthouse while they are all away. The problem is how do we get in without being noticed? Further more, if any of them should return whilst we are still up there we are going to be in serious trouble'

Rusty nodded his head and said, 'do you remember the old stick and brick method of climbing over a wall or getting over a parapet?'

Rusty was referring to a method taught in the Para's during basic training where a large stone or brick was tied to the end of a pole about five feet long. The stick and brick were thrown over the wall/parapet and the brick plus the length of the stick produced sufficient leverage to support the weight of a man enabling him to climb up the wall with the aid of the rope.

'You have got it Rusty. If we can contact Chris and Tony and arrange for them to get some rope and a broom handle we can cast the stick and brick over the penthouse parapet, climb the rope and get a detailed survey of the rooms, the love nest where the guards stay etc. If we can wrap some sacking around the brick it won't make too much noise when it lands on the roof especially as all the occupants are out'.

Rusty was on the phone to Chris and Tony before Niles had even finished talking.

'That's right Chris and get it round here as soon as possible – thanks a lot'

'All done Sandy! Chris says give them an hour and they will have the kit. Tony knew what I meant as soon as I mentioned the stick and brick method. He said he'll wise Chris up to the situation. I tell you what Sandy if we can find somewhere to hide the rope say along side a down drain pipe from the upper floor we could leave the rope in position. We will have to ensure that the rope cannot be seen from the roof. I suspect the attachment point will be the most difficult thing to disguise'.

'You've a good point there Rusty if we can keep the rope attached up there it means we have a clandestine method of getting to Domingo – all we have to work out now is how the hell we get him out without any one seeing us'.

The two them discussed the problem for the next half an hour when the arrival of Tony and Chris interrupted their train of thoughts.

Tony and Chris arrived in a bloody great four ton truck with an open back with all sorts of building materials in the back.

As Chris and Tony made their way up to the room where Niles and Irons were, Niles stood at the window looking down at the large truck. Rusty's face creased with a big grin as he thought to himself. That bastard has already worked out how we are going to get Domingo out of those apartments - I can see it in his face.

Chris burst into the room full of 'get up and go'.

'Right Sandy - Tony has told me how your Stick and Brick works and I presume you're going to use it to get into the apartment. But if you get in without being seen how the hell are you going to get that bastard Domingo out without any of his goons seeing us?'

Niles gave a big grin and motioned every one to have a seat.

'I have a plan and I would like to run it past you guys whilst we are all here together. Firstly we are going to use the Stick and Brick method to get up into the apartments and have an initially recce' tonight whilst the top floor is unoccupied. And then Rusty came up with an excellent idea, that we keep the rope concealed but still attached to the parapet. This gives us the clandestine means to get to Domingo without his goons knowing. The arrival of you two with the truck has just given me the last part of the puzzle on how to get Domingo out the apartments without any one knowing how it was achieved'.

The other three looked at Niles in a puzzled manner.

'First things first – Chris can you get your hands on any of the local drug called 'Burundanga' and a couple of hypodermic needles; we will need them by tomorrow night?'

Chris nodded his head. 'You can get Burundanga off a street dealer any time of the day or night, the needles I can get from the Embassy medical staff any time tomorrow, certainly by this time tomorrow night'.

'That's great', continued Niles. 'The next thing that has to be arranged is that the Pizza boy tomorrow evening when he is delivering the Pizzas for the top floor is going to have a small accident, two of us will help him to his feet and whilst one dusts him down and distracts him the other is going to contaminate all the drinks with the Burundanga drug. At the moment, it would appear that the Pizzas arrive about half an hour after Domingo and his goons arrive and so far, it is the only deliveries made to the apartments. Now this is where things might get tricky. We have to access the building hopefully using the rope which we have attached to the parapet - kill Domingo take him up onto the roof of the penthouse and then, tip him over the edge into the open truck which has some form of soft material in the back to deaden the noise of Domingo's body falling from three floors into it. We then make sure that we've a slip knot on the rope that can be released from the ground after the three of us have shinned our way down. If there is a drain pipe that is strong enough we may be able to throw the rope down after two of us has descended then the third man comes down the drain pipe. If all goes according to plan we can then drive Domingo off to the airport board the chopper – depart first thing in the morning - weigh the body with chains/ weights and dump him in the sea. Heh presto! Domingo has disappeared off the face of this earth and nobody knows where he has gone. How does that sound?'

Chris Brooker was the first to speak.

'You are positively evil Sandy. There are quite a few things that can go wrong but the main problem is what do we do to the girl? Domingo and her are going to be sleeping in the same bed are we going to remove her as well?'

'No! I've no intentions of killing any innocent parties and whilst I wouldn't hesitate to gun down Domingo's goons I'm not prepared to kill any innocent people to achieve our aim. I'm hoping that the, Burundanga will have knocked her unconscious. As far as I know the girl's only crime is to have slept with Domingo and once he had set his sights on her I suspect she had little to say in the matter. I am presuming that you can get some silencers for our Berettas Chris?'

Chris just grinned and nodded. 'Done'

Tony came up with the next suggestion. 'Supposing we rang the Pizza store, said we were at the apartment and asked what time the pizzas were arriving. This would ensure that we knock the right delivery motor cyclist. We could get a nasty surprise if we arrived at the penthouse and found them all conscious'.

'Good suggestion Tony, and if we can arrange the accident to happen just up the street from here but out of sight from the apartments we could be fairly certain that we were doping the right Pizzas'. Niles looked around to see if there were any further suggestions.

Rusty interjected with the next question. 'Who is going to do the actual shooting – I've never shot a person in cold blood before and the chances are that Domingo is going to be unconscious when he gets it?'

There was an uncomfortable silence as they all looked expectantly at one another. Chris was the first to break the silence.

'I think we should draw lots and the guy that draws the short straw does the killing'.

They all nodded their heads in agreement when Tony suddenly had a brain wave

'That sounds fair but that still leaves one guy to wrestle with his conscience. How about us all shooting him at the same time then we will never know for sure who's bullet actually killed him?'

The other three all looked nonplussed for a few seconds and then Niles grinned.

'Talk about a problem shared is a problem halved this way we will quarter the problem. I think it 's the best way to solve the issue - we all know what a bastard he is but there is something quite distasteful about shooting an unconscious man – I think you have the best solution there Tony'.

'It's agreed then', said Chris. 'When the time comes to dispatch him we all let him have it together'.

Tony, Rusty and Niles remained in the rented room whilst Chris departed to arrange for the stores and the drug Burundanga.

The three that remained discussed the plan making several small adjustments. Rusty had suggested that they try and swap the drinks and the Pizzas after they knocked the delivery boy over but that raised the problem of knowing what Domingo and his goons had ordered.

Suddenly Niles came up with one of his inspirations.

'We know that the Pizzas arrive about half an hour after

the goons arrive at the apartments so they must place an order within five minutes of arriving there. If we wait for about another ten minutes then Phone the Pizza Parlour and get them to confirm what we had ordered then swap them with ones that we have already doctored'.

Tony looked grim. 'Sandy; how the hell are we going to know what Pizzas the goons have ordered in time to have replacements ready to swap them with. If we replace the wrong Pizzas there's every chance that they will phone the Parlour and demand to know what's happen to the Pizza they ordered'.

Niles scratched his head and grinned.

'I screwed up there Tony, we could end up with over a thousand different combinations – the only way to avoid it is to try and get a look at the previous orders on the books of the Pizza parlour to see if there is much deviation in what the goons eat'.

'The problem is Sandy that we are running out of time – we don't know how long our friend Domingo is likely to remain here in Medellin, he could return to Bogotá or Barranquilla at any time. If we go firm on knocking the delivery boy over and then doctoring the food and drinks whilst one of us gets him to his feet, dusts him down and diverts his attention there is a strong chance we will get away with it, but trying to swap food and drinks in the middle of the road whilst dusting the poor bastard down has all the potential hallmarks of an old Charlie Chaplin movie'.

'I hate to admit it but your right Tony we're going to have to doctor the drinks and food when we knock the boy over, the fact that the goons ate a certain type of Pizza one night does not mean that they are necessarily going to make the same order the following night. I also think that tomorrow we will have to keep an eye on what's happening at Domingo's Hacienda just in case he ups and returns home leaving us here like a bunch of lemons'.

Rusty looked at Tony. 'I figure you and I could take spells at that Tony. Chris is going to be busy running around getting the drugs etc. We can leave Sandy here and you and I can keep in touch with them with the com's kit or our mobiles – which would you like us to use Sandy?'

'I figure that the com's sets that Chris supplied are going to be more secure – you guys know more about this than me what's your views?'

'I think we will stick with the kit that Chris supplied', said Rusty. 'There's less chance of it being traced at a later date'.

It was a dark night with low cloud scudding across the sky resulting in periods of almost total darkness interspersed with bright starlight. These were ideal conditions as far as Rusty was concerned for his recce of the apartments.

Midnight came before Rusty used the, 'Stick and Brick', to get on top of the penthouse.- any later and there was a danger of being interrupted by the return of Domingo and his bodyguards. It took four attempts at throwing the 'Stick and Brick', before he got it over the parapet. He quickly shinned up the rope which had knots every metre or so to provide a better handhold. Once he had got to the top of the parapet he secured the rope to the top of the railing and lowered himself down to the largest window of the penthouse but found all the windows locked. However he managed to get the layout of the rooms and the first window (the biggest) was obviously Domingo's love nest. There were a double bed two arm chairs a dressing table and two huge wardrobes- much as to be expected. There were two other rooms that he could also see from this side of the building and a kitchen and what looked like a sitting room. It appeared that this room was where there was access to a corridor to the lift. Rusty was reasonably sure that this was probably where the body guard on duty would normally sit whilst those not on duties probable used the other two bedrooms. Rusty had to lower himself down the other side of the building to survey the other two bedrooms. Nothing out of the ordinary, single beds chairs and scattered rugs, again, much as expected. A brief look confirmed that they were probably used by the off duty guards for sleeping.

Further exploration was interrupted by the return of Domingo's Mercedes. Rusty also noted that there was an entrance from the roof down into the penthouse but with the arrival of Domingo's and his hoods he had no time to investigate but under the circumstances decided to remove the stick and brick with the rope. However he kept the roof entrance in mind – this could make an easier access to the Penthouse than through the windows. He swiftly shinned down the rope, pulled the running end of the slip knot to release it, gathered the rope, stick and brick and scurried round to the back of the cafe

When Rusty reported what he'd found, the consensus of opinion was that they had gained enough intelligence to go ahead. Any attempt at this late stage to force an entry might be discovered and compromise the whole operation. It was decided to use a glass cutter on the night of the entry. Then if necessary they would throw a jug or something through the window to disguise the fact that an entry had been attempted form outside. However entry through the Penthouse roof door was the leading contender.

Chapter 36

The Mercenaries

Next day John Jack Darcy and his four companions arrived at Bogotá Air port and were choppered to Domingo's Hacienda. Domingo was there to greet them at mid afternoon and ushered them into the house. Drinks were served and they got down to their macabre business.

Tony Bryant had just relieved Rusty who'd been keeping the Hacienda under surveillance. He did not like the look of the four men who had just arrived. To start with, they were not Latinos; they had Nordic complexions and from their lack of sun tan appeared to have arrived from North American or Europe. They were also men of some importance judged by the diffident manner in which Domingo received them. Tony was not close enough to be absolutely sure but he had the impression that he'd seen mug shots of some of them before but at the moment, could not put a name to them. He decided to give the others a call.

Niles answered.

'Look Sandy we've just had four unpleasant looking characters arrive at Domingo's residence and I'm pretty certain that I've seen mug shots of two of them before, but for the life of me I can't think where. Are Rusty and Chris available to come over and have a look them before the stake out tonight? If I've seen the mug shots so has Rusty and there's a good chance that Chris may have also. If they drive a van to the end of the road I'll give them a call as soon as these characters come out the house and then they can drive past and get a close up and possibly a camera shot of them'.

'I guess so', replied Niles. 'Chris is here and Rusty has just had a bite to eat after you relieved him so we can get them up there in the next half an hour – how's that?'.

'That's great Sandy tell them to give me a bell when they are at the end of the road. You do appreciate that if these guys stay all night with Domingo it may well screw up all the plans we've made for tonight'.

'Point taken Tony, we'll just have to play the cards as dealt – with a bit of luck it might be just a quick business deal on the other hand, they could be members of another hit squad that Domingo is organising. In which case we are going to have to move fast to prevent them getting to the Fields family'.

It took less than half an hour for Rusty and Chris Brooker to arrive. They positioned their Jeep about four hundred yards up the hill hidden from Domingo's Hacienda ready to be called forward by Tony. Chris Brooker had also brought a small digital camera with him to try and get some mug shots of the recently arrived gringos.

Inside the hacienda Domingo, Darcy and his men were hashing out the details of the plan to kill Jackie Fields. They had finally decided to kill Field's wife as it would cause the maximum grief to the Secretary of defence at the same time, although he might suspect that Domingo was responsible he would never be able to prove it; which Darcy claimed, would negate the USA Government from becoming actively engaged in any revenge scenarios.

'You do realise', continued Darcy, 'that it will take a least a week for us to complete the reconnaissance phase before we can take any physical action against Mrs Fields. After your last efforts up there the security is going to be tighter than a Duck's arse'.

Domingo just grunted.

'Just so long as you get the job done within the next month, I don't want to die of fucking old age before it's completed. You've got the secure communication all in hand and I've transferred half the money to your account in Switzerland, the rest to follow after the job is completed. If you've no further queries I'll arrange for you to be choppered back to Bogotá in the next hour. The less we are seen together the better'.

Darcy looked at his four associates who he'd not bothered to introduce or even name them to Domingo, 'any questions men?'

They all shook their heads in unison. They were a hard looking bunch and even Domingo who'd been teethed on violence was intimidated by their presence. None of them had spoken since their arrival. Any responses to questions asked by Darcy were greeted by nods or shakes of their heads as deemed necessary.

Domingo rang for Renaldo his giant body guard. 'Tell the pilot to get the chopper started up our guests are about to leave', he ordered

The helicopter started up and five minutes later Domingo and his guest appeared at the front door to be transported to the airport. As they came into view Tony gave Rusty and Chris a call forward. The helicopter taking off from the front lawn of the hacienda gave Rusty an Idea.

'Quick Chris this gives us a chance to get the mug shots without disclosing our hand'.

The helicopter on the front of Domingo's lawn provided the two of them with an excellent excuse to 'Rubber neck' and they slowed down as they drove past Domingo's hacienda. To any onlookers it appeared that the two of them were simple taking photographs of the helicopter. Chris Brooker was able to overtly photograph the chopper at the same time making sure that Darcy and his friends were in the shot - then they accelerated away before any of Domingo's guards had a chance to apprehend them.

'I don't like the look of those five guys and I'm sure I've mug shots of them on the file in the Embassy', murmured Brooker as he drove down the hill.

Rusty looked thoughtful. 'I have definitely seen the guy that appears to be the leader before – and it probably means that if we have both seen photos of this guy before, then chances are that he's an international crook or terrorists of some renown and is probably on the 'Interpol List. We don't keep photos of men who've been kind to old Grannies so there're definitely criminals of one sort or another. Do you think they could be the new hit team that Domingo's organising Chris?'

'I'm afraid it looks that way Rusty – Domingo is not known for consorting with gringos and that five most definitely did not look like druggies, they had all the hall marks of hit men or mercenaries'.

'Agreed', said Rusty. 'I figure that they'll be in the States by tomorrow and ready to start operations the day after. Let's give them a minimum of a week to carry out reconnaissance of the Fields residence and after which they could be taking physical action by this time next week. It doesn't allow us much time in Colombia to finish Domingo before getting back to the States to help George and his family'.

'I think it will take longer than a week to find the Fields Rusty I've been informed that they are already in hiding until we've concluded our action down here. Never the less I'm going to have to contact them and give them the details of what we have just observed'.

Rusty and Chris returned to the rented operational rooms. Chris set to and used his Laptop computer to down load digital mug shots via the operation room at the Embassy. Those taken of the hit team were blown up and compared to the latest mug shots of wanted terrorists. They were in luck; they had two photos that matched. Chris and Rusty then hared back to the rented rooms just as Tony was returning from his vigil.

They'd identified two of the five but most important of all, was they were able to name the leader; a certain John Jack Darcy. He was an ex- Foreign Legion man who was wanted for terrorist activities in three countries in Europe. He was also wanted for the murder of three black politicians in the Republic of South Africa.

Brooker shouted to Niles who was still looking out the window at the apartments opposite.

'Hey Sandy we've identified two of the guys at Domingo's place and the leader appears to be wanted for terrorist crimes and possible murder. I don't think there can be any doubt that they're a new hit team assembled to take out Field's family. I've got to get back to the op's room and get this information to the States as soon as possible. With a bit of luck they may be able to pick Darcy and his colleagues up as they arrive in the States'.

'The trouble is', said Niles. 'They may not be travelling on their own passports and for all we know Domingo may have arranged to fly them in via Cuba on one of his Drug running aircraft. Never the less the information should make it easier for the FBI to spot the team if they know who they're looking for'.

The three of them took it in turns to keep the apartments under close watch whilst Chris went back to his operations room to back load the information to the States. Chris was proving to be a valuable asset to the team. Without his local connections and his personal "get-up-and-go" their operation would have been twice as hard.

After Chris returned they got down to the detailed planning of who was going to do what.

The other three looked to Niles to take the lead. But Niles was slightly diffident and said.

'We are now moving into a sphere of operations where you and Rusty have much more experience that me.

Rusty nodded his head in agreement. 'True Sandy, we have plenty of experience in clandestine operations but when it came to planning mayhem you had a positive flair for it, so let's thrash the plan out together, okay'.

Rusty looked to Tony to start the ball rolling. 'Thanks Rusty, you and I have been exposed to the Colombians on several occasions so I figure that if you and Chris organise the knocking down and doctoring of the drinks and Pizzas. Chris speaks the local lingo like a native and you are colloquial enough to back him up. To affect entry into the apartments I suggest we set the operation in motion about three in the morning – the Burundanga will have had plenty of time to make it effects felt. The three of us', Tony indicated Sandy, Rusty and himself. 'Will effect the entry and remove Domingo and any one else that gets in the way. In the meantime Chris drives the truck and awaits our signal to appear alongside the building'.

'Actually', said Rusty. 'I think the more of us at the scene of the accident when we knock the Pizza boy over the better. We will have a better chance of getting the food doctored. I'll bump the guy over and the rest of you can pretend to be idle witnesses but rush over to help get him to his feet – with four of us milling around him he won't know if he's on his arse or elbow. We can completely unsight him whilst the drinks and food get doctored'.

Tony looked around.' Agreed - good suggestion Rusty – any one disagrees?'

He then nodded at Chris. 'What materials have we

in the back of the truck to cushion the noise of Domingo landing Chris?'

'I have three old sprung mattresses covered by about a foot of straw. It won't stop him from getting seriously hurt but it will deaden the noise of him landing from three stories up'.

'If every thing has gone according to plan he'll be dead by that stage so we're not too worried about him breaking any limbs. It's the noise of his body hitting the back of the truck we're trying to disguise'.

'Have we got the glass cutters Chris?' asked Tony. 'If they have the air conditioning on they will almost certainly have the windows closed if not locked'.

'Yep! Plus a plumber's rubber plunger which you can use to pull the cut away glass from the window without making a noise'.

'Right', continued Niles. 'We have our Berretta silencers, our drugs, now all we have to do is wait and pray that Domingo feels horny enough to pay his mistress a visit and we're in business

Their luck held and Domingo and his henchmen turned up at the usual time. Rusty who was driving the small white van that was to be used to knock down the delivery boy. Tony was to be driving the truck in which was going to block the road and Chris and Niles were acting as by-standers.

Domingo and his entourage turned up at eight in the evening and entered the apartment. The team waited with bated breath for fifteen minutes and then moved into action to intercept the Pizza boy

The pizza delivery boy appeared as if by clockwork and just as he approached the 'T' junction Tony backed out the lorry to block his path and at the same time Rusty came down the side street and gentle bumped into the back of the pizza bike spilling the rider and his pizza orders all over the road.

Quick as a flash, Chris and Niles rushed over to help pick him up, at the same time, both the drivers of the vehicles involved stopped and rushed over to the shaken delivery boy. Whilst Chris spoke to the boy in fluent Spanish Niles and Tony collected the boxes together pretending to argue which pizza went into which box and turning the whole episode into a, "Fred Carne" melee. They quickly opened the boxes and administered the drug to both the food and drinks. Rusty and Chris ensured that the delivery boy was kept unsighted by keeping their bodies between him and what Niles and Tony were up to. Although it was only eight o'clock in the evening it was dark and the chances of being observed in such poor light were minimal. In fact the only two other witnesses showed only a mild interest in what was happening.

The accident and the doctoring of the Pizzas and drinks were all over in thirty seconds. Tony kept apologising profusely until the delivery boy was fed up to listening to him. We much rapid Spanish, too fast for all but Chris to understand the Pizza boy mounted his bike and rode off still cursing the "stupid lorry driver". The team ensured that the delivery boy went off in the right direction and watched him carefully to ensure that he went to the correct apartments.

As they saw him draw up outside the apartments Tony remarked. 'I hope to Christ we've doctored the right Pizzas otherwise some strangers are going to be very confused when they wake up tomorrow'.

Niles just grinned and turned to Chris.

'How long to you reckon we ought to wait for the drug to take effect?'

'From all the accounts I've seen and read the drug kicks in within a very short time but there seems to be some controversy on how long the effects of the drug lasts'.

'If they also have a few drinks tonight that alone should exacerbate their conditions', said Rusty. 'By the way Sandy have you considered what we are going to do if the bastards decide to go out for the night? The chances are that they will fall asleep in some god dam night club, in which case we will be up a well known creek without a paddle',

Rusty's last statement had a profound shock on all the team, none of them had considered that Domingo and his mistress might go out for the night.

'Fuck!' mused Niles. 'We hadn't really considered that option although up to present he has only taken her out once in the past week that we and Alfred's men have had him under surveillance'.

Rusty gave a big grin, 'maybe the bastards hard up for cash after all the money we've cost him'.

Chris turned to the other three.

'I reckon we are safe - in another half an hour any intention they had of going out is gradually going to falter as they feel more and more tired. We watch them for the next hour and if they haven't left by then they are not going to – lets get back to the flat and get some rest'.

The four of them took it in turns to watch the apartments across the road. The only person to leave was the giant Renaldo. As he came down the steps of the apartments just before ten-o'clock to get into the waiting taxi, he was definitely walking in a very stilted manner – similar to some one who had had too much to drink and was trying to disguise it.

The team breathed a sigh of relief as the giant disappeared down the road. The thought of having to take on such a man was quite sobering.

At half past ten all the lights in the Penthouse were gradually switched off and now the top floor of the apartments was in total darkness. Rusty went round the other side of the apartments to see if there were any lights in the bedrooms that was located on the far side of the building. He reported back there was none.

'I think we will stick to the planned time of three o'clock in the morning', said Niles. 'At that time of the morning there is less chance of any one being on the street – All agree?'

They decided to take turns at keeping the apartment under survey whilst the remainder tried to get some shut eye.

At three o'clock Tony who was on duty gave the other three a shake and they started to get their kit together.

'Any sign of activity Tony?' asked Niles.

'I haven't seen any movement since I've been on watch and Rusty had seen nothing previously so I think we can assume that they are all gently tucked up in bed'.

They started to collect all their kit and belongings together. It was important that they left no clue as to who they were or where they'd gone. Not that they were expecting anyone to search the room as there was no way in which the team could have been connected in disappearance of Domingo.

They assembled at the back of the house. Their mood was sombre each deep in their own thoughts. None knew for certain what really awaited them once they got into the penthouse. The moon was beginning to wane as it shone through some mist that had sprung up during the night. There was also a gentle breeze blowing down from the mountains which was, according to Niles, Katabatic drainage; this provided just sufficient mixing to create the turbulence necessary to cause the mist.

'I'm afraid the visibility is going to get worse before it gets better', murmured Niles. 'It could even end up as fog before the night is out which means we will have to delay the movement by helicopter'.

Tony nodded his head in agreement, 'Yes but it will also reduce the chances of any one seeing the truck or identifying it.

They agreed that Chris would park the truck at the top of the hill beyond the Apartments and await the flashlight to summons him to coast silently down the hill until he was under Domingo's window. Sandy was going to flash dah dit dah dit which was 'C' in Morse so that Chris was not alerted by some spurious light. It was going to take him half an hour to pick up the truck but it would also take about half an hour for the other three to gain entrance to the apartment and subdue Domingo and possibly his girl friend.

As the three of them crept round the back of the apartment the wind was gradually increasing which was causing the mist to thicken even more but they still had over a hundred metres or more of visibility.

Tony looked at the stick and brick that Rusty was carrying. The house brick had been covered in old Hessian but even so it would still make a considerable thump as it landed on the roof.

'If the noise of this landing on the roof doesn't waken them I figure we can assume that the drug has taken effect', whispered Tony.

The other two nodded in agreement.

It was not going to be an easy task throwing the 'stick and brick up three stories high but Rusty had managed it the night before but then the apartments had been empty.

The rope was not very thick so they had tied knots in it about every metre or so to give them better purchase when using it to climb up on to the roof.

As Rusty had done it the night before Niles and Tony stood to one side with bated breath as he whirled the brick diagonally about his head and then cast it towards the roof. The first attempt failed to reach the roof and Niles had to catch the brick before it hit the ground. However Rusty's second attempt was spot on as it landed over the parapet with a dull thud.

'Now for the acid test', grunted Niles. 'I guess we wait

two or three minutes to see if the noise has woken some one up and they come to investigate'.

'I have just had an idea', whispered Niles. 'When we make our way down from the roof by the internal stairs to Domingo's bedroom, we clobber him, open the window from the inside – dump him through the window. We then close the window and lock it from the inside and exit the room the same way we came in. Climb down the rope which we can secure with a slip knot and no one will know what the hell has happened. I reckon that if the noise of that brick landing on the roof has not woken them then the chances of us tip toeing passed the body guards must be pretty good'.

Tony looked at Niles and grinned.

'As I have said before Sandy you have a positive genius for cooking up trouble. Your scheme will negate us having to break the window and as it will be locked from the inside it will appear that some how or other Domingo has just upped and left the building and disappeared off the face of this earth'.

'Aint that just what we are trying to achieve', smiled Rusty.

They waited with bated breath for all of five minute before deciding that the guards must be well under the influence of the Burundanga drug or by now some one would have come up to the roof to investigate the noise of the brick landing.

Rusty went up first followed by Tony and they used the technique of using their feet to lock the rope with their legs whilst moving the hands up the rope for a fresh grip. This reduced any marking on the wall which might arouse suspicion after the disappearance of Domingo.

As they climbed the rope the mist continued to thicken. Niles took the longest to get up the rope as he had not practiced this skill since his days with the Para's. Rusty and Tony had shot up the rope like monkeys. Without the knots in the rope Niles had serious doubts as to whether he could have made it to the top (to the uninitiated, climbing up ropes might look easy but in fact it takes considerable strength and skill to climb a rope up three stories without assistance).

Tony pointed up the hill to where Chris was parked with the lorry.

'I'm afraid we may have to use out radios to call Chris down with the lorry, the visibility has already dropped below a hundred metres and if it gets any thicker he is not going to see our flash light signal'.

'As we're intending to come up on the roof to clear the building I don't think the radio will make sufficient noise to cause any embarrassment', replied Niles.

The flat roof of the apartments was about thirty yards square fenced with the parapet they had climbed over. There were a couple of VHF and a single TV aerial otherwise apart from the small covered door to the stairs below there was nothing else on the roof.

Rusty gently tried the door and found it was locked. 'Bastard' he growled. The door frame and surrounding structure was of stout wooden planking. Any attempt to prise the planks apart to get entrance was going to leave visual evidence. Rusty turned, looked at the other two and gave a slow smile

Tony just returned the smiled and said, 'now Rusty will demonstrate one of his many ill gotten talents that he learnt whilst serving with the Parachute Engineers'.

'Don't tell me you used to belong to those bloody pirates in 9 Independent Parachute Squadron Royal Engineers?' queried Niles.

'One and the same', laughed Rusty quietly.

Niles gave a subdued chuckle. 'If that's case then, I can't see this locked door proving to be any kind of a problem'.

The door opened outwards. Rusty whipped out an evil

looking sheath knife. He jammed it into the door crack and dug its point into the locking bolt with the knife's handle at about thirty degrees towards the door hinges. Once he felt the point of the knife making firm purchase with the door's bolt he levered the knife handle towards the door frame (that's away from the door hinges)causing the door's bolt to retract from the door hasp. Rusty could feel that the bolt was not fully retracted so using the door handle he pulled the door hard outwards to grip the bolt and trap it in its partially retracted position. He then reinserted the knife as before and as soon as he felt the knife biting into the bolt he released the outward pressure on the door and repeated the previous technique. After his second attempt the bolt was clear. He grasped the door handle and opened the door, took a bow and whispered, 'please, no applause – just throw money'.

Inside the door was a metal grill which also opened outwards but much to their surprise and relief was not locked. This was most unusual; security in Colombia was an ever present problem and all doors and windows were normally screened by locked metal grills to prevent break-ins. Presumably it was reasoned that only a raving idiot would attempt to break-in to the penthouse of Domingo's mistress.

Rusty led the way down the stairs treading carefully to minimise any creaking floor steps, Tony followed with Niles bringing up the rear. At the bottom of the stairs Rusty gently and almost imperceptibly opened the door that led onto the landing of the penthouse. The other two waited, holding their breath with suppressed excitement. He turned, gave them the thumbs up and entered the hall. The first guard was slumped in an arm chair by the door clutching a pump action 12 bore shot gun. But for the chair arms the weapon would have probably fallen to the ground. The man was snoring his head off and obviously well under the influence of the Burundanga drug. Tony gently eased the gun out of his hands whilst the other two stood coiled for immediate action should he wake. Tony ejected the shells and gently placed them in his right hand jacket pocket.

They then moved quietly along the carpeted passage until they came to the second guard who was asleep outside Domingo's bedroom and positioned opposite the elevator doors thus covering both the entrance to the penthouse and Domingo's bedroom. This man was armed with a Galil 7.62/5.56mm ARM Assault Rifle. This deadly Israel weapon was capable of firing at 700rpm and with a muzzle velocity of 3,116ft/sec. It was not a good gun to be stood in front of when it went off.

Rusty gently moved the guard forward in his chair whilst Tony eased the gun out of his hand, detached the 50-round box magazine and handed it to Rusty who then slid the rounds out of it. Reinserted the magazine and gently placed the gun back in the sleeping guard's lap. The rhythm of the guards snoring had barely changed as they unloaded his weapon. It now meant that should either of the guards wake up whilst the team were in the house then it would take them at least thirty seconds to get their act together. By that time they would be dead.

A careful search of the two other bedrooms revealed a further guard in bed completely comatose and snoring his head off, His only weapon appeared to be a Colt Double Eagle, a heavy calibre automatic pistol which fire a 0.45 slug. It makes a nasty hole in any one on the receiving end. Rust slipped the magazine out and gently placed it into the bedside locker drawer. A search of sitting room and the kitchen revealed no other occupants in the penthouse. Niles gently tried the door to Domingo's bedroom half expecting it to be locked. It was.

'Sod it!' hissed Niles. 'Domingo's locked the door to prevent his goons from watching him in action'.

Rusty knelt down and looked through the keyhole. 'Ah… I see our friend has left the key in the door – one of you look for a sheet of newspaper whilst I go to the kitchen and look for a meat skewer or something like it'.

Niles noted that the guards had been reading what was basically a pornographic magazine and ripped a middle page out. Rusty appeared waving a long meat skewer in his hand, 'Just what the doctor ordered', he grinned.

He knelt down and pushed the sheet of paper that Niles had given him under the door until it was positioned just under the door's lock and then gently probed with the meat skewer, feeling for the end of the key. He made contact and gently pushed until the key fell out of the lock on the other side of the door. They heard a metallic clink as the key fell out the lock onto the paper that they'd pushed under it.

'Shit!', gasped Rusty. 'It's only just on the paper'.

Rusty very gentle eased the paper from under the door with the key only just resting on it. If it fell off they were going to have a long job trying to rescuing the dam thing. The bloody key slipped off the paper just as they were about to slide it out under the door. Tony and Niles looked at each other in undisguised dismay.

'What now'? Tony hissed.

Rusty just grunted; jammed the end of the meat skewer between the door and frame and levered it until it had a right angled bend in it. He then lay down on the floor and using the bent skewer like a Shepard's crook pulled the key from beneath the door. Picked it up and gently waved it triumphantly to his appreciative audience.

Niles and Tony looked at Rusty in admiration and Niles whispered. 'That speaks of an ill begotten youth you evil bastard. Where did you learn all these nefarious skills?'

'I was an Army Boy Apprentice before joining the Engineers – where else to you think I learnt tricks like this?' Rusty just grinned and gently inserted the key and turned it. The lock turned almost noiselessly and the door swung open. There lay Domingo and his mistress locked together like spoons in a drawer.

'Christ!' said Tony. 'We'll need a crow bar to separate them'.

Although the air conditioning was going at full tilt neither Domingo or his mistress had any bed covers on. And the noise made by the air conditioning was going to help suppress any that they made.

They carefully eased the two lovers apart and covered the girl to keep her warm thus reducing the chances of her waking up before the team had got clear with Domingo.

Domingo groaned but did not wake up but Niles looked at Tony and Rusty and whispered.

'I reckon the bastard could wake up if we tried to move him up to the roof. I think we will have to give him a good clip about the head to make sure he doesn't come round whilst we are moving him'.

Rusty reversed his Berretta and slammed the butt into Domingo's head which produced a groan but no other reaction.

'That should keep him quiet for the next hour or so', Rusty growled.

Niles bent down and grabbed Domingo's arm and leg gave a heave, and had him over his shoulder in the fireman's lift. At the same time Tony motioned to Rusty to grab Domingo's brief case which was beside the bed and bring it with them.

'Right lets get this bastard over the parapet', grunted Niles. 'Before any of his goons start to recover'.

Rusty led the way while Tony checked to ensure that the two body guards were still comatose. Although the fog had thickened it was also now lying much closer to the ground and from their elevated position on top of the apartments they had a clear view to the top of the hill where Chris was parked with the truck. Tony flashed the Morse signal for 'C' and Chris responded with a single flash.

As they searched up the road for the truck it suddenly appeared out of the fog and coasted to a halt right beneath them.

'Sandy', said Tony. 'If we drop this bastard head first I figure he is going to break his neck even allowing for the sound proofing material that Chris has in the truck'.

'I think your right Tony - it will also negate us having to shoot him and trying to get rid of the blood stains. Let's try it and if it doesn't work then we are back to having to shoot him later.

Rusty waved to Chris to get out of the way and Tony and Niles each took a leg apiece and toppled Domingo over the parapet head first.

Despite the old mattresses and straw in the back of the truck the noise of Domingo landing on his head was quite considerable. There was a definite crack that sounded like some bones breaking.

Tony and Niles shinned down the rope first while Rusty lowered the, 'stick and brick' over the side of the parapet and made sure that the slip knot was going to function properly before he followed them. Once they were on the ground Rusty pulled the free running end of the slip knot and the rope came cascading down.

Niles jumped into the back of the truck and checked Domingo. The head of the body was twisted at a strange angle and it was obvious that the man's neck was broken. Niles checked for a pulse – there was none.

'Well that saved us the unsavoury task of having to execute him', said Niles.

Chris was looking around rather anxiously.

'Any of you guys know how we are going to get to the chopper pick up point in this fog?

Now that they were down at ground level the team

could appreciate just how the visibility had decreased while they were in the apartments.

'I think our best bet is to proceed to the Airport with the body, bluff our way though the gates and load the body on there. Let's face it; in this visibility we could load a herd of elephants on board and no one would be the wiser – do you reckon you could find the airport in this Viz' Chris? ', Niles asked.

He nodded his head. 'It'll be slow progress but no trouble - all roads within the city that are orientated North to South are called Carrera with suffix number. West to East orientated roads are called Calle's with suffix numbers. I've a street map in the truck. All we need to do is follow this Calle we're on at the moment to the West until we meet the Carrera that takes us down South to the airport'.

Niles gave the thumbs up sign and the team clambered aboard – Chris driving with Niles in the cab and Tony and Rusty keeping the body of Domingo company in the back.

The actual visibility began to improve as the colder air settled to the ground forming dew rather than fog. It took them forty minutes to get to the airport during which they saw no other vehicles on the road. On arrival they were given a wave through the airport entrance by a disinterested and sleepy security guard. He couldn't even be bothered to get off his ass let alone check their documentation.

Chapter 37

Renaldo

Renaldo, Domingo's giant body guard was extremely angry. He'd been unable to perform in the bedroom. He kept falling asleep and his girl friend was beginning to suspect that he had another senora tucked away somewhere in the city. She was also trying to force him into making a commitment that was impossible. She wanted him to promise to marry her. This was difficult. His body guard duties to Domingo demanded his total presence almost twenty four hours a day. Renaldo was one of those giant men who had no idea on how to cope with emotional women.

He'd had a similar problem four years ago and had gone to Domingo for advice. A week later the girl was killed in a traffic accident. Renaldo was not sure, but thought that Domingo had something to do with the girl's death. However Renaldo had said nothing at the time but now tended to keep his own council concerning his girl friends. Domingo was well aware of the giant's physical needs but he'd supposed he was going to the various cat houses in the town. Providing his giant was available first thing in the morning Domingo had no objections to him staying out at night. However Renaldo was not sure that his boss would be very happy at him shacking up with the same woman all the time – this could be interpreted as division of loyalties.

Although the giant had drank some of the drugged coffee he'd not eaten any of the pizza before leaving the apartments therefore the small amount of the drug he'd ingested was quickly absorbed by his huge body mass resulting in little ill effect. His assignation with his mistress had not gone smoothly. After some heavy petting the giant had dropped off into a drugged sleep, much to his mistress's disgust, she had attempted to awaken him on several occasions without much success. She felt insulted and kept trying to waken him to tell him so. She eventually managed to wake him about two in the morning to continue haranguing him and eventually he'd lost his temper and stormed out.

Renaldo decided to walk back to the apartment to ease some of the aggression. He wandered down the streets muttering to himself and deliberately staring down any passers by who might challenge his right of passage. There were none prepared to take him on. He eventually arrived back at the apartment block at about three in the morning. As he was entering the front of the apartment he noticed a truck parked alongside the apartment with no lights on. He could see no movement in the vehicle so he paid scant attention to it and entered the building.

The night receptionist was dozing behind the foyer counter but immediately recognised the giant.

'Good evening senor Renaldo you are back early this morning it is only just gone three o'clock'.

'Bastard women trouble', growled the giant. 'Any movement from the boss and the boys up stairs'?

'No, I haven't heard from them since you left this evening senor'.

Renaldo pressed the button for the elevator and entered.

As he stepped out of the elevator at the penthouse floor although he was still befuddled he realised that something was wrong. The guard sitting opposite the elevator made no move to challenge or acknowledge him. The consequences for sleeping on the job were severe. He strode across the corridor and with a vicious open handed swipe hit the guard across the face. The guard just groaned and slumped to the floor but made no other movement. Renaldo looked at the other guard and immediately saw that he was also comatose.

He was now worried. He leaped across the corridor and turned the handle to Domingo's bedroom expecting it to be locked as usual. It wasn't. The giant rushed into the bedroom and saw immediately that Domingo was missing. He grabbed the sleeping girl by the shoulder and shook her vigorously. She reacted in the same way as the two guards outside. He was now certain that they had all been drugged and that Domingo had been snatched or kidnapped.

Renaldo had no particular love for Domingo but he'd enough animal cunning to appreciate that he was his meal ticket to an easy life. Therefore unless he wanted to end up on the streets again he'd better try and find his boss.

Just then he heard a truck start up in the street below and instinctively realised that this had something to do with Domingo's disappearance.

He rushed out of the room grabbing the sleeping guards Galil assault rifle in one hand and jamming his thumb into the elevator button. He stood cursing as he waited for the elevator but had enough nous to check he had a set of keys for the motorbike that was kept in the apartment's private car park.

He rushed into the car park grabbed the Honda's handle bars, leaped onto the saddle, fitted the ignition key in and cranked the bike over. It started on the second attempt and Renaldo set off to try and catch up with the departing truck. He was not a very accomplished rider at the best of times and with him still suffering from the effects of the drug he'd taken he was practically suicidal. And but for the fog would probably never have caught up with the truck. He almost came off the bike on several occasions but he finally caught up with the vehicle as it was making one of its frequent stops to enable Chris and Niles to orientate where they were. At this stage he was not even sure that the truck had anything to do with his boss's disappearance. It was pure gut instinct that kept him going. He managed to tail them as they turned south towards the city airport.

Renaldo was not sure what he was going to do but decided he would intercept the truck as soon as they got out of the built up area. However after a mile or so the truck turned into the airport entrance where a sleepy security guard could not even be bothered to look in the vehicle's cab or load tray.

The vehicle drove into the airport and disappeared into the fog.

Renaldo approached the gates and said to the security guard, 'Do you know who I am senor'?

'Se senor I have seen you on many occasions before'.

'Right! If you know what's good for you; you will forget about the truck in front and my presence here this evening –understand'!

The man looked suitable cowed - Renaldo's reputation had preceded him and the security guard had no wish to fall out with the giant. Just one blow from the giant's mighty fist was enough to kill most men, so he just nodded his head in agreement.

Niles and his team arrived at the S76 Helicopter. They got out of the truck and were just stretching them selves when this fearsome apparition appeared out of the mist carrying a Galil Assault Rifle levelled and ready for use. The size of the man alone would normally have been enough to put the fear of god up most peopled but armed as he was; he was a truly fearful sight

'Get your hands in the air hombres', snarled the giant waving the weapon around although somewhat unsteady on his feet.

Although Renaldo was speaking in Spanish he was making it abundantly clear what he wanted.

The team raised their hands and at the same time Niles adopted his obsequious pose that he had used so often during the last three years in South America when trying to avoid attracting attention to himself At the same time he lowered his right hand and gave his groin a good scratch..

Renaldo swivelled the gun in Niles direction and snarled, 'I said get you're fucking arms up and keep them'.

Nile's dyed hair and skin disguised was working and he played on this by grovelling even more,

'I'm sorry senor but I have many crabs and they are eating me alive'.

'If you don't keep your fucking arms in the air your crabs are going to be eating you dead – now leave your prick alone! And get your arms in the air'.

'Sorry senor but I am just a simple Peon truck driver hired by the gringos to transport their oil platform stores'. As Niles delivered this last sentence he contrived to look as dim witted as he could. His speech was also slow and halting enhancing his dim wittedness (Rusty said later that it was an improvement on his usual bearing!).

However Niles spoof was beginning to work. The giant was now paying more attention to the three gringos.

'Right you bastards; against the trucks and lean on your hands. Renaldo made them face the truck with their hands in the air whilst he gave them a quick frisk. As they had not been expecting any trouble the teams weapons were still in the truck except for Niles whose Berretta was, as usual, strapped to the inside of his right thigh with the pocket of the trousers cut away.

The giant gave Niles a quick cursory check but did not feel the inside of Niles thigh and missed the Berretta. For the moment the giant believed Niles story that he was nothing but a dim local peon and therefore not worth bothering with.

As Chris had got out of the truck's cab Renaldo assumed that he was the boss and began to direct all his questions to him.

'What have you got in the back of the truck gringo?'

'You have no authority to search my company's vehicles', complained Chris in a highly aggrieved manner.

'I have all the authority I need right here', replied the giant waving the Galil about. 'Further more; you and your friend are going to unload the truck so I can inspect it'.

Niles gave himself another scratch of his balls and managed to release the safety catch of his Berretta. This time, the giant just waved the gun for him to get his arms back in the air.

Chris waved his arms around in an exasperated manner and said.

'But all we have on the truck is some old mattresses that we are going to use for sleeping on out in the bush during our oil surveys'.

'Cut the crap and get aboard that truck and start unloading it', snarled the giant

The situation was now getting critical. Rusty and Chris made getting over the tail board of the truck an effort to delay the time when the giant was eventually going to check the back of the truck and find his dead boss.

As they were clambering over the tail board Niles was surreptitiously working his way round to Renaldo's flank. He'd already had another go at scratching his balls and this time the giant barely registered it.

Renaldo final lost his temper over the time Chris and Rusty were taking to get over the tail board of the truck and started to thump them with the folding stock of the Galil Rifle to move faster.

This was the small chance that Niles had been waiting for. He slowly dropped his right hand as if to have another scratch at his balls. However this time Niles slid his hand into his right hand cut out pocket and smoothly withdrew his Berretta with the silencer still attached.

'Renaldo!' he snarled. 'Drop the gun!'

Renaldo stood stock still with shock, 'how did these people know his name '?

However, he suddenly moved with incredible speed for such big man. He swivel the Galil at Niles and squeezed the trigger all in one swift fluid movement. There was just a metallic click and nothing else. For a moment every one was frozen to the spot. Then Niles realised what had happened. Renaldo had grabbed the weapon of the sleeping guard back at the apartments which Rusty had already unloaded.

A professional soldier would have realised as soon as he picked the weapon up that it was too light for the magazine to be loaded. Then again; a man of Renaldo's massive size and strength probably wouldn't notice the difference in the weight of a loaded and unloaded magazine

The giant looked down at the gun in disbelief and then two bullets from Nile's Berretta shattered the Galil breech and stock. At the same time Chris leaned over the side of the truck and smashed the giant across the head with the 'stick and brick' that they had used to gain access to the apartments. The first blow only appeared to stun the giant and he still remained standing. However, Chris's second blow was delivered with two hands and with such force that it would have killed a normal man; it knocked the giant senseless and he collapsed to the ground.

They all stood there for a moment grinning with relief.

Chris was the first to speak.

'Christ that was a close run thing. We were lucky there'.

'Not necessarily lucky', interrupted Tony. 'Niles has had the right hand pocket of all his trousers removed to facilitate the quick withdrawal of his hand gun and Rusty and I took the precaution of unloading both the guards' weapons at the apartments. I call that contingency planning'.

Chris gave a mock bow, 'I stand corrected'.

Niles then laughed and said. 'In flying we used to have a pneumonic called the five Ps. Which stands for; Prior, Planning, Prevents Pisspoor, Performance.

'I must remember that', mused Chris. 'In the meantime what are we going to do with this guy?'

Tony grabbed the rope from the, 'stick and brick', and began to tie the giant up.

'I reckon we get this guy well trusted up before he regains consciousnesses. I wouldn't like to try and tie him up when he's awake it would be like trying to secure a Rhino'.

Once the giant had been secured they stood around looking down at him.

Niles looked at Chris and pointed to the giant.

'You know what Chris, if you could recruit this guy he could prove invaluable to your intelligence operation down here'.

Chris looked thoughtful for a moment.

'That might be worth attempting Sandy. The guy is going to be unemployed now that his boss is dead and we are already aware that he doesn't have the intelligence to climb into the higher echelons of the Cartel. I think with a bit of brain washing you've a good point there. One thing for sure, we can't leave him here. He hasn't seen Domingo's body so he can never accuse us of being implicated in his disappearance'.

'How are you going to get him back to Bogotá Chris'? Tony asked.

'I guess I'll have to keep him doped on Burundanga until I can get him transferred to Bogotá but that should be no problem I can get some help from the Embassy within three hours and hire a chopper to back load him'.

Niles thought for a moment. 'We could always call back after we dumped Domingo into the sea and chopper him back to Bogotá for you Chris'.

'Yeh I appreciate that Sandy but I really feel your first priority is to get back State side to the Fields residence and help getting Darcy and his hoods under lock and key '.

Tony looked around the team and said.

'Well I guess it's time to say adieu Chris. Sandy has planned to fly this chopper back to the States after we have dumped Domingo. It means we'll have to refuel in Panama to try and save time getting back.

Niles pointed to the giant's body. 'If you guys give Chris a hand getting the hulk into the back of the truck and Domingo's into the chopper I'll go and post a flight plan with Air Traffic Control. We can dump Domingo's body on our way to Panama for our first refuelling stop. Dumping it will only add literally minutes to our flight time so no one will be any the wiser. But before we leave Chris I would like to thank you for all your assistance without it I'm not sure how we would have managed.

Chris looked at Niles with an amused smile and said, 'Think nothing of it by the way; I believe congratulations are in order Sandy'.

Niles looked puzzled. 'Why? – For a job well done; I thought this was a team effort?'

'No', Chris grinned. 'George Fields phoned whilst you were on your way down here to say that if this all went off successfully to let Sandy know that he is due to be a Father in about eight months time. Apparently Jenny knew for sure that she was pregnant before you left but didn't want you being distracted whilst you were on this operation'.

Niles looked completely nonplussed and looked at the other two stood there grinning.

'Did either of you know that I was about to become a father'?

Tony and Rusty both nodded and Tony said, 'Yes Sandy I think every body in the USA knew. They practically had a Senate meeting on whether to let you know or not before you departed for here'.

'What are you going to do now Sandy? I thought you were a confirmed bachelor', queried Rusty with a smarmy grin on his face.

'Marry the girl of course. Even without the child Jenny has only to crook her finger and my bloody hormones activate my legs and I come running. Besides which I'm very old fashion; no child of mine is going to be born out of wedlock', concluded Niles.

Chris strode over and shook their hands leaving Niles to the last.

'It was a pleasure working with you guys and if I ever get my self into trouble I'll know who to look to for help. By the way Sandy - what are the chances of getting an invitation to the wedding'?

'Pretty good Chris and if you have got the giant suitably brainwashed and on our side bring him along too. It will impress the guy's State side when they see what we were up against'.

After they had loaded the giant into the back of the truck Niles decided to pass an Airborne Flight Plan to save time. Instead he helped Tony and Rusty to wrap Domingo's body in heavy chains that Chris had supplied and lift the body onto the S76. They got their departure clearance and headed out to sea and back to the States.

Chapter 38

Riverside Estate

Darcy and his four accomplices landed at Miami International Airport mid afternoon. He was eager to get clear of the Airport as quickly as possible. Four of the team were wanted by the FBI and although they were travelling on false passports they were eager to get clear of the airport quickly. They'd shelved the idea of getting an internal flight to Washington DC as the consensus of opinion was that the security there would be much tighter than it was at Miami.

Darcy turned to Pierre Clermont. 'Pierre you and I will collect the rental car and the other three can collect our baggage from the carousel and meet us at the main arrival entrance – Pete make sure you get all our duffle bags and meet us at the main door okay'.

Pete just grunted, he never did say much.

Darcy and Clermont made their way to the 'Greyhound' car rental service. Signed for the pre- booked car, climbed in and drove off towards the main terminal entrance. As they approaching the terminal Darcy noted that there were several bystanders stood around who appeared to doing nothing definite. There were three road sweepers who were sweeping a road where the absence of litter was conspicuous. Further on was an ice cream van which didn't appear to be selling any products. None the less they were trying to look as though they were busy. Darcy could feel the hackles on the nape of his neck rising. There was something not right here. He'd not lived on his wits for the past ten years and avoided prison by ignoring his instincts. 'Bastards! We've been rumbled', he snarled to Pierre.

Pierre looked anxiously around, 'there are a lot of people stood around working hard at doing nothing'.

Darcy floored the throttle and roared off. The three road sweepers who were ostensibly sweeping the "pristine clean" road chased after them drawing side arms as they tried to intercept the speeding rental. This was all that Darcy and Clermont needed to confirm they were in trouble. Darcy kept the throttle floored until they had cleared the Airport. Their three colleagues collecting their baggage would have to look after themselves. In this game it was a case of the, 'devil takes the hindmost'. For the next twenty four hours it was going to be every man for himself. Whatever the outcome of today Darcy realised that his hit team was now reduced to the two of them. He was going to have to make alternative arrangements. Their initial plan had just disappeared out the window

After twenty hours travelling the team landed back at the riverside estate to find the area in complete confusion. The Fields family were still hiding in Oregon so at the moment still safe. But the team soon discovered that there had been a complete fiasco at Miami International Airport.

Theo, who met them as they deplaned at the Fields residence, told them the sad story of the screw up at Miami Airport. 'The FBI had received Chris Booker's warning in time to organise and lay on a trap for the incoming hit team. The intention was to grab them once they'd cleared the Arrival Terminal when there would be less chance of bystanders being hit should any gunfire develop. This was highly unlikely as there was no chance of them travelling armed and getting through airport security which was pretty tight on all arrivals from Colombia. Why this point was not registered by the FBI Theo was not sure. Apparently, on arrival the team had split into two. Darcy and one of his mercenaries went to get a car at The Greyhound Hire Company's office leaving the other three to collect the luggage from the Baggage carousel. Darcy drove the car round to the entrance of the arrival terminal to pick up the three with their luggage when he became suspicious of the number of bystanders stood around doing nothing definite'.

'I think at this stage that Darcy became very wary. Lets face it, he's a very leery character and has escaped capture for the past ten years', continued Theo. 'Because he suddenly floored the accelerator and tore away from the terminal. Unfortunately some of the FBI agents over reacted and blew their cover by drawing their side arms and rushing after the car and trying to stop it. Mind you, at this stage I'm not sure what else they could've done. Not unnaturally this confirmed to Darcy that there had been a set up and his team had been compromised. The FBI agents had managed to arrest the other three mercenaries collecting the luggage but that still left Darcy and his companion loose in the country. There is an APB broadcast out for them to be apprehended. But Darcy is an old hand at remaining under cover and he and his accomplice are going to be hard to unearth'.

Theo was clearly embarrassed over the cock up particularly as Niles and his team's operation in Colombia had been such an outstanding success and the fact that they had even been able to inform the FBI of Darcy and his team's arrival.

Niles nodded his head sympathetically.

.Tony Bryant was not so sympathetic, 'why in Gods name didn't they board the aircraft and arrest them before they deplaned? There was no place they could have run to and further more with the high security state at all Airports these days there's no way they could have been carrying guns when they emplaned'.

'I agree', Theo shrugged his shoulders. 'However it was an FBI operation so we had nothing to do with it. If we had, I would have insisted on arresting them while they were still strapped in their cabin seats'.

Niles could see how embarrassed Theo was and knew he was a first class operator. 'There's no doubt Theo the more people you have on the job the more difficult it is to control. I take it that George Fields and family are still safe'?

'Yes, and providing it doesn't take too long to get Darcy behind bars they'll remain there but eventually they're going to have to return home and try and get on with their normal lives'.

Tony Bryant chipped in, 'We managed to get some information via Chris booker and it seems that this Darcy guy is a very experienced and wily character. He's going to be difficult to locate but we may have some information that might help to winkle him out'.

Rusty Irons was abreast of what Tony was saying and quickly produced the brief case they had lifted from Domingo's apartment. They had both had a chance to study it during the flight back from Colombia whilst Niles had been piloting and they'd been amazed at its contents.

They spread the contents of the brief case on the table. It contained much of Domingo's sensitive information including Off Shore Bank Numbers mostly for the Cayman Islands but three for well known International Banks in Switzerland. And of more immediate importance was a list of all Domingo's personal telephone numbers including one listed against Darcy's name for number in the USA. And three more numbers of American Senators one whom was Senator Jackson.

Niles got all excited when he saw the number against Darcy's name.

'Do you realise that we might be able to contact Darcy through that number and set up another trap'.

'Yes and lets do the job ourselves this time', snarled Rusty. 'That way we can ensure that it wont be fucked up again'.

Theo shook his head.

'No way Rusty - this is now a Federal case and hiding the contents of this brief case from them is a criminal offence and could get you into serious trouble'.

Theo's logic was unarguable – they would have to inform the FBI.

'I tell you what though, said Niles. 'We've been hired by George Fields to protect him and his family; that surely gives us the right to help in apprehending Darcy?'

Again Theo shook his head, as an ex-FBI agent before transferring to the Secret Service he was familiar with the machinations of the FBI.

'You could offer your services to them and be asked to be kept informed but the prerogative as to whether they want your services or not is theirs and theirs alone. However, the boss man in charge of this case is an old friend of mine so I might be able to get you on an inside track'.

Theo returned in half an hour with a lugubrious looking man in tow, he was a touch over six feet and inclined to stoop but there was alertness about his eyes that belied his kindly features. His long broken nose lent an unfortunate permanent sneer to his countenance. However his large mouth displayed plenty of white teeth when he smiled. His teeth were on show now.

Theo turned round to the man. 'These are the guys I

have been telling to you about. They are about the best I have come about in our business. Sandy, Tony, Rusty - this is Jake Lester and he is heading the FBI investigation'.

Lester shook their hands in turn and said.

'I hear you guys have just successfully completed a very difficult job down in Colombia and now Theo says you have some information that might help us to get Darcy'.

They showed Lester the contents of the brief case and explained where they'd obtained it.

'Jesus', he croaked. 'The State department is just going to love to get their hands on the contents of this. We can freeze these funds and put the Domingo part of the Cartel completely out of business'.

'Can I make an alternative suggestion', said Niles.

Lester nodded, 'Sure go ahead'.

'Why don't you draw money from the off shore Bank accounts at various intervals making it look as if Domingo is still alive?. The money would have to be correctly accounted for but it could be used to set up traps etc to catch criminal elements. However, over and apart from that, the main point of our operation was to make Domingo disappear without any one knowing what had happed to him. This was to specifically deflect any vendetta reprisals against the Defence Secretary and his family. If the money is being drawn from his numbered accounts people will assume that he is alive and has flown the country'.

'I see what you are getting at', Lester murmured a little sarcastically. 'Have you got any other theories that might be useful'?

'As a matter of fact I have', continued Niles. 'This is a telephone number that is listed against Darcy's name and it is a USA one. We could contact him with a fictitious plan by pretending to be Domingo and arrange a meeting somewhere and then grab him'.

'Just like that'! Lester raised an eyebrow.

'Yeh just like that', snarled Niles who was getting pissed off with the Agents off handed manner.

Theo just grinned at Jake Lester.

'I told you that they were some of the best in the business Jake'.

Jake nodded his head in agreement. More teeth on show.

'Look I have some guys already trying to think of a way of flushing our friend Darcy out into the open – at the moment with not too much success. I'll give you an hour to come up with a workable plan and if it's a go you guys are in on the kill – okay!"

The three of them sat down and started to plan. Theo came over and said.

'Would you consider me joining you guys in the planning, George Fields and his wife mean a lot to me and the boys and we would sure appreciate it if you could include us in your scheme'.

Tony Bryant was the first to reply. 'Well I suppose it's really up to Sandy but we normally work in groups of fours, it makes it easier for communications and more workable. I think we could include you but I would personally hesitate before including any more – but as I said, it's really up to Sandy'

Niles nodded his head in agreement. 'That's fine Theo but as Tony suggested, for the moment I would rather keep it to us four. If we come up with a workable plan we will do our best to include Mike and Homer'.

They sat down for an hour and as usual, it was Niles with his convoluted mentality that came up with the skeleton of a simple and workable plan. Whilst Rusty and Tony were able to fill in most of the practical details

Theo called the FBI chief and said they thought they had a plan that stood a good chance of success.

Jake Lester sat his self down. Pulled a cigarette, lit it,

took a deep draw and blew smoke.

'Okay, Theo tells me that you have a plan that might work in flushing Darcy out. Let's hear it.

Niles cleared his throat and started.

'As we mentioned earlier we have the US telephone number for Domingo to contact Darcy in this country. Our suggestion is that we get some one to mime Domingo phoning this number for Darcy; Bear in mind that Darcy can't be aware of Domingo's disappearance yet. We pretend that one of Domingo's contacts has got to one of the Defence Secretaries chauffeurs and bribed him with a large amount of money. Domingo suggests that Darcy and the chauffeur get together and plan how they can get the Defence Secretary isolated from his body guards long enough for assassination. The real chauffeur will obviously be replaced by me. I have seen Darcy but he has never seen me. We also have the car fitted with a, 'Tracker' system', A man of Darcy's experience is almost certainly going to change the rendezvous several times so I will probably have to be tracked at a distance in order to allay his suspicions. Okay so far'?

Lester nodded his head. 'Carry on'.

'My biggest problem', continued Niles. 'Is where I hide or carry a gun? In order to talk to Darcy he is going to have me frisked first; although I can insist that he also comes unarmed as I know no more about him that he does about me. Further more, if he tries to screw me around I'll pretend that I'm getting fed up and threaten to tell him to take a running hike. I'll make it clear that he stands to gain more from our liaison than I do. That way he won't be so inclined to mess me around too much'.

Lester again nodded his head in agreement. 'That's a good point Sandy – you've got to convince him that he needs your help more that you need his, otherwise he'll have you running all over the States trying to ascertain whether it's a trap or not'.

Niles continued. 'Now we come to the tricky bit and this is where we're going to have to be very flexible and react fast. He'll almost certainly insist on designating the meeting point, now this could be any where – but I must stipulate that I can only meet him at a specified and given time for so long because of my chauffeur duties. This will reduce the radius from Riverside that I can drive in the limited time I've available. Now, if I insist that I'm on call and can only be away from the Defence Secretaries presence for no more than an hour during the next week. We could throw a cordon around the Riverside Estate area up to fifteen miles radius and establish Quick Reaction teams at various points with choppers ready to fly them to any location at a minutes notice'.

Jake Lester sat there for a minute deep in thought. 'It could work Sandy, in fact once we get the final rendezvous there is no need for you to meet up with him – we just surround the area and grab them'.

Niles concurred with a nod of his head and continued.

'The trouble is he could place himself in such a position as to keep the meeting point under surveillance until he was sure that no one was following me – therefore we must make sure that he's at the location and the only way we can do that is if I can actually identify him. I've seen him before so I'll be able to recognise whether or not it's him. The wily bastard might well pay some cretin to turn up in his place just to see what transpires. We are only going to get one bite of the cherry at this. Once he realises the telephone number has been compromised we've lost all chance of flushing him out into the open'.

'You realise that this could be a one way ticket for you Sandy. If Darcy smells a rat he's going to attempt to waste you', Said Lester.

'I don't waste easy'.

Rusty and Tony both laughed and Tony said, 'I can

vouch for that'.

'Okay you guys - this is the best scenario we've had up to present so I think we'll run with it, further more I think you've qualified to be in at the kill'. Lester stood up and straightens his trousers. 'My only reservation at the moment Sandy is your safety. I think you and your team should consider on how to improve your chances of surviving. In the meantime, I'm going to start the ball rolling by getting the Swat teams organised into Quick Reaction Teams as you suggested and ensuring all the communications are compatible'.

Rusty looked at Niles and said, 'You know Sandy, Jake is absolutely right, and you're putting your self in grave danger. We've got to consider what we can do to reduce the risks. Further more why not let Tony or I act as the chauffeur '.

Niles thought for a minute. 'I take your point Rusty and admit that you and Tony are better soldiers than me but I figure that this charade involves more acting than soldiering and I've just spent three years doing exactly that down in Venezuela'.

Theo and Tony nodded their heads in agreement.

'Right', said Theo. 'Let's start by looking at the various problems that Sandy might be faced with, we can then work out the best way of nullifying them.

They sat in a huddle for over an hour before they agreed that they'd just about covered every contingency that Sandy could be faced with.

Jake Lester had rustled up a Latino agent from the FBI who was fluent in Spanish and could do a first class imitation of Domingo. They finally made contact with Darcy using the number secured from the brief case.

Darcy was eager to meet up with the chauffeur as he and his colleague were getting no where in trying to locate Fields and his family. When Darcy initially made contact with Niles he made it clear that he was not keen to meet personally but would rather discuss the plan over the phone. Niles refused, saying it was too dangerous to discuss over the phone, in fact they had already said too much and unless Darcy was prepared to meet him personally the plan was off. Darcy finally agreed but as Niles had suspected Darcy reserved the right to arrange the meeting between the two. He also insisted that the chauffeur (Niles) carried a mobile and Darcy be given the number so he could contact him whilst on the road.

Niles had been fitted out with a bullet proof vest and carried his usual Berretta plus a Browning Hi Power 9mm in a shoulder holster as was to be expected for a chauffeur driving the Defence Secretary. He was driving a Range Rover fitted with a, 'Tracking Device' and a large cross had been painted on the top of the vehicle that was only visible in the infra red spectrum. All the helicopters involved with the surveillance had been kitted out with infra red sights.

It was seven o'clock in the evening before they got the message from Darcy to make the meeting. Niles was informed to drive to the small town of Oxon Hill which was just east off the main highway to the south on the eastern side of the Potomac River.

Niles left the Riverside Estate and drove north up the main highway, Washington Street, turned right onto Route 95 to cross the Potomac. As he crossed the Potomac and was approaching the junction of the Indian Head Highway he got another call on the mobile telling him of a change in location. He was told to proceed to a small town called Palmers Corner.

He tuned south down the Indian Head Highway and then turned off south east towards Palmers Corner only to be given another location at a place called Oaklawn. Niles agreed to comply but made it obvious from the intonation of his voice that he was getting annoyed at being jerked around with all the changes.

He finally arrived at the Oaklawn location and checked that he was at the exact grid reference. He was. He noted that about 200metres to the north that there was a small knoll which was about 300ft higher than his present location. It would be the obvious place to keep his present location under surveillance. He'd driven over a small bridge into the location. It was surrounded by small woods on three sides but open to the north. Apart from a small derelict stone building on the west of the clearing it was completely bare except for two large oak trees.

Another call on the mobile. Darcy now wanted him to move to a place called Pagetts Corner.

Niles pretended to lose his temper.

'Look Darcy what the fuck do you think you are playing at? You've already jerked me around the country to three different locations. I'm not moving again. If you can't get here in the next five minutes I'm buggering off. My money has already been paid into my bank so its no skin off my nose it you don't show up. Take it or leave it!'

'How do I know you haven't been followed', countered Darcy.

'Because I've been checking my rear since leaving the estate, remember, I've as much to lose as you do if we get caught'.

'Okay', snarled Darcy in exasperation. 'Remain where you are and I'll join you in about five minutes'.

'You'd better be because after five minutes I'm off' and Niles switched the mobile off before Darcy could answer.

Niles went behind the Rover so that he was screen from the higher ground and called Jake Lester back at control.

'Jake, did you get all that?'

'Affirmative Sandy and we have two Reaction groups closing in on the area already'.

'Good; be advised that there is some high ground about 200 metres to the north of my present location which I think Darcy and his mate have been observing me. I suspect that Darcy's mate will stay on the high ground and keep us covered. As its already getting dark I suspect that they must have some form of night vision aid'.

'Roger that Sandy - Rusty, Tony and Theo have been following you on scramble bikes. I'll direct them to the high ground as soon as Darcy shows up at your location'.

'Thanks – out'.

Niles switched the mobile off and noted that clouds were beginning to roll in and the ambient light was already getting poor. Niles considered his options. It was going be almost dark when Darcy arrived and he was not likely to advertise his approach so, Niles was going to have to react quickly. He had a sudden thought; He pretended to be looking at the front right hand wheel of the Rover and then sat in the Rover, started the engine and re- positioned the vehicle so that it faced the high ground to the north.

He climbed out the Rover puts both hands in his trouser pockets slips the safety catch OFF on the Berretta and leans casually against the vehicle to await for Darcy's arrival

Darcy suddenly appeared out of the gloom with a nine millimetre automatic in his hand.

'Right! Get yourself spread against that Range Rover whilst I frisk you', growled Darcy.

Niles decided that he was going to have to continue where he'd left off with Darcy by pretending not to put up with any nonsense.

'Bugger off Darcy! Let's stop playing bloody soldiers and get down to the business in hand. You want to know where you can get to the Defence Secretary isolated from his guards and I can give you the time and location with about an hour's notice. Now! We either get down to discussing the details or you can search me and then I'm going to fuck off – make your mind up!'

'Why do you object to being searched if you've nothing

to hide? - you could be carrying a gun for all I know.'

'Of course I'm carrying a gun, its part of our uniform for all chauffeurs driving Political figures around. I tell you what - if you put your gun to one side I'll do the same with mine'. Niles opened his jacket and gentle laid his Browning 9mm automatic on the bonnet of the Rover as a good will gesture.

Darcy nodded and followed suit. 'Okay what have you got for me'? He asked.

Before Niles could answer a helicopter flew across the clearing which spooked Darcy. Quick as a flash he whipped a second gun out from trouser waist band and rammed it into Niles stomached and said.

'I don't trust you, that's the second chopper we have seen this evening now what the fuck's going on'?

Niles shrugged his shoulders, 'What in gods name are you talking about. Washington International Airport is only about four miles across the river. There are dozens of choppers flying in and out of the Airport every day'.

But Darcy hadn't lived for this long without being extremely careful.' Get turned round against the vehicle'.

Niles had no option but to comply. Darcy's search was quick and thorough and he quickly discovered Nile's Berretta that was strapped to his thigh.

'Ah', he exclaimed. 'A very clever ploy cutting your right hand pocket out to facilitate getting to your gun. I think it's an idea I might well copy'.

As Darcy was lifting the Berretta out another chopper clattered overhead and Darcy looked up. Niles whirled to his left. Grabbed Darcy's gun hand (his right) with his left and rammed his right knee up into Darcy's groin. Although Nile's knee did not catch Darcy exactly in the groin it caused him sufficient pain to double up. Niles held onto Darcy's gun hand and smashed it against the Rover causing him to drop it. Both hand guns were now in the grass plus the two that had originally been placed on the bonnet. As Niles looked down trying desperately to locate one of the guns in the dark Darcy butted Niles in the face and he staggered back temporally stunned. This enabled Darcy to break free and he whipped out an evil looking stiletto that had been strapped to his left wrist.

Christ!, thought Niles, the man was a fucking walking arsenal.

Darcy brandished the knife backwards and forwards.

'I don't know who or what you are but your time on this earth is just about to end'.

Niles back-pedalled to keep space between himself and Darcy at the same time he slid his jacket off and then held it in front of him as though it was a bull fighter's cape. This was a trick he had used during his hectic days in Caracas, Venezuela.

Darcy had obviously never come up against this kind of knife defence before. Every time he lunged at Niles he found his jacket between them. He tried to slash the jacket and although he had managed to cut it twice his knife had almost become tangled up in the jacket and he had nearly lost it. Darcy was beginning to appreciate why Niles was using his jacket as a defence.

As they were manoeuvring around each other Niles almost slipped on a pile of loose dirt that some burrowing animal had thrown up. Quick as a flash Darcy feinted with a slash to Niles midriff changed direction and cut into Niles scalp. Although the wound was not deep or serious he was starting to lose blood and unless he quickly got the upper hand he was going to weaken if the struggle was prolonged. Niles sidled round to where he had slipped on the mound of earth. As soon as he felt it he dug the toe of his right shoe into it and pretended to stumble. Darcy sensed his chance and lunged with the stiletto. Niles flicked the loose earth of the mound with his right toe up into the eyes of Darcy temporally blinding him. Darcy slashed at Niles who parried his thrust by throwing his jacket over the knife. Niles then let go of the jacket and grabbed Darcy's knife wrist with both of his hands and clamped hard. He then twisted hard and stepped in between Darcy's body and his knife arm which forced Darcy to double over towards his knees to prevent his arm from being broken. Then Niles delivered a tremendous kick to Darcy's solar plexus. The blow was so powerful that it caused Darcy's heart to arrest momentarily and he sagged to his knees. He then followed up with a vicious chop to the back of Darcy's unprotected neck. His blow was so powerful that it crushed Darcy's neck vertebrae killing him instantly. The follow through from the blow was so violent it caused him to fall over Darcy's body onto the ground. This saved his life.

A high velocity shot screamed over where Niles had been standing and tore a huge hole in the body work of the Range Rover. He looked at the size of the hole in disbelief. The round had passed straight through the vehicle and ended up some where in the woods to the south. What in Gods name were they shooting at him with? It must be something like a Barrett Light fifty to make a hole that size!

He grabbed hold of Darcy's body hoping to use it as a shield and shuffled round to the back of the Range Rover. He realised that the muzzle velocity of the weapon being used was so high that the bullet would probably pass straight through Darcy's body and his own body armour and still kill him with no problem. But at the moment the shooter may not have realised that Darcy was dead so he might hesitate before shooting through his boss's body.

He was stumped on what to do next. The sniper was obviously using a night scope so he could certainly see what Niles was up to. If he tried to run across the clearing to the stone building to west of his location the sniper might get him before he got to cover. And even if he did make it, he was not sure that the walls would be thick enough to offer him any protection. The woods and the two large oak trees were too far away, so they were out of the question. He also had the added problem that he was still bleeding. If he didn't get medical assistance soon there was a danger of him passing out.

Niles suddenly remembered why he had faced the Range Rover towards the high ground where the shot came from. He gently opened the back door of the Rover and folding the seats down as he crawled forward until he could reach the ignition switch. He turned the engine on and then switched the headlights onto main beam.

He then jumped out the Rover and high tailed as fast as he could to the derelict stone, "out house" to the west of the clearing.

Pierre Clermont crouched behind the STEYR 15.2mm IWS 2000 Rifle. This enormous beast weighed all of forty lbs and without some means of transport it was a real bastard to carry. The barrel was supported in a ring cradle which incorporated a hydro-pneumatic recoil system which in conjunction with its highly efficient muzzle brake reduced the recoil loads to that of a heavy sporting rifle. It had a smoothbore barrel and fired an Armoured Piercing Fin Stabilised Discarding Sabot (APFSDS) tungsten steel dart at 4757ft/sec. The round weighing 308grains was capable of piercing 40mm of steel at 1000mtrs. Its muzzle velocity was so high that to all intents and purposes there was no gravity drop. It basically had a flat trajectory. The gun was normally fitted with a 10 x telescopic sight but this evening it was fitted with one of the latest Starlight scopes for night vision.

Pierre had seen the fight between his boss and Niles but during the tussle had been unable to get a clear shot without fear of hitting his boss. Not that he was too worried about killing Darcy but he was the conduit through which their money was being paid. He'd seen Niles deliver the fateful chop but at this range could not be sure if the blow had been fatal or not. He'd fired as soon as he saw the blow delivered and if Niles had not tripped over the shot would have blown him apart.

As Niles dragged the body of Darcy round the back of the Rover Pierre was still not sure whether to shoot or not. He knew that Darcy's body would not stop the round from killing his assailant but at this stage was not sure if his boss was dead or not. As the gun was semi automatic and its magazine held five rounds he could quite easily have shot Niles before he got to cover behind the Range Rover. Even now, behind the Rover, he was convinced that the rifle had the power to penetrate the Rover and still kill anyone behind it.

Pierre was just about to take another shot at the Rover when the Starlight Scope became absolutely saturated with white light. The sensitive optics of the scope was flooded when Niles turned the head lights of the vehicle on. This rendered the scope completely useless for night vision.

Pierre took a couple of seconds to work out why the sight had been saturated with light and a further three to get the Starlight Scope off. He then used the blade sights of the gun for aiming to put two thunderous rounds into the Range Rover between the headlights. The force of the rounds slamming into the engine casing caused it to blow up and the Rover lights were reduced to side lights only. Even this illumination was too much for the night sight so Pierre took the side lights out with some very fancy shooting.

By the time Pierre had got the night sight back on the gun and functioning Niles was hiding behind the stone wall of the small building. He was however not very happy. The front wall facing the snipers location was completely broken down which left him hiding behind the back wall that was only eight inches thick. And he was not sure that even this would prevent one of the high velocity tungsten darts from penetrating it. Further more, he was still bleeding like a stuck pig.

As he scanned round the Range Rover Pierre could only make out the one body motionless on the ground behind it. The only other cover available in the clearing was the little stone house and two trees. The woods and two trees to the south and east were possibly too far for the assailant to have got to while his night sight was out of commission.

'Well cover from view is not necessarily cover from fire', murmured Pierre to himself so he put two speculative rounds through the wall of the stone building.

Niles assumption had been right! The walls of the building were not thick enough to stop the tungsten Bullets/Darts. Two rounds had passed through the wall, one about a foot to his left and the other three feet to his right. They had both left holes almost big enough to fit your head in. Niles realised that a dozen rounds could just about reduce this wall to rubble. He realised he was now in serious trouble. He quickly dialled up Jake Lester.

'Jake for Christ sake get some one up to that fucking Knoll. There's a bastard up there with something like a cannon and he has me pinned down. He is actually shooting the bloody wall I'm hiding behind to pieces. Be advised I've also got a knife wound in my scalp – it's not serious but I'm loosing blood and it needs attention'.

'Roger that Sandy help is already on the way. They should be there in thirty seconds'.

Meanwhile Niles was left in the unenviable position of trying to out guess the gunman as to where the next rounds were going to strike. He decided to put himself in the enemy's shoes and surmised that the guy hiding behind the wall would lie down to offer the most difficult target. Niles then shoved his foot through the hole created by the first shot. He then levered his torso up so that it was lying parallel just beneath the top of the wall. He'd guessed correctly. Three shots thundered out in quick succession striking the wall at three foot intervals about six inches above its base. Any one lying on the ground behind the wall would now be dead or suffering seriously hideous wounds. However, Niles was losing blood and knew he could not hold his position for much longer. Finally Niles could hold out no longer, he let go and crashed to the ground, as he did so another two rounds crashed through the wall exactly where he had been clinging. The bastard was beginning to out guess him.

Theo, Rusty and Tony were all together and had the grid reference of Niles location and were trying to find the Knoll when their attention was drawn to sound of the STEYR's firing. They couldn't find the road up there but lost no time in making their way up behind the knoll with their scramble bikes. Rusty reckoned that the firer must be wearing some form of earmuffs to deaden the sound of the shooting. However they ditch their bikes and ran the last hundred yards just in time to catch Pierre loading another magazine of five rounds. He was so engrossed in what he was doing that he never saw or heard the butt of Rusty's Berretta until it crashed into his scull rendering him unconscious. A few seconds' later two quick reaction choppers landed at Niles location to render first aid to his cut scalp. Theo then phoned Niles on his Mobile and told him that it was all over. They had secured Darcy's accomplice.

It was decided to hold a, "wash-up", in George Fields study three days after the shooting incident so that the Defence Secretary could attend. Those present included George Fields, Jake Lester the FBI chief in charge of the operations, Theo, Rusty, Tony and Niles (with his forehead swathed in bandages). The local chief of the police was also present for the first five minutes but thereafter the FBI took control of the proceedings and insisted that the numbers present be reduced to the absolute minimum. This was in essence to keep secret what had happened to Francesco Domingo.

The only new information to come out of the wash-up as far as Niles and his team were concerned was how John Jack Darcy and Pierre Clermont had got their hands on such a potent weapon as the STEYR 15.02mm IWS 2000. It appeared that the FBI was able to trace the purchase through the Austrian Authorities to a known illegal Arms Dealer - one Mr Chase. Apparently, the FBI was now able to tie Mr Chase into the supply of the weapon to Darcy and his accomplish and he would be charged accordingly. The three telephone numbers of the three American Senators was going to be investigated at a later date but the FBI were already gathering evidence. The future did not look good for them.

Pierre Clermont was also offering to cooperate with a view to getting a reduced prison sentence and confirmed that the weapon was provided by Chase. Apparently Darcy and Clermont had decided that their only chance of killing Jackie Fields would be from an extreme range, possible at a mile or so. Hence the purchase of such a large weapon, even at a range of 1000mtrs the tungsten dart was still capable of piercing armoured plate Chase was also being investigated into allegations that he had illegally supplied weapons to FARC rebels and the Drug Cartels in Colombia.

All present at the meeting were sworn to keep the secret of Domingo's disappearance. It was agreed that this was the only way to prevent a potential vendetta being created against the Defence Secretary in the future. In the mean time, money was going to be siphoned off Domingo's Off Shore and Swiss accounts at various intervals to foster the illusion that he was still alive somewhere.

The good news was that the Fields would be entertaining all people involved and the immediate family.

As the meeting was breaking up George turned to Niles and his team and said.

'I can't thank you enough for what you have done for my family and me. Although you guys have played down the danger aspect of the adventure we all know that your lives were at risk on many occasions during the past two weeks. Make no mistake about it gentlemen I will be making many calls on your Security Company when it is up and running – by the way, have thought of what you are going to call it?'

The three of them stood there looking bemused at one another. Suddenly Niles said, how about 'Bryons', a combination of Tony's name and Rusty's? It's an easy name to remember and it rolls off the tongue nice and smoothly'.

'What about your name Sandy? I thought you were coming in with us?' Queried Tony.

'Sure thing Tony and as an equal partner but to try include part of my name will make the title too cumbersome'.

'Right' laughed George Fields.' Bryons it is and I'll see you all tonight. Don't be late Sandy - Karen's anxious to see you plus another young lady'.

The party was small and intimate. They were also informed that Edward Lance and Maria would be arriving from the UK in the next week.

Alfred and Helen Mendoza accompanied by Jenny Valdez were also present. Jenny looked absolutely radiant. Pregnancy although not physically visible at this stage had made her positively bloom. She quickly settled onto Niles arm and at the first possible moment she shepherded him into a small room where they could be alone.

She looked absolutely gorgeous and she knew it. Gave him the eyebrow treatment and with surprising frankness said.

'You have heard the news about my condition Sandy?'

Niles cleared his throat, 'er..... Yes - Chris Booker informed me of your conditions and offered me his congratulations. Although we knew this is what you wanted I'm still trying to get used to the idea'.

'Sandy – I've told you how I feel about you and the fact that initially I'd no plans to inveigle you into marriage and I'll understand if you don't wish to make any commitment. If you don't I would still like to think of you as a friend'.

Sandy Niles realised that this woman was reading him like a book.

'You daft bitch. You know I'm crazy about you. My only reservation is that I was married once before and it didn't work and that was mainly my fault. I'm frightened of making the same mistakes'.

'I know you are a very committed man to any task you do which means that there'll be times when you are away. Particularly as you, Rusty and Tony are starting out on a new venture but I'm willing to take the risk that the separations won't destroy our marriage – how about you?'

He pretended to stand there and think about it but the charade was quickly terminated when Jenny gave him a swift kick in the shins. 'Its make up your mind time arsehole'. And she shrieked with laughter.

'What can a man do?'

Printed in the United Kingdom
by Lightning Source UK Ltd.
126154UK00001B/31-36/A

CN00862808

LAVENGRO AND THE ROMANY RYE

By GEORGE BORROW

DESIGNED TO BE READ AS A MODERN NOVEL

E. M. HALE AND COMPANY

Eau Claire, Wisconsin

PRINTED IN THE UNITED STATES OF AMERICA
AMERICAN BOOK–STRATFORD PRESS, INC., NEW YORK

CHAPTER I

I HAVE been a wanderer the greater part of my life; indeed I remember only two periods, and these by no means lengthy, when I was, strictly speaking, stationary. I was a soldier's son, and as the means of my father were by no means sufficient to support two establishments, his family invariably attended him wherever he went, so that from my infancy I was accustomed to travelling and wandering, and looked upon a monthly change of scene and residence as a matter of course. Sometimes we lived in barracks, sometimes in lodgings, but generally in the former, always eschewing the latter from motives of economy, save when the barracks were inconvenient and uncomfortable; and they must have been highly so indeed to have discouraged us from entering them; for though we were gentry (pray bear that in mind, gentle reader), gentry by birth, and incontestably so by my father's bearing the commission of good old George the Third, we were not *fine gentry*, but people who could put up with as much as any genteel Scotch family who find it convenient to live on a third floor in London, or on a sixth at Edinburgh or Glasgow. It was not a little that could discourage us. We once lived within the canvas walls of a camp, at a place called Pett, in Sussex; and I believe it was at this place that occurred the first circumstance, or adventure, call it which you will, that I can remember in connection with myself: it was a strange one, and I will relate it.

It happened that my brother and myself were playing one evening in a sandy lane, in the neighbourhood of this Pett camp; our mother was at a slight distance. All of a sudden, a bright yellow, and, to my infantine eye, beautiful and glorious object made its appearance at the top of the bank from between the thick quickset, and, gliding down, began to move across the lane to the other side, like a line of golden light. Uttering a cry of pleasure, I sprang forward, and seized it nearly by the middle. A strange sensation of numbing coldness seemed to pervade my whole arm, which surprised me the more as the object to the eye appeared so warm and sunlike. I did not drop it, however, but, holding it up, looked at it intently, as its head dangled about a foot from my hand. It made no resistance; I felt not even the slightest struggle; but now my brother began to scream and shriek like one possessed. "O mother, mother!" said he, "the viper! my brother has a viper in his hand!" He then, like one frantic, made an effort to snatch the creature away from me. The viper now hissed amain, and raised its head, in which were eyes like hot coals, menacing, not myself, but my brother. I dropped my captive, for I saw my mother running towards me; and the reptile, after standing for a moment nearly erect, and still hissing furiously, made off, and disappeared. The whole scene is now before me, as vividly as if it occurred yesterday—the gorgeous viper, my poor dear frantic brother, my agitated parent, and a frightened hen clucking under the bushes—and yet I was not three years old.

It is my firm belief that certain individuals possess an inherent power, or fascination, over certain creatures, otherwise I should be unable to account for many feats which I have witnessed, and, indeed, borne a share in, connected with the taming of brutes and reptiles. I have known a savage and vicious mare, whose stall it was dangerous to approach, even when bearing provender, welcome, nevertheless, with every appearance of pleasure, an uncouth, wiry-headed man, with a frightfully seamed face, and an iron hook supplying the place of his right hand, one whom the animal had never seen before, playfully bite his hair and cover his face with gentle and endearing kisses; and I have already stated how a viper would permit, without resentment, one child to take it up in his hand, whilst it showed its dislike to the approach of another by the fiercest hissings. Philosophy can explain many strange things, but there are some which are a far pitch above her, and this is one.

Another circumstance connected with my infancy, and I have done. I need offer no apology for relating it, as it subsequently exercised considerable influence over my pursuits. We were, if I remember right, in the vicinity of a place called Hythe, in Kent. One sweet evening, in the latter part of summer, our mother took her two little boys by the hand, for a wander about the fields. In the course of our stroll we came to the village church; an old grey-headed sexton stood in the porch, who, perceiving that we were strangers, invited us to enter. We were presently in the interior, wandering about the aisles, looking on the walls, and inspecting the monuments of the notable dead. I can scarcely state what we saw; how should I? I was a child not yet four years old, and yet I think I remember the evening sun streaming in through a stained window upon the dingy mahogany pulpit, and flinging a rich lustre upon the faded tints of an ancient banner. And now once more we were outside the building, where, against the wall, stood a low-eaved pent-house, into which we looked. It was half-filled with substances of some kind, which at first looked like large grey stones. The greater part were lying in layers; some, however, were seen in confused and mouldering heaps, and two or three, which had perhaps rolled down from the rest, lay separately on the floor. "Skulls, madam," said the sexton; "skulls of the old Danes! Long ago they came pirating into these parts; and then there chanced a mighty shipwreck, for God was angry with them, and He sunk them; and their skulls, as they came ashore, were placed here as a memorial. There were many more when I was young, but now they are fast disappearing.

Some of them must have belonged to strange fellows, madam. Only see that one; why, the two young gentry can scarcely lift it!" And, indeed, my brother and myself had entered the Golgotha, and commenced handling these grim relics of mortality. One enormous skull, lying in a corner, had fixed our attention, and we had drawn it forth. Spirit of eld, what a skull was yon!

I still seem to see it, the huge grim thing; many of the others were large, strikingly so, and appeared fully to justify the old man's conclusion that their owners must have been strange fellows; but, compared with this mighty mass of bone, they looked small and diminutive, like those of pigmies; it must have belonged to a giant, one of those red-haired warriors of whose strength and stature such wondrous tales are told in the ancient chronicles of the north, and whose grave-hills. when ransacked, occasionally reveal secrets which fill the minds of puny moderns with astonishment and awe. Reader, have you ever pored days and nights over the pages of Snorro? probably not, for he wrote in a language which few of the present day understand, and few would be tempted to read him tamed down by Latin dragomans. A brave old book is that of Snorro, containing the histories and adventures of old northern kings and champions, who seemed to have been quite different men, if we may judge from the feats which they performed, from those of these days. One of the best of his histories is that which describes the life of Harald Haardraade, who, after manifold adventures by land and sea, now a pirate, now a mercenary of the Greek emperor, became King of Norway, and eventually perished at the battle of Stanford Bridge, whilst engaged in a gallant onslaught upon England. Now, I have often thought that the old Kemp, whose mouldering skull in the golgotha of Hythe my brother and myself could scarcely lift. must have resembled in one respect at least this Harald, whom Snorro describes as a great and wise ruler and a determined leader, dangerous in battle, of fair presence, and measuring in height just *five ells*,[1] neither more nor less.

I never forgot the Daneman's skull; like the apparition of the viper in the sandy lane, it dwelt in the mind of the boy, affording copious food for the exercise of imagination. From that moment with the name of Dane were associated strange ideas of strength, daring, and superhuman stature; and an undefinable curiosity for all that is connected with the Danish race began to pervade me; and if, long after, when I became a student, I devoted myself with peculiar zest to Danish lore and the acquirement of the old Norse tongue and its dialects, I can only explain the matter by the early impression received at Hythe from the tale of the old sexton, beneath the pent-house, and the sight of the Danish skull.

And thus we went on straying from place to place, at Hythe to-day, and perhaps within a week looking out from our hostel-window upon the streets of old Winchester, our motions ever in accordance with the "route" of the

[1]Norwegian ells—about eight feet.

regiment, so habituated to change of scene that it had become almost necessary to our existence. Pleasant were those days of my early boyhood; and a melancholy pleasure steals over me as I recall them. Those were stirring times of which I am speaking, and there was much passing around me calculated to captivate the imagination. The dreadful struggle which so long convulsed Europe, and in which England bore so prominent a part, was then at its hottest; we were at war, and determination and enthusiasm shone in every face; man, woman and child were eager to fight the Frank, the hereditary, but, thank God, never dreaded enemy of the Anglo-Saxon race. "Love your country and beat the French, and then never mind what happens," was the cry of entire England.

But to return to my own history. I had now attained the age of six. Shall I state what intellectual progress I had been making up to this period? Alas! upon this point I have little to say calculated to afford either pleasure or edification. I had increased rapidly in size and in strength; the growth of the mind, however, had by no means corresponded with that of the body. It is true, I had acquired my letters, and was by this time able to read imperfectly, but this was all; and even this poor triumph over absolute ignorance would never have been effected but for the unremitting attention of my parents, who, sometimes by threats, sometimes by entreaties, endeavoured to rouse the dormant energies of my nature, and to bend my wishes to the acquisition of the rudiments of knowledge; but in influencing the wish lay the difficulty. Let but the will of a human being be turned to any particular object, and it is ten to one that sooner or later he achieves it. At this time I may safely say that I harboured neither wishes nor hopes; I had as yet seen no object calculated to call them forth, and yet I took pleasure in many things which perhaps unfortunately were all within my sphere of enjoyment. I loved to look upon the heavens, and to bask in the rays of the sun, or to sit beneath hedgerows and listen to the chirping of the birds, indulging the while in musing and meditation as far as my very limited circle of ideas would permit; but, unlike my brother, who was at this time at school, and whose rapid progress in every branch of instruction astonished and delighted his preceptors, I took no pleasure in books, whose use, indeed, I could scarcely comprehend, and bade fair to be as arrant a dunce as ever brought the blush of shame into the cheeks of anxious and affectionate parents.

But the time was now at hand when the ice which had hitherto bound the mind of the child with its benumbing power was to be thawed, and a world of sensations and ideas awakened to which it had hitherto been an entire stranger. One day a young lady, an intimate acquaintance of our family, and godmother to my brother, drove up to the house in which we dwelt; she staid some time conversing with my mother, and on rising to depart she put down on the table a small packet, exclaiming: "I have brought a little present for each of the boys: the one is a History of England, which I intend for my godson when he returns from school, the other is—" and here she said something which escaped my ear, as I sat at some distance, moping in a corner: "I intend it for the youngster yonder," pointing to myself; she then departed, and, my mother going out shortly after, I was left alone.

I remember for some time sitting motionless in my corner, with my eyes bent upon the ground; at last I lifted my head and looked upon the packet as it lay on the table. All at once a strange sensation came over me, such as I had never experienced before—a singular blending of curiosity, awe and pleasure, the remembrance of which, even at this distance of time, produces a remarkable effect upon my nervous system. What strange things are the nerves—I mean those more secret and mysterious ones in which I have some notion that the mind or soul, call it which you will, has its habitation; how they occasionally tingle and vibrate before any coming event closely connected with the future weal or woe of the human being. Such a feeling was now within me, certainly independent of what the eye had seen or the ear had heard. A book of some description had been brought for me, a present by no means calculated to interest me; what cared I for books? I had already many into which I never looked but from compulsion; friends, moreover, had presented me with similar things before, which I had entirely disregarded, and what was there in this particular book, whose very title I did not know, calculated to attract me more than the rest? yet something within told me that my fate was connected with the book which had been last brought; so, after looking on the packet from my corner for a considerable time, I got up and went to the table.

The packet was lying where it had been left—I took it up; had the envelope, which consisted of whitish brown paper, been secured by a string or a seal, I should not have opened it, as I should have considered such an act almost in the light of a crime; the books, however, had been merely folded up, and I therefore considered that there could be no possible harm in inspecting them, more especially as I had received no injunction to the contrary. Perhaps there was something unsound in this reasoning, something sophistical; but a child is sometimes as ready as a grown-up person in finding excuses for doing that which he is inclined to. But whether the action was right or wrong, and I am afraid it was not altogether right, I undid the packet. It contained three books, two from their similarity seemed to be separate parts of one and the same work; they were handsomely bound, and to them I first turned my attention. I opened them successively and endeavoured to make out their meaning; their contents, however, as far as I was able to understand them, were by no means interesting: whoever pleases may read these books for me, and keep them too, into the bargain, said I to myself.

I now took up the third book. It did not resemble the others, being longer and considerably thicker; the binding was of dingy calf-skin. I opened it, and as I did so another strange thrill of pleasure shot through my frame. The first object on which my eyes rested was a picture; it was exceedingly well executed, at least the scene which it represented made a vivid impression upon me, which would hardly have been the case had the artist not been faithful to nature. A wild scene it was—a heavy sea and rocky shore, with mountains in the background, above which the moon was peering. Not far from the shore, upon the water, was a boat with two figures in it, one of which stood at the bow, pointing with what I knew to be a gun at a dreadful shape in the water; fire was flashing from the muzzle of the gun, and the monster appeared to be transfixed. I almost thought I heard its cry. I remained motionless, gazing upon the picture, scarcely daring to draw my breath, lest the new and wondrous world should vanish of which I had now obtained a glimpse. "Who are those people, and what could have brought them into that strange situation?" I asked of myself; and now the seed of curiosity, which had so long lain dormant, began to expand, and I vowed to myself to become speedily acquainted with the whole history of the people in the boat. After looking on the picture till every mark and line in it were familiar to me, I turned over various leaves till I came to another engraving; a new source of wonder—a low sandy beach on which the furious sea was breaking in mountain-like billows; cloud and rack deformed the firmament, which wore a dull and leaden-like hue; gulls and other aquatic fowls were toppling upon the blast, or skimming over the tops of the maddening waves —"Mercy upon him! he must be drowned!" I exclaimed, as my eyes fell upon a poor wretch who appeared to be striving to reach the shore; he was upon his legs but was evidently half-smothered with the brine; high above his head curled a horrible billow, as if to engulf him for ever. "He must be drowned! he must be drowned!" I almost shrieked, and dropped the book. I soon snatched it up again, and now my eye lighted on a third picture: again a shore, but what a sweet and lovely one, and how I wished to be treading it; there were beautiful shells lying on the smooth white sand, some were empty like those I had occasionally seen on marble mantelpieces, but out of others peered the heads and bodies of wondrous crayfish; a wood of thick green trees skirted the beach and partly shaded it from the rays of the sun, which shone hot above, while blue waves slightly crested with foam were gently curling against it; there was a human figure upon the beach, wild and uncouth, clad in the skins of animals, with a huge cap on his head, a hatchet at his girdle, and in his hand a gun; his feet and legs were bare; he stood in an attitude of horror and surprise; his body was bent far back, and his eyes, which seemed starting out of his head, were fixed upon a mark on the sand—a large distinct mark—a human footprint!

Reader, is it necessary to name the book which now stood open in my hand, and whose very prints, feeble expounders of its wondrous lines, had produced within me emotions strange and novel? Scarcely, for it was a book which has exerted over the minds of Englishmen an influence certainly greater than any other of modern times, which has been in most people's hands, and with the contents of which even those who cannot read are to a certain extent acquainted; a book from which the most luxuriant and fertile of our modern prose writers have drunk inspiration; a book, moreover, to which, from the hardy deeds which it narrates, and the spirit of strange and romantic enterprise which it tends to awaken, England owes many of her astonishing discoveries both by sea and land, and no inconsiderable part of her naval glory.

Hail to thee, spirit of De Foe! What does not my own poor self owe to thee? England has better bards than either Greece or Rome, yet I could spare them easier far than De Foe, "unabashed De Foe," as the hunchbacked rhymer styled him.

The true chord had now been touched; a raging curiosity with respect to the contents of the volume, whose engravings had fascinated my eye, burned within me, and I never rested until I had fully satisfied it; weeks succeeded weeks, months followed months, and the wondrous volume was my only study and principal source of amusement. For hours together I would sit poring over a page till I had become acquainted with the import of every line. My progress, slow enough at first, became by degrees more rapid, till at last, under "a shoulder of mutton sail," I found myself cantering before a steady breeze over an ocean of enchantment, so well pleased with my voyage that I cared not how long it might be ere it reached its termination.

And it was in this manner that I first took to the paths of knowledge.

CHAPTER II

At length my father was recalled to his regiment, which at that time was stationed at a place called Norman Cross, in Lincolnshire, or rather Huntingdonshire, at some distance from the old town of Peterborough.

And a strange place it was, this Norman Cross, and, at the time of which I am speaking, a sad cross to many a Norman, being what was then styled a French prison, that is, a receptacle for captives made in the French war.

Much had the poor inmates to endure, and much to complain of, to the disgrace of England be it said—of England, in general so kind and bountiful. Rations of carrion meat, and bread from which I have seen the very hounds occasionally turn away, were unworthy entertainment even for the most ruffian enemy, when helpless and a captive. And then, those visits, or rather ruthless inroads, called in the slang of the place "straw-plait hunts," when, in pursuit of a contraband article, which the prisoners, in order to procure themselves a few of the necessaries and comforts of existence, were in the habit of making, red-coated battalions were marched into the prisons, who, with the bayonet's point, carried havoc and ruin into every poor convenience which ingenious wretchedness had been endeavouring to raise around it; and then the triumphant exit with the miserable booty; and, worst of all, the accursed bonfire, on the barrack parade, of the plait contraband, beneath the view of the glaring eyeballs from those lofty roofs, amidst the hurrahs of the troops, frequently drowned in the curses poured down from above like a tempest-shower, or in the terrific war-whoop of "*Vive l'Empereur!*"

It was midsummer when we arrived at this place, and the weather, which had for a long time been wet and gloomy, now became bright and glorious. I was subjected to but little control, and passed my time pleasantly enough, principally in wandering about the neighbouring country. It was flat and somewhat fenny, a district more of pasture than agriculture, and not very thickly inhabited. I soon became well acquainted with it. At the distance of two miles from the station was a large lake, styled in the dialect of the country a "mere," about whose borders tall reeds were growing in abundance. This was a frequent haunt of mine; but my favourite place of resort was a wild sequestered spot at a somewhat greater distance. Here, surrounded with woods, and thick groves, was the seat of some ancient family, deserted by the proprietor, and only inhabited by a rustic servant or two. A place more solitary and wild could scarcely be imagined; the garden and walks were overgrown with weeds and briars, and the unpruned woods were so tangled as to be almost impervious. About this domain I would wander till overtaken by fatigue, and then I would sit down with my back against some beech, elm or stately alder tree, and, taking out my book, would pass hours in a state of unmixed enjoyment, my eyes now fixed on the wondrous pages, now glancing at the sylvan scene around; and sometimes I would drop the book and listen to the voice of the rooks and wild pigeons, and not unfrequently to the croaking of multitudes of frogs from the neighbouring swamps and fens.

In going to and from this place I frequently passed a tall, elderly individual, dressed in rather a quaint fashion, with a skin cap on his head and stout gaiters on his legs; on his shoulders hung a moderate sized leathern sack; he seemed fond of loitering near sunny banks, and of groping amidst furze and low scrubby bramble bushes, of which there were plenty in the neighbourhood of Norman Cross. Once I saw him standing in the middle of a dusty road, looking intently at a large mark which seemed to have been drawn across it, as if by a walking-stick. "He must have been a large one," the old man muttered half to himself, "or he would not have left such a trail, I wonder if he is near; he seems to have moved this way." He then went behind some bushes which grew on the right side of the road, and appeared to be in quest of something, moving behind the bushes with his head downwards, and occasionally striking their roots with his foot. At length he exclaimed, "Here he is!" and forthwith I saw him dart amongst the bushes. There was a kind of scuffling noise, the rustling of branches, and the crackling of dry sticks. "I have him!" said the man at last; "I have got him!" and presently he made his appearance about twenty yards down the road, holding a large viper in his hand. "What do you think of that, my boy?" said he, as I went up to him; "what do you think of catching such a thing as that with the naked hand?" "What do I think?" said I. "Why, that I could do as much myself." "You do," said the man, "do you? Lord! how the young people in these days are given to conceit; it did not use to be so in my time; when I was a child, childer knew how to behave themselves; but the childer of these days are full of conceit, full of froth, like the mouth of this viper"; and with his forefinger and thumb he squeezed a considerable quantity of foam from the jaws of the viper down upon the road. "The childer of these days are a generation of—God forgive me, what was I about to say!" said the old man; and opening his bag he thrust the reptile into it, which appeared far from empty. I passed on. As I was returning, towards the evening, I overtook the old man, who was wending in the same direction. "Good-evening to you, sir," said I, taking off a cap which I wore on my head. "Good-evening," said the old man; and then, looking at me, "How's this?" said he, "you ar'n't, sure, the child I met in the morning?" "Yes," said I, "I am; what makes you doubt it?" "Why, you were then all froth and conceit," said the old man, "and now you take off your cap to me." "I beg your pardon," said I, "if I was frothy and conceited; it ill becomes a child like me to be so." "That's true, dear," said the old man; "well, as you have begged my pardon, I truly forgive you." "Thank you," said I; "have you caught any more of those things?" "Only four or five," said the old man; "they are getting scarce, though this used to be a great neighbourhood for them." "And what do you do with them?" said I; "do you carry them home and play with them!" "I sometimes play with one or two that I tame," said the old man; "but I hunt them mostly for the fat which they contain, out of which I make unguents which are good for various sore troubles, especially for the rheumatism." "And do you get your living by hunting these creatures?" I demanded. "Not altogether," said the old man; "besides being a viper-hunter, I am what they call a herbalist, one who knows the virtue of particular herbs; I gather them at the proper season, to make medicines with for the sick." "And do you live in the neighbourhood?" I demanded. "You seem very fond of asking questions, child. No, I do not live in this neighbourhood in particular, I travel about; I have not been in this neighbourhood till lately for some years."

From this time the old man and myself formed an acquaintance; I often accompanied him in his wanderings about the neighbourhood, and on two or three occasions assisted him in catching the reptiles which he hunted. He generally carried a viper with him which he had made quite tame, and from which he had extracted the poisonous fangs; it would dance and perform various kinds of tricks. He was fond of telling me anecdotes connected with his adventures with the reptile species. "But," said he one day, sighing, "I must shortly give up this business, I am no longer the man I was, I am become timid, and when a person is timid in viper-hunting he had better leave off, as it is quite clear his virtue is leaving him. I got a fright some years ago, which I am quite sure I shall never get the better of; my hand has been shaky more or less ever since." "What frightened you?" said I. "I had better not tell you," said the old man, "or you may be frightened too, lose your virtue, and be no longer good for the business." "I don't care," said I; "I don't intend to follow the business; I dare say I shall be an officer, like my father." "Well," said the old man, "I once saw the king of the vipers, and since then—" "The king of the vipers!" said I, interrupting him; "have the vipers a king?" "As sure as we have," said the old man, "as sure as we have King George to rule over us, have these reptiles a king to rule over them." "And where did you see him?" said I.

"I will tell you," said the old man, "though I don't like talking about the matter. It may be about seven years ago that I happened to be far down yonder to the west, on the other side of England, nearly two hundred miles from here. following my business. It was a very sultry day, I remember, and I had been out several hours catching creatures. It might be about three o'clock in the afternoon, when I found myself on some heathy land near the sea, on the ridge of a hill, the side of which, nearly as far down as the sea, was heath; but on the top there was arable ground, which had been planted, and from which the harvest had been gathered—oats or barley, I know not which—but I remember that the ground was covered with stubble. Well, about three o'clock, as I told you before, what with the heat of the day and from having walked about for hours in a lazy way, I felt very tired; so I determined to have a sleep, and I laid myself down, my head just on the ridge of the hill, towards the field, and my body over the side down amongst the heath; my bag, which was nearly filled with creatures, lay at a little distance from my face; the creatures were struggling in it, I remember, and I thought to myself, how much more comfortably off I was than they; I was taking my ease on the nice open hill, cooled with the breezes, whilst they were in the nasty close bag, coiling about one another, and breaking their very hearts, all to no purpose; and I felt quite comfortable and happy in the thought, and little by little closed my eyes, and fell into the sweetest snooze that ever I was in in all my life; and there I lay over the hill's side, with my head half in the field, I don't know how long, all dead asleep. At last it seemed to me that I heard a noise in my sleep, something like a thing moving, very faint, however, far away; then it died, and then it came again upon my ear as I slept, and now it appeared almost as if I heard crackle, crackle; then it died again, or I became yet more dead asleep than before, I know not which, but I certainly lay some time without hearing it.

"All of a sudden I became awake, and there was I, on the ridge of the hill, with my cheek on the ground towards the stubble, with a noise in my ear like that of something moving towards me, amongst the stubble of the field; well, I lay a moment or two listening to the noise, and then I became frightened, for I did not like the noise at all, it sounded so odd; so I rolled myself on my belly, and looked towards the stubble. Mercy upon us! there was a huge snake, or rather a dreadful viper, for it was all yellow and gold, moving towards me, bearing its head about a foot and a half above the ground, the dry stubble crackling beneath its outrageous belly. It might be about five yards off when I first saw it, making straight towards me, child, as if it would devour me. I lay quite still, for I was stupefied with horror, whilst the creature came still nearer; and now it was nearly upon me, when it suddenly drew back a little, and then—what do you think?—it lifted its head and chest high in the air, and high over my face as I looked up, flickering at me with its tongue as if it would fly at my face.

"Child, what I felt at that moment I can scarcely say, but it was a sufficient punishment for all the sins I ever committed; and there we two were, I looking up at the viper, and the viper looking down upon me, flickering at me with its tongue. It was only the kindness of God that saved me: all at once there was a loud noise, the report of a gun, for a fowler was shooting at a covey of birds, a little way off in the stubble. Whereupon the viper sunk its head, and immediately made off over the ridge of the hill, down in the direction of the sea. As it passed by me, however—and it passed close by me—it hesitated a moment, as if it was doubtful whether it should not seize me; it did not, however, but made off down the hill. It has often struck me that he was angry with me, and came upon me unawares for presuming to meddle with his people, as I have always been in the habit of doing."

"But," said I, "how do you know that it was the king of the vipers?"

"How do I know?" said the old man, "who else should it be? There was as much difference between it and other reptiles as between King George and other people."

"Is King George, then, different from other people?" I demanded.

"Of course," said the old man; "I have never seen him myself, but I have heard people say that he is a ten times greater man than other folks; indeed, it stands to reason that he must be different from the rest, else people would not be so eager to see him. Do you think, child, that people would be fools enough to run a matter of twenty or thirty miles to see the king, provided King George—"

"Haven't the French a king?" I demanded.

"Yes," said the old man, "or something much the same, and a queer one he is; not quite so big as King George, they say, but quite as terrible a fellow. What of him?"

"Suppose he should come to Norman Cross!"

"What should he do at Norman Cross, child?"

"Why, you were talking about the vipers in your bag breaking their hearts, and so on, and their king coming to help them. Now, suppose the French king should hear of his people being in trouble at Norman Cross, and—"

"He can't come, child," said the old man, rubbing his hands, "the water lies between. The French don't like the water; neither vipers nor Frenchmen take kindly to the water, child."

When the old man left the country, which he did a few days after the conversation which I have just related, he left me the reptile which he had tamed and rendered quite harmless by removing the fangs. I was in the habit of feeding it with milk, and frequently carried it abroad with me in my walks.

One day it happened that, being on my rambles, I entered a green lane which I had never seen before; at first it was rather narrow, but as I advanced it became considerably wider; in the middle was a drift-way with deep ruts, but right and left was a space carpeted with a sward of trefoil and clover; there was no lack of trees, chiefly ancient oaks, which, flinging out their arms from either side, nearly formed a canopy, and afforded a pleasing shelter from the rays of the sun, which was burning fiercely above. Suddenly a group of objects attracted my attention. Beneath one of the largest of the trees, upon the grass, was a kind of low tent or booth, from the top of which a thin smoke was curling; beside it stood a couple of light carts, whilst two or three lean horses or ponies were cropping the herbage which was growing nigh. Wondering to whom this odd tent could belong, I advanced till I was close before it, when I found that it consisted of two tilts, like those of waggons, placed upon the ground and fronting each other, connected behind by a sail or large piece of canvas, which was but partially drawn across the top; upon the ground, in the intervening space, was a fire, over which, supported by a kind of iron crowbar, hung a caldron. My advance had been so noiseless as not to alarm the inmates, who consisted of a man and woman, who sat apart, one on each side of the fire; they were both busily employed —the man was carding plaited straw, whilst the woman seemed to be rubbing something with a white powder, some of which lay on a plate beside her. Suddenly the man looked up, and, perceiving me, uttered a strange kind of cry, and the next moment both the woman and himself were on their feet and rushing upon me.

I retreated a few steps, yet without turning to flee. I was not, however, without apprehension, which, indeed, the appearance of these two people was well calculated to inspire. The woman was a stout figure, seemingly between thirty and forty; she wore no cap, and her long hair fell on either side of her head, like horse-tails, half-way down her waist; her skin was dark and swarthy, like that of a toad, and the expression of her countenance was particularly evil; her arms were bare, and her bosom was but half-concealed by a slight bodice, below which she wore a coarse petticoat, her only other article of dress. The man was somewhat younger, but of a figure equally wild; his frame was long and lathy, but his arms were remarkably short, his neck was rather bent, he squinted slightly, and his mouth was much awry; his complexion was dark, but, unlike that of the woman, was more ruddy than livid; there was a deep scar on his cheek, something like the impression of a halfpenny. The dress was quite in keeping with the figure: in his hat, which was slightly peaked, was stuck a peacock's feather; over a waistcoat of hide, untanned and with the hair upon it, he wore a rough jerkin of russet hue; smallclothes of leather, which had probably once belonged to a soldier, but with which pipeclay did not seem to have come in contact for many a year, protected his lower man as far as the knee; his legs were cased in long stockings of blue worsted, and on his shoes he wore immense old-fashioned buckles.

Such were the two beings who now came rushing upon me; the man was rather in advance, brandishing a ladle in his hand.

"So I have caught you at last," said he; "I'll teach ye, you young highwayman, to come skulking about my properties!"

Young as I was, I remarked that his manner of speaking was different from that of any people with whom I had been in the habit of associating. It was quite as strange as his appearance, and yet it nothing resembled the foreign English which I had been in the habit of hearing through the palisades of the prison; he could scarcely be a foreigner.

"Your properties!" said I; "I am in the King's Lane. Why did you put them there, if you did not wish them to be seen?"

"On the spy," said the woman, "hey? I'll drown him in the sludge in the toad-pond over the hedge."

"So we will," said the man, "drown him anon in the mud!"

"Drown me, will you?" said I; "I should like to see you! What's all this about? Was it because I saw you with your hands full of straw plait, and my mother there——"

"Yes," said the woman; "what was I about?"

Myself. How should I know? Making bad money, perhaps!

And it will be as well here to observe, that at this time there was much bad money in circulation in the neighbourhood, generally supposed to be fabricated by the prisoners, so that this false coin and straw plait formed the standard subjects of conversation at Norman Cross.

"I'll strangle thee," said the beldame, dashing at me. "Bad money, is it?"

"Leave him to me, wifelkin," said the man, interposing; "you shall now see how I'll baste him down the lane."

Myself. I tell you what, my chap, you had better put down that thing of yours; my father lies concealed within my tepid breast, and if to me you offer any harm or wrong, I'll call him forth to help me with his forked tongue.

Man. What do you mean, ye Bengui's bantling? I never heard such discourse in all my life; playman's speech or Frenchman's talk—which, I wonder? Your father! tell the mumping villain that if he comes near my fire I'll serve him out as I will you. Take that—Tiny Jesus! what have we got here? Oh, delicate Jesus! What is the matter with the child?

I had made a motion which the viper understood; and now, partly disengaging itself from my bosom, where it had lain perdu, it raised its head to a level with my face, and stared upon my enemy with its glittering eyes.

The man stood like one transfixed, and the ladle with which he had aimed a blow at me, now hung in the air like the hand which held it; his mouth was extended, and his cheeks became of a pale yellow, save alone that place which bore the mark which I have already described, and this shone now portentously, like fire. He stood in this manner for some time; at last the ladle fell from his hand, and its falling appeared to rouse him from his stupor.

"I say, wifelkin," said he in a faltering tone, "did you ever see the like of this here?"

But the woman had retreated to the tent, from the entrance of which her loathly face was now thrust, with an expression partly of terror and partly of curiosity. After gazing some time longer at the viper and myself, the man stooped down and took up the ladle; then, as if somewhat more assured, he moved to the tent, where he entered into conversation with the beldame in a low voice. Of their discourse, though I could hear the greater part of it, I understood not a single word; and I wondered what it could be, for I knew by the sound that it was not French. At last the man, in a somewhat louder tone, appeared to put a question to the woman, who nodded her head affirmatively, and in a moment or two produced a small stool, which she delivered to him. He placed it on the ground, close by the door of the tent, first rubbing it with his sleeve, as if for the purpose of polishing its surface.

Man. Now, my precious little gentleman, do sit down here by the poor people's tent; we wish to be civil in our slight way. Don't be angry, and say no; but look kindly upon us, and satisfied, my precious little God Almighty.

Woman. Yes, my gorgious angel, sit down by the poor bodies' fire, and eat a sweetmeat. We want to ask you a question or two; only first put that serpent away.

Myself. I can sit down, and bid the serpent go to sleep, that's easy enough; but as for eating a sweetmeat, how can I do that? I have not got one, and where am I to get it?

Woman. Never fear, my tiny tawny, we can give you one, such as you never ate, I dare say, however far you may have come from.

The serpent sunk into its usual resting-place, and I sat down on the stool. The woman opened a box, and took out a strange little basket or hamper, not much larger than a man's fist, and formed a delicate kind of matting. It was sewed at the top; but, ripping it open with a knife, she held it to me, and I saw, to my surprise, that it contained candied fruits of a dark green hue, tempting enough to one of my age. "There, my tiny," said she; "taste, and tell me how you like them."

"Very much," said I; "where did you get them?"

The beldame leered upon me for a moment, then, nodding her head thrice, with a knowing look, said: "Who knows better than yourself, my tawny?"

Now, I knew nothing about the matter; but I saw that these strange people had conceived a very high opinion of the abilities of their visitor, which I was nothing loath to encourage. I therefore answered boldly, "Ah! who indeed!"

"Certainly," said the man; "who should know better than yourself, or who so well? And now my tiny one, let me ask you one thing—you didn't come to do us any harm?"

"No," said I, "I had no dislike to you; though, if you were to meddle with me——"

Man. Of course, my gorgious, of course you would; and quite right too. Meddle with you!—what right have we? I should say it would not be quite safe. I see how it is; you are one of them there;—and he bent his head towards his left shoulder.

Myself. Yes, I am one of them—for I thought he was alluding to the soldiers,—you had best mind what you are about, I can tell you.

Man. Don't doubt we will for our own sake; Lord bless you, wifelkin, only think that we should see one of them there when we least thought about it. Well, I have heard of such things, though I never thought to see one: however, seeing is believing. Well! now you are come, and are not going to do us any mischief, I hope you will stay; you can do us plenty of good if you will.

Myself. What good can I do you?

Man. What good? plenty! Would you not bring us luck? I have heard say, that one of them there always does, if it will but settle down. Stay with us, you shall have a tilted cart all to yourself if you like. We'll make you our little God Almighty, and say our prayers to you every morning!

Myself. That would be nice; and if you were to give me plenty of these things, I should have no objection. But what would my father say? I think he would hardly let me.

Man. Why not? he would be with you; and kindly would we treat him. Indeed, without your father you would be nothing at all.

Myself. That's true; but I do not think he could be spared from his regiment. I have heard him say that they could do nothing without him.

Man. His regiment! What are you talking about?—what does the child mean?

Myself. What do I mean! why, that my father is an officerman at the barracks yonder, keeping guard over the French prisoners.

Man. Oh! then that sap is not your father!

Myself. What, the snake? Why, no! Did you think he was?

Man. To be sure we did. Didn't you tell me so?

Myself. Why, yes; but who would have thought you would have believed it? It is a tame one. I hunt vipers and tame them.

Man. O—h!

"O—h!" grunted the woman. "That's it, is it?"

The man and woman, who during this conversation had resumed their former positions within the tent, looked at each other with a queer look of surprise, as if somewhat disconcerted at what they now heard. They then entered into discourse with each other in the same strange tongue which had already puzzled me. At length the man looked me in the face, and said, somewhat hesitatingly, "so you are not one of them there, after all?"

Myself. One of them there? I don't know what you mean.

Man. Why, we have been thinking you were a goblin—a devilkin! However, I see how it is: you are a sap-engro, a chap who catches snakes, and plays tricks with them! Well, it comes very nearly to the same thing; and if you please to list with us, and bear us pleasant company, we shall be glad of you. I'd take my oath upon it that we might make a mort of money by you and that sap, and the tricks it could do; and, as you seem fly to everything, I shouldn't wonder if you would make a prime hand at telling fortunes.

"I shouldn't wonder," said I.

Man. Of course. And you might still be our God Almighty, or at any rate our clergyman, so you should live in a tilted cart by yourself and say prayers to us night and morning—to wifelkin here, and all our family; there's plenty of us when we are all together; as I said before, you seem fly, I shouldn't wonder if you could read?

"Oh, yes!" said I, "I can read"; and, eager to display my accomplishments, I took my book out of my pocket, and opening it at random, proceeded to read how a certain man whilst wandering about a certain solitary island, entered a cave, the mouth of which was overgrown with brushwood, and how he was nearly frightened to death in that cave by something which he saw.

"That will do," said the man; "that's the kind of prayers for me and my family, ar'n't they, wifelkin? I never heard more delicate prayers in all my life! Why, they beat the rubricals hollow!—and here comes my son Jasper. I say, Jasper, here's a young sap-engro that can read, and is more fly than yourself. Shake hands with him; I wish ye to be two brothers."

With a swift but stealthy pace Jasper came towards us from the farther part of the lane; on reaching the tent he stood still, and looked fixedly upon me as I sat upon the stool; I looked fixedly upon him. A queer look had Jasper; he was a lad of some twelve or thirteen years, with long arms, unlike the singular being who called himself his father; his complexion was ruddy, but his face was seamed, though it did not bear the peculiar scar which disfigured the countenance of the other; nor, though roguish enough, a certain evil expression which that of the other bore, and which the face of the woman possessed in a yet more remarkable degree. For the rest, he wore drab breeches, with certain strings at the knee, a rather gay waistcoat, and tolerably white shirt; under his arm he bore a mighty whip of whalebone with a brass knob, and upon his head was a hat without either top or brim.

"There, Jasper! shake hands, with the sap-engro."

"Can he box, father?" said Jasper, surveying me rather contemptuously. "I should think not, he looks so puny and small."

"Hold your peace, fool!" said the man; "he can do more than that—I tell you he's fly; he carries a sap about, which would sting a ninny like you to dead."

"What, a sap-engro!" said the boy, with a singular whine, and, stooping down, he leered curiously in my face, kindly, however, and then patted me on the head. "A sap-engro," he ejaculated; "lor!"

"Yes, and one of the right sort," said the man; "I am glad we have met with him; he is going to list with us, and be our clergyman and God Almighty, a'n't you, my tawny?"

"I don't know," said I; "I must see what my father will say."

"Your father; bah!"——but here he stopped, for a sound was heard like the rapid galloping of a horse, not loud and distinct as on a road, but dull and heavy as if upon a grass sward; nearer and nearer it came, and the man, starting up, rushed out of the tent, and looked around anxiously. I arose from the stool upon which I had been seated, and just at that moment, amidst a crashing of boughs and sticks, a man on horseback bounded over the hedge into the lane at a few yards' distance from where we were; from the impetus of the leap the horse was nearly down on his knees; the rider, however, by dint of vigorous handling of the reins, prevented him from falling, and then rode up to the tent. " 'Tis Nat," said the man; "what brings him here?"

The new comer was a stout, burly fellow, about the middle age; he had a savage, determined look, and his face was nearly covered over with carbuncles; he wore a broad slouching hat, and was dressed in a grey coat, cut in a fashion which I afterwards learnt to be the genuine Newmarket cut, the skirts being exceedingly short; his waistcoat was of red plush, and he wore broad corduroy breeches and white top-boots. The steed which carried him was of iron grey, spirited and powerful, but covered with sweat and foam. The fellow glanced fiercely and suspiciously around, and said something to the man of the tent in a harsh and rapid voice. A short and hurried conversation ensued in the strange tongue. I could not take my eyes off this new comer. Oh, that half-jockey, half-bruiser countenance, I never forgot it! More than fifteen years afterwards I found myself amidst a crowd before Newgate; a gallows was erected, and beneath it stood a criminal, a notorious malefactor. I recognised him at once; the horseman of the lane is now beneath the fatal tree, but nothing altered; still the same man; jerking his head to the right and left with the same fierce and under glance, just as if the affairs of this world had the same kind of interest to the last; grey coat of Newmarket cut, plush waistcoat, corduroys, and boots, nothing altered; but the head, alas! is bare and so is the neck. Oh, crime and virtue, virtue and crime!—it was old John Newton, I think, who, when he saw a man going to be hanged, said: "There goes John Newton, but for the grace of God!"

But the lane, the lane, all was now in confusion in the lane; the man and woman were employed in striking the tents and in making hurried preparations for departure; the boy Jasper was putting the harness upon the ponies and attaching them to the carts; and, to increase the singularity of the scene, two or three wild-looking women and girls, in red cloaks and immense black beaver bonnets, came from I know not what direction, and, after exchanging a few words with the others, commenced with fierce and agitated gestures to assist them in their occupation. The rider meanwhile sat upon his horse, but evidently in a state of great impatience; he muttered curses between his teeth, spurred the animal furiously, and then reined it in, causing it to rear itself up nearly perpendicular. At last he said: "Curse ye, for Romans, how slow ye are! well, it is no business of mine, stay here all day if you like; I have given ye warning, I am off to the big north road. However, before I go, you had better give me all you have of that."

"Truly spoken, Nat, my pal," said the man; "give it him, mother. There it is; now be off as soon as you please, and rid us of evil company."

The woman had handed him two bags formed of stocking, half full of something heavy, which looked through them for all the world like money of some kind. The fellow, on receiving them, thrust them without ceremony into the pockets of his coat, and then, without a word of farewell salutation, departed at a tremendous rate, the hoofs of his horse thundering for a long time on the hard soil of the neighbouring road, till the sound finally died away in the distance. The strange people were not slow in completing their preparations, and then, flogging their animals terrifically, hurried away seemingly in the same direction.

The boy Jasper was last of the band. As he was following the rest, he stopped suddenly, and looked on the ground appearing to muse; then, turning round, he came up to me where I was standing, leered in my face, and then, thrusting out his hand, he said, "Good-bye, Sap, I dare say we shall meet again, remember we are brothers, two gentle brothers."

Then whining forth, "What a sap-engro, lor!" he gave me a parting leer, and hastened away.

I remained standing in the lane gazing after the retreating company. "A strange set of people," said I at last, "I wonder who they can be."

CHAPTER III

YEARS passed on, even three years; during this period I had increased considerably in stature and in strength, and, let us hope, improved in mind; for I had entered on the study of the Latin language. The very first person to whose care I was entrusted for the acquisition of Latin was an old friend of my father's, a clergyman who kept a seminary at a town the very next we visited after our departure from "the Cross." Under his instruction, however, I continued only a few weeks, as we speedily left the place. "Captain," said this divine, when my father came to take leave of him on the eve of our departure, "I have a friendship for you, and therefore wish to give you a piece of advice concerning this son of yours. You are now removing him from my care; you do wrong, but we will let that pass. Listen to me: there is but one good school book in the world—the one I use in my seminary—Lilly's Latin Grammar, in which your son has already made some progress. If you are anxious for the success of your son in life, for the correctness of his conduct and the soundness of his principles, keep him to Lilly's Grammar. If you can by any means, either fair or foul, induce him to get by heart Lilly's Latin Grammar, you may set your heart at rest with respect to him; I, myself, will be his warrant. I never yet knew a boy that was induced, either by fair means or foul, to learn Lilly's Latin Grammar by heart, who did not turn out a man, provided he lived long enough."

My father, who did not understand the classical languages, received with respect the advice of his old friend, and from that moment conceived the highest opinion of Lilly's Latin Grammar. During three years I studied Lilly's

Latin Grammar under the tuition of various schoolmasters, for I travelled with the regiment, and in every town in which we were stationary I was invariably (God bless my father!) sent to the classical academy of the place.

It was not long before we found ourselves at Edinburgh, or rather in the Castle, into which the regiment marched with drums beating, colours flying, and a long train of baggage-waggons behind. The Castle was, as I suppose it is now, a garrison for soldiers. Two other regiments were already there; the one an Irish, if I remember right, the other a small Highland corps.

It is hardly necessary to say much about this Castle, which everybody has seen; on which account, doubtless, nobody has ever yet thought fit to describe it—at least that I am aware. Be this as it may, I have no intention of describing it, and shall content myself with observing, that we took up our abode in that immense building, or caserne, of modern erection, which occupies the entire eastern side of the bold rock on which the Castle stands. A gallant caserne it was—the best and roomiest that I had hitherto seen—rather cold and windy, it is true, especially in the winter, but commanding a noble prospect of a range of distant hills, which I was told were "the hieland hills," and of a broad arm of the sea, which I heard somebody say was the Firth of Forth.

My brother, who, for some years past, had been receiving his education in a certain celebrated school in England, was now with us; and it came to pass, that one day my father, as he sat at table, looked steadfastly on my brother and myself, and then addressed my mother: "During my journey down hither I have lost no opportunity of making inquiries about these people, the Scotch, amongst whom we now are, and since I have been here I have observed them attentively. From what I have heard and seen, I should say that upon the whole they are a very decent set of people; they seem acute and intelligent, and I am told that their system of education is so excellent, that every person is learned—more or less acquainted with Greek and Latin. There is one thing, however, connected with them, which is a great drawback—the horrid jargon which they speak. However learned they may be in Greek and Latin, their English is execrable; and yet I'm told it is not so bad as it was. I was in company the other day with an Englishman who has resided here many years. We were talking about the country and its people. 'I should like both very well,' said I, 'were it not for the language. I wish sincerely our Parliament, which is passing so many foolish acts every year, would pass one to force these Scotch to speak English.' 'I wish so too,' said he. 'The language is a disgrace to the British Government; but, if you had heard it twenty years ago, Captain!—if you had heard it as it was spoken when I first came to Edinburgh!' "

"Only custom," said my mother. "I dare say the language is now what it was then."

"I don't know," said my father; "though I dare say you are right; it could never have been worse than it is at present. But now to the point. Were it not for the language, which, if the boys were to pick it up, might ruin their prospects in life,—were it not for that, I should very much like to send them to a school there is in this place, which everybody talks about—the High School, I think they call it. 'Tis said to be the best school in the whole island; but the idea of one's children speaking Scotch—broad Scotch! I must think the matter over."

And he did think the matter over; and the result of his deliberation was a determination to send us to the school. Let me call thee up before my mind's eye, High School, to which, every morning, the two English brothers took their way from the proud old Castle through the lofty streets of the Old Town. High School!—called so, I scarcely know why; neither lofty in thyself, nor by position, being situated in a flat bottom; oblong structure of tawny stone, with many windows fenced with iron netting—with thy long hall below, and thy five chambers above, for the reception of the five classes, into which the eight hundred urchins, who styled thee instructress, were divided. Thy learned rector and his four subordinate dominies; thy strange old porter of the tall form and grizzled hair, hight Boee, and doubtless of Norse ancestry, as his name declares; perhaps of the blood of Bui hin Digri, the hero of northern song—the Jomsborg Viking who clove Thorsteinn Midlangr asunder in the dread sea battle of Horunga Vog, and who, when the fight was lost and his own two hands smitten off, seized two chests of gold with his bloody stumps, and, springing with them into the sea, cried to the scanty relics of his crew, "Overboard now, all Bui's lads!" Yes, I remember all about thee, and how at eight of every morn we were all gathered together with one accord in the long hall, from which, after the litanies had been read (for so I will call them, being an Episcopalian), the five classes from the five sets of benches trotted off in long files, one boy after the other, up the five spiral staircases of stone, each class to its destination; and well do I remember how we of the third sat hushed and still, watched by the eye of the dux, until the door opened, and in walked that model of a good Scotchman, the shrewd, intelligent, but warm-hearted and kind dominie, the respectable Carson.

And in this school I began to construe the Latin language, which I had never done before, notwithstanding my long and diligent study of Lilly, which illustrious grammar was not used at Edinburgh, nor indeed known. Greek was only taught in the fifth or highest class, in which my brother was; as for myself, I never got beyond the third during the two years that I remained at this seminary. I certainly acquired here a considerable insight in the Latin tongue; and, to the scandal of my father and horror of my mother, a thorough proficiency in the Scotch, which, in less than two months, usurped the place of the English, and so obstinately maintained its ground, that I still can occasionally detect its lingering remains. I did not spend my time unpleasantly at this school, though, first of all, I had to pass through an ordeal.

"Scotland is a better country than England," said an ugly, blear-eyed lad, about a head and shoulders taller than myself, the leader of a gang of varlets who surrounded me in the playground, on the first day, as soon as the morning lesson was over. "Scotland is a far better country than England, in every respect."

"Is it?" said I. "Then you ought to be very thankful for not having been born in England."

"That's just what I am, ye loon; and every morning when I say my prayers, I thank God for not being an Englishman. The Scotch are a much better and braver people than the English."

"It may be so," said I, "for what I know—indeed, till I came here, I never heard a word either about the Scotch or their country."

"Are ye making fun of us, ye English puppy?" said the blear-eyed lad; "take that!" and I was presently beaten black and blue. And thus did I first become aware of the difference of races and their antipathy to each other.

"Bow to the storm, and it shall pass over you." I held my peace, and silently submitted to the superiority of the Scotch—*in numbers*. This was enough; from an object of persecution I soon became one of patronage, especially amongst the champions of the class. "The English," said the blear-eyed lad, "though a wee bit behind the Scotch in strength and fortitude, are nae to be sneezed at, being far ahead of the Irish, to say nothing of the French, a pack of cowardly scoundrels. And with regard to the English country, it is na Scotland, it is true, but it has its gude properties; and, though there is ne'er a haggis in a' the land, there's an unco deal o' gowd and siller. I respect England, for I have an auntie married there."

One day I was standing on the ramparts of the castle on the south-western side which overhangs the green brae, where it slopes down into what was in those days the green swamp or morass, called by the natives of Auld Reekie the Nor Loch; it was a dark gloomy day, and a thin veil of mist was beginning to settle down upon the brae and the morass. I could perceive, however, that there was a skirmish taking place in the latter spot. I had an indistinct view of two parties—apparently of urchins—and I heard whoops and shrill cries. Eager to know the cause of this disturbance, I left the castle, and descending the brae reached the borders of the morass, where was a runnel of water and the remains of an old wall, on the other side of which a narrow path led across the swamp; upon this path at a little distance before me there was "a bicker." I pushed forward, but had scarcely crossed the ruined wall and runnel, when the party nearest to me gave way, and in great confusion came running in my direction. As they drew nigh, one of them shouted to me, "Wha are ye, mon? are ye o' the Auld Toon?" I made no answer. "Ha! ye are o' the New Toon; De'il tak ye, we'll moorder ye"; and the next moment a huge stone sung past my head. "Let me be, ye fule bodies," said I, "I'm no of either of ye, I live yonder aboon in the castle." "Ah! ye live in the castle; then ye're an auld tooner; come gie us your help, mon, and dinna stand there staring like a dunnot, we want help sair eneugh. Here are stanes."

For my own part I wished for nothing better, and, rushing forward, I placed myself at the head of my new associates, and commenced flinging stones fast and desperately. The other party now gave way in their turn, closely followed by ourselves; I was in the van and about to stretch out my hand to seize the hindermost boy of the enemy, when, not being acquainted with the miry and difficult paths of the Nor Loch, and in my eagerness taking no heed of my footing, I plunged into a quagmire, into which I sank as far as my shoulders. Our adversaries no sooner perceived this disaster, than, setting up a shout, they wheeled round and attacked us most vehemently. Had my comrades now deserted me, my life had not been worth a straw's purchase, I should either have been smothered in the quag, or, what is more probable, had my brains beaten out with stones; but they behaved like true Scots, and fought stoutly around their comrade, until I was extricated, whereupon both parties retired, the night being near at hand.

"Ye are na a bad hand at flinging stanes," said the lad who first addressed me as we now returned up the brae; "your aim is right dangerous, mon, I saw how ye skelpit them, ye maun help us agin thae New Toon blackguards at our next bicker."

After we had sojourned in Scotland nearly two years, the long continental war had been brought to an end; Napoleon was humbled for a time, and the Bourbons restored to a land which could well have dispensed with them. We returned to England, where the corps was disbanded, and my parents with their family retired to private life. Suddenly, however, the sound of war was heard again: Napoleon had broken forth from Elba, and everything was in confusion. Vast military preparations were again made, our own corps was levied anew, and my brother became an officer in it; but the danger was soon over, Napoleon was once more quelled and chained for ever, like Prometheus, to his rock. As the corps, however, though so recently levied, had already become a very fine one, thanks to my father's energetic drilling, the Government very properly determined to turn it to some account, and, as disturbances were apprehended in Ireland about this period, it occurred to them that they could do no better than despatch it to that country.

In the autumn of the year 1815 we set sail from a port in Essex; we were some eight hundred strong, and were embarked in two ships, very large, but old and crazy; a storm overtook us when off Beachy Head, in which we had nearly foundered. I was awakened early in the morning by the howling of the wind, and the uproar on deck. I kept myself close, however, as is still my constant practice on similar occasions, and waited the result with that apathy and indifference which violent seasickness is sure to produce. We shipped several seas, and once the vessel missing stays—which, to do it justice, it generally did at every third or fourth tack—we escaped almost by a miracle from being dashed upon the foreland. On the eighth day of our voyage we were in sight of Ireland. The weather was now calm and serene, the sun shone brightly on the sea and on certain green hills in the distance, on which I descried what at first sight I believed to be two ladies gathering flowers, which, however, on our nearer approach, proved to be two tall white towers, doubtless built for some purpose or other, though I did not learn for what.

We entered a kind of bay, or cove, by a narrow inlet; it was a beautiful and romantic place this cove, very spacious, and being nearly land-locked, was sheltered from every wind. A small island, every inch of which was covered with fortifications, appeared to swim upon the waters, whose dark blue denoted their immense depth; tall green hills, which ascended gradually from the shore, formed the background to the west; they were carpeted to the top with turf of the most vivid green, and studded here and there with woods, seemingly of oak; there was a strange old castle half-way up the ascent, a village on a crag—but the mists of morning were half veiling the scene when I surveyed it, and the mists of time are now hanging densely between it and my no longer youthful eye; I may not describe it;—nor will I try.

Leaving the ship in the cove, we passed up a wide river in boats till we came to a city where we disembarked. It was a large city, as large as Edinburgh to my eyes; there were plenty of fine houses, but little neatness; the streets were full of impurities; handsome equipages rolled along, but the greater part of the population were in rags; beggars abounded; there was no lack of merriment, however; boisterous shouts of laughter were heard on every side. It appeared a city of contradictions. After a few days' rest we marched from this place in two divisions. My father commanded the second; I walked by his side.

Our route lay up the country; the country at first offered no very remarkable feature; it was pretty, but tame. On the second day, however, its appearance had altered, it had become more wild; a range of distant mountains bounded the horizon. We passed through several villages, as I suppose I may term them, of low huts, the walls formed of rough stones without mortar, the roof of flags laid over wattles and wicker-work; they seemed to be inhabited solely by women and children; the latter were naked, the former, in general, blear-eyed beldames, who sat beside the doors on low stools, spinning. We saw, however, both men and women working at a distance in the fields.

I was thirsty; and going up to an ancient crone, employed in the manner which I have described, I asked her for water; she looked me in the face, appeared to consider for a moment, then tottering into her hut, presently reappeared with a small pipkin of milk, which she offered to me with a trembling hand. I drank the milk; it was sour, but I found it highly refreshing. I then took out a penny and offered it to her, whereupon she shook her head, smiled, and, patting my face with her skinny hand, murmured some words in a tongue which I had never heard before.

I walked on by my father's side, holding the stirrup-leather of his horse; presently several low uncouth cars passed by, drawn by starved cattle; the drivers were tall fellows, with dark features and athletic frames—they wore long loose blue cloaks with sleeves, which last, however, dangled unoccupied; these cloaks appeared in tolerably good condition, not so their under garments. On their heads were broad slouching hats; the generality of them were bare-footed. As they passed, the soldiers jested with them in the patois of East Anglia, whereupon the fellows laughed and appeared to jest with the soldiers; but what they said who knows, it being in a rough guttural language, strange and wild. The soldiers stared at each other, and were silent.

"A strange language that!" said a young officer to my father, "I don't understand a word of it; what can it be?"

"Irish," said my father, with a loud voice, "and a bad language it is; I have known it of old, that is, I have often heard it spoken when I was a guardsman in London. There's one part of London where all the Irish live—at least all the worst of them—and there they hatch their villainies and speak this tongue; it is that which keeps them together and makes them dangerous. I was once sent there to seize a couple of deserters—Irish—who had taken refuge among their companions; we found them in what was in my time called a *ken*, that is, a house where only thieves and desperadoes are to be found. Knowing on what kind of business I was bound, I had taken with me a sergeant's party; it was well I did so. We found the deserters in a large room, with at least thirty ruffians, horrid looking fellows, seated about a long table, drinking, swearing, and talking Irish. Ah! we had a tough battle, I remember; the two fellows did nothing, but sat still, thinking it best to be quiet; but the rest, with an ubbubboo, like the blowing up of a powder-magazine, sprang up, brandishing their sticks; for these fellows always carry sticks with them, even to bed, and not unfrequently spring up in their sleep, striking left and right."

"And did you take the deserters?" said the officer.

"Yes," said my father; "for we formed at the end of the room, and charged with fixed bayonets, which compelled the others to yield notwithstanding their numbers; but the worst was when we got out into the street; the whole district had become alarmed, and hundreds came pouring down upon us—men, women, and children. Women, did I say!—they looked fiends, half naked, with their hair hanging down over their bosoms; they tore up the very pavement to hurl at us, sticks rang about our ears, stones, and Irish—I liked the Irish worst of all, it sounded so horrid, especially as I did not understand it. It's a bad language."

"A queer tongue," said I, "I wonder if I could learn it?"

"Learn it!" said my father; "what should you learn it for?—however, I am not afraid of that. It is not like Scotch; no person can learn it, save those who are born to it, and even in Ireland the respectable people do not speak it, only the wilder sort, like those we have passed."

We continued at this place for some months, during which time the soldiers performed their duties, whatever they were; and I, having no duties to perform, was sent to school. I had been to English schools, and to the celebrated one of Edinburgh; but my education, at the present day, would not be what it is—perfect, had I never had the honour of being *alumnus* in an Irish seminary.

And there I made acquaintance, notwithstanding the hint of the landlord, with the Papist "gasoons," as they were called, the farmers' sons from the country; and of these gasoons, of which there were three, two might be reckoned as nothing at all; in the third, however, I soon discovered that there was something extraordinary.

He was about sixteen years old, and above six feet high, dressed in a grey suit; the coat, from its size, appeared to have been made for him some ten years before. He was remarkably narrow-chested and round-shouldered, owing, perhaps, as much to the tightness of his garment as to the hand of nature. His face was long, and his complexion swarthy, relieved, however, by certain freckles, with which the skin was plentifully studded. He had strange wandering eyes, grey, and somewhat unequal in size; they seldom rested on the book, but were generally wandering about the room from one object to another. Sometimes he would fix them intently on the wall; and then suddenly starting, as if from a reverie, he would commence making certain mysterious movements with his thumbs and forefingers, as if he were shuffling something from him.

One morning, as he sat by himself on a bench, engaged in this manner, I went up to him and said, "Good day, Murtagh; you do not seem to have much to do?"

"Faith, you may say that, Shorsha dear! it is seldom much to do that I have."

"And what are you doing with your hands?"

"Faith, then, if I must tell you, I was e'en dealing with the cards."

"Do you play much at cards?"

"Sorra a game, Shorsha, have I played with the cards since my uncle Phelim, the thief, stole away the ould pack, when he went to settle in the county Waterford!"

"But you have other things to do?"

"Sorra anything else has Murtagh to do that he cares about; and that makes me dread so going home at nights."

"I should like to know all about you; where do you live, joy?"

"Faith, then, ye shall know all about me, and where I live. It is at a place called the Wilderness that I live, and they call it so, because it is a fearful wild place, without any house near it but my father's own; and that's where I live when at home."

"And your father is a farmer, I suppose?"

"You may say that; and it is a farmer I should have been, like my brother Denis, had not my uncle Phelim, the thief! tould my father to send me to school, to learn Greek letters, that I might be made a saggart of and sent to Paris and Salamanca."

"And you would rather be a farmer than a priest?"

"You may say that! for, were I a farmer, like the rest, I should have something to do, like the rest, something that I cared for, and I should come home tired at night and fall asleep. as the rest do, before the fire; but when I comes home at night I am not tired, for I have been doing nothing all day that I care for; and then I sits down and stares about me, and at the fire, till I become frighted; and then I shouts to my brother Denis, or to the gasoons, 'Get up, I say, and let's be doing something; tell us a tale of Finn-ma-Coul, and how he lay down in the Shannon's bed and let the river flow down his jaws!' Arrah, Shorsha, I wish you would come and stay with us, and tell us some o' your sweet stories of your ownself and the snake ye carried about wid ye. Faith, Shorsha dear! that snake bates anything about Finn-ma-Coul or Brian Boroo, the thieves two, bad luck to them!"

"And do they get up and tell you stories?"

"Sometimes they does, but oftenmost they curses me and bids me be quiet! But I can't be quiet, either before the fire or abed; so I runs out of the house, and stares at the rocks, at the trees, and sometimes at the clouds, as they run a race across the bright moon; and the more I stares, the more frighted I grows, till I screeches and holloas. And last night I went into the barn and hid my face in the straw; and there, as I lay and shivered in the straw, I heard a voice above my head singing out 'To whit, to whoo!' and then up I starts and runs into the house, and falls over my brother Denis, as he lies at the fire. 'What's that for?' says he. 'Get up, you thief!' says I, 'and be helping me. I have been out in the barn, and an owl has crow'd at me!' "

"And what has this to do with playing cards?"

"Little enough, Shorsha dear!—If there were card-playing, I should not be frighted."

"And why do you not play at cards?"

"Did I not tell you that the thief, my uncle Phelim, stole away the pack? If we had the pack, my brother Denis and the gasoons would be ready enough to get up from their sleep before the fire, and play cards with me for ha'pence, or eggs, or nothing at all; but the pack is gone—bad luck to the thief who took it!"

"And why don't you buy another?"

"Is it of buying you are speaking? And where am I to get the money?"

"Ah! that's another thing!"

"Faith it is, honey!—And now the Christmas holidays is coming, when I shall be at home by day as well as night, and then what am I to do? Since I have been a saggarting, I have been good for nothing at all—neither for work nor Greek—only to play cards! Faith, it's going mad I will be!"

"I say, Murtagh!"

"Yes, Shorsha dear!"

"I have a pack of cards."

"You don't say so, Shorsha mavourneen! you don't say that you have cards fifty-two?"

"I do. though; and they are quite new—never been once used."

"And you'll be lending them to me, I warrant?"

"Don't think it! But I'll sell them to you, joy, if you like."

"*Hanam mon Dioul!* am I not after telling you that I have no money at all?"

"But you have as good as money, to me, at least; and I'll take it in exchange."

"What's that, Shorsha dear?"

"Irish!"

"Irish?"

"Yes, you speak Irish; I heard you talking it the other day to the cripple. You shall teach me Irish."

"And is it a language-master you'd be making of me?"

"To be sure!—what better can you do?—it would help you to pass your time at school. You can't learn Greek, so you must teach Irish!"

Before Christmas, Murtagh was playing at cards with his brother Denis, and I could speak a considerable quantity of broken Irish.

CHAPTER IV

FROM the wild scenes which I have attempted to describe in the latter pages I must now transport the reader to others of a widely different character. He must suppose himself no longer in Ireland, but in the eastern corner of merry England.

"I have been writing to the Duke," said my father one day to my excellent mother, after we had been at home somewhat better than a year, "I have been writing to the Duke of York about a commission for that eldest boy of ours. He, however, affords me no hopes; he says that his list is crammed with names, and that the greater number of the candidates have better claims than my son."

"I do not see how that can be," said my mother.

"Nor do I," replied my father. "I see the sons of bankers and merchants gazetted every month, and I do not see what claims they have to urge, unless they be golden ones. However, I have not served my king fifty years to turn grumbler at this time of life. I suppose that the people at the head of affairs know what is most proper and convenient; perhaps when the lad sees how difficult, nay, how impossible it is that he should enter the army, he will turn his mind to some other profession; I wish he may!"

"I think he has already," said my mother; "you see how fond he is of the arts, of drawing and painting, and, as far as I can judge, what he has already done is very respectable; his mind seems quite turned that way, and I heard him say the other day that he would sooner be a Michael Angelo than a general officer. But you are always talking of him; what do you think of doing with the other child?"

"What, indeed!" said my father; "that is a consideration which gives me no little uneasiness. I am afraid it will be much more difficult to settle him in life than his brother. What is he fitted for, even were it in my power to provide for him? God help the child! I bear him no ill-will, on the contrary all love and affection; but I cannot shut my eyes; there is something so strange about him! How he behaved in Ireland! I sent him to school to learn Greek, and he picked up Irish!"

"And Greek as well," said my mother. "I heard him say the other day that he could read St. John in the original tongue."

"You will find excuses for him, I know," said my father. "You tell me I am always talking of my first-born; I might retort by saying you are always thinking of the other; but it is the way of women always to side with the second-born. There's what's-her-name in the Bible, by whose wiles the old blind man was induced to give to his second son the blessing which was the birthright of the other. I wish I had been in his place! I should not have been so easily deceived! no disguise would ever have caused me to mistake an impostor for my first-born. Though I must say for this boy that he is nothing like Jacob; he is neither smooth nor sleek, and, though my second-born, is already taller and larger than his brother."

"Just so," said my mother, "his brother would make a far better Jacob than he."

"I will hear nothing against my first-born," said my father, "even in the way of insinuation: he is my joy and pride—the very image of myself in my youthful days, long before I fought Big Ben, though perhaps not quite so tall or strong built. As for the other, God bless the child! I love him, I'm sure; but I must be blind not to see the difference between him and his brother. Why, he has neither my hair nor my eyes; and then his countenance! why, 'tis absolutely swarthy, God forgive me! I had almost said like that of a gypsy, but I have nothing to say against that; the boy is not to be blamed for the colour of his face, nor for his hair and eyes; but, then, his ways and manners! I confess I do not like them, and that they give me no little uneasiness. I know that he kept very strange company when he was in Ireland; people of evil report, of whom terrible things were said—horse-witches and the like. I questioned him once or twice upon the matter, and even threatened him, but it was of no use; he put on a look as if he did not understand me, a regular Irish look, just such a one as those rascals assume when they wish to appear all innocence and simplicity, and they full of malice and deceit all the time. I don't like them; they are no friends to old England, or its old king, God bless him! That ever son of mine should have been intimate with the Papist Irish, and have learnt their language!"

"But he thinks of other things now," said my mother.

"Other languages, you mean," said my father. "It is strange that he has conceived such a zest for the study of languages; no sooner did he come home than he persuaded me to send him to that old priest to learn French and Italian, and, if I remember right, you abetted him; but, as I said before, it is in the nature of women invariably to take the part of the second-born. Well, there is no harm in learning French and Italian, perhaps much good in his case, as they may drive the other tongue out of his head. Irish! why, he might go to the university but for that; but how would he look when, on being examined with respect to his attainments, it was discovered that he understood Irish? How did you learn it? they would ask him; how did you become acquainted with the language of Papists and rebels? The boy would be sent away in disgrace."

"Be under no apprehension, I have no doubt that he has long since forgotten it."

"I am glad to hear it," said my father; "for, between ourselves, I love the poor child; ay, quite as well as my first-born. I trust they will do well, and that God will be their shield and guide; I have no doubt He will, for I have read something in the Bible to that effect. What is that text about the young ravens being fed?"

"I know a better than that," said my mother; "one of David's own words, 'I have been young and now am grown old, yet never have I seen the righteous man forsaken, or his seed begging their bread.' "

I have heard talk of the pleasures of idleness, yet it is my own firm belief that no one ever yet took pleasure in it. Mere idleness is the most disagreeable state of existence, and both mind and body are continually making efforts to escape from it. It has been said that idleness is the parent of mischief, which is very true; but mischief itself is merely an attempt to escape from the dreary vacuum of idleness. There are many tasks and occupations which a man is unwilling to perform, but let no one think that he is therefore in love with idleness; he turns to something which is more agreeable to his inclination, and doubtless more suited to his nature; but he is not in love with idleness. A boy may play the truant from school because he dislikes books and study; but, depend upon it, he intends doing something the while—to go fishing, or perhaps to take a walk; and who knows but that from such excursions both his mind and body may derive more benefit than from books and school?

I was standing on the castle hill in the midst of a fair of horses.

I had long since conceived a passion for the equine race, a passion in which circumstances had of late not permitted me to indulge. I had no horses to ride, but I took pleasure in looking at them; and I had already attended more than one of these fairs: the present was lively enough, indeed, horse fairs are seldom dull. There was shouting and whooping, neighing and braying; there was galloping and trotting; fellows with highlows and white stockings, and with many a string dangling from the knees of their tight breeches, were running desperately, holding horses by the halter, and in some cases dragging them along; there were long-tailed steeds, and dock-tailed steeds of every degree and breed; there were droves of wild ponies, and long rows of sober cart horses; there were donkeys, and even mules: the last rare things to be seen in damp, misty England, for the mule pines in mud and rain, and thrives best with a hot sun above and a burning sand below. There were—oh, the gallant creatures! I hear their neigh upon the wind; there were—goodliest sight of all—certain enormous quadrupeds only seen to perfection in our native isle, led about by dapper grooms, their manes ribanded and their tails curiously clubbed and balled. Ha! ha!—how distinctly do they say, ha! ha!

Now during all this time I had a kind of consciousness that I had been the object of some person's observation; that eyes were fastened upon me from somewhere in the crowd. Sometimes I thought myself watched from before, sometimes from behind; and occasionally methought that, if I just turned my head to the right or left, I should meet a peering and inquiring glance; and, indeed, once or twice I did turn, expecting to see somebody whom I knew, yet always without success; though it appeared to me that I was but a moment too late, and that some one had just slipped away from the direction to which I turned, like the figure in a magic lanthorn.

Two or three men on horseback are hurrying through the crowd, they are widely different in their appearance from the other people of the fair; not so much in dress, for they are clad something after the fashion of rustic jockeys, but in their look—no light brown hair have they, no ruddy cheeks, no blue quiet glances belong to them; their features are dark, their locks long, black and shining, and their eyes are wild; they are admirable horsemen, but they do not sit the saddle in the manner of common jockeys, they seem to float or hover upon it, like gulls upon the waves; two of them are mere striplings, but the third is a very tall man with a countenance heroically beautiful, but wild, wild, wild. As they rush along, the crowd give way on all sides, and now a kind of ring or circus is formed, within which the strange men exhibit their horsemanship, rushing past each other, in and out, after the manner of a reel, the tall man occasionally balancing himself upon the saddle, and standing erect on one foot. He had just regained his seat after the latter feat, and was about to push his horse to a gallop, when a figure started forward close from beside me, and laying his hand on his neck, and pulling him gently downward, appeared to whisper something into his ear; presently the tall man raised his head, and, scanning the crowd for a moment in the direction in which I was standing, fixed his eyes full upon me, and anon the countenance of the whisperer was turned, but only in part, and the side-glance of another pair of wild eyes was directed towards my face, but the entire visage of the big black man half stooping as he was, was turned full upon mine.

But now, with a nod to the figure who had stopped him, and with another inquiring glance at myself, the big man once more put his steed into motion, and after riding round the ring a few more times darted through a lane in the crowd, and followed by his two companions disappeared, whereupon the figure who had whispered to him and had subsequently remained in the middle of the space, came towards me, and cracking a whip which he held in his hand so loudly that the report was nearly equal to that of a pocket pistol, he cried in a strange tone:

"What! the sap-engro? Lor! the sap-engro upon the hill!"

"I remember that word," said I, "and I almost think I remember you. You can't be——"

"Jasper, your pal! Truth, and no lie, brother."

"It is strange that you should have known me," said I. "I am certain, but for the word you used, I should never have recognised you."

"Not so strange as you may think, brother; there is something in your face which would prevent people from forgetting you, even though they might wish it; and your face is not much altered since the time you wot of, though you are so much grown. I thought it was you, but to make sure I dodged about, inspecting you. I believe you felt me, though I never touched you; a sign, brother, that we are akin, that we are dui palor—two relations. Your blood beat when mine was near, as mine always does at the coming of a brother; and we became brothers in that lane."

"And where are you staying?" said I; "in this town?"

"Not in the town; the like of us don't find it exactly wholesome to stay in towns; we keep abroad. But I have little to do here—come with me and I'll show you where we stay."

We descended the hill in the direction of the north, and passing along the suburb reached the old Norman bridge, which we crossed; the chalk precipice, with the ruin on its top, was now before us; but turning to the left we walked swiftly along, and presently came to some rising ground, which ascending, we found ourselves upon a wild moor or heath.

"You are one of them," said I, "whom people call——"

"Just so," said Jasper; "but never mind what people call us."

"And that tall handsome man on the hill, whom you whispered? I suppose he's one of ye. What is his name?"

"Tawno Chikno," said Jasper, "which means the small one; we call him such because he is the biggest man of all our nation. You say he is handsome, that is not the word, brother; he's the beauty of the world. Women run wild at the sight of Tawno. An earl's daughter, near London—a fine young lady with diamonds round her neck—fell in love with Tawno. I have seen that lass on a heath, as this may be, kneel down to Tawno, clasp his feet, begging to be his wife—or anything else—if she might go with him. But Tawno would have nothing to do with her. 'I have a wife of my own,' said he, 'a lawful Rommany wife, whom I love better than the whole world, jealous though she sometimes be.' "

"And is she very beautiful?" said I.

"Why, you know, brother, beauty is frequently a matter of taste; however, as you ask my opinion, I should say not quite so beautiful as himself."

We had now arrived at a small valley between two hills or downs, the sides of which were covered with furze. In the midst of this valley were various carts and low tents forming a rude kind of encampment; several dark children were playing about, who took no manner of notice of us. As we passed one of the tents, however, a canvas screen was lifted up, and a woman supported upon a crutch hobbled out. She was about the middle age, and, besides being lame, was bitterly ugly; she was very slovenly dressed, and on her swarthy features ill nature was most visibly stamped. She did not deign me a look, but addressing Jasper in a tongue which I did not understand, appeared to put some eager questions to him.

"He's coming," said Jasper, and passed on. "Poor fellow," said he to me, "he has scarcely been gone an hour and she's jealous already. Well," he continued, "what do you think of her? you have seen her now and can judge for yourself—that 'ere woman is Tawno Chikno's wife!"

CHAPTER V

We went to the farthest of the tents, which stood at a slight distance from the rest, and which exactly resembled the one which I have described on a former occasion; we went in and sat down, one on each side of a small fire which was smouldering on the ground, there was no one else in the tent but a tall tawny woman of middle age, who was busily knitting. "Brother," said Jasper, "I wish to hold some pleasant discourse with you."

"As much as you please," said I, "provided you can find anything pleasant to talk about."

"Never fear," said Jasper; "and first of all we will talk of yourself. Where have you been all this long time?"

"Here and there," said I, "and far and near, going about with the soldiers; but there is no soldiering now, so we have sat down, father and family, in the town there."

"And do you still hunt snakes?" said Jasper.

"No," said I, "I have given up that long ago; I do better now: read books and learn languages."

"Well, I am sorry you have given up your snake-hunting; many's the strange talk I have had with our people about your snake and yourself, and how you frightened my father and mother in the lane."

"And where are your father and mother?"

"Where I shall never see them, brother; at least, I hope so."

"Not dead?"

"No, not dead; they are bitchadey pawdel."

"What's that?"

"Sent across—banished."

"Ah! I understand; I am sorry for them. And so you are here alone?"

"Not quite alone, brother!"

"No, not alone; but with the rest—Tawno Chikno takes care of you."

"Takes care of me, brother!"

"Yes, stands to you in the place of a father—keeps you out of harm's way."

"What do you take me for, brother?"

"For about three years older than myself."

"Perhaps; but you are of the Gorgios, and I am a Rommany Chal. Tawno Chikno take care of Jasper Petulengro!"

"Is that your name?"

"Don't you like it?"

"Very much, I never heard a sweeter; it is something like what you call me."

"The horse-shoe master and the snake-fellow, I am the first."

"Who gave you that name?"

"Ask Pharaoh."

"I would, if he were here, but I do not see him."

"I am Pharaoh."

"Then you are a king."

"Chachipen, pal."

"I do not understand you."

"Where are your languages? You want two things, brother: mother sense and gentle Rommany."

"What makes you think that I want sense?"

"That, being so old, you can't yet guide yourself!"

"I can read Dante, Jasper."

"Anan, brother."

"I can charm snakes, Jasper."

"I know you can, brother."

"Yes, and horses too; bring me the most vicious in the land, if I whisper he'll be tame."

"Then the more shame for you—a snake-fellow—a horse-witch—and a lil-reader—yet you can't shift for yourself. I laugh at you, brother!"

"Then you can shift for yourself?"

"For myself and for others, brother."

"And what does Chikno?"

"Sells me horses, when I bid him. Those horses on the chong were mine."

"And has he none of his own?"

"Sometimes he has; but he is not so well off as myself. When my father and mother were bitchadey pawdel, which, to tell you the truth, they were, for chiving wafodo dloovu, they left me all they had, which was not a little, and I became the head of our family, which was not a small one. I was not older than you when that happened; yet our people said they had never a better krallis to contrive and plan for them and to keep them in order. And this is so well known, that many Rommany Chals, not of our family, come and join themselves to us, living with us for a time, in order to better themselves, more especially those of the poorer sort, who have little of their own. Tawno is one of these."

"Is that fine fellow poor?"

"One of the poorest, brother. Handsome as he is, he has not a horse of his own to ride on. Perhaps we may put it down to his wife, who cannot move about, being a cripple, as you saw."

"And you are what is called a Gypsy King?"

"Ay, ay; a Rommany Kral."

"Are there other kings?"

"Those who call themselves so; but the true Pharaoh is Petulengro."

"Did Pharaoh make horse-shoes?"

"The first who ever did, brother."

"Pharaoh lived in Egypt."

"So did we once, brother."

"And you left it?"

"My fathers did, brother."

"And why did they come here?"

"They had their reasons, brother."

"And you are not English?"

"We are not Gorgios."

"And you have a language of your own?"

"Avali."

"This is wonderful."

"Ha, ha!" cried the woman, who had hitherto sat knitting at the farther end of the tent, without saying a word, though not inattentive to our conversation, as I could perceive by certain glances which she occasionally cast upon us both. "Ha, ha!" she screamed, fixing upon me two eyes, which shone like burning coals, and which were filled with an expression both of scorn and malignity, "It is wonderful, is it, that we should have a language of our own? What, you grudge the poor people the speech they talk among themselves? That's just like you Gorgios, you would have everybody stupid, single-tongued idiots, like yourselves. We are taken before the Poknees of the gav, myself and sister, to give an account of ourselves. So I says to my sister's little boy, speaking Rommany, I says to the little boy who is with us, 'Run to my son Jasper, and the rest, and tell them to be off, there are hawks abroad.' So the Poknees questions us, and lets us go, not being able to make anything of us; but, as we are going, he calls us back. 'Good woman,' says the Poknees, 'what was that I heard you say just now to the little boy?' 'I was telling him, your worship, to go and see the time of day, and, to save trouble, I said it in our own language.' 'Where did you get that language?' says the Poknees. ' 'Tis our own language, sir,' I tells him, 'we did not steal it.' 'Shall I tell you what it is, my good woman?' says the Poknees. 'I would thank you, sir,' says I, 'for 'tis often we are asked about it.' 'Well, then,' says the Poknees, 'it is no language at all, merely a made-up gibberish.' 'Oh, bless your wisdom,' says I, with a curtsey, 'you can tell us what our language is without understanding it!' Another time we meet a parson. 'Good woman,' says he, 'what's that you are talking? Is it broken language?' 'Of course, your reverence,' says I, 'we are broken people; give a shilling, your reverence, to the poor broken woman.' Oh, these Gorgios! they grudge us our very language!"

"She called you her son, Jasper?"

"I am her son, brother."

"I thought you said your parents were——"

"Bitchadey pawdel; you thought right, brother. This is my wife's mother."

"Then you are married, Jasper?"

"Ay, truly; I am husband and father. You will see wife and chabo anon."

"Where are they now?"

"In the gav, penning dukkerin."

"We were talking of language, Jasper?"

"True, brother."

"Yours must be a rum one?"

"'Tis called Rommany."

"I would gladly know it."

"You need it sorely."

"Would you teach it me?"

"None sooner."

"Suppose we begin now."

"Suppose we do, brother."

"Not whilst I am here," said the woman, flinging her knitting down, and starting upon her feet; "not whilst I am here shall this Gorgio learn Rommany. A pretty manœuvre, truly; and what would be the end of it? I goes to the farming ker with my sister, to tell a fortune, and earn a few sixpences for the chabes. I sees a jolly pig in the yard, and I says to my sister, speaking Rommany, 'Do so and so,' says I; which the farming man hearing, asks what we are talking about. 'Nothing at all, master,' says I; 'something about the weather'; when who should start up from behind a pale, where he has been listening, but this ugly Gorgio, crying out, 'They are after poisoning your pigs, neighbour!' so that we are glad to run, I and my sister, with perhaps the farm-engro shouting after us. Says my sister to me, when we have got fairly off, 'How came that ugly one to know what you said to me?' Whereupon I answers, 'It all comes of my son Jasper, who brings the Gorgio to our fire, and must needs be teaching him.' 'Who was fool there?' says my sister. 'Who, indeed, but my son Jasper,' I answers. And here should I be a greater fool to sit still and suffer it; which I will not do. I do not like the look of him; he looks over-gorgious. An ill day to the Romans when he masters Rommany; and when I says that, I pens a true dukkerin."

"What do you call God, Jasper?"

"You had better be jawing," said the woman, raising her voice to a terrible scream; "you had better be moving off, my Gorgio; hang you for a keen one, sitting there by the fire, and stealing my language before my face. Do you know whom you have to deal with? Do you know that I am dangerous? My name is Herne, and I comes of the hairy ones!"

And a hairy one she looked! She wore her hair clubbed upon her head, fastened with many strings and ligatures; but now, tearing these off, her locks, originally jet black, but now partially grizzled with age, fell down on every side of her, covering her face and back as far down as her knees. No she-bear of Lapland ever looked more fierce and hairy than did that woman, as, standing in the open part of the tent, with her head bent down, and her shoulders drawn up, seemingly about to precipitate herself upon me, she repeated, again and again,—

"My name is Herne, and I comes of the hairy ones!——"

"I call God Duvel, brother."

"It sounds very like Devil."

"It doth, brother, it doth."

"And what do you call divine, I mean godly?"

"Oh! I call that duvelskoe."

"I am thinking of something, Jasper."

"What are you thinking of, brother?"

"Would it not be a rum thing if divine and devilish were originally one and the same word?"

"It would, brother, it would——"

* * * * *

From this time I had frequent interviews with Jasper, sometimes in his tent, sometimes on the heath, about which we would roam for hours, discoursing on various matters. Sometimes mounted on one of his horses, of which he had several, I would accompany him to various fairs and markets in the neighbourhood, to which he went on his own affairs, or those of his tribe. I soon found that I had become acquainted with a most singular people, whose habits and pursuits awakened within me the highest interest. Of all connected with them, however, their language was doubtless that which exercised the greatest influence over my imagination. I had at first some suspicion that it would prove a mere made-up gibberish. But I was soon undeceived. Broken, corrupted, and half in ruins as it was, it was not long before I found that it was an original speech, far more so, indeed, than one or two others of high name and celebrity, which, up to that time, I had been in the habit of regarding with respect and veneration. Indeed, many obscure points connected with the vocabulary of these languages, and to which neither classic nor modern lore afforded any clue, I thought I could now clear up by means of this strange broken tongue, spoken by people who dwelt among thickets and furze bushes, in tents as tawny as their faces, and whom the generality of mankind designated, and with much semblance of justice, as thieves and vagabonds. But where did this speech come from, and who were they who spoke it? These were questions which I could not solve, and which Jasper himself, when pressed, confessed his inability to answer. "But, whoever we be, brother," said he, "we are an old people, and not what folks in general imagine, broken Gorgios; and, if we are not Egyptians, we are at any rate Rommany chals!"

"Rommany chals! I should not wonder after all," said I, "that these people had something to do with the founding of Rome. Rome, it is said, was built by vagabonds; who knows but that some tribe of the kind settled down thereabouts, and called the town which they built after their name; but whence did they come originally? ah! there is the difficulty."

But abandoning these questions, which at that time were far too profound for me, I went on studying the language, and at the same time the characters and manners of these strange people. My rapid progress in the former astonished, while it delighted, Jasper. "We'll no longer call you Sap-engro, brother," said he; "but rather Lav-engro, which in the language of the Gorgios meaneth Word Master." "Nay, brother," said Tawno Chikno, with whom I had become very intimate, "you had better call him Cooro-mengro, I have put on *the gloves* with him, and find him a pure fist master; I like him for that, for I am a Cooro-mengro myself, and was born at Brummagem."

"I likes him for his modesty," said Mrs. Chikno; "I never hears any ill words come from his mouth, but, on the contrary, much sweet language. His talk is golden, and he has taught my eldest to say his prayers in Rommany, which my rover had never the grace to do." "He is the pal of my rom," said Mrs. Petulengro, who was a very handsome woman, "and therefore I likes him, and not less for his being a rye; folks calls me high-minded, and perhaps I have reason to be so; before I married Pharaoh I had an offer from a lord—I likes the young rye, and, if he chooses to follow us, he shall have my sister. What say you, mother? should not the young rye have my sister Ursula?"

"I am going to my people," said Mrs. Herne, placing a bundle upon a donkey, which was her own peculiar property; "I am going to Yorkshire, for I can stand this no longer. You say you like him; in that we differs: I hates the Gorgio, and would like, speaking Romanly, to mix a little poison with his waters. And now go to Lundra, my children, I goes to Yorkshire. Take my blessing with ye, and a little bit of a gillie to cheer your hearts with when ye are weary. In all kinds of weather have we lived together; but now we are parted, I goes broken-hearted. I can't keep you company; ye are no longer Rommany. To gain a bad brother, ye have lost a good mother."

CHAPTER VI

So the gypsies departed; Mrs. Herne to Yorkshire, and the rest to London. As for myself, I continued in the house of my parents, passing my time in much the same manner as I have already described, principally in philological pursuits. But I was now sixteen, and it was highly necessary that I should adopt some profession, unless I intended to fritter away my existence, and to be a useless burden to those who had given me birth. But what profession was I to choose? there being none in the wide world perhaps for which I was suited; nor was there any one for which I felt any decided inclination, though perhaps there existed within me a lurking penchant for the profession of arms, which was natural enough, as, from my earliest infancy, I had been accustomed to military sights and sounds; but this profession was then closed, as I have already hinted, and, as I believe, it has since continued, to those who, like myself, had no better claims to urge than the services of a father.

My father, who, for certain reasons of his own, had no very high opinion of the advantages resulting from his career, would have gladly seen me enter the Church. His desire was, however, considerably abated by one or two passages of my life, which occurred to his recollection. He particularly dwelt on the unheard-of manner in which I had picked up the Irish language, and drew from thence the conclusion that I was not fitted by nature to cut a respectable figure at an English university. "He will fly off in a tangent," said he, "and, when called upon to exhibit his skill in Greek, will be found proficient in Irish; I have observed the poor lad attentively, and really do not know what to make of him; but I am afraid he will never make a churchman!" And I have no doubt that my excellent father was right, both in his premises and the conclusion at which he arrived. I had undoubtedly, at one period of my life, forsaken Greek for Irish, and the instructions of a learned Protestant divine for those of a Papist gasoon, the card-fancying Murtagh; and of late though I kept it a strict secret, I had abandoned in a great measure the study of the beautiful Italian, and the recitation of the sonorous terzets of the Divine Comedy, in which at one time I took the greatest delight, in order to become acquainted with the broken speech, and yet more broken songs, of certain houseless wanderers whom I had met at a horse fair. Such an erratic course was certainly by no means in consonance with the sober and unvarying routine of college study. And my father, who was a man of excellent common sense, displayed it, in not pressing me to adopt a profession which required qualities of mind which he saw I did not possess.

"My father has given me a hundred and fifty pounds," said my brother to me one morning, "and something which is better—his blessing. I am going to leave you."

"Where are you going?"

"Where? to the great city; to London, to be sure."

"I should like to go with you."

"Pooh," said my brother, "what should you do there? But don't be discouraged, I dare say a time will come when you too will go to London."

And, sure enough, so it did, and all but too soon.

There was one question which I was continually asking myself at this period, and which has more than once met the eyes of the reader who has followed me through the last chapter. "What is truth?" I had involved myself imperceptibly in a dreary labyrinth of doubt, and, whichever way I turned, no reasonable prospect of extricating myself appeared. The means by which I had brought myself into this situation may be very briefly told; I had inquired into many matters, in order that I might become wise, and I had read and pondered over the words of the wise, so called, till I had made myself master of the sum of human wisdom; namely, that everything is enigmatical and that man is an enigma to himself; thence the cry of "What is truth?" I had ceased to believe in the truth of that in which I had hitherto trusted, and yet could find nothing in which I could put any fixed or deliberate belief. I was, indeed, in a labyrinth! In what did I not doubt? With respect to crime and virtue I was in doubt; I doubted that the one was blameable and the other praiseworthy. Are not all things subjected to the law of necessity? Assuredly; time and chance govern all things: yet how can this be? alas!

Then there was myself; for what was I born? Are not all things born to be forgotten? That's incomprehensible: yet is it not so? Those butterflies fall and are forgotten. In what is man better than a butterfly? All then is born to be forgotten. Ah! that was a pang indeed; 'tis at such a moment that a man wishes to die. The wise king of Jerusalem, who sat in his shady arbours beside his sunny fishpools, saying so many fine things, wished to die, when he saw that not only all was vanity, but that he himself was vanity. Will a time come when all will be forgotten that now is beneath the sun? If so, of what profit is life?

In truth, it was a sore vexation of spirit to me when I saw, as the wise man saw of old. that whatever I could hope to perform must necessarily be of very temporary duration; and if so, why do it? I said to myself, whatever name I can acquire, will it endure for eternity? scarcely so. A thousand years? Let me see! What have I done already? I have learnt Welsh, and have translated the songs of Ab Gwilym, some ten thousand lines, into English rhyme; I have also learnt Danish, and have rendered the old book of ballads cast by the tempest upon the beach into corresponding English metre. Good! have I done enough already to secure myself a reputation of a thousand years? No, no! certainly not; I have not the slightest ground for hoping that my translations from the Welsh and Danish will be read at the end of a thousand years. Well, but I am only eighteen, and I have not stated all that I have done; I have learnt many other tongues, and have acquired some knowledge even of Hebrew and Arabic. Should I go on in this way till I am forty, I must then be very learned; and perhaps, among other things, may have translated the Talmud, and some of the great works of the Arabians. Pooh! all this is mere learning and translation, and such will never secure immortality. Translation is at best an echo, and it must be a wonderful echo to be heard after the lapse of a thousand years. No! all I have already done, and all I may yet do in the same way, I may reckon as nothing—mere pastime; something else must be done. I must either write some grand original work, or conquer an empire; the one just as easy as the other. But am I competent to do either? Yes, I think I am, under favourable circumstances. Yes, I think I may promise myself a reputation of a thousand years, if I do but give myself the necessary trouble. Well! but what's a thousand years after all, or twice a thousand years? Woe is me! I may just as well sit still.

"Would I had never been born!" I said to myself; and a thought would occasionally intrude. But was I ever born? Is not all that I see a lie—a deceitful phantom? Is there a world, and earth, and sky? Berkeley's doctrine—Spinoza's doctrine! Dear reader, I had at that time never read either Berkeley or Spinoza. I have still never read them; who are they, men of yesterday? "All is a lie—all a deceitful phantom," are old cries; they come naturally from the mouths of those, who, casting aside that choicest shield against madness, simplicity, would fain be wise as God, and can only know that they are naked. This doubting in the "universal all" is almost coeval with the human race: wisdom, so called, was early sought after. All is a lie—a deceitful phantom—was said when the world was yet young; its surface, save a scanty portion, yet untrodden by human foot, and when the great tortoise yet crawled about. All is a lie, was the doctrine of Buddh; and Buddh lived thirty centuries before the wise king of Jerusalem, who sat in his arbours, beside his sunny fishpools, saying many fine things, and, amongst others, "There is nothing new under the sun!"

* * * * *

One day, whilst I bent my way to the heath of which I have spoken on a former occasion, at the foot of the hills which formed it I came to a place where a wagon was standing, but without horses, the shafts resting on the ground; there was a crowd about it, which extended half-way up the side of the neighbouring hill. The wagon was occupied by some half a dozen men; some sitting, others standing. They were dressed in sober-coloured habiliments of black or brown, cut in plain and rather uncouth fashion, and partially white with dust; their hair was short, and seemed to have been smoothed down by the application of the hand; all were bare-headed—sitting or standing, all were bare-headed. One of them, a tall man, was speaking, as I arrived; ere, however, I could distinguish what he was saying, he left off, and then there was a cry for a hymn "to the glory of God"—that was the word. It was a strange-sounding hymn, as well it might be, for everybody joined in it: there were voices of all kinds, of men, of women, and of children—of those who could sing and of those who could not—a thousand voices all joined, and all joined heartily; no voice of all the multitude was silent save mine. The crowd consisted entirely of the lower classes, labourers, and mechanics, and their wives and children—dusty people, unwashed people, people of no account whatever, and yet they did not look a mob. And when that hymn was over—and here let me observe that, strange as it sounded, I have recalled that hymn to mind, and it has seemed to tingle in my ears on occasions when all that pomp and art could do to enhance religious solemnity was being done—in the Sistine Chapel, what time the papal band was in full play, and the choicest choristers of Italy poured forth their melodious tones in presence of Batuschca and his cardinals—on the ice of the Neva, what time the long train of stately priests, with their noble beards and their flowing robes of crimson and gold, with their ebony and ivory staves, stalked along, chanting their Sclavonian litanies in advance of the mighty Emperor of the North and his Priberjensky guard of giants, towards the orifice through which the river, running below in its swiftness, is to receive the baptismal lymph—when the hymn was over, another man in the wagon proceeded to address the people; he was a much younger man than the last speaker; somewhat square built and about the middle height; his face was rather broad, but expressive of much intelligence, and with a peculiar calm and serious look; the accent in which he spoke indicated that he was not of these parts, but from some distant district. The subject of his address was faith, and how it could remove mountains. It was a plain address, without any attempt at ornament, and delivered in a tone which was neither loud nor vehement. The speaker was evidently not a practised one—once or twice he hesitated as if for words to express his meaning, but still he held on, talking of faith, and how it could remove mountains: "It is the only thing we want, brethren, in this world; if we have that, we are indeed rich, as it will enable us to do our duty under all circumstances, and to bear our lot, however hard it may be—and the lot of all mankind is hard—the lot of the poor is hard, brethren—and who knows more of the poor than I?—a poor man myself, and the son of a poor man: but are the rich better off? not so, brethren, for God is just. The rich have their trials too: I am not rich myself, but I have seen the rich with careworn countenances; I have also seen them in mad-houses; from which you may learn, brethren, that the lot of all mankind is hard; that is, till we lay hold of faith, which makes us comfortable under all circumstances; whether we ride in gilded chariots or walk barefooted in quest of bread; whether we be ignorant, whether we be wise—for riches and poverty, ignorance and wisdom, brethren, each brings with it its peculiar temptations. Well, under all these troubles, the thing which I would recommend you to seek is one and the same—faith; faith in our Lord Jesus Christ, who made us and allotted to each his station. Each has something to do, brethren. Do it, therefore, but always in faith; without faith we shall find ourselves sometimes at fault; but with faith never—for faith can remove the difficulty. It will teach us to love life, brethren, when life is becoming bitter, and to prize the blessings around us; for as every man has his cares, brethren, so has each man his blessings. It will likewise teach us not to love life over much, seeing that we must one day part with it. It will teach us to face death with resignation, and will preserve us from sinking amidst the swelling of the river Jordan."

And when he had concluded his address, he said: "Let us sing a hymn, one composed by Master Charles Wesley—he was my countryman, brethren.

'Jesus, I cast my soul on Thee,
Mighty and merciful to save;
Thou shalt to death go down with me
And lay me gently in the grave.

This body then shall rest in hope,
This body which the worms destroy;
For Thou shalt surely raise me up,
To glorious life and endless joy.'"

Farewell, preacher with the plain coat, and the calm, serious look! I saw thee once again, and that was lately—only the other day. It was near a fishing hamlet, by the sea-side, that I saw the preacher again. He stood on the top of a steep monticle, used by pilots as a look-out for vessels approaching that coast, a dangerous one, abounding in rocks and quicksands. There he stood on the monticle, preaching to weather-worn fishermen and mariners gathered below upon the sand. "Who is he?" said I to an old fisherman, who stood beside me with a book of hymns in his hand; but the old man put his hand to his lips, and that was the only answer I received. Not a sound was heard but the voice of the preacher and the roaring of the waves; but the voice was heard loud above the roaring of the sea, for the preacher now spoke with power, and his voice was not that of one who hesitates. There he stood—no longer a young man, for his black locks were become grey, even like my own; but there was the intelligent face, and the calm, serious look which had struck me of yore. There stood the preacher, one of those men—and, thank God, their number is not few—who, animated by the spirit of Christ, amidst much poverty, and, alas! much contempt, persist in carrying the light of the Gospel amidst the dark parishes of what, but for their instrumentality, would scarcely be Christian England. I would have waited till he had concluded, in order that I might speak to him and endeavour to bring back the ancient scene to his recollection, but suddenly a man came hurrying towards the monticle, mounted on a speedy horse, and holding by the bridle one yet more speedy, and he whispered to me: "Why loiterest thou here?—knowest thou not all that is to be done before midnight?" and he flung me the bridle; and I mounted on the horse of great speed, and I followed the other, who had already galloped off. And as I departed, I waved my hand to him on the monticle, and I shouted, "Farewell, brother! the seed came up at last, after a long period!" and then I gave the speedy horse his way, and leaning over the shoulder of the galloping horse, I said: "Would that my life had been like his—even like that man's!"

I now wandered along the heath, till I came to a place where, beside a thick furze, sat a man, his eyes fixed intently on the red ball of the setting sun.

"That's not you, Jasper?"

"Indeed, brother!"

"I've not seen you for years."
"How should you, brother?"
"What brings you here?"
"The fight, brother."
"Where are the tents?"
"On the old spot, brother."
"Any news since we parted?"
"Two deaths, brother."
"Who are dead, Jasper?"
"Father and mother, brother."
"Where did they die?"
"Where they were sent, brother."
"And Mrs. Herne?"
"She's alive, brother."
"Where is she now?"
"In Yorkshire, brother."
"What is your opinion of death, Mr. Petulengro?" said I, as I sat down beside him.

"My opinion of death, brother, is much the same as that in the old song of Pharaoh, which I have heard my grandam sing:—

> 'Cana marel o manus chivios andé puv,
> Ta rovel pa leste o chavo ta romi.'

When a man dies, he is cast into the earth, and his wife and child sorrow over him. If he has neither wife nor child, then his father and mother, I suppose; and if he is quite alone in the world, why, then, he is cast into the earth, and there is an end of the matter."

"And do you think that is the end of a man?"
"There's an end of him, brother, more's the pity."
"Why do you say so?"
"Life is sweet, brother."
"Do you think so?"
"Think so! There's night and day, brother, both sweet things; sun, moon and stars, brother, all sweet things; there's likewise the wind on the heath. Life is very sweet, brother; who would wish to die?"

"I would wish to die——"

"You talk like a Gorgio—which is the same as talking like a fool—were you a Rommany Chal you would talk wiser. Wish to die, indeed! A Rommany Chal would wish to live for ever!"

"In sickness, Jasper?"
"There's the sun and stars, brother."
"In blindness, Jasper?"
"There's the wind on the heath, brother; if I could only feel that, I would gladly live for ever. Dosta, we'll now go to the tents and put on the gloves; and I'll try to make you feel what a sweet thing it is to be alive, brother!"

CHAPTER VII

"One-and-ninepence, sir, or the things which you have brought with you will be taken away from you!"

Such were the first words which greeted my ears, one damp, misty morning in March, as I dismounted from the top of a coach in the yard of a London inn.

I turned round, for I felt that the words were addressed to myself. Plenty of people were in the yard—porters, passengers, coachmen, ostlers, and others, who appeared to be intent on anything but myself, with the exception of one individual whose business appeared to lie with me, and who now confronted me at the distance of about two yards.

I looked hard at the man—and a queer kind of individual he was to look at—a rakish figure, about thirty, and of the middle size, dressed in a coat smartly cut, but threadbare, very tight pantaloons of blue stuff, tied at the ankles, dirty white stockings, and thin shoes, like those of a dancing-master; his features were not ugly, but rather haggard, and he appeared to owe his complexion less to nature than carmine; in fact, in every respect, a very queer figure.

"One-and-ninepence, sir, or your things will be taken away from you!" he said, in a kind of lisping tone, coming yet nearer to me.

I still remained staring fixedly at him, but never a word answered. Our eyes met; whereupon he suddenly lost the easy impudent air which he before wore. He glanced, for a moment, at my fist, which I had by this time clenched, and his features became yet more haggard; he faltered; a fresh "one-and-ninepence" which he was about to utter, died on his lips; he shrank back, disappeared behind a coach, and I saw no more of him.

"One-and-ninepence, or my things will be taken away from me!" said I to myself, musingly, as I followed the porter to whom I had delivered my scanty baggage; "am I to expect many of these greetings in the big world? Well, never mind; I think I know the counter-sign!" And I clenched my fist yet harder than before.

So I followed the porter through the streets of London, to a lodging which had been prepared for me by an acquaintance. The morning, as I have before said, was gloomy, and the streets through which I passed were dank and filthy; the people, also, looked dank and filthy; and so, probably, did I, for the night had been rainy, and I had come upwards of a hundred miles on the top of a coach; my heart had sunk within me by the time we reached a dark narrow street in which was the lodging.

"Cheer up, young man," said the porter, "we shall have a fine afternoon!"

And presently I found myself in the lodging which had been prepared for me. It consisted of a small room, up two pair of stairs, in which I was to sit, and another still smaller above it, in which I was to sleep. I remember that I sat down, and looked disconsolate about me—everything seemed so cold and dingy. Yet how little is required to make a situation—however cheerless at first sight—cheerful and comfortable. The people of the house, who looked kindly upon me, lighted a fire in the dingy grate; and then, what a change!—the dingy room seemed dingy no more! Oh, the luxury of a cheerful fire after a chill night's journey! I drew near to the blazing grate, rubbed my hands and felt glad.

And, when I had warmed myself, I turned to the table, on which, by this time, the people of the house had placed my breakfast; and I ate and I drank; and, as I ate and drank, I mused within myself. and my eyes were frequently directed to a small green box, which constituted part of my luggage, and which, with the rest of my things, stood in one corner of the room, till at last, leaving my breakfast unfinished, I rose, and, going to the box, unlocked it, and took out two or three bundles of papers tied with red tape, and, placing them on the table, I resumed my seat and my breakfast, my eyes intently fixed upon the bundles of papers all the time.

And when I had drained the last cup of tea out of a dingy teapot, and ate the last slice of the dingy loaf, I untied one of the bundles, and proceeded to look over the papers, which were closely written over in a singular hand, and I read for some time, till at last I said to myself, "It will do." And then I looked at the other bundle for some time, without untying it; and at last I said, "It will do also." And then I turned to the fire, and, putting my feet against the sides of the grate, I leaned back on my chair, and, with my eyes upon the fire, fell into deep thought.

And there I continued in thought before the fire, until my eyes closed, and I fell asleep; which was not to be wondered at, after the fatigue and cold which I had lately undergone on the coach-top; and, in my sleep, I imagined myself still there, amidst darkness and rain, hurrying now over wild heaths, and now along roads overhung with thick and umbrageous trees, and sometimes methought I heard the horn of the guard, and sometimes the voice of the coachman, now chiding, now encouraging his horses, as they toiled through the deep and miry ways. At length a tremendous crack of a whip saluted the tympanum of my ear, and I started up broad awake, nearly oversetting the chair on which I reclined—and, lo! I was in the dingy room before the fire, which was by this time half-extinguished. In my dream I had confounded the noise of the street with those of my night journey; the crack which had aroused me I soon found proceeded from the whip of a carter, who, with many oaths, was flogging his team below the window.

Looking at a clock which stood upon the mantel-piece, I perceived that it was past eleven; whereupon I said to myself, "I am wasting my time foolishly and unprofitably, forgetting that I am now in the big world, without anything to depend upon save my own exertions"; and then I adjusted my dress, and, locking up the bundle of papers which I had not read, I tied up the other, and, taking it under my arm, I went down stairs; and, after asking a question or two of the people of the house, I sallied forth into the street with a determined look, though at heart I felt somewhat timorous at the idea of venturing out alone into the mazes of the mighty city, of which I had heard much, but of which, of my own knowledge, I knew nothing.

I had, however, no great cause for anxiety in the present instance; I easily found my way to the place which I was in quest of—one of the many new squares on the northern side of the metropolis, and which was scarcely ten minutes' walk from the street in which I had taken up my abode. Arriving before the door of a tolerably large house which bore a certain number, I stood still for a moment in a kind of trepidation, looking anxiously at the door; I then slowly passed on till I came to the end of the square, where I stood still and pondered for awhile. Suddenly, however, like one who has formed a resolution, I clenched my right hand, flinging my hat somewhat on one side, and, turning back with haste to the door before which I had stopped, I sprang up the steps, and gave a loud rap, ringing at the same time the bell of the area. After the lapse of a minute the door was opened by a maid-servant of no very cleanly or prepossessing appearance, of whom I demanded, in a tone of some *hauteur*, whether the master of the house was at home. Glancing for a moment at the white paper bundle beneath my arm, the handmaid made no reply in words, but, with a kind of toss of her head, flung the door open, standing on one side as if to let me enter. I did enter; and the handmaid, having opened another door on the right hand, went in, and said something which I could not hear; after a considerable pause, however, I heard the voice of a man say, "Let him come in"; whereupon the handmaid, coming out, motioned me to enter, and, on my obeying, instantly closed the door behind me.

There were two individuals in the room in which I now found myself; it was a small study, surrounded with bookcases, the window looking out upon the square. Of these individuals he who appeared to be the principal stood with his back to the fire-place. He was a tall, stout man, about sixty, dressed in a loose morning gown. The expression of his countenance would have been bluff but for a certain sinister glance, and his complexion might have been called rubicund but for a considerable tinge of bilious yellow. He eyed me askance as I entered. The other, a pale, shrivelled-looking person, sat at a table apparently engaged with an account-book; he took no manner of notice of me, never once lifting his eyes from the page before him.

"Well, sir, what is your pleasure?" said the big man, in a rough tone, as I stood there looking at him wistfully—as well I might—for upon that man, at the time of which I am speaking, my principal, I may say my only, hopes rested.

"Sir," said I, "my name is so-and-so, and I am the bearer of a letter to you from Mr. so-and-so, an old friend and correspondent of yours."

The countenance of the big man instantly lost the suspicious and lowering expression which it had hitherto exhibited; he strode forward and, seizing me by the hand, gave me a violent squeeze.

"My dear sir," said he, "I am rejoiced to see you in London. I have been long anxious for the pleasure—we are old friends, though we have never before met. Taggart," said he to the man who sat at the desk, "this is our excellent correspondent, the friend and pupil of our other excellent correspondent."

The pale, shrivelled-looking man slowly and deliberately raised his head from the account-book, and surveyed me for a moment or two; not the slightest emotion was observable in his countenance. It appeared to me, however, that I could detect a droll twinkle in his eye; his curiosity, if he had any, was soon gratified; he made me a kind of bow, pulled out a snuff-box, took a pinch of snuff, and again bent his head over the page.

"And now, my dear sir," said the big man, "pray sit down, and tell me the cause of your visit. I hope you intend to remain here a day or two."

"More than that," said I, "I am come to take up my abode in London."

"Glad to hear it; and what have you been about of late? got anything which will suit me? Sir, I admire your style of writing, and your manner of thinking; and I am much obliged to my good friend and correspondent for sending me some of your productions. I inserted them all, and wished there had been more of them—quite original, sir, quite; took with the public, especially the essay about the non-existence of anything. I don't exactly agree with you, though; I have my own peculiar ideas about matter—as you know, of course, from the book I have published. Nevertheless, a very pretty piece of speculative philosophy—no such thing as matter—impossible that there should be—*ex nihilo*—what is the Greek? I have forgot—very pretty indeed; very original."

"I am afraid, sir, it was very wrong to write such trash, and yet more to allow it to be published."

"Trash! not at all; a very pretty piece of speculative philosophy; of course you were wrong in saying there is no world. The world must exist, to have the shape of a pear; and that the world is shaped like a pear, and not like an apple, as the fools of Oxford say, I have satisfactorily proved in my book. Now, if there were no world, what would become of my system? But what do you propose to do in London?"

"Here is the letter, sir," said I, "of our good friend, which I have not yet given to you; I believe it will explain to you the circumstances under which I come."

He took the letter, and perused it with attention. "Hem!" said he, with a somewhat altered manner, "my friend tells me that you are come up to London with the view of turning your literary talents to account, and desires me to assist you in my capacity of publisher in bringing forth two or three works which you have prepared. My good friend is perhaps not aware that for some time past I have given up publishing—was obliged to do so—had many severe losses—do nothing at present in that line, save sending out the Magazine once a month; and, between ourselves, am thinking of disposing of that—wish to retire—high time at my age—so you see——"

"I am very sorry, sir, to hear that you cannot assist me," (and I remember that I felt very nervous); "I had hoped——"

"A losing trade, I assure you, sir; literature is a drug. Taggart, what o'clock is it?"

"Well, sir!" said I, rising, "as you cannot assist me, I will now take my leave; I thank you sincerely for your kind reception, and will trouble you no longer."

"Oh, don't go. I wish to have some further conversation with you; and perhaps I may hit upon some plan to benefit you. I honour merit, and always make a point to encourage it when I can; but—— Taggart, go to the bank, and tell them to dishonour the bill twelve months after date for thirty pounds which becomes due to-morrow. I am dissatisfied with that fellow who wrote the fairy tales, and intend to give him all the trouble in my power. Make haste."

Taggart did not appear to be in any particular haste. First of all, he took a pinch of snuff, then, rising from his chair, slowly and deliberately drew his wig, for he wore a wig of a brown colour, rather more over his forehead than it had previously been, buttoned his coat, and, taking his hat, and an umbrella which stood in a corner, made me a low bow, and quitted the room.

"Well, sir, where were we? Oh, I remember, we were talking about merit. Sir, I always wish to encourage merit, especially when it comes so highly recommended as in the present instance. Sir, my good friend and correspondent speaks of you in the highest terms. Sir, I honour my good friend, and have the highest respect for his opinion in all matters connected with literature—rather eccentric though. Sir, my good friend has done my periodical more good and more harm than all the rest of my correspondents. Sir, I shall never forget the sensation caused by the appearance of his article about a certain personage whom he proved—and I think satisfactorily—to have been a legionary soldier—rather startling, was it not? The S—— of the world a common soldier, in a marching regiment!—original, but startling; sir, I honour my good friend."

"So you have renounced publishing, sir," said I, "with the exception of the Magazine?"

"Why, yes; except now and then, under the rose; the old coachman, you know, likes to hear the whip. Indeed, at the present moment, I am thinking of starting a Review on an entirely new and original principle; and it just struck me that you might be of high utility in the undertaking—what do you think of the matter?"

"I should be happy, sir, to render you any assistance, but I am afraid the employment you propose requires other qualifications than I possess; however, I can make the essay. My chief intention in coming to London was to lay before the world what I had prepared; and I had hoped by your assistance——"

"Ah! I see, ambition! Ambition is a very pretty thing; but, sir, we must walk before we run, according to the old saying—what is that you have got under your arm?"

"One of the works to which I was alluding; the one, indeed, which I am most anxious to lay before the world, as I hope to derive from it both profit and reputation."

"Indeed! what do you call it?"

"Ancient songs of Denmark, heroic and romantic, translated by myself, with notes philological, critical and historical."

"Then, sir, I assure you that your time and labour have been entirely flung away; nobody would read your ballads, if you were to give them to the world to-morrow."

"I am sure, sir, that you would say otherwise if you would permit me to read one to you"; and, without waiting for the answer of the big man; nor indeed so much as looking at him, to see whether he was inclined or not to hear me, I undid my manuscript, and with a voice trembling with eagerness, I read to the following effect:—

"Buckshank bold and Elfinstone,
And more than I can mention here,
They caused to be built so stout a ship,
And unto Iceland they would steer.

They launched the ship upon the main,
Which bellowed like a wrathful bear;
Down to the bottom the vessel sank,
A laidly Trold has dragged it there.

Down to the bottom sank young Roland,
And round about he groped awhile;
Until he found the path which led
Unto the bower of Ellenlyle."

"Stop!" said the publisher; "very pretty, indeed, and very original; beats Scott hollow, and Percy too: but, sir, the day for these things is gone by; nobody at present cares for Percy, nor for Scott, either, save as a novelist; sorry to discourage merit, sir, but what can I do? What else have you got?"

"The songs of Ab Gwilym, the Welsh bard, also translated by myself, with notes critical, philological and historical."

"Pass on—what else?"

"Nothing else," said I, folding up my manuscript with a sigh, "unless it be a romance in the German style; on which, I confess, I set very little value."

"Wild?"

"Yes, sir, very wild."

"Like the Miller of the Black Valley?"

"Yes, sir, very much like the Miller of the Black Valley."

"Well, that's better," said the publisher; "and yet, I don't know, I question whether any one at present cares for the miller himself. No, sir, the time for those things is also gone by; German, at present, is a drug; and, between ourselves, nobody has contributed to make it so more than my good friend and correspondent; but, sir, I see you are a young gentleman of infinite merit, and I always wish to encourage merit. Don't you think you could write a series of evangelical tales?"

"Evangelical tales, sir?"

"Yes, sir, evangelical novels."

"Something in the style of Herder?"

"Herder is a drug, sir; nobody cares for Herder—thanks to my good friend. Sir, I have in yon drawer a hundred pages about Herder, which I dare not insert in my periodical; it would sink it, sir. No, sir, something in the style of the *Dairyman's Daughter*."

"I never heard of the work till the present moment."

"Then, sir, procure it by all means. Sir, I could afford as much as ten pounds for a well-written tale in the style of the *Dairyman's Daughter;* that is the kind of literature, sir, that sells at the present day! It is not the Miller of the Black Valley—no, sir, nor Herder either, that will suit the present taste; the evangelical body is becoming very strong, sir—the canting scoundrels——"

"But, sir, surely you would not pander to a scoundrelly taste?"

"Then, sir, I must give up business altogether. Sir, I have a great respect for the goddess Reason—an infinite respect, sir; indeed, in my time, I have made a great many sacrifices for her; but, sir, I cannot altogether ruin myself for the goddess Reason. Sir, I am a friend to Liberty, as is well known; but I must also be a friend to my own family. It is with the view of providing for a son of mine that I am about to start the Review of which I was speaking. He has taken it into his head to marry, sir, and I must do something for him, for he can do but little for himself. Well, sir, I am a friend to Liberty, as I said before, and likewise a friend to Reason; but I tell you frankly that the Review which I intend to get up under the rose, and present him with when it is established, will be conducted on Oxford principles."

"Orthodox principles, I suppose you mean, sir?"

"I do, sir; I am no linguist, but I believe the words are synonymous."

Much more conversation passed between us, and it was agreed that I should become a contributor to the Oxford Review. I stipulated, however, that, as I knew little of politics, and cared less, no other articles should be required from me than such as were connected with belles-lettres and philology; to this the big man readily assented. "Nothing will be required from you," said he, "but what you mention; and now and then, perhaps, a paper on metaphysics. You understand German, and perhaps it would be desirable that you should review Kant; and in a review of Kant, sir, you could introduce to advantage your peculiar notions about *ex nihilo*." He then reverted to the subject of the *Dairyman's Daughter*, which I promised to take into consideration. As I was going away, he invited me to dine with him on the ensuing Sunday.

"That's a strange man!" said I to myself, after I had left the house, "he is evidently very clever; but I cannot say that I like him much, with his Oxford Reviews and Dairyman's Daughters. But what can I do? I am almost without a friend in the world. I wish I could find some one who would publish my ballads, or my songs of Ab Gwilym. In spite of what the big man says, I am convinced that, once published, they would bring me much fame and profit. But how is this?—what a beautiful sun!—the porter was right in saying that the day would clear up—I will now go to my dingy lodging, lock up my manuscripts and then take a stroll about the big city."

CHAPTER VIII

So I set out on my walk to see the wonders of the big city, and, as chance would have it, I directed my course to the east. The day, as I have already said, had become very fine, so that I saw the great city to advantage, and the wonders thereof, and much I admired all I saw; and, amongst other things, the huge cathedral, standing so proudly on the most commanding ground in the big city; and I looked up to the mighty dome, surmounted by a golden cross, and I said within myself: "That dome must needs be the finest in the world"; and I gazed upon it till my eyes reeled, and my brain became dizzy, and I thought that the dome would fall and crush me; and I shrank within myself, and struck yet deeper into the heart of the big city.

"O Cheapside! Cheapside!" said I, as I advanced up that mighty thoroughfare, "truly thou art a wonderful place for hurry, noise and riches! Men talk of the bazaars of the East—I have never seen them, but I dare say that, compared with thee, they are poor places, silent places, abounding with empty boxes. O thou pride of London's east!—mighty mart of old renown!—for thou art not a place of yesterday: long before the Roses red and white battled in fair England, thou didst exist—a place of throng and bustle—a place of gold and silver, perfumes and fine linen. Centuries ago thou couldst extort the praises even of the fiercest foes of England. Fierce bards of Wales, sworn foes of England, sang thy praises centuries ago; and even the fiercest of them all, Red Julius himself, wild Glendower's bard, had a word of praise for London's 'Cheape,' for so the bards of Wales styled thee in their flowing odes. Then, if those who were not English, and hated England, and all connected therewith, had yet much to say in thy praise, when thou wast far inferior to what thou art now, why should true-born Englishmen, or those who call themselves so, turn up their noses at thee, and scoff thee at the present day, as I believe they do? But, let others do as they will, I, at least, who am not only an Englishman, but an East Englishman, will not turn up my nose at thee, but will praise and extol thee, calling thee mart of the world —a place of wonder and astonishment!—and, were it right and fitting to wish that anything should endure for ever, I would say prosperity to Cheapside, throughout all ages—may it be the world's resort for merchandise, world without end."

And when I had passed through the Cheape I entered another street, which led up a kind of ascent, and which proved to be the street of the Lombards, called so from the name of its founders; and I walked rapidly up the street of the Lombards, neither looking to the right nor left, for it had no interest for me, though I had a kind of consciousness that mighty things were being transacted behind its walls; but it wanted the throng, bustle and outward magnificence of the Cheape, and it had never been spoken of by "ruddy bards!" And, when I had got to the end of the street of the Lombards, I stood still for some time, deliberating within myself whether I should turn to the right or the left, or go straight forward, and at last I turned to the right, down a street of rapid descent, and presently found myself upon a bridge which traversed the river which runs by the big city.

A strange kind of bridge it was; huge and massive, and seemingly of great antiquity. It had an arched back, like that of a hog, a high balustrade, and at either side, at intervals, were stone bowers bulking over the river, but open on the other side, and furnished with a semicircular bench. Though the bridge was wide—very wide—it was all too narrow for the concourse upon it. Thousands of human beings were pouring over the bridge. But what chiefly struck my attention was a double row of carts and wagons, the generality drawn by horses as large as elephants, each row striving hard in a different direction, and not unfrequently brought to a standstill. Oh the cracking of whips, the shouts and oaths of the carters, and the grating of wheels upon the enormous stones that formed the pavement! In fact, there was a wild hurly-burly upon the bridge, which nearly deafened me. But, if upon the bridge there was a confusion, below it there was a confusion ten times confounded. The tide, which was fast ebbing, obstructed by the immense piers of the old bridge, poured beneath the arches with a fall of several feet, forming in the river below as many whirlpools as there were arches. Truly tremendous was the roar of the descending waters, and the bellow of the tremendous gulfs, which swallowed them for a time, and then cast them forth, foaming and frothing from their horrid wombs. Slowly advancing along the bridge, I came to the highest point, and there I stood still, close beside one of the stone bowers, in which, beside a fruitstall, sat an old woman, with a pan of charcoal at her feet, and a book in her hand, in which she appeared to be reading intently. There I stood, just above the principal arch, looking through the balustrade at the scene that presented itself—and such a scene! Towards the left bank of the river, a forest of masts, thick and close, as far as the eye could reach; spacious wharfs, surmounted with gigantic edifices; and, far away, Cæsar's Castle, with its White

Tower. To the right, another forest of masts, and a maze of buildings, from which, here and there, shot up to the sky chimneys taller than Cleopatra's Needle, vomiting forth huge wreaths of that black smoke which forms the canopy—occasionally a gorgeous one—of the more than Babel city. Stretching before me, the troubled breast of the mighty river, and, immediately below, the main whirlpool of the Thames—the Maëlstrom of the bulwarks of the middle arch—a grisly pool, which, with its superabundance of horror, fascinated me. Who knows but I should have leapt into its depths?—I have heard of such things—but for a rather startling occurrence which broke the spell. As I stood upon the bridge, gazing into the jaws of the pool, a small boat shot suddenly through the arch beneath my feet. There were three persons in it; an oarsman in the middle, whilst a man and a woman sat at the stern. I shall never forget the thrill of horror which went through me at this sudden apparition. What!—a boat—a small boat—passing beneath that arch into yonder roaring gulf! Yes, yes, down through that awful waterway, with more than the swiftness of an arrow, shot the boat, or skiff, right into the jaws of the pool. A monstrous breaker curls over the prow—there is no hope; the boat is swamped, and all drowned in that strangling vortex. No! the boat, which appeared to have the buoyancy of a feather, skipped over the threatening horror, and the next moment was out of danger, the boatman—a true boatman of Cockaigne that—elevating one of his sculls in sign of triumph, the man hallooing, and the woman, a true Englishwoman that—of a certain class—waving her shawl. Whether any one observed them save myself, or whether the feat was a common one, I know not; but nobody appeared to take any notice of them. As for myself, I was so excited, that I strove to clamber up the balustrade of the bridge, in order to obtain a better view of the daring adventurers. Before I could accomplish my design, however, I felt myself seized by the body, and, turning my head, perceived the old fruit-woman, who was clinging to me.

"Nay, dear! don't—don't!" said she. "Don't fling yourself over—perhaps you may have better luck next time!"

"I was not going to fling myself over," said I, dropping from the balustrade; "how came you to think of such a thing?"

"Why, seeing you clamber up so fiercely, I thought you might have had ill luck, and that you wished to make away with yourself."

"Ill luck," said I, going into the stone bower and sitting down. "What do you mean? ill luck in what?"

"Why, no great harm, dear! cly-faking, perhaps."

"Are you coming over me with dialects," said I, "speaking unto me in fashions I wot nothing of?"

"Nay, dear! don't look so strange with those eyes of your'n, nor talk so strangely; I don't understand you."

"Nor I you; what do you mean by cly-faking?"

"Lor, dear! no harm; only taking a handkerchief now and then."

"Do you take me for a thief?"

"Nay, dear! don't make use of bad language; we never calls them thieves here, but prigs and fakers: to tell you the truth, dear, seeing you spring at that railing put me in mind of my own dear son, who is now at Bot'ny: when he had bad luck, he always used to talk of flinging himself over the bridge; and, sure enough, when the traps were after him, he did fling himself into the river, but that was off the bank; nevertheless, the traps pulled him out, and he is now suffering his sentence; so you see you may speak out, if you have done anything in the harmless line, for I am my son's own mother, I assure you."

"So you think there's no harm in stealing?"

"No harm in the world, dear! Do you think my own child would have been transported for it, if there had been any harm in it? and what's more, would the blessed woman in the book here have written her life as she has done, and given it to the world, if there had been any harm in faking? She, too, was what they call a thief and a cut-purse; ay, and was transported for it, like my dear son; and do you think she would have told the world so, if there had been any harm in the thing? Oh, it is a comfort to me that the blessed woman was transported, and came back—for come back she did, and rich too—for it is an assurance to me that my dear son, who was transported too, will come back like her."

"What was her name?"

"Her name, blessed Mary Flanders."

"Will you let me look at the book?"

"Yes, dear, that I will, if you promise me not to run away with it."

I took the book from her hand; a short thick volume, at least a century old, bound with greasy black leather. I turned the yellow and dog's-eared pages, reading here and there a sentence. Yes, and no mistake! *His* pen, his style, his spirit might be observed in every line of the uncouth-looking old volume—the air, the style, the spirit of the writer of the book which first taught me to read. I covered my face with my hand, and thought of my childhood——

"This is a singular book," said I at last; "but it does not appear to have been written to prove that thieving is no harm, but rather to show the terrible consequences of crime: it contains a deep moral."

"A deep what, dear?"

"A—— but no matter, I will give you a crown for this volume."

"No, dear, I will not sell the volume for a crown."

"I am poor," said I; "but I will give you two silver crowns for your volume."

"No, dear, I will not sell my volume for two silver crowns; no, nor for the golden one in the King's tower down there; without my book I should mope and pine, and perhaps fling myself into the river; but I am glad you like it, which shows that I was right about you, after all; you are one of our party, and you have a flash about that eye of yours which puts me just in mind of my dear son. No, dear, I won't sell you my book; but, if you like, you may have a peep into it whenever you come this way. I shall be glad to see you; you are one of the right sort, for, if you had been a common one, you would have run away with the thing; but you scorn such behaviour, and, as you are so flash of your money, though you say you are poor, you may give me a tanner to buy a little baccy with; I love baccy, dear, more by token that it comes from the plantations to which the blessed woman was sent."

"What's a tanner?" said I.

"Lor! don't you know, dear? Why, a tanner is sixpence; and, as you were talking just now about crowns, it will be as well to tell you that those of our trade never calls them crowns, but bulls; but I am talking nonsense, just as if you did not know all that already, as well as myself; you are only shamming—I'm no trap, dear, nor more was the blessed woman in the book. Thank you, dear—thank you for the tanner; if I don't spend it, I'll keep it in remembrance of your sweet face. What, you are going?—well, first let me whisper a word to you. If you have any clies to sell at any time, I'll buy them of you; all safe with me; I never 'peach, and scorns a trap; so now, dear, God bless you! and give you good luck. Thank you for your pleasant company, and thank you for the tanner."

"Tanner!" said I musingly, as I left the bridge; "Tanner! what can the man who cures raw skins by means of a preparation of oak bark and other materials have to do with the name which these fakers, as they call themselves, bestow on the smallest silver coin in these dominions? Tanner! I can't trace the connection between the man of bark and the silver coin, unless journeymen tanners are in the habit of working for sixpence a day. But I have it," I continued, flourishing my hat over my head, "tanner, in this instance, is not an English word." Is it not surprising that the language of Mr. Petulengro and of Tawno Chikno, is continually coming to my assistance whenever I appear to be at a nonplus with respect to the derivation of crabbed words? I have made out crabbed words in Æschylus by means of the speech of Chikno and Petulengro, and even in my Biblical researches I have derived no slight assistance from it. It appears to be a kind of picklock, an open sesame, Tanner—Tawno! the one is but a modification of the other; they were originally identical, and have still much the same signification. Tanner, in the language of the apple-woman, meaneth the smallest of English silver coins; and Tawno, in the language of the Petulengros, though bestowed upon the biggest of the Romans, according to strict interpretation, signifieth a little child.

So I left the bridge, retracing my steps for a considerable way, as I thought I had seen enough in the direction in which I had hitherto been wandering; I should say that I scarcely walked less than thirty miles about the big city on the day of my first arrival. Night came on, but still I was walking about, my eyes wide open, and admiring everything that presented itself to them. Everything was new to me, for everything is different in London from what it is elsewhere—the people, their language, the horses, the *tout ensemble*—

even the stones of London are different from others—at least it appeared to me that I had never walked with the same ease and facility on the flag-stones of a country town as on those of London; so I continued roving about till night came on, and then the splendour of some of the shops particularly struck me. "A regular Arabian Nights' entertainment!" said I, as I looked into one on Cornhill, gorgeous with precious merchandise, and lighted up with lustres, the rays of which were reflected from a hundred mirrors.

But, notwithstanding the excellence of the London pavement, I began about nine o'clock to feel myself thoroughly tired; painfully and slowly did I drag my feet along. I also felt very much in want of some refreshment, and I remembered that since breakfast I had taken nothing. I was now in the Strand, and, glancing about, I perceived that I was close by an hotel, which bore over the door the somewhat remarkable name of Holy Lands. Without a moment's hesitation I entered a well-lighted passage, and, turning to the left, I found myself in a well-lighted coffee-room, with a well-dressed and frizzled waiter before me. "Bring me some claret," said I, for I was rather faint than hungry, and I felt ashamed to give a humbler order to so well-dressed an individual. The waiter looked at me for a moment; then, making a low bow, he bustled off, and I sat myself down in the box nearest to the window. Presently the waiter returned, bearing beneath his left arm a long bottle, and between the fingers of his right hand two large purple glasses; placing the latter on the table, he produced a cork-screw, drew the cork in a twinkling, set the bottle down before me with a bang, and then, standing still, appeared to watch my movements. You think I don't know how to drink a glass of claret, thought I to myself. I'll soon show you how we drink claret where I come from; and, filling one of the glasses to the brim, I flickered it for a moment between my eyes and the lustre, and then held it to my nose; having given that organ full time to test the bouquet of the wine, I applied the glass to my lips, taking a large mouthful of the wine, which I swallowed slowly and by degrees, that the palate might likewise have an opportunity of performing its functions. A second mouthful I disposed of more summarily; then, placing the empty glass upon the table, I fixed my eyes upon the bottle, and said—nothing; whereupon the waiter, who had been observing the whole process with considerable attention, made me a bow yet more low than before, and turning on his heel, retired with a smart chuck of his head, as much as to say, It is all right; the young man is used to claret.

And when the waiter had retired I took a second glass of the wine, which I found excellent; and, observing a newspaper lying near me, I took it up and began perusing it. It has been observed somewhere that people who are in the habit of reading newspapers every day are not unfrequently struck with the excellence of style and general talent which they display. Now, if that be the case, how must I have been surprised, who was reading a newspaper for the first time, and that one of the best of the London Journals! Yes, strange as it may seem, it was nevertheless true, that, up to the moment of which I am speaking, I had never read a newspaper of any description.

I of course had frequently seen journals, and even handled them; but, as for reading them, what were they to me?—I cared not for news. But here I was now with my claret before me, perusing, perhaps, the best of all the London Journals—it was not the——and I was astonished: an entirely new field of literature appeared to be opened to my view. It was a discovery, but I confess rather an unpleasant one; for I said to myself, if literary talent is so very common in London, that the journals, things which, as their very name denotes, are ephemeral, are written in a style like the article I have been perusing, how can I hope to distinguish myself in this big town, when, for the life of me, I don't think I could write anything half so clever as what I have been reading. And then I laid down the paper, and fell into deep musing; rousing myself from which, I took a glass of wine, and pouring out another, began musing again. What I have been reading, thought I, is certainly very clever and very talented; but talent and cleverness I think I have heard some one say are very commonplace things, only fitted for everyday occasions. I question whether the man who wrote the book I saw this day on the bridge was a clever man; but, after all, was he not something much better? I don't think he could have written this article, but then he wrote the book which I saw on the bridge. Then, if he could not have written the article on which I now hold my fore-finger—and I do not believe he could —why should I feel discouraged at the consciousness that I, too, could not write it? I certainly could no more have written the article than he could; but then, like him, though I would not compare myself to the man who wrote the book I saw upon the bridge, I think I could—and here I emptied the glass of claret—write something better.

Thereupon I resumed the newspaper; and, as I was before struck with the fluency of style and the general talent which it displayed, I was now equally so with its common-placeness and want of originality on every subject; and it was evident to me that, whatever advantage these newspaper-writers might have over me in some points, they had never studied the Welsh bards, translated Kæmpe Viser, or been under the pupilage of Mr. Petulengro and Tawno Chikno.

And as I sat conning the newspaper three individuals entered the room, and seated themselves in the box at the farther end of which I was. They were all three very well dressed; two of them elderly gentlemen, the third a young man about my own age, or perhaps a year or two older. They called for coffee; and, after two or three observations, the two eldest commenced a conversation in French, which, however, though they spoke it fluently enough, I perceived at once was not their native language; the young man, however, took no part in their conversation, and when they addressed a portion to him, which indeed was but rarely, merely replied by a monosyllable. I have never been a listener, and I paid but little heed to their discourse, nor indeed to themselves; as I occasionally looked up, however, I could perceive that the features of the young man, who chanced to be seated exactly opposite to me, wore an air of constraint and vexation. This circumstance caused me to observe him more particularly, than I otherwise should have done: his features were handsome and prepossessing; he had dark brown hair, and a high-arched forehead. After the lapse of half an hour, the two elder individuals, having finished their coffee, called for the waiter, and then rose as if to depart, the young man, however, still remaining seated in the box. The others, having reached the door, turned round, and, finding that the youth did not follow them, one of them called to him with a tone of some authority; whereupon the young man rose, and pronouncing half audibly the word "botheration," rose and followed them. I now observed that he was remarkably tall. All three left the house. In about ten minutes, finding nothing more worth reading in the newspaper, I laid it down, and though the claret was not yet exhausted, I was thinking of betaking myself to my lodgings, and was about to call the waiter, when I heard a step in the passage, and in another moment, the tall young man entered the room, advanced to the same box, and, sitting down nearly opposite to me, again pronounced to himself, but more audibly than before, the same word.

"A troublesome world this, sir," said I, looking at him.

"Yes," said the young man, looking fixedly at me; "but I am afraid we bring most of our troubles on our own heads—at least I can say so of myself," he added, laughing. Then, after a pause, "I beg pardon," he said, "but am I not addressing one of my own country?"

"Of what country are you?" said I.

"Ireland."

"I am not of your country, sir; but I have an infinite veneration for your country, as Strap said to the French soldier. Will you take a glass of wine?"

"*Ah, de tout mon cœur*, as the parasite said to Gil Blas," cried the young man, laughing. "Here's to our better acquaintance!"

And better acquainted we soon became; and I found that, in making the acquaintance of the young man, I had, indeed, made a valuable acquisition; he was accomplished, highly connected, and bore the name of Francis Ardry. Frank and ardent he was, and in a very little time had told me much that related to himself, and in return I communicated a general outline of my own history; he listened with profound attention, but laughed heartily when I told him some particulars of my visit in the morning to the publisher, whom he had frequently heard of.

We left the house together.

"We shall soon see each other again," said he, as we separated at the door of my lodging.

CHAPTER IX

On the Sunday I was punctual to my appointment to dine with the publisher. As I hurried along the square in which his house stood, my thoughts were fixed so intently on the great man that I passed by him without seeing him. He had observed me, however, and joined me just as I was about to knock at the door. "Let us take a turn in the square," said he, "we shall not dine for half an hour."

"Well," said he, as we were walking in the square, "what have you been doing since I last saw you?"

"I have been looking about London," said I, "and I have bought the *Dairyman's Daughter;* here it is."

"Pray put it up," said the publisher; "I don't want to look at such trash. Well, do you think you could write anything like it?"

"I do not," said I.

"How is that?" said the publisher, looking at me.

"Because," said I, "the man who wrote it seems to be perfectly well acquainted with his subject; and, moreover, to write from the heart."

"By the subject you mean——"

"Religion."

"And a'n't you acquainted with religion?"

"Very little."

"I am sorry for that," said the publisher seriously, "for he who sets up for an author ought to be acquainted not only with religion, but religions, and indeed with all subjects, like my good friend in the country. It is well that I have changed my mind about the *Dairyman's Daughter*, or I really don't know whom I could apply to on the subject at the present moment, unless to himself; and after all, I question whether his style is exactly suited for an evangelical novel."

"Then you do not wish for an imitation of the *Dairyman's Daughter?*"

"I do not, sir; I have changed my mind, as I told you before; I wish to employ you in another line, but will communicate to you my intentions after dinner."

At dinner, besides the publisher and myself, were present his wife and son, with his newly-married bride; the wife appeared a quiet, respectable woman, and the young people looked very happy and good-natured; not so the publisher, who occasionally eyed both with contempt and dislike. Connected with this dinner there was one thing remarkable; the publisher took no animal food, but contented himself with feeding voraciously on rice and vegetables, prepared in various ways.

"You eat no animal food, sir?" said I.

"I do not, sir," said he; "I have forsworn it upwards of twenty years. In one respect, sir, I am a Brahmin. I abhor taking away life—the brutes have as much right to live as ourselves."

"But," said I, "if the brutes were not killed, there would be such a superabundance of them, that the land would be overrun with them."

"I do not think so, sir; few are killed in India, and yet there is plenty of room."

"But," said I, "Nature intended that they should be destroyed, and the brutes themselves prey upon one another, and it is well for themselves and the world that they do so. What would be the state of things if every insect, bird and worm were left to perish of old age?"

"We will change the subject," said the publisher; "I have never been a friend to unprofitable discussions."

I looked at the publisher with some surprise, I had not been accustomed to be spoken to so magisterially; his countenance was dressed in a portentous frown, and his eye looked more sinister than ever; at that moment he put me in mind of some of those despots of whom I had read in the history of Morocco, whose word was law. He merely wants power, thought I to myself, to be a regular Muley Mehemet; and then I sighed, for I remembered how very much I was in the power of that man.

The dinner over, the publisher nodded to his wife, who departed, followed by her daughter-in-law. The son looked as if he would willingly have attended them; he, however, remained seated; and, a small decanter of wine being placed on the table, the publisher filled two glasses, one of which he handed to myself, and the other to his son, saying: "Suppose you two drink to the success of the Review. I would join you," said he, addressing himself to me, "but I drink no wine; if I am a Brahmin with respect to meat, I am a Mahometan with respect to wine."

So the son and I drank success to the Review, and then the young man asked me various questions; for example—how I liked London?—Whether I did not think it a very fine place?—Whether I was at the play the night before?—and whether I was in the park that afternoon? He seemed preparing to ask me some more questions; but, receiving a furious look from his father, he became silent, filled himself a glass of wine, drank it off, looked at the table for about a minute, then got up, pushed back his chair, made me a bow, and left the room.

"Is that young gentleman, sir," said I, "well versed in the principles of criticism?"

"He is not, sir," said the publisher; "and, if I place him at the head of the Review ostensibly, I do it merely in the hope of procuring him a maintenance; of the principle of a thing he knows nothing, except that the principle of bread is wheat, and that the principle of that wine is grape. Will you take another glass?"

I looked at the decanter; but not feeling altogether so sure as the publisher's son with respect to the principle of what it contained, I declined taking any more.

"No, sir," said the publisher, adjusting himself in his chair, "he knows nothing about criticism, and will have nothing more to do with the reviewals than carrying about the books to those who have to review them; the real conductor of the Review will be a widely different person, to whom I will, when convenient, introduce you. And now we will talk of the matter which we touched upon before dinner: I told you then that I had changed my mind with respect to you; I have been considering the state of the market, sir, the book market, and I have come to the conclusion that, though you might be profitably employed upon evangelical novels, you could earn more money for me, sir, and consequently for yourself, by a compilation of Newgate lives and trials."

"Newgate lives and trials!"

"Yes, sir," said the publisher, "Newgate lives and trials; and now, sir, I will briefly state to you the services which I expect you to perform, and the terms I am willing to grant. I expect you, sir, to compile six volumes of Newgate lives and trials, each volume to contain by no manner of means less than one thousand pages; the remuneration which you will receive when the work is completed will be fifty pounds, which is likewise intended to cover any expenses you may incur in procuring books, papers and manuscripts necessary for the compilation. Such will be one of your employments, sir, —such the terms. In the second place, you will be expected to make yourself useful in the Review—generally useful, sir—doing whatever is required of you; for it is not customary, at least with me, to permit writers, especially young writers, to choose their subjects. In these two departments, sir, namely, compilation and reviewing, I had yesterday, after due consideration, determined upon employing you. I had intended to employ you no further, sir—at least for the present; but, sir, this morning I received a letter from my valued friend in the country, in which he speaks in terms of strong admiration (I don't overstate) of your German acquirements. Sir, he says that it would be a thousand pities if your knowledge of the German language should be lost to the world, or even permitted to sleep, and he entreats me to think of some plan by which it may be turned to account. Sir, I am at all times willing, if possible, to oblige my worthy friend, and likewise to encourage merit and talent; I have, therefore, determined to employ you in German."

"Sir," said I, rubbing my hands, "you are very kind, and so is our mutual friend; I shall be happy to make myself useful in German; and if you think a good translation from Goethe—his 'Sorrows' for example, or more particularly his 'Faust'——"

"Sir," said the publisher, "Goethe is a drug; his 'Sorrows' are a drug, so is his 'Faustus,' more especially the last, since that fool——rendered him into English. No, sir, I do not want you to translate Goethe or anything belonging to him; nor do I want you to translate anything from the German; what I want you to do, is to translate into German. I am willing to encourage merit, sir; and, as my good friend in his last letter has spoken very highly of your German acquirements, I have determined that you shall translate my book of philosophy into German."

"Your book of philosophy into German, sir?"

"Yes, sir; my book of philosophy into German. I am not a drug, sir, in Germany, as Goethe is here, no more is my book. I intend to print the translation at Leipzig, sir; and if it turns out a profitable speculation, as I make no doubt it will, provided the translation be well executed, I will make you some remuneration. Sir, your remuneration will be determined by the success of your translation."

"But, sir——"

"Sir," said the publisher, interrupting me, "you have heard my intentions; I consider that you ought to feel yourself highly gratified by my intentions towards you; it is not frequently that I deal with a writer, especially a young writer, as I have done with you. And now, sir, permit me to inform you that I wish to be alone. This is Sunday afternoon, sir; I never go to church, but I am in the habit of spending part of every Sunday afternoon alone—profitably, I hope, sir—in musing on the magnificence of nature and the moral dignity of man."

Two or three days after our last interview, the publisher made his appearance in my apartment; he bore two tattered volumes under his arm, which he placed on the table. "I have brought you two volumes of lives, sir," said he, "which I yesterday found in my garret; you will find them of service for your compilation. As I always wish to behave liberally and encourage talent, especially youthful talent, I shall make no charge for them, though I should be justified in so doing, as you are aware that, by our agreement, you are to provide any books and materials which may be necessary. Have you been in quest of any?"

"No," said I, "not yet."

"Then, sir, I would advise you to lose no time in doing so; you must visit all the bookstalls, sir, especially those in the by-streets and blind alleys. It is in such places that you will find the description of literature you are in want of. You must be up and doing, sir; it will not do for an author, especially a young author, to be idle in this town. To-night you will receive my book of philosophy, and likewise books for the Review. And, by-the-bye, sir, it will be as well for you to review my book of philosophy for the Review, the other Reviews not having noticed it. Sir, before translating it, I wish you to review my book of philosophy for the Review."

"I shall be happy to do my best, sir."

"Very good, sir; I should be unreasonable to expect anything beyond a person's best. And now, sir, if you please, I will conduct you to the future editor of the Review. As you are to co-operate, sir, I deem it right to make you acquainted."

The intended editor was a little old man, who sat in a kind of wooden pavilion in a small garden behind a house in one of the purlieus of the city, composing tunes upon a piano. The walls of the pavilion were covered with fiddles of various sizes and appearances, and a considerable portion of the floor occupied by a pile of books all of one size. The publisher introduced him to me as a gentleman scarcely less eminent in literature than in music, and me to him as an aspirant critic—a young gentleman scarcely less eminent in philosophy than in philology. The conversation consisted entirely of compliments till just before we separated, when the future editor inquired of me whether I had ever read Quintilian; and, on my replying in the negative, expressed his surprise that any gentleman should aspire to become a critic who had never read Quintilian, with the comfortable information, however, that he could supply me with a Quintilian at half-price, that is, a translation made by himself some years previously, of which he had, pointing to the heap on the floor, still a few copies remaining unsold. For some reason or other, perhaps a poor one, I did not purchase the editor's translation of Quintilian.

"Sir," said the publisher, as we were returning from our visit to the editor, "you did right in not purchasing a drug. I am not prepared, sir, to say that Quintilian is a drug, never having seen him; but I am prepared to say that man's translation is a drug, judging from the heap of rubbish on the floor; besides, sir, you will want any loose money you may have to purchase the description of literature which is required for your compilation."

The publisher presently paused before the entrance of a very forlorn-looking street. "Sir," said he, after looking down it with attention, "I should not wonder if in that street you find works connected with the description of literature which is required for your compilation. It is in streets of this description, sir, and blind alleys, where such works are to be found. You had better search that street, sir, whilst I continue my way."

I searched the street to which the publisher had pointed, and, in the course of the three succeeding days, many others of a similar kind. I did not find the description of literature alluded to by the publisher to be a drug, but, on the contrary, both scarce and dear. I had expended much more than my loose money long before I could procure materials even for the first volume of my compilation.

CHAPTER X

One evening I was visited by the tall young gentleman, Francis Ardry, whose acquaintance I had formed at the coffee-house. As it is necessary that the reader should know something more about this young man, who will frequently appear in the course of these pages, I will state in a few words who and what he was. He was born of an ancient Roman Catholic family in Ireland; his parents, whose only child he was, had long been dead. His father, who had survived his mother several years, had been a spendthrift, and at his death had left the family property considerably embarrassed. Happily, however, the son and the estate fell into the hands of careful guardians, near relations of the family, by whom the property was managed to the best advantage, and every means taken to educate the young man in a manner suitable to his expectations. At the age of sixteen he was taken from a celebrated school in England at which he had been placed, and sent to a small French University, in order that he might form an intimate and accurate acquaintance with the grand language of the continent. There he continued three years, at the end of which he went, under the care of a French abbé, to Germany and Italy. It was in this latter country that he first began to cause his guardians serious uneasiness. He was in the hey-day of youth when he visited Italy, and he entered wildly into the various delights of that fascinating region, and, what was worse, falling into the hands of certain sharpers, not Italian, but English, he was fleeced of considerable sums of money. The abbé, who, it seems, was an excellent individual of the old French school, remonstrated with his pupil on his dissipation and extravagance; but, finding his remonstrances vain, very properly informed the guardians of the manner of life of his charge. They were not slow in commanding Francis Ardry home; and, as he was entirely in their power, he was forced to comply. He had been about three months in London when I met him in the coffee-room, and the two elderly gentlemen in his company were his guardians. At this time they were very solicitous that he should choose for himself a profession, offering to his choice either the army or law—he was calculated to shine in either of these professions—for, like many others of his countrymen, he was brave and eloquent; but he did not wish to shackle himself with a profession. As, however, his minority did not terminate till he was three-and-twenty, of which age he wanted nearly two years, during which he would be entirely dependent on his guardians, he deemed it expedient to conceal, to a certain degree, his sentiments, temporising with the old gentlemen, with whom, notwithstanding his many irregularities, he was a great favourite, and at whose death he expected to come into a yet greater property than that which he inherited from his parents.

Such is a brief account of Francis Ardry—of my friend Francis Ardry; for the acquaintance, commenced in the singular manner with which the reader is acquainted, speedily ripened into a friendship which endured through many long years of separation, and which still endures certainly on my part, and on his—if he lives; but it is many years since I have heard from Francis Ardry.

And yet many people would have thought it impossible for our friendship to have lasted a week, for in many respect no two people could be more dissimilar. He was an Irishman, I an Englishman; he fiery, enthusiastic and open-hearted, I neither fiery, enthusiastic nor open-hearted; he fond of pleasure and dissipation, I of study and reflection. Yet it is of such dissimilar elements that the most lasting friendships are formed: we do not like counterparts of ourselves. "Two great talkers will not travel far together," is a Spanish saying; I will add, "Nor two silent people"; we naturally love our opposites.

So Francis Ardry came to see me, and right glad I was to see him, for I had just flung my books and papers aside, and was wishing for a little social converse; and when we had conversed for some little time together, Francis Ardry proposed that we should go to the play to see Kean; so we went to the play, and saw—not Kean, who at that time was ashamed to show himself, but—a man who was not ashamed to show himself, and who people said was a much better man than Kean—as I have no doubt he was—though whether he was a better actor I cannot say, for I never saw Kean.

Two or three evenings after, Francis Ardry came to see me again, and again we went out together, and Francis Ardry took me to—shall I say?—why not?—a gaming house, where I saw people playing, and where I saw Francis Ardry play and lose five guineas, and where I lost nothing, because I did not play, though I felt somewhat inclined; for a man with a white hat and a sparkling eye held up a box which contained something which rattled, and asked me to fling the bones. "There is nothing like flinging the bones!" said he, and then I thought I should like to know what kind of thing flinging the bones was; I, however, restrained myself. "There is nothing like flinging the bones!" shouted the man, as my friend and myself left the room.

Long life and prosperity to Francis Ardry! but for him I should not have obtained knowledge which I did of the strange and eccentric places of London. Some of the places to which he took me were very strange places indeed! but, however strange the places were, I observed that the inhabitants thought there were no places like their several places, and no occupations like their several occupations; and among other strange places to which Francis Ardry conducted me, was a place not far from the abbey church of Westminster.

Before we entered this place our ears were greeted by a confused hubbub of human voices, squealing of rats, barking of dogs, and the cries of various other animals. Here we beheld a kind of cock-pit, around which a great many people, seeming of all ranks, but chiefly of the lower, were gathered. and in it we saw a dog destroy a great many rats in a very small period; and when the dog had destroyed the rats, we saw a fight between a dog and a bear, then a fight between two dogs, then——

After the diversions of the day were over, my friend introduced me to the genius of the place, a small man of about five feet high, with a very sharp countenance, and dressed in a brown jockey coat, and top boots. "Joey," said he, "this is a friend of mine." Joey nodded to me with a patronising air. "Glad to see you, sir!—want a dog?"

"No," said I.

"You have got one, then—want to match him?"

"We have a dog at home," said I, "in the country; but I can't say I should like to match him. Indeed, I do not like dog-fighting."

"Not like dog-fighting!" said the man, staring.

"The truth is, Joe, that he is just come to town."

"So I should think; he looks rather green—not like dog-fighting!"

"Nothing like it, is there, Joey?"

"I should think not; what is like it? A time will come, and that speedily, when folks will give up everything else, and follow dog-fighting."

"Do you think so?" said I.

"Think so? Let me ask what there is that a man wouldn't give up for it?"

"Why," said I, modestly, "there's religion."

"Religion! How you talk. Why, there's myself, bred and born an Independent, and intended to be a preacher, didn't I give up religion for dog-fighting? Religion, indeed! If it were not for the rascally law, my pit would fill better on Sundays than any other time. Who would go to church when they could come to my pit? Religion! why, the parsons themselves come to my pit; and I have now a letter in my pocket from one of them, asking me to send him a dog."

"Well, then, politics," said I.

"Politics! Why, the gemmen in the House would leave Pitt himself, if he were alive, to come to my pit. There were three of the best of them here to-night, all great horators. Get on with you, what comes next?"

"Why, there's learning and letters."

"Pretty things, truly, to keep people from dog-fighting! Why, there's the young gentlemen from the Abbey School comes here in shoals, leaving books, and letters, and masters too. To tell you the truth, I rather wish they would mind their letters, for a more precious set of young blackguards I never seed. It was only the other day I was thinking of calling in a constable for my own protection, for I thought my pit would have been torn down by them."

Scarcely knowing what to say, I made an observation at random. "You show by your own conduct," said I, "that there are other things worth following besides dog-fighting. You practise rat-catching and badger-baiting as well."

The dog-fancier eyed me with supreme contempt.

"Your friend here," said he, "might well call you a new one. When I talks of dog-fighting, I of course means rat-catching and badger-baiting, ay, and bull-baiting too, just as when I speaks religiously, when I says one I means not one but three. And talking of religion puts me in mind that I have something else to do besides chaffing here, having a batch of dogs to send off by this night's packet to the Pope of Rome."

But at last I had seen enough of what London had to show, whether strange or common-place, so at least I thought, and I ceased to accompany my friend in his rambles about town, and to partake of his adventures. Our friendship, however, still continued unabated, though I saw, in consequence, less of him. I reflected that time was passing on, that the little money I had brought to town was fast consuming, and that I had nothing to depend upon but my own exertions for a fresh supply; and I returned with redoubled application to my pursuits.

I compiled the *Chronicles of Newgate;* I reviewed books for the Review established on an entirely new principle; and I occasionally tried my best to translate into German portions of the publisher's philosophy. In this last task I experienced more than one difficulty. I was a tolerable German scholar, it is true, and I had long been able to translate from German into English with considerable facility; but to translate from a foreign language into your own, is a widely different thing from translating from your own into a foreign language; and, in my first attempt to render the publisher into German, I was conscious of making miserable failures, from pure ignorance of German grammar; however, by the assistance of grammars and dictionaries, and by extreme perseverance, I at length overcame all the difficulties connected with the German language. But alas! another difficulty remained, far greater than any connected with German—a difficulty connected with the language of the publisher—the language which the great man employed in his writings was very hard to understand; I say in his writings, for his colloquial English was plain enough. Though not professing to be a scholar, he was much addicted, when writing, to the use of Greek and Latin terms, not as other people used them, but in a manner of his own, which set the authority of dictionaries at defiance; the consequence was, that I was sometimes utterly at a loss to understand the meaning of the publisher. Many a quarter of an hour did I pass at this period staring at periods of the publisher, and wondering what he could mean, but in vain, till at last, with a shake of the head, I would snatch up the pen, and render the publisher literally into German. Sometimes I was almost tempted to substitute something of my own for what the publisher had written, but my conscience interposed; the awful words *Traduttore traditore* commenced ringing in my ears, and I asked myself whether I should be acting honourably towards the publisher, who had committed to me the delicate task of translating him into German; should I be acting honourably towards him, in making him speak in German in a manner different from that in which he expressed himself in English? No, I could not reconcile such conduct with any principle of honour; by substituting something of my own in lieu of these mysterious passages of the publisher, I might be giving a fatal blow to his whole system of philosophy. Besides, when translating into English, had I treated foreign authors in this manner? Had I treated the minstrels of the Kæmpe Viser in this manner? No. Had I treated Ab Gwilym in this manner? Even when translating his Ode to the Mist, in which he is misty enough, had I attempted to make Ab Gwilym less misty? No; on referring to my translation, I found that Ab Gwilym in my hands was quite as misty as in his own. Then, seeing that I had not ventured to take liberties with people who had never put themselves into my hands for the purpose of being rendered, how could I venture to substitute my own thoughts and ideas for the publisher's, who had put himself into my hands for that purpose? Forbid it every proper feeling!—so I told the Germans in the publisher's own way, the publisher's tale of an apple and a pear.

I at first felt much inclined to be of the publisher's opinion with respect to the theory of the pear. After all, why should the earth be shaped like an apple, and not like a pear?—it would certainly gain in appearance by being shaped like a pear. A pear being a handsomer fruit than an apple, the publisher is probably right, thought I, and I will say that he is right on this point in the notice which I am about to write of his publication for the

Review. And yet I don't know, said I, after a long fit of musing—I don't know but what there is more to be said for the Oxford theory. The world may be shaped like a pear, but I don't know that it is; but one thing I know, which is, that it does not taste like a pear; I have always liked pears, but I don't like the world. The world to me tastes much more like an apple, and I have never liked apples. I will uphold the Oxford theory; besides, I am writing in an Oxford Review, and am in duty bound to uphold the Oxford theory. So in my notice I asserted that the world was round; I quoted Scripture, and endeavoured to prove that the world was typified by the apple in Scripture, both as to shape and properties. "An apple is round," said I, "and the world is round; the apple is a sour, disagreeable fruit, and who has tasted much of the world without having his teeth set on edge?" I, however, treated the publisher, upon the whole, in the most urbane and Oxford-like manner; complimenting him upon his style, acknowledging the general soundness of his views, and only differing with him in the affair of the apple and pear.

I did not like reviewing at all—it was not to my taste; it was not in my way; I liked it far less than translating the publisher's philosophy, for that was something in the line of one whom a competent judge had surnamed "Lavengro." I never could understand why reviews were instituted; works of merit do not require to be reviewed, they can speak for themselves, and require no praising; works of no merit at all will die of themselves, they require no killing. The Review to which I was attached was, as has been already intimated, established on an entirely new plan; it professed to review all new publications, which certainly no Review had ever professed to do before, other Reviews never pretending to review more than one-tenth of the current literature of the day. When I say it professed to review all new publications, I should add, which should be sent to it; for, of course, the Review would not acknowledge the existence of publications, the authors of which did not acknowledge the existence of the Review. I don't think, however, that the Review had much cause to complain of being neglected; I have reason to believe that at least nine-tenths of the publications of the day were sent to the Review, and in due time reviewed. I had good opportunity of judging. I was connected with several departments of the Review, though more particularly with the poetical and philosophic ones. An English translation of Kant's philosophy made its appearance on my table the day before its publication. In my notice of this work, I said that the English shortly hoped to give the Germans a *quid pro quo*. I believe at that time authors were much in the habit of publishing at their own expense. All the poetry which I reviewed appeared to be published at the expense of the authors. If I am asked how I comported myself, under all circumstances, as a reviewer, I answer, I did not forget that I was connected with a Review established on Oxford principles, the editor of which had translated Quintilian. All the publications which fell under my notice I treated in a gentlemanly and Oxford-like manner, no personalities—no vituperation—no shabby insinuations; decorum, decorum was the order of the day. Occasionally a word of admonition, but gently expressed, as an Oxford under-graduate might have expressed it, or master of arts. How the authors whose publications were consigned to my colleagues were treated by them I know not; I suppose they were treated in an urbane and Oxford-like manner, but I cannot say; I did not read the reviewals of my colleagues, I did not read my own after they were printed. I did not like reviewing.

Of all my occupations at this period I am free to confess I liked that of compiling the *Newgate Lives and Trials* the best; that is, after I had surmounted a kind of prejudice which I originally entertained. The trials were entertaining enough; but the lives—how full were they of wild and racy adventures, and in what racy, genuine language were they told. What struck me most with respect to these lives was the art which the writers, whoever they were, possessed of telling a plain story. It is no easy thing to tell a story plainly and distinctly by mouth; but to tell one on paper is difficult indeed, so many snares lie in the way. People are afraid to put down what is common on paper, they seek to embellish their narratives, as they think, by philosophic speculations and reflections; they are anxious to shine, and people who are anxious to shine can never tell a plain story. "So I went with them to a music booth, where they made me almost drunk with gin, and began to talk their flash language, which I did not understand," says, or is made to say, Henry Simms, executed at Tyburn some seventy years before the time of which I am speaking. I have always looked upon this sentence as a masterpiece of the narrative style, it is so concise and yet so very clear. As I gazed on passages like this, and there were many nearly as good in the *Newgate Lives*, I often sighed that it was not my fortune to have to render these lives into German rather than the publisher's philosophy—his tale of an apple and pear.

Mine was an ill-regulated mind at this period. As I read over the lives of these robbers and pickpockets, strange doubts began to arise in my mind about virtue and crime. Years before, when quite a boy, as in one of the early chapters I have hinted, I had been a necessitarian; I had even written an essay on crime (I have it now before me, penned in a round, boyish hand), in which I attempted to prove that there is no such thing as crime or virtue, all our actions being the result of circumstances or necessity. These doubts were now again reviving in my mind; I could not for the life of me imagine how, taking all circumstances into consideration, these highwaymen, these pickpockets, should have been anything else than highwaymen and pickpockets; any more than how, taking all circumstances into consideration, Bishop Latimer (the reader is aware that I had read Fox's *Book of Martyrs*) should have been anything else than Bishop Latimer. I had a very ill-regulated mind at that period.

My own peculiar ideas with respect to everything being a lying dream began also to revive. Sometimes at midnight, after having toiled for hours at my occupations, I would fling myself back on my chair, look about the poor apartment, dimly lighted by an unsnuffed candle, or upon the heaps of books and papers before me, and exclaim: "Do I exist? Do these things, which I think I see about me, exist, or do they not? Is not everything a dream—a deceitful dream? Is not this apartment a dream—the furniture a dream? The publisher a dream—his philosophy a dream? Am I not myself a dream—dreaming about translating a dream? I can't see why all should not be a dream; what's the use of the reality?" And then I would pinch myself, and snuff the burdened smoky light. "I can't see, for the life of me, the use of all this; therefore, why should I think that it exists? If there was a chance, a probability of all this tending to anything, I might believe; but——" and then I would stare and think, and after some time shake my head and return again to my occupations for an hour or two; and then I would perhaps shake, and shiver, and yawn, and look wistfully in the direction of my sleeping apartment; and then, but not wistfully, at the papers and books before me; and sometimes I would return to my papers and books; but oftener I would arise, and, after another yawn and shiver, take my light, and proceed to my sleeping chamber.

They say that light fare begets light dreams; my fare at that time was light enough, but I had anything but light dreams, for at that period I had all kind of strange and extravagant dreams, and amongst other things I dreamt that the whole world had taken to dog-fighting; and that I, myself, had taken to dog-fighting, and that in a vast circus I backed an English bulldog against the bloodhound of the Pope of Rome.

CHAPTER XI

One day I found myself about noon at the bottom of Oxford Street, where it forms a right angle with the road which leads or did lead to Tottenham Court. Happening to cast my eyes around, it suddenly occurred to me that something uncommon was expected; people were standing in groups on the pavement—the upstair windows of the houses were thronged with faces, especially those of women, and many of the shops were partly, and not a few entirely closed. What could be the reason of all this? All at once I bethought me that this street of Oxford was no other than the far-famed Tyburn way. Oh, oh, thought I, an execution; some handsome young robber is about to be executed at the farther end; just so, see how earnestly the women are peering; perhaps another Harry Simms—Gentleman Harry as they called him—is about to be carted along this street to Tyburn tree; but then I remembered that Tyburn tree had long since been cut down, and that criminals, whether young or old, good-looking or ugly, were executed before the big stone gaol, which I had looked at with a kind of shudder during my short rambles in the city. What could be the matter? Just then I heard various voices cry "There it comes!" and all heads were turned up Oxford

Street, down which a hearse was slowly coming: nearer and nearer it drew; presently it was just opposite the place where I was standing, when, turning to the left, it proceeded slowly along Tottenham Road; immediately behind the hearse were three or four mourning coaches, full of people, some of which, from the partial glimpse which I caught of them, appeared to be foreigners; behind these came a very long train of splendid carriages, all of which, without one exception, were empty.

"Whose body is in that hearse?" said I to a dapper-looking individual seemingly a shopkeeper, who stood beside me on the pavement, looking at the procession.

"The mortal relics of Lord Byron," said the dapper-looking individual, mouthing his words and smirking, "the illustrious poet, which have been just brought from Greece, and are being conveyed to the family vault in ——shire."

"An illustrious poet, was he?" said I.

"Beyond all criticism," said the dapper man; "all we of the rising generation are under incalculable obligation to Byron; I myself in particular, have reason to say so; in all my correspondence my style is formed on the Byronic model."

I looked at the individual for a moment, who smiled and smirked to himself applause, and then I turned my eyes upon the hearse proceeding slowly up the almost endless street. This man, this Byron, had for many years past been the demigod of England, and his verses the daily food of those who read, from the peer to the draper's assistant; all were admirers, or rather worshippers, of Byron, and all doated on his verses; and then I thought of those who, with genius as high as his, or higher, had lived and died neglected. I thought of Milton abandoned to poverty and blindness; of witty and ingenious Butler consigned to the tender mercies of bailiffs; and starving Otway: they had lived neglected and despised, and, when they died, a few poor mourners only had followed them to the grave; but this Byron had been made a half-god of when living, and now that he was dead he was followed by worshipping crowds, and the very sun seemed to come out on purpose to grace his funeral. And, indeed, the sun, which for many days past had hidden its face in clouds, shone out that morn with wonderful brilliancy, flaming upon the black hearse and its tall ostrich plumes, the mourning coaches, and the long train of aristocratic carriages which followed behind.

"Great poet, sir," said the dapper-looking man, "great poet, but unhappy."

Unhappy? yes, I had heard that he had been unhappy; that he had roamed about a fevered, distempered man, taking pleasure in nothing—that I had heard; but was it true? was he really unhappy? was not this unhappiness assumed, with the view of increasing the interest which the world took in him? and yet who could say? He might be unhappy and with reason. Was he a real poet, after all? might he not doubt himself? might he not have a lurking consciousness that he was undeserving of the homage which he was receiving? that it could not last? that he was rather at the top of fashion than of fame? He was a lordling, a glittering, gorgeous lordling: and he might have had a consciousness that he owed much of his celebrity to being so; he might have felt that he was rather at the top of fashion than of fame. Fashion soon changes, thought I eagerly to myself; a time will come, and that speedily, when he will be no longer in the fashion; when this idiotic admirer of his, who is still grinning at my side, shall have ceased to mould his style on Byron's; and this aristocracy, squirearchy, and what not, who now send their empty carriages to pay respect to the fashionable corpse, shall have transferred their empty worship to some other animate or inanimate thing. Well, perhaps after all it was better to have been mighty Milton in his poverty and blindness—witty and ingenious Butler consigned to the tender mercies of bailiffs, and starving Otway; they might enjoy more real pleasure than this lordling; they must have been aware that the world would one day do them justice—fame after death is better than the top of fashion in life. They have left a fame behind them which shall never die, whilst this lordling—a time will come when he will be out of fashion and forgotten. And yet I don't know; didn't he write "Childe Harold" and that ode? Yes, he wrote "Childe Harold" and that ode. Then a time will scarcely come when he will be forgotten. Lords, squires and cockneys may pass away, but a time will scarcely come when "Childe Harold" and that ode will be forgotten. He was a poet, after all, and he must have known it; a real poet, equal to——to——what a destiny! rank, beauty, fashion, immortality—he could not be unhappy; what a difference in the fate of men—I wish I could think he was unhappy.

I turned away.

"Great poet, sir," said the dapper man, turning away too, "but unhappy —fate of genius, sir; I, too, am frequently unhappy."

Hurrying down the street to the right, I encountered Francis Ardry.

"What means the multitude yonder?" he demanded.

"They are looking after the hearse which is carrying the remains of Byron up Tottenham Road."

"I have seen the man," said my friend, as he turned back the way he had come, "so I can dispense with seeing the hearse—I saw the living man at Venice—ah, a great poet."

"Yes," said I, "a great poet, it must be so, everybody says so—what a destiny! What a difference in the fate of men; but 'tis said he was unhappy; you have seen him, how did he look?"

"Oh, beautiful!"

"But did he look happy?"

"Why, I can't say he looked very unhappy; I saw him with two——very fair ladies; but what is it to you whether the man was unhappy or not? Come, where shall we go—to Joey's? His hugest bear——"

"Oh, I have had enough of bears, I have just been worried by one."

"The publisher?"

"Yes."

"Then come to Joey's, three dogs are to be launched at his bear: as they pin him, imagine him to be the publisher."

"No," said I, "I am good for nothing; I think I shall stroll to London Bridge."

"That's too far for me—farewell!"

So I went to London Bridge, and again took my station on the spot by the booth where I had stood on the former occasion. The booth, however, was empty; neither the apple-woman nor her stall were to be seen. I looked over the balustrade upon the river; the tide was now, as before, rolling beneath the arch with frightful impetuosity. As I gazed upon the eddies of the whirlpool, I thought within myself how soon human life would become extinct there; a plunge, a convulsive flounder, and all would be over. When I last stood over that abyss I had felt a kind of impulse—a fascination: I had resisted it—I did not plunge into it. At present I felt a kind of impulse to plunge; but the impulse was of a different kind; it proceeded from a loathing of life. I looked wistfully at the eddies—what had I to live for?—what, indeed! I thought of Brandt and Struensee, and Yeoman Patch—should I yield to the impulse—why not? My eyes were fixed on the eddies. All of a sudden I shuddered; I thought I saw heads in the pool; human bodies wallowing confusedly; eyes turned up to heaven with hopeless horror; was that water, or—— Where was the impulse now? I raised my eyes from the pool, I looked no more upon it—I looked forward, far down the stream in the distance. "Ha! what is that? I thought I saw a kind of Fata Morgana, green meadows, waving groves, a rustic home; but in the far distance—I stared—I stared—a Fata Morgana—it was gone——"

I left the balustrade and walked to the farther end of the bridge, where I stood for some time contemplating the crowd; I then passed over to the other side with the intention of returning home; just half-way over the bridge, in a booth immediately opposite the one in which I had formerly beheld her, sat my friend, the old apple-woman, huddled up behind her stall.

"Well, mother," said I, "how are you?" The old woman lifted her head with a startled look.

"Don't you know me?" said I.

"Yes, I think I do. Ah, yes," said she, as her features beamed with recollection, "I know you, dear; you are the young lad that gave me the tanner. Well, child, got anything to sell?"

"Nothing at all," said I.

"Bad luck?"

"Yes," said I, "bad enough, and ill usage."

"Ah, I suppose they caught ye; well, child, never mind, better luck next time; I am glad to see you."

"Thank you," said I, sitting down on the stone bench; "I thought you had left the bridge—why have you changed your side?"

The old woman shook.

"What is the matter with you," said I, "are you ill?"

"No, child, no; only——"

"Only what? Any bad news of your son?"

"No, child, no; nothing about my son. Only low, child—every heart has its bitters."

"That's true," said I; "well, I don't want to know your sorrows; come, where's the book?"

The apple-woman shook more violently than before, bent herself down, and drew her cloak more closely about her than before. "Book, child, what book?"

"Why, blessed Mary, to be sure."

"Oh, that; I ha'n't got it, child—I have lost it, have left it at home."

"Lost it," said I; "left it at home—what do you mean? Come, let me have it."

"I ha'n't got it, child."

"I believe you have got it under your cloak."

"Don't tell any one, dear; don't—don't," and the apple-woman burst into tears.

"What's the matter with you?" said I, staring at her.

"You want to take my book from me?"

"Not I, I care nothing about it; keep it, if you like, only tell me what's the matter?"

"Why, all about that book."

"The book?"

"Yes, they wanted to take it from me."

"Who did?"

"Why, some wicked boys. I'll tell you all about it. Eight or ten days ago, I sat behind my stall, reading my book; all of a sudden I felt it snatched from my hand; up I started, and see three rascals of boys grinning at me; one of them held the book in his hand. 'What book is this?' said he, grinning at it. 'What do you want with my book?' said I, clutching at it over my stall, 'give me my book.' 'What do you want a book for?' said he, holding it back; 'I have a good mind to fling it into the Thames.' 'Give me my book,' I shrieked; and, snatching at it, I fell over my stall, and all my fruit was scattered about. Off ran the boys—off ran the rascal with my book. Oh dear, I thought I should have died; up I got, however, and ran after them as well as I could. I thought of my fruit; but I thought more of my book. I left my fruit and ran after my book. 'My book! my book!' I shrieked, 'murder! theft! robbery!' I was near being crushed under the wheels of a cart; but I didn't care—I followed the rascals. 'Stop them! stop them!' I ran nearly as fast as they—they couldn't run very fast on account of the crowd. At last some one stopped the rascal, whereupon he turned round, and flinging the book at me, it fell into the mud; well, I picked it up and kissed it, all muddy as it was. 'Has he robbed you?' said the man. 'Robbed me, indeed; why, he had got my book.' 'Oh, your book,' said the man, and laughed, and let the rascal go. Ah, he might laugh, but——"

"Well, go on."

"My heart beats so. Well, I went back to my booth and picked up my stall and my fruits, what I could find of them. I couldn't keep my stall for two days, I got such a fright, and when I got round I couldn't bide the booth where the thing had happened, so I came over to the other side. Oh, the rascals, if I could but see them hanged."

"For what?"

"Why for stealing my book."

"I thought you didn't dislike stealing, that you were ready to buy things—there was your son, you know——"

"Yes, to be sure."

"He took things."

"To be sure he did."

"But you don't like a thing of yours to be taken."

"No, that's quite a different thing; what's stealing handkerchiefs, and that kind of thing, to do with taking my book; there's a wide difference—don't you see?"

"Yes, I see."

"Do you, dear? well, bless your heart, I'm glad you do. Would you like to look at the book?"

"Well, I think I should."

"Honour bright?" said the apple-woman, looking me in the eyes.

"Honour bright," said I, looking the apple-woman in the eyes.

"Well then, dear, here it is," said she, taking it from under her cloak; "read it as long as you like, only get a little farther into the booth. Don't sit so near the edge—you might——"

I went deep into the booth, and the apple-woman, bringing her chair round, almost confronted me. I commenced reading the book, and was soon engrossed by it; hours passed away, once or twice I lifted up my eyes, the apple-woman was still confronting me: at last my eyes began to ache, whereupon I returned the book to the apple-woman, and giving her another tanner, walked away.

CHAPTER XII

Time passed away, and with it the Review, which, contrary to the publisher's expectation, did not prove a successful speculation. About four months after the period of its birth it expired, as all Reviews must for which there is no demand. My money was growing short, and I one day asked pay for my labours in the deceased publication.

"Sir," said the publisher, "what do you want the money for?"

"Merely to live on," I replied; "it is very difficult to live in this town without money."

"How much money did you bring with you to town?" demanded the publisher.

"Some twenty or thirty pounds," I replied.

"And you have spent it already?"

"No," said I, "not entirely; but it is fast disappearing."

"Sir," said the publisher, "I believe you to be extravagant; yes, sir, extravagant!"

"On what grounds do you suppose me to be so?"

"Sir," said the publisher, "you eat meat."

"Yes," said I, "I eat meat sometimes: what should I eat?"

"Bread, sir," said the publisher; "bread and cheese."

"So I do, sir, when I am disposed to indulge; but I cannot often afford it—it is very expensive to dine on bread and cheese, especially when one is fond of cheese, as I am. My last bread and cheese dinner cost me fourteen pence. There is drink, sir; with bread and cheese one must drink porter, sir."

"Then, sir, eat bread—bread alone. As good men as yourself have eaten bread alone; they have been glad to get it, sir. If with bread and cheese you must drink porter, sir, with bread alone you can, perhaps, drink water, sir."

However, I got paid at last for my writings in the Review, not, it is true, in the current coin of the realm, but in certain bills; there were two of them, one payable at twelve, and the other at eighteen months after date. It was a long time before I could turn these bills to any account; at last I found a person who, at a discount of only thirty per cent., consented to cash them; not, however, without sundry grimaces, and, what was still more galling, holding, more than once, the unfortunate papers high in air between his forefinger and thumb. So ill, indeed, did I like this last action, that I felt much inclined to snatch them away. I restrained myself, however, for I remembered that it was very difficult to live without money, and that, if the present person did not discount the bills, I should probably find no one else that would.

But if the treatment which I had experienced from the publisher, previous to making this demand upon him, was difficult to bear, that which I subsequently underwent was far more so; his great delight seemed to consist in causing me misery and mortification; if, on former occasions, he was continually sending me in quest of lives and trials difficult to find, he now was continually demanding lives and trials which it was impossible to find, the personages whom he mentioned never having lived, nor consequently been tried. Moreover, some of my best lives and trials which I had corrected and edited with particular care, and on which I prided myself no little, he caused to be cancelled after they had passed through the press. Amongst these was the life of "Gentleman Harry." "They are drugs, sir," said the publisher, "drugs; that life of Harry Simms has long been the greatest drug in the calendar—has it not, Taggart?"

Taggart made no answer save by taking a pinch of snuff. The reader has,

I hope, not forgotten Taggart, whom I mentioned whilst giving an account of my first morning's visit to the publisher. I beg Taggart's pardon for having been so long silent about him; but he was a very silent man—yet there was much in Taggart—and Taggart had always been civil and kind to me in his peculiar way.

"Well, young gentleman," said Taggart to me one morning, when we chanced to be alone a few days after the affair of the cancelling, "how do you like authorship?"

"I scarcely call authorship the drudgery I am engaged in," said I.

"What do you call authorship?" said Taggart.

"I scarcely know," said I; "that is, I can scarcely express what I think it."

"Shall I help you out?" said Taggart, turning round his chair, and looking at me.

"If you like," said I.

"To write something grand," said Taggart, taking snuff; "to be stared at —lifted on people's shoulders——"

"Well," said I, "that is something like it."

Taggart took snuff. "Well," said he, "why don't you write something grand?"

"I have," said I.

"What?" said Taggart.

"Why," said I, "there are those ballads."

Taggart took snuff.

"And those wonderful versions from Ab Gwilym."

Taggart took snuff again.

"You seem to be very fond of snuff," said I, looking at him angrily.

Taggart tapped his box.

"Have you taken it long?"

"Three-and-twenty years."

"What snuff do you take?"

"Universal mixture."

"And you find it of use?"

Taggart tapped his box.

"In what respect?" said I.

"In many—there is nothing like it to get a man through; but for snuff I should scarcely be where I am now."

"Have you been long here?"

"Three-and-twenty years."

"Dear me," said I; "and snuff brought you through? Give me a pinch—pah, I don't like it," and I sneezed.

"Take another pinch," said Taggart.

"No," said I, "I don't like snuff."

"Then you will never do for authorship—at least for this kind."

"So I begin to think—what shall I do?"

Taggart took snuff.

"You were talking of a great work—what shall it be?"

Taggart took snuff.

"Do you think I could write one?"

Taggart uplifted his two forefingers as if to tap; he did not, however.

"It would require time," said I, with half a sigh.

Taggart tapped his box.

"A great deal of time; I really think that my ballads——"

Taggart took snuff.

"If published would do me credit. I'll make an effort, and offer them to some other publisher."

Taggart took a double quantity of snuff.

By the month of October I had, in spite of all difficulties and obstacles, accomplished about two-thirds of the principal task which I had undertaken, the compiling of the Newgate lives; I had also made some progress in translating the publisher's philosophy into German. But about this time I began to see very clearly that it was impossible that our connection should prove of long duration; yet, in the event of my leaving the big man, what other resource had I? another publisher? But what had I to offer? There were my ballads, my Ab Gwilym; but then I thought of Taggart and his snuff, his pinch of snuff. However, I determined to see what could be done, so I took my ballads under my arm, and went to various publishers; some took snuff, others did not, but none took my ballads or Ab Gwilym, they would not even look at them. One asked me if I had anything else—he was a snuff-taker—I said yes; and going home returned with my translation of the German novel, to which I have before alluded. After keeping it for a fortnight, he returned it to me on my visiting him, and, taking a pinch of snuff, told me it would not do. There were marks of snuff on the outside of the manuscript, which was a roll of paper bound with red tape, but there were no marks of snuff on the interior of the manuscript, from which I concluded that he had never opened it.

I had often heard of one Glorious John, who lived at the western end of the town; on consulting Taggart, he told me that it was possible that Glorious John would publish my ballads and Ab Gwilym, that is, said he, taking a pinch of snuff, provided you can see him; so I went to the house where Glorious John resided, and a glorious house it was, but I could not see Glorious John. I called a dozen times, but I never could see Glorious John. Twenty years after, by the greatest chance in the world, I saw Glorious John, and sure enough Glorious John published my books, but they were different books from the first; I never offered my ballads or Ab Gwilym to Glorious John. Glorious John was no snuff-taker. He asked me to dinner, and treated me with superb Rhenish wine. Glorious John is now gone to his rest, but I—what was I going to say?—the world will never forget Glorious John.

So I returned to my last resource for the time then being—to the publisher, persevering doggedly in my labour. One day, on visiting the publisher, I found him stamping with fury upon certain fragments of paper.

"Sir," said he, "you know nothing of German; I have shown your translation of the first chapter of my Philosophy to several Germans: it is utterly unintelligible to them." "Did they see the Philosophy?" I replied. "They did, sir, but they did not profess to understand English." "No more do I," I replied, "if that Philosophy be English."

The publisher was furious—I was silent. For want of a pinch of snuff, I had recourse to something which is no bad substitute for a pinch of snuff to those who can't take it, silent contempt; at first it made the publisher more furious, as perhaps a pinch of snuff would; it, however, eventually calmed him, and he ordered me back to my occupations, in other words, the compilation. To be brief, the compilation was completed, I got paid in the usual manner, and forthwith left him.

He was a clever man, but what a difference in clever men!

CHAPTER XIII

It was past mid-winter, and I sat on London Bridge, in company with the old apple-woman: she had just returned to the other side of the bridge to her place in the booth where I had originally found her. This she had done after repeated conversations with me; "she liked the old place best," she said, which she would never have left but for the terror which she experienced when the boys ran away with her book. So I sat with her at the old spot, one afternoon past mid-winter, reading the book, of which I had by this time come to the last pages. I had observed that the old woman for some time past had shown much less anxiety about the book than she had been in the habit of doing. I was, however, not quite prepared for her offering to make me a present of it, which she did that afternoon; when, having finished it, I returned it to her, with many thanks for the pleasure and instruction I had derived from its perusal. "You may keep it, dear," said the old woman, with a sigh; "you may carry it to your lodging, and keep it for your own."

Looking at the old woman with surprise, I exclaimed: "Is it possible that you are willing to part with the book which has been your source of comfort so long?"

Whereupon the old woman entered into a long history, from which I gathered that the book had become distasteful to her; she hardly ever opened it of late, she said, or if she did, it was only to shut it again; also, that other things which she had been fond of, though of a widely different kind, were now distasteful to her. Porter and beef-steaks were no longer grateful to her palate, her present diet chiefly consisting of tea, and bread and butter.

"Ah," said I, "you have been ill, and when people are ill, they seldom like the things which give them pleasure when they are in health." I learned, moreover, that she slept little at night, and had all kinds of strange thoughts; that as she lay awake many things connected with her youth, which she had quite forgotten, came into her mind. There were certain words that came into her mind the night before the last, which were continually humming in her ears: I found that the words were, "Thou shalt not steal."

On inquiring where she had first heard these words, I learned that she had read them at school, in a book called the primer; to this school she had been sent by her mother, who was a poor widow, who followed the trade of apple-selling in the very spot where her daughter followed it now. It seems that the mother was a very good kind of woman, but quite ignorant of letters, the benefit of which she was willing to procure for her child; and at the school the daughter learned to read, and subsequently experienced the pleasure and benefit of letters, in being able to read the book which she found in an obscure closet of her mother's house, and which had been her principal companion and comfort for many years of her life.

But, as I have said before, she was now dissatisfied with the book, and with most other things in which she had taken pleasure; she dwelt much on the words, "Thou shalt not steal"; she had never stolen things herself, but then she had bought things which other people had stolen, and which she knew had been stolen; and her dear son had been a thief, which he perhaps would not have been but for the example which she set him in buying things from characters, as she called them, who associated with her.

On inquiring how she had become acquainted with these characters, I learned that times had gone hard with her; that she had married, but her husband had died after a long sickness, which had reduced them to great distress; that her fruit trade was not a profitable one, and that she had bought and sold things which had been stolen to support herself and her son. That for a long time she supposed there was no harm in doing so, as her book was full of entertaining tales of stealing; but she now thought that the book was a bad book, and that learning to read was a bad thing; her mother had never been able to read, but had died in peace, though poor.

So here was a woman who attributed the vices and follies of her life to being able to read; her mother, she said, who could not read, lived respectably, and died in peace; and what was the essential difference between the mother and daughter, save that the latter could read? But for her literature she might in all probability have lived respectably and honestly, like her mother, and might eventually have died in peace, which at present she could scarcely hope to do. Education had failed to produce any good in this poor woman; on the contrary, there could be little doubt that she had been injured by it. Then was education a bad thing? Rousseau was of opinion that it was; but Rousseau was a Frenchman, at least wrote in French, and I cared not the snap of my fingers for Rousseau. But education has certainly been of benefit in some instances; well, what did that prove, but that partiality existed in the management of the affairs of the world. If education was a benefit to some, why was it not a benefit to others? Could some avoid abusing it, any more than others could avoid turning it to a profitable account? I did not see how they could; this poor simple woman found a book in her mother's closet; a book, which was a capital book for those who could turn it to the account for which it was intended; a book, from the perusal of which I felt myself wiser and better, but which was by no means suited to the intellect of this poor simple woman, who thought that it was written in praise of thieving; yet she found it, she read it, and—and I felt myself getting into a maze; what is right? thought I; what is wrong? Do I exist? Does the world exist? if it does, every action is bound up with necessity.

"Necessity!" I exclaimed, and cracked my finger joints.

"Ah, it is a bad thing," said the old woman.

"What is a bad thing?" said I.

"Why, to be poor, dear."

"You talk like a fool," said I, "riches and poverty are only different forms of necessity."

"You should not call me a fool, dear; you should not call your own mother a fool."

"You are not my mother," said I.

"Not your mother, dear?—no, no more I am; but your calling me fool put me in mind of my dear son, who often used to call me fool—and you just now looked as he sometimes did, with a blob of foam on your lip."

"After all, I don't know that you are not my mother."

"Don't you, dear? I'm glad of it; I wish you would make it out."

"How should I make it out? who can speak from his own knowledge as to the circumstances of his birth? Besides, before attempting to establish our relationship, it would be necessary to prove that such people exist."

"What people, dear?"

"You and I."

"Lord, child, you are mad; that book has made you so."

"Don't abuse it," said I; "the book is an excellent one, that is, provided it exists."

"I wish it did not," said the old woman; "but it shan't long; I'll burn it, or fling it into the river—the voices of night tell me to do so."

"Tell the voices," said I, "that they talk nonsense; the book, if it exists, is a good book, it contains a deep moral; have you read it all?"

"All the funny parts, dear; all about taking things, and the manner it was done; as for the rest, I could not exactly make it out."

"Then the book is not to blame; I repeat that the book is a good book, and contains deep morality, always supposing that there is such a thing as morality, which is the same thing as supposing that there is anything at all."

"Anything at all! Why, a'n't we here on this bridge, in my booth, with my stall and my——"

"Apples and pears, baked hot, you would say—I don't know; all is a mystery, a deep question. It is a question, and probably always will be, whether there is a world, and consequently apples and pears; and, provided there be a world, whether that world be like an apple or a pear."

"Don't talk so, dear."

"I won't; we will suppose that we all exist—world, ourselves, apples, and pears: so you wish to get rid of the book?"

"Yes, dear, I wish you would take it."

"I have read it, and have no further use for it; I do not need books: in a little time, perhaps, I shall not have a place wherein to deposit myself, far less books."

"Then I will fling it into the river."

"Don't do that; here, give it me. Now what shall I do with it? you were so fond of it."

"I am so no longer."

"But how will you pass your time? what will you read?"

"I wish I had never learned to read, or, if I had, that I had only read the books I saw at school: the primer or the other."

"What was the other?"

"I think they called it the Bible: all about God, and Job, and Jesus."

"Ah, I know it."

"You have read it? is it a nice book—all true?"

"True, true—I don't know what to say; but if the world be true, and not all a lie, a fiction, I don't see why the Bible, as they call it, should not be true. By-the-bye, what do you call Bible in your tongue, or, indeed, book of any kind? as Bible merely means a book."

"What do I call the Bible in my language, dear?"

"Yes, the language of those who bring you things."

"The language of those who *did*, dear; they bring them now no longer. They call me fool, as you did, dear, just now; they call kissing the Bible, which means taking a false oath, smacking calf-skin."

"That's metaphor," said I, "English, but metaphorical; what an odd language! So you would like to have a Bible—shall I buy you one?"

"I am poor, dear—no money since I left off the other trade."

"Well, then, I'll buy you one."

"No, dear, no; you are poor, and may soon want the money; but if you can take me one conveniently on the sly, you know—I think you may, for, as it is a good book, I suppose there can be no harm in taking it."

"That will never do," said I, "more especially as I should be sure to be caught, not having made taking of things my trade; but I'll tell you what I'll do—try and exchange this book of yours for a Bible; who knows for what great things this same book of yours may serve?"

"Well, dear," said the old woman, "do as you please; I should like to see the—what do you call it?—Bible, and to read it, as you seem to think it true."

"Yes," said I, "seem; that is the way to express yourself in this maze of doubt—I seem to think—these apples and pears seem to be—and here seems to be a gentleman who wants to purchase either one or the other."

A person had stopped before the apple-woman's stall, and was glancing now at the fruit, now at the old woman and myself; he wore a blue mantle, and had a kind of fur cap on his head; he was somewhat above the middle stature; his features were keen, but rather hard; there was a slight obliquity in his vision. Selecting a small apple, he gave the old woman a penny; then, after looking at me scrutinizingly for a moment, he moved from the booth in the direction of Southwark.

"Do you know who that man is?" said I to the old woman.

"No," said she, "except that he is one of my best customers: he frequently stops, takes an apple, and gives me a penny; his is the only piece of money I have taken this blessed day. I don't know him, but he has once or twice sat down in the booth with two strange-looking men—Mulattos, or Lascars, I think they call them."

In pursuance of my promise to the old woman, I set about procuring her a Bible with all convenient speed, placing the book which she had intrusted to me for the purpose of exchange in my pocket. I went to several shops, and asked if Bibles were to be had: I found that there were plenty. When, however, I informed the people that I came to barter, they looked blank, and declined treating with me, saying that they did not do business in that way. At last I went into a shop over the window of which I saw written, "Books bought and exchanged": there was a smartish young fellow in the shop, with black hair and whiskers. "You exchange?" said I. "Yes," said he, "sometimes, but we prefer selling; what book do you want?" "A Bible," said I. "Ah," said he, "there's a great demand for Bibles just now; all kinds of people are become very pious of late," he added, grinning at me; "I am afraid I can't do business with you, more especially as the master is not at home. What book have you brought?" Taking the book out of my pocket, I placed it on the counter. The young fellow opened the book, and inspecting the title-page, burst into a loud laugh. "What do you laugh for?" said I, angrily, and half clenching my fist. "Laugh!" said the young fellow; "laugh! who could help laughing?" "I could," said I; "I see nothing to laugh at; I want to exchange this book for a Bible." "You do?" said the young fellow; "well, I dare say there are plenty who would be willing to exchange, that is, if they dared. I wish master were at home; but that would never do, either. Master's a family man, the Bibles are not mine, and master being a family man, is sharp, and knows all his stock; I'd buy it of you, but, to tell you the truth, I am quite empty here," said he, pointing to his pocket, "so I am afraid we can't deal."

Whereupon, looking anxiously at the young man, "What am I to do?" said I; "I really want a Bible."

"Can't you buy one?" said the young man; "have you no money?"

"Yes," said I, "I have some, but I am merely the agent of another; I came to exchange, not to buy; what am I to do?"

"I don't know," said the young man, thoughtfully, laying down the book on the counter; "I don't know what you can do; I think you will find some difficulty in this bartering job, the trade are rather precise." All at once he laughed louder than before; suddenly stopping, however, he put on a very grave look. "Take my advice," said he; "there is a firm established in this neighbourhood which scarcely sells any books but Bibles; they are very rich, and pride themselves on selling their books at the lowest possible price; apply to them, who knows but what they will exchange with you?"

Thereupon I demanded with some eagerness of the young man the direction to the place where he thought it possible that I might effect the exchange—which direction the young fellow cheerfully gave me, and, as I turned away, had the civility to wish me success.

I had no difficulty in finding the house to which the young fellow directed me; it was a very large house, situated in a square, and upon the side of the house was written in large letters, "Bibles, and other religious books."

At the door of the house were two or three tumbrils, in the act of being loaded with chests, very much resembling teachests; one of the chests falling down, burst, and out flew, not tea, but various books, in a neat, small size, and in neat leather covers; Bibles, said I,—Bibles, doubtless. I was not quite right, nor quite wrong; picking up one of the books, I looked at it for a moment, and found it to be the New Testament. "Come, young lad," said a man who stood by, in the dress of a porter, "put that book down, it is none of yours; if you want a book, go in and deal for one."

Deal, thought I, deal—the man seems to know what I am coming about—and going in, I presently found myself in a very large room. Behind a counter two men stood with their backs to a splendid fire, warming themselves, for the weather was cold.

Of these men one was dressed in brown, and the other was dressed in black; both were tall men—he who was dressed in brown was thin, and had a particularly ill-natured countenance; the man dressed in black was bulky, his features were noble, but they were those of a lion.

"What is your business, young man?" said the precise personage, as I stood staring at him and his companion.

"I want a Bible," said I.

"What price, what size?" said the precise-looking man.

"As to size," said I, "I should like to have a large one—that is, if you can afford me one—I do not come to buy."

"Oh, friend," said the precise-looking man, "if you come here expecting to have a Bible for nothing, you are mistaken—we——"

"I would scorn to have a Bible for nothing," said I, "or anything else; I came not to beg, but to barter; there is no shame in that, especially in a country like this, where all folks barter."

"Oh, we don't barter," said the precise man, "at least Bibles; you had better depart."

"Stay, brother," said the man with the countenance of a lion, "let us ask a few questions; this may be a very important case; perhaps the young man has had convictions."

"Not I," I exclaimed, "I am convinced of nothing, and with regard to the Bible—I don't believe——"

"Hey!" said the man with the lion countenance, and there he stopped. But with that "Hey," the walls of the house seemed to shake, the windows rattled, and the porter whom I had seen in front of the house came running up the steps, and looked into the apartment through the glass of the door.

There was silence for about a minute—the same kind of silence which succeeds a clap of thunder.

At last the man with the lion countenance, who had kept his eyes fixed upon me, said calmly: "Were you about to say that you don't believe in the Bible, young man?"

"No more than in anything else," said I; "you were talking of convictions—I have no convictions. It is not easy to believe in the Bible till one is convinced that there is a Bible."

"He seems to be insane," said the prim-looking man, "we had better order the porter to turn him out."

"I am by no means certain," said I, "that the porter could turn me out; always provided there is a porter, and this system of ours be not a lie, and a dream."

"Come," said the lion-looking man, impatiently, "a truce with this nonsense. If the porter cannot turn you out, perhaps some other person can; but to the point—you want a Bible?"

"I do," said I, "but not for myself; I was sent by another person to offer something in exchange for one."

"And who is that person?"

"A poor old woman, who has had what you call convictions—heard voices, or thought she heard them—I forgot to ask her whether they were loud ones."

"What has she sent to offer in exchange?" said the man, without taking any notice of the concluding part of my speech.

"A book," said I.

"Let me see it."

"Nay, brother," said the precise man, "this will never do; if we once adopt the system of barter, we shall have all the holders of useless rubbish in the town applying to us."

"I wish to see what he has brought," said the other; "perhaps Baxter, or Jewell's Apology, either of which would make a valuable addition to our collection. Well, young man, what's the matter with you?"

I stood like one petrified; I had put my hand into my pocket—the book was gone.

"What's the matter?" repeated the man with the lion countenance, in a voice very much resembling thunder.

"I have it not—I have lost it!"

"A pretty story, truly," said the precise-looking man, "lost it!"

"You had better retire," said the other.

"How shall I appear before the party who intrusted me with the book? She will certainly think that I have purloined it, notwithstanding all I can say; nor, indeed, can I blame her—appearances are certainly against me."

"They are so—you had better retire."

I moved towards the door. "Stay, young man, one word more; there is only one way of proceeding which would induce me to believe that you are sincere."

"What is that?" said I, stopping and looking at him anxiously.

"The purchase of a Bible."

"Purchase!" said I, "purchase! I came not to purchase, but to barter; such was my instruction, and how can I barter if I have lost the book?"

The other made no answer, and turning away I made for the door; all of a sudden I started, and turning round, "Dear me," said I, "it has just come into my head, that if the book was lost by my negligence, as it must have been, I have clearly a right to make it good."

No answer.

"Yes," I repeated, "I have clearly a right to make it good; how glad I am! see the effect of a little reflection. I will purchase a Bible instantly, that is, if I have not lost—" and with considerable agitation I felt in my pocket.

The prim-looking man smiled: "I suppose," said he, "that he has lost his money as well as book."

"No," said I, "I have not"; and pulling out my hand I displayed no less sum than three half-crowns.

"O, noble goddess of the Mint!" as Dame Charlotta Nordenflycht, the Swede, said a hundred and fifty years ago, "great is thy power; how energetically the possession of thee speaks in favour of man's character!"

"Only half a crown for this Bible?" said I, putting down the money, "it is worth three"; and bowing to the man of the noble features, I departed with my purchase.

"Queer customer," said the prim-looking man, as I was about to close the door—"don't like him."

"Why, as to that, I scarcely know what to say," said he of the countenance of a lion.

CHAPTER XIV

A FEW DAYS after the occurrence of what is recorded in the last chapter, as I was wandering in the City, chance directed my footsteps to an alley leading from one narrow street to another in the neighbourhood of Cheapside. Just before I reached the mouth of the alley, a man in a greatcoat, closely followed by another, passed it; and, at the moment in which they were passing, I observed the man behind snatch something from the pocket of the other; whereupon, darting into the street, I seized the hindermost man by the collar, crying at the same time to the other, "My good friend, this person has just picked your pocket."

The individual whom I addressed, turning round with a start, glanced at me, and then at the person whom I held. London is the place for strange rencounters. It appeared to me that I recognised both individuals—the man whose pocket had been picked and the other; the latter now began to struggle violently; "I have picked no one's pocket," said he. "Rascal," said the other, "you have got my pocket-book in your bosom." "No, I have not," said the other; and struggling more violently than before, the pocket-book dropped from his bosom upon the ground.

The other was now about to lay hands upon the fellow, who was still struggling. "You had better take up your book," said I; "I can hold him." He followed my advice, and, taking up his pocket-book, surveyed my prisoner with a ferocious look, occasionally glaring at me. Yes, I had seen him before—it was the stranger whom I had observed on London Bridge, by the stall of the old apple-woman, with the cap and cloak; but, instead of these, he now wore a hat and greatcoat. "Well," said I, at last, "what am I to do with this gentleman of ours?" nodding to the prisoner, who had now left off struggling. "Shall I let him go?"

"Go!" said the other; "go! The knave—the rascal; let him go, indeed! Not so, he shall go before the Lord Mayor. Bring him along."

"Oh, let me go," said the other; "let me go; this is the first offence, I assure ye—the first time I ever thought to do anything wrong."

"Hold your tongue," said I, "or I shall be angry with you. If I am not very much mistaken, you once attempted to cheat me."

"I never saw you before in all my life," said the fellow, though his countenance seemed to belie his words.

"That is not true," said I; " you are the man who attempted to cheat me of one-and-ninepence in the coach-yard, on the first morning of my arrival in London."

"I don't doubt it," said the other; "a confirmed thief"; and here his tones became peculiarly sharp; "I would fain see him hanged—crucified. Drag him along."

"I am no constable," said I; "you have got your pocket-book—I would rather you would bid me let him go."

"Bid you let him go!" said the other almost furiously, "I command—stay, what was I going to say? I was forgetting myself," he observed more gently; "but he stole my pocket-book; if you did but know what it contained."

"Well," said I, "if it contains anything valuable, be the more thankful that you have recovered it; as for the man, I will help you to take him where you please; but I wish you would let him go."

The stranger hesitated, and there was an extraordinary play of emotion in his features; he looked ferociously at the pick-pocket, and, more than once, somewhat suspiciously at myself; at last his countenance cleared, and, with a good grace, he said, "Well, you have done me a great service, and you have my consent to let him go; but the rascal shall not escape with impunity," he exclaimed suddenly, as I let the man go, and starting forward, before the fellow could escape, he struck him a violent blow on the face. The man staggered, and had nearly fallen; recovering himself, however, he said: "I tell you what, my fellow, if I ever meet you in this street in a dark night, and I have a knife about me, it shall be the worse for you; as for you, young man," said he to me; but, observing that the other was making towards him, he left whatever he was about to say unfinished, and, taking to his heels, was out of sight in a moment.

The stranger and myself walked in the direction of Cheapside, the way in which he had been originally proceeding; he was silent for a few moments, at length he said: "You have really done me a great service, and I should be ungrateful not to acknowledge it. I am a merchant; and a merchant's pocket-book, as you perhaps know, contains many things of importance; but young man," he exclaimed. "I think I have seen you before; I thought so at first, but where I cannot exactly say: where was it?" I mentioned London Bridge and the old apple-woman. "Oh," said he, and smiled, and there was something peculiar in his smile, "I remember now. Do you frequently sit on London Bridge?" "Occasionally," said I; "that old woman is an old friend of mine." "Friend?" said the stranger, "I am glad of it, for I shall know where to find you. At present I am going to 'Change; time you know is precious to a merchant." We were by this time close to Cheapside. "Farewell," said he, "I shall not forget this service. I trust we shall soon meet again." He then shook me by the hand and went his way.

The next day, as I was seated beside the old woman in the booth, the stranger again made his appearance, and after a word or two, sat down beside me; the old woman was sometimes reading the Bible, which she had already had two or three days in her possession, and sometimes discoursing with me. Our discourse rolled chiefly on philological matters.

"What do you call bread in your language?" said I.

"You mean the language of those who bring me things to buy, or who did; for, as I told you before, I sha'n't buy any more; it's no language of mine, dear—they call bread pannam in their language."

"Pannam!" said I, "pannam! evidently connected with, if not derived from, the Latin panis; even as the word tanner, which signifieth a sixpence, is connected with, if not derived from, the Latin tener, which is itself connected with, if not derived from, tawno or tawner, which, in the language of Mr. Petulengro, signifieth a sucking child. Let me see, what is the term for bread in the language of Mr. Petulengro? Morro, or manro, as I have sometimes heard it called; is there not some connection between these words and panis? Yes, I think there is; and I should not wonder if morro, manro, and panis were connected, perhaps derived from the same root; but what is that root? I don't know—I wish I did; though, perhaps, I should not be the happier. Morro—manro! I rather think morro is the oldest form; it is easier to say morro than manro. Morro! Irish, aran; Welsh, bara; English, bread. I can see a resemblance between all the words, and pannam too; and I rather think that the Petulengrian word is the elder. How odd it would be if the language of Mr. Petulengro should eventually turn out to be the mother of all the languages in the world; yet it is certain that there are some languages in which the terms for bread have no connection with the word used by Mr. Petulengro, notwithstanding that those languages, in many other points, exhibit a close affinity to the language of the horseshoe master: for example, bread, in Hebrew, is Laham, which assuredly exhibits little similitude to the word used by the aforesaid Petulengro. In Armenian it is—"

"Zhats!" said the stranger starting up. "By the Patriarch and the Three Holy Churches, this is wonderful! How came you to know aught of Armenian?"

Just as I was about to reply to the interrogation of my new-formed acquaintance, a man, with a dusky countenance, probably one of the Lascars, or Mulattos, of whom the old woman had spoken, came up and whispered to him, and with this man he presently departed, not however before he had told me the place of his abode, and requested me to visit him.

After the lapse of a few days, I called at the house which he had indicated. It was situated in a dark and narrow street, in the heart of the city, at no great distance from the Bank. I entered a counting-room, in which a solitary clerk, with a foreign look, was writing. The stranger was not at home; returning the next day, however, I met him at the door as he was about to enter; he shook me warmly by the hand. "I am glad to see you," said he, "follow me. I was just thinking of you." He led me through the counting-room to an apartment up a flight of stairs; before ascending, however, he looked into the book in which the foreign-visaged clerk was writing, and, seemingly not satisfied with the manner in which he was executing his task, he gave him two or three cuffs, telling him at the same time that he deserved crucifixion.

The apartment above stairs, to which he led me, was large, with three windows which opened upon the street. The walls were hung with wired cases, apparently containing books. There was a table and two or three chairs; but the principal article of furniture was a long sofa, extending from the door by which we entered to the farther end of the apartment. Seating himself upon the sofa, my new acquaintance motioned me to a seat beside him, and then, looking me full in the face, repeated his former inquiry. "In the name of all that is wonderful, how came you to know aught of my language?"

"There is nothing wonderful in that," said I; "we are at the commencement of a philological age, every one studies languages: that is, every one who is fit for nothing else; philology being the last resource of dulness and ennui, I have got a little in advance of the throng, by mastering the Armenian alphabet; but I foresee the time when every unmarriageable miss, and desperate blockhead, will likewise have acquired the letters of Mesroub, and will know the term for bread, in Armenian, and perhaps that for wine."

"Kini," said my companion; "and that and the other word put me in mind of the duties of hospitality. Will you eat bread and drink wine with me?"

"Willingly," said I. Whereupon my companion, unlocking a closet, produced on a silver salver, a loaf of bread, with a silver-handled knife, and wine in a silver flask, with cups of the same metal. "I hope you like my fare," said he, after we had both eaten and drunk.

"I like your bread," said I, "for it is stale; I like not your wine, it is sweet, and I hate sweet wine."

"It is wine of Cyprus," said my entertainer; and, when I found that it was wine of Cyprus, I tasted it again, and the second taste pleased me much better than the first, notwithstanding that I still thought it somewhat sweet. "So," said I, after a pause, looking at my companion, "you are an Armenian."

"Yes," said he, "an Armenian born in London, but not less an Armenian on that account. My father was a native of Ispahan, one of the celebrated Armenian colony which was established there shortly after the time of the dreadful hunger, which drove the children of Haik in swarms from their original country, and scattered them over most parts of the eastern and western world. In Ispahan he passed the greater portion of his life, following mercantile pursuits with considerable success. Certain enemies, however, having accused him to the despot of the place, of using seditious language, he was compelled to flee, leaving most of his property behind. Travelling in the direction of the west, he came at last to London, where he established himself, and where he eventually died, leaving behind a large property and myself, his only child, the fruit of a marriage with an Armenian English woman, who did not survive my birth more than three months."

The Armenian then proceeded to tell me that he had carried on the business of his father, which seemed to embrace most matters, from buying silks of Lascars, to speculating in the funds, and that he had considerably increased the property which his father had left him. He candidly confessed that he was wonderfully fond of gold, and said there was nothing like it for giving a person respectability and consideration in the world; to which assertion I made no answer, being not exactly prepared to contradict it.

And, when he had related to me his history, he expressed a desire to know something more of myself, whereupon I gave him the outline of my history, concluding with saying: "I am now a poor author, or rather a philologist, upon the streets of London, possessed of many tongues, which I find of no use in the world."

"Learning without money is anything but desirable," said the Armenian, "as it unfits a man for humble occupations. It is true that it may occasionally beget him friends; I confess to you that your understanding something of my language weighs more with me than the service you rendered me in rescuing my pocket-book the other day from the claws of that scoundrel whom I yet hope to see hanged, if not crucified, notwithstanding there were in that pocket-book papers and documents of considerable value. Yes, that circumstance makes my heart warm towards you, for I am proud of my language—as I indeed well may be—what a language, noble and energetic! quite original, differing from all others both in words and structure."

"You are mistaken," said I; "many languages resemble the Armenian both in structure and words."

"For example?" said the Armenian.

"For example," said I, "the English."

"The English," said the Armenian; "show me one word in which the English resembles the Armenian."

"You walk on London Bridge," said I.

"Yes," said the Armenian.

"I saw you look over the balustrade the other morning."

"True," said the Armenian.

"Well, what did you see rushing up through the arches with noise and foam?"

"What was it?" said the Armenian. "What was it?—you don't mean the *tide?*"

"Do I not?" said I.

"Well, what has the tide to do with the matter?"

"Much," said I; "what is the tide?"

"The ebb and flow of the sea," said the Armenian.

"The sea itself; what is the Haik word for sea?"

The Armenian gave a strong gasp; then, nodding his head thrice, "you are right," said he, "the English word tide is the Armenian for sea; and now I begin to perceive that there are many English words which are Armenian; there is — and — and there again in French there is — and — derived from the Armenian. How strange, how singular—I thank you. It is a proud thing to see that the language of my race has had so much influence over the languages of the world."

I saw that all that related to his race was the weak point of the Armenian. I did not flatter the Armenian with respect to his race or language. "An inconsiderable people," said I, "shrewd and industrious, but still an inconsiderable people. A language bold and expressive, and of some antiquity, derived, though perhaps not immediately, from some much older tongue. I do not think that the Armenian has had any influence over the formation of the languages of the world. I am not much indebted to the Armenian for the solution of any doubts; whereas to the language of Mr. Petulengro—"

"I have heard you mention that name before," said the Armenian; "who is Mr. Petulengro?"

And then I told the Armenian who Mr. Petulengro was. The Armenian spoke contemptuously of Mr. Petulengro and his race. "Don't speak contemptuously of Mr. Petulengro," said I, "nor of anything belonging to him. He is a dark, mysterious personage; all connected with him is a mystery, especially his language; but I believe that his language is doomed to solve a great philological problem—Mr. Petulengro——"

"You appear agitated," said the Armenian; "take another glass of wine; you possess a great deal of philological knowledge, but it appears to me that the language of this Petulengro is your foible: but let us change the subject; I feel much interested in you, and would fain be of service to you. Can you cast accounts?"

I shook my head.

"Keep books?"

"I have an idea that I could write books," said I; "but, as to keeping them——" and here again I shook my head.

The Armenian was silent some time; all at once, glancing at one of the wire cases, with which, as I have already said, the walls of the room were hung, he asked me if I was well acquainted with the learning of the Haiks. "The books in these cases," said he, "contain the masterpieces of Haik learning."

"No," said I, "all I know of the learning of the Haiks is their translation of the Bible."

"You have never read Z——?"

"No," said I, "I have never read Z——."

"I have a plan," said the Armenian; "I think I can employ you agreeably and profitably; I should like to see Z—— in an English dress: you shall translate Z——. If you can read the Scriptures in Armenian, you can translate Z——. He is our Esop, the most acute and clever of all our moral writers—his philosophy——"

"I will have nothing to do with him," said I.

"Wherefore?" said the Armenian.

"There is an old proverb," said I, "that 'a burnt child avoids the fire.' I have burnt my hands sufficiently with attempting to translate philosophy, to make me cautious of venturing upon it again"; and then I told the Armenian how I had been persuaded by the publisher to translate his philosophy into German, and what sorry thanks I had received; "and who knows," said I, "but the attempt to translate Armenian philosophy into English might be attended with yet more disagreeable consequences."

The Armenian smiled. "You would find me very different from the publisher."

"In many points I have no doubt I should," I replied; "but at the present moment I feel like a bird which has escaped from a cage, and, though hungry, feels no disposition to return. Of what nation is the dark man below stairs, whom I saw writing at the desk?"

"He is a Moldave," said the Armenian; "the dog (and here his eyes sparkled) deserves to be crucified, he is continually making mistakes."

The Armenian again renewed his proposition about Z——, which I again refused, as I felt but little inclination to place myself beneath the jurisdiction of a person who was in the habit of cuffing those whom he employed, when they made mistakes. I presently took my departure; not, however, before I had received from the Armenian a pressing invitation to call upon him whenever I should feel disposed.

CHAPTER XV

Occasionally I called on Francis Ardry. This young gentleman resided in handsome apartments in the neighbourhood of a fashionable square, kept a livery servant, and upon the whole, lived in very good style. Going to see him one day, between one and two, I was informed by the servant that his master was engaged for the moment, but that, if I pleased to wait a few minutes, I should find him at liberty. Having told the man that I had no objection, he conducted me into a small apartment which served as ante-chamber to a drawing-room; the door of this last being half-open, I could see Francis Ardry at the farther end, speechifying and gesticulating in a very impressive manner. The servant, in some confusion, was hastening to close the door, but, ere he could effect his purpose, Francis Ardry, who had caught a glimpse of me, exclaimed, "Come in—come in by all means," and then proceeded, as before, speechifying and gesticulating. Filled with some surprise, I obeyed his summons.

On entering the room I perceived another individual to whom Francis Ardry appeared to be addressing himself; this other was a short, spare man of about sixty; his hair was of a badger grey, and his face was covered with wrinkles—without vouchsafing me a look, he kept his eye, which was black and lustrous, fixed full on Francis Ardry, as if paying the deepest attention to his discourse. All of a sudden, however, he cried with a sharp, cracked voice, "that won't do, sir; that won't do—more vehemence—your argument is at present particularly weak; therefore, more vehemence—you must confuse them, stun them, stultify them, sir"; and, at each of these injunctions, he struck the back of his right hand sharply against the palm of the left. "Good, sir—good!" he occasionally uttered, in the same sharp, cracked tone, as the voice of Francis Ardry became more and more vehement. "Infinitely good!" he exclaimed, as Francis Ardry raised his voice to the highest pitch; "and now, sir, abate; let the tempest of vehemence decline—gradually, sir; not too fast. Good, sir—very good!" as the voice of Francis Ardry declined gradually in vehemence. "And now a little pathos, sir—try them with a little pathos. That won't do, sir—that won't do,"—as Francis Ardry made an attempt to become pathetic—"that will never pass for pathos—with tones and gesture of that description you will never redress the wrongs of your country. Now, sir, observe my gestures, and pay attention to the tone of my voice, sir."

Thereupon, making use of nearly the same terms which Francis Ardry had employed, the individual in black uttered several sentences in tones and with gestures which were intended to express a considerable degree of pathos, though it is possible that some people would have thought both the one and the other highly ludicrous. After a pause, Francis recommenced imitating the tones and the gestures of his monitor in the most admirable manner. Before he had proceeded far, however, he burst into a fit of laughter, in which I should, perhaps, have joined, provided it were ever my wont to laugh. "Ha, ha!" said the other, good-humouredly, "you are laughing at me. Well, well, I merely wished to give you a hint; but you saw very well what I meant; upon the whole, I think you improve. But I must now go, having two other pupils to visit before four."

Then taking from the table a kind of three-cornered hat, and a cane headed with amber, he shook Francis Ardry by the hand; and, after glancing at me for a moment, made me a half-bow, attended with a strange grimace, and departed.

"Who is that gentleman?" said I to Francis Ardry as soon as we were alone.

"Oh, that is—" said Frank smiling, "the gentleman who gives me lessons in elocution."

"And what need have you of elocution?"

"Oh, I merely obey the commands of my guardians," said Francis, "who insist that I should, with the assistance of —, qualify myself for Parliament; for which they do me the honour to suppose that I have some natural talent. I dare not disobey them, for, at the present moment, I have particular reasons for wishing to keep on good terms with them."

"But," said I, "you are a Roman Catholic, and I thought that persons of your religion were excluded from Parliament?"

"Why, upon that very thing the whole matter hinges; people of our religion are determined to be no longer excluded from Parliament, but to have a share in the government of the nation. Not that I care anything about the matter; I merely obey the will of my guardians; my thoughts are fixed on something better than politics."

"I understand you," said I; "dog-fighting—well, I can easily conceive that to some minds dog-fighting—"

"I was not thinking of dog-fighting," said Francis Ardry, interrupting me.

"Not thinking of dog-fighting!" I ejaculated.

"No," said Francis Ardry, "something higher and much more rational than dog-fighting at present occupies my thoughts."

"Dear me," said I, "I thought I heard you say, that there was nothing like it!"

"Like what?" said Francis Ardry.

"Dog-fighting, to be sure," said I.

"Pooh," said Francis Ardry; "who but the gross and unrefined care anything for dog-fighting? That which at present engages my waking and sleeping thoughts is love—divine love—there is nothing like *that*. Listen to me, I have a secret to confide to you."

And then Francis Ardry proceeded to make me his confidant. It appeared that he had had the good fortune to make the acquaintance of the most delightful young Frenchwoman imaginable, Annette La Noire by name, who had just arrived from her native country with the intention of obtaining the situation of governess in some English family; a position which, on account of her many accomplishments, she was eminently qualified to fill. Francis Ardry had, however, persuaded her to relinquish her intention for the present, on the ground that, until she had become acclimated in England, her health would probably suffer from the confinement inseparable from the occupation in which she was desirous of engaging; he had, moreover—for it appeared that she was the most frank and confiding creature in the world—succeeded in persuading her to permit him to hire for her a very handsome first floor in his own neighbourhood, and to accept a few inconsiderable presents in money and jewellery. "I am looking out for a handsome gig and horse," said Francis Ardry, at the conclusion of his narration; "it were a burning shame that so divine a creature should have to go about a place like London on foot, or in a paltry hackney coach."

"But," said I, "will not the pursuit of politics prevent your devoting much time to this fair lady?"

"It will prevent me devoting all my time," said Francis Ardry, "as I gladly would; but what can I do? My guardians wish me to qualify myself for a political orator, and I dare not offend them by a refusal. If I offend my guardians, I should find it impossible to support Annette, present her with articles of dress and jewellery, and purchase a horse and cabriolet worthy of conveying her angelic person through the streets of London."

Anxious thoughts frequently disturbed me at this time with respect to what I was to do, and how support myself in the Great City. My future prospects were gloomy enough, and I looked forward and feared; sometimes I felt half disposed to accept the offer of the Armenian, and to commence forthwith, under his superintendence, the translation of the Haik Esop; but the remembrance of the cuffs which I had seen him bestow upon the Moldavian, when glancing over my shoulder into the ledger or whatever it was on which he was employed, immediately drove the inclination from my mind. I could not support the idea of the possibility of his staring over my shoulder upon my translation of the Haik Esop, and, dissatisfied with my attempts, treating me as he had treated the Moldavian clerk; placing myself in a position which exposed me to such treatment, would indeed be plunging into the fire after escaping from the frying pan. The publisher, insolent and overbearing as he was, whatever he might have wished or thought, had never lifted his hand against me, or told me that I merited crucifixion.

What was I to do? turn porter? I was strong; but there was something besides strength required to ply the trade of a porter—a mind of a particularly phlegmatic temperament, which I did not possess. What should I do?—enlist as a soldier? I was tall enough; but something besides height is required to make a man play with credit the part of soldier, I mean a private one—a spirit, if spirit it can be called, which will not only enable a man to submit with patience to insolence and abuse, and even to cuffs and kicks, but occasionally to the lash. I felt that I was not qualified to be a soldier, at least a private one; far better be a drudge to the most ferocious of publishers, editing Newgate lives, and writing in eighteenpenny reviews—better to translate the Haik Esop, under the superintendence of ten Armenians, than be a private soldier in the English service; I did not decide rashly—I knew something of soldiering. What should I do? I thought that I would make a last and desperate attempt to dispose of the ballads and of Ab Gwilym.

But I found the publishers as untractable as ever, and to this day the public has never had an opportunity of doing justice to the glowing fire of my ballad versification, and the alliterative euphony of my imitations of Ab Gwilym.

I had not seen Francis Ardry since the day I had seen him taking lessons in elocution. One afternoon, as I was seated at my table, my head resting on my hands, he entered my apartment; sitting down, he inquired of me why I had not been to see him.

"I might ask the same question of you," I replied. "Wherefore have you not been to see me?" Whereupon Francis Ardry told me that he had been much engaged in his oratorical exercises, also in escorting the young Frenchwoman about to places of public amusement; he then again questioned me as to the reason of my not having been to see him.

I returned an evasive answer. The truth was, that for some time past my appearance, owing to the state of my finances, had been rather shabby; and I did not wish to expose a fashionable young man like Francis Ardry, who lived in a fashionable neighbourhood, to the imputation of having a shabby acquaintance. I was aware that Francis Ardry was an excellent fellow; but, on that very account, I felt, under existing circumstances, a delicacy in visiting him.

It is very possible that he had an inkling of how matters stood, as he presently began to talk of my affairs and prospects. I told him of my late ill success with the booksellers, and inveighed against their blindness to their own interest in refusing to publish my translations. "The last that I addressed myself to," said I, "told me not to trouble him again, unless I could bring him a decent novel or a tale."

"Well," said Frank, "and why did you not carry him a decent novel or a tale?"

"Because I have neither," said I; "and to write them is, I believe, above my capacity. At present I feel divested of all energy—heartless and almost hopeless."

"I see how it is," said Francis Ardry, "you have overworked yourself, and, worst of all, to no purpose. Take my advice; cast all care aside, and only think of diverting yourself for a month at least."

"Divert myself," said I; "and where am I to find the means?"

"Be that care on my shoulders," said Francis Ardry. "Listen to me—my uncles have been so delighted with the favourable accounts which they have lately received from T— of my progress in oratory, that, in the warmth of their hearts, they made me a present yesterday of two hundred pounds. This is more money than I want, at least for the present; do me the favour to take half of it as a loan—hear me," said he, observing that I was about to interrupt him, "I have a plan in my head—one of the prettiest in the world. The sister of my charmer is just arrived from France; she cannot speak a word of English; and, as Annette and myself are much engaged in our own matters, we cannot pay her the attention which we should wish, and which she deserves, for she is a truly fascinating creature, although somewhat differing from my charmer, having blue eyes and flaxen hair; whilst Annette, on the contrary— But I hope you will shortly see Annette. Now my plan is this: Take the money, dress yourself fashionably, and conduct Annette's sister to Bagnigge Wells."

"And what should we do at Bagnigge Wells?"

"Do!" said Francis Ardry. "Dance!"

"But," said I, "I scarcely know anything of dancing."

"Then here's an excellent opportunity of improving yourself. Like most Frenchwomen, she dances divinely; however, if you object to Bagnigge Wells and dancing, go to Brighton, and remain there a month or two, at the end of which time you can return with your mind refreshed and invigorated, and materials, perhaps, for a tale or novel."

"I never heard a more foolish plan," said I, "or one less likely to terminate profitably or satisfactorily. I thank you, however, for your offer, which is, I dare say, well meant. If I am to escape from my cares and troubles, and find my mind refreshed and invigorated, I must adopt other means than conducting a French demoiselle to Brighton or Bagnigge Wells, defraying the expense by borrowing from a friend."

CHAPTER XVI

The Armenian! I frequently saw this individual, availing myself of the permission which he had given me to call upon him. A truly singular personage was he, with his love of amassing money, and his nationality so strong as to be akin to poetry. Many an Armenian I have subsequently known fond of money-getting, and not destitute of national spirit; but never another, who, in the midst of his schemes of lucre, was at all times willing to enter into a conversation on the structure of the Haik language, or who ever offered me money to render into English the fables of Z— in the hope of astonishing the stock-jobbers of the Exchange with the wisdom of the Haik Esop.

But he was fond of money, very fond. Within a little time I had won his confidence to such a degree that he informed me that the grand wish of his heart was to be possessed of two hundred thousand pounds.

"I think you might satisfy yourself with the half," said I. "One hundred thousand pounds is a large sum."

"You are mistaken," said the Armenian, "a hundred thousand pounds is nothing. My father left me that or more at his death. No; I shall never be satisfied with less than two."

"And what will you do with your riches," said I, "when you have obtained them? Will you sit down and muse upon them, or will you deposit them in a cellar, and go down once a day to stare at them? I have heard say that the fulfilment of one's wishes is invariably a precursor of extreme misery, and forsooth I can scarcely conceive a more horrible state of existence than to be without a hope or wish."

"It is bad enough, I dare say," said the Armenian; "it will, however, be time enough to think of disposing of the money when I have procured it. I still fall short by a vast sum of the two hundred thousand pounds."

I had occasionally much conversation with him on the state and prospects of his nation, especially of that part of it which still continued in the original country of the Haiks–Ararat and its confines, which, it appeared, he had frequently visited. He informed me that since the death of the last Haik monarch, which occurred in the eleventh century, Armenia had been governed both temporally and spiritually by certain personages called patriarchs; their temporal authority, however, was much circumscribed by the Persian and Turk, especially the former, of whom the Armenian spoke with much hatred, whilst their spiritual authority had at various times been considerably undermined by the emissaries of the Papa of Rome, as the Armenian called him.

"The Papa of Rome sent his emissaries at an early period amongst us," said the Armenian, "seducing the minds of weak-headed people, persuading them that the hillocks of Rome are higher than the ridges of Ararat; that the Roman Papa has more to say in heaven than the Armenian patriarch, and that puny Latin is a better language than nervous and sonorous Haik."

"They are both dialects," said I, "of the language of Mr. Petulengro, one of whose race I believe to have been the original founder of Rome; but, with respect to religion, what are the chief points of your faith? you are Christians, I believe."

"Yes," said the Armenian, "we are Christians in our way; we believe in God, the Holy Spirit, and Saviour, though we are not prepared to admit that the last personage is not only himself, but the other two. We believe——" and then the Armenian told me of several things which the Haiks believed or disbelieved.

The Armenian had occasionally reverted to the subject of the translation of the Haik Esop, which he had still a lurking desire that I should execute; but I had invariably declined the undertaking, without, however, stating my reasons. On one occasion, when we had been conversing on the subject, the Armenian, who had been observing my countenance for some time with much attention, remarked, "Perhaps, after all, you are right, and you might employ your time to better advantage. Literature is a fine thing, especially Haik literature, but neither that nor any other would be likely to serve as a foundation to a man's fortune: and to make a fortune should be the principal aim of every one's life; therefore listen to me. Accept a seat at the desk opposite to my Moldavian clerk, and receive the rudiments of a merchant's education. You shall be instructed in the Armenian way of doing business —I think you would make an excellent merchant."

"Why do you think so?"

"Because you have something of the Armenian look."

"I understand you," said I; "you mean to say that I squint?"

"Not exactly," said the Armenian, "but there is certainly a kind of irregularity in your features. One eye appears to me larger than the other —never mind, but rather rejoice; in that irregularity consists your strength. All people with regular features are fools; it is very hard for them, you'll say, but there is no help: all we can do, who are not in such a predicament, is to pity those who are. Well! will you accept my offer? No! you are a singular individual; but I must not forget my own concerns. I must now go forth, having an appointment by which I hope to make money."

The fulfilment of the Armenian's grand wish was nearer at hand than either he or I had anticipated. Partly owing to the success of a bold speculation, in which he had some time previously engaged, and partly owing to the bequest of a large sum of money by one of his nation who died at this period in Paris, he found himself in the possession of a fortune somewhat exceeding two hundred thousand pounds; this fact he communicated to me one evening about an hour after the close of 'Change, the hour at which I generally called, and at which I mostly found him at home.

"Well," said I, "and what do you intend to do next?"

"I scarcely know," said the Armenian. "I was thinking of that when you came in. I don't see anything that I can do, save going on in my former course. After all, I was perhaps too moderate in making the possession of two hundred thousand pounds the summit of my ambition; there are many individuals in this town who possess three times that sum, and are not yet satisfied. No, I think I can do no better than pursue the old career; who knows but I may make the two hundred thousand three or four?—there is already a surplus, which is an encouragement; however, we will consider the matter over a goblet of wine; I have observed of late that you have become partial to my Cyprus."

And it came to pass that, as we were seated over the Cyprus wine, we heard a knock at the door. "*Adelante!*" cried the Armenian; whereupon the door opened, and in walked a somewhat extraordinary figure—a man in a long loose tunic of a stuff striped with black and yellow; breeches of plush velvet, silk stockings, and shoes with silver buckles. On his head he wore a high-peaked hat; he was tall, had a hooked nose, and in age was about fifty.

"Welcome, Rabbi Manasseh," said the Armenian. "I know your knock —you are welcome; sit down."

"I am welcome," said Manasseh, sitting down; "he—he—he! you know my knock—I bring you money—*bueno!*"

There was something very peculiar in the sound of that *bueno*—I never forgot it.

Thereupon a conversation ensued between Rabbi Manasseh and the Armenian, in a language which I knew to be Spanish, though a peculiar dialect. It related to a mercantile transaction. The Rabbi sighed heavily as he delivered to the other a considerable sum of money.

"It is right," said the Armenian, handing a receipt. "It is right; and I am quite satisfied."

"You are satisfied—you have taken money. *Bueno*, I have nothing to say against your being satisfied."

"Come, Rabbi," said the Armenian, "do not despond; it may be your turn next to take money; in the meantime, can't you be persuaded to taste my Cyprus?"

"He—he—he! senor, you know I do not love wine. I love Noah when he is himself; but, as Janus, I love him not. But you are merry, *bueno;* you have a right to be so."

"Excuse me," said I, "but does Noah ever appear as Janus?"

"He—he—he!" said the Rabbi, "he only appeared as Janus once—*una vez quando estuvo borracho;* which means——"

"I understand," said I; "when he was——" and I drew the side of my right hand sharply across my left wrist.

"Are you one of our people?" said the Rabbi.

"No," said I, "I am one of the Goyim; but I am only half-enlightened. Why should Noah be Janus, when he was in that state?"

"He—he—he! you must know that in Lasan akhades wine is janin."

"In Armenian, kini," said I; "in Welsh, gwin; Latin, vinum; but do you think that Janus and janin are one?"

"Do I think? Don't the commentators say so? Does not Master Leo Abarbenel say so in his *Dialogues of Divine Love?*"

"But," said I, "I always thought that Janus was a god of the ancient Romans, who stood in a temple open in time of war, and shut in time of peace; he was represented with two faces, which—which——"

"He—he—he!" said the Rabbi, rising from his seat; "he had two faces, had he? And what did those two faces typify? You do not know; no, nor did the Romans who carved him with two faces know why they did so; for they were only half-enlightened, like you and the rest of the Goyim. Yet they were right in carving him with two faces looking from each other—they were right, though they knew not why; there was a tradition among them that the *Janinoso* had two faces, but they knew not that one was for the world which was gone, and the other for the world before him—for the drowned world, and for the present, as Master Leo Abarbenel says in his *Dialogues of Divine Love*. He—he—he!" continued the Rabbi, who had by this time advanced to the door, and, turning round, waved the two fore-fingers of his right hand in our faces; "the Goyim and Epicouraiyim are clever men, they know how to make money better than we of Israel. My good friend there is a clever man, I bring him money, he never brought me any, *bueno:* I do not blame him, he knows much, very much; but one thing there is my friend does not know, nor any of the Epicureans, he does not know the sacred thing—he has never received the gift of interpretation which God alone gives to the seed—he has his gift, I have mine—he is satisfied, I don't blame him, *bueno*."

And with this last word in his mouth, he departed.

"Is that man a native of Spain?" I demanded.

"Not a native of Spain," said the Armenian, "though he is one of those who call themselves Spanish Jews, and who are to be found scattered throughout Europe, speaking the Spanish language transmitted to them by their ancestors, who were expelled from Spain in the time of Ferdinand and Isabella."

"The Jews are a singular people," said I.

"A race of cowards and dastards," said the Armenian, "without a home or country; servants to servants; persecuted and despised by all."

"And what are the Haiks?" I demanded.

"Very different from the Jews," replied the Armenian; "the Haiks have a home—a country, and can occasionally use a good sword; though it is true they are not what they might be."

"Then it is a shame that they do not become so," said I; "but they are too fond of money. There is yourself, with two hundred thousand pounds in your pocket, craving for more, whilst you might be turning your wealth to the service of your country."

"In what manner?" said the Armenian.

"I have heard you say that the grand oppressor of your country is the Persian; why not attempt to free your country from his oppression—you have two hundred thousand pounds, and money is the sinew of war?"

"Would you, then, have me attack the Persian?"

"I scarcely know what to say; fighting is a rough trade, and I am by no means certain that you are calculated for the scratch. It is not every one who has been brought up in the school of Mr. Petulengro and Tawno Chikno. All I can say is, that if I were an Armenian, and had two hundred thousand pounds to back me, I would attack the Persian."

"Hem!" said the Armenian.

One morning on getting up I discovered that my whole worldly wealth was reduced to one half-crown—throughout that day I walked about in considerable distress of mind: it was now requisite that I should come to a speedy decision with respect to what I was to do; I had not many alternatives, and, before I had retired to rest on the night of the day in question, I had determined that I could do no better than accept the first proposal of the Armenian, and translate, under his superintendence, the Haik Esop into English.

I reflected, for I made a virtue of necessity, that, after all, such an employment would be an honest and honourable one; honest, inasmuch as by engaging in it I should do harm to nobody; honourable, inasmuch as it was a literary task, which not every one was capable of executing. It was not every one of the booksellers' writers of London who was competent to translate the Haik Esop. I determined to accept the offer of the Armenian.

Once or twice the thought of what I might have to undergo in the translation from certain peculiarities of the Armenian's temper almost unsettled me; but a mechanical diving of my hand into my pocket, and the feeling of the solitary half-crown, confirmed me; after all this was a life of trial and tribulation, and I had read somewhere or other that there was much merit in patience, so I determined to hold fast in my resolution of accepting the offer of the Armenian.

But all of a sudden I remembered that the Armenian appeared to have altered his intentions towards me: he appeared no longer desirous that I should render the Haik Esop into English for the benefit of the stock-jobbers on Exchange, but rather that I should acquire the rudiments of doing business in the Armenian fashion, and accumulate a fortune, which would enable me to make a figure upon 'Change with the best of the stock-jobbers. "Well," thought I, withdrawing my hand from my pocket, whither it had again mechanically dived, "after all, what would the world, what would this city be, without commerce? I believe the world, and particularly this city, would cut a very poor figure without commerce; and then there is something poetical in the idea of doing business after the Armenian fashion, dealing with dark-faced Lascars and Rabbins of the Sephardim. Yes, should the Armenian insist upon it, I will accept a seat at the desk, opposite the Moldavian clerk. I do not like the idea of cuffs similar to those the Armenian bestowed upon the Moldavian clerk; whatever merit there may be in patience, I do not think that my estimation of the merit of patience would be sufficient to induce me to remain quietly sitting under the infliction of cuffs. I think I should, in the event of his cuffing me, knock the Armenian down. Well, I think I have heard it said somewhere, that a knock-down blow is a great cementer of friendship; I think I have heard of two people being better friends than ever after the one had received from the other a knock-down blow."

That night I dreamed I had acquired a colossal fortune, some four hundred thousand pounds, by the Armenian way of doing business, but suddenly awoke in dreadful perplexity as to how I should dispose of it.

About nine o'clock next morning I set off to the house of the Armenian; I had never called upon him so early before, and certainly never with a heart beating with so much eagerness; but the situation of my affairs had become very critical, and I thought that I ought to lose no time in informing the Armenian that I was at length perfectly willing either to translate the Haik Esop under his superintendence, or to accept a seat at the desk opposite to the Moldavian clerk, and acquire the secrets of Armenian commerce. With a quick step I entered the counting-room, where, notwithstanding the earliness of the hour, I found the clerk busied as usual at his desk.

He had always appeared to me a singular being, this same Moldavian clerk. A person of fewer words could scarcely be conceived. Provided his master were at home, he would, on my inquiring, nod his head; and, provided he were not, he would invariably reply with the monosyllable "no," delivered in a strange guttural tone. On the present occasion, being full of eagerness and impatience, I was about to pass by him to the apartment above, without my usual inquiry, when he lifted his head from the ledger in which he was writing, and, laying down his pen, motioned to me with his forefinger, as if to arrest my progress; whereupon I stopped, and, with a palpitating heart, demanded whether the master of the house was at home? The Moldavian clerk replied with his usual guttural, and, opening his desk ensconced his head therein.

"It does not much matter," said I, "I suppose I shall find him at home after 'Change; it does not much matter, I can return."

I was turning away with the intention of leaving the room; at this moment, however, the head of the Moldavian clerk became visible, and I observed a letter in his hand, which he had inserted in the desk at the same time with his head; this he extended towards me, making at the same time a side-long motion with his head, as much as to say that it contained something which interested me.

I took the letter, and the Moldavian clerk forthwith resumed his occupation. The back of the letter bore my name, written in Armenian characters. With a trembling hand I broke the seal, and, unfolding the letter, I beheld several lines also written in the letters of Mesroub, the Cadmus of the Armenians.

I stared at the lines, and at first could not make out a syllable of their meaning; at last, however, by continued staring, I discovered that, though the letters were Armenian, the words were English; in about ten minutes I had contrived to decipher the sense of the letter; it ran somewhat in this style:

"MY DEAR FRIEND,—

"The words which you uttered in our last conversation have made a profound impression upon me; I have thought them over day and night, and have come to the conclusion that it is my bounden duty to attack the Persians. When these lines are delivered to you, I shall be on the route to Ararat. A mercantile speculation will be to the world the ostensible motive of my journey, and it is singular enough that one which offers considerable prospect of advantage has just presented itself on the confines of Persia. Think not, however, that motives of lucre would have been sufficiently powerful to tempt me to the East at the present moment. I may speculate, it is true; but I should scarcely have undertaken the journey but for your pungent words inciting me to attack the Persians. Doubt not that I will attack them on the first opportunity. I thank you heartily for putting me in mind of my duty. I have hitherto, to use your own words, been too fond of money-getting, like all my countrymen. I am much indebted to you; farewell! and may every prosperity await you."

For some time after I had deciphered the epistle, I stood as if rooted to the floor. I felt stunned—my last hope was gone; presently a feeling arose in my mind—a feeling of self-reproach. Whom had I to blame but myself for the departure of the Armenian? Would he have ever thought of attacking the Persians had I not put the idea into his head? he had told me in his epistle that he was indebted to me for the idea. But for that, he might at the present moment have been in London, increasing his fortune by his usual methods, and I might be commencing under his auspices the translation of the Haik Esop, with the promise, no doubt, of a considerable remuneration for my trouble; or I might be taking a seat opposite the Moldavian clerk, and imbibing the first rudiments of doing business after the Armenian fashion, with the comfortable hope of realising in a short time, a fortune of three or four hundred thousand pounds; but the Armenian was now gone, and farewell to the fine hopes I had founded upon him the day before. What was I to do? I looked wildly around, till my eyes rested on the Moldavian clerk, who was writing away in his ledger with particular vehemence. Not knowing well what to do or to say, I thought I might as well ask the Moldavian clerk when the Armenian had departed, and when he thought he would return. It is true it mattered little to me when he departed seeing that he was gone, and it was evident that he would not be back soon; but I knew not what to do, and in pure helplessness thought I might as well ask; so I went up to the Moldavian clerk and asked him when the Armenian had departed, and whether he had been gone two days or three? Whereupon the Moldavian clerk looking up from his ledger, made certain signs, which I could by no means understand. I stood astonished, but presently recovering myself, inquired when he considered it probable that the master would return, and whether he thought it would be two months or—my tongue faltered—two years; whereupon the Moldavian clerk made more signs than before, and yet more unintelligible; as I persisted, however, he flung down his pen, and, putting his thumb into his mouth moved it rapidly, causing the nail to sound against the lower jaw; whereupon I saw that he was dumb, and hurried away, for I had always entertained a horror of dumb people, having once heard my mother say, when I was a child, that dumb people were half demoniacs, or little better.

CHAPTER XVII

Leaving the house of the Armenian, I strolled about for some time; almost mechanically my feet conducted me to London Bridge, to the booth in which stood the stall of the old apple-woman; the sound of her voice aroused me, as I sat in a kind of stupor on the stone bench beside her; she was inquiring what was the matter with me.

At first, I believe, I answered her very incoherently, for I observed alarm beginning to depict itself upon her countenance. Rousing myself, however, I in my turn put a few questions to her upon her present condition and prospects. The old woman's countenance cleared up instantly; she informed me that she had never been more comfortable in her life; that her trade, her *honest* trade—laying an emphasis on the word honest—had increased of late wonderfully; that her health was better, and, above all, that she felt no fear and horror "here," laying her hand on her breast.

On my asking her whether she still heard voices in the night, she told me that she frequently did; but that the present were mild voices, sweet voices, encouraging voices, very different from the former ones; that a voice only the night previous, had cried out about "the peace of God," in particularly sweet accents; a sentence which she remembered to have read in her early youth in the primer, but which she had clean forgotten till the voice the night before brought it to her recollection.

After a pause, the old woman said to me: "I believe, dear, that it is the blessed book you brought me which has wrought this goodly change. How glad I am now that I can read; but oh what a difference between the book you brought to me and the one you took away. I believe the one you brought is written by the finger of God, and the other by——"

"Don't abuse the book," said I, "it is an excellent book for those who can understand it; it was not exactly suited to you, and perhaps it had been better that you had never read it—and yet, who knows? Peradventure, if you had not read that book, you would not have been fitted for the perusal of the one which you say is written by the finger of God"; and, pressing my hand to my head, I fell into a deep fit of musing. "What, after all," thought I, "if there should be more order and system in the working of the moral world than I have thought? Does there not seem in the present instance to be something like the working of a Divine hand? I could not conceive why this woman, better educated than her mother, should have been, as she certainly was, a worse character than her mother. Yet perhaps this woman may be better and happier than her mother ever was; perhaps she is so already—perhaps this world is not a wild, lying dream, as I have occasionally supposed it to be."

But the thought of my own situation did not permit me to abandon myself much longer to these musings. I started up. "Where are you going, child?" said the woman anxiously. "I scarcely know," said I; "anywhere." "Then stay here, child," said she; "I have much to say to you." "No," said I, "I shall be better moving about"; and I was moving away, when it suddenly occurred to me that I might never see this woman again; and turning round I offered her my hand, and bade her good-bye. "Farewell, child," said the old woman, "and God bless you!" I then moved along the bridge until I reached the Southwark side, and, still holding on my course, my mind again became quickly abstracted from all surrounding objects.

At length I found myself in a street or road, with terraces on either side, and seemingly of interminable length, leading, as it would appear, to the south-east. I was walking at a great rate—there were likewise a great number of people, also walking at a great rate; also carts and carriages driving at a great rate; and all, men, carts and carriages, going in the selfsame direction, namely, to the south-east. I stopped for a moment and deliberated whether or not I should proceed. What business had I in that direction? I could not say that I had any particular business in that direction, but what could I do were I to turn back? only walk about well-known streets; and, if I must walk, why not continue in the direction in which I was to see whither the road and its terraces led? I was here in a terra incognita, and an unknown place had always some interest for me; moreover, I had a desire to know whither all this crowd was going, and for what purpose. I thought they could not be going far, as crowds seldom go far, especially at such a rate; so I walked on more lustily than before, passing group after group of the crowd, and almost vieing in speed with some of the carriages, especially the hackney-coaches; and by dint of walking at this rate, the terraces and houses becoming somewhat less frequent as I advanced, I reached in about three-quarters of an hour a kind of low dingy town, in the neighbourhood of the river; the streets were swarming with people, and I concluded, from the number of wild-beast shows, caravans, gingerbread stalls, and the like, that a fair was being held. Now, as I had always been partial to fairs, I felt glad that I had fallen in with the crowd which had conducted me to the present one, and, casting away as much as I was able all gloomy thoughts, I did my best to enter into the diversions of the fair; staring at the wonderful representations of animals on canvas hung up before the shows of wild beasts, which, by-the-bye, are frequently found much more worthy of admiration than the real beasts themselves; listening to the jokes of the merry-andrews from the platforms in front of the temporary theatres, or admiring the splendid tinsel dresses of the performers who thronged the stages in the intervals of the entertainments; and in this manner, occasionally gazing and occasionally listening, I passed through the town till I came in front of a large edifice looking full upon the majestic bosom of the Thames.

It was a massive stone edifice, built in an antique style, and black with age, with a broad esplanade between it and the river, on which, mixed with a few people from the fair, I observed moving about a great many individuals in quaint dresses of blue, with strange three-cornered hats on their heads; most of them were mutilated; this had a wooden leg—this wanted an arm; some had but one eye; and as I gazed upon the edifice, and the singular-looking individuals who moved before it, I guessed where I was. "I am at——" said I; "these individuals are battered tars of Old England, and this edifice, once the favourite abode of Glorious Elizabeth, is the refuge which a grateful country has allotted to them. Here they can rest their weary bodies; at their ease talk over the actions in which they have been injured; and, with the tear of enthusiasm flowing from their eyes, boast how they have trod the deck of fame with Rodney, or Nelson, or others whose names stand emblazoned in the naval annals of their country."

Turning to the right, I entered a park or wood consisting of enormous trees, occupying the foot, sides, and top of a hill, which rose behind the town; there were multitudes of people among the trees, diverting themselves in various ways. Coming to the top of the hill, I was presently stopped by a lofty wall, along which I walked, till, coming to a small gate, I passed through and found myself on an extensive green plain, on one side bounded in part by the wall of the park, and on the others, in the distance, by extensive ranges of houses; to the south-east was a lofty eminence, partially clothed with wood. The plain exhibited an animated scene, a kind of continuation of the fair below; there were multitudes of people upon it, many tents, and shows; there was also horse-racing, and much noise and shouting, the sun shining brightly overhead. After gazing at the horse-racing for a little time, feeling myself somewhat tired, I went up to one of the tents, and laid myself down on the grass. There was much noise in the tent. "Who will stand me?" said a voice with a slight tendency to lisp. "Will you, my lord?" "Yes," said another voice. Then there was a sound as of a piece of money banging on a table. "Lost! lost! lost!" cried several voices; and then the banging down of the money, and the "lost! lost! lost!" were frequently repeated; at last the second voice exclaimed: "I will try no more; you have cheated me." "Never cheated any one in my life, my lord—all fair—all chance. Them that finds, wins—them that can't find, loses. Any one else try? Who'll try? Will you, my lord?" and then it appeared that some other lord tried, for I heard more money flung down. Then again the cry of "Lost! lost!"—then again the sound of money, and so on. Once or twice, but not more, I heard "Won! won!" but the predominant cry was "Lost! lost!" At last there was a considerable hubbub, and the words "Cheat!" "Rogue!" and "You filched away the pea!" were used freely by more voices than one, to which the voice with the tendency to lisp replied; "Never filched a pea in my life; would scorn it. Always glad when folks wins; but, as those here don't appear to be civil, nor to wish to play any more, I shall take myself off with my table; so, good-day, gentlemen."

Presently a man emerged from the tent, bearing before him a rather singular table; it appeared to be of white deal, was exceedingly small at the top, and with very long legs. At a few yards from the entrance he paused, and looked round, as if to decide on the direction which he should take; presently, his eye glancing on me as I lay upon the ground, he started, and appeared for a moment inclined to make off as quick as possible, table and all. In a moment, however, he seemed to recover assurance, and, coming up to the place where I was, the long legs of the table projecting before him, he cried: "Glad to see you here, my lord."

"Thank you," said I, "it's a fine day."

"Very fine, my lord; will your lordship play? Them that finds, wins—them that don't find, loses."

"Play at what?" said I.

"Only at the thimble and pea, my lord."

"I never heard of such a game."

"Didn't you? Well, I'll soon teach you," said he, placing the table down. "All you have to do is to put a sovereign down on my table, and to find the pea, which I put under one of my thimbles. If you find it—and it is easy enough to find it—I give you a sovereign besides your own: for them that finds, wins."

"And them that don't find, loses," said I; "no, I don't wish to play."

"Why not, my lord?"

"Why, in the first place, I have no money."

"Oh, you have no money; that of course alters the case. If you have no money, you can't play. Well, I suppose I must be seeing after my customers," said he, glancing over the plain.

"Good-day," said I.

"Good-day," said the man slowly, but without moving, and as if in reflection. After a moment or two, looking at me inquiringly, he added: "Out of employ?"

"Yes," said I, "out of employ."

The man measured me with his eye as I lay on the ground. At length he said: "May I speak a word or two to you, my lord?"

"As many as you please," said I.

"Then just come a little out of hearing, a little farther on the grass, if you please, my lord."

"Why do you call me my lord?" said I, as I arose and followed him.

"We of the thimble always calls our customers lords," said the man; "but I won't call you such a foolish name any more; come along."

The man walked along the plain till he came to the side of a dry pit, when looking round to see that no one was nigh, he laid his table on the grass, and, sitting down with his legs over the side of the pit, he motioned me to do the same. "So you are in want of employ," said he, after I had sat down beside him.

"Yes," said I, "I am very much in want of employ."

"I think I can find you some."

"What kind?" said I.

"Why," said the man, "I think you would do to be my bonnet."

"Bonnet!" said I, "what is that?"

"Don't you know? However, no wonder, as you had never heard of the thimble-and-pea game, but I will tell you. We of the game are very much exposed; folks when they have lost their money, as those who play with us mostly do, sometimes uses rough language, calls us cheats, and sometimes knocks our hats over our eyes; and what's more, with a kick under our table, cause the top deals to fly off; this is the third table I have used this day, the other two being broken by uncivil customers: so we of the game generally like to have gentlemen go about with us to take our part, and encourage us, though pretending to know nothing about us; for example, when the customer says, 'I'm cheated,' the bonnet must say, 'No, you a'n't, it is all right'; or, when my hat is knocked over my eyes, the bonnet must square, and say, 'I never saw the man before in all my life, but I won't see him ill-used'; and so, when they kicks at the table, the bonnet must say, 'I won't see the table ill-used, such a nice table, too; besides, I want to play myself'; and then I would say to the bonnet, 'Thank you, my lord, them that finds, wins'; and then the bonnet plays, and I lets the bonnet win."

"In a word," said I, "the bonnet means the man who covers you, even as the real bonnet covers the head."

"Just so," said the man, "I see you are awake, and would soon make a first-rate bonnet."

"Bonnet," said I, musingly; "bonnet; it is metaphorical."

"Is it?" said the man.

"Yes," said I, "like the cant words——"

"Bonnet is cant," said the man; "we of the thimble, as well as all clyfakers and the like, understand cant, as, of course, must every bonnet; so, if you are employed by me, you had better learn it as soon as you can, that we may discourse together without being understood by every one. Besides covering his principal, a bonnet must have his eyes about him, for the trade of the pea, though a strictly honest one, is not altogether lawful; so it is the duty of the bonnet, if he sees the constable coming, to say, the Gorgio's welling."

"That is not cant," said I, "that is the language of the Rommany Chals."

"Do you know those people?" said the man.

"Perfectly," said I, "and their language too."

"I wish I did," said the man, "I would give ten pounds and more to know the language of the Rommany Chals. There's some of it in the language of the pea and thimble; how it came there I don't know, but so it is. I wish I knew it, but it is difficult. You'll make a capital bonnet; shall we close?"

"What would the wages be?" I demanded.

"Why, to a first-rate bonnet, as I think you would prove, I could afford to give from forty to fifty shillings a week."

"Is it possible?" said I.

"Good wages, a'n't they?" said the man.

"First rate," said I; "bonneting is more profitable than reviewing."

"Anan?" said the man.

"Or translating; I don't think the Armenian would have paid me at that rate for translating his Esop."

"Who is he?" said the man.

"Esop?"

"No, I know what that is, Esop's cant for a hunchback; but t'other?"

"You should know," said I.

"Never saw the man in all my life."

"Yes, you have," said I, "and felt him too; don't you remember the individual from whom you took the pocket-book?"

"Oh, that was he; well, the less said about that matter the better; I have left off that trade, and taken to this, which is a much better. Between ourselves, I am not sorry that I did not carry off that pocket-book; if I had, it might have encouraged me in the trade, in which, had I remained, I might have been lagged, sent abroad, as I had been already imprisoned; so I determined to leave it off at all hazards, though I was hard up, not having a penny in the world."

"And wisely resolved," said I, "it was a bad and dangerous trade; I wonder you should ever have embraced it."

"It is all very well talking," said the man, "but there is a reason for everything; I am the son of a Jewess, by a military officer,"—and then the man told me his story. I shall not repeat the man's story, it was a poor one, a vile one; at last he observed: "So that affair which you know of determined me to leave the filching trade, and take up with a more honest and safe one; so at last I thought of the pea and thimble, but I wanted funds, especially to pay for lessons at the hands of a master, for I knew little about it."

"Well," said I, "how did you get over that difficulty?"

"Why," said the man, "I thought I should never have got over it. What funds could I raise? I had nothing to sell; the few clothes I had I wanted, for we of the thimble must always appear decent, or nobody would come near us. I was at my wits' end; at last I got over my difficulty in the strangest way in the world."

"What was that?"

"By an old thing which I had picked up some time before—a book."

"A book?" said I.

"Yes, which I had taken out of your lordship's pocket one day as you were walking the streets in a great hurry. I thought it was a pocket-book at first, full of bank notes, perhaps," continued he, laughing. "It was well for me, however, that it was not, for I should have soon spent the notes; as it was, I had flung the old thing down with an oath, as soon as I brought it home. When I was so hard up, however, after the affair with that friend of yours, I took it up one day, and thought I might make something by it to support myself a day with. Chance or something else led me into a grand shop; there was a man there who seemed to be the master, talking to a jolly, portly old gentleman, who seemed to be a country squire. Well, I went up to the first, and offered it for sale; he took the book, opened it at the title-page, and then all of a sudden his eyes glistened, and he showed it to the fat, jolly gentleman, and his eyes glistened too, and I heard him say 'How singular!' and then the two talked together in a speech I didn't understand—I rather thought it was French, at any rate it wasn't cant; and presently the first asked me what I would take for the book. Now I am not altogether a fool nor am I blind, and I had narrowly marked all that passed, and it came into my head that now was the time for making a man of myself, at any rate I could lose nothing by a little confidence; so I looked the man boldly in the face, and said: 'I will have five guineas for that book, there a'n't such another in the whole world.' 'Nonsense,' said the first man, 'there are plenty of them, there have been nearly fifty editions to my knowledge; I will give you five shillings.' 'No,' said I, 'I'll not take it, for I don't like to be cheated, so give me my book again'; and I attempted to take it away from the fat gentleman's hand. 'Stop,' said the younger man, 'are you sure that you won't take less?' 'Not a farthing,' said I; which was not altogether true, but I said so. 'Well,' said the fat gentleman, 'I will give you what you ask'; and sure enough he presently gave me the money; so I made a bow, and was leaving the shop, when it came into my head that there was something odd in all this, and, as I had got the money in my pocket, I turned back, and, making another bow, said: 'May I be so bold as to ask why you gave me all this money for that 'ere dirty book? When I came into the shop, I should have been glad to get a shilling for it; but I saw you wanted it, and asked five guineas.' Then they looked at one another, and smiled, and shrugged up their shoulders. Then the first man, looking at me, said: 'Friend, you have been a little too sharp for us; however, we can afford to forgive you, as my friend here has long been in quest of this particular book; there are plenty of editions, as I told you, and a common copy is not worth five shillings; but this is a first edition, and a copy of the first edition is worth its weight in gold.' "

"So, after all, they outwitted you," I observed.

"Clearly," said the man; "I might have got double the price, had I known the value; but I don't care, much good may it do them, it has done me plenty. By means of it I have got into an honest, respectable trade, in which there's little danger and plenty of profit, and got out of one which would have got me lagged sooner or later."

"But," said I, "you ought to remember that the thing was not yours; you took it from me, who had been requested by a poor old apple-woman to exchange it for a Bible."

"Well," said the man, "did she ever get her Bible?"

"Yes," said I, "she got her Bible."

"Then she has no cause to complain; and, as for you, chance or something else has sent you to me, that I may make you reasonable amends for any loss you may have had. Here am I ready to make you my bonnet, with forty or fifty shillings a week, which you say yourself are capital wages."

"I find no fault with the wages," said I, "but I don't like the employ."

"Not like bonneting," said the man; "ah, I see, you would like to be principal; well, a time may come—those long white fingers of yours would just serve for the business."

"Is it a difficult one?" I demanded.

"Why, it is not very easy: two things are needful—natural talent, and constant practice; but I'll show you a point or two connected with the game"; and, placing his table between his knees as he sat over the side of the pit, he produced three thimbles, and a small brown pellet, something resembling a pea. He moved the thimble and pellet about, now placing it to all appearance under one, and now under another; "Under which is it now?" he said at last. "Under that," said I, pointing to the lower most of the thimbles, which, as they stood, formed a kind of triangle. "No," said he, "it is not, but lift it up"; and, when I lifted up the thimble, the pellet, in truth, was not under it. "It was under none of them," said he, "it was pressed by my little finger against my palm"; and then he showed me how he did the trick, and asked me if the game was not a funny one; and, on my answering in the affirmative, he said: "I am glad you like it, come along and let us win some money."

Thereupon, getting up, he placed the table before him, and was moving away; observing, however, that I did not stir, he asked me what I was staying for. "Merely for my own pleasure," said I, "I like sitting here very well." "Then you won't close?" said the man. "By no means," I replied, "your proposal does not suit me." "You may be principal in time," said the man. "That makes no difference," said I; and, sitting with my legs over the pit, I forthwith began to decline an Armenian noun. "That a'n't cant," said the man; "no, nor gypsy either. Well, if you won't close, another will, I can't lose any more time," and forthwith he departed.

And after I had declined four Armenian nouns, of different declensions, I rose from the side of the pit, and wandered about amongst the various groups of people scattered over the green. Presently I came to where the man of the thimbles was standing, with the table before him, and many people about him. "Them who finds, wins, and them who can't find, loses," he cried. Various individuals tried to find the pellet, but all were unsuccessful, till at last considerable dissatisfaction was expressed, and the terms rogue and cheat were lavished upon him. "Never cheated anybody in all my life," he cried; and, observing me at hand, "didn't I play fair, my lord?" he inquired. But I made no answer. Presently some more played, and he permitted one or two to win, and the eagerness to play with him became greater. After I had looked on for some time, I was moving away; just then I perceived a short, thick personage, with a staff in his hand, advancing in a great hurry; whereupon with a sudden impulse, I exclaimed:—

Shoon thimble-engro;
Avella Gorgio.

The man who was in the midst of his pea-and-thimble process, no sooner heard the last word of the distich, than he turned an alarmed look in the direction of where I stood; then, glancing around, and perceiving the constable, he slipped forthwith his pellet and thimbles into his pocket, and, lifting up his table, he cried to the people about him, "Make way!" and with a motion of his head to me, as if to follow him, he darted off with a swiftness which the short, pursy constable could by no means rival; and whither he went, or what became of him, I know not, inasmuch as I turned away in another direction.

And, as I wandered along the green, I drew near to a place where several men, with a cask beside them, sat carousing in the neighbourhood of a small tent. "Here he comes," said one of them, as I advanced, and standing up he raised his voice and sang:—

Here the Gypsy gemman see,
With his Roman jib and his rome and dree—
Rome and dree, rum and dry
Rally round the Rommany Rye.

It was Mr. Petulengro, who was here diverting himself with several of his comrades; they all received me with considerable frankness. "Sit down, brother," said Mr. Petulengro, "and take a cup of good ale."

I sat down. "Your health, gentlemen," said I, as I took the cup which Mr. Petulengro handed to me.

"Aukko tu pios adrey Rommanis. Here is your health in Rommany, brother," said Mr. Petulengro; who, having refilled the cup, now emptied it at a draught.

"Your health in Rommany, brother," said Tawno Chikno, to whom the cup came next.

"The Rommany Rye," said a third.

"The Gypsy gentleman," exclaimed a fourth, drinking.

And then they all sang in chorus:—

Here the Gypsy gemman see,
With his Roman jib and his rome and dree—
Rome and dree, rum and dry
Rally round the Rommany Rye.

"And now, brother," said Mr. Petulengro, "seeing that you have drunk and been drunken, you will perhaps tell us where you have been, and what about?"

"I have been in the Big City," said I, "writing lils."

"How much money have you got in your pocket, brother?" said Mr. Petulengro.

"Eighteen pence," said I; "all I have in the world."

"I have been in the Big City, too," said Mr. Petulengro; "but I have not written lils—I have fought in the ring—I have fifty pounds in my pocket—I have much more in the world. Brother, there is considerable difference between us."

"I would rather be the lil-writer, after all," said the tall, handsome, black man; "indeed, I would wish for nothing better."

"Why so?" said Mr. Petulengro.

"Because they have so much to say for themselves," said the black man, "even when dead and gone. When they are laid in the churchyard, it is their own fault if people a'n't talking of them. Who will know, after I am dead, or bitchadey pawdel, that I was once the beauty of the world, or that you, Jasper, were——"

"The best man in England of my inches. That's true, Tawno—however, here's our brother will perhaps let the world know something about us."

"Not he," said the other, with a sigh; "he'll have quite enough to do in writing his own lils, and telling the world how handsome and clever he was; and who can blame him? Not I. If I could write lils, every word should be about myself and my own tacho Rommanis—my own lawful wedded wife, which is the same thing. I tell you what, brother, I once heard a wise man say in Brummagem, that 'there is nothing like blowing one's own horn,' which I conceived to be much the same thing as writing one's own lil."

After a little more conversation, Mr. Petulengro arose, and motioned me to follow him. "Only eighteen pence in the world, brother!" said he, as we walked together.

"Nothing more, I assure you. How came you to ask me how much money I had?"

"Because there was something in your look, brother, something very much resembling that which a person showeth who does not carry much money in his pocket. I was looking at my own face this morning in my wife's looking-glass—I did not look as you do, brother."

"I believe your sole motive for inquiring," said I, "was to have an opportunity of venting a foolish boast, and to let me know that you were in possession of fifty pounds."

"What is the use of having money unless you let people know you have it?" said Mr. Petulengro. "It is not every one can read faces, brother; and, unless you knew I had money, how could you ask me to lend you any?"

"I am not going to ask you to lend me any."

"Then you may have it without asking; as I said before, I have fifty pounds, all lawfully earnt money, got by fighting in the ring—I will lend you that, brother."

"You are very kind," said I; "but I will not take it."

"Then the half of it?"

"Nor the half of it; but it is getting towards evening, I must go back to the Great City."

"And what will you do in the Boro Foros?"

"I know not," said I.

"Earn money?"

"If I can."

"And if you can't?"

"Starve!"

"You look ill, brother," said Mr. Petulengro.

"I do not feel well; the Great City does not agree with me. Should I be so fortunate as to earn some money, I would leave the Big City, and take to the woods and fields."

"You may do that, brother," said Mr. Petulengro, "whether you have money or not. Our tents and horses are on the other side of yonder wooded hill, come and stay with us; we shall all be glad of your company, but more especially myself and my wife Pakomovna."

"What hill is that?" I demanded.

And then Mr. Petulengro told me the name of the hill. "We shall stay on t'other side of the hill a fortnight," he continued; "and as you are fond of lil writing, you may employ yourself profitably whilst there. You can write the lil of him whose dook gallops down that hill every night, even as the living man was wont to do long ago."

"Who was he?" I demanded.

"Jemmy Abershaw," said Mr. Petulengro; "one of those whom we call Boro-drom-engroes, and the Gorgios highwaymen. I once heard a rye say that the life of that man would fetch much money; so come to the other side of the hill, and write the lil in the tent of Jasper and his wife Pakomovna."

At first I felt inclined to accept the invitation of Mr. Petulengro; a little consideration, however, determined me to decline it. I had always been on excellent terms with Mr. Petulengro, but I reflected that people might be excellent friends when they met occasionally in the street, or on the heath, or in the wood; but that these very people when living together in a house, to say nothing of a tent, might quarrel. I reflected, moreover, that Mr. Petulengro had a wife. I had always, it is true, been a great favourite with Mrs. Petulengro, who had frequently been loud in her commendation of the young rye, as she called me, and his turn of conversation; but this was at a time when I stood in need of nothing, lived under my parents' roof, and only visited at the tents to divert and to be diverted. The times were altered, and I was by no means certain that Mrs. Petulengro, when she should discover that I was in need both of shelter and subsistence, might not alter her opinion both with respect to the individual and what he said–stigmatising my conversation as saucy discourse, and myself as a scurvy companion; and that she might bring over her husband to her own way of thinking, provided, indeed, he should need any conducting. I therefore, though without declaring my reasons, declined the offer of Mr. Petulengro, and presently, after shaking him by the hand, bent again my course towards the Great City.

I crossed the river at a bridge considerably above that hight of London; for not being acquainted with the way, I missed the turning which should have brought me to the latter. Suddenly I found myself in a street of which I had some recollection, and mechanically stopped before the window of a shop at which various publications were exposed; it was that of the bookseller to whom I had last applied in the hope of selling my ballads or Ab

Gwilym, and who had given me hopes that in the event of my writing a decent novel, or a tale, he would prove a purchaser. As I stood listlessly looking at the window, and the publications which it contained, I observed a paper affixed to the glass by wafers with something written upon it. I drew yet nearer for the purpose of inspecting it; the writing was in a fair round hand —"A Novel or Tale is much wanted," was what was written.

CHAPTER XVIII

"I MUST do something," said I, as I sat that night in my lonely apartment, with some bread and a pitcher of water before me.

Thereupon taking some of the bread, and eating it, I considered what I was to do. "I have no idea what I am to do," said I, as I stretched my hand towards the pitcher, "unless—and here I took a considerable draught—I write a tale or a novel—— That bookseller," I continued, speaking to myself, "is certainly much in need of a tale or novel, otherwise he would not advertise for one. Suppose I write one, I appear to have no other chance of extricating myself from my present difficulties; surely it was Fate that conducted me to his window.

"I will do it," said I, as I struck my hand against the table; "I will do it." Suddenly a heavy cloud of despondency came over me. Could I do it? Had I the imagination requisite to write a tale or a novel? "Yes, yes," said I, as I struck my hand again against the table, "I can manage it; give me fair play, and I can accomplish anything."

But should I have fair play? I must have something to maintain myself with whilst I wrote my tale, and I had but eighteen pence in the world. Would that maintain me whilst I wrote my tale? Yes, I thought it would, provided I ate bread, which did not cost much, and drank water, which cost nothing; it was poor diet, it was true, but better men than myself had written on bread and water; had not the big man told me so, or something to that effect, months before?

It was true there was my lodging to pay for; but up to the present time I owed nothing, and perhaps, by the time the people of the house asked me for money, I should have written a tale or a novel, which would bring me in money; I had paper, pens and ink, and, let me not forget them, I had candles in my closet, all paid for, to light me during my night work. Enough, I would go doggedly to work upon my tale or novel.

But what was the tale or novel to be about? Was it to be a tale of fashionable life, about Sir Harry Somebody, and the Countess Something? But I knew nothing about fashionable people, and cared less; therefore how should I attempt to describe fashionable life? What should the tale consist of? The life and adventures of some one. Good—but of whom? Did not Mr. Petulengro mention one Jemmy Abershaw? Yes. Did he not tell me that the life and adventures of Jemmy Abershaw would bring in much money to the writer? Yes, but I knew nothing of that worthy. I heard, it is true, from Mr. Petulengro, that when alive he committed robberies on the hill, on the side of which Mr. Petulengro had pitched his tents, and that his ghost still haunted the hill at midnight; but those were scant materials out of which to write the man's life. It is probable, indeed, that Mr. Petulengro would be able to supply me with further materials if I should apply to him, but I was in a hurry, and could not afford the time which it would be necessary to spend in passing to and from Mr. Petulengro, and consulting him. Moreover, my pride revolted at the idea of being beholden to Mr. Petulengro for the materials of the history. No, I would not write the history of Abershaw. Whose then—Harry Simms? Alas, the life of Harry Simms had been already much better written by himself than I could hope to do it; and, after all, Harry Simms, like Jemmy Abershaw, was merely a robber. Both, though bold and extraordinary men, were merely highwaymen. I questioned whether I could compose a tale likely to excite any particular interest out of the exploits of a mere robber. I want a character for my hero, thought I, something higher than a mere robber; some one like—like Colonel B——. By the way, why should I not write the life and adventures of Colonel B—— of Londonderry, in Ireland?

A truly singular man was this same Colonel B—— of Londonderry, in Ireland; a personage of most strange and incredible feats and daring, who had been a partisan soldier, a bravo—who, assisted by certain discontented troopers, nearly succeeded in stealing the crown and regalia from the Tower of London; who attempted to hang the Duke of Ormond, at Tyburn; and whose strange eventful career did not terminate even with his life, his dead body, on the circulation of an unfounded report that he did not come to his death by fair means, having been exhumed by the mob of his native place, where he had retired to die, and carried in the coffin through the streets.

Of his life I had inserted an account in the *Newgate Lives and Trials;* it was bare and meagre, and written in the stiff, awkward style of the seventeenth century; it had, however, strongly captivated my imagination and I now thought that out of it something better could be made; that, if I added to the adventures, and purified the style, I might fashion out of it a very decent tale or novel. On a sudden, however, the proverb of mending old garments with new cloth occurred to me. "I am afraid," said I, "any new adventures which I can invent will not fadge well with the old tale; one will but spoil the other." I had better have nothing to do with Colonel B——, thought I, but boldly and independently sit down and write the life of Joseph Sell.

This Joseph Sell, dear reader, was a fictitious personage who had just come into my head. I had never even heard of the name, but just at that moment it happened to come into my head; I would write an entirely fictitious narrative, called the *Life and Adventures of Joseph Sell, the Great Traveller.*

I had better begin at once, thought I; and removing the bread and the jug, which latter was now empty, I seized pen and paper, and forthwith essayed to write the life of Joseph Sell, but soon discovered that it is much easier to resolve upon a thing than to achieve it, or even to commence it; for the life of me I did not know how to begin, and, after trying in vain to write a line, I thought it would be as well to go to bed, and defer my projected undertaking till the morrow.

So I went to bed, but not to sleep. During the greater part of the night I lay awake, musing upon the work which I had determined to execute. For a long time my brain was dry and unproductive; I could form no plan which appeared feasible. At length I felt within my brain a kindly glow; it was the commencement of inspiration; in a few minutes I had formed my plan; I then began to imagine the scenes and the incidents. Scenes and incidents flitted before my mind's eye so plentifully that I knew not how to dispose of them; I was in a regular embarrassment. At length I got out of the difficulty in the easiest manner imaginable, namely, by consigning to the depths of oblivion all the feebler and less stimulant scenes and incidents, and retaining the better and more impressive ones. Before morning I had sketched the whole work on the tablets of my mind, and then resigned myself to sleep in the pleasing conviction that the most difficult part of my undertaking was achieved.

Rather late in the morning I awoke; for a few minutes I lay still, perfectly still; my imagination was considerably sobered; the scenes and situations which had pleased me so much over night appeared to me in a far less captivating guise that morning. I felt languid and almost hopeless—the thought, however, of my situation soon roused me—I must make an effort to improve the posture of my affairs; there was no time to be lost; so I sprang out of bed, breakfasted on bread and water, and then sat down doggedly to write the life of Joseph Sell.

It was a great thing to have formed my plan, and to have arranged the scenes in my head, as I had done on the preceding night. The chief thing requisite at present was the mere mechanical act of committing them to paper. This I did not find at first so easy as I could wish—I wanted mechanical skill; but I persevered, and before evening I had written ten pages. I partook of some bread and water; and, before I went to bed that night, I had completed fifteen pages of my life of Joseph Sell.

The next day I resumed my task—I found my power of writing considerably increased; my pen hurried rapidly over the paper—my brain was in a wonderfully teeming state; many scenes and visions which I had not thought of before were evolved, and, as fast as evolved, written down; they seemed to be more pat to my purpose, and more natural to my history, than many others which I had imagined before, and which I made now give place to these newer creations: by about midnight I had added thirty fresh pages to my *Life and Adventures of Joseph Sell.*

The third day arose—it was dark and dreary out of doors, and I passed it drearily enough within; my brain appeared to have lost much of its former glow, and my pen much of its power; I, however, toiled on, but at midnight had only added seven pages to my history of Joseph Sell.

On the fourth day the sun shone brightly—I arose, and, having breakfasted as usual, I fell to work. My brain was this day wonderfully prolific, and my pen never before or since glided so rapidly over the paper; towards night I began to feel strangely about the back part of my head, and my whole system was extraordinarily affected. I likewise occasionally saw double—a tempter now seemed to be at work within me.

"You had better leave off now for a short space," said the tempter, "and go out and drink a pint of beer; you have still one shilling left—if you go on at this rate, you will go mad—go out and spend sixpence, you can afford it, more than half your work is done." I was about to obey the suggestion of the tempter, when the idea struck me that, if I did not complete the work whilst the fit was on me, I should never complete it; so I held on. I am almost afraid to state how many pages I wrote that day of the life of Joseph Sell.

From this time I proceeded in a somewhat more leisurely manner; but, as I drew nearer and nearer to the completion of my task, dreadful fears and despondencies came over me. It will be too late, thought I; by the time I have finished the work, the bookseller will have been supplied with a tale or a novel. Is it probable that, in a town like this, where talent is so abundant—hungry talent too—a bookseller can advertise for a tale or a novel, without being supplied with half a dozen in twenty-four hours? I may as well fling down my pen—I am writing to no purpose. And these thoughts came over my mind so often, that at last, in utter despair, I flung down the pen. Whereupon the tempter within me said: "And, now you have flung down the pen, you may as well fling yourself out of the window; what remains for you to do?" Why, to take it up again, thought I to myself, for I did not like the latter suggestion at all—and then forthwith I resumed the pen, and wrote with greater vigour than before, from about six o'clock in the evening until I could hardly see, when I rested for awhile, when the tempter within me again said, or appeared to say: "All you have been writing is stuff, it will never do—a drug—a mere drug"; and methought these last words were uttered in the gruff tones of the big publisher. "A thing merely to be sneezed at," a voice like that of Taggart added; and then I seemed to hear a sternutation—as I probably did, for, recovering from a kind of swoon, I found myself shivering with cold. The next day I brought my work to a conclusion.

But the task of revision still remained; for an hour or two I shrank from it, and remained gazing stupidly at the pile of paper which I had written over. I was all but exhausted, and I dreaded, on inspecting the sheets, to find them full of absurdities which I had paid no regard to in the furor of composition. But the task, however trying to my nerves, must be got over; at last, in a kind of desperation, I entered upon it. It was far from an easy one; there were, however, fewer errors and absurdities than I had anticipated. About twelve o'clock at night I had got over the task of revision. "To-morrow, for the bookseller," said I, as my head sank on the pillow. "Oh me!"

On arriving at the bookseller's shop, I cast a nervous look at the window, for the purpose of observing whether the paper had been removed or not. To my great delight the paper was in its place; with a beating heart I entered, there was nobody in the shop; as I stood at the counter, however, deliberating whether or not I should call out, the door of what seemed to be a back-parlour opened, and out came a well-dressed lady-like female, of about thirty, with a good-looking and intelligent countenance. "What is your business, young man?" said she to me, after I had made her a polite bow. "I wish to speak to the gentleman of the house," said I. "My husband is not within at present," she replied; "what is your business?" "I have merely brought something to show him," said I, "but I will call again." "If you are the young gentleman who has been here before," said the lady, "with poems and ballads, as, indeed, I know you are," she added, smiling, "for I have seen you through the glass door, I am afraid it will be useless; that is," she added with another smile, "if you bring us nothing else." "I have not brought you poems and ballads now," said I, "but something widely different; I saw your advertisement for a tale or a novel, and have written something which I think will suit; and here it is," I added, showing the roll of paper which I held in my hand. "Well," said the bookseller's wife, "you may leave it, though I cannot promise you much chance of its being accepted. My husband has already had several offered to him; however, you may leave it; give it me. Are you afraid to entrust it to me?" she demanded somewhat hastily, observing that I hesitated. "Excuse me," said I, "but it is all I have to depend upon in the world; I am chiefly apprehensive that it will not be read." "On that point I can reassure you," said the good lady, smiling, and there was now something sweet in her smile. "I give you my word that it shall be read; come again to-morrow morning at eleven, when, if not approved, it shall be returned to you."

I returned to my lodging, and forthwith betook myself to bed, notwithstanding the earliness of the hour. I felt tolerably tranquil; I had now cast my last stake, and was prepared to abide by the result. Whatever that result might be, I could have nothing to reproach myself with; I had strained all the energies which nature had given me in order to rescue myself from the difficulties which surrounded me. I presently sank into a sleep, which endured during the remainder of the day, and the whole of the succeeding night. I awoke about nine on the morrow, and spent my last threepence on a breakfast somewhat more luxurious than the immediately preceding ones, for one penny of the sum was expended on the purchase of milk.

At the appointed hour I repaired to the house of the bookseller; the bookseller was in his shop. "Ah," said he, as soon as I entered, "I am glad to see you." There was an unwonted heartiness in the bookseller's tones, an unwonted benignity in his face. "So," said he, after a pause, "you have taken my advice, written a book of adventure; nothing like taking the advice, young man, of your superiors in age. Well, I think your book will do, and so does my wife, for whose judgment I have a great regard; as well I may, as she is the daughter of a first-rate novelist, deceased. I think I shall venture on sending your book to the press." "But," said I, "we have not yet agreed upon terms." "Terms, terms," said the bookseller; "ahem! well, there is nothing like coming to terms at once. I will print the book, and give you half the profit when the edition is sold." "That will not do," said I; "I intend shortly to leave London: I must have something at once." "Ah, I see," said the bookseller, "in distress; frequently the case with authors, especially young ones. Well, I don't care if I purchase it of you, but you must be moderate; the public are very fastidious, and the speculation may prove a losing one, after all. Let me see, will five——hem"—he stopped. I looked the bookseller in the face; there was something peculiar in it. Suddenly it appeared to me as if the voice of him of the thimble sounded in my ear: "Now is your time, ask enough, never such another chance of establishing yourself; respectable trade, pea and thimble." "Well," said I at last, "I have no objection to take the offer which you were about to make, though I really think five-and-twenty guineas to be scarcely enough, everything considered." "Five-and-twenty guineas!" said the bookseller; "are you—what was I going to say—I never meant to offer half as much—I mean a quarter; I was going to say five guineas—I mean pounds; I will, however, make it up guineas." "That will not do," said I; "but, as I find we shall not deal, return me my manuscript, that I may carry it to some one else." The bookseller looked blank. "Dear me," said he, "I should never have supposed that you would have made any objection to such an offer; I am quite sure that you would have been glad to take five pounds for either of the two huge manuscripts of songs and ballads that you brought me on a former occasion." "Well," said I, "if you will engage to publish either of those two manuscripts, you shall have the present one for five pounds." "God forbid that I should make any such bargain," said the bookseller; "I would publish neither on any account; but, with respect to this last book, I have really an inclination to print it, both for your sake and mine; suppose we say ten pounds." "No," said I, "ten pounds will not do; pray restore me my manuscript." "Stay," said the bookseller, "my wife is in the next room, I will go and consult her." Thereupon he went into his back-room, where I heard him conversing with his wife in a low tone; in about ten minutes he returned. "Young gentleman," said he, "perhaps you will take tea with us this evening, when we will talk further over the matter."

That evening I went and took tea with the bookseller and his wife, both of whom, particularly the latter, overwhelmed me with civility. It was not long before I learned that the work had been already sent to the press, and was intended to stand at the head of a series of entertaining narratives, from which my friends promised themselves considerable profit. The subject of terms was again brought forward. I stood firm to my first demand for a long time; when, however, the bookseller's wife complimented me on my production in the highest terms, and said that she discovered therein the germs of genius, which she made no doubt would some day prove ornamental to my native land, I consented to drop my demand to twenty pounds, stipulating, however, that I should not be troubled with the correction of the work.

Before I departed I received the twenty pounds, and departed with a light heart to my lodgings.

Reader, amidst the difficulties and dangers of this life, should you ever be tempted to despair, call to mind these latter chapters of the life of Lavengro. There are few positions, however difficult, from which dogged resolution and perseverance may not liberate you.

CHAPTER XIX

I HAD long ago determined to leave London as soon as the means should be in my power, and now that they were, I determined to leave the Great City; yet I felt some reluctance to go. I would fain have pursued the career of original authorship which had just opened itself to me, and have written other tales of adventure. The bookseller had given me encouragement enough to do so; he had assured me that he should be always happy to deal with me for an article (that was the word) similar to the one I had brought him, provided my terms were moderate; and the bookseller's wife, by her complimentary language, had given me yet more encouragement. But for some months past I had been far from well, and my original indisposition, brought on partly by the peculiar atmosphere of the Big City, partly by anxiety of mind, had been much increased by the exertions which I had been compelled to make during the last few days. I felt that, were I to remain where I was, I should die, or become a confirmed valetudinarian. I would go forth into the country, travelling on foot, and, by exercise and inhaling pure air, endeavour to recover my health, leaving my subsequent movements to be determined by Providence.

But whither should I bend my course? Once or twice I thought of walking home to the old town, stay some time with my mother and my brother, and enjoy the pleasant walks in the neighbourhood; but, though I wished very much to see my mother and my brother, and felt much disposed to enjoy the said pleasant walks, the old town was not exactly the place to which I wished to go at this present juncture. I was afraid the people would ask, Where are your Northern Ballads? Where are your alliterative translations from Ab Gwilym—of which you were always talking, and with which you promised to astonish the world? Now, in the event of such interrogations, what could I answer? It is true I had compiled *Newgate Lives and Trials*, and had written the life of Joseph Sell, but I was afraid that the people of the old town would scarcely consider these as equivalents for the Northern

Ballads and the songs of Ab Gwilym. I would go forth and wander in any direction but that of the old town.

But how one's sensibility on any particular point diminishes with time! At present, I enter the old town perfectly indifferent as to what the people may be thinking on the subject of the songs and ballads. With respect to the people themselves, whether, like my sensibility, their curiosity has altogether evaporated, or whether, which is at least equally probable, they never entertained any, one thing is certain, that never in a single instance have they troubled me with any remarks on the subject of the songs and ballads.

As it was my intention to travel on foot, with a bundle and a stick, I despatched my trunk containing some few clothes and books to the old town. My preparations were soon made; in about three days I was in readiness to start.

Before departing, however, I bethought me of my old friend the apple-woman of London Bridge. Apprehensive that she might be labouring under the difficulties of poverty, I sent her a piece of gold by the hands of a young maiden in the house in which I lived. The latter punctually executed her commission, but brought me back the piece of gold. The old woman would not take it; she did not want it, she said. "Tell the poor thin lad," she added, "to keep it for himself, he wants it more than I."

Rather late one afternoon I departed from my lodging, with my stick in one hand and a small bundle in the other, shaping my course to the south-west. When I first arrived, somewhat more than a year before, I had entered the city by the north-east. As I was not going home, I determined to take my departure in the direction the very opposite to home.

Just as I was about to cross the street called the Haymarket at the lower part, a cabriolet, drawn by a magnificent animal, came dashing along at a furious rate; it stopped close by the curb-stone where I was, a sudden pull of the reins nearly bringing the spirited animal upon its haunches. The Jehu who had accomplished this feat was Francis Ardry. A small beautiful female, with flashing eyes, dressed in the extremity of fashion, sat beside him.

"Holloa, friend," said Francis Ardry, "whither bound?"

"I do not know," said I; "all I can say is, that I am about to leave London."

"And the means?" said Francis Ardry.

"I have them," said I, with a cheerful smile.

"*Qui est celui-ci?*" demanded the small female impatiently.

"*C'est—mon ami le plus intime;* so you were about to leave London without telling me a word," said Francis Ardry somewhat angrily.

"I intended to have written to you," said I: "what a splendid mare that is!"

"Is she not?" said Francis Ardry, who was holding in the mare with difficulty; "she cost a hundred guineas."

"*Qu'est-ce qu'il dit?*" demanded his companion.

"*Il dit que le jument est bien beau.*"

"*Allons, mon ami, il est tard,*" said the beauty, with a scornful toss of her head; "*allons!*"

"*Encore un moment*," said Francis Ardry; "and when shall I see you again?"

"I scarcely know," I replied: "I never saw a more splendid turn-out."

"*Qu'est-ce qu'il dit?*" said the lady again.

"*Il dit que tout l'équipage est en assez bon goût.*"

"*Allons, c'est un ours*," said the lady; "*le cheval même en a peur*," added she, as the mare reared up on high.

"Can you find nothing else to admire but the mare and the equipage?" said Francis Ardry reproachfully, after he had with some difficulty brought the mare to order.

Lifting my hand, in which I held my stick, I took off my hat. "How beautiful!" said I, looking the lady full in the face.

"*Comment?*" said the lady inquiringly.

"*Il dit que vous êtes belle comme un ange*," said Francis Ardry emphatically.

"*Mais à la bonne heure! arrêtez, mon ami*," said the lady to Francis Ardry, who was about to drive off; "*je voudrais bien causer un moment avec lui; arrêtez, il est délicieux. Est-ce bien ainsi que vous traitez vos amis?*" said she passionately, as Francis Ardry lifted up his whip. "*Bonjour, Monsieur, bonjour*," said she, thrusting her head from the side and looking back, as Francis Ardry drove off at the rate of thirteen miles an hour.

In about two hours I had cleared the Great City, and got beyond the suburban villages, or rather towns, in the direction in which I was travelling; I was in a broad and excellent road, leading I knew not whither. I now slackened my pace, which had hitherto been great. Presently, coming to a milestone on which was graven nine miles, I rested against it, and looking round towards the vast city, which had long ceased to be visible, I fell into a train of meditation.

I thought of all my ways and doings since the day of my first arrival in that vast city. I had worked and toiled, and, though I had accomplished nothing at all commensurate with the hopes which I had entertained previous to my arrival, I had achieved my own living, preserved my independence, and become indebted to no one. I was now quitting it, poor in purse, it is true, but not wholly empty; rather ailing, it may be, but not broken in health; and, with hope within my bosom, had I not cause upon the whole to be thankful? Perhaps there were some who, arriving at the same time under not more favourable circumstances, had accomplished much more, and whose future was far more hopeful—Good! But there might be others who, in spite of all their efforts, had been either trodden down in the press, never more to be heard of, or were quitting that mighty town broken in purse, broken in health, and, oh! with not one dear hope to cheer them. Had I not, upon the whole, abundant cause to be grateful? Truly, yes!

My meditation over, I left the milestone and proceeded on my way in the same direction as before until the night began to close in. I had always been a good pedestrian; but now, whether owing to indisposition or to not having for some time past been much in the habit of taking such lengthy walks, I began to feel not a little weary. Just as I was thinking of putting up for the night at the next inn or public-house I should arrive at, I heard what sounded like a coach coming up rapidly behind me. Induced, perhaps, by the weariness which I felt, I stopped and looked wistfully in the direction of the sound; presently up came a coach, seemingly a mail, drawn by four bounding horses—there was no one upon it but the coachman and the guard; when nearly parallel with me it stopped. "Want to get up?" sounded a voice in the true coachman-like tone—half-querulous, half-authoritative. I hesitated; I was tired, it is true, but I had left London bound on a pedestrian excursion, and I did not much like the idea of having recourse to a coach after accomplishing so very inconsiderable a distance. "Come, we can't be staying here all night," said the voice, more sharply than before. "I can ride a little way, and get down whenever I like," thought I; and springing forward I clambered up the coach, and was going to sit down upon the box, next the coachman. "No, no," said the coachman, who was a man about thirty, with a hooked nose and red face, dressed in a fashionably cut greatcoat, with a fashionable black castor on his head. "No, no, keep behind—the box a'n't for the like of you," said he, as he drove off; "the box is for lords, or gentlemen at least." I made no answer. "D—— that off-hand leader," said the coachman, as the right-hand front horse made a desperate start at something he saw in the road; and, half rising, he with great dexterity hit with his long whip the off-hand leader a cut on the off cheek. "These seem to be fine horses," said I. The coachman made no answer. "Nearly thorough-bred," I continued; the coachman drew his breath, with a kind of hissing sound, through his teeth. "Come, young fellow, none of your chaff. Don't you think, because you ride on my mail, I'm going to talk to you about 'orses. I talk to nobody about 'orses except lords." "Well," said I, "I have been called a lord in my time." "It must have been by a thimble-rigger, then," said the coachman, bending back, and half-turning his face round with a broad leer. "You have hit the mark wonderfully," said I. "You coachmen, whatever else you may be, are certainly no fools." "We a'n't, a'n't we?" said the coachman. "There you are right; and, to show you that you are, I'll now trouble you for your fare. If you have been amongst the thimble-riggers you must be tolerably well cleared out. Where are you going?—to ——? I think I have seen you there. The fare is sixteen shillings. Come, tip us the blunt; them that has no money can't ride on my mail."

Sixteen shillings was a large sum, and to pay it would make a considerable inroad on my slender finances; I thought, at first, that I would say I did not want to go so far; but then the fellow would ask at once where I wanted to go, and I was ashamed to acknowledge my utter ignorance of the road. I determined, therefore, to pay the fare, with a tacit determination not to mount a coach in future without knowing whither I was going. So I paid the man the money, who, turning round, shouted to the guard—"All right,

Jem; got fare to ——," and forthwith whipped on his horses, especially the off-hand leader, for whom he seemed to entertain a particular spite, to greater speed than before—the horses flew.

A young moon gave a feeble light, partially illuminating a line of road which, appearing by no means interesting, I the less regretted having paid my money for the privilege of being hurried along it in the flying vehicle. We frequently changed horses; and at last my friend the coachman was replaced by another, the very image of himself—hawk nose, red face, with narrow-rimmed hat and fashionable benjamin. After he had driven about fifty yards, the new coachman fell to whipping one of the horses. "D—— this near-hand wheeler," said he, "the brute has got a corn." "Whipping him won't cure him of his corn," said I. "Who told you to speak?" said the driver, with an oath; "mind your own business; 'tisn't from the like of you I am to learn to drive 'orses." Presently I fell into a broken kind of slumber. In an hour or two I was aroused by a rough voice—"Got to ——, young man; get down if you please." I opened my eyes—there was a dim and indistinct light, like that which precedes dawn; the coach was standing still in something like a street; just below me stood the guard. "Do you mean to get down," said he, "or will you keep us here till morning? other fares want to get up." Scarcely knowing what I did, I took my bundle and stick and descended, whilst two people mounted. "All right, John," said the guard to the coachman, springing up behind; whereupon off whisked the coach, one or two individuals who were standing by disappeared, and I was left alone.

CHAPTER XX

After standing still a minute or two, considering what I should do, I moved down what appeared to be the street of a small straggling town; presently I passed by a church, which rose indistinctly on my right hand; anon there was the rustling of foliage and the rushing of waters. I reached a bridge, beneath which a small stream was running in the direction of the south. I stopped and leaned over the parapet, for I have always loved to look upon streams, especially at the still hours. "What stream is this, I wonder?" said I, as I looked down from the parapet into the water, which whirled and gurgled below.

Leaving the bridge, I ascended a gentle acclivity, and presently reached what appeared to be a tract of moory undulating ground. It was now tolerably light, but there was a mist or haze abroad which prevented my seeing objects with much precision. I felt chill in the damp air of the early morn, and walked rapidly forward. In about half an hour I arrived where the road divided into two at an angle or tongue of dark green sward. "To the right or the left?" said I, and forthwith took, without knowing why, the left-hand road, along which I proceeded about a hundred yards, when, in the midst of the tongue of sward formed by the two roads, collaterally with myself, I perceived what I at first conceived to be a small grove of blighted trunks of oaks, barked and grey. I stood still for a moment, and then, turning off the road, advanced slowly towards it over the sward; as I drew nearer, I perceived that the objects which had attracted my curiosity, and which formed a kind of circle, were not trees, but immense upright stones. A thrill pervaded my system; just before me were two, the mightiest of the whole, tall as the stems of proud oaks, supporting on their tops a huge transverse stone, and forming a wonderful doorway. I knew now where I was, and laying down my stick and bundle, and taking off my hat, I advanced slowly, and cast myself—it was folly, perhaps, but I could not help what I did—cast myself, with my face on the dewy earth, in the middle of the portal of giants, beneath the transverse stone.

The spirit of Stonehenge was strong upon me!

And after I had remained with my face on the ground for some time, I arose, placed my hat on my head, and taking up my stick and bundle, wandered around the wondrous circle, examining each individual stone, from the greatest to the least and then entering by the great door, seated myself upon an immense broad stone, one side of which was supported by several small ones, and the other slanted upon the earth; and there in deep meditation I sat for an hour or two, till the sun shone in my face above the tall stones of the eastern side.

And as I still sat there, I heard the noise of bells, and presently a large number of sheep came browzing past the circle of stones; two or three entered, and grazed upon what they could find, and soon a man also entered the circle at the northern side.

"Early here, sir," said the man, who was tall, and dressed in a dark green slop, and had all the appearance of a shepherd; "a traveller, I suppose?"

"Yes," said I, "I am a traveller; are these sheep yours?"

"They are, sir; that is, they are my master's. A strange place this, sir," said he, looking at the stones; "ever here before?"

"Never in body, frequently in mind."

"Heard of the stones, I suppose; no wonder—all the people of the plain talk of them."

"What do the people of the plain say of them?"

"Why, they say—How did they ever come here?"

"Do they not suppose them to have been brought?"

"Who should have brought them?"

"I have read that they were brought by many thousand men."

"Where from?"

"Ireland."

"How did they bring them?"

"I don't know."

"And what did they bring them for?"
"To form a temple, perhaps."
"What is that?"
"A place to worship God in."
"A strange place to worship God in."
"Why?"
"It has no roof."
"Yes, it has."
"Where?" said the man looking up.
"What do you see above you?"
"The sky."
"Well?"
"Well!"
"Have you anything to say?"
"How did these stones come here?"
"Are there other stones like these on the plains?" said I.
"None; and yet there are plenty of strange things on these downs."
"What are they?"
"Strange heaps, and barrows, and great walls of earth built on the tops of hills."
"Do the people of the plain wonder how they came there?"
"They do not."
"Why?"
"They were raised by hands."
"And these stones?"
"How did they ever come here?"
"I wonder whether they are here?" said I.
"These stones?"
"Yes."
"So sure as the world," said the man; "and, as the world, they will stand as long."
"I wonder whether there is a world."
"What do you mean?"
"An earth and sea, moon and stars, sheep and men."
"Do you doubt it?"
"Sometimes."
"I never heard it doubted before."
"It is impossible there should be a world."
"It a'n't possible there shouldn't be a world."
"Just so." At this moment a fine ewe attended by a lamb, rushed into the circle and fondled the knees of the shepherd. "I suppose you would not care to have some milk," said the man.
"Why do you suppose so?"
"Because, so be, there be no sheep, no milk, you know; and what there ben't is not worth having."

"You could not have argued better," said I; "that is, supposing you have argued; with respect to the milk, you may do as you please."

"Be still, Nanny," said the man; and producing a tin vessel from his scrip, he milked the ewe into it. "Here is milk of the plains, master," said the man, as he handed the vessel to me.

"Where are those barrows and great walls of earth you were speaking of," said I, after I had drank some of the milk; "are there any near where we are?"

"Not within many miles; the nearest is yonder away," said the shepherd, pointing to the south-east. "It's a grand place, that, but not like this; quite different, and from it you have a sight of the finest spire in the world."

"I must go to it," said I, and I drank the remainder of the milk, "yonder, you say."

"Yes, yonder; but you cannot get to it in that direction, the river lies between."

"What river?"

"The Avon."

"Avon is British," said I.

"Yes," said the man, "we are all British here."

"No, we are not," said I.

"What are we then?"

"English."

"A'n't they one?"

"No."

"Who were the British?"

"The men who are supposed to have worshipped God in this place, and who raised these stones."

"Where are they now?"

"Our forefathers slaughtered them, spilled their blood all about, especially in this neighbourhood, destroyed their pleasant places, and left not, to use their own words, one stone upon another."

"Yes, they did," said the shepherd, looking aloft at the transverse stone.

"And it is well for them they did; whenever that stone, which English hands never raised, is by English hands thrown down, woe, woe, woe to the English race; spare it, English! Hengist spared it!—Here is sixpence."

"I won't have it," said the man.

"Why not?"

"You talk so prettily about these stones; you seem to know all about them."

"I never receive presents; with respect to the stones, I say with yourself, How did they ever come here?"

"How did they ever come here?" said the shepherd.

Leaving the shepherd, I bent my way in the direction pointed out by him as that in which the most remarkable of the strange remains of which he had spoken lay. I proceeded rapidly, making my way over the downs covered with coarse grass and fern; with respect to the river of which he had spoken,

I reflected that, either by wading or swimming, I could easily transfer myself and what I bore to the opposite side. On arriving at its banks, I found it a beautiful stream, but shallow, with here and there a deep place, where the water ran dark and still.

Always fond of the pure lymph, I undressed, and plunged into one of these gulfs, from which I emerged, my whole frame in a glow, and tingling with delicious sensations. After conveying my clothes and scanty baggage to the farther side, I dressed, and then with hurried steps bent my course in the direction of some lofty ground; I at length found myself on a high road, leading over wide and arid downs; following the road for some miles without seeing anything remarkable, I supposed at length that I had taken the wrong path, and wended on slowly and disconsolately for some time, till, having nearly surmounted a steep hill, I knew at once, from certain appearances, that I was near the object of my search. Turning to the right near the brow of the hill, I proceeded along a path which brought me to a causeway leading over a deep ravine, and connecting the hill with another which had once formed part of it, for the ravine was evidently the work of art. I passed over the causeway, and found myself in a kind of gateway which admitted me into a square space of many acres, surrounded on all sides by mounds or ramparts of earth. Though I had never been in such a place before, I knew that I stood within the precincts of what had been a Roman encampment, and one probably of the largest size, for many thousand warriors might have found room to perform their evolutions in that space, in which corn was now growing, the green ears waving in the morning wind.

After I had gazed about the space for a time, standing in the gateway formed by the mounds, I clambered up the mound to the left hand, and on the top of that mound I found myself at a great altitude; beneath, at the distance of a mile, was a fair old city, situated amongst verdant meadows, watered with streams, and from the heart of that old city, from amidst mighty trees, I beheld towering to the sky the finest spire in the world.

After I had looked from the Roman rampart for a long time, I hurried away, and, retracing my steps along the causeway, regained the road, and, passing over the brow of the hill, descended to the city of the spire.

CHAPTER XXI

And in the old city I remained two days, passing my time as I best could—inspecting the curiosities of the place, eating and drinking when I felt so disposed, which I frequently did, the digestive organs having assumed a tone to which for many months they had been strangers—enjoying at night balmy sleep in a large bed in a dusky room, at the end of a corridor, in a certain hostelry in which I had taken up my quarters—receiving from the people of the hostelry such civility and condescension as people who travel on foot with bundle and stick, but who nevertheless are perceived to be not altogether destitute of coin, are in the habit of receiving. On the third day, on a fine sunny afternoon, I departed from the city of the spire.

As I was passing through one of the suburbs, I saw, all on a sudden, a respectable-looking female fall down in a fit; several persons hastened to her assistance. "She is dead," said one. "No, she is not," said another. "I am afraid she is," said a third. "Life is very uncertain," said a fourth. "It is Mrs.—" said a fifth; "let us carry her to her own house." Not being able to render any assistance, I left the poor female in the hands of her townsfolk, and proceeded on my way. I had chosen a road in the direction of the north-west, it led over downs where corn was growing, but where neither tree nor hedge were to be seen; two or three hours' walking brought me to a beautiful valley, abounding with trees of various kinds, with a delightful village at its farthest extremity; passing through it I ascended a lofty acclivity, on the top of which I sat down on a bank, and taking off my hat, permitted a breeze, which swept coolly and refreshingly over the downs, to dry my hair, dripping from the effects of exercise and the heat of the day.

And as I sat there, gazing now at the blue heavens, now at the downs before me, a man came along the road in the direction in which I had hitherto been proceeding: just opposite to me he stopped, and, looking at me, cried: "Am I right for London, master?"

He was dressed like a sailor, and appeared to be between twenty-five and thirty years of age; he had an open manly countenance, and there was a bold and fearless expression in his eye.

"Yes," said I, in reply to his question; "this is one of the ways to London. Do you come from far?"

"From —," said the man, naming a well-known seaport.

"Is this the direct road to London from that place?" I demanded.

"No," said the man; "but I had to visit two or three other places on certain commissions I was entrusted with; amongst others to —, where I had to take a small sum of money. I am rather tired, master; and, if you please, I will sit down beside you."

"You have as much right to sit down here as I have," said I, "the road is free for every one; as for sitting down beside me, you have the look of an honest man, and I have no objection to your company."

"Why, as for being honest, master," said the man, laughing and sitting down by me, "I hav'n't much to say–many is the wild thing I have done when I was younger; however, what is done, is done. To learn, one must live, master; and I have lived long enough to learn the grand point of wisdom."

"What is that?" said I.

"That honesty is the best policy, master."

"You appear to be a sailor," said I, looking at his dress.

"I was not bred a sailor," said the man, "though, when my foot is on the salt water, I can play the part—and play it well too. I am now from a long voyage."

"From America?" said I.

"Farther than that," said the man.

"Have you any objection to tell me?" said I.

"From New South Wales," said the man, looking me full in the face.

"Dear me," said I.

"Why do you say 'Dear me'?" said the man.

"It is a very long way off," said I.

"Was that your reason for saying so?" said the man.

"Not exactly," said I.

"No," said the man, with something of a bitter smile; "it was something else that made you say so; you were thinking of the convicts."

"Well," said I, "what then—you are no convict."

"How do you know?"

"You do not look like one."

"Thank you, master," said the man cheerfully; "and, to a certain extent, you are right—bygones are bygones—I am no longer what I was, nor ever will be again; the truth, however, is the truth—a convict I have been—a convict at Sydney Cove."

"And you have served out the period for which you were sentenced, and are now returned?"

"As to serving out my sentence," replied the man, "I can't say that I did; I was sentenced for fourteen years, and I was in Sydney Cove little more than half that time. The truth is that I did the Government a service. There was a conspiracy amongst some of the convicts to murder and destroy—I overheard and informed the Government; mind one thing, however, I was not concerned in it; those who got it up were no comrades of mine, but a bloody gang of villains. Well, the Government, in consideration of the service I had done them, remitted the remainder of my sentence; and some kind gentlemen interested themselves about me, gave me good books and good advice, and, being satisfied with my conduct, procured me employ in an exploring expedition, by which I earned money. In fact, the being sent to Sydney was the best thing that ever happened to me in all my life."

"And you have now returned to your native country. Longing to see home brought you from New South Wales."

"There you are mistaken," said the man. "Wish to see England again would never have brought me so far; for, to tell you the truth, master, England was a hard mother to me, as she has proved to many. No, a wish to see another kind of mother—a poor old woman whose son I am—has brought me back."

"You have a mother, then?" said I. "Does she reside in London?"

"She used to live in London," said the man; "but I am afraid she is long since dead."

"How did she support herself?" said I.

"Support herself! with difficulty enough; she used to keep a small stall on London Bridge, where she sold fruit; I am afraid she is dead, and that she died perhaps in misery. She was a poor sinful creature; but I loved her, and she loved me. I came all the way back merely for the chance of seeing her."

"Did you ever write to her," said I, "or cause others to write to her?"

"I wrote to her myself," said the man, "about two years ago; but I never received an answer. I learned to write very tolerably over there, by the assistance of the good people I spoke of. As for reading, I could do that very well before I went—my poor mother taught me to read, out of a book that she was very fond of; a strange book it was, I remember. Poor dear! what I would give only to know that she is alive."

"Life is very uncertain," said I.

"That is true," said the man, with a sigh.

"We are here one moment, and gone the next," I continued. "As I passed through the streets of a neighbouring town, I saw a respectable woman drop down, and people said she was dead. Who knows but that she too had a son coming to see her from a distance, at that very time."

"Who knows, indeed," said the man. "Ah, I am afraid my mother is dead. Well, God's will be done."

"However," said I, "I should not wonder at your finding your mother alive."

"You wouldn't?" said the man, looking at me wistfully.

"I should not wonder at all," said I; "indeed, something within me seems to tell me you will; I should not much mind betting five shillings to five pence that you will see your mother within a week. Now, friend, five shillings to five pence——"

"Is very considerable odds," said the man, rubbing his hands; "sure you must have good reason to hope, when you are willing to give such odds."

"After all," said I, "it not unfrequently happens that those who lay the long odds lose. Let us hope, however. What do you mean to do in the event of finding your mother alive?"

"I scarcely know," said the man; "I have frequently thought that if I found my mother alive I would attempt to persuade her to accompany me to the country which I have left—it is a better country for a man—that is a free man—to live in than this; however, let me first find my mother—if I could only find my mother——"

"Farewell," said I, rising. "Go your way, and God go with you—I will go mine." "I have but one thing to ask you," said the man. "What is that?" I inquired. "That you would drink with me before we part—you have done me so much good." "How should we drink?" said I; "we are on the top of a hill where there is nothing to drink." "But there is a village below," said the man; "do let us drink before we part." "I have been through that village already," said I, "and I do not like turning back." "Ah," said the man sorrowfully, "you will not drink with me because I told you I was——"

"You are quite mistaken," said I, "I would as soon drink with a convict as with a judge. I am by no means certain that, under the same circumstances, the judge would be one whit better than the convict. Come along! I will go back to oblige you. I have an odd sixpence in my pocket, which I will change, that I may drink with you." So we went down the hill together to the village through which I had already passed, where, finding a public-house, we drank together in true English fashion, after which we parted, the sailor-looking man going his way and I mine.

After walking about a dozen miles, I came to a town, where I rested for the night. The next morning I set out again in the direction of the north-west. I continued journeying for four days, my daily journeys varying from twenty to twenty-five miles. During this time nothing occurred to me worthy of any especial notice. The weather was brilliant, and I rapidly improved both in strength and spirits. On the fifth day, about two o'clock, I arrived at a small town. Feeling hungry, I entered a decent-looking inn. Within a kind of bar I saw a huge, fat, landlord-looking person, with a very pretty, smartly-dressed maiden. Addressing myself to the fat man, "House!" said I, "house! Can I have dinner, house?"

"Young gentleman," said the huge, fat landlord, "you are come at the right time; dinner will be taken up in a few minutes, and such a dinner," he continued, rubbing his hands, "as you will not see every day in these times."

"I am hot and dusty," said I, "and should wish to cool my hands and face."

"Jenny!" said the huge landlord, with the utmost gravity, "show the gentleman into number seven that he may wash his hands and face."

"By no means," said I, "I am a person of primitive habits, and there is nothing like the pump in weather like this."

"Jenny!" said the landlord, with the same gravity as before, "go with the young gentleman to the pump in the back kitchen, and take a clean towel along with you."

Thereupon the rosy-faced clean-looking damsel went to a drawer, and producing a large, thick, but snowy-white towel, she nodded to me to follow her; whereupon I followed Jenny through a long passage into the back kitchen.

And at the end of the back kitchen there stood a pump; and going to it I placed my hands beneath the spout, and said, "Pump, Jenny," and Jenny incontinently, without laying down the towel, pumped with one hand, and I washed and cooled my heated hands.

And, when my hands were washed and cooled, I took off my neckcloth, and unbuttoning my shirt collar, I placed my head beneath the spout of the pump, and I said unto Jenny: "Now, Jenny, lay down the towel, and pump for your life."

Thereupon Jenny, placing the towel on a linen-horse, took the handle of the pump with both hands and pumped over my head as handmaid had never pumped before; so that the water poured in torrents from my head, my face, and my hair down upon the brick floor.

And after the lapse of somewhat more than a minute, I called out with a half-strangled voice, "Hold, Jenny!" and Jenny desisted. I stood for a few moments to recover my breath, then taking the towel which Jenny proffered, I dried composedly my hands and head, my face and hair; then, returning the towel to Jenny, I gave a deep sigh and said: "Surely this is one of the pleasant moments of life."

Then, having set my dress to rights, and combed my hair with a pocket comb, I followed Jenny, who conducted me back through the long passage, and showed me into a neat, sanded parlour on the ground floor.

I sat down by a window which looked out upon the dusty street; presently in came the handmaid, and commenced laying the table-cloth. "Shall I spread the table for one, sir," said she, "or do you expect anybody to dine with you?"

"I can't say that I expect anybody," said I, laughing inwardly to myself; "however, if you please you can lay for two, so that if any acquaintance of mine should chance to step in, he may find a knife and fork ready for him."

So I sat by the window, sometimes looking out upon the dusty street, and now glancing at certain old-fashioned prints which adorned the wall over against me. I fell into a kind of doze, from which I was almost instantly awakened by the opening of the door. Dinner, thought I; and I sat upright in my chair. No, a man of the middle age, and rather above the middle height dressed in a plain suit of black, made his appearance, and sat down in a chair at some distance from me, but near to the table, and appeared to be lost in thought.

"The weather is very warm, sir," said I.

"Very," said the stranger laconically, looking at me for the first time.

"Would you like to see the newspaper?" said I, taking up one which lay on the window seat.

"I never read newspapers," said the stranger, "nor, indeed——" Whatever it might be that he had intended to say he left unfinished. Suddenly he walked to the mantelpiece at the farther end of the room, before which he placed himself with his back towards me. There he remained motionless for some time; at length, raising his hand, he touched the corner of the mantelpiece with his finger, advanced towards the chair which he had left, and again seated himself.

"Have you come far?" said he, suddenly looking towards me, and speaking in a frank and open manner, which denoted a wish to enter into conversation. "You do not seem to be of this place."

"I come from some distance," said I; "indeed, I am walking for exercise, which I find as necessary to the mind as the body. I believe that by exercise people would escape much mental misery."

Scarcely had I uttered these words when the stranger laid his hand, with seeming carelessness, upon the table, near one of the glasses; after a moment or two he touched the glass with his finger as if inadvertently, then, glancing furtively at me, he withdrew his hand and looked towards the window.

"Are you from these parts?" said I at last, with apparent carelessness.

"From this vicinity," replied the stranger. "You think, then, that it is as easy to walk off the bad humours of the mind as of the body."

"I, at least, am walking in that hope," said I.

"I wish you may be successful," said the stranger; and here he touched one of the forks which lay on the table near him.

Here the door, which was slightly ajar, was suddenly pushed open with some fracas, and in came the stout landlord, supporting with some difficulty an immense dish, in which was a mighty round mass of smoking meat garnished all round with vegetables; so high was the mass that it probably obstructed his view, for it was not until he had placed it upon the table that he appeared to observe the stranger; he almost started, and quite out of breath exclaimed: "God bless me, your honour; is your honour the acquaintance that the young gentleman was expecting?"

"Is the young gentleman expecting an acquaintance?" said the stranger.

There is nothing like putting a good face upon these matters, thought I to myself; and, getting up, I bowed to the unknown.

"Sir," said I, "when I told Jenny that she might lay the table-cloth for two, so that in the event of any acquaintance dropping in he might find a knife and fork ready for him, I was merely jocular, being an entire stranger in these parts, and expecting no one. Fortune, however, it would seem, has been unexpectedly kind to me; I flatter myself, sir, that since you have been in this room I have had the honour of making your acquaintance; and in the strength of that hope I humbly entreat you to honour me with your company to dinner, provided you have not already dined."

The stranger laughed outright.

"Sir," I continued, "the round of beef is a noble one, and seems exceedingly well boiled, and the landlord was just right when he said I should have such a dinner as is not seen every day. A round of beef, at any rate such a round of beef as this, is seldom seen smoking upon the table in these degenerate times. Allow me, sir," said I, observing that the stranger was about to speak, "allow me another remark. I think I saw you just now touch the fork, I venture to hail it as an omen that you will presently seize it and apply it to its proper purpose, and its companion the knife also."

The stranger changed colour, and gazed upon me in silence.

"Do, sir," here put in the landlord; "do, sir, accept the young gentleman's invitation. Your honour has of late been looking poorly, and the young gentleman is a funny young gentleman, and a clever young gentleman; and I think it will do your honour good to have a dinner's chat with the young gentleman."

"It is not my dinner hour," said the stranger; "I dine considerably later; taking anything now would only discompose me; I shall, however, be most happy to sit down with the young gentleman: reach me that paper, and, when the young gentleman has satisfied his appetite, we may perhaps have a little chat together."

The landlord handed the stranger the newspaper, and, bowing, retired with his maid Jenny. I helped myself to a portion of the smoking round, and commenced eating with no little appetite. The stranger appeared to be soon engrossed with the newspaper. We continued thus a considerable time —the one reading and the other dining. Chancing suddenly to cast my eyes upon the stranger, I saw his brow contract; he gave a slight stamp with his foot, and flung the newspaper to the ground, then stooping down he picked it up, first moving his forefinger along the floor, seemingly slightly scratching it with his nail.

"Do you hope, sir," said I, "by that ceremony with the finger to preserve yourself from the evil chance?"

The stranger started; then, after looking at me for some time in silence, he said: "Is it possible that you——?"

"Ay, ay," said I, helping myself to some more of the round, "I have touched myself in my younger days, both for the evil chance and the good. Can't say, though, that I ever trusted much in the ceremony."

The stranger made no reply, but appeared to be in deep thought; nothing further passed between us until I had concluded the dinner, when I said to him: "I shall now be most happy, sir, to have the pleasure of your conversation over a pint of wine."

The stranger rose; "No, my young friend," said he, smiling, "that would scarce be fair. It is my turn now—pray do me the favour to go home with me, and accept what hospitality my poor roof can offer; to tell you the truth, I wish to have some particular discourse with you which would hardly be possible in this place. As for wine, I can give you some much better than you can get here; the landlord is an excellent fellow, but he is an innkeeper, after all. I am going out for a moment, and will send him in, so that you may settle your account; I trust you will not refuse me, I only live about two miles from here."

I looked in the face of the stranger—it was a fine intelligent face, with a cast of melancholy in it. "Sir," said I, "I would go with you though you lived four miles instead of two."

"Who is that gentleman?" said I to the landlord, after I had settled his bill; "I am going home with him."

"I wish I were going too," said the fat landlord, laying his hand upon his stomach. "Young gentleman, I shall be a loser by his honour's taking you away; but, after all, the truth is the truth—there are few gentlemen in these parts like his honour, either for learning or welcoming his friends. Young gentleman, I congratulate you."

CHAPTER XXII

I FOUND the stranger awaiting me at the door of the inn. "Like yourself, I am fond of walking," said he, "and when any little business calls me to this place I generally come on foot."

We were soon out of the town, and in a very beautiful country. After proceeding some distance on the high road, we turned off, and were presently in one of those mazes of lanes for which England is famous; the stranger at first seemed inclined to be taciturn; a few observations, however, which I made, appeared to rouse him, and he soon exhibited not only considerable powers of conversation, but stores of information which surprised me. So pleased did I become with my new acquaintance, that I soon ceased to pay the slightest attention either to place or distance. At length the stranger was silent, and I perceived that we had arrived at a handsome iron gate and a lodge; the stranger having rung a bell, the gate was opened by an old man, and we proceeded along a gravel path, which in about five minutes brought us to a large brick house, built something in the old French style, having a spacious lawn before it, and immediately in front a pond in which were golden fish, and in the middle a stone swan discharging quantities of water from its bill. We ascended a spacious flight of steps to the door, which was at once flung open, and two servants with powdered hair, and in livery of blue plush, came out and stood one on either side as we passed the threshold. We entered a large hall, and the stranger, taking me by the hand, welcomed me to his poor home, as he called it, and then gave orders to another servant, but out of livery, to show me to an apartment, and give me whatever assistance I might require in my toilette. Notwithstanding the plea as to primitive habits which I had lately made to my other host in the town, I offered no objection to this arrangement, but followed the bowing domestic to a spacious and airy chamber, where he rendered me all those little nameless offices which the somewhat neglected state of my dress required. When everything had been completed to my perfect satisfaction, he told me that if I pleased he would conduct me to the library, where dinner would be speedily served.

In the library I found a table laid for two; my host was not there, having as I supposed not been quite so speedy with his toilette as his guest. Left alone, I looked round the apartment with inquiring eyes; it was long and tolerably lofty, the walls from the top to the bottom were lined with cases containing books of all sizes and bindings; there was a globe or two, a couch, and an easy chair. Statues and busts there were none, and only one painting, a portrait, that of my host, but not him of the mansion. Over the mantelpiece, the features staringly like, but so ridiculously exaggerated that they scarcely resembled those of a human being, daubed evidently by the hand of the commonest sign-artist, hung a half-length portrait of him of round of beef celebrity—my sturdy host of the town.

I had been in the library about ten minutes, amusing myself as I best could, when my friend entered; he seemed to have resumed his taciturnity—scarce a word escaped his lips till dinner was served, when he said, smiling: "I suppose it would be merely a compliment to ask you to partake?"

"I don't know," said I, seating myself; "your first course consists of troutlets. I am fond of troutlets, and I always like to be companionable."

The dinner was excellent, though I did but little justice to it from the circumstance of having already dined; the stranger also, though without my excuse, partook but slightly of the good cheer; he still continued taciturn, and appeared lost in thought, and every attempt which I made to induce him to converse was signally unsuccessful.

And now dinner was removed, and we sat over our wine, and I remember that the wine was good, and fully justified the encomiums of my host of the town. Over the wine I made sure that my entertainer would have loosened the chain which seemed to tie his tongue—but no! I endeavoured to tempt him by various topics, and talked of geometry and the use of the globes, of the heavenly sphere, and the star Jupiter, which I said I had heard was a very large star, also of the evergreen tree, which, according to Olaus, stood of old before the heathen temple of Upsal, and which I affirmed was a yew—but no, nothing that I said could induce my entertainer to relax his taciturnity.

It grew dark, and I became uncomfortable; "I must presently be going," I at last exclaimed.

At these words he gave a sudden start; "Going," said he, "are you not my guest, and an honoured one?"

"You know best," said I; "but I was apprehensive I was an intruder; to several of my questions you have returned no answer."

"Ten thousand pardons!" he exclaimed, seizing me by the hand; "but you cannot go now, I have much to talk to you about—there is one thing in particular——"

"If it be the evergreen tree at Upsal," said I, interrupting him, "I hold it to have been a yew—what else? The evergreens of the south, as the old bishop observes, will not grow in the north, and a pine was unfitted for such a locality, being a vulgar tree. What else could it have been but the yew—the sacred yew which our ancestors were in the habit of planting in their churchyards? Moreover, I affirm it to have been the yew for the honour of the tree; for I love the yew, and had I home and land, I would have one growing before my front windows."

"You would do right; the yew is indeed a venerable tree, but it is not about the yew."

"The star Jupiter, perhaps?"

"Nor the star Jupiter, nor its moons; an observation which escaped you at the inn has made a considerable impression upon me."

"But I really must take my departure," said I; "the dark hour is at hand."

And as I uttered these last words, the stranger touched rapidly something which lay near him, I forget what it was. It was the first action of the kind which I had observed on his part since we sat down to table.

"You allude to the evil chance," said I; "but it is getting both dark and late."

"I believe we are going to have a storm," said my friend, "but I really hope that you will give me your company for a day or two; I have, as I said before, much to talk to you about."

"Well," said I, "I shall be most happy to be your guest for this night; I am ignorant of the country, and it is not pleasant to travel unknown paths by night—dear me, what a flash of lightning!"

It had become very dark; suddenly a blaze of sheet-lightning illumed the room. By the momentary light I distinctly saw my host touch another object upon the table.

"Will you allow me to ask you a question or two?" said he at last.

"As many as you please," said I; "but shall we not have lights?"

"Not unless you particularly wish it," said my entertainer; "I rather like the dark, and though a storm is evidently at hand, neither thunder nor lightning have any terrors for me. It is other things I quake at—I should rather say ideas. Now, permit me to ask you——"

And then my entertainer asked me various questions, to all of which I answered unreservedly; he was then silent for some time, at last he exclaimed: "I should wish to tell you the history of my life; though not an adventurous one, I think it contains some things which will interest you."

Without waiting for my reply he began. Amidst darkness and gloom, occasionally broken by flashes of lightning, the stranger related to me, as we sat at the table in the library, his truly touching history.

"Before proceeding to relate the events of my life, it will not be amiss to give you some account of my ancestors. My great-grandfather on the male side was a silk mercer, in Cheapside, who, when he died, left his son, who was his only child, a fortune of one hundred thousand pounds, and a splendid business; the son, however, had no inclination for trade, the summit of his ambition was to be a country gentleman, to found a family, and to pass the remainder of his days in rural ease and dignity, and all this he managed to accomplish; he disposed of his business, purchased a beautiful and extensive estate for four score thousand pounds, built upon it the mansion to which I had the honour of welcoming you to-day, married the daughter of a neighbouring squire, who brought him a fortune of five thousand pounds, became a magistrate, and only wanted a son and heir to make him completely happy; this blessing, it is true, was for a long time denied him; it came, however, at last, as is usual, when least expected. His lady was brought to bed of my father, and then who so happy a man as my grandsire; he gave away two thousand pounds in charities, and in the joy of his heart made a speech at the next quarter sessions; the rest of his life was spent in ease, tranquillity and rural dignity; he died of apoplexy on the day that my father came of age; perhaps it would be difficult to mention a man who in all respects was so fortunate as my grandfather; his death was sudden, it is true, but I am not one of those who pray to be delivered from á sudden death.

"I should not call my father a fortunate man; it is true that he had the advantage of a first-rate education; that he made the grand tour with a private tutor, as was the fashion at that time; that he came to a splendid fortune on the very day that he came of age; that for many years he tasted all the diversions of the capital; that, at last determined to settle, he married the sister of a baronet, an amiable and accomplished lady, with a large fortune; that he had the best stud of hunters in the county, on which, during the season, he followed the fox gallantly; had he been a fortunate man he would never have cursed his fate, as he was frequently known to do; ten months after his marriage his horse fell upon him, and so injured him, that he expired in a few days in great agony. My grandfather was, indeed, a fortunate man; when he died he was followed to the grave by the tears of the poor—my father was not.

"Two remarkable circumstances are connected with my birth—I am a posthumous child, and came into the world some weeks before the usual time, the shock which my mother experienced at my father's death having brought on the pangs of premature labour; both my mother's life and my own were at first despaired of; we both, however, survived the crisis. My mother loved me with the most passionate fondness, and I was brought up in this house under her own eye—I was never sent to school.

"I have already told you that mine is not a tale of adventure; my life has not been one of action, but of wild imaginings and strange sensations; I was born with excessive sensibility, and that has been my bane. I have not been a fortunate man.

"No one is fortunate unless he is happy, and it is impossible for a being constructed like myself to be happy for an hour, or even enjoy peace and tranquillity; most of our pleasures and pains are the effects of imagination, and wherever the sensibility is great, the imagination is great also. No sooner has my imagination raised up an image of pleasure, than it is sure to conjure up one of distress and gloom; these two antagonistic ideas instantly commence a struggle in my mind, and the gloomy one generally, I may say invariably, prevails. How is it possible that I should be a happy man?

"It has invariably been so with me from the earliest period that I can remember: the first playthings that were given me caused me for a few minutes excessive pleasure; they were pretty and glittering; presently, however, I became anxious and perplexed, I wished to know their history, how they were made, and what of—were the materials precious; I was not satisfied with their outward appearance. In less than an hour I had broken the playthings in an attempt to discover what they were made of.

"When I was eight years of age my uncle the baronet, who was also my godfather, sent me a pair of Norway hawks, with directions for managing them; he was a great fowler. Oh, how rejoiced was I with the present which had been made me, my joy lasted for at least five minutes; I would let them breed, I would have a house of hawks; yes, that I would—but—and here came the unpleasant idea—suppose they were to fly away, how very annoying! Ah, but, said hope, there's little fear of that; feed them well and they will never fly away, or if they do they will come back, my uncle says so; so sunshine triumphed for a little time. Then the strangest of all doubts came into my head; I doubted the legality of my tenure of these hawks; how did I come by them? why, my uncle gave them to me, but how did they come into his possession? what right had he to them? after all, they might not be his to give,—I passed a sleepless night. The next morning I found that the man who brought the hawks had not departed. 'How came my uncle by these hawks?' I anxiously inquired. 'They were sent to him from Norway, master, with another pair.' 'And who sent them?' 'That I don't know, master, but I suppose his honour can tell you.' I was even thinking of scrawling a letter to my uncle to make inquiry on this point, but shame restrained me, and I likewise reflected that it would be impossible for him to give my mind entire satisfaction; it is true he could tell who sent him the hawks, but how was he to know how the hawks came into the possession of those who sent them to him, and by what right they possessed them or the parents of the hawks. In a word, I wanted a clear valid title, as lawyers would say, to my hawks, and I believe no title would have satisfied me that did not extend up to the time of the first hawk, that is, prior to Adam; and, could I have obtained such a title, I make no doubt that, young as I was, I should have suspected that it was full of flaws.

"I was now disgusted with the hawks, and no wonder, seeing all the disquietude they had caused me; I soon totally neglected the poor birds, and they would have starved had not some of the servants taken compassion upon them and fed them. My uncle, soon hearing of my neglect, was angry, and took the birds away; he was a very good-natured man, however, and soon sent me a fine pony; at first I was charmed with the pony, soon, however, the same kind of thoughts arose which had disgusted me on a former occasion. How did my uncle become possessed of the pony? This question I asked him the first time I saw him. Oh, he had bought it of a gypsy, that I might learn to ride upon it. A gypsy; I had heard that gypsies were great thieves, and I instantly began to fear that the gypsy had stolen the pony, and it is probable that for this apprehension I had better grounds than for many others. I instantly ceased to set any value upon the pony, but for that reason, perhaps, I turned it to some account; I mounted it, and rode it about, which I don't think I should have done had I looked upon it as a secure possession. Had I looked upon my title as secure, I should have prized it so much that I should scarcely have mounted it for fear of injuring the animal; but now, caring not a straw for it, I rode it most unmercifully, and soon became a capital rider. This was very selfish in me, and I tell the fact with shame.

I was punished, however, as I deserved; the pony had a spirit of its own, and, moreover, it had belonged to gypsies; once, as I was riding it furiously over the lawn, applying both whip and spur, it suddenly lifted up its heels, and flung me at least five yards over its head. I received some desperate contusions, and was taken up for dead; it was many months before I perfectly recovered.

"But it is time for me to come to the touching part of my story. There was one thing that I loved better than the choicest gift which could be bestowed upon me, better than life itself—my mother; at length she became unwell, and the thought that I might possibly lose her now rushed into my mind for the first time; it was terrible, and caused me unspeakable misery, I may say horror. My mother became worse, and I was not allowed to enter her apartment, lest by my frantic exclamations of grief I might aggravate her disorder. I rested neither day nor night, but roamed about the house like one distracted. Suddenly I found myself doing that which even at the time struck me as being highly singular; I found myself touching particular objects that were near me, and to which my fingers seemed to be attracted by an irresistible impulse. It was now the table or the chair that I was compelled to touch; now the bell-rope; now the handle of the door; now I would touch the wall, and the next moment stooping down, I would place the point of my finger upon the floor: and so I continued to do day after day; frequently I would struggle to resist the impulse, but invariably in vain. I have even rushed away from the object, but I was sure to return, the impulse was too strong to be resisted: I quickly hurried back, compelled by the feeling within me to touch the object. Now, I need not tell you that what impelled me to these actions was the desire to prevent my mother's death; whenever I touched any particular object, it was with the view of baffling the evil chance, as you would call it—in this instance my mother's death.

"A favourable crisis occurred in my mother's complaint, and she recovered; this crisis took place about six o'clock in the morning; almost simultaneously with it there happened to myself a rather remarkable circumstance connected with the nervous feeling which was rioting in my system. I was lying in bed in a kind of uneasy doze, the only kind of rest which my anxiety, on account of my mother, permitted me at this time to take, when all at once I sprang up as if electrified, the mysterious impulse was upon me, and it urged me to go without delay, and climb a stately elm behind the house, and touch the topmost branch; otherwise—you know the rest—the evil chance would prevail. Accustomed for some time as I had been, under this impulse, to perform extravagant actions, I confess to you that the difficulty and peril of such a feat startled me; I reasoned against the feeling, and strove more strenuously than I had ever done before; I even made a solemn vow not to give way to the temptation, but I believe nothing less than chains, and those strong ones, could have restrained me. The demoniac influence, for I can call it nothing else, at length prevailed; it compelled me to rise, to dress myself, to descend the stairs, to unbolt the door, and to go forth; it drove me to the foot of the tree, and it compelled me to climb the trunk; this was a tremendous task, and I only accomplished it after repeated falls and trials. When I had got amongst the branches, I rested for a time, and then set about accomplishing the remainder of the ascent; this for some time was not so difficult, for I was now amongst the branches; as I approached the top, however, the difficulty became greater, and likewise the danger; but I was a light boy, and almost as nimble as a squirrel, and, moreover, the nervous feeling was within me, impelling me upward. It was only by means of a spring, however, that I was enabled to touch the top of the tree; I sprang, touched the top of the tree, and fell a distance of at least twenty feet, amongst the branches; had I fallen to the bottom I must have been killed, but I fell into the middle of the tree, and presently found myself astride upon one of the boughs; scratched and bruised all over, I reached the ground, and regained my chamber unobserved; I flung myself on my bed quite exhausted; presently they came to tell me that my mother was better—they found me in the state which I have described, and in a fever besides. The favourable crisis must have occurred just about the time that I performed the magic touch; it certainly was a curious coincidence, yet I was not weak enough, even though a child, to suppose that I had baffled the evil chance of my daring feat.

"Indeed, all the time that I was performing these strange feats, I knew them to be highly absurd, yet the impulse to perform them was irresistible—a mysterious dread hanging over me till I had given way to it; even at that early period I frequently used to reason within myself as to what could be the cause of my propensity to touch, but of course I could come to no satisfactory conclusion respecting it; being heartily ashamed of the practice, I never spoke of it to any one, and was at all times highly solicitous that no one should observe my weakness."

After a short pause my host resumed his narration. "Though I was never sent to school, my education was not neglected on that account; I had tutors in various branches of knowledge, under whom I made a tolerable progress; by the time I was eighteen I was able to read most of the Greek and Latin authors with facility; I was likewise, to a certain degree, a mathematician. I cannot say that I took much pleasure in my studies; my chief aim in endeavouring to accomplish my tasks was to give pleasure to my beloved parent, who watched my progress with anxiety truly maternal. My life at this period may be summed up in a few words; I pursued my studies, roamed about the woods, walked the green lanes occasionally, cast my fly in a trout stream, and sometimes, but not often, rode a hunting with my uncle. A considerable part of my time was devoted to my mother, conversing with her and reading to her; youthful companions I had none, and as to my mother, she lived in the greatest retirement, devoting herself to the superintendence of my education, and the practice of acts of charity; nothing could be more innocent than this mode of life, and some people say that in innocence there is happiness, yet I can't say that I was happy. A continual dread overshadowed my mind, it was the dread of my mother's death. Her constitution had never been strong, and it had been considerably shaken by her last illness; this I knew, and this I saw—for the eyes of fear are marvellously keen. Well, things went on in this way till I had come of age; my tutors were then dismissed, and my uncle the baronet took me in hand, telling my mother that it was high time for him to exert his authority; that I must see something of the world, for that, if I remained much longer with her, I should be ruined. 'You must consign him to me,' said he, 'and I will introduce him to the world.' My mother sighed and consented; so my uncle the baronet introduced me to the world, took me to horse races and to London, and endeavoured to make a man of me according to his idea of the term, and in part succeeded. I became moderately dissipated—I say moderately, for dissipation had but little zest for me.

"In this manner four years passed over. It happened that I was in London in the height of the season with my uncle, at his house; one morning he summoned me into the parlour, he was standing before the fire, and looked very serious. 'I have had a letter,' said he; 'your mother is very ill.' I staggered, and touched the nearest object to me; nothing was said for two or three minutes, and then my uncle put his lips to my ear and whispered something. I fell down senseless. My mother was—— I remember nothing for a long time—for two years I was out of my mind; at the end of this time I recovered, or partly so. My uncle the baronet was very kind to me; he advised me to travel, he offered to go with me. I told him he was very kind, but I would rather go by myself. So I went abroad, and saw, amongst other things, Rome and the Pyramids. By frequent change of scene my mind became not happy, but tolerably tranquil. I continued abroad some years, when, becoming tired of travelling, I came home, found my uncle the baronet alive, hearty, and unmarried, as he still is. He received me very kindly, took me to Newmarket, and said that he hoped by this time I was become quite a man of the world; by his advice I took a house in town, in which I lived during the season. In summer I strolled from one watering-place to another; and, in order to pass the time, I became very dissipated.

"At last I became as tired of dissipation as I had previously been of travelling, and I determined to retire to the country, and live on my paternal estate; this resolution I was not slow in putting into effect; I sold my house in town, repaired and refurnished my country house, and for at least ten years, lived a regular country life; I gave dinner parties, prosecuted poachers, was charitable to the poor, and now and then went into my library; during this time I was seldom or never visited by the magic impulse, the reason being, that there was nothing in the wide world for which I cared sufficiently to move a finger to preserve it. When the ten years, however, were nearly ended, I started out of bed one morning in a fit of horror, exclaiming, 'Mercy, mercy! what will become of me? I am afraid I shall go mad. I have lived thirty-five years and upwards without doing anything; shall I pass through life in this manner? Horror!' And then in rapid succession I touched three different objects.

"I dressed myself and went down, determining to set about something; but what was I to do?—there was the difficulty. I ate no breakfast, but walked about the room in a state of distraction; at last I thought that the easiest way to do something was to get into Parliament, there would be no difficulty in that. I had plenty of money, and could buy a seat: but what was I to do in Parliament? Speak, of course—but could I speak? 'I'll try at once,' said I, and forthwith I rushed into the largest dining-room, and, locking the door, I commenced speaking; 'Mr. Speaker,' said I, and then I went on speaking for about ten minutes as I best could, and then I left off, for I was talking nonsense. No, I was not formed for Parliament; I could do nothing there. What—what was I to do?

"Many, many times I thought this question over, but was unable to solve it; a fear now stole over me that I was unfit for anything in the world, save the lazy life of vegetation which I had for many years been leading; yet, if that were the case. thought I, why the craving within me to distinguish myself? Surely it does not occur fortuitously, but is intended to rouse and call into exercise certain latent powers that I possess? and then with infinite eagerness I set about attempting to discover these latent powers. I tried an infinity of pursuits, botany and geology amongst the rest, but in vain; I was fitted for none of them. I became very sorrowful and despondent, and at one time I had almost resolved to plunge again into the whirlpool of dissipation; it was a dreadful resource, it was true, but what better could I do?

"But I was not doomed to return to the dissipation of the world. One morning a young nobleman, who had for some time past shown a wish to cultivate my acquaintance, came to me in a considerable hurry. 'I am come to beg an important favour of you,' said he; 'one of the county memberships is vacant—I intend to become a candidate; what I want immediately is a spirited address to the electors. I have been endeavouring to frame one all the morning, but in vain; I have, therefore, recourse to you as a person of infinite genius; pray, my dear friend, concoct me one by the morning.' 'What you require of me,' I replied, 'is impossible; I have not the gift of words; did I possess it I would stand for the county myself, but I can't speak. Only the other day I attempted to make a speech, but left off suddenly, utterly ashamed, although I was quite alone. of the nonsense I was uttering.' 'It is not a speech that I want,' said my friend, 'I can talk for three hours without hesitating, but I want an address to circulate through the county, and I find myself utterly incompetent to put one together; do oblige me by writing one for me, I know you can; and, if at any time you want a person to speak for you, you may command me not for three but for six hours. Good morning; to-morrow I will breakfast with you.' In the morning he came again. 'Well,' said he, 'what success?' 'Very poor,' said I; 'but judge for yourself'; and I put into his hand a manuscript of several pages. My friend read it through with considerable attention. 'I congratulate you,' said he, 'and likewise myself; I was not mistaken in my opinion of you; the address is too long by at least two-thirds, or I should rather say it is longer by two-thirds than addresses generally are; but it will do—I will not curtail it of a word. I shall win my election.' And in truth he did win his election; and it was not only his own but the general opinion that he owed it to the address.

"But, however that might be, I had, by writing the address, at last discovered what had so long eluded my search—what I was able to do. I, who had neither the nerve nor the command of speech necessary to constitute the orator—who had not the power of patient research required by those who would investigate the secrets of nature, had, nevertheless, a ready pen and teeming imagination. This discovery decided my fate—from that moment I became an author."

"An author," said I, "is it possible that I am under the roof of an author?"

"Yes," said my host, sighing, "my name is so and so, and I am the author of so and so; it is more than probable that you have heard both of my name and works. I will not detain you much longer with my history; the night is advancing, and the storm appears to be upon the increase. My life since the period of my becoming an author may be summed briefly as an almost uninterrupted series of doubts, anxieties and trepidations. I see clearly that it is not good to love anything immoderately in this world, but it has been my misfortune to love immoderately everything on which I have set my heart. This is not good, I repeat—but where is the remedy? The ancients were always in the habit of saying, 'Practise moderation,' but the ancients appear to have considered only one portion of the subject. It is very possible to practise moderation in some things, in drink and the like—to restrain the appetites—but can a man restrain the affections of his mind, and tell them, so far you shall go, and no farther? Alas, no! for the mind is a subtle principle, and cannot be confined. The winds may be imprisoned; Homer says that Odysseus carried certain winds in his ship, confined in leathern bags, but Homer never speaks of confining the affections. It were but right that those who exhort us against inordinate affections, and setting our hearts too much upon the world and its vanities, would tell us how to avoid doing so.

"I need scarcely tell you, that no sooner did I become an author, than I gave myself up immoderately to my vocation. It became my idol, and, as a necessary consequence, it has proved a source of misery and disquietude to me, instead of pleasure and blessing. I had trouble enough in writing my first work, and I was not long in discovering that it was one thing to write a stirring and spirited address to a set of county electors, and another widely different to produce a work at all calculated to make an impression upon the great world. I felt, however, that I was in my proper sphere, and by dint of unwearied diligence and exertion I succeeded in evolving from the depths of my agitated breast a work which, though it did not exactly please me, I thought would serve to make an experiment upon the public; so I laid it before the public, and the reception which it met with was far beyond my wildest expectations. The public were delighted with it, but what were my feelings? Anything, alas! but those of delight. No sooner did the public express its satisfaction at the result of my endeavours, than my perverse imagination began to conceive a thousand chimerical doubts; forthwith I sat down to analyse it; and my worst enemy, and all people have their enemies, especially authors—my worst enemy could not have discovered or sought to discover a tenth part of the faults which I, the author and creator of the unfortunate production, found or sought to find in it. It has been said that love makes us blind to the faults of the loved object—common love does, perhaps—the love of a father to his child, or that of a lover to his mistress, but not the inordinate love of an author to his works, at least not the love which one like myself bears to his works: to be brief, I discovered a thousand faults in my work, which neither public nor critics discovered. However, I was beginning to get over this misery, and to forgive my work all its imperfections, when—and I shake when I mention it—the same kind of idea which perplexed me with regard to the hawks and the gypsy pony rushed into my mind, and I forthwith commenced touching the objects around me, in order to baffle the evil chance, as you call it: it was neither more nor less than a doubt of the legality of my claim to the thoughts, expressions and situations contained in the book; that is, to all that constituted the book. How did I get them? How did they come into my mind? Did I invent them? Did they originate with myself? Are they my own, or are they some other body's? You see into what difficulty I had got; I won't trouble you by relating all that I endured at that time, but will merely say that after eating my own heart, as the Italians say, and touching every object that came in my way for six months, I at length flung my book, I mean the copy of it which I possessed, into the fire, and began another.

"But, not to tire you, it fared with my second work as it did with my first; I flung it aside and, in order to forget it, I began a third, on which I am now occupied; but the difficulty of writing it is immense, my extreme desire to be original sadly cramping the powers of my mind; my fastidiousness being so great that I invariably reject whatever ideas I do not think to be legitimately my own. But there is one circumstance to which I cannot help alluding, here, as it serves to show what miseries this love of originality must needs bring upon an author. I am constantly discovering that, however original I may wish to be, I am continually producing the same things which other people say or write. Whenever, after producing something which gives me perfect satisfaction, and which has cost me perhaps days and nights of brooding, I chance to take up a book for the sake of a little relaxation, a book which I never saw before, I am sure to find in it something more or less resembling some part of what I have been just composing. You will easily conceive the distress which then comes over me; 'tis then that I am almost tempted to execrate the chance which, by discovering my latent powers, induced me to adopt a profession of such anxiety and misery.

"For some time past I have given up reading almost entirely, owing to the dread which I entertain of lighting upon something similar to what I myself have written. I scarcely ever transgress without having almost instant reason to repent. To-day, when I took up the newspaper, I saw in a speech of the Duke of Rhododendron, at an agricultural dinner, the very same ideas, and almost the same expressions which I had put into the mouth of an imaginary personage of mine, on a widely different occasion; you saw how I dashed the newspaper down—you saw how I touched the floor; the touch was to baffle the evil chance, to prevent the critics detecting any similarity between the speech of the Duke of Rhododendron at the agricultural dinner, and the speech of my personage. My sensibility on the subject of my writings is so great, that sometimes a chance word is sufficient to unman me; I apply it to them in a superstitious sense; for example, when you said some time ago that the dark hour was coming on, I applied it to my works—it appeared to bode them evil fortune; you saw how I touched, it was to baffle the evil chance; but I do not confine myself to touching when the fear of the evil chance is upon me. To baffle it I occasionally perform actions which must appear highly incomprehensible; I have been known, when riding in company with other people, to leave the direct road, and make a long circuit by a miry lane to the place to which we were going. I have also been seen attempting to ride across a morass, where I had no business whatever, and in which my horse finally sank up to its saddle-girths, and was only extricated by the help of a multitude of hands. I have, of course, frequently been asked the reason for such conduct, to which I have invariably returned no answer, for I scorn duplicity; whereupon people have looked mysteriously, and sometimes put their fingers to their foreheads. 'And yet it can't be,' I once heard an old gentleman say; 'don't we know what he is capable of?' and the old man was right; I merely did these things to avoid the evil chance, impelled by the strange feeling within me; and this evil chance is invariably connected with my writings, the only things at present which render life valuable to me. If I touch various objects, and ride into miry places, it is to baffle any mischance befalling me as an author, to prevent my books getting into disrepute; in nine cases out of ten to prevent any expressions, thoughts or situations in any work which I am writing from resembling the thoughts, expressions and situations of other authors, for my great wish, as I told you before, is to be original.

"I have now related my history, and have revealed to you the secrets of my inmost bosom. I should certainly not have spoken so unreservedly as I have done, had I not discovered in you a kindred spirit. I have long wished for an opportunity of discoursing on the point which forms the peculiar feature of my history with a being who could understand me; and truly it was a lucky chance which brought you to these parts; you who seem to be acquainted with all things strange and singular, and who are as well acquainted with the subject of the magic touch as with all that relates to the star Jupiter, or the mysterious tree at Upsal."

Such was the story which my host related to me in the library, amidst the darkness, occasionally broken by flashes of lightning.

CHAPTER XXIII

During the greater part of that night my slumbers were disturbed by strange dreams. Amongst other things, I fancied that I was my host; my head appeared to be teeming with wild thoughts and imaginations, out of which I was endeavouring to frame a book. And now the book was finished and given to the world, and the world shouted; and all eyes were turned upon me, and I shrunk from the eyes of the world. And, when I got into retired places, I touched various objects in order to baffle the evil chance. In short, during the whole night, I was acting over the story which I had heard before I went to bed.

At about eight o'clock I awoke. The storm had long since passed away, and the morning was bright and shining; my couch was so soft and luxurious that I felt loth to quit it, so I lay some time, my eyes wandering about the magnificent room to which fortune had conducted me in so singular a manner; at last I heaved a sigh; I was thinking of my own homeless condition, and imagining where I should find myself on the following morning. Unwilling, however, to indulge in melancholy thoughts, I sprang out of bed and proceeded to dress myself, and, whilst dressing, I felt an irresistible inclination to touch the bed-post.

I finished dressing and left the room, feeling compelled, however, as I left it, to touch the lintel of the door. It is possible, thought I, that from what I have lately heard the long-forgotten influence should have possessed me again? but I will not give way to it; so I hurried down stairs, resisting as I went a certain inclination which I occasionally felt to touch the rail of the bannister. I was presently upon the gravel walk before the house: it was indeed a glorious morning. I stood for some time observing the golden fish disporting in the waters of the pond, and then strolled about amongst the noble trees of the park; the beauty and freshness of the morning—for the air had been considerably cooled by the late storm—soon enabled me to cast away the gloomy ideas which had previously taken possession of my mind, and, after a stroll of about half an hour, I returned towards the house in high spirits. It is true that once I felt very much inclined to go and touch the leaves of a flowery shrub which I saw at some distance, and had even moved two or three paces towards it; but, bethinking myself, I manfully resisted the temptation. "Begone!" I exclaimed, "ye sorceries, in which I formerly trusted—begone for ever vagaries which I had almost forgotten; good luck is not to be obtained, or bad averted, by magic touches; besides, two wizards in one parish would be too much, in all conscience."

I returned to the house, and entered the library; breakfast was laid on the table, and my friend was standing before the portrait which I have already said hung above the mantelpiece; so intently was he occupied in gazing at it that he did not hear me enter, nor was aware of my presence till I advanced close to him and spoke, when he turned round, and shook me by the hand.

"What can possibly have induced you to hang that portrait up in your library? it is a staring likeness, it is true, but it appears to me a wretched daub."

"Daub as you call it," said my friend, smiling, "I would not part with it for the best piece of Raphael. For many a happy thought I am indebted to that picture—it is my principal source of inspiration; when my imagination flags, as of course it occasionally does, I stare upon those features, and forthwith strange ideas of fun and drollery begin to flow into my mind; these I round, amplify, or combine into goodly creations, and bring forth as I find an opportunity. It is true that I am occasionally tormented by the thought that, by doing this, I am committing plagiarism; though in that case, all thoughts must be plagiarisms, all that we think being the result of what we hear, see or feel. What can I do? I must derive my thoughts from some source or other; and, after all, it is better to plagiarise from the features of my landlord than from the works of Butler and Cervantes. My works, as you are aware, are of a serio-comic character. My neighbours are of opinion that I am a great reader and so I am, but only of those features—my real library is that picture."

"But how did you obtain it?"

"Some years ago a travelling painter came into this neighbourhood, and my jolly host, at the request of his wife, consented to sit for his portrait; she highly admired the picture, but she soon died, and then my fat friend, who is of an affectionate disposition, said he could not bear the sight of it, as it put him in mind of his poor wife. I purchased it of him for five pounds—I would not take five thousand for it; when you called that picture a daub, you did not see all the poetry of it."

We sat down to breakfast; my entertainer appeared to be in much better spirits than on the preceding day; I did not observe him touch once; ere breakfast was over a servant entered—"The Reverend Mr. Platitude, sir," said he.

A shade of dissatisfaction came over the countenance of my host. "What does the silly pestilent fellow mean by coming here?" said he, half to himself; "let him come in," said he to the servant.

The servant went out, and in a moment reappeared, introducing the Reverend Mr. Platitude. The Reverend Mr. Platitude, having what is vulgarly called a game leg, came shambling into the room; he was about thirty years of age, and about five feet three inches high; his face was of the colour of pepper, and nearly as rugged as a nutmeg grater; his hair was black; with his eyes he squinted, and grinned with his lips, which were very much apart, disclosing two very irregular rows of teeth; he was dressed in the true Levitical fashion, in a suit of spotless black, and a neckerchief of spotless white.

The Reverend Mr. Platitude advanced winking and grinning to my entertainer, who received him politely but with evident coldness; nothing daunted, however, the Reverend Mr. Platitude took a seat by the table, and, being asked to take a cup of coffee, winked, grinned and consented.

In company I am occasionally subject to fits of what is generally called absence; my mind takes flight and returns to former scenes, or presses forward into the future. One of these fits of absence came over me at this time —I looked at the Reverend Mr. Platitude for a moment, heard a word or two that proceeded from his mouth, and saying to myself, "You are no man for me," fell into a fit of musing—into the same train of thought as in the morning, no very pleasant one—I was thinking of the future.

I continued in my reverie for some time, and probably should have continued longer, had I not been suddenly aroused by the voice of Mr. Platitude raised to a very high key. "Yes, my dear sir," said he, "it is but too true; I have it on good authority—a gone church—a lost church—a ruined church—a demolished church is the Church of England. Toleration to Dissenters! oh, monstrous!"

"I suppose," said my host, "that the repeal of the Test Acts will be merely a precursor of the emancipation of the Papists?"

"Of the Catholics," said the Reverend Mr. Platitude. "Ahem. There was a time, as I believe you are aware, my dear sir, when I was as much opposed to the emancipation of the Catholics as it was possible for any one to be; but I was prejudiced, my dear sir, labouring under a cloud of most unfortunate prejudice; but I thank my Maker I am so no longer. I have travelled, as you are aware. It is only by travelling that one can rub off prejudices; I think you will agree with me there. I am speaking to a traveller. I left behind all my prejudices in Italy. The Catholics are at least our fellow-Christians. I thank Heaven that I am no longer an enemy to Catholic emancipation."

"And yet you would not tolerate Dissenters?"

"Dissenters, my dear sir; I hope you would not class such a set as the Dissenters with Catholics?"

"Perhaps it would be unjust," said my host, "though to which of the two parties is another thing; but permit me to ask you a question: Does it not smack somewhat of paradox to talk of Catholics, whilst you admit there are Dissenters? If there are Dissenters, how should there be Catholics?"

"It is not my fault that there are Dissenters," said the Reverend Mr. Platitude; "if I had my will I would neither admit there were any, nor permit any to be."

"Of course you would admit there were such as long as they existed; but how would you get rid of them?"

"I would have the Church exert its authority."

"What do you mean by exerting its authority?"

"I would not have the Church bear the sword in vain."

"What, the sword of St. Peter? You remember what the founder of the religion which you profess said about the sword, 'He who striketh with it—' I think those who have called themselves the Church have had enough of the sword. Two can play with the sword, Mr. Platitude. The Church of Rome tried the sword with the Lutherans: how did it fare with the Church of Rome? The Church of England tried the sword, Mr. Platitude, with the Puritans: how did it fare with Laud and Charles?"

"Oh, as for the Church of England," said Mr. Platitude, "I have little to say. Thank God I left all my Church of England prejudices in Italy. Had the Church of England known its true interests, it would long ago have sought a reconciliation with its illustrious mother. If the Church of England had not been in some degree a schismatic church, it would not have fared so ill at the time of which you are speaking; the rest of the Church would have come to its assistance. The Irish would have helped it, so would the French, so would the Portuguese. Disunion has always been the bane of the Church."

Once more I fell into a reverie. My mind now reverted to the past; methought I was in a small, comfortable room wainscoted with oak; I was seated on one side of a fireplace, close by a table on which were wine and fruit; on the other side of the fire sat a man in a plain suit of brown, with the hair combed back from his somewhat high forehead; he had a pipe in his mouth, which for some time he smoked gravely and placidly, without saying a word; at length, after drawing at the pipe for some time rather vigorously, he removed it from his mouth, and emitting an accumulated cloud of smoke, he exclaimed in a slow and measured tone: "As I was telling you just now, my good chap, I have always been an enemy to humbug."

When I awoke from my reverie the Reverend Mr. Platitude was quitting the apartment.

"Who is that person?" said I to my entertainer, as the door closed behind him.

"Who is he?" said my host; "why, the Rev. Mr. Platitude."

"Does he reside in this neighbourhood?"

"He holds a living about three miles from here; his history, as far as I am acquainted with it, is as follows: His father was a respectable tanner in the neighbouring town, who, wishing to make his son a gentleman, sent him to college. Having never been at college myself, I cannot say whether he took the wisest course; I believe it is more easy to unmake than to make a gentleman; I have known many gentlemanly youths go to college, and return anything but what they went. Young Mr. Platitude did not go to college a gentleman, but neither did he return one; he went to college an ass, and returned a prig; to his original folly was superadded a vast quantity of conceit. He told his father that he had adopted high principles, and was determined to discountenance everything low and mean; advised him to eschew trade, and to purchase him a living. The old man retired from business, purchased his son a living, and shortly after died, leaving him what remained of his fortune. The first thing the Reverend Mr. Platitude did after his father's decease, was to send his mother and sister into Wales to live upon a small annuity, assigning as a reason that he was averse to anything low and that they talked ungrammatically. Wishing to shine in the pulpit, he now preached high sermons, as he called them, interspersed with scraps of learning. His sermons did not, however, procure him much popularity; on the contrary, his church soon became nearly deserted, the greater part of his flock going over to certain dissenting preachers, who had shortly before made their appearance in the neighbourhood. Mr. Platitude was filled with wrath, and abused Dissenters in most unmeasured terms. Coming in contact with some of the preachers at a public meeting, he was rash enough to enter into argument with them. Poor Platitude! he had better have been quiet, he appeared like a child, a very infant in their grasp; he attempted to take shelter under his college learning, but found, to his dismay, that his opponents knew more Greek and Latin than himself. These illiterate boors, as he had supposed them, caught him at once in a false concord, and Mr. Platitude had to slink home overwhelmed with shame. To avenge himself he applied to the ecclesiastical court, but was told that the Dissenters could not be put down by the present ecclesiastical law. He found the Church of England, to use his own expression, a poor, powerless, restricted Church. He now thought to improve his consequence by marriage, and made up to a rich and beautiful young lady in the neighbourhood; the damsel measured him from head to foot with a pair of very sharp eyes, dropped a curtsey, and refused him. Mr. Platitude, finding England a very stupid place, determined to travel; he went to Italy; how he passed his time there he knows best, to other people it is a matter of little importance. At the end of two years he returned with a real or assumed contempt for everything English, and especially for the Church to which he belongs, and out of which he is supported. He forthwith gave out that he had left behind him all his Church of England prejudices, and, as a proof thereof, spoke against sacerdotal wedlock and the toleration of schismatics. In an evil hour for myself he was introduced to me by a clergyman of my acquaintance, and from that time I have been pestered, as I was this morning, at least once a week."

After some further conversation, the subjects being, if I remember right, college education, priggism, church authority, tomfoolery, and the like, I rose and said to my host, "I must now leave you."

"Whither are you going?"

"I do not know."

"Stay here, then—you shall be welcome as many days, months, and years as you please to stay."

"Do you think I would hang upon another man? No, not if he were Emperor of all the Chinas. I will now make my preparations, and then bid you farewell."

I retired to my apartment and collected the handful of things which I carried with me on my travels.

"I will walk a little way with you," said my friend on my return.

He walked with me to the park gate; neither of us said anything by the way. When we had come upon the road, I said: "Farewell now; I will not permit you to give yourself any further trouble on my account. Receive my best thanks for your kindness; before we part, however, I should wish to ask you a question. Do you think you shall ever grow tired of authorship?"

"I have my fears," said my friend, advancing his hand to one of the iron bars of the gate.

"Don't touch," said I, "it is a bad habit. I have but one word to add: should you ever grow tired of authorship follow your first idea of getting into Parliament; you have words enough at command."

I departed. At the distance of twenty yards I turned round suddenly; my friend was just withdrawing his finger from the bar of the gate.

CHAPTER XXIV

After walking some time, I found myself on the great road, at the same spot where I had turned aside the day before with my new-made acquaintance, in the direction of his house. I now continued my journey as before, towards the north. The weather, though beautiful, was much cooler than it had been for some time past; I walked at a great rate, with a springing and elastic step. In about two hours I came to where a kind of cottage stood a little way back from the road, with a huge oak before it, under the shade of which stood a little pony and cart, which seemed to contain various articles. I was going past, when I saw scrawled over the door of the cottage, "Good beer sold here"; upon which, feeling myself all of a sudden very thirsty, I determined to go in and taste the beverage.

I entered a well-sanded kitchen, and seated myself on a bench, on one side of a long white table; the other side, which was nearest to the wall, was occupied by a party, or rather family, consisting of a grimy-looking man, somewhat under the middle size, dressed in faded velveteens, and wearing a leather apron—a rather pretty-looking woman, but sun-burnt, and meanly dressed, and two ragged children, a boy and girl, about four or five years old. The man sat with his eyes fixed upon the table, supporting his chin with both his hands; the woman, who was next to him, sat quite still, save that occasionally she turned a glance upon her husband with eyes that appeared to have been lately crying. The children had none of the vivacity so general at their age. A more disconsolate family I had never seen; a mug, which, when filled, might contain half a pint, stood empty before them; a very disconsolate party indeed.

"House!" said I; "House!" and then as nobody appeared, I cried again as loud as I could, "House! do you hear me House!"

"What's your pleasure, young man?" said an elderly woman, who now made her appearance from a side apartment.

"To taste your ale," said I.

"How much?" said the woman, stretching out her hand towards the empty mug upon the table.

"The largest measure-full in your house," said I, putting back her hand gently. "This is not the season for half-pint mugs."

"As you will, young man," said the landlady, and presently brought in an earthen pitcher which might contain about three pints, and which foamed and frothed withal.

"Will this pay for it?" said I, putting down sixpence.

"I have to return you a penny," said the landlady, putting her hand into her pocket.

"I want no change," said I, flourishing my hand with an air.

"As you please, young gentleman," said the landlady, and then making a kind of curtsey, she again retired to the side apartment.

"Here is your health, sir," said I to the grimy-looking man, as I raised the pitcher to my lips.

The tinker, for such I supposed him to be, without altering his posture, raised his eyes, looked at me for a moment, gave a slight nod, and then once more fixed his eyes upon the table. I took a draught of the ale, which I found excellent; "Won't you drink?" said I, holding the pitcher to the tinker.

The man again lifted his eyes, looked at me, and then at the pitcher, and then at me again. I thought at one time that he was about to shake his head in sign of refusal, but no, he looked once more at the pitcher, and the temptation was too strong. Slowly removing his head from his arms, he took the pitcher, sighed, nodded, and drank a tolerable quantity, and then set the pitcher down before me upon the table.

"You had better mend your draught," said I to the tinker; "it is a sad heart that never rejoices."

"That's true," said the tinker, and again raising the pitcher to his lips, he mended his draught as I had bidden him, drinking a larger quantity than before.

"Pass it to your wife," said I.

The poor woman took the pitcher from the man's hand: before, however, raising it to her lips, she looked at the children. True mother's heart, thought I to myself, and taking the half-pint mug, I made her fill it, and then held it to the children, causing each to take a draught. The woman wiped her eyes with the corner of her gown before she raised the pitcher and drank to my health.

In about five minutes none of the family looked half so disconsolate as before, and the tinker and I were in deep discourse.

Oh, genial and gladdening is the power of good ale, the true and proper drink of Englishmen. He is not deserving of the name of Englishman who speaketh against ale, that is good ale, like that which has just made merry the hearts of this poor family; and yet there are beings, calling themselves Englishmen, who say that it is a sin to drink a cup of ale, and who, on coming to this passage will be tempted to fling down the book and exclaim: "The man is evidently a bad man, for behold, by his own confession, he is not only fond of ale himself, but is in the habit of tempting other people with it." Alas! alas! what a number of silly individuals there are in this world.

"Well," said the tinker, after we had discoursed some time, "I little thought when I first saw you, that you were of my own trade."

Myself. Nor am I, at least not exactly. There is not much difference, 'tis true, between a tinker and a smith.

Tinker. You are a whitesmith, then?

Myself. Not I, I'd scorn to be anything so mean; no, friend, black's the colour; I am a brother of the horseshoe. Success to the hammer and tongs.

Tinker. Well, I shouldn't have thought you were a blacksmith by your hands.

Myself. I have seen them, however, as black as yours. The truth is, I have not worked for many a day.

Tinker. Where did you serve first?

Myself. In Ireland.

Tinker. That's a good way off, isn't it?

Myself. Not very far; over those mountains to the left, and the run of salt water that lies behind them, there's Ireland.

Tinker. It's a fine thing to be a scholar.

Myself. Not half so fine as to be a tinker.

Tinker. How you talk!

Myself. Nothing but the truth; what can be better than to be one's own master? Now, a tinker is his own master, a scholar is not. Let us suppose the best of scholars, a schoolmaster, for example, for I suppose you will admit that no one can be higher in scholarship than a schoolmaster; do you call his a pleasant life? I don't; we should call him a school-slave, rather than a schoolmaster. Only conceive him in blessed weather like this, in his close school, teaching children to write in copy-books, "Evil communication corrupts good manners," or "You cannot touch pitch without defilement," or to spell out of Abedariums, or to read out of Jack Smith, or Sandford and Merton. Only conceive him, I say, drudging in such guise from morning till night, without any rational enjoyment but to beat the children. Would you compare such a dog's life as that with your own—the happiest under heaven—true Eden life, as the Germans would say—pitching your tent under the pleasant hedge-row, listening to the song of the feathered tribes, collecting all the leaky kettles in the neighbourhood, soldering and joining, earning your honest bread by the wholesome sweat of your brow—making ten holes—hey, what's this? what's the man crying for?

Suddenly the tinker had covered his face with his hands, and begun to sob and moan like a man in the deepest distress; the breast of his wife was heaved with emotion; even the children were agitated, the youngest began to roar.

Myself. What's the matter with you; what are you all crying about?

Tinker (uncovering his face). Lord, why to hear you talk; isn't that enough to make anybody cry—even the poor babes? Yes, you said right, 'tis life in the garden of Eden—the tinker's; I see so now that I'm about to give it up.

Myself. Give it up! you must not think of such a thing.

Tinker. No, I can't bear to think of it, and yet I must; what's to be done? How hard to be frightened to death, to be driven off the roads.

Myself. Who has driven you off the roads?

Tinker. Who! the Flaming Tinman.

Myself. Who is he?

Tinker. The biggest rogue in England, and the cruelest, or he wouldn't have served me as he has done—I'll tell you all about it. I was born upon the roads, and so was my father before me, and my mother too; and I worked with them as long as they lived, as a dutiful child, for I have nothing to reproach myself with on their account; and when my father died I took up the business, and went his beat, and supported my mother for the little time she lived; and when she died I married this young woman, who was not born upon the roads, but was a small tradesman's daughter, at Glo'ster. She had a kindness for me, and, notwithstanding her friends were against the match, she married the poor tinker, and came to live with him upon the roads. Well, young man, for six or seven years I was the happiest fellow breathing, living just the life you described just now—respected by everybody in this beat; when in an evil hour comes this Black Jack, this flaming tinman, into these parts, driven as they say out of Yorkshire—for no good, you may be sure. Now, there is no beat will support two tinkers, as you doubtless know; mine was a good one, but it would not support the flying tinker and myself, though if it would have supported twenty it would have been all the same to the flying villain, who'll brook no one but himself; so he presently finds me out, and offers to fight me for the beat. Now, being bred upon the roads, I can fight a little, that is with anything like my match, but I was not going to fight him, who happens to be twice my size, and so I told him; whereupon he knocks me down, and would have done me further mischief had not some men been nigh and prevented him; so he threatened to cut my throat, and went his way. Well, I did not like such usage at all, and was woundily frightened, and tried to keep as much out of his way as possible, going anywhere but where I thought I was likely to meet him; and sure enough for several months I contrived to keep out of his way. At last somebody told me he was gone back to Yorkshire, whereupon I was glad at heart, and ventured to show myself, going here and there as I did before. Well, young man, it was yesterday that I and mine set ourselves down in a lane, about five miles from here, and lighted our fire, and had our dinner, and after dinner I sat down to mend three kettles and a frying pan which the people in the neighbourhood had given me to mend—for, as I told you before, I have a good connection, owing to my honesty. Well, as I sat there hard at work, happy as the day's long, and thinking of anything but what was to happen, who should come up but this Black Jack, this king of the tinkers, rattling along in his cart, with his wife, that they call Grey Moll, by his side—for the villain has got a wife, and a maid-servant too; the last I never saw, but they that has, says that she is as big as a house, and young, and well to look at, which can't be all said of Moll, who, though she's big enough in all conscience, is neither young nor handsome. Well, no sooner does he see me and mine, than giving the reins to Grey Moll, he springs out of his cart, and comes straight at me; not a word did he say, but on he comes straight at me like a wild bull. I am a quiet man, young fellow, but I saw now that quietness would be of no use, so I sprang up upon my legs, and being bred upon the roads, and able to fight a little, I squared as he came running in upon me, and had a round or two with him. Lord bless you, young man, it was like a fly fighting with an elephant—one of those big beasts the show-folks carry about. I had not a chance with the fellow, he knocked me here, he knocked me there, knocked me into the hedge, and knocked me out again. I was at my last shifts, and my poor wife saw it. Now, my poor wife, though she is as gentle as a pigeon, has yet a spirit of her own, and though she wasn't bred upon the roads, can scratch a little, so when she saw me at my last shifts, she flew at the villain—she couldn't bear to see her partner murdered—and she scratched the villain's face. Lord bless you, young man, she had better have been quiet: Grey Moll no sooner saw what she was about, than springing out of the cart, where she had sat all along perfectly quiet, save a little whooping and screeching to encourage her blade—Grey Moll, I say (my flesh creeps when I think of it—for I am a kind husband, and love my poor wife)——

Myself. Take another draught of the ale; you look frightened, and it will do you good. Stout liquor makes stout heart, as the man says in the play.

Tinker. That's true, young man; here's to you—where was I? Grey Moll no sooner saw what my wife was about, than springing out of the cart, she flew at my poor wife, clawed off her bonnet in a moment, and seized hold of her hair. Lord bless you, young man, my poor wife, in the hands of Grey Moll, was nothing better than a pigeon in the claws of a buzzard hawk, or I in the hands of the Flaming Tinman, which when I saw, my heart was fit to burst, and I determined to give up everything—everything to save my poor wife out of Grey Moll's claws. "Hold!" I shouted. "Hold, both of you—Jack, Moll. Hold, both of you, for God's sake, and I'll do what you will: give up trade and business, connection, bread, and everything, never more travel the roads, and go down on my knees to you in the bargain." Well, this had some effect: Moll let go my wife, and the Blazing Tinman stopped for a moment; it was only for a moment, however, that he left off—all of a sudden he hit me a blow which sent me against a tree; and what did the villain then? why the flying villain seized me by the throat, and almost throttled me, roaring—what do you think, young man, that the flaming villain roared out?

Myself. I really don't know—something horrible, I suppose.

Tinker. Horrible, indeed; you may well say horrible, young man; neither more nor less than the Bible—"a Bible, a Bible!" roared the Blazing Tinman; and he pressed my throat so hard against the tree that my senses began to dwaul away—a Bible, a Bible, still ringing in my ears. Now, young man, my poor wife is a Christian woman, and though she travels the roads, carries a Bible with her at the bottom of her sack, with which sometimes she teaches the children to read—it was the only thing she brought with her from the place of her kith and kin, save her own body and the clothes on her back; so my poor wife, half-distracted, runs to her sack, pulls out the Bible, and puts it into the hand of the Blazing Tinman, who then thrusts the end of it into my mouth with such fury that it made my lips bleed, and broke short one of my teeth which happened to be decayed. "Swear," said he, "swear you mumping villain, take your Bible oath that you will quit and give up the beat altogether, or I'll"—and then the hard-hearted villain made me swear by the Bible, and my own damnation, half-throttled as I was—to—to—I can't go on——

Myself. Take another draught—stout liquor——

Tinker. I can't, young man, my heart's too full, and what's more, the pitcher is empty.

Myself. And so he swore you, I suppose, on the Bible, to quit the roads?

Tinker. You are right, he did so, the gypsy villain.

Myself. Gypsy! Is he a gypsy?

Tinker. Not exactly; what they call a half and half. His father was a gypsy, and his mother, like mine, one who walked the roads.

Myself. Is he of the Smiths—the Petulengres?

Tinker. I say, young man, you know a thing or two; one would think, to hear you talk, you had been bred upon the roads. I thought none but those bred upon the roads knew anything of that name—Petulengres! No, not he, he fights the Petulengres whenever he meets them; he likes nobody but himself, and wants to be king of the roads. I believe he is a Boss, or a——at any rate he's a bad one, as I know to my cost.

Myself. And what are you going to do?

Tinker. Do! you may well ask that; I don't know what to do. My poor wife and I have been talking of that all the morning, over that half-pint mug of beer; we can't determine on what's to be done. All we know is, that we must quit the roads. The villain swore that the next time he saw us on the roads he'd cut all our throats, and seize our horse and bit of a cart that are now standing out there under the tree.

Myself. And what do you mean to do with your horse and cart?

Tinker. Another question! What shall we do with our cart and pony? they are of no use to us now. Stay on the roads I will not, both for my oath's sake and my own. If we had a trifle of money, we were thinking of going to Bristol, where I might get up a little business, but we have none; our last three farthings we spent about the mug of beer.

Myself. But why don't you sell your horse and cart?

Tinker. Sell them? And who would buy them, unless some one who wished to set up in my line; but there's no beat, and what's the use of the horse and cart and the few tools without the beat?

Myself. I'm half-inclined to buy your cart and pony, and your beat too.

Tinker. You! How came you to think of such a thing?

Myself. Why, like yourself, I hardly know what to do. I want a home and work. As for a home, I suppose I can contrive to make a home out of your tent and cart; and as for work, I must learn to be a tinker, it would not be hard for one of my trade to learn to tinker; what better can I do? Would you have me go to Chester and work there now? I don't like the thoughts of it. If I go to Chester and work there, I can't be my own man; I must work under a master, and perhaps he and I should quarrel, and when I quarrel I am apt to hit folks, and those that hit folks are sometimes sent to prison; I don't like the thought either of going to Chester or to Chester prison. What do you think I could earn at Chester?

Tinker. A matter of eleven shillings a week, if anybody would employ you, which I don't think they would with those hands of yours. But whether they would or not, if you are of a quarrelsome nature, you must not go to Chester; you would be in the castle in no time. I don't know how to advise you. As for selling you my stock, I'd see you farther first, for your own sake.

Myself. Why?

Tinker. Why! you would get your head knocked off. Suppose you were to meet him?

Myself. Pooh, don't be afraid on my account; if I were to meet him I could easily manage him one way or other. I know all kinds of strange words and names, and, as I told you before, I sometimes hit people when they put me out.

Here the tinker's wife, who for some minutes past had been listening attentively to our discourse, interposed, saying, in a low, soft tone: "I really don't see, John, why you shouldn't sell the young man the things, seeing that he wishes for them, and is so confident; you have told him plainly how matters stand, and if anything ill should befall him, people couldn't lay the blame on you; but I don't think any ill will befall him, and who knows but God has sent him to our assistance in time of need."

"I'll hear of no such thing," said the tinker; "I have drunk at the young man's expense, and though he says he's quarrelsome, I would not wish to sit in pleasanter company. A pretty fellow I should be, now, if I were to let him follow his own will. If he once sets up on my beat, he's a lost man, his ribs will be stove in, and his head knocked off his shoulders. There, you are crying, but you shan't have your will, though; I won't be the young man's destruction—— If, indeed, I thought he could manage the tinker—but he never can; he says he can hit, but it's no use hitting the tinker; crying still! you are enough to drive one mad. I say, young man, I believe you understand a thing or two; just now you were talking of knowing hard words and names—I don't wish to send you to your mischief—you say you know hard words and names, let us see. Only on one condition I'll sell you the pony and things; as for the beat, it's gone, isn't mine—sworn away by my own mouth. Tell me what's my name; if you can't, may I——"

Myself. Don't swear, it's a bad habit, neither pleasant nor profitable. Your name is Slingsby—Jack Slingsby. There, don't stare, there's nothing in my telling you your name: I've been in these parts before, at least not very far from here. Ten years ago, when I was little more than a child, I was about twenty miles from here in a post-chaise at the door of an inn, and as I looked from the window of the chaise, I saw you standing by a gutter, with a big tin ladle in your hand, and somebody called you Jack Slingsby. I never forget anything I hear or see; I can't, I wish I could. So there's nothing strange in my knowing your name; indeed, there's nothing strange in anything, provided you examine it to the bottom. Now, what am I to give you for the things?

I paid Slingsby five pounds ten shillings for his stock in trade, cart, and pony—purchased sundry provisions of the landlady, also a wagoner's frock, which had belonged to a certain son of hers, deceased, gave my little animal a feed of corn, and prepared to depart.

"God bless you, young man," said Slingsby, shaking me by the hand, "you are the best friend I've had for many a day: I have but one thing to tell you: Don't cross that fellow's path if you can help it; and stay—should the pony refuse to go, just touch him so, and he'll fly like the wind."

CHAPTER XXV

It was two or three hours past noon when I took my departure from the place of the last adventure, walking by the side of my little cart; the pony, invigorated by the corn, to which he was probably not much accustomed, proceeded right gallantly; so far from having to hasten him forward by the particular application which the tinker had pointed out to me, I had rather to repress his eagerness, being, though an excellent pedestrian, not unfrequently left behind. The country through which I passed was beautiful and interesting, but solitary: few habitations appeared. As it was quite a matter of indifference to me in what direction I went, the whole world being before me, I allowed the pony to decide upon the matter; it was not long before he left the high road, being probably no friend to public places. I followed him I knew not whither, but, from subsequent observation, have reason to suppose that our course was in a north-west direction. At length night came upon us, and a cold wind sprang up, which was succeeded by a drizzling rain.

I had originally intended to pass the night in the cart, or to pitch my little tent on some convenient spot by the road's side; but, owing to the alteration in the weather, I thought that it would be advisable to take up my quarters in any hedge alehouse at which I might arrive. To tell the truth, I was not very sorry to have an excuse to pass the night once more beneath a roof. I had determined to live quite independent, but I had never before passed a night by myself abroad, and felt a little apprehensive at the idea; I hoped, however, on the morrow, to be a little more prepared for the step, so I determined for one night—only for one night longer—to sleep like a Christian; but human determinations are not always put into effect, such a thing as opportunity is frequently wanting, such was the case here. I went on for a considerable time, in expectation of coming to some rustic hostelry, but nothing of the kind presented itself to my eyes; the country in which I now was seemed almost uninhabited, not a house of any kind was to be seen —at least I saw none—though it is true houses might be near without my seeing them, owing to the darkness of the night, for neither moon nor star was abroad. I heard, occasionally, the bark of dogs; but the sound appeared to come from an immense distance. The rain still fell, and the ground beneath my feet was wet and miry; in short, it was a night in which even a tramper by profession would feel more comfortable in being housed than abroad. I followed in the rear of the cart, the pony still proceeding at a sturdy pace, till methought I heard other hoofs than those of my own nag; I listened for a moment, and distinctly heard the sound of hoofs approaching at a great rate, and evidently from the quarter towards which I and my little caravan were moving. We were in a dark lane—so dark that it was impossible for me to see my own hand. Apprehensive that some accident might occur, I ran forward, and, seizing the pony by the bridle, drew him as near as I could to the hedge. On came the hoofs—trot, trot, trot; and evidently more than those of one horse; their speed as they advanced appeared to slacken—it was only, however, for a moment. I heard a voice cry, "Push on, this is a desperate robbing place, never mind the dark"; and the hoofs came on quicker than before. "Stop!" said I, at the top of my voice; "stop! or——" Before I could finish what I was about to say there was a stumble, a heavy fall, a cry, and a groan, and putting out my foot I felt what I conjectured to be the head of a horse stretched upon the road. "Lord have mercy upon us! what's the matter?" exclaimed a voice. "Spare my life," cried another voice, apparently from the ground; "only spare my life, and take all I have." "Where are you, Master Wise?" cried the other voice. "Help! here, Master Bat," cried the voice from the ground, "help me up or I shall be murdered." "Why, what's the matter?" said Bat. "Some one has knocked me down, and is robbing me," said the voice from the ground. "Help! murder!" cried Bat; and, regardless of the entreaties of the man on the ground that he would stay and help him up, he urged his horse forward and galloped away as fast as he could. I remained for some time quiet, listening to various groans and exclamations uttered by the person on the ground; at length I said, "Holloa! are you hurt?" "Spare my life, and take all I have!" said the voice from the ground. "Have they not done robbing you yet?" said I; "when they have finished let me know, and I will come and help you." "Who is that?" said the voice; "pray come and help me, and do me no mischief." "You were saying that some one was robbing you," said I, "don't think I shall come till he is gone away." "Then you ben't he?" said the voice. "Ar'n't you robbed?" said I. "Can't say I be," said the voice; "not yet at any rate; but who are you? I don't know you." "A traveller whom you and your partner were going to run over in this dark lane; you almost frightened me out of my senses." "Frightened!" said the voice, in a louder tone; "frightened! oh!" and thereupon I heard somebody getting upon his legs. This accomplished, the individual proceeded to attend to his horse, and with a little difficulty raised him upon his legs also. "Ar'n't you hurt?" said I. "Hurt!" said the voice; "not I; don't think it, whatever the horse may be. I tell you what, my fellow, I thought you were a robber, and now I find you are not; I have a good mind——" "To do what?" "To serve you out; ar'n't you ashamed——?" "At what?" said I; "not to have robbed you? Shall I set about it now?" "Ha, ha!" said the man, dropping the bullying tone which he had assumed; "you are joking—robbing! who talks of robbing? I wonder how my horse's knees are; not much hurt, I think—only mired." The man, whoever he was, then got upon his horse; and, after moving him about a little, said, "Good-night, friend; where are you?" "Here I am," said I, "just behind you." "You are, are you? Take that." I know not what he did, but probably pricking his horse with the spur the animal kicked out violently; one of his heels struck me on the shoulder, but luckily missed my face; I fell back with the violence of the blow, whilst the fellow scampered off at a great rate. Stopping at some distance, he loaded me with abuse, and then, continuing his way at a rapid trot, I heard no more of him.

"What a difference!" said I, getting up; "last night I was *fêted* in the hall of a rich genius, and to-night I am knocked down and mired in a dark lane by the heel of Master Wise's horse—I wonder who gave him that name? And yet he was wise enough to wreak his revenge upon me, and I was not wise enough to keep out of his way. Well, I am not much hurt, so it is of little consequence."

I now bethought me that, as I had a carriage of my own, I might as well make use of it; I therefore got into the cart, and, taking the reins in my hand, gave an encouraging cry to the pony, whereupon the sturdy little animal started again at as brisk a pace as if he had not already come many a long mile. I lay half-reclining in the cart, holding the reins lazily, and allowing the animal to go just where he pleased, often wondering where he would conduct me. At length I felt drowsy, and my head sank upon my breast; I soon aroused myself, but it was only to doze again; this occurred several times. Opening my eyes after a doze somewhat longer than the others, I found that the drizzling rain had ceased, a corner of the moon was apparent in the heavens, casting a faint light; I looked around for a moment or two, but my eyes and brain were heavy with slumber, and I could scarcely distinguish where we were. I had a kind of dim consciousness that we were traversing an uninclosed country—perhaps a heath; I thought, however, that I saw certain large black objects looming in the distance, which I had a confused idea might be woods or plantations; the pony still moved at his usual pace. I did not find the jolting of the cart at all disagreeable; on the contrary, it had quite a somniferous effect upon me. Again my eyes closed; I opened them once more, but with less perception in them than before, looked forward, and, muttering something about woodlands, I placed myself in an easier posture than I had hitherto done, and fairly fell asleep.

How long I continued in that state I am unable to say, but I believe for a considerable time; I was suddenly awakened by the ceasing of the jolting to which I had become accustomed, and of which I was perfectly sensible in my sleep. I started up and looked around me, the moon was still shining, and the face of the heaven was studded with stars; I found myself amidst a maze of bushes of various kinds, but principally hazel and holly, through which was a path or driftway with grass growing on either side, upon which the pony was already diligently browsing. I conjectured that this place had been one of the haunts of his former master, and, on dismounting and looking about, was strengthened in that opinion by finding a spot under an ash tree which, from its burnt and blackened appearance, seemed to have been frequently used as a fireplace. I will take up my quarters here, thought I; it is an excellent spot for me to commence my new profession in; I was quite right to trust myself to the guidance of the pony. Unharnessing the animal without delay, I permitted him to browse at free will on the grass, convinced that he would not wander far from a place to which he was so much attached; I then pitched the little tent close beside the ash tree to which I have alluded, and conveyed two or three articles into it, and instantly felt that I had commenced housekeeping for the first time in my life. Housekeeping, however, without a fire is a very sorry affair, something like the housekeeping of children in their toy houses; of this I was the more sensible from feeling very cold and shivering, owing to my late exposure to the rain, and sleeping in the night air. Collecting, therefore, all the dry sticks and furze I could find, I placed them upon the fireplace, adding certain chips and a billet which I found in the cart, it having apparently been the habit of Slingsby to carry with him a small store of fuel. Having then struck a spark in a tinder-box and lighted a match, I set fire to the combustible heap, and was not slow in raising a cheerful blaze; I then drew my cart near the fire, and, seating myself on one of the shafts, hung over the warmth with feelings of intense pleasure and satisfaction. Having continued in this posture for a considerable time, I turned my eyes to the heaven in the direction of a particular star; I, however, could not find the star, nor indeed many of the starry train, the greater number having fled, from which circumstance, and from the appearance of the sky, I concluded that morning was nigh. About this time I again began to feel drowsy; I therefore arose, and having prepared for myself a kind of couch in the tent, I flung myself upon it and went to sleep.

I will not say that I was awakened in the morning by the carolling of birds, as I perhaps might if I were writing a novel; I awoke because, to use vulgar language, I had slept my sleep out, not because the birds were carolling around me in numbers, as they had probably been for hours without my hearing them. I got up and left my tent; the morning was yet more bright than that of the preceding day. Impelled by curiosity, I walked about, endeavouring to ascertain to what place chance, or rather the pony, had brought me; following the driftway for some time, amidst bushes and stunted trees, I came to a grove of dark pines, through which it appeared to lead; I tracked it a few hundred yards, but seeing nothing but trees, and the way being wet and sloughy, owing to the recent rain, I returned on my steps, and, pursuing the path in another direction, came to a sandy road leading over a common, doubtless the one I had traversed the preceding night. My curiosity satisfied, I returned to my little encampment, and on the way beheld a small footpath on the left winding through the bushes, which had before escaped my observation. Having reached my tent and cart, I breakfasted on some of the provisions which I had procured the day before, and then proceeded to take a regular account of the stock formerly possessed by Slingsby the tinker, but now become my own by right of lawful purchase.

Besides the pony, the cart, and the tent, I found I was possessed of a mattress stuffed with straw on which to lie, and a blanket to cover me, the last quite clean and nearly new; then there was a frying-pan and a kettle, the first for cooking any food which required cooking, and the second for heating any water which I might wish to heat. I likewise found an earthen teapot and two or three cups; of the first I should rather say I found the remains, it being broken in three parts, no doubt since it came into my possession, which would have precluded the possibility of my asking anybody to tea for the present, should anybody visit me, even supposing I had tea and sugar, which was not the case. I then overhauled what might more strictly be called the stock in trade; this consisted of various tools, an iron ladle, a chafing pan and small bellows, sundry pans and kettles, the latter being of tin, with the exception of one which was of copper, all in a state of considerable dilapidation—if I may use the term; of these first Slingsby had spoken in particular, advising me to mend them as soon as possible, and to endeavour to sell them, in order that I might have the satisfaction of receiving some return upon the outlay which I had made. There was likewise a small quantity of block tin, sheet tin, and solder. "This Slingsby," said I, "is certainly a very honest man, he has sold me more than my money's worth; I believe, however, there is something more in the cart." Thereupon I rummaged the farther end of the cart, and, amidst a quantity of straw, I found a small anvil and bellows of that kind which are used in forges, and two hammers such as smiths use, one great, and the other small.

The sight of these last articles caused me no little surprise, as no word which had escaped from the mouth of Slingsby had given me reason to suppose that he had ever followed the occupation of a smith; yet, if he had not, how did he come by them? I sat down upon the shaft, and pondered the question deliberately in my mind; at length I concluded that he had come by them by one of those numerous casualties which occur upon the roads, of which I, being a young hand upon the roads, must have a very imperfect conception; honestly, of course—for I scouted the idea that Slingsby would have stolen this blacksmith's gear—for I had the highest opinion of his honesty, which opinion I still retain at the present day, which is upwards of twenty years from the time of which I am speaking, during the whole of which period I have neither seen the poor fellow, nor received any intelligence of him.

CHAPTER XXVI

I PASSED the greater part of the day in endeavouring to teach myself the mysteries of my new profession. I cannot say that I was very successful, but the time passed agreeably, and was therefore not ill spent. Towards evening I flung my work aside, took some refreshment, and afterwards a walk.

This time I turned up the small footpath, of which I have already spoken. It led in a zigzag manner through thickets of hazel, elder and sweet briar; after following its windings for somewhat better than a furlong, I heard a gentle sound of water, and presently came to a small rill, which ran directly across the path. I was rejoiced at the sight, for I had already experienced the want of water, which I yet knew must be nigh at hand, as I was in a place to all appearance occasionally frequented by wandering people, who I was aware never take up their quarters in places where water is difficult to be obtained. Forthwith I stretched myself on the ground, and took a long and delicious draught of the crystal stream, and then, seating myself in a bush, I continued for some time gazing on the water as it purled tinkling away in its channel through an opening in the hazels, and should have probably continued much longer had not the thought that I had left my property unprotected compelled me to rise and return to my encampment.

Two or three days passed by in much the same manner as the first. During the morning I worked upon my kettles, and employed the remaining part of the day as I best could. The whole of this time I only saw two individuals, rustics, who passed by my encampment without vouchsafing me a glance; they probably considered themselves my superiors, as perhaps they were.

One very brilliant morning, as I sat at work in very good spirits, for by this time I had actually mended in a very creditable way, as I imagined, two kettles and a frying-pan, I heard a voice which seemed to proceed from the path leading to the rivulet; at first it sounded from a considerable distance, but drew nearer by degrees. I soon remarked that the tones were exceedingly sharp and shrill, with yet something of childhood in them. Once or twice I distinguished certain words in the song which the voice was singing; the words were—but no, I thought again I was probably mistaken—and then the voice ceased for a time; presently I heard it again, close to the entrance of the footpath; in another moment I heard it in the lane or glade in which stood my tent, where it abruptly stopped, but not before I had heard the very words which I at first thought I had distinguished.

I turned my head; at the entrance of the footpath, which might be about thirty yards from the place where I was sitting, I perceived the figure of a young girl; her face was turned towards me, and she appeared to be scanning me and my encampment; after a little time she looked in the other direction, only for a moment, however; probably observing nothing in that quarter, she again looked towards me, and almost immediately stepped forward; and, as she advanced, sang the song which I had heard in the wood, the first words of which were those which I have already alluded to:

The Rommany chi
And the Rommany chal,
Shall jaw tasaulor
To drab the bawlor,
And dook the gry
Of the farming rye.

A very pretty song, thought I, falling again hard to work upon my kettle; a very pretty song, which bodes the farmers much good. Let them look to their cattle.

"All alone here, brother?" said a voice close by me, in sharp but not disagreeable tones.

I made no answer, but continued my work, click, click, with the gravity which became one of my profession. I allowed at least half a minute to elapse before I even lifted up my eyes.

A girl of about thirteen was standing before me; her features were very pretty, but with a peculiar expression; her complexion was a clear olive, and her jet black hair hung back upon her shoulders. She was rather scantily dressed, and her arms and feet were bare; round her neck, however, was a handsome string of corals, with ornaments of gold: in her hand she held a bulrush.

"All alone here, brother?" said the girl, as I looked up; "all alone here, in the lane; where are your wife and children?"

"Why do you call me brother?" said I; "I am no brother of yours. Do you take me for one of your people? I am no gypsy; not I, indeed!"

"Don't be afraid, brother, you are no Roman—Roman indeed, you are not handsome enough to be a Roman; not black enough, tinker though you be. If I called you brother, it was because I didn't know what else to call you. Marry, come up, brother, I should be sorry to have you for a brother."

"Then you don't like me?"

"Neither like you, nor dislike you, brother; what will you have for that kekaubi?"

"What's the use of talking to me in that unchristian way; what do you mean, young gentlewoman?"

"Lord, brother, what a fool you are; every tinker knows what a kekaubi is. I was asking you what you would have for that kettle."

"Three-and-sixpence, young gentlewoman; isn't it well mended?"

"Well mended! I could have done it better myself; three-and-sixpence! it's only fit to be played at football with."

"I will take no less for it, young gentlewoman; it has caused me a world of trouble."

"I never saw a worse mended kettle. I say, brother, your hair is white."

" 'Tis nature; your hair is black; nature, nothing but nature."

"I am young, brother; my hair is black—that's nature: you are young, brother; your hair is white—that's not nature."

"I can't help it if it be not, but it is nature after all; did you never see grey hair on the young?"

"Never! I have heard it is true of a grey lad, and a bad one he was. Oh, so bad."

"Sit down on the grass, and tell me all about it, sister; do to oblige me, pretty sister."

"Hey, brother, you don't speak as you did—you don't speak like a Gorgio, you speak like one of us, you call me sister."

"As you call me brother; I am not an uncivil person after all, sister."

"I say, brother, tell me one thing, and look me in the face—there—do you speak Rommany?"

"Rommany! Rommany! what is Rommany?"

"What is Rommany? our language, to be sure; tell me, brother, only one thing, you don't speak Rommany?"

"You say it."

"I don't say it, I wish to know. Do you speak Rommany?"

"Do you mean thieves' slang—cant? no, I don't speak cant, I don't like it, I only know a few words; they call a sixpence a tanner, don't they?"

"I don't know," said the girl, sitting down on the ground, "I was almost thinking—well, never mind, you don't know Rommany. I say, brother, I think I should like to have the kekaubi."

"I thought you said it was badly mended?"

"Yes, yes, brother, but——"

"I thought you said it was only fit to be played at football with?"

"Yes, yes, brother, but——"

"What will you give for it?"

"Brother, I am the poor person's child, I will give you sixpence for the kekaubi."

"Poor person's child; how came you by that necklace?"

"Be civil, brother; am I to have the kekaubi?"

"Not for sixpence; isn't the kettle nicely mended?"

"I never saw a nicer mended kettle, brother; am I to have the kekaubi, brother?"

"You like me then?"

"I don't dislike you—I dislike no one; there's only one, and him I don't dislike, him I hate."

"Who is he?"

"I scarcely know, I never saw him, but 'tis no affair of yours, you don't speak Rommany; you will let me have the kekaubi, pretty brother?"

"You may have it, but not for sixpence. I'll give it to you."

"Parraco tute, that is, I thank you, brother; the rikkeni kekaubi is now mine. O, rare! I thank you kindly, brother."

Starting up, she flung the bulrush aside which she had hitherto held in her hand, and seizing the kettle, she looked at it for a moment, and then began a kind of dance, flourishing the kettle over her head the while, and singing—

The Rommany chi
And the Rommany chal,
Shall jaw tasaulor
To drab the bawlor,
And dook the gry
Of the farming rye.

"Good-bye, brother, I must be going."

"Good-bye, sister; why do you sing that wicked song?"

"Wicked song, hey, brother! you don't understand the song!"

"Ha, ha! gypsy daughter," said I, starting up and clapping my hands, "I don't understand Rommany, don't I? You shall see; here's the answer to your gillie—

"The Rommany chi
And the Rommany chal
Love Luripen
And dukkeripen,
And hokkeripen,
And every pen
But Lachipen
And tatchipen."

The girl, who had given a slight start when I began, remained for some time after I had concluded the song, standing motionless as a statue, with the kettle in her hand. At length she came towards me, and stared me full in the face. "Grey, tall, and talks Rommany," said she to herself. In her countenance there was an expression which I had not seen before—an expression which struck me as being composed of fear, curiosity and the deepest hate. It was momentary, however, and was succeeded by one smiling, frank, and open. "Ha, ha, brother," said she, "well, I like you all the better for talking Rommany; it is a sweet language, isn't it? especially as you sing it. How did you pick it up? But you picked it up upon the roads, no doubt? Ha, it was funny in you to pretend not to know it, and you so flush with it all the time; it was not kind in you, however, to frighten the poor person's child so by screaming out, but it was kind in you to give the rikkeni kekaubi to the child of the poor person. She will be grateful to you; she will bring you her little dog to show you, her pretty juggal; the poor person's child will come and see you again; you are not going away to-day, I hope, or to-morrow, pretty brother, grey-hair'd brother—you are not going away to-morrow, I hope?"

"Nor the next day," said I, "only to take a stroll to see if I can sell a kettle; good-bye, little sister, Rommany sister, dingy sister."

"Good-bye, tall brother," said the girl, as she departed, singing:—

The Rommany chi, etc.

"There's something about that girl that I don't understand," said I to myself; "something mysterious. However, it is nothing to me, she knows not who I am, and if she did, what then?"

Late that evening as I sat on the shaft of my cart in deep meditation, with my arms folded, I thought I heard a rustling in the bushes over against me. I turned my eyes in that direction, but saw nothing. "Some bird," said I; "an owl, perhaps"; and once more I fell into meditation; my mind wandered from one thing to another—musing now on the structure of the Roman tongue—now on the rise and fall of the Persian power—and now on the powers vested in recorders at quarter sessions. I was thinking what a fine thing it must be to be a recorder of the peace, when lifting up my eyes, I saw right opposite, not a culprit at the bar, but, staring at me through a gap in the bush, a face wild and strange, half-covered with grey hair; I only saw it a moment, the next it had disappeared.

CHAPTER XXVII

The next day at an early hour I harnessed my little pony, and, putting my things in my cart, I went on my projected stroll. Crossing the moor, I arrived in about an hour at a small village, from which, after a short stay, I proceeded to another, and from thence to a third. I found that the name of Slingsby was well known in these parts.

"If you are a friend of Slingsby you must be an honest lad," said an ancient crone; "you shall never want for work whilst I can give it you. Here, take my kettle, the bottom came out this morning, and lend me that of yours till you bring it back. I'm not afraid to trust you—not I. Don't hurry yourself, young man; if you don't come back for a fortnight I sha'n't have the worse opinion of you."

I returned to my quarters at evening, tired but rejoiced at heart; I had work before me for several days, having collected various kekaubies which required mending, in place of those which I left behind me—those which I had been employed upon during the last few days. I found all quiet in the lane or glade, and, unharnessing my little horse, I once more pitched my tent in the old spot beneath the ash, lighted my fire, ate my frugal meal, and then, after looking for some time at the heavenly bodies, and more particularly at the star Jupiter, I entered my tent, lay down upon my pallet, and went to sleep.

Nothing occurred on the following day which requires any particular notice, nor indeed on the one succeeding that. It was about noon on the third day that I sat beneath the shade of the ash tree; I was not at work, for the weather was particularly hot, and I felt but little inclination to make any exertion. Leaning my back against the tree, I was not long in falling into a slumber. I particularly remember that slumber of mine beneath the ash tree, for it was about the sweetest that I ever enjoyed; how long I continued in it I do not know; I could almost have wished that it had lasted to the present time. All of a sudden it appeared to me that a voice cried in my ear, "Danger! danger! danger!" Nothing seemingly could be more distinct than the words which I heard; then an uneasy sensation came over me, which I strove to get rid of, and at last succeeded, for I awoke. The gypsy girl was standing just opposite to me, with her eyes fixed upon my countenance; a singular kind of little dog stood beside her.

"Ha!" said I, "was it you that cried danger? What danger is there?"

"Danger, brother, there is no danger; what danger should there be. I called to my little dog, but that was in the wood; my little dog's name is not danger, but stranger; what danger should there be, brother?"

"What, indeed, except in sleeping beneath a tree; what is that you have got in your hand?"

"Something for you," said the girl, sitting down and proceeding to untie a white napkin; "a pretty manricli, so sweet, so nice; when I went home to my people I told my grandbebee how kind you had been to the poor person's child, and when my grandbebee saw the kekaubi, she said: 'Hir mi devlis, it won't do for the poor people to be ungrateful; by my God, I will bake a cake for the young harko mescro.'"

"But there are two cakes."

"Yes, brother, two cakes, both for you; my grandbebee meant them both for you—but list, brother, I will have one of them for bringing them. I know you will give me one, pretty brother, grey-haired brother—which shall I have, brother?"

In the napkin were two round cakes, seemingly made of rich and costly compounds, and precisely similar in form, each weighing about half a pound.

"Which shall I have, brother?" said the gypsy girl.

"Whichever you please."

"No, brother, no, the cakes are yours, not mine, it is for you to say."

"Well, then, give me the one nearest you, and take the other."

"Yes, brother, yes," said the girl; and taking the cakes, she flung them into the air two or three times, catching them as they fell, and singing the while. "Pretty brother, grey-haired brother—here, brother," said she, "here is your cake, this other is mine."

"Are you sure," said I, taking the cake, "that this is the one I chose?"

"Quite sure, brother; but if you like you can have mine; there's no difference; however—shall I eat?"

"Yes, sister, eat."

"See, brother, I do; now, brother, eat pretty brother, grey-haired brother."

"I am not hungry."

"Not hungry! well, what then—what has being hungry to do with the matter? It is my grandbebee's cake which was sent because you were kind to the poor person's child; eat, brother, eat, and we shall be like the children in the wood that the Gorgios speak of."

"The children in the wood had nothing to eat."

"Yes, they had hips and haws; we have better. Eat, brother."

"See, sister, I do," and I ate a piece of the cake.

"Well, brother, how do you like it?" said the girl, looking fixedly at me.

"It is very rich and sweet, and yet there is something strange about it; I don't think I shall eat any more."

"Fie, brother, fie, to find fault with the poor person's cake; see, I have nearly eaten mine."

"That's a pretty little dog."

"Is it not, brother? that's my juggal, my little sister, as I call her."

"Come here, Juggal," said I to the animal.

"What do you want with my juggal?" said the girl.

"Only to give her a piece of cake," said I, offering the dog a piece which I had just broken off.

"What do you mean?" said the girl, snatching the dog away; "my grandbebee's cake is not for dogs."

"Why, I just now saw you give the animal a piece of yours."

"You lie, brother, you saw no such thing; but I see how it is, you wish to affront the poor person's child. I shall go to my house."

"Keep still, and don't be angry; see, I have eaten the piece which I offered the dog. I meant no offence. It is a sweet cake after all."

"Isn't it, brother? I am glad you like it. Offence! brother, no offence at all! I am so glad you like my grandbebee's cake, but she will be wanting me at home. Eat one piece more of grandbebee's cake and I will go."

"I am not hungry, I will put the rest by."

"One piece more before I go, handsome brother, grey-haired brother."

"I will not eat any more, I have already eaten more than I wished to oblige you; if you must go, good-day to you."

The girl rose upon her feet, looked hard at me, then at the remainder of the cake which I held in my hand, and then at me again, and then stood for a moment or two, as if in deep thought; presently an air of satisfaction came over her countenance, she smiled and said: "Well, brother, well, do as you please; I merely wished you to eat because you have been so kind to the poor person's child. She loves you so, that she could have wished to have seen you eat it all; good-bye, brother, I dare say when I am gone you will eat some more of it, and if you don't I dare say you have eaten enough to—to—show your love for us. After all, it was a poor person's cake, a Rommany manricli, and all you Gorgios are somewhat gorgious. Farewell, brother, pretty brother, grey-haired brother. Come, juggal."

I remained under the ash tree seated on the grass for a minute or two, and endeavoured to resume the occupation in which I had been engaged before I fell asleep, but I felt no inclination for labour. I then thought I would sleep again, and once more reclined against the tree, and slumbered for some little time, but my sleep was more agitated than before. Something appeared to bear heavy on my breast. I struggled in my sleep, fell on the grass, and awoke; my temples were throbbing, there was a burning in my eyes, and my mouth felt parched; the oppression about the chest which I had felt in my sleep still continued. "I must shake off these feelings," said I, "and get upon my legs." I walked rapidly up and down upon the green sward; at length, feeling my thirst increase, I directed my steps down the narrow path to the spring which ran amidst the bushes; arriving there, I knelt down and drank of the water, but on lifting up my head I felt thirstier than before; again I drank, but with like results; I was about to drink for the third time, when I felt a dreadful qualm which instantly robbed me of nearly all my strength. What can be the matter with me, thought I; but I suppose I have made myself ill by drinking cold water. I got up and made the best of my way back to my tent; before I reached it the qualm had seized me again, and I was deadly sick. I flung myself on my pallet; qualm succeeded qualm, but in the intervals my mouth was dry and burning, and I felt a frantic desire to drink, but no water was at hand, and to reach the spring once more was impossible; the qualms continued, deadly pains shot through my whole frame; I could bear my agonies no longer, and I fell into a trance or swoon. How long I continued therein I know not; on recovering, however, I felt somewhat better, and attempted to lift my head off my couch; the next moment, however, the qualms and pains returned, if possible, with greater violence than before. I am dying, thought I, like a dog, without any help; and then methought I heard a sound at a distance like people singing, and then once more I relapsed into my swoon.

I revived just as a heavy blow sounded upon the canvas of the tent. I started, but my condition did not permit me to rise; again the same kind of blow sounded upon the canvas; I thought for a moment of crying out and requesting assistance, but an inexplicable something chained my tongue, and now I heard a whisper on the outside of the tent. "He does not move, bebee," said a voice which I knew. "I should not wonder if it has done for him already; however, strike again with your ran"; and then there was another blow, after which another voice cried aloud in a strange tone: "Is the gentleman of the house asleep, or is he taking his dinner?" I remained quite silent and motionless, and in another moment the voice continued: "What, no answer? what can the gentleman of the house be about that he makes no answer? Perhaps the gentleman of the house may be darning his stockings?" Thereupon a face peered into the door of the tent, at the farther extremity of which I was stretched. It was that of a woman, but owing to the posture in which she stood, with her back to the light, and partly owing to a large straw bonnet, I could distinguish but very little of the features of her countenance. I had, however, recognised her voice; it was that of my old acquaintance, Mrs. Herne. "Ho, ho, sir!" said she, "here you are. Come here, Leonora," said she to the gypsy girl, who pressed in at the other side of the door; "here is the gentleman, not asleep, but only stretched out after dinner. Sit down on your ham, child, at the door; I shall do the same. There—you have seen me before, sir, have you not?"

"The gentleman makes no answer, bebee; perhaps he does not know you."

"I have known him of old, Leonora," said Mrs. Herne; "and, to tell you the truth, though I spoke to him just now, I expected no answer."

"It's a way he has, bebee, I suppose?"

"Yes, child, it's a way he has."

"Take off your bonnet, bebee; perhaps he cannot see your face."

"I do not think that will be of much use, child; however, I will take off my bonnet—there—and shake out my hair—there—you have seen this hair before, sir, and this face——"

"No answer, bebee."

"Though the one was not quite so grey, nor the other so wrinkled."

"How came they so, bebee?"

"All along of this Gorgio, child."

"The gentleman in the house, you mean, bebee."

"Yes, child, the gentleman in the house. God grant that I may preserve my temper. Do you know, sir, my name? My name is Herne, which signifies a hairy individual, though neither grey-haired nor wrinkled. It is not the nature of the Hernes to be grey or wrinkled, even when they are old, and I am not old."

"How old are you, bebee?"

"Sixty-five years, child—an inconsiderable number. My mother was a hundred and one—a considerable age—when she died, yet she had not one grey hair, and not more than six wrinkles—an inconsiderable number."

"She had no griefs, bebee?"

"Plenty, child, but not like mine."

"Not quite so hard to bear, bebee?"

"No, child; my head wanders when I think of them. After the death of my husband, who came to his end untimeously, I went to live with a daughter of mine, married out among certain Romans who walk about the eastern counties, and with whom for some time I found a home and pleasant society, for they lived right Romanly, which gave my heart considerable satisfaction, who am a Roman born, and hope to die so. When I say right Romanly, I mean that they kept to themselves, and were not much given to blabbing about their private matters in promiscuous company. Well, things went on in this way for some time, when one day my son-in-law brings home a young Gorgio of singular and outrageous ugliness, and without much preamble, says to me and mine, 'This is my pal, a'n't he a beauty? fall down and worship him.' 'Hold,' said I, 'I for one will never consent to such foolishness.' "

"That was right, bebee, I think I should have done the same."

"I think you would, child; but what was the profit of it? The whole party makes an almighty of this Gorgio, lets him into their ways, says prayers of his making, till things come to such a pass that my own daughter says to me: 'I shall buy myself a veil and fan, and treat myself to a play and sacrament.' 'Don't,' says I; says she, 'I should like for once in my life to be courtesied to as a Christian gentlewoman.' "

"Very foolish of her, bebee."

"Wasn't it, child? Where was I? At the fan and sacrament; with a heavy heart I put seven score miles between us, came back to the hairy ones, and found them over-given to gorgious companions; said I, 'foolish manners is catching, all this comes of that there Gorgio.' Answers the child Leonora, 'Take comfort, bebee, I hate the Gorgios as much as you do.' "

"And I say so again, bebee, as much or more."

"Time flows on, I engage in many matters, in most miscarry. Am sent to prison; says I to myself, I am become foolish. Am turned out of prison, and go back to the hairy ones, who receive me not over courteously; says I, for their unkindness, and my own foolishness, all the thanks to that Gorgio. Answers to me the child, 'I wish I could set eyes upon him, bebee.' "

"I did so, bebee; go on."

" 'How shall I know him, bebee?' says the child. 'Young and grey, tall, and speaks Romanly.' Runs to me the child, and says, 'I've found him, bebee.' 'Where, child?' says I. 'Come with me, bebee,' says the child. 'That's he,' says I, as I looked at my gentleman through the hedge."

"Ha, ha! bebee, and here he lies, poisoned like a hog."

"You have taken drows, sir," said Mrs. Herne; "do you hear, sir? drows; tip him a stave, child, of the song of poison."

And thereupon the girl clapped her hands, and sang—

> The Rommany churl
> And the Rommany girl,
> To-morrow shall hie
> To poison the sty,
> And bewitch on the mead
> The farmer's steed.

"Do you hear that, sir?" said Mrs. Herne; "the child has tipped you a stave of the song of poison: that is, she has sung it Christianly, though perhaps you would like to hear it Romanly; you were always fond of what was Roman. Tip it him Romanly, child."

"He has heard it Romanly already, bebee; 'twas by that I found him out, as I told you."

"Halloo, sir, are you sleeping? you have taken drows; the gentleman makes no answer. God give me patience!"

"And what if he doesn't, bebee; isn't he poisoned like a hog? Gentleman! indeed, why call him gentleman? If he ever was one he's broke, and is now a tinker, a worker of blue metal."

"That's his way, child, to-day a tinker, to-morrow something else; and as for being drabbed, I don't know what to say about it."

"Not drabbed! what do you mean, bebee? but look there, bebee; ha, ha, look at the gentleman's motions."

"He is sick, child, sure enough. Ho, ho! sir, you have taken drows; what, another throe! writhe, sir, writhe, the hog died by the drow of gypsies; I saw him stretched at evening. That's yourself, sir. There is no hope, sir, no help, you have taken drow; shall I tell you your fortune, sir, your dukkerin? God bless you, pretty gentleman, much trouble will you have to suffer, and much water to cross; but never mind, pretty gentleman, you shall be fortunate at the end, and those who hate shall take off their hats to you."

"Hey, bebee!" cried the girl; "what is this? what do you mean? you have blessed the Gorgio!"

"Blessed him! no, sure; what did I say? Oh, I remember, I'm mad; well, I can't help it, I said what the dukkerin dook told me; woe's me; he'll get up yet."

"Nonsense, bebee! Look at his motions, he's drabbed, spite of dukkerin."

"Don't say so, child; he's sick, 'tis true, but don't laugh at dukkerin, only folks do that that know no better. I, for one, will never laugh at the dukkerin dook. Sick again; I wish he was gone."

"He'll soon be gone, bebee; let's leave him. He's as good as gone; look there, he's dead."

"No, he's not, he'll get up—I feel it; can't we hasten him?"

"Hasten him! yes, to be sure; set the dog upon him. Here, juggal, look in there, my dog."

The dog made its appearance at the door of the tent, and began to bark and tear up the ground.

"At him, juggal, at him; he wished to poison, to drab you. Halloo!"

The dog barked violently, and seemed about to spring at my face, but retreated.

"The dog won't fly at him, child; he flashed at the dog with his eye, and scared him. He'll get up."

"Nonsense, bebee! you make me angry; how should he get up?"

"The dook tells me so, and, what's more, I had a dream. I thought I was at York, standing amidst a crowd to see a man hung, and the crowd shouted, 'There he comes!' and I looked, and lo! it was the tinker; before I could cry with joy I was whisked away, and I found myself in Ely's big church, which was chock full of people to hear the dean preach, and all eyes were turned to the big pulpit; and presently I heard them say, 'There he mounts!' and I looked up to the big pulpit, and, lo! the tinker was in the pulpit, and he raised his arm and began to preach. Anon, I found myself at York again, just as the drop fell, and I looked up, and I saw, not the tinker, but my own self hanging in the air."

"You are going mad, bebee; if you want to hasten him, take your stick and poke him in the eye."

"That will be of no use, child, the dukkerin tells me so; but I will try what I can do. Halloo, tinker! you must introduce yourself into a quiet family, and raise confusion—must you? You must steal its language, and what was never done before, write it down Christianly—must you? Take that—and that"; and she stabbed violently with her stick towards the end of the tent.

"That's right, bebee, you struck his face; now, once more, and let it be in the eye. Stay, what's that? get up, bebee."

"What's the matter, child?"

"Some one is coming, come away."

"Let me make sure of him, child; he'll be up yet." And thereupon, Mrs. Herne, rising, leaned forward into the tent, and supporting herself against the pole, took aim in the direction of the farther end. "I will thrust out his eye," said she; and, lunging with her stick, she would probably have accomplished her purpose had not at that moment the pole of the tent given way, whereupon she fell to the ground, the canvas falling upon her and her intended victim.

"Here's a pretty affair, bebee," screamed the girl.

"He'll get up yet," said Mrs. Herne, from beneath the canvas.

"Get up!—get up yourself; where are you? where is your—— Here, there, bebee, here's the door; there, make haste, they are coming."

"He'll get up yet," said Mrs. Herne, recovering her breath; "the dook tells me so."

"Never mind him or the dook; he is drabbed; come away, or we shall be grabbed—both of us."

"One more blow, I know where his head lies."

"You are mad, bebee; leave the fellow—Gorgio avella."

And thereupon the females hurried away.

A vehicle of some kind was evidently drawing nigh; in a little time it came alongside of the place where lay the fallen tent, and stopped suddenly. There was a silence for a moment, and then a parley ensued between two voices, one of which was that of a woman. It was not in English, but in a deep guttural tongue.

"*Peth yw hono sydd yn gorwedd yna ar y ddaear?*" said a masculine voice.

"*Yn wirionedd*—I do not know what it can be," said the female voice, in the same tongue.

"Here is a cart, and there are tools; but what is that on the ground?"

"Something moves beneath it; and what was that—a groan?"

"Shall I get down?"

"Of course, Peter, some one may want your help."

"Then I will get down, though I do not like this place, it is frequented by Egyptians, and I do not like their yellow faces, nor their clibberty clabber, as Master Ellis Wyn says. Now, I am down. It is a tent, Winifred, and see, here is a boy beneath it. Merciful father! what a face!"

A middle-aged man, with a strongly marked and serious countenance, dressed in sober-coloured habiliments, had lifted up the stifling folds of the tent and was bending over me. "Can you speak, my lad?" said he in English, "what is the matter with you? If you could but tell me, I could perhaps help you—— What is it that you say? I can't hear you. I will kneel down"; and he flung himself on the ground, and placed his ear close to my mouth. "Now speak if you can. Hey! what! no, sure, God forbid!" then starting up, he cried to a female who sat in the cart, anxiously looking on—"*Gwenwyn! Gwenwyn! yw y gwas wedi ei gwenwynaw*. The oil! Winifred, the oil!"

CHAPTER XXVIII

The oil, which the strangers compelled me to take, produced the desired effect, though, during at least two hours, it was very doubtful whether or not my life would be saved. At the end of that period the man said, that with the blessing of God, he would answer for my life. He then demanded whether I thought I could bear to be removed from the place in which we were? "For I like it not," he continued, "as something within me tells me that it is not good for any of us to be here." I told him, as well as I was able, that I, too, should be glad to leave the place; whereupon, after collecting my things, he harnessed my pony, and, with the assistance of the woman, he contrived to place me in the cart; he then gave me a draught out of a small phial, and we set forward at a slow pace, the man walking by the side of the cart in which I lay. It is probable that the draught consisted of a strong opiate, for after swallowing it I fell into a deep slumber; on my awaking, I found that the shadows of night had enveloped the earth—we were still moving on. Shortly, however, after descending a declivity, we turned into a lane, at the entrance of which was a gate. This lane conducted to a meadow, through the middle of which ran a small brook; it stood between two rising grounds, that on the left, which was on the farther side of the water, was covered with wood, whilst the one on the right, which was not so high, was crowned with the white walls of what appeared to be a farm-house.

Advancing along the meadow, we presently came to a place where grew three immense oaks, almost on the side of the brook, over which they flung their arms, so as to shade it as with a canopy; the ground beneath was bare of grass, and nearly as hard and smooth as the floor of a barn. Having led his own cart on one side of the midmost tree, and my own on the other, the stranger said to me: "This is the spot where my wife and myself generally tarry in the summer season, when we come into these parts. We are about to pass the night here. I suppose you will have no objection to do the same? Indeed, I do not see what else you could do under present circumstances." After receiving my answer, in which I, of course, expressed my readiness to assent to his proposal, he proceeded to unharness his horse, and, feeling myself much better, I got down, and began to make the necessary preparations for passing the night beneath the oak.

Whilst thus engaged, I felt myself touched on the shoulder, and, looking round, perceived the woman, whom the stranger called Winifred, standing close to me. The moon was shining brightly upon her, and I observed that she was very good-looking, with a composed, yet cheerful expression of countenance; her dress was plain and primitive, very much resembling that of a Quaker. She held a straw bonnet in her hand. "I am glad to see thee moving about, young man," said she, in a soft, placid tone; "I could scarcely have expected it. Thou must be wondrous strong; many, after what thou hast suffered, would not have stood on their feet for weeks and months. What do I say?—Peter, my husband, who is skilled in medicine, just now told me that not one in five hundred would have survived what thou hast this day undergone; but allow me to ask thee one thing, Hast thou returned thanks to God for thy deliverance?" I made no answer, and the woman, after a pause, said: "Excuse me, young man, but do you know anything of God?"

"Very little," I replied, "but I should say He must be a wondrous strong person, if He made all those big bright things up above there, to say nothing of the ground on which we stand, which bears beings like these oaks, each of which is fifty times as strong as myself, and will live twenty times as long."

The woman was silent for some moments, and then said: "I scarcely know in what spirit thy words are uttered. If thou art serious, however, I would caution thee against supposing that the power of God is more manifested in these trees, or even in those bright stars above us, than in thyself—they are things of time, but thou art a being destined to an eternity; it depends upon thyself whether thy eternity shall be one of joy or sorrow."

"Poor fellow, he seems to be almost brutally ignorant," said Peter, addressing his wife in their native language, after they had bidden me farewell for the night.

"I am afraid he is," said Winifred; "yet my heart warms to the poor lad, he seems so forlorn."

I slept soundly during that night, partly owing to the influence of the opiate. Early in the morning I was awakened by the voices of Peter and his wife, who were singing a morning hymn in their own language. Both subsequently prayed long and fervently. I lay still till their devotions were completed, and then left my tent. "Good-morning," said Peter, "how dost thou feel?" "Much better," said I, "than I could have expected." "I am glad of it," said Peter. "Art thou hungry? yonder comes our breakfast," pointing to the same young woman I had seen the preceding night, who was again descending the hill, bearing the tray upon her head.

"What dost thou intend to do, young man, this day?" said Peter, when we had about half finished breakfast. "Do," said I, "as I do other days, what I can." "And dost thou pass this day as thou dost other days?" said Peter. "Why not?" said I; "what is there in this day different from the rest? It seems to be of the same colour as yesterday." "Art thou aware," said the wife interposing, "what day it is? that it is Sabbath? that it is Sunday?" "No," said I, "I did not know that it was Sunday." "And how did that happen?" said Winifred with a sigh. "To tell you the truth," said I, "I live very much alone, and pay very little heed to the passing of time." "And yet of what infinite importance is time," said Winifred. "Art thou not aware that every year brings thee nearer to thy end?" "I do not think," said I, "that I am so near my end as I was yesterday." "Yes thou art," said the woman; "thou wast not doomed to die yesterday; an invisible hand was watching over thee yesterday; but thy day will come, therefore improve the time; be grateful that thou wast saved yesterday; and, oh! reflect on one thing; if thou hadst died yesterday, where wouldst thou have been now?" "Cast into the earth, perhaps," said I. "I have heard Mr. Petulengro say that to be cast into the earth is the natural end of man."

"Who is Mr. Petulengro?" said Peter, interrupting his wife, as she was about to speak. "Master of the horse-shoe," said I, "and, according to his own account, king of Egypt." "I understand," said Peter, "head of some family of wandering Egyptians—they are a race utterly godless. Art thou of them?—but no, thou art not, thou hast not their yellow blood. I suppose thou belongest to the family of wandering artisans called—— I do not like you the worse for belonging to them. A mighty speaker of old sprang up from amidst that family."

"Who was he?" said I. "John Bunyan," replied Peter, reverently, "and the mention of his name reminds me that I have to preach this day; wilt thou go and hear? the distance is not great, only half a mile." "No," said I, "I will not go and hear." "Wherefore?" said Peter. "I belong to the church," said I, "and not to the congregations." "Oh! the pride of that church," said Peter, addressing his wife in their own tongue, "exemplified even in the lowest and most ignorant of its members." "Then thou, doubtless, meanest to go to church," said Peter, again addressing me; "there is a church on the other side of that wooded hill." "No," said I, "I do not mean to go to church." "May I ask thee wherefore?" said Peter. "Because," said I, "I prefer remaining beneath the shade of these trees, listening to the sound of the leaves, and the tinkling of the waters."

"Then thou intendest to remain here?" said Peter, looking fixedly at me. "If I do not intrude," said I; "but if I do, I will wander away; I wish to be beholden to nobody—perhaps you wish me to go?" "On the contrary," said Peter, "I wish you to stay. I begin to see something in thee which has much interest for me; but we must now bid thee farewell for the rest of the day, the time is drawing nigh for us to repair to the place of preaching; before we leave thee alone, however, I should wish to ask thee a question: Didst thou seek thy own destruction yesterday, and didst thou wilfully take that poison?" "No," said I; "had I known there had been poison in the cake, I certainly should not have taken it." "And who gave it thee?" said Peter. "An enemy of mine," I replied. "Who is thy enemy?" "An Egyptian sorceress and poisonmonger." "Thy enemy is a female. I fear thou hadst given her cause to hate thee—of what did she complain?" "That I had stolen the tongue out of her head." "I do not understand thee—is she young?" "About sixty-five."

Here Winifred interposed. "Thou didst call her just now by hard names, young man," said she; "I trust thou dost bear no malice against her." "No," said I, "I bear no malice against her." "Thou art not wishing to deliver her into the hand of what is called justice?" "By no means," said I, "I have lived long enough upon the roads not to cry out for the constable when my finger is broken. I consider this poisoning as an accident of the roads; one of those to which those who travel are occasionally subject." "In short, thou forgivest thine adversary?" "Both now and for ever," said I. "Truly," said Winifred, "the spirit which the young man displayeth pleases me much: I should be loth that he left us yet. I have no doubt, with the blessing of God, and a little of thy exhortation, he will turn out a true Christian before he leaveth us." "My exhortation!" said Peter, and a dark shade passed over his countenance; "thou forgettest what I am—I—I—but I am forgetting myself; the Lord's will be done; and now put away the things, for I perceive that our friends are coming to attend us to the place of meeting."

Again the family which I had seen the night before descended the hill from their abode. They were now dressed in their Sunday's best. The master of the house led the way. They presently joined us, when a quiet, sober greeting ensued on each side. After a little time Peter shook me by the hand and bade me farewell till the evening; Winifred did the same, adding, that she hoped I should be visited by sweet and holy thoughts. The whole party then moved off in the direction by which we had come the preceding night, Peter and the master leading the way, followed by Winifred and the mistress of the family. As I gazed on their departing forms, I felt almost inclined to follow them to their place of worship. I did not stir, however, but remained leaning against my oak with my hands behind me.

And after a time I sat me down at the foot of the oak with my face turned towards the water, and, folding my hands, I fell into deep meditation. I thought on the early Sabbaths of my life, and the manner in which I was wont to pass them. How carefully I said my prayers when I got up on the

Sabbath morn, and how carefully I combed my hair and brushed my clothes in order that I might do credit to the Sabbath day. I thought of the old church at pretty D——, the dignified rector, and yet more dignified clerk. I thought of England's grand Liturgy, and Tate and Brady's sonorous minstrelsy. I thought of the Holy Book, portions of which I was in the habit of reading between service. I thought, too, of the evening walk which I sometimes took in fine weather like the present, with my mother and brother —a quiet, sober walk, during which I would not break into a run, even to chase a butterfly, or yet more a honey-bee, being fully convinced of the dread importance of the day which God had hallowed. And how glad I was when I had got over the Sabbath day without having done anything to profane it. And how soundly I slept on the Sabbath night after the toil of being very good throughout the day.

And when I had mused on those times a long while, I sighed and said to myself, I am much altered since then; am I altered for the better? And then I looked at my hands and my apparel, and sighed again. I was not wont of yore to appear thus on the Sabbath day.

For a long time I continued in a state of deep meditation, till at last I lifted up my eyes to the sun, which, as usual during that glorious summer, was shining in unclouded majesty; and then I lowered them to the sparkling water, in which hundreds of the finny brood were disporting themselves, and then I thought what a fine thing it was to be a fish on such a fine summer day, and I wished myself a fish, or at least amongst the fishes; and then I looked at my hands again, and then, bending over the water, I looked at my face in the crystal mirror, and started when I saw it, for it looked squalid and miserable.

Forthwith I started up, and said to myself, I should like to bathe and cleanse myself from the squalor produced by my late hard life and by Mrs. Herne's drow. I wonder if there is any harm in bathing on the Sabbath day. I will ask Winifred when she comes home; in the meantime I will bathe, provided I can find a fitting place.

But the brook, though a very delightful place for fish to disport in, was shallow, and by no means adapted for the recreation of so large a being as myself; it was, moreover, exposed, though I saw nobody at hand, nor heard a single human voice or sound. Following the winding of the brook I left the meadow, and, passing through two or three thickets, came to a place where between lofty banks the water ran deep and dark, and there I bathed, imbibing new tone and vigour into my languid and exhausted frame.

Having put on my clothes, I returned by the way I had come to my vehicle beneath the oak tree. From thence, for want of something better to do, I strolled up the hill, on the top of which stood the farm-house; it was a large and commodious building built principally of stone, and seeming of some antiquity, with a porch, on either side of which was an oaken bench. On the right was seated a young woman with a book in her hand, the same who had brought the tray to my friends and myself.

"Good-day," said I, "pretty damsel, sitting in the farm porch.

"Good-day," said the girl, looking at me for a moment, and then fixing her eyes on her book.

"That's a nice book you are reading," said I.

The girl looked at me with surprise. "How do you know what book it is?" said she.

"How do I know—never mind; but a nice book it is—no love, no fortune-telling in it."

The girl looked at me half offended. "Fortune-telling!" said she, "I should think not. But you know nothing about it"; and she bent her head once more over the book.

"I tell you what, young person," said I, "I know all about that book; what will you wager that I do not?"

"I never wager," said the girl.

"Shall I tell you the name of it," said I, "O daughter of the dairy?"

The girl half started. "I should never have thought," said she, half timidly, "that you could have guessed it."

"I did not guess it," said I, "I knew it; and meet and proper it is that you should read it."

"Why so?" said the girl.

"Can the daughter of the dairy read a more fitting book than the *Dairyman's Daughter?*"

"Where do you come from?" said the girl.

"Out of the water," said I. "Don't start, I have been bathing; are you fond of the water?"

"No," said the girl, heaving a sigh; "I am not fond of the water, that is, of the sea"; and here she sighed again.

"The sea is a wide gulf," said I, "and frequently separates hearts."

The girl sobbed.

"Why are you alone here?" said I.

"I take my turn with the rest," said the girl, "to keep at home on Sunday."

"And you are——" said I.

"The master's niece!" said the girl. "How came you to know it? But why did you not go with the rest and with your friends?"

"Who are those you call my friends?" said I.

"Peter and his wife."

"And who are they?" said I.

"Do you not know?" said the girl; "you came with them."

"They found me ill by the way," said I; "and they relieved me: I know nothing about them."

"I thought you knew everything," said the girl.

"There are two or three things which I do not know, and this is one of them. Who are they?"

"Did you never hear of the great Welsh preacher, Peter Williams?"

"Never," said I.

"Well," said the girl, "this is he, and Winifred is his wife, and a nice person she is. Some people say, indeed, that she is as good a preacher as her husband, though of that matter I can say nothing, having never heard her preach. So these two wander over all Wales and the greater part of England, comforting the hearts of the people with their doctrine, and doing all the good they can. They frequently come here, for the mistress is a Welsh woman, and an old friend of both, and then they take up their abode in the cart beneath the old oaks down there by the stream."

"And what is their reason for doing so?" said I; "would it not be more comfortable to sleep beneath a roof?"

"I know not their reasons," said the girl, "but so it is; they never sleep beneath a roof unless the weather is very severe. I once heard the mistress say that Peter had something heavy upon his mind; perhaps that is the cause. If he is unhappy, all I can say is, that I wish him otherwise, for he is a good man and a kind——"

"Thank you," said I, "I will now depart."

"Hem!" said the girl, "I was wishing——"

"What? to ask me a question?"

"Not exactly; but you seem to know everything; you mentioned, I think, fortune-telling."

"Do you wish me to tell your fortune?"

"By no means; but I have a friend at a distance at sea, and I should wish to know——"

"When he will come back? I have told you already there are two or three things which I do not know—this is another of them. However, I should not be surprised if he were to come back some of these days; I would, if I were in his place. In the meantime be patient, attend to the dairy, and read the *Dairyman's Daughter* when you have nothing better to do."

It was late in the evening when the party of the morning returned. The farmer and his family repaired at once to their abode, and my two friends joined me beneath the tree. Peter sat down at the foot of the oak, and said nothing. Supper was brought by a servant, not the damsel of the porch. We sat round the tray, Peter said grace, but scarcely anything else; he appeared sad and dejected, his wife looked anxiously upon him. I was as silent as my friends; after a little time we retired to our separate places of rest.

About midnight I was awakened by a noise; I started up and listened; it appeared to me that I heard voices and groans. In a moment I had issued from my tent—all was silent—but the next moment I again heard groans and voices; they proceeded from the tilted cart where Peter and his wife lay; I drew near, again there was a pause, and then I heard the voice of Peter, in an accent of extreme anguish, exclaim: "*Pechod Ysprydd Glan—O pechod Ysprydd Glan!*" and then he uttered a deep groan. Anon, I heard the voice of Winifred, and never shall I forget the sweetness and gentleness of the tones of her voice in the stillness of that night. I did not understand all she said—she spoke in her native language, and I was some way apart;

she appeared to endeavour to console her husband, but he seemed to refuse all comfort, and, with many groans, repeated—"*Pechod Ysprydd Glan—O pechod Ysprydd Glan!*" I felt I had no right to pry into their afflictions, and retired.

Now, "*pechod Ysprydd Glan,*" interpreted, is the sin against the Holy Ghost.

CHAPTER XXIX

PETER and his wife did not proceed on any expedition during the following day. The former strolled gloomily about the fields, and the latter passed many hours in the farm-house. Towards evening, without saying a word to either, I departed with my vehicle, and finding my way to a small town at some distance, I laid in a store of various articles, with which I returned. It was night, and my two friends were seated beneath the oak; they had just completed their frugal supper. "We waited for thee some time," said Winifred, "but finding that thou didst not come, we began without thee; but sit down, I pray thee, there is still enough for thee." "I will sit down," said I, "but I require no supper, for I have eaten where I have been." Nothing more particular occurred at the time. Next morning the kind pair invited me to share their breakfast. "I will not share your breakfast," said I. "Wherefore not?" said Winifred anxiously. "Because," said I, "it is not proper that I be beholden to you for meat and drink." "But we are beholden to other people," said Winifred. "Yes," said I, "but you preach to them, and give them ghostly advice, which considerably alters the matter; not that I would receive anything from them, if I preached to them six times a day." "Thou art not fond of receiving favours, then, young man," said Winifred. "I am not," said I. "And of conferring favours?" "Nothing affords me greater pleasure," said I, "than to confer favours." "What a disposition!" said Winifred, holding up her hands; "and this is pride, genuine pride—that feeling which the world agrees to call so noble. Oh, how mean a thing is pride! never before did I see all the meanness of what is called pride!"

"But how wilt thou live, friend?" said Peter; "dost thou not intend to eat?" "When I went out last night," said I, "I laid in a provision." "Thou hast laid in a provision!" said Peter, "pray let us see it. Really, friend," said he, after I had produced it, "thou must drive a thriving trade; here are provisions enough to last three people for several days. Here are butter and eggs, here is tea, here is sugar, and there is a flitch. I hope thou wilt let us partake of some of thy fare." "I should be very happy if you would," said I. "Doubt not but we shall," said Peter; "Winifred shall have some of thy flitch cooked for dinner. In the meantime, sit down, young man, and breakfast at our expense—we will dine at thine."

On the evening of that day, Peter and myself sat alone beneath the oak. We fell into conversation; Peter was at first melancholy, but he soon became more cheerful, fluent and entertaining. I spoke but little, but I observed that sometimes what I said surprised the good Methodist. We had been silent some time. At length, lifting up my eyes to the broad and leafy canopy of the trees, I said, having nothing better to remark, "What a noble tree! I wonder if the fairies ever dance beneath it?"

"Fairies!" said Peter, "fairies! how came you, young man, to know anything about the fair family?"

"I am an Englishman," said I, "and of course know something about fairies; England was once a famous place for them."

"Was once, I grant you," said Peter, "but is so no longer. I have travelled for years about England, and never heard them mentioned before; the belief in them has died away, and even their name seems to be forgotten. If you had said you were a Welshman, I should not have been surprised. The Welsh have much to say of the *Tylwyth Teg*, or fair family, and many believe in them."

"And do you believe in them?" said I.

"I scarcely know what to say. Wise and good men have been of opinion that they are nothing but devils, who, under the form of pretty and amiable spirits, would fain allure poor human beings; I see nothing irrational in the supposition."

"Do you believe in devils, then?"

"Do I believe in devils, young man!" said Peter, and his frame was shaken as if by convulsions. "If I do not believe in devils, why am I here at the present moment?"

"You know best," said I: "but I don't believe that fairies are devils, and I don't wish to hear them insulted. What learned men have said they are devils?"

"Many have said it, young man, and, amongst others, Master Ellis Wyn, in that wonderful book of his, the *Bardd Cwsg*."

"The *Bardd Cwsg*," said I; "what kind of book is that? I have never heard of that book before."

"Heard of it before; I suppose not; how should you have heard of it before! By-the-bye, can you read?"

"Very tolerably," said I; "so there are fairies in this book. What do you call it—the *Bardd Cwsg?*"

"Yes, the *Bardd Cwsg*. You pronounce Welsh very fairly; have you ever been in Wales?"

"Never," said I.

"Not been in Wales; then, of course, you don't understand Welsh; but we were talking of the *Bardd Cwsg*—yes, there are fairies in the *Bardd Cwsg* —the author of it, Master Ellis Wyn, was carried away in his sleep by them over mountains and valleys, rivers and great waters, incurring mighty perils at their hands, till he was rescued from them by an angel of the Most High, who subsequently showed him many wonderful things."

"I would sooner hear your own tale," said I, "than all the visions of the *Bardd Cwsg*."

Peter shook, bent his form nearly double, and covered his face with his hands. I sat still and motionless, with my eyes fixed upon him. Presently Winifred descended the hill, and joined us. "What is the matter?" said she, looking at her husband, who still remained in the posture I have described. He made no answer; whereupon, laying her hand gently on his shoulder, she said, in the peculiar soft and tender tone which I had heard her use on a former occasion, "Take comfort, Peter; what has happened now to afflict thee?" Peter removed his hands from his face. "The old pain, the old pain," said he; "I was talking with this young man, and he would fain know what brought me here, he would fain hear my tale, Winifred—my sin: *O pechod Ysprydd Glan! O pechod Ysprydd Glan!*"

Two evenings later, when we were again seated beneath the oak, Peter took the hand of his wife in his own, and then, in tones broken and almost inarticulate, commenced telling me his tale—the tale of the *Pechod Ysprydd Glan*.

"I was born in the heart of North Wales, the son of a respectable farmer, and am the youngest of seven brothers.

"My father was a member of the Church of England, and was what is generally called a serious man. He went to church regularly, and read the Bible every Sunday evening; in his moments of leisure he was fond of holding religious discourse both with his family and his neighbours.

"One autumn afternoon, on a week day, my father sat with one of his neighbours taking a cup of ale by the oak table in our stone kitchen. I sat near them, and listened to their discourse. I was at that time seven years of age. They were talking of religious matters. 'It is a hard matter to get to heaven,' said my father. 'Exceedingly so,' said the other. 'However. I don't despond, none need despair of getting to heaven, save those who have committed the sin against the Holy Ghost.'

"'Ah!' said my father, 'thank God I never committed that—how awful must be the state of a person who has committed the sin against the Holy Ghost! I can scarcely think of it without my hair standing on end'; and then my father and his friend began talking of the nature of the sin against the Holy Ghost, and I heard them say what it was, as I sat with greedy ears listening to their discourse.

"I lay awake the greater part of the night musing upon what I had heard. When I awoke in the morning the first thing I thought of was the mysterious sin, and a voice within me seemed to say, 'Commit it'; and I felt a strong temptation to do so, even stronger than in the night.

"After breakfast I went to school, and endeavoured to employ myself upon my tasks, but all in vain; I could think of nothing but the sin against the Holy Ghost; my eyes, instead of being fixed upon my book, wandered in vacancy. My master observed my inattention, and chid me. The time came for saying my task, and I had not acquired it. My master reproached me, and, yet more, he beat me; I felt shame and anger, and I went home with a full determination to commit the sin against the Holy Ghost.

"Awaking in the night, I determined that nothing should prevent my committing the sin. Arising from my bed, I went out upon the wooden gallery, and having stood for a few moments looking at the stars, with which the heavens were thickly strewn, I laid myself down, and supporting my face with my hand, I murmured out words of horror—words not to be repeated—and in this manner I committed the sin against the Holy Ghost.

"I awoke several times during the night, each time with the dim idea that something strange and monstrous had occurred, but presently I fell asleep again; in the morning I awoke with the same vague feeling, but presently recollection returned, and I remembered that I had committed the sin against the Holy Ghost.

"I went to school, but sat stupefied. I was again chidden, again beaten by my master. I felt no anger this time, and scarcely heeded the strokes. I looked, however, at my master's face, and thought to myself, you are beating me for being idle, as you suppose; poor man, what would you do if you knew I had committed the sin against the Holy Ghost?

"Days and weeks passed by. I had once been cheerful, and fond of the society of children of my own age; but I was now reserved and gloomy. It seemed to me that a gulf separated me from all my fellow-creatures. I used to look at my brothers and schoolfellows, and think how different I was from them; they had not done what I had. I seemed, in my own eyes, a lone, monstrous being, and yet, strange to say, I felt a kind of pride in being so. I was unhappy, but I frequently thought to myself, I have done what no one else would dare to do; there was something grand in the idea; I had yet to learn the horror of my condition.

"Shortly after this my father fell sick; the progress of the disorder was rapid; feeling his end approaching, he called his children before him. After tenderly embracing us, he said: 'God bless you, my children; I am going from you, but take comfort, I trust that we shall all meet again in heaven.'

"As he uttered these last words, horror took entire possession of me. Meet my father in heaven—how could I ever hope to meet him there? I looked wildly at my brethren and at my mother; they were all bathed in tears, but how I envied them! They might hope to meet my father in heaven, but how different were they from me—they had never committed the unpardonable sin.

"In a few days my father died; he left his family in comfortable circumstances, at least such as would be considered so in Wales, where the wants of the people are few. My elder brother carried on the farm for the benefit of my mother and us all. In course of time my brothers were put out to various trades. I still remained at school, but without being a source of expense to my relations, as I was by this time able to assist my master in the business of the school.

"At church I was constant, and when there listened with deepest attention to every word which proceeded from the mouth of the minister. In a little time it appeared to me that I had become a good, a very good young man. At times the recollection of the sin would return, and I would feel a momentary chill; but the thought quickly vanished, and I again felt happy and secure.

"One Sunday morning, after I had said my prayers, I felt particularly joyous. I thought of the innocent and virtuous life I was leading; and when the recollection of the sin intruded for a moment, I said, 'I am sure God will never utterly cast away so good a creature as myself.' I went to church, and was as usual attentive. The subject of the sermon was on the duty of searching the Scriptures: all I knew of them was from the Liturgy. I now, however, determined to read them, and perfect the good work which I had begun. My father's Bible was upon the shelf, and on that evening I took it with me to my chamber. I placed it on the table, and sat down. My heart was filled with pleasing anticipation. I opened the book at random, and began to read; the first passage on which my eyes lighted was the following:

" 'He who committeth the sin against the Holy Ghost shall not be forgiven, either in this world or the next.' "

Here Peter was seized with convulsive tremors. Winifred sobbed violently. I got up, and went away. Returning in about a quarter of an hour, I found him more calm; he motioned me to sit down; and, after a short pause, continued his narration.

"Where was I, young man? Oh, I remember, at the fatal passage which removed all hope. I will not dwell on what I felt. I closed my eyes, and wished that I might be dreaming; but it was no dream, but a terrific reality. I will not dwell on that period, I should only shock you. I could not bear my feelings; so, bidding my friends a hasty farewell, I abandoned myself to horror and despair, and ran wild through Wales, climbing mountains and wading streams.

"On one occasion I found myself near the sea; instantly the idea came into my head that I would cast myself into it, and thus anticipate my final doom. I hesitated a moment, but a voice within me seemed to tell me that I could do no better; the sea was near, and I could not swim, so I determined to fling myself into the sea. As I was running along at great speed, in the direction of a lofty rock, which beetled over the waters, I suddenly felt myself seized by the coat. I strove to tear myself away, but in vain; looking round, I perceived a venerable, hale old man, who had hold of me. 'Let me go!' said I fiercely. 'I will not let thee go,' said the old man; and now, instead of with one, he grappled me with both hands. 'In whose name dost thou detain me?' said I, scarcely knowing what I said. 'In the name of my Master, who made thee and yonder sea, and has said to the sea, so far shalt thou come, and no farther, and to thee, thou shalt do no murder.' 'Has not a man a right to do what he pleases with his own?' said I. 'He has,' said the old man, 'but thy life is not thy own; thou art accountable for it to thy God. Nay, I will not let thee go,' he continued, as I again struggled; 'if thou struggle with me the whole day I will not let thee go, as Charles Wesley says in his *Wrestlings of Jacob;* and see, it is of no use struggling, for I am, in the strength of my Master, stronger than thou'; and indeed, all of a sudden I had become very weak and exhausted; whereupon the old man, beholding my situation, took me by the arm and led me gently to a neighbouring town, which stood behind a hill, and which I had not before observed; presently he opened the door of a respectable-looking house, which stood beside a large building having the appearance of a chapel, and conducted me into a small room, with a great many books in it. Having caused me to sit down, he stood looking at me for some time, occasionally heaving a sigh. I was, indeed, haggard and forlorn.

" 'Who art thou?' he said at last. 'A miserable man,' I replied. 'What makes thee miserable?' said the old man. 'A hideous crime,' I replied. 'I can find no rest; like Cain, I wander here and there.' The old man turned pale. 'Hast thou taken another's life?' said he; 'if so, I advise thee to surrender thyself to the magistrate; thou canst do no better; thy doing so will be the best proof of thy repentance; and though there be no hope for thee in this world there may be much in the next.' 'No,' said I, 'I have never taken another's life.' 'What then, another's goods? If so, restore them seven-fold if possible: or, if it be not in thy power, and thy conscience accuse thee, surrender thyself to the magistrate, and make the only satisfaction thou art able.' 'I have taken no one's goods,' said I. 'Of what art thou guilty, then?' said he. 'Art thou a drunkard? a profligate?' 'Alas, no,' said I; 'I am neither of these; would that I were no worse!'

"Thereupon the old man looked steadfastly at me for some time; then, after appearing to reflect, he said: 'Young man, I have a great desire to know your name.' 'What matters it to you what is my name?' said I; 'you know nothing of me.' 'Perhaps you are mistaken,' said the old man, looking kindly at me; 'but at all events tell me your name.' I hesitated a moment, and then told him who I was, whereupon he exclaimed with much emotion, 'I thought so; how wonderful are the ways of Providence! I have heard of thee, young man, and know thy mother well. Only a month ago, when upon a journey, I experienced much kindness from her. She was speaking to me of her lost child, with tears; she told me that you were one of the best of sons, but that some strange idea appeared to have occupied your mind. Despair not, my son. If thou hast been afflicted, I doubt not but that thy affliction will eventually turn out to thy benefit; I doubt not but that thou wilt be preserved, as an example of the great mercy of God. I will now kneel down and pray for thee, my son.'

"And when we had risen from our knees, the old man left me for a short time, and on his return led me into another room, where were two females; one was an elderly person, the wife of the old man, the other was a young woman of very prepossessing appearance (hang not down thy head, Winifred), who I soon found was a distant relation of the old man. Both received me with great kindness.

"I staid several days in the good man's house. I had still the greater portion of a small sum which I happened to have about me when I departed on my dolorous wandering, and with this I purchased clothes, and altered my appearance considerably. On the evening of the second day, my friend said: 'I am going to preach, perhaps you will come and hear me.' I consented, and we all went, not to a church, but to the large building next the house; for the old man, though a clergyman, was not of the established persuasion, and there the old man mounted a pulpit, and began to preach. 'Come unto Me, all ye that labour and are heavy laden.' etc., etc., was his text. His sermon was long, but I still bear the greater portion of it in my mind.

"The substance of it was that Jesus was at all times ready to take upon Himself the burden of our sins, provided we came to Him with a humble and contrite spirit, and begged His help.

"I staid several days in the family, during which time I more than once heard my venerable friend preach; each time he preached he exhorted his hearers not to despair. The whole family were kind to me; his wife frequently discoursed with me, and also the young person to whom I have already alluded. It appeared to me that the latter took a peculiar interest in my fate.

"At last my friend said to me: 'It is now time thou shouldst return to thy mother and thy brother.' So I arose, and departed to my mother and my brother; and at my departure my old friend gave me his blessing, and his wife and the young person shed tears, the last especially. And when my mother saw me, she shed tears, and fell on my neck and kissed me, and my brother took me by the hand and bade me welcome; and when our first emotions were subsided, my mother said: 'I trust thou art come in a lucky hour. A few weeks ago my cousin (whose favourite thou always wast) died and left thee his heir—left thee the goodly farm in which he lived. I trust, my son, that thou wilt now settle, and be a comfort to me in my old days.' And I answered: 'I will, if so please the Lord'; and I said to myself, 'God grant that this bequest be a token of the Lord's favour.'

"And in a few days I departed to take possession of my farm; it was about twenty miles from my mother's house, in a beautiful but rather wild district; I arrived at the fall of the leaf. All day long I busied myself with my farm, and thus kept my mind employed. At night, however, I felt rather solitary, and I frequently wished for a companion. Each night and morning I prayed fervently unto the Lord; for His hand had been very heavy upon me, and I feared Him.

"I shrank from searching the Scriptures; the remembrance of the fatal passage was still too vivid in my mind to permit me. But occasionally, when I had nothing else to do, I renewed my studies. Many is the book I read, especially in my native language, for I was always fond of my native language, and proud of being a Welshman. Amongst the books I read were the odes of the great Ab Gwilym, whom thou, friend, hast never heard of; no, nor any of thy countrymen, for you are an ignorant race, you Saxons, at least with respect to all that relates to Wales and Welshmen. I likewise read the book of Master Ellis Wyn. The latter work possessed a singular fascination for me, on account of its wonderful delineations of the torments of the nether world.

"But man does not love to be alone; indeed, the Scripture says that it is not good for man to be alone. I occupied my body with the pursuits of husbandry, and I improved my mind with the perusal of good and wise books; but, as I have already said, I frequently sighed for a companion with whom I could exchange ideas, and who could take an interest in my pursuits; the want of such a one I more particularly felt in the long winter evenings. It was then that the image of the young person whom I had seen in the house of the preacher frequently rose up distinctly before my mind's eye, decked with quiet graces—hang not down your head, Winifred—and I thought that of all the women in the world I should wish her to be my partner, and then I considered whether it would be possible to obtain her. I am ready to acknowledge, friend, that it was both selfish and wicked in me to wish to fetter any human being to a lost creature like myself, conscious of having committed a crime for which the Scriptures told me there is no pardon. I had, indeed, a long struggle as to whether I should make the attempt or not—selfishness, however, prevailed. With respect to the young person, she did not ask many questions; and I soon found that I had won her heart. To be brief, I married her; and here she is, the truest wife that ever man had, and the kindest.

"One night, after I had been reading to my wife a portion of Ellis Wyn, my wife said: 'This is a wonderful book, and containing much true and pleasant doctrine; but how is it that you, who are so fond of good books, and good things in general, never read the Bible? You read me the book of Master Ellis Wyn, you read me sweet songs of your own composition, you edify me with your gift of prayer, but yet you never read the Bible.' And when I heard her mention the Bible I shook, for I thought of my own condemnation. However, I dearly loved my wife, and as she pressed me, I commenced on that very night reading the Bible. All went on smoothly for a long time; for months and months I did not find the fatal passage, so that I almost thought that I had imagined it. My affairs prospered much the while, so that I was almost happy, taking pleasure in everything around me—in my wife, in my farm, my books and compositions, and the Welsh language; till one night, as I was reading the Bible, feeling particularly comfortable, a thought having just come into my head that I would print some of my compositions, and purchase a particular field of a neighbour—oh, God—God! I came to the fatal passage.

"Friend, friend, what shall I say? I rushed out. My wife followed me, asking me what was the matter. I could only answer with groans—for three days and three nights I did little else than groan. Oh, the kindness and solicitude of my wife! 'What is the matter, husband, dear husband?' she was continually saying."

"And so I still say," said Winifred, sobbing. "Let us retire to rest, dear husband; your fears are groundless. I had hoped long since that your affliction would have passed away, and I still hope that it eventually will; so take heart, Peter, and let us retire to rest, for it is getting late."

"Rest!" said Peter; "there is no rest for the wicked!"

"We are all wicked," said Winifred; "but you are afraid of a shadow. How often have I told you that the sin of your heart is not the sin against the Holy Ghost: the sin of your heart is its natural pride, of which you are scarcely aware, to keep down which God in His mercy permitted you to be terrified with the idea of having committed a sin which you never committed."

"Then you will still maintain," said Peter, "that I never committed the sin against the Holy Spirit?"

"I will," said Winifred; "you never committed it. How should a child seven years old commit a sin like that?"

"Have I not read my own condemnation?" said Peter. "Did not the first words which I read in the Holy Scripture condemn me? 'He who committeth the sin against the Holy Ghost shall never enter into the kingdom of God.'"

"You never committed it," said Winifred.

"But the words! the words! the words!" said Peter.

"The words are true words," said Winifred, sobbing; "but they were not meant for you, but for those who have broken their profession, who, having embraced the cross, have receded from their Master."

"And what sayest thou to the effect which the words produced upon me?" said Peter. "Did they not cause me to run wild through Wales for years, like Merddin Wyllt of yore? Thinkest thou that I opened the book at that particular passage by chance?"

"No," said Winifred, "not by chance; it was the hand of God directed you, doubtless for some wise purpose. You had become satisfied with yourself. The Lord wished to rouse thee from thy state of carnal security, and therefore directed your eyes to that fearful passage."

"I see thou wouldst comfort me," said Peter, "as thou hast often before attempted to do. I would fain ask the young man his opinion."

"I am thinking of London Bridge," said I.

"Of London Bridge!" said Peter and his wife.

"Yes," said I, "of London Bridge. I am indebted for much wisdom to London Bridge; it was there that I completed my studies. But to the point. I was once reading on London Bridge a book which an ancient gentlewoman, who kept the bridge, was in the habit of lending me; and there I found written, 'Each one carries in his breast the recollection of some sin which presses heavy upon him. O! if men could but look into each other's hearts, what blackness would they find there!'"

"That's true," said Peter. "What is the name of the book?"

"*The Life of Blessed Mary Flanders.*"

"Some popish saint, I suppose," said Peter.

"As much of a saint, I dare say," said I, "as most popish ones; but you interrupted me. One part of your narrative brought the passage which I have quoted into my mind. You said that after you had committed this same sin of yours you were in the habit, at school, of looking upon your schoolfellows with a kind of gloomy superiority, considering yourself a lone, monstrous being who had committed a sin far above the daring of any of them. Are you sure that many others of your schoolfellows were not looking upon you and the others with much the same eyes with which you were looking upon them?"

"How!" said Peter, "dost thou think that they had divined my secret?"

"Not they," said I; "they were, I dare say, thinking too much of themselves and of their own concerns to have divined any secrets of yours. All I mean to say is, they had probably secrets of their own, and who knows that the secret sin of more than one of them was not the very sin which caused you so much misery?"

"Dost thou then imagine," said Peter, "the sin against the Holy Ghost to be so common an occurrence?"

"As you have described it," said I, "of very common occurrence, especially amongst children, who are, indeed, the only beings likely to commit it."

"Truly," said Winifred, "the young man talks wisely."

Peter was silent for some moments, and appeared to be reflecting; at last, suddenly raising his head, he looked me full in the face, and, grasping my hand with vehemence, he said: "Tell me, young man, only one thing, hast thou, too, committed the sin against the Holy Ghost?"

"I am neither Papist nor Methodist," said I, "but of the Church, and, being so, confess myself to no one, but keep my own counsel; I will tell thee, however, had I committed, at the same age, twenty such sins as that which you committed, I should feel no uneasiness at these years—but I am sleepy, and must go to rest."

"God bless thee, young man," said Winifred.

CHAPTER XXX

Before I sank to rest I heard Winifred and her husband conversing in the place where I had left them; both their voices were low and calm. I soon fell asleep, and slumbered for some time. On my awakening I again heard them conversing, but they were now in their cart; still the voices of both were calm. I heard no passionate bursts of wild despair on the part of the man. Methought I occasionally heard the word *Pechod* proceeding from the lips of each, but with no particular emphasis. I supposed they were talking of the innate sin of both their hearts.

"I wish that man were happy," said I to myself, "were it only for his wife's sake, and yet he deserves to be happy for his own."

Sunday came, fine and glorious as the last. Again my friends and myself breakfasted together, again the good family of the house on the hill above, headed by the respectable master, descended to the meadow. Peter and his wife were ready to receive them. Again Peter placed himself at the side of the honest farmer, and Winifred by the side of her friend. "Wilt thou not come?" said Peter, looking towards me with a face in which there was much emotion. "Wilt thou not come?" said Winifred, with a face beaming with kindness. But I made no answer, and presently the party moved away, in the same manner in which it had moved on the preceding Sabbath, and I was again left alone.

The hours of the Sabbath passed slowly away. I sat gazing at the sky, the trees and the water. At last I strolled up to the house and sat down in the porch. It was empty; there was no modest maiden there, as on the preceding Sabbath. The damsel of the book had accompanied the rest. I had seen her in the procession, and the house appeared quite deserted. The owners had probably left it to my custody, so I sat down in the porch, quite alone. The hours of the Sabbath passed heavily away.

At last evening came, and with it the party of the morning. I was now at my place beneath the oak. I went forward to meet them. Peter and his wife received me with a calm and quiet greeting, and passed forward. The rest of the party had broke into groups. There was a kind of excitement amongst them, and much eager whispering. I went to one of the groups; the young girl of whom I have spoken more than once, was speaking: "Such a sermon," said she, "it has never been our lot to hear; Peter never before spoke as he has done this day—he was always a powerful preacher; but oh, the unction of the discourse of this morning, and yet more of that of the afternoon, which was the continuation of it." "What was the subject?" said I, interrupting her. "Ah! you should have been there, young man, to have heard it; it would have made a lasting impression upon you. I was bathed in tears all the time; those who heard it will never forget the preaching of the good Peter Williams on the Power, Providence and Goodness of God."

On the morrow I said to my friends: "I am about to depart; farewell!" "Depart!" said Peter and his wife simultaneously, "whither wouldst thou go?" "I can't stay here all my days," I replied. "Of course not," said Peter, "but we had no idea of losing thee so soon: we had almost hoped that thou wouldst join us, become one of us. We are under infinite obligations to thee." "You mean I am under infinite obligations to you," said I. "Did you not save my life?" "Perhaps so, under God," said Peter; "and what hast thou not done for me? Art thou aware that, under God, thou hast preserved my soul from despair? But, independent of that, we like thy company, and feel a deep interest in thee, and would fain teach thee the way that is right. Hearken, to-morrow we go into Wales; go with us." "I have no wish to go into Wales," said I. "Why not?" said Peter with animation. "Wales is a goodly country; as the Scripture says—a land of brooks of water, of fountains and depths, that spring out of valleys and hills, a land whose stones are iron, and out of whose hills thou mayest dig lead."

"I dare say it is a very fine country," said I, "but I have no wish to go there just now; my destiny seems to point in another direction, to say nothing of my trade." "Thou dost right to say nothing of thy trade," said Peter, smiling, "for thou seemest to care nothing about it; which has led Winifred and myself to suspect that thou are not altogether what thou seemest; but, setting that aside, we should be most happy if thou wouldst go with us into Wales." "I cannot promise to go with you into Wales," said I; "but, as you depart to-morrow, I will stay with you through the day, and on the morrow accompany you part of the way." "Do," said Peter. "I have many people to see to-day, and so has Winifred; but we will both endeavour to have some serious discourse with thee, which, perhaps, will turn to thy profit in the end."

On the next day everything was ready for our departure. The good family of the house came to bid us farewell. There were shaking of hands, and kisses, as on the night of our arrival.

And as I stood somewhat apart, the young girl of whom I have spoken so often came up to me, and, holding out her hand, said: "Farewell, young man, wherever thou goest." Then, after looking around her, she said: "It was all true you told me. Yesterday I received a letter from him thou wottest of, he is coming soon. God bless you, young man; who would have thought thou knewest so much!"

So after we had taken our farewell of the good family, we departed, proceeding in the direction of Wales. Peter was very cheerful, and enlivened the way with godly discourse and spiritual hymns, some of which were in the Welsh language.

We were now drawing very near the hills, and Peter said, "If you are to go into Wales, you must presently decide, for we are close upon the border."

"Which is the border?" said I.

"Yon small brook," said Peter, "into which the man on horseback, who is coming towards us, is now entering."

"I see it," said I, "and the man; he stops in the middle of it, as if to water his steed."

We proceeded till we had nearly reached the brook. "Well," said Peter, "will you go into Wales?"

"What should I do in Wales?" I demanded.

"Do!" said Peter, smiling. "Learn Welsh."

I stopped my little pony. "Then I need not go into Wales; I already know Welsh."

"Know Welsh!" said Peter, staring at me.

"Know Welsh!" said Winifred, stopping her cart.

"How and when did you learn it?" said Peter.

"From books, in my boyhood."

"Read Welsh!" said Peter, "is it possible?"

"Read Welsh!" said Winifred, "is it possible?"

"Well, I hope you will come with us," said Peter.

"Come with us, young man," said Winifred; "let me, on the other side of the brook, welcome you into Wales."

"Thank you both," said I, "but I will not come."

"Wherefore?" exclaimed both simultaneously.

"Because it is neither fit nor proper that I cross into Wales at this time, and in this manner. When I go into Wales, I should wish to go in a new suit of superfine black, with hat and beaver, mounted on a powerful steed, black and glossy, like that which bore Greduv to the fight of Catraeth. I should wish, moreover, to see the Welshmen assembled on the border ready to welcome me with pipe and fiddle, and much whooping and shouting, and to attend me to Wrexham, or even as far as Machynllaith, where I should wish to be invited to a dinner at which all the bards should be present, and to be seated at the right hand of the president, who, when the cloth was removed should arise, and, amidst cries of silence, exclaim—'Brethren and Welshmen, allow me to propose the health of my most respectable friend the translator of the odes of the great Ab Gwilym, the pride and glory of Wales.' "

"How!" said Peter; "hast thou translated the works of the mighty Dafydd?"

"With notes critical, historical and explanatory."

"Come with us, friend," said Peter. "I cannot promise such a dinner as thou wishest, but neither pipe nor fiddle shall be wanting."

"Come with us, young man," said Winifred, "even as thou art, and the daughters of Wales shall bid thee welcome."

"I will not go with you," said I. "Dost thou see that man in the ford?"

"Who is staring at us so, and whose horse has not yet done drinking? Of course I see him."

"I shall turn back with him. God bless you!"

"Go back with him not," said Peter, "he is one of those whom I like not, one of the clibberty-clabber, as Master Ellis Wyn observes—turn not with that man."

"Go not back with him," said Winifred. "If thou goest with that man, thou wilt soon forget all our profitable counsels; come with us."

"I cannot; I have much to say to him. Kosko Divvus, Mr. Petulengro."

"Kosko Divvus, Pal," said Mr. Petulengro, riding through the water; "are you turning back?"

I turned back with Mr. Petulengro.

Peter came running after me: "One moment, young man, who and what are you?"

"I must answer in the words of Taliesin," said I; "none can say with positiveness whether I be fish or flesh, least of all myself. God bless you both!"

"Take this," said Peter; and he thrust his Welsh Bible into my hand.

CHAPTER XXXI

So I turned back with Mr. Petulengro. We travelled for some time in silence; at last we fell into discourse. "You have been in Wales, Mr. Petulengro?"

"Ay, truly, brother."

"What have you been doing there?"

"Assisting at a funeral."

"At whose funeral?"

"Mrs. Herne's, brother."

"Is she dead, then?"

"As a nail, brother."

"How did she die?"

"By hanging, brother."

"I am lost in astonishment," said I; whereupon Mr. Petulengro, lifting his sinister leg over the neck of his steed, and adjusting himself sideways in the saddle, replied with great deliberation: "Two days ago, I happened to be at a fair not very far from here; I was all alone by myself, for our party were upwards of forty miles off, when who should come up but a chap that I knew, a relation, or rather, a connection of mine—one of those Hernes. 'Ar'n't you going to the funeral?' said he; and then, brother, there passed between him and me, in the way of questioning and answering, much the same as has just now passed between I and you; but when he mentioned hanging, I thought I could do no less than ask who hanged her, which you forgot to do. 'Who hanged her?' said I; and then the man told me that she had done it herself—been her own hinjiri; and then I thought to myself what a sin and shame it would be if I did not go to the funeral, seeing that she was my own mother-in-law. I would have brought my wife, and, indeed, the whole of our party, but there was no time for that; they were too far off, and the dead was to be buried early the next morning, so I went with the man, and he led me into Wales, where his party had lately retired, and when there, through many wild and desolate places to their encampment, and there I found the Hernes, and the dead body—the last laid out on a mattress, in a tent, dressed Romaneskoenaes, in a red cloak and big bonnet of black beaver. I must say for the Hernes that they took the matter very coolly: some were eating, others drinking, and some were talking about their small affairs; there was one, however, who did not take the matter so coolly, but took on enough for the whole family, sitting beside the dead woman, tearing her hair, and refusing to take either meat or drink; it was the child Leonora. I arrived at nightfall, and the burying was not to take place till the morning, which I was rather sorry for, as I am not very fond of them Hernes, who are not very fond of anybody. They never asked me to eat or drink, notwithstanding I had married into the family; one of them, however, came up and offered to fight me for five shillings; had it not been for them, I should have come back as empty as I went—he didn't stand up five minutes. Brother, I passed the night as well as I could, beneath a tree, for the tents were full, and not over clean; I slept little, and had my eyes about me, for I knew the kind of people I was among.

"Early in the morning the funeral took place. The body was placed not in a coffin but on a bier, and carried not to a churchyard but to a deep dell close by; and there it was buried beneath a rock, dressed just as I have told you; and this was done by the bidding of Leonora, who had heard her bebee say that she wished to be buried, not in gorgious fashion, but like a Roman woman of the old blood, the kosko puro rati, brother. When it was over, and we had got back to the encampment, I prepared to be going. Before mounting my gry, however, I bethought me to ask what could have induced the dead woman to make away with herself, a thing so uncommon amongst Romanies; whereupon one squinted with his eyes, a second spirted saliver into the air, and a third said that he neither knew nor cared; she was a good riddance, having more than once been nearly the ruin of them all, from the quantity of brimstone she carried about her. One, however, I suppose, rather ashamed of the way in which they had treated me, said at last, that if I wanted to know all about the matter, none could tell me better than the child, who was in all her secrets, and was not a little like her; so I looked about for the child, but could find her nowhere. At last the same man told me that he shouldn't wonder if I found her at the grave; so I went back to the grave, and sure enough there I found the child, Leonora, seated on the ground above the body, crying and taking on; so I spoke kindly to her, and said, how came all this, Leonora? tell me all about it. It was a long time before I could get any answer; at last she opened her mouth, and spoke, and these were the words she said: 'It was all along of your pal,' and then she told me all about the matter. How Mrs. Herne could not abide you, which I knew before, and that she had sworn your destruction, which I did not know before. And then she told me how she found you living in the wood by yourself, and how you were enticed to eat a poisoned cake; and she told me many other things that you wot of, and she told me what perhaps you don't wot, namely, that finding you had been removed, she, the child, had tracked you a long way, and found you at last well and hearty, and no ways affected by the poison, and heard you, as she stood concealed, disputing about religion with a Welsh Methody. Well, brother, she told me all this; and, moreover, that when Mrs. Herne heard of it, she said that a dream of hers had come to pass. I don't know what it was, but something about herself, a tinker, and a dean; and then she added, that it was all up with her, and that she must take a long journey. Well, brother, that same night Leonora, waking from her sleep in the tent, where Mrs. Herne and she were wont to sleep, missed her bebee, and, becoming alarmed, went in search of her, and at last found her hanging from a branch; and when the child had got so far, she took on violently, and I could not get another word from her; so I left her, and here I am."

"And I am glad to see you, Mr. Petulengro; but this is sad news which you tell me about Mrs. Herne."

"Somewhat dreary, brother; yet, perhaps, after all, it is a good thing that she is removed; she carried so much Devil's tinder about with her, as the man said."

"I am sorry for her," said I; "more especially as I am the cause of her death—though the innocent one."

"She could not bide you, brother, that's certain; but that is no reason"—said Mr. Petulengro, balancing himself upon the saddle—"that is no reason why she should prepare drow to take away your essence of life, and, when disappointed, to hang herself upon a tree: if she was dissatisfied with you, she might have flown at you, and scratched your face; or, if she did not judge herself your match, she might have put down five shillings for a turn-up between you and some one she thought could beat you—myself, for example, and so the matter might have ended comfortably; but she was always too fond of covert ways, drows and brimstones. This is not the first poisoning affair she has been engaged in."

"You allude to drabbing bawlor."

"Bah!" said Mr. Petulengro; "there's no harm in that. No, no! she has cast drows in her time for other guess things than bawlor; both Gorgios and Romans have tasted of them, and died. Did you never hear of the poisoned plum pudding?"

"Never."

"Then I will tell you about it. It happened about six years ago, a few months after she had quitted us—she had gone first among her own people, as she called them; but there was another small party of Romans, with whom she soon became very intimate. It so happened that this small party got into trouble; whether it was about a horse or an ass, or passing bad money, no matter to you and me, who had no hand in the business; three or four of them were taken and lodged in —— Castle, and amongst them was a woman; but the sherengro, or principal man of the party, and who it seems had most hand in the affair, was still at large. All of a sudden a rumour was spread abroad that the woman was about to play false, and to peach the rest. Said the principal man, when he heard it, 'If she does, I am nashkado.' Mrs. Herne was then on a visit to the party, and when she heard the principal man take on so, she said: 'But I suppose you know what to do?' 'I do not,' said he. 'Then hir mi devlis,' said she, 'you are a fool. But leave the matter to me, I know how to dispose of her in Roman fashion.' Why she wanted to interfere in the matter, brother, I don't know, unless it was from pure brimstoneness of disposition—she had no hand in the matter which had brought the party into trouble, she was only on a visit, and it had happened before she came; but she was always ready to give dangerous advice. Well, brother, the principal man listened to what she had to say, and let her do what she would; and she made a pudding, a very nice one, no doubt—for, besides plums, she put in drows and all the Roman condiments that she knew of; and she gave it to the principal man, and the principal man put it into a basket and directed it to the woman in —— Castle, and the woman in the castle took it and——"

"Ate of it," said I, "just like my case?"

"Quite different, brother; she took it, it is true, but instead of giving way to her appetite as you might have done, she put it before the rest whom she was going to impeach—perhaps she wished to see how they liked it before she tasted it herself—and all the rest were poisoned, and one died, and there was a precious outcry, and the woman cried loudest of all; and she said: 'It was my death was sought for; I know the man, and I'll be revenged,' and then the Poknees spoke to her and said, 'Where can we find him?' and she said, 'I am awake to his motions; three weeks from hence, the night before the full moon, at such and such an hour, he will pass down such a lane with such a man.' "

"Well," said I, "and what did the Poknees do?"

"Do, brother, sent for a plastramengro from Bow Street, quite secretly, and told him what the woman had said; and the night before the full moon, the plastramengro went to the place which the juwa had pointed out, all alone, brother; and, in order that he might not be too late, he went two hours before his time. I know the place well, brother, where the plastramengro placed himself behind a thick holly tree, at the end of a lane, where a gate leads into various fields, through which there is a path for carts and horses. The lane is called the dark lane by the Gorgios, being much shaded by trees; so the plastramengro placed himself in the dark lane behind the holly tree; it was a cold February night, dreary, though; the wind blew in gusts, and the moon had not yet risen, and the plastramengro waited behind a tree till he was tired, and thought he might as well sit down; so he sat down and was not long in falling to sleep, and there he slept for some hours; and when he awoke, the moon had risen, and was shining bright, so that there was a kind of moonlight even in the dark lane; and the plastramengro pulled out his watch, and contrived to make out that it was just two hours beyond the time when the men should have passed by. Brother, I do not know what the plastramengro thought of himself, but I know, brother, what I should have thought of myself in his situation. I should have thought, brother, that I was a drowsy scoppelo, and that I had let the fellow pass by whilst I was sleeping behind a bush. As it turned out, however, his going to sleep did no harm, but quite the contrary; just as he was going away, he heard a gate slam in the direction of the fields, and then he heard the low stumping of horses, as if on soft ground, for the path in those fields is generally soft, and at that time it had been lately ploughed up. Well, brother, presently he saw two men on horseback coming towards the lane through the field behind the gate; the man who rode foremost was a tall, big fellow, the very man he was in quest of: the other was a smaller chap, not so small either, but a light, wiry fellow, and a proper master of his hands when he sees occasion for using them. Well, brother, the foremost man came to the gate, reached at the hank, undid it, and rode through, holding it open for the other. Before, however, the other could follow into the lane, out bolted the plastramengro from behind the tree, kicked the gate to with his foot, and, seizing the big man on horseback, 'You are my prisoner,' said he. I am of opinion, brother, that the plastramengro, notwithstanding he went to sleep, must have been a regular fine fellow."

"I am entirely of your opinion," said I; "but what happened then?"

"Why, brother, the Rommany chal, after he had somewhat recovered from his surprise, for it is rather uncomfortable to be laid hold of at night-time, and told you are a prisoner; more especially when you happen to have two or three things on your mind, which, if proved against you, would carry you to the nashky. The Rommany chal, I say, clubbed his whip, and aimed a blow at the plastramengro, which, if it had hit him on the skull, as was intended, would very likely have cracked it. The plastramengro, however, received it partly on his staff, so that it did him no particular damage. Whereupon seeing what kind of customer he had to deal with, he dropped his staff, and seized the chal with both his hands who forthwith spurred his horse, hoping by doing so, either to break away from him, or fling him down; but it would not do—the plastramengro held on like a bulldog, so that the Rommany chal, to escape being hauled to the ground, suddenly flung himself off the saddle, and then happened in that lane, close by the gate, such a struggle between those two—the chal and the runner—as I suppose will never happen again. But you must have heard of it; every one has heard of it; every one has heard of the fight between the Bow Street engro and the Rommany chal."

"I never heard of it till now."

"All England rung of it, brother. There never was a better match than between those two. The runner was somewhat the stronger of the two—all these engros are strong fellows—and a great deal cooler, for all of that sort are wondrous cool people—he had, however, to do with one who knew full well how to take his own part. The chal fought the engro, brother, in the old Roman fashion. He bit, he kicked, and screamed like a wild cat of Benygant; casting foam from his mouth, and fire from his eyes. Sometimes he was beneath the engro's legs, and sometimes he was upon his shoulders. What the engro found the most difficult, was to get a firm hold of the chal, for no sooner did he seize the chal by any part of his wearing apparel, than the chal either tore himself away, or contrived to slip out of it; so that in a little time the chal was three parts naked; and as for holding him by the body, it was out of the question, for he was as slippery as an eel. At last the engro seized the chal by the Belcher's handkerchief, which he wore in a knot round his neck, and do whatever the chal could, he could not free himself; and when the engro saw that, it gave him fresh heart, no doubt; 'It's of no use,' said he; 'you had better give in; hold out your hands for the darbies, or I will throttle you.' "

"And what did the other fellow do, who came with the chal?" said I.

"I sat still on my horse, brother."

"You?" said I. "Were you the man?"

"I was he, brother."

"And why did you not help your comrade?"

"I have fought in the ring, brother."

"And what had fighting in the ring to do with fighting in the lane?"

"You mean not fighting. A great deal, brother; it taught me to prize fair play. When I fought Staffordshire Dick, t'other side of London. I was alone, brother. Not a Rommany chal to back me, and he had all his brother pals about him; but they gave me fair play, brother; and I beat Staffordshire Dick, which I couldn't have done had they put one finger on his side the scale; for he was as good a man as myself, or nearly so. Now, brother, had I but bent a finger in favour of the Rommany chal the plastramengro would never have come alive out of the lane; but I did not, for I thought to myself fair play is a precious stone; so you see, brother——"

"That you are quite right, Mr. Petulengro; I see that clearly; and now, pray proceed with your narration; it is both moral and entertaining."

But Mr. Petulengro did not proceed with his narration, neither did he proceed upon his way; he had stopped his horse, and his eyes were intently fixed on a broad strip of grass beneath some lofty trees, on the left side of the road. It was a pleasant enough spot, and seemed to invite wayfaring people, such as we were, to rest from the fatigues of the road, and the heat and vehemence of the sun. After examining it for a considerable time, Mr. Petulengro said: "I say, brother, that would be a nice place for a tuzzle!"

"I dare say it would," said I, "if two people were inclined to fight."

"The ground is smooth," said Mr. Petulengro; "without holes or ruts, and the trees cast much shade. I don't think, brother, that we could find a better place," said Mr. Petulengro, springing from his horse.

"But you and I don't want to fight!"

"Speak for yourself, brother," said Mr. Petulengro. "However, I will tell you how the matter stands. There is a point at present between us. There can be no doubt that you are the cause of Mrs. Herne's death, innocently, you will say, but still the cause. Now, I shouldn't like it to be known that I went up and down the country with a pal who was the cause of my mother-in-law's death—that's to say, unless he gave me satisfaction. Now, if I and my pal have a tuzzle, he gives me satisfaction; and if he knocks my eyes out, which I know you can't do, it makes no difference at all, he gives me satisfaction; and he who says to the contrary, knows nothing of gypsy law, and is a dinelo into the bargain."

"But we have no gloves!"

"Gloves!" said Mr. Petulengro contemptuously, "gloves! I tell you what, brother, I always thought you were a better hand at the gloves than the naked fist; and, to tell you the truth, besides taking satisfaction for Mrs. Herne's death, I wish to see what you can do with your morleys; so now is your time, brother, and this is your place, grass and shade, no ruts or holes; come on, brother, or I shall think you what I should not like to call you."

And when I heard Mr. Petulengro talk in this manner, which I had never heard him do before, and which I can only account for by his being fasting and ill-tempered, I had of course no other alternative than to accept his challenge; so I put myself into a posture which I deemed the best both for offence and defence, and the tuzzle commenced; and when it had endured for about half an hour, Mr. Petulengro said: "Brother, there is much blood on your face, you had better wipe it off"; and when I had wiped it off, and again resumed my former attitude, Mr. Petulengro said: "I think enough has been done, brother, in the affair of the old woman; I have, moreover, tried what you are able to do, and find you as I thought, less apt with the naked morleys than the stuffed gloves; nay, brother, put your hands down; I'm satisfied; blood has been shed, which is all that can be reasonably expected for an old woman, who carried so much brimstone about her as Mrs. Herne."

So the struggle ended, and we resumed our route, Mr. Petulengro sitting sideways upon his horse as before, and I driving my little pony-cart; and when we had proceeded about three miles, we came to a small public-house, which bore the sign of the Silent Woman, where we stopped to refresh our cattle and ourselves; and as we sat over our bread and ale, it came to pass that Mr. Petulengro asked me various questions, and amongst others, how I intended to dispose of myself; I told him that I did not know; whereupon with considerable frankness, he invited me to his camp, and told me that if I chose to settle down amongst them, and become a Rommany chal, I should have his wife's sister, Ursula, who was still unmarried, and occasionally talked of me.

I declined his offer, assigning as a reason the recent death of Mrs. Herne, of which I was the cause, although innocent. "A pretty life I should lead with those two," said I, "when they came to know it." "Pooh," said Mr. Petulengro, "they will never know it. I sha'n't blab, and as for Leonora, that girl has a head on her shoulders." "Unlike the woman in the sign," said I, "whose head is cut off. You speak nonsense, Mr. Petulengro; as long as a woman has a head on her shoulders she'll talk—but, leaving women out of the case, it is impossible to keep anything a secret; an old master of mine told me so long ago. I have moreover another reason for declining your offer. I am at present not disposed for society. I am become fond of solitude. I wish I could find some quiet place to which I could retire to hold communion with my own thoughts, and practise, if I thought fit, either of my trades." "What trades?" said Mr. Petulengro. "Why, the one which I have lately been engaged in, or my original one, which I confess I should like better, that of kaulomescro." "Ah, I have frequently heard you talk of making horse-shoes," said Mr. Petulengro. "I, however, never saw you make one, and no one else that I am aware. I don't believe—come, brother, don't be angry, it's quite possible that you may have done things which neither I nor any one else has seen you do, and that such things may some day or other come to light, as you say nothing can be kept secret. Be that, however, as it may, pay the reckoning and let us be going; I think I can advise you to just such a kind of place as you seem to want."

"And how do you know that I have got wherewithal to pay the reckoning?" I demanded. "Brother," said Mr. Petulengro, "I was just now looking in your face, which exhibited the very look of a person conscious of the possession of property; there was nothing hungry or sneaking in it. Pay the reckoning, brother."

And when we were once more upon the road Mr. Petulengro began to talk of the place which he conceived would serve me as a retreat under present circumstances. "I tell you frankly, brother, that it is a queer kind of place, and I am not very fond of pitching my tent in it, it is so surprisingly dreary. It is a deep dingle in the midst of a large field, on an estate about which there has been a lawsuit for some years past. I dare say you will be quiet enough, for the nearest town is five miles distant, and there are only a few huts and hedge public-houses in the neighbourhood. Brother, I am fond of solitude myself, but not that kind of solitude; I like a quiet heath, where I can pitch my house, but I always like to have a gay, stirring place not far off, where the women can pen dukkerin, and I myself can sell or buy a horse, if needful—such a place as the Chong Gav. I never feel so merry as when there, brother, or on the heath above it, where I taught you Rommany."

Shortly after this discourse we reached a milestone, and a few yards from the milestone, on the left hand, was a cross-road. Thereupon Mr. Petulengro said: "Brother, my path lies to the left; if you choose to go with me to my camp, good, if not, Chal Devlehi." But I again refused Mr. Petulengro's invitation, and, shaking him by the hand, proceeded forward alone, and about ten miles farther on I reached the town of which he had spoken, and following certain directions which he had given, discovered, though not without some difficulty, the dingle which he had mentioned. It was a deep hollow in the midst of a wide field, the shelving sides were overgrown with trees and bushes, a belt of sallows surrounded it on the top, a steep winding path led down into the depths, practicable, however, for a light cart, like mine; at the bottom was an open space, and there I pitched my tent, and there I contrived to put up my forge. "I will here ply the trade of kaulomescro," said I.

CHAPTER XXXII

It has always struck me that there is something highly poetical about a forge. I am not singular in this opinion: various individuals have assured me that they can never pass by one, even in the midst of a crowded town, without experiencing sensations which they can scarcely define, but which are highly pleasurable. I have a decided *penchant* for forges, especially rural ones, placed in some quaint, quiet spot—a dingle, for example, which is a poetical place, or at a meeting of four roads, which is still more so; for how many a superstition—and superstition is the soul of poetry—is connected with these cross-roads! I love to light upon such a one, especially after nightfall, as everything about a forge tells to most advantage at night; the hammer sounds more solemnly in the stillness; the glowing particles scattered by the strokes sparkle with more effect in the darkness, whilst the sooty visage of the sastramescro, half in shadow, and half-illumed by the red and partial blaze of the forge, looks more mysterious and strange. On such occasions I draw in my horse's rein, and, seated in the saddle, endeavour to associate with the picture before me—in itself a picture of romance—whatever of the wild and wonderful I have read of in books, or have seen with my own eyes in connection with forges.

I am in the dingle making a horse-shoe. Having no other horses on whose hoofs I could exercise my art, I made my first essay on those of my own horse, if that could be called horse which horse was none, being only a pony. Perhaps if I had sought all England, I should scarcely have found an animal more in need of the kind offices of the smith. On three of his feet there were no shoes at all, and on the fourth only a remnant of one, on which account his hoofs were sadly broken and lacerated by his late journeys over the hard and flinty roads. "You belonged to a tinker before," said I, addressing the animal, "but now you belong to a smith. It is said that the household of the shoemaker invariably go worse shod than that of any other craft. That may be the case of those who make shoes of leather, but it sha'n't be said of the household of him who makes shoes of iron; at any rate, it sha'n't be said of mine. I tell you what, my gry, whilst you continue with me, you shall both be better shod, and better fed, than you were with your last master."

I am in the dingle making a petul; and I must here observe, that whilst I am making a horse-shoe, the reader need not be surprised if I speak occasionally in the language of the lord of the horse-shoe—Mr. Petulengro. I have for some time past been plying the peshota, or bellows, endeavouring to raise up the yag, or fire, in my primitive forge. The angar, or coals, are now burning fiercely, casting forth sparks and long vagescoe chipes, or tongues of flame; a small bar of sastra, or iron, is lying in the fire, to the length of ten or twelve inches, and so far it is hot, very hot, exceedingly hot, brother. And now you see me, prala, snatch the bar of iron, and place the heated end of it upon the covantza, or anvil, and forthwith I commence cooring the sastra as hard as if I had been just engaged by a master at the rate of dui caulor or two shillings a day, brother; and when I have beaten the iron till it is nearly cool, and my arm tired, I place it again in the angar, and begin again to rouse the fire with the pudamengro, which signifies the blowing thing, and is another and more common word for bellows, and whilst thus employed I sing a gypsy song, the sound of which is wonderfully in unison with the hoarse moaning of the pudamengro, and ere the song is finished, the iron is again hot and malleable. Behold, I place it once more on the covantza, and recommence hammering; and now I am somewhat at fault; I am in want of assistance; I want you, brother, or some one else, to take the bar out of my hand and support it upon the covantza, whilst I, applying a chinomescro, or kind of chisel, to the heated iron, cut off with a lusty stroke or two of the shukaro baro, or big hammer, as much as is required for the petul. But having no one to help me, I go on hammering till I have fairly knocked off as much as I want, and then I place the piece in the fire, and again apply the bellows, and take up the song where I left it off; and when I have finished the song, I take out the iron, but this time with my plaistra, or pincers, and then I recommence hammering, turning the iron round and round with my pincers: and now I bend the iron, and lo, and behold, it has assumed something the outline of a petul.

I am not going to enter into further details with respect to the process—it was rather a wearisome one. I had to contend with various disadvantages; my forge was a rude one, my tools might have been better; I was in want of one or two highly necessary implements, but, above all, manual dexterity. Though free of the forge, I had not practised the albeytarian art for very many years, never since—but stay, it is not my intention to tell the reader, at least in this place, how and when I became a blacksmith. There was one thing, however, which stood me in good stead in my labour, the same thing which through life has ever been of incalculable utility to me, and has not unfrequently supplied the place of friends, money, and many other things of almost equal importance—iron perseverance, without which all the advantages of time and circumstance are of very little avail in any undertaking. I was determined to make a horse-shoe, and a good one, in spite of every obstacle—ay, in spite of dukkerin. At the end of four days, during which I had fashioned and refashioned the thing at least fifty times, I had made a petul such as no master of the craft need have been ashamed of; with the second shoe I had less difficulty, and, by the time I had made the fourth, I would have scorned to take off my hat to the best smith in Cheshire.

But I had not yet shod my little gry; this I proceeded now to do. After having first well pared the hoofs with my churi, I applied each petul hot, glowing hot to the pindro. Oh, how the hoofs hissed; and, oh, the pleasant, pungent odour which diffused itself through the dingle, an odour good for an ailing spirit.

I shod the little horse bravely—merely pricked him once, slightly, with a cafi, for doing which, I remember, he kicked me down; I was not disconcerted, however, but, getting up, promised to be more cautious in future; and having finished the operation, I filed the hoof well with the rin baro; then dismissed him to graze amongst the trees, and, putting my smaller tools into the muchtar, I sat down on my stone, and, supporting my arm upon my knee, leaned my head upon my hand. Heaviness had come over me.

Two mornings after I sat by my fire at the bottom of the dingle. I had just breakfasted, and had finished the last morsel of food which I had brought with me to that solitude.

"What shall I now do?" said I to myself; "shall I continue here, or decamp? This is a sad, lonely spot; perhaps I had better quit it; but whither should I go? the wide world is before me, but what can I do therein? I have been in the world already without much success. No, I had better remain here; the place is lonely, it is true, but here I am free and independent, and can do what I please; but I can't remain here without food. Well, I will find my way to the nearest town, lay in a fresh supply of provision, and come back, turning my back upon the world, which has turned its back upon me. I don't see why I should not write a little sometimes; I have pens and an ink-horn, and for a writing-desk I can place the Bible on my knee. I shouldn't wonder if I could write a capital satire on the world on the back of that Bible; but first of all I must think of supplying myself with food."

I rose up from the stone on which I was seated, determining to go to the nearest town with my little horse and cart, and procure what I wanted. The nearest town, according to my best calculation, lay about five miles distant; I had no doubt, however, that by using ordinary diligence I should be back before evening. In order to go lighter, I determined to leave my tent standing as it was, and all the things which I had purchased of the tinker, just as they were. "I need not be apprehensive on their account," said I to myself; "nobody will come here to meddle with them; the great recommendation of this place is its perfect solitude; I dare say that I could live here six months without seeing a single human visage. I will now harness my little gry and be off to the town."

At a whistle which I gave, the little gry, which was feeding on the bank near the uppermost part of the dingle, came running to me: for by this time he had become so accustomed to me, that he would obey my call for all the world as if he had been one of the canine species. "Now," said I to him, "we are going to the town to buy bread for myself, and oats for you. I am in a hurry to be back; therefore, I pray you to do your best, and to draw me and the cart to the town with all possible speed, and to bring us back; if you do your best, I promise you oats on your return. You know the meaning of oats, Ambrol?"

Ambrol whinnied as if to let me know that he understood me perfectly well, as indeed he well might, as I had never once fed him during the time he had been in my possession without saying the word in question to him. Now, ambrol, in the gypsy tongue, signifieth a pear.

So I caparisoned Ambrol, and then, going to the cart, I removed two or three things from out it into the tent; I then lifted up the shafts, and was just going to call to the pony to come and be fastened to them, when I thought I heard a noise.

I stood stock still supporting the shaft of the little cart in my hand, and bending the right side of my face slightly towards the ground; but I could hear nothing. The noise which I thought I had heard was not one of those sounds which I was accustomed to hear in that solitude: the note of a bird, or the rustling of a bough; it was—there I heard it again, a sound very much resembling the grating of a wheel amongst gravel. Could it proceed from the road? Oh no, the road was too far distant for me to hear the noise of anything moving along it. Again I listened, and now I distinctly heard the sound of wheels, which seemed to be approaching the dingle; nearer and nearer they drew, and presently the sound of wheels was blended with the murmur of voices. Anon I heard a boisterous shout, which seemed to proceed from the entrance of the dingle. "Here are folks at hand," said I, letting the shaft of the cart fall to the ground, "is it possible that they can be coming here?"

My doubts on that point, if I entertained any, were soon dispelled; the wheels, which had ceased moving for a moment or two, were once again in motion, and were now evidently moving down the winding path which led to my retreat. Leaving my cart, I came forward and placed myself near the entrance of the open space, with my eyes fixed on the path down which my unexpected, and I may say unwelcome, visitors were coming. Presently I heard a stamping or sliding, as if of a horse in some difficulty; and then a loud curse, and the next moment appeared a man and a horse and cart; the former holding the head of the horse up to prevent him from falling, of which he was in danger, owing to the precipitous nature of the path. Whilst thus occupied, the head of the man was averted from me. When, however, he had reached the bottom of the descent, he turned his head, and perceiving me, as I stood bareheaded, without either coat or waistcoat, about two yards from him, he gave a sudden start, so violent, that the backward motion of his hand had nearly flung the horse upon his haunches.

"Why don't you move forward?" said a voice from behind, apparently that of a female, "you are stopping up the way, and we shall be all down upon one another"; and I saw the head of another horse overtopping the back of the cart.

"Why don't you move forward, Jack?" said another voice, also of a female, yet higher up the path.

The man stirred not, but remained staring at me in the posture which he had assumed on first perceiving me, his body very much drawn back, his left foot far in advance of his right, and with his right hand still grasping the halter of the horse, which gave way more and more, till it was clean down on his haunches.

"What's the matter?" said the voice which I had last heard.

"Get back with you, Belle, Moll," said the man, still staring at me, "here's something not over-canny or comfortable."

"What is it?" said the same voice; "let me pass, Moll, and I'll soon clear the way," and I heard a kind of rushing down the path.

"You need not be afraid," said I, addressing myself to the man, "I mean you no harm; I am a wanderer like yourself—come here to seek for shelter—you need not be afraid; I am a Roman chabo by matriculation—one of the right sort, and no mistake. Good-day to ye, brother; I bid ye welcome."

The man eyed me suspiciously for a moment, then turning to his horse with a loud curse, he pulled him up from his haunches and led him and the cart farther down to one side of the dingle, muttering as he passed me, "Afraid. Hm!"

I do not remember ever to have seen a more ruffianly-looking fellow; he was about six feet high, with an immensely athletic frame; his face was black and bluff, and sported an immense pair of whiskers, but with here and there a grey hair, for his age could not be much under fifty. He wore a faded blue frock-coat, corduroys, and highlows; on his black head was a kind of red night-cap; round his bull neck a Barcelona handkerchief—I did not like the look of the man at all.

"Afraid," growled the fellow, proceeding to unharness his horse; "that was the word, I think."

But other figures were now already upon the scene. Dashing past the other horse and cart, which by this time had reached the bottom of the pass, appeared an exceedingly tall woman, or rather girl, for she could scarcely have been above eighteen; she was dressed in a tight bodice, and a blue stuff gown; hat, bonnet or cap she had none, and her hair, which was flaxen, hung down on her shoulders unconfined; her complexion was fair, and her features handsome, with a determined but open expression. She was followed by another female, about forty, stout and vulgar-looking, at whom I scarcely glanced, my whole attention being absorbed by the tall girl.

"What's the matter, Jack?" said the latter, looking at the man.

"Only afraid, that's all," said the man, still proceeding with his work.

"Afraid at what—at that lad? why, he looks like a ghost. I would engage to thrash him with one hand."

"You might beat me with no hands at all," said I, "fair damsel, only by looking at me; I never saw such a face and figure, both regal. Why, you look like Ingeborg, Queen of Norway; she had twelve brothers, you know, and could lick them all, though they were heroes:—

> 'On Dovrefield in Norway,
> Were once together seen,
> The twelve heroic brothers
> Of Ingeborg the queen.'"

"None of your chaffing, young fellow," said the tall girl, "or I will give you what shall make you wipe your face; be civil, or you will rue it."

"Well, perhaps I was a peg too high," said I; "I ask your pardon—here's something a bit lower:—

> 'As I was jawing to the gav yeck divvus
> I met on the drom miro Rommany chi—'"

"None of your Rommany chies, young fellow," said the tall girl, looking more menacingly than before and clenching her fist, "you had better be civil, I am none of your chies; and though I keep company with gypsies, or, to speak more proper, half and halfs, I would have you to know that I come of Christian blood and parents, and was born in the great house of Long Melford."

"I have no doubt," said I, "that it was a great house judging from your size, I shouldn't wonder if you were born in a church."

"Stay, Belle," said the man, putting himself before the young virago, who was about to rush upon me, "my turn is first"; then, advancing to me in a menacing attitude, he said, with a look of deep malignity, "Afraid was the word, wasn't it?"

"It was," said I, "but I think I wronged you; I should have said, aghast, you exhibited every symptom of one labouring under uncontrollable fear."

The fellow stared at me with a look of stupid ferocity, and appeared to be hesitating whether to strike or not; ere he could make up his mind, the tall girl started forward, crying, "He's chaffing, let me at him"; and, before I could put myself on my guard, she struck me a blow on the face which had nearly brought me to the ground.

"Enough," said I, putting my hand to my cheek; "you have now performed your promise, and made me wipe my face; now be pacified, and tell me fairly the grounds of this quarrel."

"Grounds!" said the fellow; "didn't you say I was afraid? and if you hadn't, who gave you leave to camp on my ground?"

"Is it your ground?" said I.

"A pretty question," said the fellow; "as if all the world didn't know that. Do you know who I am?"

"I guess I do," said I; "unless I am much mistaken, you are he whom folks call the 'Flaming Tinman.' To tell you the truth, I'm glad we have met, for I wished to see you. These are your two wives, I suppose; I greet them. There's no harm done—there's room enough here for all of us—we shall soon be good friends, I dare say; and when we are a little better acquainted, I'll tell you my history."

"Well, if that doesn't beat all," said the fellow.

"I don't think he's chaffing now," said the girl, whose anger seemed to have subsided on a sudden; "the young man speaks civil enough."

"Civil," said the fellow with an oath; "but that's just like you; with you it is a blow, and all over. Civil! I suppose you would have him stay here, and get into all my secrets, and hear all I may have to say to my two morts."

"Two morts!" said the girl, kindling up, "where are they? Speak for one, and no more. I am no mort of yours, whatever some one else may be. I tell you one thing, Black John, or Anselo, for t'other an't your name, the same thing I told the young man here: be civil, or you will rue it."

The fellow looked at the girl furiously, but his glance soon quailed before hers; he withdrew his eyes, and cast them on my little horse, which was feeding amongst the trees. "What's this?" said he, rushing forward and seizing the animal. "Why, as I am alive, this is the horse of that mumping villain Slingsby."

"It's his no longer; I bought it and paid for it."

"It's mine now," said the fellow; "I swore I would seize it the next time I found it on my beat; ay, and beat the master too."

"I am not Slingsby."

"All's one for that."

"You don't say you will beat me?"

"Afraid was the word."

"I'm sick and feeble."

"Hold up your fists."

"Won't the horse satisfy you?"

"Horse nor bellows either."

"No mercy, then."

"Here's at you."

"Mind your eyes, Jack. There, you've got it. I thought so," shouted the girl, as the fellow staggered back from a sharp blow in the eye. "I thought he was chaffing at you all along."

"Never mind, Anselo. You know what to do—go in," said the vulgar woman, who had hitherto not spoken a word, but who now came forward with all the look of a fury; "go in apopli; you'll smash ten like he."

The Flaming Tinman took her advice, and came in, bent on smashing, but stopped short on receiving a left-handed blow on the nose.

"You'll never beat the Flaming Tinman in that way," said the girl, looking at me doubtfully.

And so I began to think myself, when, in the twinkling of an eye, the Flaming Tinman disengaging himself of his frock-coat, and, dashing off his red night-cap, came rushing in more desperately than ever. To a flush hit which he received in the mouth he paid as little attention as a wild bull would have done; in a moment his arms were around me, and in another, he had hurled me down, falling heavily upon me. The fellow's strength appeared to be tremendous.

"Pay him off now," said the vulgar woman. The Flaming Tinman made no reply, but planting his knee on my breast, seized my throat with two huge horny hands. I gave myself up for dead, and probably should have been so in another minute but for the tall girl, who caught hold of the handkerchief which the fellow wore round his neck with a grasp nearly as powerful as that with which he pressed my throat.

"Do you call that fair play?" said she.

"Hands off, Belle," said the other woman; "do you call it fair play to interfere? hands off, or I'll be down upon you myself."

But Belle paid no heed to the injunction, and tugged so hard at the handkerchief that the Flaming Tinman was nearly throttled; suddenly relinquishing his hold of me, he started on his feet, and aimed a blow at my fair preserver, who avoided it, but said coolly:—

"Finish t'other business first, and then I'm your woman whenever you like; but finish it fairly—no foul play when I'm by—I'll be the boy's second, and Moll can pick you up when he happens to knock you down."

The battle during the next ten minutes raged with considerable fury; but it so happened that during this time I was never able to knock the Flaming Tinman down, but on the contrary received six knock-down blows myself. "I can never stand this," said I, as I sat on the knee of Belle, "I am afraid I must give in; the Flaming Tinman hits very hard," and I spat out a mouthful of blood.

"Sure enough you'll never beat the Flaming Tinman in the way you fight—it's of no use flipping at the Flaming Tinman with your left hand; why don't you use your right?"

"Because I'm not handy with it," said I; and then getting up, I once more confronted the Flaming Tinman, and struck him six blows for his one, but they were all left-handed blows, and the blow which the Flaming Tinman gave me knocked me off my legs.

"Now, will you use Long Melford?" said Belle, picking me up.

"I don't know what you mean by Long Melford," said I, gasping for breath.

"Why, this long right of yours," said Belle, feeling my right arm—"if you do, I shouldn't wonder if you yet stand a chance."

And now the Flaming Tinman was once more ready, much more ready than myself. I, however, rose from my second's knee as well as my weakness would permit me; on he came, striking left and right, appearing almost as fresh as to wind and spirit as when he first commenced the combat, though his eyes were considerably swelled, and his nether lip was cut in two; on he came, striking left and right, and I did not like his blows at all, or even the wind of them, which was anything but agreeable, and I gave way before him. At last he aimed a blow which, had it taken full effect, would doubtless have ended the battle, but owing to his slipping, the fist only grazed my left shoulder, and came with terrific force against a tree, close to which I had been driven; before the Tinman could recover himself, I collected all my strength, and struck him beneath the ear, and then fell to the ground completely exhausted, and it so happened that the blow which I struck the tinker beneath the ear was a right-handed blow.

"Hurrah for Long Melford!" I heard Belle exclaim; "there is nothing like Long Melford for shortness all the world over."

At these words I turned round my head as I lay, and perceived the Flaming Tinman stretched upon the ground apparently senseless. "He is dead," said the vulgar woman, as she vainly endeavoured to raise him up; "he is dead; the best man in all the north country, killed in this fashion, by a boy." Alarmed at these words, I made shift to get on my feet; and, with the assistance of the woman, placed my fallen adversary in a sitting posture. I put my hand to his heart, and felt a slight pulsation. "He's not dead," said I, "only stunned; if he were let blood, he would recover presently." I produced a penknife which I had in my pocket, and, baring the arm of the Tinman, was about to make the necessary incision, when the woman gave me a violent blow, and, pushing me aside, exclaimed: "I'll tear the eyes out of your head, if you offer to touch him. Do you want to complete your work, and murder him outright, now he's asleep? you have had enough of his blood already." "You are mad," said I, "I only seek to do him service. Well, if you won't let him be blooded, fetch some water and fling it in his face, you know where the pit is."

"A pretty manœuvre," said the woman; "leave my husband in the hands of you and that limmer, who has never been true to us; I should find him strangled or his throat cut when I came back." "Do you go," said I, to the tall girl, "take the can and fetch some water from the pit." "You had better go yourself," said the girl, wiping a tear as she looked on the yet senseless form of the tinker; "you had better go yourself, if you think water will do him good." I had by this time somewhat recovered my exhausted powers, and, taking the can, I bent my steps as fast as I could to the pit; arriving there, I lay down on the brink, took a long draught, and then plunged my head into the water; after which I filled the can, and bent my way back to the dingle. Before I could reach the path which led down into its depths, I had to pass some way along its side; I had arrived at a part immediately over the scene of the last encounter, where the bank, overgrown with trees, sloped precipitously down. Here I heard a loud sound of voices in the dingle; I stopped, and laying hold of a tree, leaned over the bank and listened. The two women appeared to be in hot dispute in the dingle. "It was all owing to you, you limmer," said the vulgar woman to the other; "had you not interfered, the old man would soon have settled the boy."

"I'm for fair play and Long Melford," said the other. "If your old man, as you call him, could have settled the boy fairly, he might, for all I should have cared, but no foul work for me; and as for sticking the boy with our gulleys when he comes back, as you proposed, I am not so fond of your old man or you that I should oblige you in it, to my soul's destruction." "Hold your tongue, or I'll—"; I listened no farther, but hastened as fast as I could to the dingle. My adversary had just begun to show signs of animation; the vulgar woman was still supporting him, and occasionally cast glances of anger at the tall girl who was walking slowly up and down. I lost no time in dashing the greater part of the water into the Tinman's face, whereupon he sneezed, moved his hands, and presently looked round him. At first his looks were dull and heavy, and without any intelligence at all; he soon, however, began to recollect himself, and to be conscious of his situation; he cast a scowling glance at me, then one of the deepest malignity at the tall girl, who was still walking about without taking much notice of what was going forward. At last he looked at his right hand, which had evidently suffered from the blow against the tree, and a half-stifled curse escaped his lips. The vulgar woman now said something to him in a low tone, whereupon he looked at her for a moment, and then got upon his legs. Again the vulgar woman said something to him; her looks were furious, and she appeared to be urging him on to attempt something. I observed that she had a clasped knife in her hand. The fellow remained standing for some time as if hesitating what to do; at last he looked at his hand, and, shaking his head, said something to the woman which I did not understand. The tall girl, however, appeared to overhear him, and, probably repeating his words, said: "No, it won't do; you are right there, and now hear what I have to say—let bygones be bygones, and let us all shake hands, and camp here, as the young man was saying just now." The man looked at her, and then, without any reply, went to his horse, which was lying down among the trees, and kicking it up, led it to the cart, to which he forthwith began to harness it. The other cart and horse had remained standing motionless during the whole affair which I have been recounting, at the bottom of the pass. The woman now took the horse by the head, and leading it with the cart into the open part of the dingle turned both round, and then led them back, till the horse and cart had mounted a little way up the ascent; she then stood still and appeared to be expecting the man. During this proceeding Belle had stood looking on without saying anything; at last, perceiving that the man had harnessed his horse to the other cart, and that both he and the woman were about to take their departure, she said: "You are not going, are you?" Receiving no answer, she continued: "I tell you what, both of you, Black John, and you Moll, his mort, this is not treating me over civilly—however, I am ready to put up with it, and to go with you if you like, for I bear no malice. I'm sorry for what has happened, but you have only yourselves to thank for it. Now, shall I go with you, only tell me?" The man made no manner of reply, but flogged his horse. The woman, however, whose passions were probably under less control, replied, with a screeching tone: "Stay where you are, you jade, and may the curse of Judas cling to you—stay with the bit of a mullo whom you helped, and my only hope is that he may gulley you before he comes to be—— Have you with us, indeed! after what's past, no, nor nothing belonging to you. Fetch down your mailla go-cart and live here with your chabo." She then whipped on the horse, and ascended the pass, followed by the man. The carts were light, and they were not long in ascending the winding path. I followed to see that they took their departure. Arriving at the top, I found near the entrance a small donkey cart, which I concluded belonged to the girl. The tinker and his mort were already at some distance; I stood looking after them for a little time, then taking the donkey by the reins I led it with the cart to the bottom of the dingle. Arrived there, I found Belle seated on the stone by the fireplace. Her hair was all dishevelled, and she was in tears.

"They were bad people," said she, "and I did not like them, but they were my only acquaintance in the wide world."

In the evening of that same day the tall girl and I sat at tea by the fire, at the bottom of the dingle; the girl on a small stool, and myself, as usual, upon my stone.

The water which served for the tea had been taken from a spring of pellucid water in the neighbourhood, which I had not had the good fortune to discover, though it was well known to my companion, and to the wandering people who frequented the dingle.

"This tea is very good," said I, "but I cannot enjoy it as much as if I were well: I feel very sadly."

"How else should you feel," said the girl, "after fighting with the Flaming Tinman? All I wonder at is that you can feel at all! As for the tea, it ought to be good, seeing that it cost me ten shillings a pound."

"That's a great deal for a person in your station to pay."

"In my station! I'd have you to know, young man—however, I haven't the heart to quarrel with you, you look so ill; and after all, it is a good sum for one to pay who travels the roads; but if I must have tea, I like to have the best; and tea I must have, for I am used to it, though I can't help thinking that it sometimes fills my head with strange fancies—what some folks call vapours, making me weep and cry."

"Dear me," said I, "I should never have thought that one of your size and fierceness would weep and cry!"

"My size and fierceness! I tell you what, young man, you are not over civil this evening; but you are ill, as I said before, and I sha'n't take much notice of your language, at least for the present; as for my size, I am not so much bigger than yourself; and as for being fierce, you should be the last one to fling that at me. It is well for you that I can be fierce sometimes. If I hadn't taken your part against Blazing Bosville, you wouldn't be now taking tea with me."

"It is true that you struck me in the face first; but we'll let that pass. So that man's name is Bosville; what's your own?"

"Isopel Berners."

"How did you get that name?"

"I say, young man, you seem fond of asking questions! will you have another cup of tea?"

"I was just going to ask for another."

"Well, then, here it is, and much good may it do you; as for my name, I got it from my mother."

"Your mother's name, then, was Isopel?"

"Isopel Berners."

"But had you never a father?"

"Yes, I had a father," said the girl, sighing, "but I don't bear his name."

"Is it the fashion, then, in your country for children to bear their mother's name?"

"If you ask such questions, young man, I shall be angry with you. I have told you my name, and whether my father's or mother's, I am not ashamed of it."

"It is a noble name."

"There you are right, young man. The chaplain in the great house where I was born, told me it was a noble name; it was odd enough, he said, that the only three noble names in the country were to be found in the great house; mine was one; the other two were Devereux and Bohun."

"What do you mean by the great house?"

"The workhouse."

"Is it possible that you were born there?"

"Yes, young man; and as you now speak softly and kindly, I will tell you my whole tale. My father was an officer of the sea, and was killed at sea as he was coming home to marry my mother, Isopel Berners. He had been acquainted with her, and had left her; but after a few months he wrote her a letter, to say that he had no rest, and that he repented, and that as soon as his ship came to port he would do her all the reparation in his power. Well, young man, the very day before they reached port they met the enemy, and there was a fight, and my father was killed, after he had struck down six of the enemy's crew on their own deck; for my father was a big man, as I have heard, and knew tolerably well how to use his hands. And when my mother heard the news, she became half distracted, and ran away into the fields and forests, totally neglecting her business, for she was a small milliner; and so she ran demented about the meads and forests for a long time, now sitting under a tree, and now by the side of a river—at last she flung herself into some water, and would have been drowned, had not some one been at hand and rescued her, whereupon she was conveyed to the great house, lest she should attempt to do herself further mischief, for she had neither friends nor parents—and there she died three months after, having first brought me into the world. She was a sweet, pretty creature, I'm told, but hardly fit for this world, being neither large, nor fierce, nor able to take her own part. So I was born and bred in the great house, where I learnt to read and sew, to fear God, and to take my own part. When I was fourteen I was put out to service to a small farmer and his wife, with whom, however, I did not stay long, for I was half starved, and otherwise ill-treated, especially by my mistress, who one day attempting to knock me down with a besom, I knocked her down with my fist, and went back to the great house."

"And how did they receive you in the great house?"

"Not very kindly, young man—on the contrary, I was put into a dark room, where I was kept a fortnight on bread and water; I did not much care, however, being glad to have got back to the great house at any rate, the place where I was born, and where my poor mother died, and in the great house I continued two years longer, reading and sewing, fearing God, and taking my own part when necessary. At the end of the two years I was again put out to service, but this time to a rich farmer and his wife, with whom, however, I did not live long, less time, I believe, than with the poor ones, being obliged to leave for——"

"Knocking your mistress down?"

"No, young man, knocking my master down, who conducted himself improperly towards me. This time I did not go back to the great house, having a misgiving that they would not receive me, so I turned my back to the great house where I was born, and where my poor mother died, and wandered for several days, I know not whither, supporting myself on a few halfpence which I chanced to have in my pocket. It happened one day, as I sat under a hedge crying, having spent my last farthing, that a comfortable-looking elderly woman came up in a cart, and seeing the state in which I was, she stopped and asked what was the matter with me; I told her some part of my story, whereupon she said: 'Cheer up, my dear, if you like you shall go with me, and wait upon me.' Of course I wanted little persuasion, so I got into the cart and went with her. She took me to London and various other places, and I soon found that she was a travelling woman, who went about the country with silks and linen. I was of great use to her, more especially in those places where we met evil company. Once, as we were coming from Dover, we were met by two sailors, who stopped our cart, and would have robbed and stripped us. 'Let me get down,' said I; so I got down, and fought with them both, till they turned round and ran away. Two years I lived with the old gentlewoman who was very kind to me, almost as kind as a mother; at last she fell sick at a place in Lincolnshire, and after a few days died, leaving me her cart and stock in trade, praying me only to see her decently buried, which I did, giving her a funeral fit for a gentlewoman. After which I travelled the country melancholy enough for want of company, but so far fortunate, that I could take my own part when anybody was uncivil to me. At last, passing through the valley of Todmorden, I formed the acquaintance of Blazing Bosville and his wife, with whom I occasionally took journeys for company's sake, for it is melancholy to travel about alone, even when one can take one's own part. I soon found they were evil people; but, upon the whole, they treated me civilly, and I sometimes lent them a little money, so that we got on tolerably well together. He and I, it is true, had once a dispute, and nearly came to blows, for once, when we were alone, he wanted me to marry him, promising if I would, to turn off Grey Moll, or if I liked it better, to make her wait upon me as a maid-servant; I never liked him much, but from that hour less than ever. Of the two, I believe Grey Moll to be the best, for she is at any rate true and faithful to him, and I like truth and constancy, don't you, young man?"

"Yes," said I, "they are very nice things. I feel very strangely."

"How do you feel, young man?"

"Very much afraid."

"Afraid, at what? At the Flaming Tinman? Don't be afraid of him. He won't come back, and if he did, he shouldn't touch you in this state. I'd fight him for you, but he won't come back, so you needn't be afraid of him."

"I'm not afraid of the Flaming Tinman."

"What, then, are you afraid of?"

"The evil one."

"The evil one!" said the girl, "where is he?"

"Coming upon me."

"Never heed," said the girl, "I'll stand by you."

CHAPTER XXXIII

The kitchen of the public-house was a large one, and many people were drinking in it; there was a confused hubbub of voices.

I sat down on a bench behind a deal table, of which there were three or four in the kitchen; presently a bulky man, in a green coat, of the Newmarket cut, and without a hat, entered, and observing me, came up, and in rather a gruff tone cried: "Want anything, young fellow?"

"Bring me a jug of ale," said I, "if you are the master, as I suppose you are, by that same coat of yours, and your having no hat on your head."

"Don't be saucy, young fellow," said the landlord, for such he was, "don't be saucy, or——" Whatever he intended to say, he left unsaid, for fixing his eyes upon one of my hands, which I had placed by chance upon the table, he became suddenly still.

This was my left hand, which was raw and swollen, from the blows dealt on a certain hard skull in a recent combat. "What do you mean by staring at my hand so?" said I, withdrawing it from the table.

"No offence, young man, no offence," said the landlord, in a quite altered tone; "but the sight of your hand——" Then observing that our conversation began to attract the notice of the guests in the kitchen, he interrupted himself, saying in an undertone: "But mum's the word for the present, I will go and fetch the ale."

In about a minute he returned, with a jug of ale foaming high. "Here's your health," said he, blowing off the foam, and drinking; but perceiving that I looked rather dissatisfied, he murmured: "All's right, I glory in you; but mum's the word." Then placing the jug on the table, he gave me a confidential nod, and swaggered out of the room.

What can the silly, impertinent fellow mean, thought I, but the ale was now before me, and I hastened to drink, for my weakness was great, and my mind was full of dark thoughts, the remains of the indescribable horror of the preceding night. It may kill me, thought I, as I drank deep, but who cares, anything is better than what I have suffered. I drank deep, and then leaned back against the wall; it appeared as if a vapour was stealing up into my brain, gentle and benign, soothing and stilling the horror and the fear; higher and higher it mounted, and I felt nearly overcome; but the sensation was delicious, compared with that I had lately experienced, and now I felt myself nodding; and bending down I laid my head on the table on my folded hands.

And in that attitude I remained some time, perfectly unconscious. At length, by degrees, perception returned, and I lifted up my head. I felt somewhat dizzy and bewildered, but the dark shadow had withdrawn itself from me. And now, once more, I drank of the jug; this second draught did not produce an overpowering effect upon me—it revived and strengthened me. I felt a new man.

I looked around me: the kitchen had been deserted by the greater part of the guests; besides myself, only four remained; these were seated at the farther end. One was haranguing fiercely and eagerly; he was abusing England, and praising America. At last he exclaimed: "So when I gets to New York, I will toss up my hat, and damn the King."

That man must be a Radical, thought I.

The individual whom I supposed to be a Radical, after a short pause, again uplifted his voice: he was rather a strong-built fellow of about thirty, with an ill-favoured countenance, a white hat on his head, a snuff-coloured coat on his back, and, when he was not speaking, a pipe in his mouth. "Who would live in such a country as England?" he shouted.

"There is no country like America," said his nearest neighbour, a man also in a white hat, and of a very ill-favoured countenance, "there is no country like America," said he, withdrawing a pipe from his mouth; "I think I shall"—and here he took a draught from a jug, the contents of which he appeared to have in common with the other—"go to America one of these days myself."

"Poor old England is not such a bad country, after all," said a third, a simple-looking man in a labouring dress, who sat smoking a pipe without anything before him. "If there was but a little more work to be got, I should have nothing to say against her. I hope, however——"

"You hope, who cares what you hope?" interrupted the first, in a savage tone; "you are one of those sneaking hounds who are satisfied with dog's wages, a bit of bread and a kick. Work, indeed! who, with the spirit of a man, would work for a country where there is neither liberty of speech, nor of action? a land full of beggarly aristocracy, hungry borough-mongers, insolent parsons, and 'their——wives and daughters,' as William Cobbett says, in his *Register*."

"Ah, the Church of England has been a source of incalculable mischief to these realms," said another.

"You are quite right," said the first, alluding to what this last had said, "the Church of England has done incalculable mischief here. I value no religion three halfpence, for I believe in none; but the one that I hate most is the Church of England; so when I get to New York, after I have shown the fine fellows on the quay a spice of me, by——the King, I'll toss up my hat again, and——the Church of England too."

"And suppose the people of New York should clap you in the stocks?" said I.

The Radical and his companion stared at me ferociously; the simple-looking man in the labouring dress laughed.

"What are you laughing at, you fool?" said the Radical, turning and looking at the other, who appeared to be afraid of him, "hold your noise;

and a pretty fellow, you," said he, looking at me, "to come here, and speak against the great American nation."

"I speak against the great American nation?" said I, "I rather paid them a compliment."

"By supposing they would put me in the stocks. Well, I call it abusing them, to suppose they would do any such thing—stocks, indeed!—there are no stocks in all the land. Put me in the stocks? why, the President will come down to the quay, and ask me to dinner, as soon as he hears what I have said about the King and the Church."

"I shouldn't wonder," said I, "if you got to America, you will say of the President and country what now you say of the King and Church, and cry out for somebody to send you back to England."

The Radical dashed his pipe to pieces against the table. "I tell you what, young fellow, you are a spy of the aristocracy, sent here to kick up a disturbance."

"Kicking up a disturbance," said I, "is rather inconsistent with the office of spy. If I were a spy, I should hold my head down, and say nothing."

"Well, if you ar'n't sent to spy, you are sent to bully, to prevent people speaking, and to run down the great American nation; but you sha'n't bully me. I say down with the aristocracy, the beggarly aristocracy. Come, what have you to say to that?"

"Nothing," said I.

"Nothing!" repeated the Radical.

"No," said I, "down with them as soon as you can."

"As soon as I can! I wish I could. But I can down with a bully of theirs. Come, will you fight for them?"

"No," said I.

"You won't?"

"No," said I; "though from what I have seen of them I should say they are tolerably able to fight for themselves."

"You won't fight for them," said the Radical, triumphantly; "I thought so; all bullies, especially those of the aristocracy, are cowards. Here, landlord," said he, raising his voice, and striking against the table with the jug, "some more ale—he won't fight for his friends."

"A white feather," said his companion.

"Landlord, landlord," shouted the Radical, striking the table with the jug louder than before. "Who called?" said the landlord, coming in at last. "Fill this jug again," said the other, "and be quick about it."

"I don't care for the young fellow," said the man in the snuff-coloured coat.

"I know you don't," said the other, "so get up, and serve him out."

"I could serve out three like him," said the man in the snuff-coloured coat.

"So much the better for you," said the other, "the present work will be all the easier for you, get up, and serve him out at once."

The man in the snuff-coloured coat did not stir.

"Who shows the white feather now?" said the simple-looking man.

"Come, Hunter," said the other, "get up, and fight against the Church of England."

"I have no particular quarrel against the Church of England," said the man in the snuff-coloured coat, "my quarrel is with the aristocracy. However," he continued suddenly, "I won't slink from the matter either; it shall never be said by the fine fellows on the quay of New York, that I wouldn't fight against the Church of England. So down with the beggarly aristocracy, the Church, and the Pope, to the bottom of the pit of Eldon, and may the Pope fall first, and the others upon him."

Thereupon, dashing his hat on the table, he placed himself in an attitude of offence, and rushed forward. He was, as I have said before, a powerful fellow, and might have proved a dangerous antagonist, more especially to myself, who, after my recent encounter with the Flaming Tinman, and my wrestlings with the evil one, was in anything but fighting order. Any collision, however, was prevented by the landlord, who, suddenly appearing, thrust himself between us. "There shall be no fighting here," said he, "no one shall fight in this house, except it be with myself; so if you two have anything to say to each other, you had better go into the field behind the house. But, you fool," said he, pushing Hunter violently on the breast, "do you know whom you are going to tackle with? this is the young chap that beat Blazing Bosville, only as late as yesterday, in Mumpers' Dingle. Grey Moll told me all about it last night, when she came for some brandy for her husband, who, she said, had been half killed; and she described the young man to me so closely, that I knew him at once, that is, as soon as I saw how his left hand was bruised, for she told me he was a left-hand hitter. Ar'n't it all true, young man? Ar'n't you he that beat Flaming Bosville in Mumpers' Dingle?" "I never beat Flaming Bosville," said I, "he beat himself. Had he not struck his hand against a tree, I shouldn't be here at the present moment." "Here! here!" said the landlord, "now that's just as it should be; I like a modest man, for, as the parson says, nothing sits better upon a young man than modesty. I remember, when I was young, fighting with Tom of Hopton, the best man that ever pulled off coat in England. I remember, too, that I won the battle; for I happened to hit Tom of Hopton, in the mark, as he was coming in, so that he lost his wind, and falling squelch on the ground, do ye see, he lost the battle, though I am free to confess that he was a better man than myself; indeed, the best man that ever fought in England; yet still I won the battle, as every customer of mine, and everybody within twelve miles round, has heard over and over again. Now, Mr. Hunter, I have one thing to say, if you choose to go into the field behind the house, and fight the young man, you can. I'll back him for ten pounds; but no fighting in my kitchen!—because why? I keeps a decent kind of an establishment."

"I have no wish to fight the young man," said Hunter; "more especially as he has nothing to say for the aristocracy. If he chose to fight for them, indeed—but he won't, I know; for I see he's a decent, respectable young man;

and, after all, fighting is a blackguard way of settling a dispute; so I have no wish to fight; however, there is one thing I'll do," said he, uplifting his fist, "I'll fight this fellow in black here for half a crown, or for nothing, if he pleases; it was he that got up the last dispute between me and the young man, with his Pope and his nonsense; so I will fight him for anything he pleases, and perhaps the young man will be my second; whilst you——"

"Come, Doctor," said the landlord, "or whatsoever you be, will you go into the field with Hunter? I'll second you, only you must back yourself. I'll lay five pounds on Hunter, if you are inclined to back yourself; and will help you to win it as far, do you see, as a second can; because why? I always likes to do the fair thing."

"Oh! I have no wish to fight," said the man in black hastily, "fighting is not my trade. If I have given any offence, I beg anybody's pardon."

"Landlord," said I, "what have I to pay?"

"Nothing at all," said the landlord; "glad to see you. This is the first time that you have been at my house, and I never charge new customers, at least customers such as you, anything for the first draught. You'll come again, I dare say; shall always be glad to see you. I won't take it," said he, as I put sixpence on the table; "I won't take it."

"Yes, you shall," said I; "but not in payment for anything I have had myself: it shall serve to pay for a jug of ale for that gentleman," said I, pointing to the simple-looking individual; "he is smoking a poor pipe. I do not mean to say that a pipe is a bad thing; but a pipe without ale, do you see——"

"Bravo!" said the landlord, "that's just the conduct I like."

"Bravo!" said Hunter. "I shall be happy to drink with the young man whenever I meet him at New York, where, do you see, things are better managed than here."

CHAPTER XXXIV

The public-house where the scenes which I have attempted to describe in the preceding chapters took place, was at the distance of about two miles from the dingle. The sun was sinking in the west by the time I returned to the latter spot. I found Belle seated by a fire, over which her kettle was suspended. During my absence she had prepared herself a kind of tent, consisting of large hoops covered over with tarpaulin, quite impenetrable to rain, however violent. "I am glad you are returned," said she, as soon as she perceived me; "I began to be anxious about you. Did you take my advice?"

"Yes," said I, "I went to the public-house and drank ale as you advised me; it cheered, strengthened, and drove away the horror from my mind—I am much beholden to you."

"I knew it would do you good," said Belle; "I remembered that when the poor women in the great house were afflicted with hysterics and fearful imaginings, the surgeon, who was a good, kind man, used to say: 'Ale, give them ale, and let it be strong.' "

"He was no advocate for tea, then?" said I.

"He had no objection to tea; but he used to say, 'Everything in its season.' Shall we take ours now—I have waited for you."

"I have no objection," said I; "I feel rather heated, and at present should prefer tea to ale—'Everything in its season,' as the surgeon said."

Thereupon Belle prepared tea, and, as we were taking it, she said: "What did you see and hear at the public-house?"

"Really," said I, "you appear to have your full portion of curiosity; what matters it to you what I saw and heard at the public-house?"

"It matters very little to me," said Belle; "I merely inquired of you, for the sake of a little conversation—you were silent, and it is uncomfortable for two people to sit together without opening their lips—at least I think so."

"One only feels uncomfortable," said I, "in being silent, when one happens to be thinking of the individual with whom one is in company. To tell you the truth, I was not thinking of my companion, but of certain company with whom I had been at the public-house."

"Really, young man," said Belle, "you are not over complimentary; but who may this wonderful company have been—some young——?" and here Belle stopped.

"No," said I, "there was no young person—if person you were going to say. There was a big portly landlord, whom I dare say you have seen; a noisy savage Radical, who wanted at first to fasten upon me a quarrel about America, but who subsequently drew in his horns."

"Was there no one else?" said Belle.

"You are mighty curious," said I. "No, none else, except a poor, simple mechanic, and some common company, who soon went away."

Belle looked at me for a moment, and then appeared to be lost in thought —"America?" said she, musingly—"America?"

"What of America?" said I.

"I have heard that it is a mighty country."

"I dare say it is," said I; "I have heard my father say that the Americans are first-rate marksmen."

"I heard nothing about that," said Belle; "what I heard was, that it is a great and goodly land, where people can walk about without jostling, and where the industrious can always find bread; I have frequently thought of going thither."

"Well," said I, "the Radical in the public-house will perhaps be glad of your company thither; he is as great an admirer of America as yourself, though I believe on different grounds."

"I shall go by myself," said Belle, "unless—unless that should happen which is not likely—I am not fond of Radicals no more than I am of scoffers and mockers."

"Do you mean to say that I am a scoffer and mocker?"

"I don't wish to say you are," said Belle; "but some of your words sound strangely like scoffing and mocking. I have now one thing to beg, which is, if you have anything to say against America, you would speak it out boldly."

"What should I have to say against America? I never was there."

"Many people speak against America who never were there."

"Many people speak in praise of America who never were there; but with respect to myself, I have not spoken for or against America."

"If you like America you would speak in its praise."

"By the same rule, if I disliked America I should speak against it."

"I can't speak with you," said Belle; "but I see you dislike the country."

"The country!"

"Well, the people—don't you?"

"I do."

"Why do you dislike them?"

"Why, I have heard my father say that the American marksmen, led on by a chap of the name of Washington, sent the English to the right-about in double-quick time."

"And that is your reason for disliking the Americans?"

"Yes," said I, "that is my reason for disliking them."

"Will you take another cup of tea?" said Belle.

I took another cup; we were again silent. "It is rather uncomfortable," said I, at last, "for people to sit together without having anything to say."

"Were you thinking of your company?" said Belle.

"What company?" said I.

"The present company."

"The present company! oh, ah!—I remember that I said one only feels uncomfortable in being silent with a companion, when one happens to be thinking of the companion. Well, I had been thinking of you the last two or three minutes, and had just come to the conclusion, that to prevent us both feeling occasionally uncomfortable towards each other, having nothing to say, it would be as well to have a standing subject, on which to employ our tongues. Belle, I have determined to give you lessons in Armenian."

"What is Armenian?"

"Did you ever hear of Ararat?"

"Yes, that was the place where the ark rested; I have heard the chaplain in the great house talk of it; besides, I have read of it in the Bible."

"Well, Armenian is the speech of people of that place, and I should like to teach it you."

"To prevent——"

"Ay, ay, to prevent our occasionally feeling uncomfortable together. Your acquiring it besides might prove of ulterior advantage to us both; for example, suppose you and I were in promiscuous company, at Court, for example, and you had something to communicate to me which you did not wish any one else to be acquainted with, how safely you might communicate it to me in Armenian."

"Would not the language of the roads do as well?" said Belle.

"In some places it would," said I, "but not at Court, owing to its resemblance to thieves' slang. There is Hebrew, again, which I was thinking of teaching you, till the idea of being presented at Court made me abandon it, from the probability of our being understood, in the event of our speaking it, by at least half a dozen people in our vicinity. There is Latin, it is true, or Greek, which we might speak aloud at Court with perfect confidence of safety, but upon the whole I should prefer teaching you Armenian, not because it would be a safer language to hold communication with at Court, but because, not being very well grounded in it myself, I am apprehensive that its words and forms may escape from my recollection, unless I have sometimes occasion to call them forth."

"I am afraid we shall have to part company before I have learnt it," said Belle; "in the meantime, if I wish to say anything to you in private, somebody being by, shall I speak in the language of the roads?"

"If no roadster is nigh, you may," said I, "and I will do my best to understand you. Belle, I will now give you a lesson in Armenian."

"I suppose you mean no harm," said Belle.

"Not in the least; I merely propose the thing to prevent our occasionally feeling uncomfortable together. Let us begin."

"Stop till I have removed the tea-things," said Belle; and, getting up, she removed them to her own encampment.

"I am ready," said Belle, returning, and taking her former seat, "to join with you in anything which will serve to pass away the time agreeably, provided there is no harm in it."

"Belle," said I, "I have determined to commence the course of Armenian lessons by teaching you the numerals; but, before I do that, it will be as well to tell you that the Armenian language is called Haik."

"I am sure that word will hang upon my memory," said Belle.

"Why hang upon it?"

"Because the old woman in the great house used to call so the chimney-hook, on which they hung the kettle; in like manner, on the hake of my memory I will hang your hake."

"Good!" said I, "you will make an apt scholar; but, mind, that I did not say hake, but haik; the words are, however, very much alike; and, as you observe, upon your hake you may hang my haik. We will now proceed to the numerals."

"What are numerals?" said Belle.

"Numbers. I will say the Haikan numbers up to ten. There, have you heard them?"—"Yes." "Well, try and repeat them."

"I only remember number one," said Belle, "and that because it is *me*."

"I will repeat them again," said I, "and pay greater attention. Now, try again."

"*Me, jergo, earache.*"

"I neither said *jergo* nor *earache.* I said *yergou* and *yerek*. Belle, I am afraid I shall have some difficulty with you as a scholar."

Time passed on, and Belle and I lived in the dingle; when I say lived, the reader must not imagine that we were always there. She went out upon her pursuits, and I went out where inclination led me; but my excursions were very short ones, and hers occasionally occupied whole days and nights. If I am asked how we passed the time when we were together in the dingle, I would answer that we passed the time very tolerably, all things considered; we conversed together, and when tired of conversing I would sometimes give Belle a lesson in Armenian; her progress was not particularly brilliant, but upon the whole satisfactory; in about a fortnight she had hung up 100 Haikan numerals upon the hake of her memory. I found her conversation highly entertaining; she had seen much of England and Wales, and had been acquainted with some of the most remarkable characters who travelled the roads at that period; and let me be permitted to say that many remarkable characters have travelled the roads of England, of whom fame has never said a word. I loved to hear her anecdotes of these people; some of whom I found had occasionally attempted to lay violent hands either upon her person or effects, and had invariably been humbled by her without the assistance of either justice or constable. I could clearly see, however, that she was rather tired of England, and wished for a change of scene; she was particularly fond of talking of America, to which country her aspirations chiefly tended. She had heard much of America, which had excited her imagination; for at that time America was much talked of, on roads and in homesteads, at least so said Belle, who had good opportunities of knowing, and most people allowed that it was a good country for adventurous English. The people who chiefly spoke against it, as she informed me, were soldiers disbanded upon pensions, the sextons of village churches, and excisemen. Belle had a craving desire to visit that country, and to wander with cart and little animal amongst its forests; when I would occasionally object, that she would be exposed to danger from strange and perverse customers, she said that she had not wandered the roads of England so long and alone, to be afraid of anything which might befall in America; and that she hoped, with God's favour, to be able to take her own part, and to give to perverse customers as good as they might bring. She had a dauntless heart, that same Belle. Such was the staple of Belle's conversation. As for mine, I would endeavour to entertain her with strange dreams of adventure, in which I figured in opaque forests, strangling wild beasts, or discovering and plundering the hordes of dragons; and sometimes I would narrate to her other things far more genuine—how I had tamed savage mares, wrestled with Satan, and had dealings with ferocious publishers. Belle had a kind heart, and would weep at the accounts I gave her of my early wrestlings with the dark monarch. She would sigh, too, as I recounted the many slights and degradations I had received at the hands of ferocious publishers; but she had the curiosity of a woman; and once, when I talked to her of the triumphs which I had achieved over unbroken mares, she lifted up her head and questioned me as to the secret of the virtue which I possessed over the aforesaid animals; whereupon I sternly reprimanded, and forthwith commanded her to repeat the Armenian numerals; and, on her demurring, I made use of words, to escape which she was glad to comply, saying the Armenian numerals from one to a hundred, which numerals, as a punishment for her curiosity, I made her repeat three times, loading her with the bitterest reproaches whenever she committed the slightest error, either in accent or pronunciation, which reproaches she appeared to bear with the greatest patience. And now I have given a very fair account of the manner in which Isopel Berners and myself passed our time in the dingle.

CHAPTER XXXV

Amongst other excursions, I went several times to the public-house, to which I introduced the reader in a former chapter. I had experienced such beneficial effects from the ale I had drunk on that occasion, that I wished to put its virtue to a frequent test; nor did the ale on subsequent trials belie the good opinion which I had at first formed of it. After each visit which I made to the public-house, I found my frame stronger, and my mind more cheerful than they had previously been. The landlord appeared at all times glad to see me, and insisted that I should sit within the bar, where, leaving his other guests to be attended to by a niece of his who officiated as his housekeeper, he would sit beside me and talk of matters concerning "the ring," indulging himself with a cigar and a glass of sherry, which he told me was his favourite wine, whilst I drank my ale. "I loves the conversation of all you coves of the ring," said he once, "which is natural, seeing as how I have fought in a ring myself. Ah, there is nothing like the ring; I wish I was not rather too old to go again into it. I often think I should like to have another rally—one more rally, and then—but there's a time for all things—youth will be served, every dog has his day, and mine has been a fine one—let me be content. After beating Tom of Hopton, there was not much more to be done in the way of reputation; I have long sat in my bar the wonder and glory of this here neighbourhood. I'm content, as far as reputation goes; I only wish money would come in a little faster; however, the next main of cocks will bring me in something handsome—comes off next Wednesday at——have ventured ten five-pound notes—shouldn't say ventured either—run no risk at all, because why? I know my birds." About ten days after this harangue, I called again at about three o'clock one afternoon. The landlord was seated on a bench by a table in the common room, which was entirely empty; he was neither smoking nor drinking, but sat with his arms folded, and his head hanging down over his breast. At the sound of my step he looked up; "Ah," said he, "I am glad you are come, I was just thinking about you." "Thank you," said I; "it was very kind of you, especially at a time like this, when your mind must be full of your good fortune. Allow me to congratulate you on the sums of money you won by the main of cocks at— I hope you brought it all safe home." "Safe home," said the landlord; "I brought myself safe home, and that was all; came home without a shilling, regularly done, cleaned out." "I am sorry for that," said I; "but after you had won the money, you ought to have been satisfied, and not risked it again—how did you lose it? I hope not by the pea and thimble." "Pea and thimble," said the landlord, "not I; those confounded cocks left me nothing to lose by the pea and thimble." "Dear me," said I; "I thought that you knew your birds." "Well, so I did," said the landlord; "I knew the birds to be good birds, and so they proved, and would have won if better birds had not been brought against them, of which I knew nothing, and so do you see I am done, regularly done." "Well," said I, "don't be cast down; there is one thing of which the cocks by their misfortune cannot deprive you—your reputation; make the most of that, give up cock-fighting, and be content with the custom of your house, of which you will always have plenty, as long as you are the wonder and glory of the neighbourhood."

The landlord struck the table before him violently with his fist. "Confound my reputation!" said he. "No reputation that I have will be satisfaction to my brewer for the seventy pounds I owe him. Reputation won't pass for the current coin of this here realm; and let me tell you, that if it a'n't backed by some of it, it a'n't a bit better than rotten cabbage, as I have found. Only three weeks since I was, as I told you, the wonder and glory of the neighbourhood; and people used to come and look at me, and worship me, but as soon as it began to be whispered about that I owed money to the brewer, they presently left off all that kind of thing; and now, during the last three days, since the tale of my misfortune with the cocks has got wind, almost everybody has left off coming to the house, and the few who does, merely comes to insult and flout me. It was only last night that fellow, Hunter, called me an old fool in my own kitchen here. He wouldn't have called me a fool a fortnight ago; 'twas I called him fool then, and last night he called me old fool; what do you think of that? the man that beat Tom of Hopton, to be called, not only a fool, but an old fool; and I hadn't heart, with one blow of this here fist into his face, to send his head ringing against the wall; for when a man's pocket is low, do you see, his heart a'n't much higher; but it is of no use talking, something must be done. I was thinking of you just as you came in, for you are just the person that can help me."

"If you mean," said I, "to ask me to lend you the money which you want, it will be to no purpose, as I have very little of my own, just enough for my own occasions; it is true, if you desired it, I would be your intercessor with the person to whom you owe the money, though I should hardly imagine that anything I could say——" "You are right there," said the landlord; "much the brewer would care for anything you could say on my behalf—your going would be the very way to do me up entirely. A pretty opinion he would have of the state of my affairs if I were to send him such a 'cessor as you, and as for your lending me money, don't think I was ever fool enough to suppose either that you had any, or if you had that you would be fool enough to lend me any. No, no, the coves of the ring knows better; I have been in the ring myself, and knows what fighting a cove is, and though I was fool enough to back those birds, I was never quite fool enough to lend anybody money. What I am about to propose is something very different from going to my landlord, or lending any capital; something which, though it will put money into my pocket, will likewise put something handsome into your own. I want to get up a fight in this here neighbourhood, which would be sure to bring plenty of people to my house, for a week before and after it takes place, and as people can't come without drinking, I think I could, during one fortnight, get off for the brewer all the sour and unsaleable liquids he now has, which people wouldn't drink at any other time, and by that means, do you see, liquidate my debt; then, by means of betting, making first all right, do you see, I have no doubt that I could put something handsome into my pocket and yours, for I should wish you to be the fighting man, as I think I can depend upon you." "You really must excuse me," said I, "I have no wish to figure as a pugilist, besides there is such a difference in our ages; you may be the stronger man of the two, and perhaps the hardest hitter, but I am in much better condition, am more active on my legs, so that I am almost sure I should have the advantage, for, as you very properly observed, 'Youth will be served.'" "Oh, I didn't mean to fight," said the landlord; "I think I could beat you if I were to train a little; but in the fight I propose I looks more to the main chance than anything else. I question whether half so many people could be brought together if you were to fight with me as the person I have in view, or whether there would be half such opportunities for betting, for I am a man, do you see, the person I wants you to fight with is not a man, but the young woman you keeps company with."

"The young woman I keep company with," said I; "pray what do you mean?"

"We will go into the bar, and have something," said the landlord, getting up. "My niece is out, and there is no one in the house, so we can talk the matter over quietly." Thereupon I followed him into the bar, where, having drawn me a jug of ale, helped himself as usual to a glass of sherry, and lighted a cigar, he proceeded to explain himself farther. "What I wants is to get up a fight between a man and a woman; there never has yet been such a thing in the ring, and the mere noise of the matter would bring thousands of people together, quite enough to drink out—for the thing should be close to my house—all the brewer's stock of liquids, both good and bad." "But," said I, "you were the other day boasting of the respectability of your house; do you think that a fight between a man and a woman close to your establishment would add to its respectability?" "Confound the respectability of my house," said the landlord, "will the respectability of my house pay the brewer, or keep the roof over my head? No, no! when respectability won't keep a man, do you see, the best thing is to let it go and wander. Only let me have my own way, and both the brewer, myself, and every one of us, will be satisfied. And then the betting—what a deal we may make by the betting—and that we shall have all to ourselves, you, I, and the young woman; the brewer will have no hand in that. I can manage to raise ten pounds, and if by flashing that about, I don't manage to make a hundred, call me horse." "But, suppose," said I, "the party should lose, on whom you sport your money, even as the birds did?" "We must first make all right," said the landlord, "as I told you before; the birds were irrational beings, and therefore couldn't come to an understanding with the others, as you and the young woman can. The birds fought fair; but I intend you and the young woman should fight cross." "What do you mean by cross?" said I. "Come, come," said the landlord, "don't attempt to gammon me; you in the ring, and pretend not to know what fighting cross is. That won't do, my fine fellow; but as no one is near us, I will speak out. I intend that you and the young woman should understand one another and agree beforehand which should be beat; and if you take my advice you will determine between you that the young woman shall be beat, as I am sure that the odds will run high upon her, her character as a fist woman being spread far and wide, so that all the flats who think it will be all right, will back her, as I myself would, if I thought it would be a fair thing." "Then," said I, "you would not have us fight fair." "By no means," said the landlord, "because why? I conceives that a cross is a certainty to those who are in it, whereas by the fair thing one may lose all he has." "But," said I, "you said the other day, that you liked the fair thing." "That was by way of gammon," said the landlord; "just, do you see, as a Parliament cove might say speechifying from a barrel to a set of flats, whom he means to sell. Come, what do you think of the plan?"

"It is a very ingenious one," said I.

"A'n't it," said the landlord. "The folks in this neighbourhood are beginning to call me old fool, but if they don't call me something else, when they sees me friends with the brewer, and money in my pocket, my name is not Catchpole. Come, drink your ale, and go home to the young gentlewoman."

"I am going," said I, rising from my seat, after finishing the remainder of the ale.

"Do you think she'll have any objection?" said the landlord.

"To do what?" said I.

"Why, to fight cross."

"Yes, I do," said I.

"But you will do your best to persuade her?"

"No, I will not," said I.

"Are you fool enough to wish to fight fair?"

"No," said I, "I am wise enough to wish not to fight at all."

CHAPTER XXXVI

NEARLY three days elapsed without anything of particular moment occurring. Belle drove the little cart containing her merchandise about the neighbourhood, returning to the dingle towards the evening. As for myself, I kept within my wooded retreat, working during the periods of her absence leisurely at my forge. Having observed that the quadruped which my companion drove was as much in need of shoes as my own had been some time previously, I had determined to provide it with a set, and during the aforesaid periods occupied myself in preparing them. As I was employed three mornings and afternoons about them, I am sure that the reader will agree that I worked leisurely, or rather lazily. On the third day Belle arrived somewhat later than usual; I was lying on my back at the bottom of the dingle, employed in tossing up the shoes, which I had produced, and catching them as they fell, some being always in the air mounting or descending, somewhat after the fashion of the waters of a fountain.

"Why have you been absent so long?" said I to Belle, "it must be long past four by the day."

"I have been almost killed by the heat," said Belle; "I was never out in a more sultry day—the poor donkey, too, could scarcely move along."

"He shall have fresh shoes," said I, continuing my exercise; "here they are, quite ready; to-morrow I will tack them on."

"And why are you playing with them in that manner?" said Belle.

"Partly in triumph at having made them, and partly to show that I can do something besides making them; it is not every one who, after having made a set of horse-shoes, can keep them going up and down in the air, without letting one fall."

"One has now fallen on your chin," said Belle.

"And another on my cheek," said I, getting up; "it is time to discontinue the game, for the last shoe drew blood."

Belle went to her own little encampment; and as for myself, after having flung the donkey's shoes into my tent, I put some fresh wood on the fire, which was nearly out, and hung the kettle over it. I then issued forth from the dingle, and strolled round the wood that surrounded it; for a long time I was busied in meditation, looking at the ground, striking with my foot, half unconsciously, the tufts of grass and thistles that I met in my way. After some time, I lifted up my eyes to the sky, at first vacantly, and then with more attention, turning my head in all directions for a minute or two; after which I returned to the dingle. Isopel was seated near the fire, over which the kettle was now hung; she had changed her dress—no signs of the dust and fatigue of her late excursion remained; she had just added to the fire a small billet of wood, two or three of which I had left beside it; the fire cracked, and a sweet odour filled the dingle.

"I am fond of sitting by a wood fire," said Belle, "when abroad, whether it be hot or cold; I love to see the flames dart out of the wood; but what kind is this, and where did you get it?"

"It is ash," said I, "green ash. Somewhat less than a week ago, whilst I was wandering along the road by the side of a wood, I came to a place where some peasants were engaged in cutting up and clearing away a confused mass of fallen timber: a mighty-aged oak had given way the night before, and in its fall had shivered some smaller trees; the upper part of the oak, and the fragments of the rest, lay across the road. I purchased, for a trifle, a bundle or two, and the wood on the fire is part of it—ash, green ash."

"That makes good the old rhyme," said Belle, "which I have heard sung by the old woman in the great house:—

'Ash, when green,
Is fire for a queen.'"

"And on fairer form of queen, ash fire never shone," said I, "than on thine, O beauteous queen of the dingle."

"I am half disposed to be angry with you, young man," said Belle.

"And why not entirely?" said I.

Belle made no reply.

"Shall I tell you?" I demanded. "You had no objection to the first part of the speech, but you did not like being called queen of the dingle. Well, if I had the power, I would make you queen of something better than the dingle —Queen of China. Come, let us have tea."

"Something less would content me," said Belle, sighing, as she rose to prepare our evening meal.

So we took tea together, Belle and I. "How delicious tea is after a hot summer's day, and a long walk," said she.

"I dare say it is most refreshing then," said I; "but I have heard people say that they most enjoy it on a cold winter's night, when the kettle is hissing on the fire, and their children playing on the hearth."

Belle sighed. "Where does tea come from?" she presently demanded.

"From China," said I; "I just now mentioned it, and the mention of it put me in mind of tea."

"What kind of country is China?"

"I know very little about it; all I know is, that it is a very large country far to the East, but scarcely large enough to contain its inhabitants, who are so numerous, that though China does not cover one-ninth part of the world, its inhabitants amount to one-third of the population of the world."

"And do they talk as we do?"

"Oh no! I know nothing of their language; but I have heard that it is quite different from all others, and so difficult that none but the cleverest people amongst foreigners can master it, on which account, perhaps, only the French pretend to know anything about it."

"Are the French so very clever, then?" said Belle.

"They say there are no people like them, at least in Europe. But talking of Chinese reminds me that I have not for some time past given you a lesson in Armenian. The word for tea in Armenian is—by-the-bye, what is the Armenian word for tea?"

"That's your affair, not mine," said Belle; "it seems hard that the master should ask the scholar."

"Well," said I, "whatever the word may be in Armenian, it is a noun; and as we have never yet declined an Armenian noun together, we may as well take this opportunity of declining one. Belle, there are ten declensions in Armenian!"

"What's a declension?"

"The way of declining a noun."

"Then, in the civilest way imaginable, I decline the noun. Is that a declension?"

"You should never play on words; to do so is low, vulgar, smelling of the pothouse, the workhouse. Belle, I insist on your declining an Armenian noun."

"I have done so already," said Belle.

"If you go on in this way," said I, "I shall decline taking any more tea with you. Will you decline an Armenian noun?"

"I don't like the language," said Belle. "If you must teach me languages, why not teach me French or Chinese?"

"I know nothing of Chinese; and as for French, none but a Frenchman is clever enough to speak it—to say nothing of teaching; no, we will stick to Armenian, unless, indeed, you would prefer Welsh!"

"Welsh, I have heard, is vulgar," said Belle; "so, if I must learn one of the two, I will prefer Armenian, which I never heard of till you mentioned it to me; though of the two, I really think Welsh sounds best."

"The Armenian noun," said I, "which I propose for your declension this night, is . . . which signifieth master."

"I neither like the word nor the sound," said Belle.

"I can't help that," said I; "it is the word I choose; master, with all its variations, being the first noun, the sound of which I would have you learn from my lips. Come, let us begin—

"A master . . . Of a master, etc. Repeat—"

"I am not much used to say the word," said Belle. "But, to oblige you, I will decline it as you wish"; and thereupon Belle declined master in Armenian.

"You have declined the noun very well," said I; "that is in the singular number; we will now go to the plural."

"What is the plural?" said Belle.

"That which implies more than one, for example, masters; you shall now go through masters in Armenian."

"Never," said Belle, "never; it is bad to have one master, but more I would never bear, whether in Armenian or English."

"You do not understand," said I; "I merely want you to decline masters in Armenian."

"I do decline them; I will have nothing to do with them, nor with master either; I was wrong to— What sound is that?"

"I did not hear it, but I dare say it is thunder; in Armenian—"

"Never mind what it is in Armenian; but why do you think it is thunder?"

"Ere I returned from my stroll, I looked up into the heavens, and by their appearance I judged that a storm was nigh at hand."

"And why did you not tell me so?"

"You never asked me about the state of the atmosphere, and I am not in the habit of giving my opinion to people on any subject, unless questioned. But, setting that aside, can you blame me for not troubling you with forebodings about storm and tempest, which might have prevented the pleasure you promised yourself in drinking tea, or perhaps a lesson in Armenian, though you pretend to dislike the latter."

"My dislike is not pretended," said Belle; "I hate the sound of it, but I love my tea, and it was kind of you not to wish to cast a cloud over my little pleasures; the thunder came quite time enough to interrupt it without being anticipated—there is another peal—I will clear away, and see that my tent is in a condition to resist the storm, and I think you had better bestir yourself."

Isopel departed, and I remained seated on my stone, as nothing belonging to myself required any particular attention; in about a quarter of an hour she returned, and seated herself upon her stool.

"How dark the place is become since I left you," said she; "just as if night were just at hand."

"Look up at the sky," said I, "and you will not wonder; it is all of a deep olive. The wind is beginning to rise; hark how it moans among the branches; and see how their tops are bending—it brings dust on its wings—I felt some fall on my face; and what is this, a drop of rain?"

"We shall have plenty anon," said Belle; "do you hear? it already begins to hiss upon the embers; that fire of ours will soon be extinguished."

"It is not probable that we shall want it," said I, "but we had better seek shelter; let us go into my tent."

"Go in," said Belle, "but you go in alone; as for me, I will seek my own."

"You are right," said I, "to be afraid of me; I have taught you to decline master in Armenian."

"You almost tempt me," said Belle, "to make you decline mistress in English."

"To make matters short," said I, "I decline a mistress."

"What do you mean?" said Belle angrily.

"I have merely done what you wished me," said I, "and in your own style; there is no other way of declining anything in English, for in English there are no declensions."

"The rain is increasing," said Belle.

"It is so," said I; "I shall go to my tent; you may come, if you please; I do assure you I am not afraid of you."

"Nor I of you," said Belle; "so I will come. Why should I be afraid? I can take my own part; that is—"

We went into the tent and sat down, and now the rain began to pour with vehemence. "I hope we shall not be flooded in this hollow," said I to Belle. "There is no fear of that," said Belle; "the wandering people, amongst other names, call it the dry hollow. I believe there is a passage somewhere or other by which the wet is carried off. There must be a cloud right above us, it is so dark. Oh! what a flash!"

"And what a peal," said I; "that is what the Hebrews call *Koul Adonai*—the voice of the Lord. Are you afraid?"

"No," said Belle, "I rather like to hear it."

"You are right," said I; "I am fond of the sound of thunder myself. There is nothing like it; *Koul Adonai behadar;* the voice of the Lord is a glorious voice, as the prayer-book version hath it."

"There is something awful in it," said Belle; "and then the lightning, the whole dingle is now in a blaze."

" 'The voice of the Lord maketh the hinds to calve, and discovereth the thick bushes.' As you say, there is something awful in thunder."

"There are all kinds of noises above us," said Belle; "surely I heard the crashing of a tree?"

" 'The voice of the Lord breaketh the cedar trees,' " said I, "but what you hear is caused by a convulsion of the air; during a thunderstorm there are occasionally all kinds of aërial noises. Ab Gwilym, who, next to King David, has best described a thunderstorm, speaks of these aërial noises in the following manner:—

'Astonied now I stand at strains,
As of ten thousand clanking chains;
And once, methought, that overthrown,
The welkin's oaks came whelming down;

Upon my head up starts my hair:
Why hunt abroad the hounds of air?
What cursed hag is screeching high,
Whilst crash goes all her crockery?'

You would hardly believe, Belle, that though I offered at least ten thousand lines nearly as good as those to the booksellers in London, the simpletons were so blind to their interest as to refuse purchasing them."

"I don't wonder at it," said Belle, "especially if such dreadful expressions frequently occur as that towards the end; surely that was the crash of a tree?"

"Ah!" said I, "there falls the cedar tree—I mean the sallow; one of the tall trees on the outside of the dingle has been snapped short."

"What a pity," said Belle, "that the fine old oak, which you saw the peasants cutting up, gave way the other night, when scarcely a breath of air was stirring; how much better to have fallen in a storm like this, the fiercest I remember."

"I don't think so," said I; "after braving a thousand tempests, it was meeter for it to fall of itself than to be vanquished at last. But to return to Ab Gwilym's poetry, he was above culling dainty words, and spoke boldly his mind on all subjects. Enraged with the thunder for parting him and Morfydd, he says, at the conclusion of his ode:—

'My curse, O Thunder, cling to thee,
For parting my dear pearl and me.' "

"You and I shall part; that is, I shall go to my tent if you persist in repeating from him. The man must have been a savage. A poor wood-pigeon has fallen dead."

"Yes," said I, "there he lies just outside the tent; often have I listened to his note when alone in this wilderness. So you do not like Ab Gwilym; what say you to old Goethe:—

'Mist shrouds the night, and rack;
Hear, in the woods, what an awful crack!
Wildly the owls are flitting,
Hark to the pillars splitting
Of palaces verdant ever,
The branches quiver and sever.

The mighty stems are creaking,
The poor roots breaking and shrieking,
In wild mixt ruin down dashing,
O'er one another they're crashing;
Whilst 'midst the rocks so hoary,
Whirlwinds hurry and worry,
Hear'st not, sister——' "

"Hark!" said Belle, "hark!"

" 'Hear'st not, sister, a chorus
Of voices——?' "

"No," said Belle, "but I hear a voice."

I listened attentively, but I could hear nothing but the loud clashing of branches, the pattering of rain, and the muttered growl of thunder. I was about to tell Belle that she must have been mistaken, when I heard a shout, indistinct it is true, owing to the noises aforesaid, from some part of the field above the dingle. "I will soon see what's the matter," said I to Belle, starting up. "I will go, too," said the girl. "Stay where you are," said I; "if

I need you, I will call"; and, without waiting for any answer, I hurried to the mouth of the dingle. I was about a few yards only from the top of the ascent, when I beheld a blaze of light, from whence I know not; the next moment there was a loud crash, and I appeared involved in a cloud of sulphurous smoke. "Lord have mercy upon us," I heard a voice say, and methought I heard the plunging and struggling of horses. I had stopped short on hearing the crash, for I was half stunned; but I now hurried forward, and in a moment stood upon the plain. Here I was instantly aware of the cause of the crash and the smoke. One of those balls, generally called fire-balls, had fallen from the clouds, and was burning on the plain at a short distance; and the voice which I had heard, and the plunging, were as easily accounted for. Near the left-hand corner of the grove which surrounded the dingle, and about ten yards from the fire-ball, I perceived a chaise, with a postillion on the box, who was making efforts, apparently useless, to control his horses, which were kicking and plunging in the highest degree of excitement. I instantly ran towards the chaise, in order to offer what help was in my power. "Help me," said the poor fellow, as I drew nigh; but, before I could reach the horses, they had turned rapidly round, one of the fore-wheels flew from its axle-tree, the chaise was overset, and the postillion flung violently from his seat upon the field. The horses now became more furious than before, kicking desperately, and endeavouring to disengage themselves from the fallen chaise. As I was hesitating whether to run to the assistance of the postillion, or endeavour to disengage the animals, I heard the voice of Belle exclaiming: "See to the horses, I will look after the man." She had, it seems, been alarmed by the crash which accompanied the fire-bolt, and had hurried up to learn the cause. I forthwith seized the horses by the heads, and used all the means I possessed to soothe and pacify them, employing every gentle modulation of which my voice was capable. Belle, in the meantime, had raised up the man, who was much stunned by his fall; but presently recovering his recollection to a certain degree, he came limping to me, holding his hand to his right thigh. "The first thing that must now be done," said I, "is to free these horses from the traces; can you undertake to do so?" "I think I can," said the man, looking at me somewhat stupidly. "I will help," said Belle, and without loss of time laid hold of one of the traces. The man, after a short pause, also set to work, and in a few minutes the horses were extricated. "Now," said I to the man, "what is next to be done?" "I don't know," said he; "indeed, I scarcely know anything; I have been so frightened by this horrible storm, and so shaken by my fall." "I think," said I, "that the storm is passing away, so cast your fears away too; and as for your fall, you must bear it as lightly as you can. I will tie the horses amongst those trees, and then we will all betake us to the hollow below." "And what's to become of my chaise?" said the postillion, looking ruefully on the fallen vehicle. "Let us leave the chaise for the present," said I; "we can be of no use to it." "I don't like to leave my chaise lying on the ground in this weather," said the man; "I love my chaise, and him whom it belongs to." "You are quite right to be fond of yourself," said I, "on which account I advise you to seek shelter from the rain as soon as possible." "I was not talking of myself," said the man, "but my master, to whom the chaise belongs." "I thought you called the chaise yours," said I. "That's my way of speaking," said the man; "but the chaise is my master's, and a better master does not live. Don't you think we could manage to raise up the chaise?" "And what is to become of the horses?" said I. "I love my horses well enough," said the man; "but they will take less harm than the chaise. We two can never lift up that chaise." "But we three can," said Belle; "at least, I think so; and I know where to find two poles which will assist us." "You had better go to the tent," said I, "you will be wet through." "I care not for a little wetting," said Belle; "moreover, I have more gowns than one—see you after the horses." Thereupon, I led the horses past the mouth of the dingle, to a place where a gap in the hedge afforded admission to the copse or plantation, on the southern side. Forcing them through the gap, I led them to a spot amidst the trees, which I deemed would afford them the most convenient place for standing; then, darting down into the dingle, I brought up a rope, and also the halter of my own nag, and with these fastened them each to a separate tree in the best manner I could. This done, I returned to the chaise and the postillion. In a minute or two Belle arrived with two poles, which, it seems, had long been lying, overgrown with brushwood, in a ditch or hollow behind the plantation. With these both she and I set to work in endeavouring to raise the fallen chaise from the ground.

We experienced considerable difficulty in this undertaking; at length, with the assistance of the postillion, we saw our efforts crowned with success—the chaise was lifted up, and stood upright on three wheels.

"We may leave it here in safety," said I, "for it will hardly move away on three wheels, even supposing it could run by itself; I am afraid there is work here for a wheelwright, in which case I cannot assist you; if you were in need of a blacksmith it would be otherwise." "I don't think either the wheel or the axle is hurt," said the postillion, who had been handling both; "it is only the linch-pin having dropped out that caused the wheel to fly off; if I could but find the linch-pin! though, perhaps, it fell out a mile away." "Very likely," said I; "but never mind the linch-pin, I can make you one, or something that will serve: but I can't stay here any longer, I am going to my place below with this young gentlewoman, and you had better follow us." "I am ready," said the man; and after lifting up the wheel and propping it against the chaise, he went with us, slightly limping, and with his hand pressed to his thigh.

As we were descending the narrow path, Belle leading the way, and myself the last of the party, the postillion suddenly stopped short, and looked about him. "Why do you stop?" said I. "I don't wish to offend you," said the man, "but this seems to be a strange place you are leading me into; I hope you and the young gentlewoman, as you call her, don't mean me any harm—you seemed in a great hurry to bring me here." "We wished to get you out of the rain," said I, "and ourselves too; that is, if we can, which I rather doubt, for the canvas of a tent is slight shelter in such a rain; but what harm should we wish to do you?" "You may think I have money," said the man, "and I have some, but only thirty shillings, and for a sum like that it would be hardly worth while to—" "Would it not?" said I; "thirty shillings, after all, are thirty shillings, and for what I know, half a dozen throats may have been cut in this place for that sum at the rate of five shillings each; moreover, there are the horses, which would serve to establish this young gentlewoman and myself in housekeeping, provided we were thinking of such a thing." "Then I suppose I have fallen into pretty hands," said the man, putting himself in a posture of defence; "but I'll show no craven heart; and if you attempt to lay hands on me, I'll try to pay you in your own coin. I'm rather lamed in the leg, but I can still use my fists; so come on both of you, man and woman, if woman this be, though she looks more like a grenadier."

"Let me hear no more of this nonsense," said Belle; "if you are afraid, you can go back to your chaise—we only seek to do you a kindness."

"Why, he was just now talking of cutting throats," said the man. "You brought it on yourself," said Belle; "you suspected us, and he wished to pass a joke upon you; he would not hurt a hair of your head, were your coach laden with gold, nor would I." "Well," said the man, "I was wrong—here's my hand to both of you," shaking us by the hands; "I'll go with you where you please, but I thought this a strange, lonesome place, though I ought not much to mind strange, lonesome places, having been in plenty of such when I was a servant in Italy, without coming to any harm—come, let us move on, for 'tis a shame to keep you two in the rain."

So we descended the path which led into the depths of the dingle; at the bottom I conducted the postillion to my tent, which, though the rain dripped and trickled through it, afforded some shelter; there I bade him sit down on the log of wood, while I placed myself as usual on my stone. Belle in the meantime had repaired to her own place of abode. After a little time, I produced a bottle of the cordial of which I have previously had occasion to speak, and made my guest take a considerable draught. I then offered him some bread and cheese, which he accepted with thanks. In about an hour the rain had much abated: "What do you now propose to do?" said I. "I scarcely know," said the man; "I suppose I must endeavour to put on the wheel with your help." "How far are you from your home?" I demanded. "Upwards of thirty miles," said the man; "my master keeps an inn on the great north road, and from thence I started early this morning with a family which I conveyed across the country to a hall at some distance from here. On my return I was beset by the thunderstorm, which frightened the horses, who dragged the chaise off the road to the field above, and overset it as you saw. I had proposed to pass the night at an inn about twelve miles from here on my way back, though how I am to get there to-night I scarcely know, even if we can put on the wheel, for, to tell you the truth,

I am shaken by my fall, and the smoulder and smoke of that fire-ball have rather bewildered my head; I am, moreover, not much acquainted with the way."

"The best thing you can do," said I, "is to pass the night here; I will presently light a fire, and endeavour to make you comfortable—in the morning we will see to your wheel." "Well," said the man, "I shall be glad to pass the night here, provided I do not intrude, but I must see to the horses." Thereupon I conducted the man to the place where the horses were tied. "The trees drip very much upon them," said the man, "and it will not do for them to remain here all night; they will be better out on the field picking the grass, but first of all they must have a good feed of corn"; thereupon he went to his chaise, from which he presently brought two small bags, partly filled with corn; into them he inserted the mouths of the horses, tying them over their heads. "Here we will leave them for a time," said the man; "when I think they have had enough, I will come back, tie their fore-legs, and let them pick about."

CHAPTER XXXVII

It might be about ten o'clock at night. Belle, the postillion, and myself, sat just within the tent, by a fire of charcoal which I had kindled in the chafing-pan. The man had removed the harness from his horses, and, after tethering their legs, had left them for the night in the field above, to regale themselves on what grass they could find. The rain had long since entirely ceased, and the moon and stars shone bright in the firmament, up to which, putting aside the canvas, I occasionally looked from the depths of the dingle. Large drops of water, however, falling now and then upon the tent from the neighbouring trees, would have served, could we have forgotten it, to remind us of the recent storm, and also a certain chilliness in the atmosphere, unusual to the season, proceeding from the moisture with which the ground was saturated; yet these circumstances only served to make our party enjoy the charcoal fire the more. There we sat bending over it: Belle, with her long beautiful hair streaming over her magnificent shoulders; the postillion smoking his pipe, in his shirt-sleeves and waistcoat, having flung aside his greatcoat, which had sustained a thorough wetting; and I without my wagoner's slop, of which, it being in the same plight, I had also divested myself.

The new comer was a well-made fellow of about thirty, with an open and agreeable countenance. I found him very well informed for a man in his station, and with some pretensions to humour. After we had discoursed for some time on indifferent subjects, the postillion, who had exhausted his pipe, took it from his mouth, and, knocking out the ashes upon the ground, exclaimed: "I little thought, when I got up in the morning, that I should spend the night in such agreeable company, and after such a fright."

"Well," said I, "I am glad that your opinion of us has improved; it is not long since you seemed to hold us in rather a suspicious light."

"And no wonder," said the man, "seeing the place you were taking me to. I was not a little, but very much afraid of ye both; and so I continued for some time, though, not to show a craven heart, I pretended to be quite satisfied; but I see I was altogether mistaken about ye. I thought you vagrant gypsy folks and trampers; but now——"

"Vagrant gypsy folks and trampers," said I; "and what are we but people of that stamp?"

"Oh," said the postillion, "if you wish to be thought such, I am far too civil a person to contradict you, especially after your kindness to me, but——"

"But!" said I; "what do you mean by but? I would have you to know that I am proud of being a travelling blacksmith: look at these donkey-shoes, I finished them this day."

The postillion took the shoes and examined them. "So you made these shoes?" he cried at last.

"To be sure I did; do you doubt it?"

"Not in the least," said the man.

"Ah! ah!" said I, "I thought I should bring you back to your original opinion. I am, then, a vagrant gypsy body, a tramper, a wandering blacksmith."

"Not a blacksmith, whatever else you may be," said the postillion laughing.

"Then how do you account for my making those shoes?"

"By your not being a blacksmith," said the postillion; "no blacksmith would have made shoes in that manner. Besides, what did you mean just now by saying you had finished these shoes to-day? A real blacksmith would have flung off three or four sets of donkey-shoes in one morning, but you, I will be sworn, have been hammering at these for days, and they do you credit, but why? because you are no blacksmith; no, friend, your shoes may do for this young gentlewoman's animal, but I shouldn't like to have my horses shod by you, unless at a great pinch indeed."

"Then," said I, "for what do you take me?"

"Why, for some runaway young gentleman," said the postillion. "No offence, I hope?"

"None at all; no one is offended at being taken or mistaken for a young gentleman, whether runaway or not; but from whence do you suppose I have run away?"

"Why, from college," said the man: "no offence?"

"None whatever; and what induced me to run away from college?"

"A love affair, I'll be sworn," said the postillion. "You had become acquainted with this young gentlewoman, so she and you——"

"Mind how you get on, friend," said Belle, in a deep serious tone.

"Pray proceed," said I; "I dare say you mean no offence."

"None in the world," said the postillion; "all I was going to say was that you agreed to run away together, you from college, and she from boarding-school. Well, there's nothing to be ashamed of in a matter like that, such things are done every day by young folks in high life."

"Are you offended?" said I to Belle.

Belle made no answer; but, placing her elbows on her knees buried her face in her hands.

"So we ran away together?" said I.

"Ay, ay," said the postillion, "to Gretna Green, though I can't say that I drove ye, though I have driven many a pair."

"And from Gretna Green we came here?"

"I'll be bound you did," said the man, "till you could arrange matters at home."

"And the horse-shoes?" said I.

"The donkey-shoes, you mean," answered the postillion; "why, I suppose you persuaded the blacksmith who married you to give you, before you left, a few lessons in his trade."

"And we intend to stay here till we have arranged matters at home?"

"Ay, ay," said the postillion, "till the old people are pacified and they send you letters directed to the next post town, to be left till called for, beginning with, 'Dear children,' and enclosing you each a cheque for one hundred pounds, when you will leave this place, and go home in a coach like gentlefolks, to visit your governors; I should like nothing better than to have the driving of you: and then there will be a grand meeting of the two families, and after a few reproaches, the old people will agree to do something handsome for the poor thoughtless things; so you will have a genteel house taken for you, and an annuity allowed you. You won't get much the first year, five hundred at the most, in order that the old folks may let you feel that they are not altogether satisfied with you, and that you are yet entirely in their power; but the second, if you don't get a cool thousand, may I catch cold, especially should young madam here present a son and heir for the old people to fondle, destined one day to become sole heir of the two illustrious houses, and then all the grand folks in the neighbourhood, who have, bless their prudent hearts! kept rather aloof from you till then, for fear you should want anything from them—I say, all the carriage people in the neighbourhood, when they see how swimmingly matters are going on, will come in shoals to visit you."

"Really," said I, "you are getting on swimmingly."

"Oh," said the postillion, "I was not a gentleman's servant nine years without learning the ways of gentry, and being able to know gentry when I see them."

"And what do you say to all this?" I demanded of Belle.

"Stop a moment," interposed the postillion, "I have one more word to say:

and when you are surrounded by your comforts, keeping your nice little barouche and pair, your coachman and livery servant, and visited by all the carriage people in the neighbourhood—to say nothing of the time when you come to the family estates on the death of the old people—I shouldn't wonder if now and then you look back with longing and regret to the days when you lived in the damp, dripping dingle, had no better equipage than a pony or donkey-cart, and saw no better company than a tramper or gypsy, except once, when a poor postillion was glad to seat himself at your charcoal fire."

"Pray," said I, "did you ever take lessons in elocution?"

"Not directly," said the postillion; "but my old master who was in Parliament, did, and so did his son, who was intended to be an orator. A great professor used to come and give them lessons, and I used to stand and listen, by which means I picked up a considerable quantity of what is called rhetoric. In what I last said, I was aiming at what I have heard him frequently endeavouring to teach my governors as a thing indispensably necessary in all oratory, a graceful pere—pere—peregrination."

"Peroration, perhaps?"

"Just so," said the postillion; "and now I am sure I am not mistaken about you; you have taken lessons yourself, at first hand, in the college vacations, and a promising pupil you were, I make no doubt. Well, your friends will be all the happier to get you back. Has your governor much borough interest?"

"I ask you once more," said I, addressing myself to Belle, "what do you think of the history which this good man has made for us?"

"What should I think of it," said Belle, still keeping her face buried in her hands, "but that it is mere nonsense?"

"Nonsense!" said the postillion.

"Yes," said the girl, "and you know it."

"May my leg always ache, if I do," said the postillion, patting his leg with his hand; "will you persuade me that this young man has never been at college?"

"I have never been at college, but——"

"Ay, ay," said the postillion; "but——"

"I have been to the best schools in Britain, to say nothing of a celebrated one in Ireland."

"Well, then, it comes to the same thing," said the postillion, "or perhaps you know more than if you had been at college—and your governor?"

"My governor, as you call him," said I, "is dead."

"And his borough interest?"

"My father had no borough interest," said I; "had he possessed any, he would perhaps not have died as he did, honourably poor."

"No, no," said the postillion; "if he had had borough interest, he wouldn't have been poor, nor honourable, though perhaps a right honourable. However, with your grand education and genteel manners, you made all right at last by persuading this noble young gentlewoman to run away from boarding-school with you."

"I was never at boarding-school," said Belle, "unless you call——"

"Ay, ay," said the postillion, "boarding-school is vulgar, I know: I beg your pardon, I ought to have called it academy, or by some other much finer name—you were in something much greater than a boarding-school."

"There you are right," said Belle, lifting up her head and looking the postillion full in the face by the light of the charcoal fire; "for I was bred in the workhouse."

"Wooh!" said the postillion.

"It is true that I am of good——"

"Ay, ay," said the postillion, "let us hear——"

"Of good blood," continued Belle; "my name is Berners, Isopel Berners, though my parents were unfortunate. Indeed, with respect to blood, I believe I am of better blood than the young man."

"There you are mistaken," said I; "by my father's side I am of Cornish blood, and by my mother's of brave French Protestant extraction. Now, with respect to the blood of my father—and to be descended well on the father's side is the principal thing—it is the best blood in the world, for the Cornish blood, as the proverb says——"

"I don't care what the proverb says," said Belle; "I say my blood is the best—my name is Berners, Isopel Berners—it was my mother's name, and is better, I am sure, than any you bear, whatever that may be; and though you say that the descent on the father's side is the principal thing—and I know why you say so," she added with some excitement—"I say that descent on the mother's side is of most account, because the mother——"

"Just come from Gretna Green, and already quarrelling," said the postillion.

"We do not come from Gretna Green," said Belle.

"Ah, I had forgot," said the postillion, "none but great people go to Gretna Green. Well, then, from church, and already quarrelling about family, just like two great people."

"We have never been to church," said Belle, "and, to prevent any more guessing on your part, it will be as well for me to tell you, friend, that I am nothing to the young man, and he, of course, nothing to me. I am a poor travelling girl, born in a workhouse: journeying on my occasions with certain companions, I came to this hollow, where my company quarrelled with the young man, who had settled down here, as he had a right to do, if he pleased; and not being able to drive him out, they went away after quarrelling with me, too, for not choosing to side with them; so I stayed here along with the young man, there being room for us both, and the place being as free to me as to him."

"And, in order that you may be no longer puzzled with respect to myself," said I, "I will give you a brief outline of my history. I am the son of honourable parents, who gave me a first-rate education, as far as literature and languages went, with which education I endeavoured, on the death of my father, to advance myself to wealth and reputation in the big city; but failing in the attempt, I conceived a disgust for the busy world, and determined to retire from it. After wandering about for some time, and meeting with various adventures, in one of which I contrived to obtain a pony, cart and certain tools, used by smiths and tinkers, I came to this place, where I amused myself with making horse-shoes, or rather pony-shoes, having acquired the art of wielding the hammer and tongs from a strange kind of smith—not him of Gretna Green—whom I knew in my childhood. And here I lived, doing harm to no one, quite lonely and solitary, till one fine morning the premises were visited by this young gentlewoman and her companions. She did herself anything but justice when she said that her companions quarrelled with her because she would not side with them against me; they quarrelled with her, because she came most heroically to my assistance as I was on the point of being murdered; and she forgot to tell you, that after they had abandoned her she stood by me in the dark hour, comforting and cheering me, when unspeakable dread, to which I am occasionally subject, took possession of my mind. She says she is nothing to me, even as I am nothing to her. I am of course nothing to her, but she is mistaken in thinking she is nothing to me. I entertain the highest regard and admiration for her, being convinced that I might search the whole world in vain for a nature more heroic and devoted."

"And for my part," said Belle, with a sob, "a more quiet, agreeable partner in a place like this I would not wish to have; it is true he has strange ways, and frequently puts words into my mouth very difficult to utter; but —but—" and here she buried her face once more in her hands.

"Well," said the postillion, "I have been mistaken about you; that is, not altogether, but in part. You are not rich folks, it seems, but you are not common people, and that I could have sworn. What I call a shame is, that some people I have known are not in your place and you in theirs—you with their estates and borough interest, they in this dingle with these carts and animals; but there is no help for these things. Were I the great Mumbo Jumbo above, I would endeavour to manage matters better; but being a simple postillion, glad to earn three shillings a day, I can't be expected to do much."

"Who is Mumbo Jumbo?" said I.

"Ah!" said the postillion, "I see there may be a thing or two I know better than yourself. Mumbo Jumbo is a god of the black coast, to which people go for ivory and gold."

"Were you ever there?" I demanded.

"No," said the postillion, "but I heard plenty of Mumbo Jumbo when I was a boy."

I awoke at the first break of day, and, leaving the postillion fast asleep, stepped out of the tent. The dingle was dank and dripping. I lighted a fire of coals, and got my forge in readiness. I then ascended to the field, where the chaise was standing as we had left it on the previous evening. After looking at the cloud-stone near it, now cold, and split into three pieces, I set about prying narrowly into the condition of the wheel and axle-tree—the latter had sustained no damage of any consequence, and the wheel, as far as I was able to judge, was sound, being only slightly injured in the box. The only thing requisite to set the chaise in a travelling condition appeared to be a linch-pin, which I determined to make. Going to the companion wheel, I took out the linch-pin, which I carried down with me to the dingle, to serve as a model.

I found Belle by this time dressed, and seated near the forge: with a slight nod to her like that which a person gives who happens to see an acquaintance when his mind is occupied with important business, I forthwith set about my work. Selecting a piece of iron which I thought would serve my purpose, I placed it in the fire, and plying the bellows in a furious manner, soon made it hot; then seizing it with the tongs, I laid it on my anvil, and began to beat it with my hammer, according to the rules of my art. The dingle resounded with my strokes. Belle sat still, and occasionally smiled, but suddenly started up, and retreated towards her encampment, on a spark which I purposely sent in her direction alighting on her knee. I found the making of a linch-pin no easy matter; it was, however, less difficult than the fabrication of a pony-shoe; my work, indeed, was much facilitated by my having another pin to look at. In about three-quarters of an hour I had succeeded tolerably well, and had produced a linch-pin which I thought would serve. During all this time, notwithstanding the noise which I was making, the postillion never showed his face. His non-appearance at first alarmed me: I was afraid he might be dead, but, on looking into the tent, I found him still buried in the soundest sleep. "He must surely be descended from one of the seven sleepers," said I, as I turned away, and resumed my work. My work finished, I took a little oil, leather, and sand, and polished the pin as well as I could; then, summoning Belle, we both went to the chaise, where, with her assistance, I put on the wheel. The linch-pin which I had made fitted its place very well, and having replaced the other, I gazed at the chaise for some time with my heart full of that satisfaction which results from the consciousness of having achieved a great action; then, after looking at Belle in the hope of obtaining a compliment from her lips, which did not come, I returned to the dingle, without saying a word, followed by her.

Belle set about making preparations for breakfast; and I taking the kettle, went and filled it at the spring. Having hung it over the fire, I went to the tent in which the postillion was still sleeping, and called upon him to arise. He awoke with a start, and stared around him at first with the utmost surprise, not unmixed, I could observe, with a certain degree of fear. At last, looking in my face, he appeared to recollect himself. "I had quite forgot," said he, as he got up, "where I was, and all that happened yesterday. However, I remember now the whole affair, thunder-storm, thunder-bolt, frightened horses, and all your kindness. Come, I must see after my coach and horses; I hope we shall be able to repair the damage." "The damage is already quite repaired," said I, "as you will see, if you come to the field above." "You don't say so," said the postillion, coming out of the tent; "well, I am mightily beholden to you. Good morning, young gentlewoman," said he, addressing Belle, who, having finished her preparations, was seated near the fire. "Good morning, young man," said Belle, "I suppose you would be glad of some breakfast; however, you must wait a little, the kettle does not boil." "Come and look at your chaise," said I; "but tell me how it happened that the noise which I have been making did not awake you; for three-quarters of an hour at least I was hammering close at your ear." "I heard you all the time," said the postillion, "but your hammering made me sleep all the sounder; I am used to hear hammering in my morning sleep. There's a forge close by the room where I sleep when I'm at home, at my inn; for we have all kinds of conveniences at my inn—forge, carpenter's shop, and wheelwright's—so that when I heard you hammering I thought, no doubt, that it was the old noise, and that I was comfortable in my bed at my own inn."

We now ascended to the field, where I showed the postillion his chaise. He looked at the pin attentively, rubbed his hands, and gave a loud laugh. "Is it not well done?" said I. "It will do till I get home," he replied. "And that is all you have to say?" I demanded. "And that's a good deal," said he, "considering who made it. But don't be offended," he added, "I shall prize it all the more for its being made by a gentleman, and no blacksmith; and so will my governor, when I show it to him. I shan't let it remain where it is, but will keep it, as a remembrance of you, as long as I live." He then again rubbed his hands with great glee, and said, "I will now go and see after my horses, and then to breakfast, partner, if you please." Suddenly, however, looking at his hands, he said, "Before sitting down to breakfast I am in the habit of washing my hands and face: I suppose you could not furnish me with a little soap and water." "As much water as you please," said I, "but if you want soap, I must go and trouble the young gentlewoman for some." "By no means," said the postillion, "water will do at a pinch."

"Follow me," said I, and leading him to the pond of the frogs and newts, I said, "this is my ewer; you are welcome to part of it—the water is so soft that it is scarcely necessary to add soap to it"; then lying down on the bank, I plunged my head into the water, then scrubbed my hands and face, and afterwards wiped them with some long grass which grew on the margin of the pond. "Bravo," said the postillion, "I see you know how to make a shift:" he then followed my example, declared he never felt more refreshed in his life, and, giving a bound, said, "he would go and look after his horses."

We then went to look after the horses, which we found not much the worse for having spent the night in the open air. My companion again inserted their heads in the corn-bags, and, leaving the animals to discuss their corn, returned with me to the dingle, where we found the kettle boiling. We sat down, and Belle made tea and did the honours of the meal. The postillion was in high spirits, ate heartily, and, to Belle's evident satisfaction, declared that he had never drank better tea in his life, or indeed any half so good. Breakfast over, he said that he must go now and harness his horses, as it was high time for him to return to his inn. Belle gave him her hand and wished him farewell: the postillion shook her hand warmly, and was advancing close up to her—for what purpose I cannot say—whereupon Belle, withdrawing her hand, drew herself up with an air which caused the postillion to retreat a step or two with an exceedingly sheepish look. Recovering himself, however, he made a low bow, and proceeded up the path. I attended him, and helped to harness his horses and put them to the vehicle; he then shook me by the hand, and taking the reins and whip mounted to his seat; ere he drove away he thus addressed me: "If ever I forget your kindness and that of the young woman below, dash my buttons. If ever either of you should enter my inn you may depend upon a warm welcome, the best that can be set before you, and no expense to either, for I will give both of you the best of characters to the governor, who is the very best fellow upon all the road. As for your linch-pin, I trust it will serve till I get home, when I will take it out and keep it in remembrance of you all the days of my life"; then giving the horses a jerk with his reins, he cracked his whip and drove off.

I returned to the dingle, Belle had removed the breakfast things. and was busy in her own encampment: nothing occurred, worthy of being related, for two hours, at the end of which time Belle departed on a short expedition, and I again found myself alone in the dingle.

CHAPTER XXXVIII

On the following morning, as I was about to leave my tent, I heard the voice of Belle at the door, exclaiming, "Sleepest thou, or wakest thou?" "I was never more awake in my life," said I, going out. "What is the matter?" "He of the horse-shoe," said she, "Jasper, of whom I have heard you talk, is above there on the field with all his people; I went out about a quarter of an hour ago to fill the kettle at the spring, and saw them arriving." "It is well," said I; "have you any objection to asking him and his wife to breakfast?" "You can do as you please," said she; "I have cups enough, and have no objection to their company." "We are the first occupiers of the ground," said I, "and, being so, should consider ourselves in the light of hosts, and do our best to practise the duties of hospitality." "How fond you are of using that word," said Belle; "if you wish to invite the man and his wife, do so, without more ado; remember, however, that I have not cups enough, nor indeed tea enough, for the whole company." Thereupon hurrying up the ascent, I presently found myself outside the dingle. It was as usual a brilliant morning, the dewy blades of the rye-grass which covered the plain sparkled brightly in the beams of the sun, which had probably been about two hours above the horizon. A rather numerous body of my ancient friends and allies occupied the ground in the vicinity of the mouth of the dingle. About five yards on the right I perceived Mr. Petulengro busily employed in erecting his tent; he held in his hand an iron bar, sharp at the bottom, with a kind of arm projecting from the top for the purpose of supporting a kettle or cauldron over the fire, and which is called in the Romanian language "Kekauviskoe saster." With the sharp end of this Mr. Petulengro was making holes in the earth, at about twenty inches distant from each other, into which he inserted certain long rods with a considerable bend towards the top, which constituted no less than the timber of the tent, and the supporters of the canvas. Mrs. Petulengro, and a female with a crutch in her hand, whom I recognised as Mrs. Chikno, sat near him on the ground, whilst two or three children, from six to ten years old, who composed the young family of Mr. and Mrs. Petulengro, were playing about.

"Here we are, brother," said Mr. Petulengro, as he drove the sharp end of the bar into the ground; "here we are, and plenty of us—Bute dosta Romany chals."

"I am glad to see you all," said I; "and particularly you, madam," said I, making a bow to Mrs. Petulengro; "and you also, madam," taking off my hat to Mrs. Chikno.

"Good-day to you, sir," said Mrs. Petulengro; "you look, as usual, charmingly, and speak so, too; you have not forgot your manners."

"It is not all gold that glitters," said Mrs. Chikno. "However, good-morrow to you, young rye."

"I do not see Tawno," said I, looking around; "where is he?"

"Where, indeed!" said Mrs. Chikno; "I don't know; he who countenances him in the roving line can best answer."

"He will be here anon," said Mr. Petulengro; "he has merely ridden down a by-road to show a farmer a two-year-old colt; she heard me give him directions, but she can't be satisfied."

"I can't indeed," said Mrs. Chikno.

"And why not, sister?"

"Because I place no confidence in your words, brother; as I said before, you countenances him."

"Well," said I, "I know nothing of your private concerns; I am come on an errand. Isopel Berners, down in the dell there, requests the pleasure of Mr. and Mrs. Petulengro's company at breakfast. She will be happy also to see you, madam," said I, addressing Mrs. Chikno.

"Is that young female your wife, young man?" said Mrs. Chikno.

"My wife?" said I.

"Yes, young man; your wife, your lawful certificated wife?"

"No," said I; "she is not my wife."

"Then I will not visit with her," said Mrs. Chikno; "I countenance nothing in the roving line."

"What do you mean by the roving line?" I demanded.

"What do I mean by the roving line? Why, by it I mean such conduct as is not tatcheno. When ryes and rawnies live together in dingles, without being certificated, I call such behaviour being tolerably deep in the roving line, everything savouring of which I am determined not to sanctify. I have suffered too much by my own certificated husband's outbreaks in that line to afford anything of the kind the slightest shadow of countenance."

"It is hard that people may not live in dingles together without being suspected of doing wrong," said I.

"So it is," said Mrs. Petulengro, interposing; "and, to tell you the truth, I am altogether surprised at the illiberality of my sister's remarks. I have often heard say, that it is in good company—and I have kept good company in my time—that suspicion is king's evidence of a narrow and uncultivated mind; on which account I am suspicious of nobody, not even of my own husband, whom some people would think I have a right to be suspicious of, seeing that on his account I once refused a lord; but ask him whether I am suspicious of him, and whether I seek to keep him close tied to my apron-string; he will tell you nothing of the kind; but that, on the contrary, I always allows him an agreeable latitude, permitting him to go where he pleases, and to converse with any one to whose manner of speaking he may take a fancy. But I have had the advantage of keeping good company, and therefore——"

"Meklis," said Mrs. Chikno, "pray drop all that, sister; I believe I have kept as good company as yourself; and with respect to that offer with which you frequently fatigue those who keeps company with you, I believe, after all, it was something in the roving and uncertificated line."

"In whatever line it was," said Mrs. Petulengro, "the offer was a good one. The young duke—for he was not only a lord, but a duke too—offered to keep me a fine carriage, and to make me his second wife; for it is true that he had another who was old and stout, though mighty rich, and highly good-natured; so much so, indeed, that the young lord assured me that she would have no manner of objection to the arrangement; more especially if I would consent to live in the same house with her, being fond of young and cheerful society. So you see——"

"Yes, yes," said Mrs. Chikno, "I see, what I before thought, that it was altogether in the uncertificated line."

"Meklis," said Mrs. Petulengro; "I use your own word, madam, which is Romany: for my own part, I am not fond of using Romany words, unless I can hope to pass them off for French, which I cannot in the present company. I heartily wish that there was no such language, and do my best to keep it away from my children, lest the frequent use of it should altogether confirm them in low and vulgar habits. I have four children, madam, but——"

"I suppose by talking of your four children you wish to check me for having none," said Mrs. Chikno, bursting into tears; "if I have no children, sister, it is no fault of mine, it is—but why do I call you sister?" said she, angrily; "you are no sister of mine, you are a grasni, a regular mare—a pretty sister, indeed, ashamed of your own language. I remember well that by your high-flying notions you drove your own mother——"

"We will drop it," said Mrs. Petulengro; "I do not wish to raise my voice, and to make myself ridiculous. Young gentleman," said she, "pray present my compliments to Miss Isopel Berners, and inform her that I am very sorry that I cannot accept her polite invitation. I am just arrived, and have some slight domestic matters to see to—amongst others, to wash my children's faces; but that in the course of the forenoon, when I have attended to what I have to do, and have dressed myself, I hope to do myself the honour of paying her a regular visit; you will tell her that, with my compliments. With respect to my husband he can answer for himself, as I, not being of a jealous disposition, never interferes with his matters."

"And tell Miss Berners," said Mr. Petulengro, "that I shall be happy to wait upon her in company with my wife as soon as we are regularly settled: at present I have much on my hands, having not only to pitch my own tent, but this here jealous woman's, whose husband is absent on my business."

Thereupon I returned to the dingle, and, without saying anything about Mrs. Chikno's observations, communicated to Isopel the messages of Mr. and Mrs. Petulengro; Isopel made no other reply than by replacing in her coffer two additional cups and saucers, which, in expectation of company, she had placed upon the board. The kettle was by this time boiling. We sat down, and, as we breakfasted, I gave Isopel Berners another lesson in the Armenian language.

About mid-day Mr. and Mrs. Petulengro came to the dingle to pay the promised visit. Belle, at the time of their arrival, was in her tent, but I was at the fire-place, engaged in hammering part of the outer-tire, or defence, which had come off from one of the wheels of my vehicle. On perceiving them I forthwith went to receive them. Mr. Petulengro was dressed in Roman fashion, with a somewhat smartly-cut sporting-coat, the buttons of which were half-crowns—and a waistcoat, scarlet and black, the buttons of which were spaded half-guineas; his breeches were of a stuff half velveteen, half corduroy, the cords exceedingly broad. He had leggings of buff cloth, furred at the bottom; and upon his feet were highlows. Under his left arm was a long black whalebone riding-whip, with a red lash, and an immense silver knob. Upon his head was a hat with a high peak, somewhat of the kind which the Spaniards call *calané*, so much in favour with the bravos of Seville and Madrid. Now, when I have added that Mr. Petulengro had on a very fine white holland shirt, I think I have described his array. Mrs. Petulengro—I beg pardon for not having spoken of her first—was also arrayed very much in the Roman fashion. Her hair, which was exceedingly black and lustrous, fell in braids on either side of her head. In her ears were rings, with long drops of gold. Round her neck was a string of what seemed very much like very large pearls, somewhat tarnished, however, and apparently of considerable antiquity. "Here we are, brother," said Mr. Petulengro; "here we are, come to see you—wizard and witch, witch and wizard:—

'There's a chovahanee, and a chovahano,
The nav se len is Petulengro.' "

"Hold your tongue, sir," said Mrs. Petulengro; "you make me ashamed of you with your vulgar ditties. We are come a visiting now, and everything low should be left behind."

"True," said Mr. Petulengro; "why bring what's low to the dingle, which is low enough already?"

"What, are you a catcher at words?" said I. "I thought that catching at words had been confined to the pothouse farmers and village witty bodies."

"All fools," said Mrs. Petulengro, "catch at words, and very naturally, as by so doing they hope to prevent the possibility of rational conversation. Catching at words confined to pothouse farmers. and village witty bodies! No, not to Jasper Petulengro. Listen for an hour or two to the discourse of a set they call newspaper editors, and if you don't go out and eat grass, as a dog does when he is sick, I am no female woman. The young lord whose hand I refused when I took up with wise Jasper, once brought two of them to my mother's tan, when hankering after my company; they did nothing but carp at each other's words, and a pretty hand they made of it. Ill-favoured dogs they were; and their attempts at what they called wit almost as unfortunate as their countenances."

"Well," said I, "madam, we will drop all catchings and carpings for the present. Pray take your seat on this stool, whilst I go and announce to Miss Isopel Berners your arrival."

Thereupon I went to Belle's habitation, and informed her that Mr. and Mrs. Petulengro had paid us a visit of ceremony, and were awaiting her at the fire-place. "Pray go and tell them that I am busy," said Belle, who was engaged with her needle. "I do not feel disposed to take part in any such nonsense." "I shall do no such thing," said I; "and I insist upon your coming forthwith, and showing proper courtesy to your visitors. If you do not, their feelings will be hurt, and you are aware that I cannot bear that people's feelings should be outraged. Come this moment, or——" "Or what?" said Belle, half smiling. "I was about to say something in Armenian," said I. "Well," said Belle, laying down her work, "I will come." "Stay," said I; "your hair is hanging about your ears, and your dress is in disorder; you had better stay a minute or two to prepare yourself to appear before your visitors, who have come in their very best attire." "No," said Belle, "I will make no alteration in my appearance; you told me to come this moment, and you shall be obeyed." So Belle and I advanced towards our guests. As we drew nigh Mr. Petulengro took off his hat, and made a profound obeisance to Belle, whilst Mrs. Petulengro rose from the stool, and made a profound curtsey. Belle, who had flung her hair back over her shoulders, returned their salutations by bending her head, and after slightly glancing at Mr. Petulengro, fixed her large blue eyes full upon his wife. Both these females were very handsome—but how unlike! Belle fair, with blue eyes and flaxen hair; Mrs. Petulengro with olive complexion, eyes black, and hair dark—as dark as could be. Belle, in demeanour calm and proud; the gypsy graceful, but full of movement and agitation. And then how different were those two in stature! The head of the Romany rawnie scarcely ascended to the breast of Isopel Berners. I could see that Mrs. Petulengro gazed on Belle with unmixed admiration; so did her husband. "Well," said the latter, "one thing I will say, which is, that there is only one on earth worthy to stand up in front of this she, and that is the beauty of the world, as far as man flesh is concerned, Tawno Chikno; what a pity he did not come down!"

"Tawno Chikno," said Mrs. Petulengro, flaring up; "a pretty fellow he to stand up in front of this gentlewoman, a pity he didn't come, quotha? not at all, the fellow is a sneak, afraid of his wife. He stand up against this rawnie! why, the look she has given me would knock the fellow down."

"It is easier to knock him down with a look than with a fist," said Mr. Petulengro; "that is, if the look comes from a woman: not that I am disposed to doubt that this female gentlewoman is able to knock him down either one way or the other. I have heard of her often enough, and have seen her once or twice, though not so near as now. Well, ma'am, my wife and I are come to pay our respects to you; we are both glad to find that you have left off keeping company with Flaming Bosville, and have taken up with my pal; he is not very handsome, but a better——"

"I take up with your pal, as you call him! you had better mind what you say," said Isopel Berners, "I take up with nobody."

"I merely mean taking up your quarters with him," said Mr. Petulengro; "and I was only about to say a better fellow-lodger you cannot have, or a more instructive, especially if you have a desire to be inoculated with tongues, as he calls them. I wonder whether you and he have had any tongue-work already."

"Have you and your wife anything particular to say? if you have nothing but this kind of conversation I must leave you, as I am going to make a journey this afternoon, and should be getting ready."

"You must excuse my husband, madam," said Mrs. Petulengro, "he is not overburdened with understanding, and has said but one word of sense since he has been here, which was that we came to pay our respects to you. We have dressed ourselves in our best Roman way, in order to do honour to you; perhaps you do not like it; if so, I am sorry. I have no French clothes, madam; if I had any, madam, I would have come in them, in order to do you more honour."

"I like to see you much better as you are," said Belle; "people should keep to their own fashions, and yours is very pretty."

"I am glad you are pleased to think it so, madam; it has been admired in the great city; it created what they call a sensation; and some of the great ladies, the court ladies, imitated it, else I should not appear in it so often as I am accustomed; for I am not very fond of what is Roman, having an imagination that what is Roman is ungenteel; in fact, I once heard the wife of a rich citizen say that gypsies were vulgar creatures. I should have taken her saying very much to heart, but for her improper pronunciation; she could not pronounce her words, madam, which we gypsies, as they call us, usually can, so I thought she was no very high purchase. You are very beautiful, madam, though you are not dressed as I could wish to see you, and your hair is hanging down in sad confusion; allow me to assist you in arranging your hair, madam; I will dress it for you in our fashion; I would fain see how your hair would look in our poor gypsy fashion; pray allow me, madam?" and she took Belle by the hand.

"I really can do no such thing," said Belle, withdrawing her hand; "I thank you for coming to see me, but—"

"Do allow me to officiate upon your hair, madam," said Mrs. Petulengro. "I should esteem your allowing me a great mark of condescension. You are very beautiful, madam, and I think you doubly so, because you are so fair; I have a great esteem for persons with fair complexions and hair; I have a less regard for people with dark hair and complexions, madam."

"Then why did you turn off the lord, and take up with me?" said Mr. Petulengro; "that same lord was fair enough all about him."

"People do when they are young and silly what they sometimes repent of when they are of riper years and understandings. I sometimes think that had I not been something of a simpleton, I might at this time be a great court lady. Now, madam," said she, again taking Belle by the hand, "do oblige me by allowing me to plait your hair a little?"

"I have really a good mind to be angry with you," said Belle, giving Mrs. Petulengro a peculiar glance.

"Do allow her to arrange your hair," said I; "she means no harm, and wishes to do you honour; do oblige her and me too, for I should like to see how your hair would look dressed in her fashion."

"You hear what the young rye says?" said Mrs. Petulengro. "I am sure you will oblige the young rye, if not myself. Many people would be willing to oblige the young rye, if he would but ask them; but he is not in the habit of asking favours. He has a nose of his own, which he keeps tolerably exalted; he does not think small-beer of himself, madam; and all the time I have been with him, I never heard him ask a favour before; therefore, madam, I am sure you will oblige him. My sister Ursula would be very willing to oblige him in many things, but he will not ask for anything, except for such a favour as a word, which is a poor favour after all. I don't mean for her word; perhaps he will some day ask you for your word. If so—"

"Why, here you are, after railing at me for catching at words, catching at a word yourself," said Mr. Petulengro.

"Hold your tongue, sir," said Mrs. Petulengro. "Don't interrupt me in my discourse; if I caught at a word now, I am not in the habit of doing so. I am no conceited body; no newspaper Neddy; no pothouse witty person. I was about to say, madam, that if the young rye asks you at any time for your word, you will do as you deem convenient; but I am sure you will oblige him by allowing me to braid your hair."

"I shall not do it to oblige him," said Belle; "the young rye, as you call him, is nothing to me."

"Well, then, to oblige me," said Mrs. Petulengro; "do allow me to become your poor tire-woman."

"It is great nonsense," said Belle, reddening; "however, as you came to see me, and ask the matter as a particular favour to yourself——"

"Thank you, madam," said Mrs. Petulengro, leading Belle to the stool; "please to sit down here. Thank you; your hair is very beautiful, madam," she continued, as she proceeded to braid Belle's hair; "so is your countenance. Should you ever go to the great city, among the grand folks, you would make a sensation, madam. I have made one myself, who am dark; the chi she is kauley, which last word signifies black, which I am not, though rather dark. There is no colour like white, madam; it's so lasting, so genteel. Gentility will carry the day, madam, even with the young rye. He will ask words of the black lass, but beg the word of the fair."

In the meantime Mr. Petulengro and myself entered into conversation. "Any news stirring, Mr. Petulengro?" said I. "Have you heard anything of the great religious movements?"

"Plenty," said Mr. Petulengro; "all the religious people, more especially the Evangelicals—those that go about distributing tracts—are very angry about the fight between Gentleman Cooper and White-headed Bob, which they say ought not to have been permitted to take place; and then they are trying all they can to prevent the fight between the lion and the dogs, which they say is a disgrace to a Christian country. Now I can't say that I have any quarrel with the religious party and the Evangelicals; they are always civil to me and mine, and frequently give us tracts, as they call them, which neither I nor mine can read; but I cannot say that I approve of any movements, religious or not, which have in aim to put down all life and manly sport in this here country."

"Anything else?" said I.

"People are becoming vastly sharp," said Mr. Petulengro; "and I am told that all the old-fashioned good-tempered constables are going to be set aside, and a paid body of men to be established, who are not to permit a tramper or vagabond on the roads of England—and talking of roads, puts me in mind of a strange story I heard two nights ago, whilst drinking some beer at a public-house in company with my cousin Sylvester. I had asked Tawno to go, but his wife would not let him. Just opposite me, smoking their pipes, were a couple of men, something like engineers, and they were talking of a wonderful invention which was to make a wonderful alteration in England; inasmuch as it would set aside all the old roads, which in a little time would be ploughed up, and sowed with corn, and cause all England to be laid down with iron roads, on which people would go thundering along in vehicles, pushed forward by fire and smoke. Now, brother, when I heard this, I did not feel very comfortable; for I thought to myself, what a queer place such a road would be to pitch one's tent upon, and how impossible it would be for one's cattle to find a bite of grass upon it; and I thought likewise of the danger to which one's family would be exposed in being run over and severely scorched by these same flying fiery vehicles; so I made bold to say, that I hoped such an invention would never be countenanced, because it was likely to do a great deal of harm. Whereupon, one of the men, giving me a glance, said, without taking the pipe out of his mouth, that for his part, he sincerely hoped that it would take effect; and if it did no other good than stopping the rambles of gypsies, and other like scamps, it ought to be encouraged. Well, brother, feeling myself insulted, I put my hand into my pocket. in order to pull out money, intending to challenge him to fight for a five-shilling stake, but merely found sixpence, having left all my other money at the tent; which sixpence was just sufficient to pay for the beer which Sylvester and myself were drinking, of whom I couldn't hope to borrow anything—'poor as Sylvester' being a by-word amongst us. So, not being able to back myself, I held my peace, and let the Gorgio have it all his own way, who, after turning up his nose at me, went on discoursing about the said invention, saying what a fund of profit it would be to those who knew how to make use of it, and should have the laying down of the new roads, and the shoeing of England with iron. And after he had said this, and much more of the same kind, which I cannot remember, he and his companion got up and walked away; and presently I and Sylvester got up and walked to our camp; and there I lay down in my tent by the side of my wife, where I had an ugly dream of having camped upon an iron road; my tent being overturned by a flying vehicle; my wife's leg injured; and all my affairs put into great confusion."

"Now, madam," said Mrs. Petulengro, "I have braided your hair in our fashion: you look very beautiful, madam; more beautiful, if possible, than before." Belle now rose, and came forward with her tire-woman. Mr. Petulengro was loud in his applause, but I said nothing, for I did not think Belle was improved in appearance by having submitted to the ministry of Mrs. Petulengro's hand. Nature never intended Belle to appear as a gypsy; she had made her too proud and serious. A more proper part for her was that of a heroine, a queenly heroine—that of Theresa of Hungary, for example; or, better still, that of Brynhilda the Valkyrie, the beloved of Sigurd, the serpent-killer, who incurred the curse of Odin, because, in the tumult of spears, she sided with the young king, and doomed the old warrior to die, to whom Odin had promised victory.

Belle looked at me for a moment in silence; then turning to Mrs. Petulengro, she said, "You have had your will with me; are you satisfied?" "Quite so, madam," said Mrs. Petulengro. "and I hope you will be so too, as soon as you have looked in the glass." "I have looked in one already," said Belle; "and the glass does not flatter." "You mean the face of the young rye," said Mrs. Petulengro; "never mind him, madam; the young rye, though he knows a thing or two, is not a university, nor a person of universal wisdom. I assure you, that you never looked so well before; and I hope that, from this moment, you will wear your hair in this way." "And who is to braid it in this way?" said Belle, smiling. "I, madam," said Mrs. Petulengro; "I will braid it for you every morning, if you will but be persuaded to join us. Do so, madam, and I think, if you did, the young rye would do so too." "The young rye is nothing to me, nor I to him," said Belle; "we have stayed some time together; but our paths will soon be apart. Now, farewell, for I am about to take a journey." "And you will go out with your hair as I have braided it," said Mrs. Petulengro; "if you do, everybody will be in love with you." "No," said Belle; "hitherto I have allowed you to do what you please, but henceforth I shall have my own way. Come, come," said she, observing that the gypsy was about to speak, "we have had enough of nonsense; whenever I leave this hollow, it will be wearing my hair in my own fashion." "Come, wife," said Mr. Petulengro; "we will no longer intrude upon the rye and rawnie; there is such a thing as being troublesome." Thereupon Mr. Petulengro and his wife took their leave, with many salutations. "Then you are going?" said I, when Belle and I were left alone. "Yes," said Belle; "I am going on a journey; my affairs compel me." "But you will return again?" said I. "Yes," said Belle, "I shall return once more." "Once more," said I; "what do you mean by once more? The Petulengros will soon be gone, and will you abandon me in this place?" "You were alone here," said Belle, "before I came, and I suppose, found it agreeable, or you would not have stayed in it." "Yes," said I, "that was before I knew you; but having lived with you here, I should be very loth to live here without you." "Indeed," said Belle; "I did not know that I was of so much consequence to you. Well, the day is wearing away—I must go and harness Traveller to the cart." "I will do that," said I, "or anything else you may wish me. Go and prepare yourself; I will see after Traveller and the cart." Belle departed to her tent, and I set about performing the task I had undertaken. In about half-an-hour Belle again made her appearance—she was dressed neatly and plainly. Her hair was no longer in the Roman fashion, in which Pakomovna had plaited it, but was secured by a comb; she held a bonnet in her hand. "Is there anything else I can do for you?" I demanded. "There are two or three bundles by my tent, which you can put into the cart," said Belle. I put the bundles into the cart, and then led Traveller and the cart up the winding path to the mouth of the dingle, near which was Mr. Petulengro's encampment. Belle followed. At the top, I delivered the reins into her hands; we looked at each other stedfastly for some time. Belle then departed, and I returned to the dingle, where, seating myself on my stone, I remained for upwards of an hour in thought.

CHAPTER XXXIX

On the following day there was much feasting amongst the Romany chals of Mr. Petulengro's party. Throughout the forenoon the Romany chies did scarcely anything but cook flesh, and the flesh which they cooked was swine's flesh. About two o'clock, the chals dividing themselves into various parties, sat down and partook of the fare, which was partly roasted, partly sodden. I dined that day with Mr. Petulengro and his wife and family, Ursula, Mr. and Mrs. Chikno, and Sylvester and his two children. Sylvester, it will be as well to say, was a widower, and had consequently no one to cook his victuals for him, supposing he had any, which was not always the case, Sylvester's affairs being seldom in a prosperous state. He was noted for his bad success in trafficking, notwithstanding the many hints which he received from Jasper, under whose protection he had placed himself, even as Tawno Chikno had done, who himself, as the reader has heard on a former occasion, was anything but a wealthy subject, though he was at all times better off than Sylvester, the Lazarus of the Romany tribe.

All our party ate with a good appetite, except myself, who, feeling rather melancholy that day, had little desire to eat. I did not, like the others, partake of the pork, but got my dinner entirely off the body of a squirrel which had been shot the day before by a chal of the name of Piramus, who, besides being a good shot, was celebrated for his skill in playing on the fiddle. During the dinner a horn filled with ale passed frequently around; I drank of it more than once, and felt inspirited by the draughts. The repast concluded, Sylvester and his children departed to their tent, and Mr. Petulengro, Tawno, and myself, getting up, went and lay down under a shady hedge, where Mr. Petulengro, lighting his pipe, began to smoke, and where Tawno presently fell asleep. I was about to fall asleep also, when I heard the sound of music and song. Piramus was playing on the fiddle, whilst Mrs. Chikno, who had a voice of her own, was singing in tones sharp enough, but of great power, a gypsy song:—

POISONING THE PORKER

BY MRS. CHIKNO

To mande shoon ye Romany chals
Who besh in the pus about the yag,
I'll pen how we drab the baulo,
I'll pen how we drab the baulo.

We jaws to the drab-engro ker,
Trin horsworth there of drab we lels,
And when to the swety back we wels

We pens we'll drab the baulo,
We'll have a drab at a baulo.

And then we kairs the drab opré,
And then we jaws to the farming ker,
To mang a beti habben,
A beti poggado habben.

A rinkeno baulo there we dick,
And then we pens in Romano jib;
Wust lis odoi opré ye chick,
And the baulo he will lel lis,
The baulo he will lel lis.

Coliko, coliko saulo we
Apopli to the farming ker
Will wel and mang him mullo,
Will wel and mang his truppo.

And so we kairs, and so we kairs;
The baulo in the rarde mers;
We mang him on the saulo,
And rig to the tan the baulo.

And then we toves the wendror well
Till sore the wendror iuziou se,
Till kekkeno drab's adrey lis,
Till drab there's kek adrey lis.

And then his truppo well we hatch,
Kin levinor at the kitchema,
And have a kosko habben,
A kosko Romano habben.

The boshom engro kils, he kils,
The tawnie juva gils, she gils
A puro Romano gillie,
Now shoon the Romano gillie.

Which song I had translated in the following manner, in my younger days, for a lady's album:

Listen to me ye Romanlads, who are seated in the straw about the fire, and I will tell how we poison the porker, I will tell how we poison the porker.

We go to the house of the poison-monger,[1] where we buy three pennies' worth of bane, and when we return to our people we say, we will poison the porker; we will try and poison the porker.

We then make up the poison, and then we take our way to the house of the farmer, as if to beg a bit of victuals, a little broken victuals.

[1]The apothecary.

We see a jolly porker, and then we say in Roman language, "Fling the bane yonder amongst the dirt, and the porker soon will find it, the porker soon will find it."

Early on the morrow, we will return to the farm-house, and beg the dead porker, the body of the dead porker.

And so we do, even so we do; the porker dieth during the night; on the morrow we beg the porker, and carry to the tent the porker.

And then we wash the inside well, till all the inside is perfectly clean, till there's no bane within it, not a poison grain within it.

And then we roast the body well, send for ale to the alehouse, and have a merry banquet, a merry Roman banquet.

The fellow with the fiddle plays, he plays; the little lassie sings, she sings an ancient Roman ditty; now hear the Roman ditty.

SONG OF THE BROKEN CHASTITY

By Ursula

Penn'd the Romany chi ké laki dye
"Miry dearie dye mi shom cambri!"
"And coin kerdo tute cambri,
Miry dearie chi, miry Romany chi?"
"O miry dye a boro rye,
A bovalo rye, a gorgiko rye,
Sos kistur pré a pellengo grye,
'Twas yov sos kerdo man cambri."
"Tu tawnie vassavie lubbeny,
Tu chal from miry tan abri;
Had a Romany chal kair'd tute cambri,
Then I had penn'd ke tute chie,
But tu shan a vassavie lubbeny
With gorgikie rat to be cambri."

"There's some kernel in those songs, brother," said Mr. Petulengro, when the songs and music were over.

"Yes," said I; "they are certainly very remarkable songs. I say, Jasper, I hope you have not been drabbing baulor lately."

"And suppose we have, brother, what then?"

"Why, it is a very dangerous practice, to say nothing of the wickedness of it."

"Necessity has no law, brother."

"That is true," said I; "I have always said so, but you are not necessitous, and should not drab baulor."

"And who told you we had been drabbing baulor?"

"Why, you have had a banquet of pork, and after the banquet, Mrs. Chikno sang a song about drabbing baulor, so I naturally thought you might have lately been engaged in such a thing."

"Brother, you occasionally utter a word or two of common sense. It was natural for you to suppose, after seeing that dinner of pork, and hearing that song, that we had been drabbing baulor; I will now tell you that we have not been doing so. What have you to say to that?"

"That I am very glad of it."

"Had you tasted that pork, brother, you would have found that it was sweet and tasty, which balluva that is drabbed can hardly be expected to be. We have no reason to drab baulor at present, we have money and credit; but necessity has no law. Our forefathers occasionally drabbed baulor; some of our people may still do such a thing, but only from compulsion."

"I see," said I; "and at your merry meetings you sing songs upon the compulsatory deeds of your people, alias, their villainous actions; and, after all, what would the stirring poetry of any nation be, but for its compulsatory deeds? Look at the poetry of Scotland, the heroic part, founded almost entirely on the villainous deeds of the Scotch nation; cow-stealing, for example, which is very little better than drabbing baulor; whilst the softer part is mostly about the slips of its females among the broom, so that no upholder of Scotch poetry could censure Ursula's song as indelicate, even if he understood it. What do you think, Jasper?"

"I think, brother, as I before said, that occasionally you utter a word of common sense; you were talking of the Scotch, brother; what do you think of a Scotchman finding fault with Romany!"

"A Scotchman finding fault with Romany, Jasper! Oh dear, but you joke, the thing could never be."

"Yes, and at Piramus's fiddle; what do you think of a Scotchman turning up his nose at Piramus's fiddle?"

"A Scotchman turning up his nose at Piramus's fiddle! nonsense, Jasper."

"Do you know what I most dislike, brother?"

"I do not, unless it be the constable, Jasper."

"It is not the constable; it's a beggar on horseback, brother."

"What do you mean by a beggar on horseback?"

"Why, a scamp, brother, raised above his proper place, who takes every opportunity of giving himself fine airs. About a week ago, my people and myself camped on a green by a plantation in the neighbourhood of a great house. In the evening we were making merry, the girls were dancing, while Piramus was playing on the fiddle a tune of his own composing, to which he has given his own name, Piramus of Rome, and which is much celebrated amongst our people, and from which I have been told that one of the grand Gorgio composers, who once heard it, has taken several hints. So, as we were making merry, a great many grand people, lords and ladies, I believe, came from the great house, and looked on, as the girls danced to the tune of Piramus of Rome, and seemed much pleased; and when the girls had left off dancing, and Piramus playing, the ladies wanted to have their fortunes told; so I bade Mikailia Chikno, who can tell a fortune when she pleases better than any one else, tell them a fortune, and she, being in a good mind, told them a fortune which pleased them very much. So, after they had heard their fortunes, one of them asked if any of our women could sing; and I told them several could, more particularly Leviathan—you know Leviathan, she is not here now, but some miles distant, she is our best singer, Ursula coming next. So the lady said she should like to hear Leviathan sing, whereupon Leviathan sang the Gudlo pesham, and Piramus played the tune of the same name, which as you know, means the honeycomb, the song and the tune being well entitled to the name, being wonderfully sweet. Well, everybody present seemed mighty well pleased with the song and music, with the exception of one person, a carroty-haired Scotch body; how he came there I don't know, but there he was; and, coming forward, he began in Scotch as broad as a barn-door to find fault with the music and the song, saying, that he had never heard viler stuff than either. Well, brother, out of consideration for the civil gentry with whom the fellow had come, I held my peace for a long time, and in order to get the subject changed, I said to Mikailia in Romany, 'You have told the ladies their fortunes, now tell the gentlemen theirs, quick, quick—pen lende dukkerin.' Well, brother, the Scotchman, I suppose, thinking I was speaking ill of him, fell into a greater passion than before, and catching hold of the word dukkerin—'Dukkerin,' said he, 'what's dukkerin?' 'Dukkerin,' said I, 'is fortune, a man or woman's destiny; don't you like the word?' 'Word! d'ye ca' that a word? a bonnie word,' said he. 'Perhaps, you'll tell us what it is in Scotch,' said I, 'in order that we may improve our language by a Scotch word; a pal of mine has told me that we have taken a great many words from foreign lingos.' 'Why, then, if that be the case, fellow, I will tell you; it is e'en "spaeing,"' said he, very seriously. 'Well, then,' said I, 'I'll keep my own word, which is much the prettiest—spaeing! spaeing! why, I should be ashamed to make use of the word, it sounds so much like a certain other word'; and then I made a face as if I were unwell. 'Perhaps it's Scotch also for that?' 'What do ye mean by speaking in that guise to a gentleman?' said he; 'you insolent vagabond, without a name or a country.' 'There you are mistaken,' said I; 'my country is Egypt, but we 'Gyptians, like you Scotch, are rather fond of travelling; and as for name—my name is Jasper Petulengro, perhaps you have a better; what is it?' 'Sandy Macraw.' At that, brother, the gentlemen burst into a roar of laughter, and all the ladies tittered."

"You were rather severe on the Scotchman, Jasper."

"Not at all, brother, and suppose I were, he began first; I am the civilest man in the world, and never interfere with anybody, who lets me and mine alone. He finds fault with Romany, forsooth! why, L—d A'mighty, what's Scotch? He doesn't like our songs; what are his own? I understand them as little as he mine; I have heard one or two of them, and pretty rubbish they seemed. But the best of the joke is, the fellow's finding fault with Piramus's fiddle—a chap from the land of bagpipes finding fault with Piramus's fiddle! Why, I'll back that fiddle against all the bagpipes in Scotland, and Piramus against all the bagpipers; for though Piramus weighs but ten stone, he shall flog a Scotchman of twenty."

"Scotchmen are never so fat as that," said I, "unless indeed, they have been a long time pensioners of England. I say, Jasper, what remarkable names your people have!"

"And what pretty names, brother; there's my own, for example, Jasper; then there's Ambrose and Sylvester; then there's Culvato, which signifies Claude; then there's Piramus—that's a nice name, brother."

"Then there's your wife's name, Pakomovna; then there's Ursula and Morella."

"Then, brother, there's Ercilla."

"Ercilla! the name of the great poet of Spain, how wonderful; then Leviathan."

"The name of a ship, brother; Leviathan was named after a ship, so don't make a wonder out of her. But there's Sanpriel and Synfye."

"Ay, and Clementina and Lavinia, Camillia and Lydia, Curlanda and Orlanda; wherever did they get those names?"

"Where did my wife get her necklace, brother?"

"She knows best, Jasper. I hope——"

"Come, no hoping! She got it from her grandmother, who died at the age of a hundred and three, and sleeps in Coggeshall churchyard. She got it from her mother, who also died very old, and who could give no other account of it than that it had been in the family time out of mind."

"Whence could they have got it?"

"Why, perhaps where they got their names, brother. A gentleman, who had travelled much, once told me that he had seen the sister of it about the neck of an Indian queen."

"Some of your names, Jasper, appear to be church names; your own, for example, and Ambrose, and Sylvester; perhaps you got them from the Papists, in the times of Popery; but where did you get such a name as Piramus, a name of Grecian romance? Then some of them appear to be Slavonian; for example, Mikailia and Pakomovna. I don't know much of Slavonian; but——"

"What is Slavonian, brother?"

"The family name of certain nations, the principal of which is the Russian, and from which the word slave is originally derived. You have heard of the Russians, Jasper?"

"Yes, brother; and seen some. I saw their crallis at the time of the peace; he was not a bad-looking man for a Russian."

"By-the-bye, Jasper, I'm half inclined to think that crallis is a Slavish word. I saw something like it in a lil called 'Voltaire's Life of Charles.' How you should have come by such names and words is to me incomprehensible."

"You seem posed, brother."

"I really know very little about you, Jasper."

"Very little indeed, brother. We know very little about ourselves; and you know nothing, save what we have told you; and we have now and then told you things about us which are not exactly true, simply to make a fool of you, brother. You will say that was wrong; perhaps it was. Well,

Sunday will be here in a day or two, when we will go to church, where possibly we shall hear a sermon on the disastrous consequences of lying."

CHAPTER XL

When two days had passed, Sunday came; I breakfasted by myself in the solitary dingle; and then, having set things a little to rights, I ascended to Mr. Petulengro's encampment. I could hear church-bells ringing around in the distance, appearing to say, "Come to church, come to church," as clearly as it was possible for church-bells to say. I found Mr. Petulengro seated by the door of his tent, smoking his pipe, in rather an ungenteel undress. "Well, Jasper," said I, "are you ready to go to church? for if you are, I am ready to accompany you." "I am not ready, brother," said Mr. Petulengro, "nor is my wife; the church, too, to which we shall go is three miles off; so it is of no use to think of going there this morning, as the service would be three-quarters over before we got there; if, however, you are disposed to go in the afternoon, we are your people." Thereupon I returned to my dingle, where I passed several hours in conning the Welsh Bible, which the preacher, Peter Williams, had given me.

At last I gave over reading, took a slight refreshment, and was about to emerge from the dingle, when I heard the voice of Mr. Petulengro calling me. I went up again to the encampment, where I found Mr. Petulengro, his wife, and Tawno Chikno, ready to proceed to church. Mr. and Mrs. Petulengro were dressed in Roman fashion, though not in the full-blown manner in which they had paid their visit to Isopel and myself. Tawno had on a clean white slop, with a nearly new black beaver, with very broad rims, and the nap exceedingly long. As for myself, I was dressed in much the same manner as that in which I departed from London, having on, in honour of the day, a shirt perfectly clean, having washed one on purpose for the occasion, with my own hands, the day before, in the pond of tepid water in which the newts and efts were in the habit of taking their pleasure. We proceeded for upwards of a mile, by footpaths through meadows and cornfields; we crossed various stiles; at last, passing over one, we found ourselves in a road, wending along which for a considerable distance, we at last came in sight of a church, the bells of which had been tolling distinctly in our ears for some time; before, however, we reached the church-yard, the bells had ceased their melody. It was surrounded by lofty beech-trees of brilliant green foliage. We entered the gate, Mrs. Petulengro leading the way, and proceeded to a small door near the east end of the church. As we advanced, the sound of singing within the church rose upon our ears. Arrived at the small door, Mrs. Petulengro opened it and entered, followed by Tawno Chikno. I myself went last of all, following Mr. Petulengro, who, before I entered, turned round, and, with a significant nod, advised me to take care how I behaved.

Still following Mrs. Petulengro, we proceeded down the chancel and along the aisle; notwithstanding the singing, I could distinctly hear as we passed many a voice whispering, "Here come the gypsies! here come the gypsies!" I felt rather embarrassed, with a somewhat awkward doubt as to where we were to sit; none of the occupiers of the pews, who appeared to consist almost entirely of farmers, with their wives, sons, and daughters, opened a door to admit us. Mrs. Petulengro, however, appeared to feel not the least embarrassment, but tripped along the aisle with the greatest non-chalance. We passed under the pulpit, in which stood the clergyman in his white surplice, and reached the middle of the church, where we were con-fronted by the sexton dressed in long blue coat, and holding in his hand a wand. This functionary motioned towards the lower end of the church, where were certain benches, partly occupied by poor people and boys. Mrs. Petulengro, however, with a toss of her head, directed her course to a magnificent pew, which was unoccupied, which she opened and entered, followed closely by Tawno Chikno, Mr. Petulengro, and myself. The sexton did not appear by any means to approve of the arrangement, and as I stood next the door, laid his finger on my arm, as if to intimate that my-self and companions must quit our aristocratical location. I said nothing, but directed my eyes to the clergyman, who uttered a short and expressive cough; the sexton looked at him for a moment, and then, bowing his head, closed the door—in a moment more the music ceased. I took up a prayer-book, on which was engraved an earl's coronet. The clergyman uttered, "I will arise, and go to my father." England's sublime liturgy had commenced.

Oh, what feelings came over me on finding myself again in an edifice de-voted to the religion of my country! I had not been in such a place I cannot tell for how long—certainly not for years; and now I had found my way there again, it appeared as if I had fallen asleep in the pew of the old church of pretty D——. I had occasionally done so when a child and had suddenly woke up.

The liturgy was now over, during the reading of which my companions behaved in a most unexceptionable manner, sitting down and rising up when other people sat down and rose, and holding in their hands prayer-books which they found in the pew, into which they stared intently, though I observed that, with the exception of Mrs. Petulengro, who knew how to read a little, they held the books by the top, and not the bottom, as is the usual way. The clergyman now ascended the pulpit, arrayed in his black gown. The congregation composed themselves to attention, as did also my companions, who fixed their eyes upon the clergyman with a certain strange immovable stare, which I believe to be peculiar to their race. The clergyman gave out his text, and began to preach. He was a tall, gentlemanly man, seemingly between fifty and sixty, with greyish hair; his features were very handsome, but with a somewhat melancholy cast: the tones of his voice were rich and noble, but also with somewhat of melancholy in them. The text which he gave out was the following one, "In what would a man be profited, provided he gained the whole world, and lost his own soul?"

The service over, my companions and myself returned towards the encampment, by the way we came. Some of the humble part of the congregation laughed and joked at us as we passed. Mr. Petulengro and his wife, however, returned their laughs and jokes with interest. As for Tawno and myself, we said nothing: Tawno, like most handsome fellows, having very little to say for himself at any time; and myself, though not handsome, not being particularly skilful at repartee. Some boys followed us for a considerable time, making all kinds of observations about gypsies; but as we walked at a great pace, we gradually left them behind, and at last lost sight of them. Mrs. Petulengro and Tawno Chikno walked together, even as they had come; whilst Mr. Petulengro and myself followed at a little distance.

"That was a very fine preacher we heard," said I to Mr. Petulengro, after we had crossed the stile into the fields.

"Very fine indeed, brother," said Mr. Petulengro; "he is talked of, far and wide, for his sermons; folks say that there is scarcely another like him in the whole of England."

"You seem to know all about him, Jasper. Did you ever hear him preach before?"

"Never, brother; but he has frequently been to our tent, and his daughters too, and given us tracts; for he is one of the people they call Evangelicals, who give folks tracts which they cannot read."

"You should learn to read, Jasper."

"We have no time, brother."

"Are you not frequently idle?"

"Never, brother; when we are not engaged in our traffic, we are engaged in taking our relaxation: so we have no time to learn."

"You really should make an effort. If you were disposed to learn to read, I would endeavour to assist you. You would be all the better for knowing how to read."

"In what way, brother?"

"Why, you could read the Scriptures, and, by so doing, learn your duty towards your fellow-creatures."

"We know that already, brother; the constables and justices have contrived to knock that tolerably into our heads."

"Yet you frequently break the laws."

"So, I believe, do now and then those who know how to read, brother."

"Very true, Jasper; but you really ought to learn to read, as, by so doing, you might learn your duty towards yourselves: and your chief duty is to take care of your own souls; did not the preacher say, 'In what is a man profited, provided he gain the whole world?'"

"We have not much of the world, brother."

"Very little indeed, Jasper. Did you not observe how the eyes of the whole congregation were turned towards our pew, when the preacher said, 'There are some people who lose their souls, and get nothing in exchange; who are outcast, despised, and miserable'? Now was not what he said quite applicable to the gypsies?"

"We are not miserable, brother."

"Well, then, you ought to be, Jasper. Have you an inch of ground of your own? Are you of the least use? Are you not spoken ill of by everybody? What's a gypsy?"

"What's the bird noising yonder, brother?"

"The bird! oh, that's the cuckoo tolling; but what has the cuckoo to do with the matter?"

"We'll see, brother; what's the cuckoo?"

"What is it? you know as much about it as myself, Jasper."

"Isn't it a kind of roguish, chaffing bird, brother?"

"I believe it is, Jasper."

"Nobody knows whence it comes, brother?"

"I believe not, Jasper."

"Very poor, brother, not a nest of its own?"

"So they say, Jasper."

"With every person's bad word, brother?"

"Yes, Jasper, every person is mocking it."

"Tolerably merry, brother?"

"Yes, tolerably merry, Jasper."

"Of no use at all, brother?"

"None whatever, Jasper."

"You would be glad to get rid of the cuckoos, brother?"

"Why, not exactly, Jasper; the cuckoo is a pleasant, funny bird, and its presence and voice give a great charm to the green trees and fields; no, I can't say I wish exactly to get rid of the cuckoo."

"Well, brother, what's a Romany chal?"

"You must answer that question yourself, Jasper."

"A roguish, chaffing fellow, a'n't he, brother?"

"Ay, ay, Jasper."

"Of no use at all, brother?"

"Just so, Jasper; I see—"

"Something very much like a cuckoo, brother?"

"I see what you are after, Jasper."

"You would like to get rid of us, wouldn't you?"

"Why no, not exactly."

"We are no ornament to the green lanes in spring and summer time, are we, brother? and the voices of our chies, with their cukkerin and dukkerin, don't help to make them pleasant?"

"I see what you are at, Jasper."

"You would wish to turn the cuckoos into barn-door fowls, wouldn't you?"

"Can't say I should, Jasper, whatever some people might wish."

"And the chals and chies into radical weavers and factory wenches, hey, brother?"

"Can't say that I should, Jasper. You are certainly a picturesque people, and in many respects an ornament both to town and country; painting and lil writing too are under great obligations to you. What pretty pictures are made out of your campings and groupings, and what pretty books have been written in which gypsies, or at least creatures intended to represent gypsies, have been the principal figures. I think if we were without you, we should begin to miss you."

"Just as you would the cuckoos, if they were all converted into barn-door fowls. I tell you what, brother; frequently, as I have sat under a hedge in spring or summer time, and heard the cuckoo, I have thought that we chals and cuckoos are alike in many respects, but especially in character. Everybody speaks ill of us both, and everybody is glad to see both of us again."

"Yes, Jasper, but there is some difference between men and cuckoos; men have souls, Jasper!"

"And why not cuckoos, brother?"

"You should not talk so, Jasper; what you say is little short of blasphemy. How should a bird have a soul?"

"And how should a man?"

"Oh, we know very well that a man has a soul."

"How do you know it?"

"We know very well."

"Would you take your oath of it, brother—your bodily oath?"

"Why, I think I might, Jasper!"

"Did you ever see the soul, brother?"

"No, I never saw it."

"Then how could you swear to it? A pretty figure you would make in a court of justice, to swear to a thing which you never saw. Hold up your head, fellow. When and where did you see it? Now upon your oath, fellow, do you mean to say that this Roman stole the donkey's foal? Oh, there's no one for cross-questioning like Counsellor P——. Our people when they are in a hobble always like to employ him, though he is somewhat dear. Now, brother, how can you get over the 'upon your oath, fellow, will you say that you have a soul?' "

"Well, we will take no oaths on the subject; but you yourself believe in the soul. I have heard you say that you believe in dukkerin; now what is dukkerin but the soul science?"

"When did I say that I believed in it?"

"Why, after that fight, when you pointed to the bloody mark in the cloud, whilst he you wot of was galloping in the barouche to the old town, amidst the rain-cataracts, the thunder, and flame of heaven."

"I have some kind of remembrance of it, brother."

"Then, again, I heard you say that the dook of Abershaw rode every night on horseback down the wooded hill."

"I say, brother, what a wonderful memory you have!"

"I wish I had not, Jasper; but I can't help it, it is my misfortune."

"Misfortune! well, perhaps it is; at any rate it is very ungenteel to have such a memory. I have heard my wife say that to show you have a long memory looks very vulgar; and that you can't give a greater proof of gentility than by forgetting a thing as soon as possible—more especially a promise, or an acquaintance when he happens to be shabby. Well, brother, I don't deny that I may have said that I believe in dukkerin, and in Abershaw's dook, which you say is his soul; but what I believe one moment, or say I believe, don't be certain that I shall believe the next, or say I do."

"Indeed, Jasper, I heard you say on a previous occasion, on quoting a piece of a song, that when a man dies he is cast into the earth, and there's an end of him."

"I did, did I? Lor' what a memory you have, brother. But you are not sure that I hold that opinion now."

"Certainly not, Jasper. Indeed, after such a sermon as we have been hearing, I should be very shocked if you held such an opinion."

"However, brother, don't be sure I do not, however shocking such an opinion may be to you."

"What an incomprehensible people you are, Jasper."

"We are rather so, brother; indeed, we have posed wiser heads than yours before now."

"You seem to care for so little, and yet you rove about a distinct race."

"I say, brother!"

"Yes, Jasper."

"What do you think of our women?"

"They have certainly very singular names, Jasper."

"Names! Lavengro! However, brother, if you had been as fond of things as of names, you would never have been a pal of ours."

"What do you mean, Jasper?"

"A'n't they rum animals?"

"They have tongues of their own, Jasper."

"Did you ever feel their teeth and nails, brother?"

"Never, Jasper, save Mrs. Herne's. I have always been very civil to them, so——"

"They let you alone. I say, brother, some part of the secret is in them."

"They seem rather flighty, Jasper."

"Ay, ay, brother!"

"Rather fond of loose discourse!"

"Rather so, brother."

"Can you always trust them, Jasper?"

"We never watch them, brother."

"Can they always trust you?"

"Not quite so well as we can them. However, we get on very well together, except Mikailia and her husband; but Mikailia is a cripple, and is married to the beauty of the world, so she may be expected to be jealous—though he would not part with her for a duchess, no more than I would part with my rawnie, nor any other chal with his."

"Ay, but would not the chi part with the chal for a duke, Jasper?"

"My Pakomovna gave up the duke for me, brother."

"But she occasionally talks of him, Jasper."

"Yes, brother, but Pakomovna was born on a common not far from the sign of the gammon."

"Gammon of bacon, I suppose."

"Yes, brother; but gammon likewise means——"

"I know it does, Jasper; it means fun, ridicule, jest; it is an ancient Norse word, and is found in the Edda."

"Lor', brother! how learned in lils you are!"

"Many words of Norse are to be found in our vulgar sayings, Jasper; for example—in that particularly vulgar saying of ours, 'Your mother is up,' there's a noble Norse word; mother, there, meaning not the female who bore us, but rage and choler, as I discovered by reading the Sagas, Jasper."

"Lor', brother! how book-learned you be."

"Indifferently so, Jasper. Then you think you might trust your wife with the duke?"

"I think I could, brother, or even with yourself."

"Myself, Jasper! Oh, I never troubled my head about your wife; but I suppose there have been love affairs between Gorgios and Romany chies. Why, novels are stuffed with such matters; and then even one of your own songs says so—the song which Ursula was singing the other afternoon."

"That is somewhat of an old song, brother, and is sung by the chies as a warning at our solemn festivals."

"Well! but there's your sister-in-law, Ursula, herself, Jasper."

"Ursula, herself, brother?"

"You were talking of my having her, Jasper."

"Well, brother, why didn't you have her?"

"Would she have had me?"

"Of course, brother. You are so much of a Roman, and speak Romany so remarkably well."

"Poor thing! she looks very innocent!"

"Remarkably so, brother! however, though not born on the same common with my wife, she knows a thing or two of Roman matters."

"I should like to ask her a question or two, Jasper, in connection with that song."

"You can do no better, brother. Here we are at the camp. After tea, take Ursula under a hedge, and ask her a question or two in connection with that song."

CHAPTER XLI

I TOOK tea that evening with Mr. and Mrs. Petulengro and Ursula, outside of their tent. Tawno was not present, being engaged with his wife in his own tabernacle; Sylvester was there, however, lolling listlessly upon the ground. As I looked upon this man, I thought him one of the most disagreeable fellows I had ever seen. His features were ugly, and, moreover, as dark as pepper; and, besides being dark, his skin was dirty. As for his dress, it was torn and sordid. His chest was broad, and his arms seemed powerful; but, upon the whole, he looked a very caitiff. "I am sorry that man has lost his wife," thought I; "for I am sure he will never get another." What surprises me is, that he ever found a woman disposed to unite her lot with his!

After tea I got up and strolled about the field. My thoughts were upon Isopel Berners. I wondered where she was, and how long she would stay away. At length becoming tired and listless, I determined to return to the dingle, and resume the reading of the Bible at the place where I had left off. "What better could I do," methought, "on a Sunday evening?" I was then near the wood which surrounded the dingle, but at that side which was farthest from the encampment, which stood near the entrance. Suddenly, on turning round the southern corner of the copse, which surrounded the dingle, I perceived Ursula seated under a thornbush. I thought I never saw her look prettier than then, dressed as she was, in her Sunday's best.

"Good evening, Ursula," said I; "I little thought to have the pleasure of seeing you here."

"Nor would you, brother," said Ursula, "had not Jasper told me that you had been talking about me, and wanted to speak to me under a hedge; so, hearing that, I watched your motions, and came here and sat down."

"I was thinking of going to my quarters in the dingle, to read the Bible, Ursula, but——"

"Oh, pray then, go to your quarters, brother, and read the Miduveleskoe lil; you can speak to me under a hedge some other time."

"I think I will sit down with you, Ursula; for, after all, reading godly books in dingles at eve, is rather sombre work. Yes, I think I will sit down with you"; and I sat down by her side.

"Well, brother, now you have sat down with me under the hedge, what have you to say to me?"

"Why, I hardly know, Ursula."

"Not know, brother; a pretty fellow you to ask young women to come and sit with you under hedges, and, when they come, not know what to say to them."

"Oh! ah! I remember; do you know, Ursula, that I take a great interest in you?"

"Thank ye, brother: kind of you, at any rate."

"You must be exposed to a great many temptations, Ursula."

"A great many indeed, brother. It is hard to see fine things, such as shawls, gold watches, and chains in the shops, behind the big glasses, and to know that they are not intended for one. Many's the time I have been tempted to make a dash at them; but I bethought myself that by so doing I should cut my hands, besides being almost certain of being grabbed and sent across the gull's bath to the foreign country."

"Then you think gold and fine things temptations, Ursula?"

"Of course, brother, very great temptations; don't you think them so?"

"Can't say I do, Ursula."

"Then more fool you, brother; but have the kindness to tell me what you would call a temptation?"

"Why, for example, the hope of honour and renown, Ursula."

"The hope of honour and renown! very good, brother; but I tell you one thing, that unless you have money in your pocket, and good broad-cloth on your back, you are not likely to obtain much honour and—what do you call it? amongst the Gorgios, to say nothing of the Romany chals."

"I should have thought, Ursula, that the Romany chals, roaming about the world as they do, free and independent, were above being led by such trifles."

"Then you know nothing of the gypsies, brother; no people on earth are fonder of those trifles, as you call them, than the Romany chals, and more disposed to respect those who have them."

"Then money and fine clothes would induce you to do anything, Ursula?"

"Ay, ay, brother, anything."

"To chore, Ursula?"

"Like enough, brother; gypsies have been transported before now for choring."

"To hokkawar?"

"Ay, ay; I was telling dukkerin only yesterday, brother."

"In fact, to break the law in everything?"

"Who knows, brother, who knows? as I said before, gold and fine clothes are great temptations."

"Well, Ursula, I am sorry for it, I should never have thought you so depraved."

"Indeed, brother."

"To think that I am seated by one who is willing to—to——"

"Go on, brother."

"To play the thief."

"Go on, brother."

"The liar."

"Go on, brother."

"The–the—"

"Go on, brother."

"The–the lubbeny."

"The what, brother?" said Ursula, starting from her seat.

"Why, the lubbeny; don't you—"

"I tell you what, brother," said Ursula, looking somewhat pale, and speaking very low, "if I had only something in my hand, I would do you a mischief."

"Why, what is the matter, Ursula?" said I; "how have I offended you?"

"How have you offended me? Why, didn't you insinivate just now that I was ready to play the–the—"

"Go on, Ursula."

"The–the— I'll not say it; but I only wish I had something in my hand."

"If I have offended, Ursula, I am very sorry for it; any offence I may have given you was from want of understanding you. Come, pray be seated. I have much to question you about–to talk to you about."

"Seated, not I! It was only just now that you gave me to understand that you was ashamed to be seated by me, a thief, a liar."

"Well, did you not almost give me to understand that you were both, Ursula?"

"I don't much care being called a thief and a liar," said Ursula; "a person may be a liar and thief, and yet a very honest woman, but—"

"Well, Ursula."

"I tell you what, brother, if you ever sinivate again that I could be the third thing, so help me duvel! I'll do you a mischief. By my God I will!"

"Well, Ursula, I assure you that I shall sinivate, as you call it, nothing of the kind about you. I have no doubt, from what you have said, that you are a very paragon of virtue–a perfect Lucretia; but—"

"My name is Ursula, brother, and not Lucretia: Lucretia is not of our family, but one of the Bucklands; she travels about Oxfordshire; yet I am as good as she any day."

"Lucretia; how odd! Where could she have got that name? Well, I make no doubt, Ursula, that you are quite as good as she, and she as her namesake of ancient Rome; but there is a mystery in this same virtue, Ursula, which I cannot fathom; how a thief and a liar should be able, or indeed willing, to preserve her virtue is what I don't understand. You confess that you are very fond of gold. Now, how is it that you don't barter your virtue for gold sometimes? I am a philosopher, Ursula, and like to know everything. You must be every now and then exposed to great temptation, Ursula; for you are of a beauty calculated to captivate all hearts. Come, sit down and tell me how you are enabled to resist such a temptation as gold and fine clothes?"

"Well, brother," said Ursula, "as you say you mean no harm, I will sit down beside you, and enter into discourse with you; but I will uphold that you are the coolest hand that I ever came nigh, and say the coolest things."

And thereupon Ursula sat down by my side.

"Well, Ursula, we will, if you please, discourse on the subject of your temptations. I suppose that you travel very much about, and show yourself in all kinds of places?"

"In all kinds, brother; I travels, as you say, very much about, attends fairs and races, and enters booths and public-houses, where I tells fortunes, and sometimes dances and sings."

"And do not people often address you in a very free manner?"

"Frequently, brother; and I give them tolerably free answers."

"Do people ever offer to make you presents? I mean presents of value, such as——"

"Silk handkerchiefs, shawls, and trinkets; very frequently, brother."

"And what do you do, Ursula?"

"I takes what people offers me, brother, and stows it away as soon as I can."

"Well, but don't people expect something for their presents? I don't mean dukkerin, dancing, and the like; but such a moderate and innocent thing as a choomer, Ursula?"

"Innocent thing, do you call it, brother?"

"The world calls it so, Ursula. Well, do the people who give you the fine things never expect a choomer in return?"

"Very frequently, brother."

"And do you ever grant it?"

"Never, brother."

"How do you avoid it?"

"I gets away as soon as possible, brother. If they follows me, I tries to baffle them, by means of jests and laughter; and if they persist, I uses bad and terrible language, of which I have plenty in store."

"But if your terrible language has no effect?"

"Then I screams for the constable, and if he comes not, I uses my teeth and nails."

"And are they always sufficient?"

"I have only had to use them twice, brother; but then I found them sufficient."

"But suppose the person who followed you was highly agreeable, Ursula? A handsome young officer of local militia, for example, all dressed in Lincoln green, would you still refuse him the choomer?"

"We makes no difference, brother; the daughters of the gypsy-father makes no difference; and what's more, sees none."

"Well, Ursula, the world will hardly give you credit for such indifference."

"What cares we for the world, brother! we are not of the world."

"But your fathers, brothers, and uncles, give you credit, I suppose, Ursula."

"Ay, ay, brother, our fathers, brothers, and cokos gives us all manner of credit; for example, I am telling lies and dukkerin in a public-house where my batu or coko—perhaps both—are playing on the fiddle; well, my batu and my coko beholds me amongst the public-house crew, talking nonsense and hearing nonsense; but they are under no apprehension; and presently they sees the good-looking officer of militia, in his greens and Lincolns, get up and give me a wink, and I go out with him abroad, into the dark night perhaps; well, my batu and my coko goes on fiddling just as if I were six miles off asleep in the tent, and not out in the dark street with the local officer, with his Lincolns and his greens."

"They know they can trust you, Ursula?"

"Ay, ay, brother; and, what's more, I knows I can trust myself."

"So you would merely go out to make a fool of him, Ursula?"

"Merely go out to make a fool of him, brother, I assure you."

"But such proceedings really have an odd look, Ursula."

"Amongst Gorgios, very so, brother."

"Well, it must be rather unpleasant to lose one's character even amongst Gorgios, Ursula; and suppose the officer, out of revenge for being tricked and duped by you, were to say of you the thing that is not, were to meet you on the race-course the next day, and boast of receiving favours which he never had, amidst a knot of jeering militia-men, how would you proceed, Ursula? would you not be abashed?"

"By no means, brother; I should bring my action of law against him."

"Your action at law, Ursula?"

"Yes, brother, I should give a whistle, whereupon all one's cokos and batus, and all my near and distant relations, would leave their fiddling, dukkerin, and horse-dealing, and come flocking about me. 'What's the matter, Ursula?' says my coko. 'Nothing at all,' I replies, 'save and except that Gorgio, in his greens and his Lincolns, says that I have played the — with him.' 'Oho, he does, Ursula,' says my coko, 'try your action of law against him, my lamb,' and he puts something privily into my hands; whereupon I goes close up to the grinning Gorgio, and staring him in the face, with my head pushed forward, I cries out: 'You say I did what was wrong with you last night when I was out with you abroad?' 'Yes,' says the local officer, 'I says you did,' looking down all the time. 'You are a liar,' says I, and forthwith I breaks his head with the stick which I holds behind me, and which my coko has conveyed privily into my hand."

"And this is your action at law, Ursula?"

"Yes, brother, this is my action at club-law."

"And would your breaking the fellow's head quite clear you of all suspicion in the eyes of your batus, cokos, and what not?"

"They would never suspect me at all, brother, because they would know that I would never condescend to be over-intimate with a Gorgio; the breaking the head would be merely intended to justify Ursula in the eyes of the Gorgios."

"And would it clear you in their eyes?"

"Would it not, brother? when they saw the blood running down from the fellow's cracked poll on his greens and Lincolns, they would be quite satisfied; why, the fellow would not be able to show his face at fair or merry-making for a year and three-quarters."

"Did you ever try it, Ursula?"

"Can't say I ever did, brother, but it would do."

"And how did you ever learn such a method of proceeding?"

"Why, 't is advised by gypsy liri, brother. It's part of our way of settling difficulties amongst ourselves; for example, if a young Roman were to say the thing which is not respecting Ursula and himself, Ursula would call a great meeting of the people, who would all sit down in a ring, the young fellow amongst them; a coko would then put a stick in Ursula's hand, who would then get up and go to the young fellow, and say, 'Did I play the — with you?' and were he to say 'Yes,' she would crack his head before the eyes of all."

"Well," said I, "Ursula, I was bread an apprentice to gorgio law, and of course ought to stand up for it, whenever I conscientiously can, but I must say the gypsy manner of bringing an action for defamation is much less tedious, and far more satisfactory, than the gorgiko one. I wish you now to clear up a certain point which is rather mysterious to me. You say that for a Romany chi to do what is unseemly with a Gorgio is quite out of the question, yet only the other day I heard you singing a song in which a Romany chi confesses herself to be cambri by a grand gorgious gentleman."

"A sad let down," said Ursula.

"Well," said I, "sad or not, there's the song that speaks of the thing, which you give me to understand is not."

"Well, if the thing ever was," said Ursula, "it was a long time ago, and perhaps, after all, not true."

"Then why do you sing the song?"

"I'll tell you, brother, we sings the song now and then to be a warning to ourselves to have as little to do as possible in the way of acquaintance with the Gorgios; and a warning it is; you see how the young woman in the song was driven out of her tent by her mother, with all kind of disgrace and bad language; but you don't know that she was afterwards buried alive by her cokos and pals, in an uninhabited place; the song doesn't say it, but the story says it, for there is a story about it, though, as I said before, it was a long time ago, and perhaps, after all, wasn't true."

"But if such a thing were to happen at present, would the cokos and pals bury the girl alive?"

"I can't say what they would do," said Ursula; "I suppose they are not so strict as they were long ago; at any rate, she would be driven from the tan, and avoided by all her family and relations as a Gorgio's acquaintance; so that, perhaps, at last, she would be glad if they would bury her alive."

"Well, I can conceive that there would be an objection on the part of the cokos and batus that a Romany chi should form an improper acquaintance with a Gorgio, but I should think that the batus and cokos could hardly object to the chi's entering into the honourable estate of wedlock with a Gorgio."

Ursula was silent.

"Marriage is an honourable estate, Ursula."

"Well, brother, suppose it be?"

"I don't see why a Romany chi should object to enter into the honourable estate of wedlock with a Gorgio."

"You don't, brother; don't you?"

"No," said I; "and, moreover, I am aware, notwithstanding your evasion, Ursula, that marriages and connections now and then occur between Gorgios and Romany chies; the result of which is the mixed breed, called half and half, which is at present travelling about England, and to which the Flaming Tinman belongs, otherwise called Anselo Herne."

"As for the half and halfs," said Ursula, "they are a bad set; and there is not a worse blackguard in England than Anselo Herne."

"All that you say may be very true, Ursula, but you admit that there are half and halfs."

"The more's the pity, brother."

"Pity, or not, you admit the fact; but how do you account for it?"

"How do I account for it? why, I will tell you, by the break up of a Roman family, brother—the father of a small family dies, and, perhaps, the mother; and the poor children are left behind; sometimes, they are gathered up by their relations, and sometimes, if they have none, by charitable Romans, who bring them up in the observance of gypsy law; but sometimes they are not so lucky, and falls into the company of Gorgios, trampers, and basket-makers, who live in caravans, with whom they take up, and so—— I hate to talk of the matter, brother; but so comes this race of the half and halfs."

"Then you mean to say, Ursula, that no Romany chi, unless compelled by hard necessity, would have anything to do with a Gorgio?"

"We are not over-fond of Gorgios, brother, and we hates basket-makers, and folks that live in caravans."

"Well," said I, "suppose a Gorgio who is not a basket-maker, a fine, handsome gorgious gentleman, who lives in a fine house——"

"We are not fond of houses, brother; I never slept in a house in my life."

"But would not plenty of money induce you?"

"I hate houses, brother, and those who live in them."

"Well, suppose such a person were willing to resign his fine house; and, for love of you, to adopt gypsy law, speak Romany, and live in a tan, would you have nothing to say to him?"

"Bringing plenty of money with him, brother?"

"Well, bringing plenty of money with him, Ursula."

"Well, brother, suppose you produce your man; where is he?"

"I was merely supposing such a person, Ursula."

"Then you don't know of such a person, brother?"

"Why, no, Ursula; why do you ask?"

"Because, brother, I was almost beginning to think that you meant yourself."

"Myself! Ursula; I have no fine house to resign; nor have I money. Moreover, Ursula, though I have a great regard for you, and though I consider you very handsome, quite as handsome, indeed, as Meridiana in——"

"Meridiana! where did you meet with her?" said Ursula, with a toss of her head.

"Why, in old Pulci's——"

"At old Fulcher's! that's not true, brother, Meridiana is a Borzlam, and travels with her own people, and not with old Fulcher, who is a Gorgio, and a basket-maker."

"I was not speaking of old Fulcher, but Pulci, a great Italian writer, who lived many hundred years ago, and who, in his poem called 'Morgante Maggiore,' speaks of Meridiana, the daughter of——"

"Old Carus Borzlam," said Ursula; "but if the fellow you mention lived so many hundred years ago, how, in the name of wonder, could he know anything of Meridiana?"

"The wonder, Ursula, is, how your people could ever have got hold of that name, and similar ones. The Meridiana of Pulci was not the daughter of old Carus Borzlam, but of Caradoro, a great pagan king of the East, who, being besieged in his capital by Manfredonio, another mighty pagan king, who wished to obtain possession of his daughter, who had refused him, was relieved in his distress by certain paladins of Charlemagne, with one of whom, Oliver, his daughter Meridiana fell in love."

"I see," said Ursula, "that it must have been altogether a different person, for I am sure that Meridiana Borzlam would never have fallen in love with Oliver. Oliver! why, that is the name of the curo-mengro, who lost the fight near the chong gav, the day of the great tempest, when I got wet through. No, no! Meridiana Borzlam would never have so far forgot her blood as to take up with Tom Oliver."

"I was not talking of that Oliver, Ursula, but of Oliver, peer of France, and paladin of Charlemagne, with whom Meridiana, daughter of Caradoro, fell in love, and for whose sake she renounced her religion and became a Christian, and finally ingravidata, or cambri, by him:—

'E nacquene un figliuol, dice la storia,
Che dette a Carlo-man poi gran vittoria;'

which means——"

"I don't want to know what it means," said Ursula; "no good, I'm sure. Well, if the Meridiana of Charles's wain's pal was no handsomer than Meridiana Borzlam, she was no great catch, brother; for though I am by no means given to vanity, I think myself better to look at than she, though I will say she is no lubbeny, and would scorn——"

"I make no doubt she would, Ursula, and I make no doubt that you are much handsomer than she, or even the Meridiana of Oliver. What I was about to say, before you interrupted me, is this: that though I have a great regard for you, and highly admire you, it is only in a brotherly way, and——"

"And you had nothing better to say to me." said Ursula, "when you wanted to talk to me beneath a hedge, than that you liked me in a brotherly way! well, I declare——"

"You seem disappointed, Ursula."

"Disappointed, brother! not I."

"You were just now saying that you disliked Gorgios, so, of course, could only wish that I, who am a Gorgio, should like you in a brotherly way: I wished to have a conversation with you beneath a hedge, but only with the view of procuring from you some information respecting the song which you sung the other day, and the conduct of Roman females, which has always struck me as being highly unaccountable; so, if you thought anything else——"

"What else should I expect from a picker-up of old words, brother? Bah! I dislike a picker-up of old words worse than a picker-up of old rags."

"Don't be angry, Ursula, I feel a great interest in you; you are very handsome, and very clever; indeed, with your beauty and cleverness, I only wonder that you have not long since been married."

"You do, do you, brother?"

"Yes. However, keep up your spirits, Ursula, you are not much past the prime of youth, so——"

"Not much past the prime of youth! Don't be uncivil, brother, I was only twenty-two last month."

"Don't be offended, Ursula, but twenty-two is twenty-two, or, I should rather say, that twenty-two in a woman is more than twenty-six in a man. You are still very beautiful, but I advise you to accept the first offer that's made to you."

"Thank you, brother, but your advice comes rather late; I accepted the first offer that was made me five years ago."

"You married five years ago, Ursula! is it possible?"

"Quite possible, brother, I assure you."

"And how came I to know nothing about it?"

"How comes it that you don't know many thousand things about the Romans, brother? Do you think they tell you all their affairs?"

"Married, Ursula, married! well, I declare!"

"You seem disappointed, brother."

"Disappointed! Oh! no, not at all; but Jasper, only a few weeks ago, told me that you were not married; and, indeed, almost gave me to understand that you would be very glad to get a husband."

"And you believed him? I'll tell you, brother, for your instruction, that there is not in the whole world a greater liar than Jasper Petulengro."

"I am sorry to hear it, Ursula; but with respect to him you married—who might he be? A Gorgio, or a Romany chal?"

"Gorgio, or Romany chal! Do you think I would ever condescend to a Gorgio! It was a Camomescro, brother, a Lovell, a distant relation of my own."

"And where is he? and what became of him! Have you any family?"

"Don't think I am going to tell you all my history, brother; and, to tell you the truth, I am tired of sitting under hedges with you, talking nonsense. I shall go to my house."

"Do sit a little longer, sister Ursula. I most heartily congratulate you on your marriage. But where is this same Lovell? I have never seen him: I wish to congratulate him too. You are quite as handsome as the Meridiana of Pulci, Ursula, ay, or the Despina of Riciardetto. Riciardetto, Ursula, is a poem written by one Fortiguerra, about ninety years ago, in imitation of the Morgante of Pulci. It treats of the wars of Charlemagne and his paladins with various barbarous nations, who came to besiege Paris. Despina was the daughter and heiress of Scricca, King of Cafria; she was the beloved of Riciardetto, and was beautiful as an angel; but I make no doubt you are quite as handsome as she."

"Brother," said Ursula, plucking a dandelion which grew at her feet, "I have always said that a more civil and pleasant-spoken person than yourself can't be found. I have a great regard for you and your learning, and am willing to do you any pleasure in the way of words or conversation. Mine is not a very happy story, but as you wish to hear it, it is quite at your service. Launcelot Lovell made me an offer, as you call it, and we were married in Roman fashion; that is, we gave each other our right hands, and promised to be true to each other. We lived together two years, travelling sometimes by ourselves, sometimes with our relations; I bore him two children, both of which were still-born, partly, I believe, from the fatigue I underwent in running about the country telling dukkerin when I was not exactly in a state to do so, and partly from the kicks and blows which my husband Launcelot was in the habit of giving me every night, provided I came home with less than five shillings, which it is sometimes impossible to make in the country, provided no fair or merry-making is going on. At the end of two years my husband, Launcelot, whistled a horse from a farmer's field, and sold it for forty-pounds; and for that horse he was taken, put in prison, tried, and condemned to be sent to the other country for life. Two days before he was to be sent away, I got leave to see him in the prison, and in the presence of the turnkey I gave him a thin cake of gingerbread, in which there was a dainty saw which could cut through iron. I then took on wonderfully, turned my eyes inside out, fell down in a seeming fit, and was carried out of the prison. That same night my husband sawed his irons off, cut through the bars of his window, and dropping down a height of fifty feet, lighted on his legs, and came and joined me on a heath where I was camped alone. We were just getting things ready to be off, when we heard people coming, and sure enough they were runners after my husband, Launcelot Lovell; for his escape had been discovered within a quarter of an hour after he had got away. My husband, without bidding me farewell, set off at full speed, and they after him, but they could not take him, and so they came back and took me, and shook me, and threatened me, and had me before the poknees, who shook his head at me, and threatened me in order to make me discover where my husband was, but I said I did not know, which was true enough; not that I would have told him if I had. So at last the poknees and the runners, not being able to make anything out of me, were obliged to let me go, and I went in search of my husband. I wandered about with my cart for several days in the direction in which I saw him run off, with my eyes bent on the ground, but could see no marks of him; at last, coming to four cross roads, I saw my husband's patteran."

"You saw your husband's patteran?"

"Yes, brother. Do you know what patteran means?"

"Of course. Ursula; the gypsy trail, the handful of grass which the gypsies strew in the roads as they travel, to give information to any of their companions who may be behind, as to the route they have taken. The gypsy patteran has always had a strange interest for me, Ursula."

"Like enough, brother; but what does patteran mean?"

"Why, the gypsy trail, formed as I told you before."

"And you know nothing more about patteran, brother?"

"Nothing at all, Ursula; do you?"

"What's the name for the leaf of a tree, brother?"

"I don't know," said I; "it's odd enough that I have asked that question of a dozen Romany chals and chies, and they always told me that they did not know."

"No more they did, brother; there's only one person in England that knows, and that's myself—the name for a leaf is patteran. Now there are two that knows it—the other is yourself."

"Dear me, Ursula, how very strange! I am much obliged to you. I think I never saw you look so pretty as you do now; but who told you?"

"My mother, Mrs. Herne, told it me one day, brother, when she was in a good humour, which she very seldom was, as no one has a better right to know than yourself, as she hated you mortally: it was one day when you had been asking our company what was the word for a leaf, and nobody could tell you, that she took me aside and told me, for she was in a good humour, and triumphed in seeing you balked. She told me the word for leaf was patteran, which our people use now for trail, having forgotten the true meaning. She said that the trail was called patteran, because the gypsies of old were in the habit of making the marks with the leaves and branches of trees, placed in a certain manner. She said that nobody knew it but herself, who was one of the old sort, and begged me never to tell the word to any one but him I should marry; and to be particularly cautious never to let you know it, whom she hated. Well, brother, perhaps I have done wrong to tell you; but, as I said before, I likes you, and am always ready to do your pleasure in words and conversation; my mother, moreover, is dead and gone, and, poor thing, will never know anything about the matter. So, when I married, I told my husband about the patteran, and we were in the habit of making our private trails with leaves and branches of trees, which none of the other gypsy people did; so, when I saw my husband's patteran, I knew it at once, and I followed it upwards of two hundred miles towards the north; and then I came to a deep, awful-looking water, with an overhanging bank, and on the bank I found the patteran, which directed me to proceed along the bank towards the east, and I followed my husband's patteran towards the east; and before I had gone half a mile, I came to a place where I saw the bank had given way, and fallen into the deep water. Without paying much heed, I passed on, and presently came to a public-house, not far from the water, and I entered the public-house to get a little beer, and perhaps to tell a dukkerin, for I saw a great many people about the door; and, when I entered, I found there was what they calls an inquest being held upon a body in that house, and the jury had just risen to go and look at the body; and being a woman, and having a curiosity, I thought I would go with them, and so I did; and no sooner did I see the body, than I knew it to be my husband's; it was much swelled and altered, but I knew it partly by the clothes, and partly by a mark on the forehead, and I cried out, 'It is my husband's body,' and I fell down in a fit, and the fit that time, brother, was not a seeming one."

"Dear me," said I, "how terrible! but tell me, Ursula, how did your husband come by his death?"

"The bank, overhanging the deep water, gave way under him, brother, and he was drowned; for, like most of our people, he could not swim, or only a little. The body, after it had been in the water a long time, came up of itself, and was found floating. Well, brother, when the people of the neighbourhood found that I was the wife of the drowned man, they were very kind to me, and made a subscription for me, with which, after having seen my husband buried, I returned the way I had come, till I met Jasper and his people, and with them I have travelled ever since: I was very melancholy for a long time, I assure you, brother; for the death of my husband preyed very much upon my mind."

"His death was certainly a very shocking one, Ursula; but, really, if he had died a natural one, you could scarcely have regretted it, for he appears to have treated you barbarously."

"Women must bear, brother; and, barring that he kicked and beat me, and drove me out to tell dukkerin when I could scarcely stand, he was not a bad husband. A man, by gypsy law, brother, is allowed to kick and beat his wife, and to bury her alive, if he thinks proper. I am a gypsy, and have nothing to say against the law."

"But what has Mikailia Chikno to say about it?"

"She is a cripple. brother, the only cripple amongst the Roman people: so she is allowed to do and say as she pleases. Moreover, her husband does not think fit to kick or beat her, though it is my opinion she would like him all the better if he were occasionally to do so, and threaten to bury her alive; at any rate, she would treat him better, and respect him more."

"Your sister does not seem to stand much in awe of Jasper Petulengro, Ursula."

"Let the matters of my sister and Jasper Petulengro alone, brother; you must travel in their company some time before you can understand them; they are a strange two, up to all kind of chaffing: but two more regular Romans don't breathe, and I'll tell you, for your instruction, that there isn't a better mare-breaker in England than Jasper Petulengro, if you can manage Miss Isopel Berners as well as——"

"Isopel Berners," said I, "how came you to think of her?"

"How should I but think of her, brother, living as she does with you in Mumper's Dingle, and travelling about with you; you will have, brother, more difficulty to manage her, than Jasper has to manage my sister Pakomovna. I should have mentioned her before, only I wanted to know what you had to say to me; and when we got into discourse, I forgot her. I say, brother, let me tell you your dukkerin, with respect to her, you will never——"

"I want to hear no dukkerin, Ursula."

"Do let me tell you your dukkerin, brother, you will never manage——"

"I want to hear no dukkerin, Ursula, in connection with Isopel Berners. Moreover, it is Sunday, we will change the subject; it is surprising to me that, after all you have undergone, you should look so beautiful. I suppose you do not think of marrying again, Ursula?"

"No, brother, one husband at a time is quite enough for any reasonable mort; especially such a good husband as I have got."

"Such a good husband! why, I thought you told me your husband was drowned?"

"Yes, brother, my first husband was."

"And have you a second?"

"To be sure, brother."

"And who is he? in the name of wonder."

"Who is he? why Sylvester, to be sure."

"I do assure you, Ursula, that I feel disposed to be angry with you; such a handsome young woman as yourself to take up with such a nasty pepper-faced good for nothing——"

"I won't hear my husband abused, brother; so you had better say no more."

"Why, is he not the Lazarus of the gypsies? has he a penny of his own, Ursula?"

"Then the more his want, brother, of a clever chi like me to take care of him and his childer. I tell you what, brother, I will chore, if necessary, and tell dukkerin for Sylvester, if even so heavy as scarcely to be able to stand. You call him lazy; you would not think him lazy if you were in a ring with him: he is a proper man with his hands; Jasper is going to back him for twenty pounds against Slammocks of the Chong gav, the brother of Roarer and Bell-metal, he says he has no doubt that he will win."

"Well, if you like him, I, of course, can have no objection. Have you been long married?"

"About a fortnight, brother; that dinner, the other day, when I sang the song, was given in celebration of the wedding."

"Were you married in a church, Ursula?"

"We were not, brother; none but Gorgios, cripples, and lubbenys are ever married in a church: we took each other's words. Brother, I have been with you near three hours beneath this hedge. I will go to my husband."

"Does he know that you are here?"

"He does, brother."

"And is he satisfied?"

"Satisfied! of course. Lor', you Gorgios! Brother, I go to my husband and my house." And, thereupon, Ursula rose and departed.

After waiting a little time I also arose; it was now dark, and I thought I could do no better than betake myself to the dingle; at the entrance of it I found Mr. Petulengro. "Well, brother," said he, "what kind of conversation have you and Ursula had beneath the hedge?"

"If you wished to hear what we were talking about, you should have come and sat down beside us; you knew where we were."

"Well, brother, I did much the same, for I went and sat down behind you."

"Behind the hedge, Jasper?"

"Behind the hedge, brother."

"And heard all our conversation."

"Every word, brother; and a rum conversation it was."

"'Tis an old saying, Jasper, that listeners never hear any good of themselves; perhaps you heard the epithet that Ursula bestowed upon you."

"If, by epitaph, you mean that she called me a liar, I did, brother, and she was not much wrong, for I certainly do not always stick exactly to truth; you, however, have not much to complain of me."

"You deceived me about Ursula, giving me to understand she was not married."

"She was not married when I told you so, brother; that is, not to Sylvester; nor was I aware that she was going to marry him. I once thought you had a kind of regard for her, and I am sure she had as much for you as a Romany chi can have for a Gorgio. I half expected to have heard you make love to her behind the hedge, but I begin to think you care for nothing in this world but old words and strange stories. Lor' to take a young woman under a hedge, and talk to her as you did to Ursula; and yet you got everything out of her that you wanted, with your gammon about old Fulcher and Meridiana. You are a cunning one, brother."

"There you are mistaken, Jasper. I am not cunning. If people think I am, it is because, being made up of art themselves, simplicity of character is a puzzle to them. Your women are certainly extraordinary creatures, Jasper."

"Didn't I say they were rum animals? Brother, we Romans shall always stick together as long as they stick fast to us."

"Do you think they always will, Jasper?"

"Can't say, brother; nothing lasts for ever. Romany chies are Romany chies still, though not exactly what they were sixty years ago. My wife, though a rum one, is not Mrs. Herne, brother. I think she is rather fond of Frenchmen and French discourse. I tell you what, brother, if ever gypsyism breaks up, it will be owing to our chies having been bitten by that mad puppy they calls gentility."

CHAPTER XLII

I DESCENDED to the bottom of the dingle. It was nearly involved in obscurity. To dissipate the feeling of melancholy which came over my mind, I resolved to kindle a fire; and having heaped dry sticks upon my hearth, and added a billet or two, I struck a light, and soon produced a blaze. Sitting down, I fixed my eyes upon the blaze, and soon fell into a deep meditation. I thought of the events of the day, the scene at church, and what I had heard at church, the danger of losing one's soul, the doubts of Jasper Petulengro as to whether one had a soul. I thought over the various arguments which I had either heard, or which had come spontaneously to my mind, for or against the probability of a state of future existence. They appeared to me to be tolerably evenly balanced. I then thought that it was at all events taking the safest part to conclude that there was a soul. It would be a terrible thing, after having passed one's life in the disbelief of the existence of a soul, to wake up after death a soul, and to find one's self a lost soul. Yes, methought I would come to the conclusion that one has a soul. Choosing the safe side, however, appeared to me to be playing a rather dastardly part. I had never been an admirer of people who chose the safe side in everything; indeed I had always entertained a thorough contempt for them. Surely it would be showing more manhood to adopt the dangerous side, that of disbelief; I almost resolved to do so—but yet in a question of so much importance, I ought not to be guided by vanity. The question was not which was the safe, but the true side? yet how was I to know which was the true side? Then I thought of the Bible—which I had been reading in the morning—that spoke of the soul and a future state; but was the Bible true? I had heard learned and moral men say that it was true but I had also heard learned and moral men say that it was not: how was I to decide? Still that balance of probabilities! If I could but see the way of truth, I would follow it, if necessary, upon hands and knees; on that I was determined; but I could not see it. Feeling my brain begin to turn round, I resolved to think of something else; and forthwith began to think of what had passed between Ursula and myself in our discourse beneath the hedge.

I mused deeply on what she had told me as to the virtue of the females of her race. How singular that virtue must be which was kept pure and immaculate by the possessor, whilst indulging in habits of falsehood and dishonesty! I had always thought the gypsy females extraordinary beings. I had often wondered at them, their dress, their manner of speaking, and, not least, at their names; but, until the present day, I had been unacquainted with the most extraordinary point connected with them. How came they possessed of this extraordinary virtue? was it because they were thievish? I remembered that an ancient thief-taker, who had retired from his useful calling, and who frequently visited the office of my master at law, the respectable S——, who had the management of his property—I remembered to have heard this worthy, with whom I occasionally held discourse, philosophic and profound, when he and I chanced to be alone together in the office, say that all first-rate thieves were sober, and of well-regulated morals, their bodily passions being kept in abeyance by their love of gain; but this axiom could scarcely hold good with respect to these women—however thievish they might be, they did care for something besides gain: they cared for their husbands. If they did thieve, they merely thieved for their husbands; and though, perhaps, some of them were vain, they merely prized their beauty because it gave them favour in the eyes of their husbands. Whatever the husbands were—and Jasper had almost insinuated that the males occasionally allowed themselves some latitude—they appeared to be as faithful to their husbands as the ancient Roman matrons were to theirs. Roman matrons! and, after all, might not these be in reality Roman matrons? They called themselves Romans; might not they be the descendants of the old Roman matrons? Might not they be of the same blood as Lucretia? And were not many of their strange names—Lucretia amongst the rest—handed down to them from old Rome? It is true their language was not that of old Rome; it was not, however, altogether different from it. After all, the ancient Romans might be a tribe of these people, who settled down and founded a village with the tilts of carts, which, by degrees, and the influx of other people, became the grand city of the world. I liked the idea of the grand city of the world owing its origin to a people who had been in the habit of carrying their houses in their carts. Why, after all, should not the Romans of history be a branch of these Romans? There were several points of similarity between them; if Roman matrons were chaste, both men and women were thieves. Old Rome was the thief of the world; yet still there were difficulties to be removed before I could persuade myself that the old Romans and my Romans were identical; and in trying to remove these difficulties, I felt my brain once more beginning to turn, and in haste took up another subject of meditation, and that was the patteran, and what Ursula had told me about it.

I had always entertained a strange interest for that sign by which in their wanderings the Romanese gave to those of their people who came behind intimation as to the direction which they took; but it now inspired me with greater interest than ever—now that I had learnt that the proper meaning of it was the leaves of trees. I had, as I had said in my dialogue with Ursula, been very eager to learn the word for leaf in the Romanian language, but had never learnt it till this day; so patteran signified leaf of a tree; and no one at present knew that but myself and Ursula, who had learnt it from Mrs. Herne, the last, it was said, of the old stock; and then I thought what strange people the gypsies must have been in the old time. They were sufficiently strange at present, but they must have been far stranger of old; they must have been a more peculiar people—their language must have been more perfect—and they must have had a greater stock of strange secrets. I almost wished that I had lived some two or three hundred years ago, that I might have observed these people when they were yet stranger than at present. I wondered whether I could have introduced myself to their company at that period, whether I should have been so fortunate as to meet such a strange, half-malicious, half-good-humoured being as Jasper, who would have instructed me in the language, then more deserving of note than at present. What might I not have done with that language, had I known it in its purity? Why, I might have written books in it; yet those who spoke it would hardly have admitted me to their society at that period, when they kept more to themselves. Yet I thought that I might possibly have gained their confidence, and have wandered about with them, and learnt their language, and all their strange ways, and then—and then—and a sigh rose from the depth of my breast; for I began to think, "Supposing I had accomplished all this, what would have been the profit of it; and in what would all this wild gypsy dream have terminated?"

Then rose another sigh, yet more profound, for I began to think, "What was likely to be the profit of my present way of life; the living in dingles, making pony- and donkey-shoes, conversing with gypsy-women under hedges, and extracting from them their odd secrets?" What was likely to be the profit of such a kind of life, even should it continue for a length of time? —a supposition not very probable, for I was earning nothing to support me, and the funds with which I had entered upon this life were gradually disappearing. I was living, it is true, not unpleasantly, enjoying the healthy air of heaven; but, upon the whole, was I not sadly misspending my time? Surely I was; and, as I looked back, it appeared to me that I had always been doing so. What had been the profit of the tongues which I had learnt? had they ever assisted me in the day of hunger? No, no! it appeared to me that I had always misspent my time, save in one instance, when by a desperate effort I had collected all the powers of my imagination, and written the "Life of Joseph Sell"; but even when I wrote the "Life of Sell," was I not in a false position? Provided I had not misspent my time, would it have been necessary to make that effort, which, after all, had only enabled me to leave London, and wander about the country for a time? But could I, taking all circumstances into consideration, have done better than I had? With my peculiar temperament and ideas, could I have pursued with advantage the profession to which my respectable parents had endeavoured to bring me up? It appeared to me that I could not, and that the hand of necessity had guided me from my earliest years, until the present night, in which I found myself seated in the dingle, staring on the brands of the fire. But ceasing to think of the past which, as irrecoverably gone, it was useless to regret, even were there cause to regret it, what should I do in future? Should I write another book like the "Life of Joseph Sell"; take it to London, and offer it to a publisher? But when I reflected on the grisly sufferings which I had undergone whilst engaged in writing the "Life of Sell," I shrank from the idea of a similar attempt; moreover, I doubted whether I possessed the power to write a similar work—whether the materials for the life of another Sell lurked within the recesses of my brain? Had I not better become in reality what I had hitherto been merely playing at—a tinker or a gypsy? But I soon saw that I was not fitted to become either in reality. It was much more agreeable to play the gypsy or the tinker than to become either in realty. I had seen enough of gypsying and tinkering to be convinced of that. All of a sudden the idea of tilling the soil came into my head; tilling the soil was a healthful and noble pursuit! but my idea of tilling the soil had no connection with Britain; for I could only expect to till the soil in Britain as a serf. I thought of tilling it in America, in which it was said there was plenty of wild, unclaimed land, of which any one, who chose to clear it of its trees, might take possession. I figured myself in America, in an immense forest, clearing the land destined, by my exertions, to become a fruitful and smiling plain. Methought I heard the crash of the huge trees as they fell beneath my axe; and then I bethought me that a man was intended to marry—I ought to marry; and if I married, where was I likely to be more happy as a husband and a father than in America, engaged in tilling the ground? I fancied myself in America, engaged in tilling the ground, assisted by an enormous progeny. Well, why not marry, and go and till the ground in America? I was young, and youth was the time to marry in, and to labour in. I had the use of all my faculties; my eyes, it is true, were rather dull from early study, and from writing the "Life of Joseph Sell"; but I could see tolerably well with them, and they were not bleared. I felt my arms, and thighs, and teeth—they were strong and sound enough; so now was the time to labour, to marry, eat strong flesh, and beget strong children—the power of doing all this would pass away with youth, which was terribly transitory. I bethought me that a time would come when my eyes would be bleared, and perhaps, sightless; my arms and thighs strengthless and sapless; when my teeth would shake in my jaws, even supposing they did not drop out. No going a wooing then—no labouring—no eating strong flesh, and begetting lusty children then; and I bethought me how, when all this should be, I should bewail the days of my youth as misspent, provided I had not in them founded for myself a home, and begotten strong children to take care of me in the days when I could not take care of myself; and thinking of these things, I became sadder and sadder, and stared vacantly upon the fire till my eyes closed in a doze.

I continued dozing over the fire, until rousing myself I perceived that the brands were nearly consumed, and I thought of retiring for the night. I arose, and was about to enter my tent, when a thought struck me. "Suppose," thought I, "that Isopel Berners should return in the midst of the night, how dark and dreary would the dingle appear without a fire! truly, I will keep up the fire, and I will do more; I have no board to spread for her, but I will fill the kettle, and heat it, so that, if she comes, I may be able to welcome her with a cup of tea, for I know she loves tea." Thereupon, I piled more wood upon the fire, and soon succeeded in procuring a better blaze than before; then, taking the kettle, I set out for the spring. On arriving at the mouth of the dingle, which fronted the east, I perceived that Charles's wain was nearly opposite to it, high above in the heavens, by which I knew that the night was tolerably well advanced. The gypsy encampment lay before me; all was hushed and still within it, and its inmates appeared to be locked in slumber; as I advanced, however, the dogs, which were fastened outside the tents, growled and barked; but presently recognising me, they were again silent, some of them wagging their tails. As I drew near a particular tent, I heard a female voice say—"Some one is coming!" and, as I was about to pass it, the cloth which formed the door was suddenly lifted up, and a black head and part of a huge naked body protruded. It was the head and upper part of the giant Tawno, who, according to the fashion of gypsy men, lay next the door wrapped in his blanket; the blanket had, however, fallen off, and the starlight shone clear on his athletic tawny body, and was reflected from his large staring eyes.

"It is only I, Tawno," said I, "going to fill the kettle, as it is possible that Miss Berners may arrive this night." "Kos-ko," drawled out Tawno, and replaced the curtain. "Good, do you call it?" said the sharp voice of his wife; "there is no good in the matter! if that young chap were not living with the rawnie in the illegal and uncertificated line, he would not be getting up in the middle of the night to fill her kettles." Passing on, I proceeded to the spring, where I filled the kettle, and then returned to the dingle.

Placing the kettle upon the fire, I watched it till it began to boil; then removing it from the top of the brands, I placed it close beside the fire, and leaving it simmering, I retired to my tent; where, having taken off my shoes, and a few of my garments, I lay down on my palliasse, and was not long in falling asleep. I believe I slept soundly for some time, thinking and dreaming of nothing; suddenly, however, my sleep became disturbed, and the subject of the patterans began to occupy my brain. I imagined that I saw Ursula tracing her husband, Launcelot Lovell, by means of his patterans; I imagined that she had considerable difficulty in doing so; that she was occasionally interrupted by parish beadles and constables, who asked her whither she was travelling, to whom she gave various answers. Presently methought that, as she was passing by a farm-yard, two fierce and savage dogs flew at her; I was in great trouble, I remember, and wished to assist her, but could not, for though I seemed to see her, I was still at a distance: and now it appeared that she had escaped from the dogs, and was proceeding with her cart along a gravelly path which traversed a wild moor; I could hear the wheels grating amidst sand and gravel. The next moment I was awake, and found myself sitting up in my tent; there was a glimmer of light through the canvas caused by the fire; a feeling of dread came over me, which was perhaps natural, on starting suddenly from one's sleep in that wild lone place; I half imagined that some one was nigh the tent; the idea made me rather uncomfortable and, to dissipate it, I lifted up the canvas of the door and peeped out, and, lo! I had a distinct view of a tall figure standing by the tent. "Who is that?" said I, whilst I felt my blood rush to my heart. "It is I," said the voice of Isopel Berners; "you little expected me, I dare say; well, sleep on, I do not wish to disturb you." "But I was expecting you," said I, recovering myself, "as you may see by the fire and kettle. I will be with you in a moment."

Putting on in haste the articles of dress which I had flung off, I came out of the tent, and addressing myself to Isopel, who was standing beside her cart, I said—"Just as I was about to retire to rest I thought it possible that you might come to-night, and got everything in readiness for you. Now, sit down by the fire whilst I lead the donkey and cart to the place where you stay; I will unharness the animal, and presently come and join you." "I need not trouble you," said Isopel; "I will go myself and see after my things." "We will go together," said I, "and then return and have some tea." Isopel made no objection, and in about half-an-hour we had arranged everything at her quarters, I then hastened and prepared tea. Presently Isopel rejoined me, bringing her stool; she had divested herself of her bonnet, and her hair fell over her shoulders; she sat down, and I poured out the beverage, handing her a cup. "Have you made a long journey to-night?" said I. "A very long one," replied Belle. "I have come nearly twenty miles since six o'clock." "I believe I heard you coming in my sleep," said I; "did the dogs above bark at you?" "Yes," said Isopel, "very violently; did you think of me in your sleep?" "No," said I, "I was thinking of Ursula and something she had told me." "When and where was that?" said Isopel. "Yesterday evening," said I, "beneath the dingle hedge." "Then you were talking with her beneath the hedge?" "I was," said I, "but only upon gypsy matters. Do you know, Belle, that she has just been married to Sylvester, so that you need not think that she and I——" "She and you are quite at liberty to sit where you please," said Isopel. "However, young man," she continued, dropping her tone, which she had slightly raised, "I believe what you said, that you were merely talking about gypsy matters, and also what you were going to say, if it was, as I suppose, that she and you had no particular acquaintance." Isopel was now silent for some time. "What are you thinking of?" said I. "I was thinking," said Belle, "how exceedingly kind it was of you to get everything in readiness for me, though you did not know that I should come." "I had a presentiment that you would come," said I; "but you forget that I have prepared the kettle for you before, though it was true that I was then certain that you would come." "I had not forgotten your doing so, young man," said Belle; "but I was beginning to think that you were utterly selfish, caring for nothing but the gratification of your own selfish whims." "I am very fond of having my own way," said I, "but utterly selfish I am not, as I dare say I shall frequently prove to you. You will often find the kettle boiling when you come home." "Not heated by you," said Isopel, with a sigh. "By whom else?" said I; "surely you are not thinking of driving me away?" "You have as much right here as myself," said Isopel, "as I have told you before; but I must be going myself." "Well," said I, "we can go together; to tell you the truth, I am rather tired of this place." "Our paths must be separate," said Belle. "Separate," said I, "what do you mean? I sha'n't let you go alone, I shall go with you; and you know the road is as free to me as to you; besides, you can't think of parting company with me, considering how much you would lose by doing so; remember that you know scarcely anything of the Armenian language; now, to learn Armenian from me would take you twenty years."

Belle faintly smiled. "Come," said I, "take another cup of tea." Belle took another cup of tea, and yet another; we had some indifferent conversation, after which I arose and gave her donkey a considerable feed of corn. Belle thanked me, shook me by the hand, and then went to her own tabernacle, and I returned to mine.

CHAPTER XLIII

On the following morning, after breakfasting with Belle, who was silent and melancholy, I left her in the dingle, and took a stroll amongst the neighbouring lanes. After some time I thought I would pay a visit to the landlord of the public-house, whom I had not seen since the day when he communicated to me his intention of changing his religion. I therefore directed my steps to the house, and on entering it found the landlord standing in the kitchen. Just then two mean-looking fellows, who had been drinking at one of the tables, and who appeared to be the only customers in the house, got up, brushed past the landlord, and saying in a surly tone, we shall pay you some time or other, took their departure. "That's the way they serve me now," said the landlord, with a sigh. "Do you know those fellows," I demanded, "since you let them go away in your debt?" "I know nothing about them," said the landlord, "save that they are a couple of scamps." "Then why did you let them go away without paying you?" said I. "I had not the heart to stop them," said the landlord; "and, to tell you the truth, everybody serves me so now, and I suppose they are right, for a child could flog me." "Nonsense," said I, "behave more like a man, and, with respect to those two fellows, run after them, I will go with you, and if they refuse to pay the reckoning I will help you to shake some money out of their clothes."

"I am half inclined to take your advice," said the landlord, "only, to tell you the truth, I feel quite low, without any heart in me." "Come into the bar," said I, "and let us have something together—you need not be afraid of my not paying for what I order."

We went into the bar-room, where the landlord and I discussed between us two bottles of strong ale. Whilst quaffing our beverage, he gave me an account of the various mortifications to which he had of late been subject, dwelling with particular bitterness on the conduct of Hunter, who he said came every night and mouthed him, and afterwards went away without paying for what he had drank or smoked, in which conduct he was closely imitated by a clan of fellows who constantly attended him. After spending several hours at the public-house I departed, not forgetting to pay for the two bottles of ale. The landlord, before I went, shaking me by the hand, declared that he had now made up his mind to stick to his religion at all hazards, the more especially as he was convinced he should derive no good by giving it up.

It might be about five in the evening, when I reached the gypsy encampment. Here I found Mr. Petulengro, Tawno Chikno, Sylvester, and others in a great bustle, clipping and trimming certain ponies and old horses which they had brought with them. On inquiring of Jasper the reason of their being so engaged, he informed me that they were getting the horses ready for a fair, which was to be held on the morrow, at a place some miles distant, at which they should endeavour to dispose of them, adding—"Perhaps, brother, you will go with us, provided you have nothing better to do?" Not having any particular engagement, I assured him that I should have great pleasure in being of the party. It was agreed that we should start early on the following morning.

Thereupon I descended into the dingle. Belle was sitting before the fire, at which the kettle was boiling. "Were you waiting for me?" I inquired. "Yes," said Belle, "I thought that you would come, and I waited for you." "That was very kind," said I. "Not half so kind," said she, "as it was of you to get everything ready for me in the dead of last night, when there was scarcely a chance of my coming." The tea-things were brought forward, and we sat down. "Have you been far?" said Belle. "Merely to that public-house," said I, "to which you directed me on the second day of our acquaintance." "Young men should not make a habit of visiting public-houses," said Belle, "they are bad places." "They may be so to some people," said I, "but I do not think the worst public-house in England could do me any harm." "Perhaps, you are so bad already," said Belle, with a smile, "that it would be impossible to spoil you."

"How dare you catch at my words?" said I; "come, I will make you pay for doing so—you shall have this evening the longest lesson in Armenian which I have yet inflicted upon you." "You may well say inflicted," said Belle, "but pray spare me. I do not wish to hear anything about Armenian, especially this evening." "Why this evening?" said I. Belle made no answer. "I will not spare you," said I; "this evening I intend to make you conjugate an Armenian verb." "Well, be it so," said Belle; "for this evening you shall command." "To command is hramahyel," said I. "Ram her ill, indeed," said Belle; "I do not wish to begin with that." "No," said I, "as we have come to the verbs, we will begin regularly; hramahyel is a verb of the second conjugation. We will begin with the first." "First of all tell me," said Belle, "what a verb is?" "A part of speech," said I, "which, according to the dictionary, signifies some action or passion; for example, I command you, or I hate you." "I have given you no cause to hate me," said Belle, looking me sorrowfully in the face.

"I was merely giving two examples," said I, "and neither was directed at you. In those examples, to command and hate are verbs. Belle, in Armenian there are four conjugations of verbs; the first ends in al, the second in yel, the third in oul, and the fourth in il. Now, have you understood me?"

"I am afraid, indeed, it will all end ill," said Belle. "Hold your tongue," said I, "or you will make me lose my patience." "You have already made me nearly lose mine," said Belle. "Let us have no unprofitable interruptions," said I; "the conjugations of the Armenian verbs are neither so numerous nor so difficult as the declensions of the nouns; hear that, and rejoice. Come, we will begin with the verb hntal, a verb of the first conjugation, which signifies to rejoice. Come along; hntam, I rejoice; hntas, thou rejoicest; why don't you follow, Belle?"

"I am sure I don't rejoice, whatever you may do," said Belle. "The chief difficulty, Belle," said I, "that I find in teaching you the Armenian grammar, proceeds from your applying to yourself and me every example I give. Rejoice, in this instance, is merely an example of an Armenian verb of the first conjugation, and has no more to do with your rejoicing than lal, which is also a verb of the first conjugation, and which signifies to weep, would have to do with your weeping, provided I made you conjugate it. Come along; hntam, I rejoice; hntas, thou rejoicest; hntà, he rejoices; hntamk, we rejoice: now, repeat those words."

"I can't," said Belle, "they sound more like the language of horses than human beings. Do you take me for——?" "For what?" said I. Belle was silent. "Were you going to say mare?" said I. "Mare! mare! by-the-bye, do you know, Belle, that mare in old English stands for woman; and that when we call a female an evil mare, the strict meaning of the term is merely a bad woman. So if I were to call you a mare without prefixing bad, you must not be offended." "But I should though," said Belle. "I was merely attempting to make you acquainted with a philological fact," said I. "If mare, which in old English, and likewise in vulgar English, signifies a woman, sounds the same as mare, which in modern and polite English signifies a female horse, I can't help it. There is no such confusion of sounds in Armenian, not, at least, in the same instance. Belle, in Armenian, woman is ghin, the same word, by-the-bye, as our queen, whereas mare is madagh tzi, which signifies a female horse; and perhaps you will permit me to add, that a hard-mouthed jade is, in Armenian, madagh tzi hsdierah."

"I can't bear this much longer," said Belle. "Keep yourself quiet," said I; "I wish to be gentle with you; and to convince you, we will skip hntal, and also for the present verbs of the first conjugation and proceed to the second. Belle, I will now select for you to conjugate the prettiest verb in Armenian; not only of the second, but also of all the four conjugations; that verb is siriel. Here is the present tense:—siriem, siries, sirè, siriemk, sirèk, sirien. You observe that it runs on just in the same manner as hntal, save and except that the e is substituted for a; and it will be as well to tell you that almost the only difference between the second, third, and fourth conjugation, and the first, is the substituting in the present, preterite and other tenses e or ou, or i for a; so you see that the Armenian verbs are by no means difficult. Come on, Belle, and say siriem." Belle hesitated. "Pray oblige me, Belle, by saying siriem!" Belle still appeared to hesitate. "You must admit, Belle, that it is much softer than hntam." "It is so," said Belle; "and to oblige you I will say siriem." "Very well indeed, Belle," said I. "No vartabied, or doctor, could have pronounced it better; and now, to show you how verbs act upon pronouns in Armenian, I will say siriem zkiez. Please to repeat siriem zkiez!" "Siriem zkiez!" said Belle; "that last word is very hard to say." "Sorry that you think so, Belle," said I. "Now please to say sirià zis." Belle did so. "Exceedingly well," said I. "Now say, yerani thè sirèir zis." "Yerani thè sirèir zis," said Belle. "Capital!" said I; "you have now said, I love you—love me—ah! would that you would love me!"

"And I have said all these things?" said Belle. "Yes," said I; "you have said them in Armenian." "I would have said them in no language that I understood," said Belle; "and it was very wrong of you to take advantage of my ignorance, and make me say such things." "Why so?" said I; "if you said them, I said them too." "You did so," said Belle; "but I believe you were merely bantering and jeering." "As I told you before, Belle," said I, "the chief difficulty which I find in teaching you Armenian proceeds from your persisting in applying to yourself and me every example I give." "Then you meant nothing after all," said Belle, raising her voice. "Let us proceed," said I; "sirietsi, I loved." "You never loved any one but yourself," said Belle; "and what's more—" "Sirietsits, I will love," said I; "sirietsies, thou wilt love." "Never one so thoroughly heartless," said Belle. "I tell you what, Belle, you are becoming intolerable, but we will change the verb; or rather I will now proceed to tell you here, that some of the Armenian conjugations have their anomalies; one species of these I wish to bring before your notice. As old Villotte says—from whose work I first contrived to pick up the rudiments of Armenian—'Est verborum transitivorum, quorum infinitivus—' but I forgot, you don't understand Latin. He says there are certain transitive verbs, whose infinitive is in outsaniel; the preterite in outsi; the imperative in oue; for example—parghatsoutsaniem, I irritate—"

"You do, you do," said Belle; "and it will be better for both of us, if you leave off doing so."

"You would hardly believe, Belle," said I, "that the Armenian is in some respects closely connected with the Irish, but so it is; for example, that word parghatsoutsaniem is evidently derived from the same root as feargaim, which, in Irish, is as much as to say I vex."

"You do, indeed," said Belle, sobbing.

"But how do you account for it?"

"O man, man!" said Belle, bursting into tears, "for what purpose do you ask a poor ignorant girl such a question, unless it be to vex and irritate her? If you wish to display your learning, do so to the wise and instructed, and not to me, who can scarcely read or write. Oh, leave off your nonsense; yet I know you will not do so, for it is the breath of your nostrils! I could have wished we should have parted in kindness, but you will not permit it. I have deserved better at your hands than such treatment. The whole time we have kept company together in this place, I have scarcely had one kind word from you, but the strangest—" and here the voice of Belle was drowned in her sobs.

"I am sorry to see you take on so, dear Belle," said I. "I really have given you no cause to be so unhappy; surely teaching you a little Armenian was a very innocent kind of diversion."

"Yes, but you went on so long, and in such a strange way, and made me repeat such strange examples, as you call them, that I could not bear it."

"Why, to tell you the truth, Belle, it's just my way; and I have dealt with you just as I would with—"

"A hard-mouthed jade," said Belle, "and you practising your horse-witchery upon her. I have been of an unsubdued spirit, I acknowledge, but I was always kind to you; and if you have made me cry, it's a poor thing to boast of."

"Boast of!" said I; "a pretty thing indeed to boast of; I had no idea of making you cry. Come, I beg your pardon; what more can I do? Come, cheer up, Belle. You were talking of parting; don't let us part, but depart, and that together."

"Our ways lie different," said Belle.

"I don't see why they should," said I. "Come, let us be off to America together."

"To America together?" said Belle, looking full at me.

"Yes," said I; "where we will settle down in some forest, and conjugate the verb siriel conjugally."

"Conjugally?" said Belle.

"Yes," said I; "as man and wife in America, air yew ghin."

"You are jesting, as usual," said Belle.

"Not I, indeed. Come, Belle, make up your mind, and let us be off to America; and leave priests, humbug, learning, and languages behind us."

"I don't think you are jesting," said Belle; "but I can hardly entertain your offers; however, young man, I thank you."

"You had better make up your mind at once," said I, "and let us be off. I sha'n't make a bad husband, I assure you. Perhaps you think I am not worthy of you? To convince you, Belle, that I am, I am ready to try a fall with you this moment upon the grass. Brynhilda, the valkyrie, swore that no one should ever marry her who could not fling her down. Perhaps you have done the same. The man who eventually married her, got a friend of his, who was called Sigurd, the serpent-killer, to wrestle with her, disguising him in his own armour. Sigurd flung her down, and won her for his friend, though he loved her himself. I shall not use a similar deceit, nor employ Jasper Petulengro to personate me—so get up, Belle, and I will do my best to fling you down."

"I require no such thing of you, or anybody," said Belle; "you are beginning to look rather wild."

"I every now and then do," said I; "come, Belle, what do you say?"

"I will say nothing at present on the subject," said Belle, "I must have time to consider."

"Just as you please," said I, "to-morrow I go to a fair with Mr. Petulengro, perhaps you will consider whilst I am away. Come, Belle, let us have some more tea. I wonder whether we shall be able to procure tea as good as this in the American forest."

It was about the dawn of day when I was awakened by the voice of Mr. Petulengro shouting from the top of the dingle, and bidding me get up. I arose instantly, and dressed myself for the expedition to the fair. On leaving my tent, I was surprised to observe Belle, entirely dressed, standing close to her own little encampment. "Dear me," said I, "I little expected to find you up so early. I suppose Jasper's call awakened you, as it did me." "I merely lay down in my things," said Belle, "and have not slept during the night." "And why did you not take off your things and go to sleep?" said I. "I did not undress," said Belle, "because I wished to be in readiness to bid you farewell when you departed; and as for sleeping, I could not." "Well, God bless you!" said I, taking Belle by the hand. Belle made no answer, and I observed that her hand was very cold. "What is the matter with you?" said I, looking her in the face. Belle looked at me for a moment in the eyes—and then cast down her own—her features were very pale. "You are really unwell," said I, "I had better not go to the fair, but stay here, and take care of you." "No," said Belle, "pray go, I am not unwell." "Then go to your tent," said I, "and do not endanger your health by standing abroad in the raw morning air. God bless you, Belle. I shall be home to-night, by which time I expect you will have made up your mind; if not, another lesson in Armenian, however late the hour be." I then wrung Belle's hand, and ascended to the plain above.

I found the Romany party waiting for me, and everything in readiness for departing. Mr. Petulengro and Tawno Chikno were mounted on two old horses. The rest, who intended to go to the fair, amongst whom were two or three women, were on foot. On arriving at the extremity of the plain, I looked towards the dingle. Isopel Berners stood at the mouth, the beams of the early morning sun shone full on her noble face and figure. I waved my hand towards her. She slowly lifted up her right arm. I turned away, and never saw Isopel Berners again.

My companions and myself proceeded on our way. In about two hours we reached the place where the fair was to be held. After breakfasting on bread and cheese and ale behind a broken stone wall, we drove our animals to the fair. The fair was a common cattle and horse fair: there was little merriment going on, but there was no lack of business. By about two o'clock in the afternoon, Mr. Petulengro and his people had disposed of their animals at what they conceived very fair prices—they were all in high spirits, and Jasper proposed to adjourn to a public-house. As we were proceeding to one, a very fine horse, led by a jockey, made its appearance on the ground. Mr. Petulengro stopped short, and looked at it stedfastly: "Fino covar dove odoy sas miro—a fine thing were that if it were but mine!" he exclaimed. "If you covet it," said I, "why do you not purchase it?" "We low 'Gyptians never buy animals of that description; if we did we could never sell them, and most likely should be had up as horse-stealers." "Then why did you say just now, 'It were a fine thing if it were but yours'?" said I. "We 'Gyptians always say so when we see anything that we admire. An animal like that is not intended for a little hare like me, but for some grand gentleman like yourself. I say, brother, do you buy that horse!" "How should I buy the horse, you foolish person?" said I. "Buy the horse, brother," said Mr. Petulengro, "if you have not the money I can lend it you, though I be of lower Egypt." "You talk nonsense," said I; "however, I wish you would ask the man the price of it." Mr. Petulengro, going up to the jockey, inquired the price of the horse—the man, looking at him scornfully, made no reply. "Young man," said I, going up to the jockey, "do me the favour to tell me the price of that horse, as I suppose it is to sell." The jockey, who was a surly-looking man, of about fifty, looked at me for a moment, then, after some hesitation, said, laconically, "Seventy." "Thank you," said I, and turned away. "Buy that horse," said Mr. Petulengro, coming after me; "the dook tells me that in less than three months he will be sold for twice seventy." "I will have nothing to do with him," said I; "besides, Jasper, I don't like his tail. Did you observe what a mean scrubby tail he has?" "What a fool you are, brother," said Mr. Petulengro; "that very tail of his shows his breeding. No good bred horse ever yet carried a fine tail—'tis your scrubby-tailed horses that are your out-and-outers. Did you ever hear of Syntax, brother? That tail of his puts me in mind of Syntax. Well, I say nothing more, have your own way—all I wonder at is, that a horse like him was ever brought to such a fair of dog cattle as this."

We then made the best of our way to a public-house, where we had some refreshment. I then proposed returning to the encampment, but Mr. Petulengro declined, and remained drinking with his companions till about six o'clock in the evening, when various jockeys from the fair came in. After some conversation a jockey proposed a game of cards; and in a little time, Mr. Petulengro and another gypsy sat down to play a game of cards with two of the jockeys.

Though not much acquainted with cards, I soon conceived a suspicion that the jockeys were cheating Mr. Petulengro and his companion, I therefore called Mr. Petulengro aside, and gave him a hint to that effect. Mr. Petulengro, however, instead of thanking me, told me to mind my own bread and butter, and forthwith returned to his game. I continued watching the players for some hours. The gypsies lost considerably, and I saw clearly that the jockeys were cheating them most confoundedly. I therefore once more called Mr. Petulengro aside, and told him that the jockeys were cheating him, conjuring him to return to the encampment. Mr. Petulengro, who was by this time somewhat the worse for liquor, now fell into a passion, swore several oaths, and asking me who had made me a Moses over him and his brethren, told me to return to the encampment by myself. Incensed at the unworthy return which my well-meant words had received, I forthwith left the house, and having purchased a few articles of provision, I set out for the dingle alone. It was a dark night when I reached it, and descending I saw the glimmer of a fire from the depths of the dingle; my heart beat with fond anticipation of a welcome. "Isopel Berners is waiting for me," said I, "and the first words that I shall hear from her lips is that she has made up her mind. We shall go to America, and be so happy together."

On reaching the bottom of the dingle, however, I saw seated near the fire, beside which stood the kettle simmering, not Isopel Berners, but a gypsy girl, who told me that Miss Berners when she went away had charged her to keep up the fire, and have the kettle boiling against my arrival. Startled at these words, I inquired at what hour Isopel had left, and whither she was gone, and was told that she had left the dingle, with her cart, about two hours after I departed; but where she was gone, she, the girl, did not know. I then asked whether she had left no message, and the girl replied that she had left none, but had merely given directions about the kettle and fire, putting, at the same time, sixpence into her hand.

"Very strange," thought I; then dismissing the gypsy girl I sat down by the fire. I had no wish for tea, but sat looking on the embers, wondering what could be the motive of the sudden departure of Isopel. "Does she mean to return?" thought I to myself. "Surely she means to return," Hope replied, "or she would not have gone away without leaving any message" —"and yet she could scarcely mean to return," muttered Foreboding, "or she assuredly would have left some message with the girl." I then thought to myself what a hard thing it would be, if, after having made up my mind to assume the yoke of matrimony, I should be disappointed of the woman of my choice. "Well, after all," thought I, "I can scarcely be disappointed; if such an ugly scoundrel as Sylvester had no difficulty in getting such a nice wife as Ursula, surely I, who am not a tenth part so ugly, cannot fail to obtain the hand of Isopel Berners, uncommonly fine damsel though she be. Husbands do not grow upon hedgerows; she is merely gone after a little business and will return to-morrow."

Comforted in some degree by these hopeful imaginings, I retired to my tent, and went to sleep.

CHAPTER XLIV

NOTHING occurred to me of any particular moment during the following day. Isopel Berners did not return; but Mr. Petulengro and his companions came home from the fair early in the morning. When I saw him, which was about mid-day, I found him with his face bruised and swelled. It appeared that, some time after I had left him, he himself perceived that the jockeys with whom he was playing cards were cheating him and his companion; a quarrel ensued, which terminated in a fight between Mr. Petulengro and one of the jockeys, which lasted some time, and in which Mr. Petulengro, though he eventually came off victor, was considerably beaten. His bruises, in conjunction with his pecuniary loss, which amounted to about seven pounds, were the cause of his being much out of humour; before night, however, he had returned to his usual philosophic frame of mind, and, coming up to me as I was walking about, apologized for his behaviour on the preceding day, and assured me that he was determined, from that time forward, never to quarrel with a friend for giving him good advice.

Two more days passed, and still Isopel Berners did not return. Gloomy thoughts and forebodings filled my mind. During the day I wandered about the neighbouring roads in the hopes of catching an early glimpse of her and her returning vehicle; and at night lay awake, tossing about on my hard couch, listening to the rustle of every leaf, and occasionally thinking that I heard the sound of her wheels upon the distant road. Once at midnight, just as I was about to fall into unconsciousness, I suddenly started up, for I was convinced that I heard the sound of wheels. I listened most anxiously, and the sound of wheels striking against stones was certainly plain enough. "She comes at last," thought I, and for a few moments I felt as if a mountain had been removed from my breast; "Here she comes at last, now, how shall I receive her? Oh," thought I, "I will receive her rather coolly, just as if I was not particularly anxious about her—that's the way to manage these women." The next moment the sound became very loud, rather too loud, I thought, to proceed from her wheels, and then by degrees became fainter.

Rushing out of my tent, I hurried up the path to the top of the dingle, where I heard the sound distinctly enough, but it was going from me, and evidently proceeded from something much larger than the cart of Isopel. I could, moreover, hear the stamping of a horse's hoof at a lumbering trot. Those only whose hopes have been wrought up to a high pitch, and then suddenly cast down, can imagine what I felt at that moment; and yet when I returned to my lonely tent, and lay down on my hard pallet, the voice of conscience told me that the misery I was then undergoing I had fully merited, for the unkind manner in which I had intended to receive her, when for a brief moment I supposed that she had returned.

It was on the morning after this affair, and the fourth, if I forget not, from the time of Isopel's departure, that, as I was seated on my stone at the bottom of the dingle, getting my breakfast, I heard an unknown voice from the path above—apparently that of a person descending—exclaim, "Here's a strange place to bring a letter to"; and presently an old woman, with a belt round her middle, to which was attached a leathern bag, made her appearance, and stood before me.

"Well, if I ever!" said she, as she looked about her. "My good gentlewoman," said I, "pray what may you please to want?" "Gentlewoman!" said the old dame, "please to want—well, I call that speaking civilly, at any rate. It is true, civil words cost nothing; nevertheless, we do not always get them. What I please to want is to deliver a letter to a young man in this place; perhaps you be he?" "What's the name on the letter?" said I, getting up, and going to her. "There's no name upon it," said she, taking a letter out of her scrip, and looking at it. "It is directed to the young man in Mumper's Dingle." "Then it is for me, I make no doubt," said I, stretching out my hand to take it. "Please to pay me ninepence first," said the old woman. "However," said she, after a moment's thought, "civility is civility, and, being rather a scarce article, should meet with some return. Here's the letter, young man, and I hope you will pay for it; for if you do not I must pay the postage myself." "You are the postwoman, I suppose," said I, as I took the letter. "I am the postman's mother," said the old woman; "but as he has a wide beat, I help him as much as I can, and I generally carry letters to places like this, to which he is afraid to come himself." "You say the postage is ninepence," said I, "here's a shilling." "Well, I call that honourable," said the old woman, taking the shilling, and putting it into her pocket —"here's your change, young man," said she, offering me threepence. "Pray keep that for yourself," said I; "you deserve it for your trouble." "Well, I call that genteel," said the old woman; "and as one good turn deserves another, since you look as if you couldn't read, I will read your letter for you. Let's see it; it's from some young woman or other, I dare say." "Thank you," said I, "but I can read." "All the better for you," said the old woman; "your being able to read will frequently save you a penny, for that's the charge I generally make for reading letters; though, as you behaved so genteelly to me, I should have charged you nothing. Well, if you can read, why don't you open the letter, instead of keeping it hanging between your finger and thumb?" "I am in no hurry to open it," said I, with a sigh. The old woman looked at me for a moment—"Well, young man," said she, "there are some—especially those who can read—who don't like to open their letters when anybody is by, more especially when they come from young women. Well, I won't intrude upon you, but leave you alone with your letter. I wish it may contain something pleasant. God bless you," and with these words she departed.

I sat down on my stone, with my letter in my hand. I knew perfectly well that it could have come from no other person than Isopel Berners; but what did the letter contain? I guessed tolerably well what its purport was—an eternal farewell! yet I was afraid to open the letter, lest my expectation should be confirmed. There I sat with the letter, putting off the evil moment as long as possible. At length I glanced at the direction, which was written in a fine bold hand, and was directed, as the old woman had said, to the young man in "Mumper's Dingle," with the addition, near ——, in the county of —— Suddenly the idea occurred to me, that, after all, the letter might not contain an eternal farewell; and that Isopel might have written, requesting me to join her. Could it be so? "Alas! no," presently said Foreboding. At last I became ashamed of my weakness. The letter must be opened sooner or later. Why not at once? So as the bather who, for a considerable time, has stood shivering on the bank, afraid to take the decisive plunge, suddenly takes it, I tore open the letter almost before I was aware. I had no sooner done so than a paper fell out. I examined it; it contained a lock of bright flaxen hair. "This is no good sign," said I, as I thrust the lock and paper into my bosom, and proceeded to read the letter, which ran as follows:—

"TO THE YOUNG MAN IN MUMPER'S DINGLE.

"SIR,—I send these lines, with the hope and trust that they will find you well, even as I am myself at this moment, and in much better spirits, for my own are not such as I could wish they were, being sometimes rather hysterical and vapourish, and at other times, and most often, very low. I am at a seaport, and am just going on shipboard; and when you get these I shall be on the salt waters, on my way to a distant country, and leaving my own behind me, which I do not expect ever to see again.

"And now, young man, I will, in the first place, say something about the manner in which I quitted you. It must have seemed somewhat singular to you that I went away without taking any leave, or giving you the slightest hint that I was going; but I did not do so without considerable reflection. I was afraid that I should not be able to support a leave-taking; and as you had said that you were determined to go wherever I did, I thought it best not to tell you at all; for I did not think it advisable that you should go with me, and I wished to have no dispute.

"In the second place, I wish to say something about an offer of wedlock which you made me; perhaps, young man, had you made it at the first period of our acquaintance, I should have accepted it, but you did not, and kept putting off and putting off, and behaving in a very strange manner, till I could stand your conduct no longer, but determined upon leaving you and Old England, which last step I had been long thinking about; so when you made your offer at last, everything was arranged—my cart and donkey engaged to be sold—and the greater part of my things disposed of. However, young man, when you did make it, I frankly tell you that I had half a mind to accept it; at last, however, after very much consideration, I thought it best to leave you for ever, because, for some time past, I had become almost convinced, that though with a wonderful deal of learning, and exceedingly shrewd in some things, you were—pray don't be offended—at the root mad! and though mad people, I have been told, sometimes make very good husbands, I was unwilling that your friends, if you had any, should say that Belle Berners, the workhouse girl, took advantage of your infirmity; for there is no concealing that I was born and bred up in a workhouse; notwithstanding that, my blood is better than your own, and as good as the best; you having yourself told me that my name is a noble name, and once, if I mistake not, that it was the same word as baron, which is the same thing as bear; and that to be called in old times a bear was considered a great compliment—the bear being a mighty strong animal, on which account our forefathers called all their great fighting-men barons, which is the same as bears.

"However, setting matters of blood and family entirely aside, many thanks to you, young man, from poor Belle, for the honour you did her in making that same offer; for, after all, it is an honour to receive an honourable offer, which she could see clearly yours was, with no floriness nor chaff in it: but, on the contrary, entire sincerity. She assures you that she shall always bear it and yourself in mind, whether on land or water; and as a proof of the good-will she bears to you, she sends you a lock of the hair which she wears on her head, which you were often looking at, and were pleased to call flax, which word she supposes you meant as a compliment, even as the old people meant to pass a compliment to their great folks, when they called them bears; though she cannot help thinking that they might have found an animal as strong as a bear, and somewhat less uncouth, to call their great folks after: even as she thinks yourself, amongst your great store of words, might have found something a little more genteel to call her hair after than flax, which, though strong and useful, is rather a coarse and common kind of article.

"And as another proof of the good-will she bears to you, she sends you, along with the lock, a piece of advice, which is worth all the hair in the world, to say nothing of the flax.

"*Fear God*, and take your own part. There's Bible in that, young man: see how Moses feared God, and how he took his own part against everybody who meddled with him. And see how David feared God, and took his own part against all the bloody enemies which surrounded him—so fear God, young man, and never give in! The world can bully, and is fond, provided it sees a man in a kind of difficulty, of getting about him, calling him coarse names, and even going so far as to hustle him: but the world, like all bullies, carries a white feather in its tail, and no sooner sees the man taking off his coat, and offering to fight its best, than it scatters here and there, and is always civil to him afterwards. So when folks are disposed to ill-treat you, young man, say, 'Lord have mercy upon me!' and then tip them to Long Melford, which, as the saying goes, there is nothing comparable for shortness all the world over; and these last words, young man, are the last you will ever have from her who is nevertheless,

"Your affectionate female servant,

"ISOPEL BERNERS."

After reading the letter I sat for some time motionless, holding it in my hand. The daydream in which I had been a little time before indulging, of marrying Isopel Berners, of going with her to America, and having by her a large progeny, who were to assist me in felling trees, cultivating the soil, and who would take care of me when I was old, was now thoroughly dispelled. Isopel had deserted me, and was gone to America by herself, where, perhaps, she would marry some other person, and would bear him a progeny, who would do for him what in my dream I had hoped my progeny by her would do for me. Then the thought came into my head that though she was gone, I might follow her to America, but then I thought that if I did I might not find her; America was a very large place, and I did not know the port to which she was bound; but I could follow her to the port from which she had sailed, and there possibly discover the port to which she was bound; but I did not even know the port from which she had set out, for Isopel had not dated her letter from any place. Suddenly it occurred to me that the post-mark on the letter would tell me from whence it came, so I forthwith looked at the back of the letter, and in the post-mark read the name of a well-known and not very distant sea-port. I then knew with tolerable certainty the port where she had embarked, and I almost determined to follow her, but I almost instantly determined to do no such thing. Isopel Berners had abandoned me, and I would not follow her; "Perhaps," whispered Pride, "if I overtook her, she would only despise me for running after her"; and it also told me pretty roundly, provided I ran after her, whether I overtook her or not, I should heartily despise myself. So I determined not to follow Isopel Berners; I took her lock of hair, and looked at it, then put it in her letter, which I folded up and carefully stowed away, resolved to keep both for ever, but I determined not to follow her. Two or three times, however, during the day, I wavered in my determination, and was again and again almost tempted to follow her, but every succeeding time the temptation was fainter.

In the evening I left the dingle, and sat down with Mr. Petulengro and his family by the door of his tent; Mr. Petulengro soon began talking of the letter which I had received in the morning. "Is it not from Miss Berners, brother?" said he. I told him it was. "Is she coming back, brother?" "Never," said I; "she is gone to America, and has deserted me." "I always knew that you two were never destined for each other," said he. "How did you know that?" I inquired. "The dook told me so, brother; you are born to be a great traveller." "Well," said I, "if I had gone with her to America, as I was thinking of doing, I should have been a great traveller." "You are to travel in another direction, brother," said he.

"I wish you would tell me all about my future wanderings," said I. "I can't, brother," said Mr. Petulengro, "there's a power of clouds before my eye." "You are a poor seer, after all," said I; and getting up, I retired to my dingle and my tent, where I betook myself to my bed, and there, knowing the worst, and being no longer agitated by apprehension, nor agonized by expectation, I was soon buried in a deep slumber, the first which I had fallen into for several nights.

CHAPTER XLV

It was rather late on the following morning when I awoke. At first I was almost unconscious of what had occurred on the preceding day; recollection, however, by degrees returned, and I felt a deep melancholy coming over me, but perfectly aware that no advantage could be derived from the indulgence of such a feeling, I sprang up, prepared my breakfast, which I ate with a tolerable appetite, and then left the dingle, and betook myself to the gypsy encampment, where I entered into discourse with various Romanies, both male and female. After some time, feeling myself in better spirits, I determined to pay another visit to the landlord of the public-house. From the position of his affairs when I had last visited him I entertained rather gloomy ideas with respect to his present circumstances. I imagined that I should either find him alone in his kitchen smoking a wretched pipe, or in company with some surly bailiff or his follower, whom his friend the brewer had sent into the house in order to take possession of his effects.

Nothing more entirely differing from either of these anticipations could have presented itself to my view than what I saw about one o'clock in the afternoon, when I entered the house. I had come, though somewhat in want of consolation myself, to offer any consolation which was at my command to my acquaintance Catchpole, and perhaps like many other people who go to a house with "drops of compassion trembling on their eyelids," I felt rather disappointed at finding that no compassion was necessary. The house was thronged with company, and cries for ale and porter, hot brandy and water, cold gin and water, were numerous; moreover, no desire to receive and not to pay for the landlord's liquids was manifested—on the contrary, everybody seemed disposed to play the most honourable part: "Landlord, here's the money for this glass of brandy and water—do me the favour to take it; all right, remember I have paid you." "Landlord, here's the money for the pint of half-and-half—fourpence halfpenny, ain't it?—here's sixpence; keep the change—confound the change!" The landlord, assisted by his niece, bustled about; his brow erect, his cheeks plumped out, and all his features exhibiting a kind of surly satisfaction. Wherever he moved, marks of the most cordial amity were shown him, hands were thrust out to grasp his, nor were looks of respect, admiration, nay, almost of adoration, wanting.

Presently the landlord, as he moved about, observing me, stopped short: "Ah!" said he, "are you here? I am glad to see you, come this way. Stand back," said he to his company, as I followed him to the bar, "stand back for me and this gentleman." Two or three young fellows were in the bar, seemingly sporting yokels, drinking sherry and smoking. "Come, gentlemen," said the landlord, "clear the bar, I must have a clear bar for me and my friend here." "Landlord, what will you take," said one, "a glass of sherry? I know you like it." "—— sherry and you too," said the landlord, "I want neither sherry nor yourself; didn't you hear what I told you?" "All right, old fellow," said the other, shaking the landlord by the hand, "all right, don't wish to intrude—but I suppose when you and your friend have done, I may come in again"; then, with a "sarvant, sir," to me, he took himself into the kitchen, followed by the rest of the sporting yokels.

Thereupon the landlord, taking a bottle of ale from a basket, uncorked it, and pouring the contents into two large glasses, handed me one, and motioning me to sit down, placed himself by me; then, emptying his own glass at a draught, he gave a kind of grunt of satisfaction, and fixing his eyes upon the opposite side of the bar, remained motionless, without saying a word, buried apparently in important cogitations. With respect to myself, I swallowed my ale more leisurely, and was about to address my friend, when his niece, coming into the bar, said that more and more customers were arriving, and how she should supply their wants she did not know, unless her uncle would get up and help her.

"The customers!" said the landlord, "let the scoundrels wait till you have time to serve them, or till I have leisure to see after them." "The kitchen won't contain half of them," said his niece. "Then let them sit out abroad," said the landlord. "But there are not benches enough, uncle," said the niece. "Then let them stand or sit on the ground," said the uncle, "what care I; I'll let them know that the man who beat Tom of Hopton stands as well again on his legs as ever." Then opening a side door which led from the bar into the back yard, he beckoned me to follow him. "You treat your customers in rather a cavalier manner," said I, when we were alone together in the yard.

"Don't I?" said the landlord; "and I'll treat them more so yet; now I have got the whiphand of the rascals I intend to keep it. I dare say you are a bit surprised with regard to the change which has come over things since you were last here. I'll tell you how it happened. You remember in what a desperate condition you found me, and I dare say you can't have forgotten how you gave me good advice. Well, after you were gone, I felt all the better for your talk, and what you had made me drink, and it was a mercy that I did feel better; for my niece was gone out. poor thing, and I was left alone in the house, without a soul to look at, or to keep me from doing myself a mischief in case I was so inclined. Well, things wore on in this way till it grew dusk, when in came that blackguard Hunter with his train to drink at my expense, and to insult me as usual; there were more than a dozen of them, and a pretty set they looked. Well, they ordered about in a very free and easy manner for upwards of an hour and a half, occasionally sneering and jeering at me, as they had been in the habit of doing for some time past; so, as I said before, things wore on, and other customers came in, who, though they did not belong to Hunter's gang, also passed off their jokes upon me; for, as you perhaps know, we English are a set of low hounds, who will always take part with the many by way of making ourselves safe, and currying favour with the stronger side. I said little or nothing, for my spirits had again become very low, and I was verily scared and afraid. All of a sudden I thought of the ale which I had drank in the morning, and of the good it did me then, so I went into the bar, opened another bottle, took a glass, and felt better; so I took another, and feeling better still, I went back into the kitchen, just as Hunter and his crew were about leaving.

"'Mr. Hunter,' said I, 'you and your people will please to pay me for what you have had?' 'What do you mean by my people?' said he, with an oath. 'Ah, what do you mean by calling us his people?' said the clan. 'We are nobody's people'; and then there was a pretty load of abuse, and threatening to serve me out. 'Well,' said I, 'I was perhaps wrong to call them your people, and beg your pardon and theirs. And now you will please to pay me for what you have had yourself, and afterwards I can settle with them.' 'I shall pay you when I think fit,' said Hunter. 'Yes,' said the rest, 'and so shall we. We shall pay you when we think fit.' 'I tell you what,' said Hunter, 'I conceives I do such an old fool as you an honour when I comes into his house and drinks his beer, and goes away without paying for it'; and then there was a roar of laughter from everybody, and almost all said the same thing. 'Now do you please to pay me, Mr. Hunter?' said I. 'Pay you!' said Hunter; 'pay you! Yes, here's the pay'; and thereupon he held out his thumb, twirling it round till it just touched my nose.

"I can't tell you what I felt that moment; a kind of madhouse thrill came upon me, and all I know is, that I bent back as far as I could, then lunging out, struck him under the ear, sending him reeling two or three yards, when he fell on the floor. I wish you had but seen how my company looked at me and at each other. One or two of the clan went to raise Hunter, and get him to fight, but it was no go; though he was not killed, he had had enough for that evening. Oh, I wish you had seen my customers; those who did not belong to the clan, but who had taken part with them, and helped to jeer and flout me, now came and shook me by the hand, wishing me joy, and saying as how 'I was a brave fellow, and had served the bully right!' As for the clan, they all said Hunter was bound to do me justice; so they made him pay me what he owed for himself, and the reckoning of those among them who said they had no money. Two or three of them then led him away, while the rest stayed behind, and flattered me, and worshipped me, and called Hunter all kinds of dogs' names. What do you think of that?"

"Why," said I, "it makes good what I read in a letter which I received yesterday. It is just the way of the world."

"A'n't it," said the landlord. "Well, God don't love them who won't strike out for themselves. So, dash my buttons if I show the ungrateful mind to you! I don't offer to knock anybody down for you, because why—I dare say you can knock a body down yourself; but I'll offer something more to the purpose; as my business is wonderfully on the increase, I shall want somebody to help me in serving my customers, and keeping them in order. If you choose to come and serve for your board, and what they'll give you, give me your fist; or if you like ten shillings a week better than their sixpences and ha'pence, only say so—though, to be open with you, I believe you would make twice ten shillings out of them—the sneaking, fawning, curry-favouring humbugs!"

"I am much obliged to you," said I, "for your handsome offer, which, however, I am obliged to decline."

"Why so?" said the landlord.

"I am not fit for service," said I; "moreover, I am about to leave this part of the country." As I spoke a horse neighed in the stable. "What horse is that?" said I.

"It belongs to a cousin of mine, who put it into my hands yesterday in the hopes that I might get rid of it for him, though he would no more have done so a week ago, when he considered me a down pin, than he would have given the horse away. Are you fond of horses?"

"Very much," said I.

"Then come and look at it." He led me into the stable, where, in a stall, stood a noble-looking animal.

"Dear me," said I, "I saw this horse at —— fair."

"Like enough," said the landlord; "he was there and was offered for seventy pounds, but didn't find a bidder at any price. What do you think of him?"

"He's a splendid creature."

"I am no judge of horses," said the landlord; "but I am told he's a first-rate trotter, good leaper, and has some of the blood of Syntax. What does all that signify?—the game is against his master, who is a down pin, is thinking of emigrating, and wants money confoundedly. He asked seventy pounds at the fair; but, between ourselves, he would be glad to take fifty here."

"I almost wish," said I, "that I were a rich squire."

"You would buy him then," said the landlord. Here he mused for some time, with a very profound look. "It would be a rum thing," said he, "if, some time or other, that horse should come into your hands. Didn't you hear how he neighed when you talked about leaving the country? My granny was a wise woman, and was up to all kinds of signs and wonders, sounds and noises, the interpretation of the language of birds and animals, crowing and lowing, neighing and braying. If she had been here, she would have said at once that that horse was fated to carry you away. On that point, however, I can say nothing, for under fifty pounds no one can have him. Are you taking that money out of your pocket to pay me for the ale? That won't do; nothing to pay; I invited you this time. Now if you are going, you had best get into the road through the yard-gate. I won't trouble you to make your way through the kitchen and my fine-weather company —confound them!"

As I returned along the road I met Mr. Petulengro and one of his companions, who told me that they were bound for the public-house; whereupon I informed Jasper how I had seen in the stable the horse which we had admired at the fair. "I shouldn't wonder if you buy that horse after all, brother," said Mr. Petulengro. With a smile at the absurdity of such a supposition, I left him and his companion, and betook myself to the dingle. In the evening I received a visit from Mr. Petulengro, who forthwith commenced talking about the horse, which he had again seen, the landlord having shown it to him on learning that he was a friend of mine. He told me that the horse pleased him more than ever, he having examined his points with more accuracy than he had an opportunity of doing on the first occasion, concluding by pressing me to buy him. I begged him to desist from such foolish importunity, assuring him that I had never so much money in all my life as would enable me to purchase the horse.

Whilst this discourse was going on, Mr. Petulengro and myself were standing together in the midst of the dingle. Suddenly he began to move round me in a very singular manner, making strange motions with his hands, and frightful contortions with his features, till I became alarmed, and asked him whether he had not lost his senses? Whereupon, ceasing his movements and contortions, he assured me that he had not, but had merely been seized with a slight dizziness, and then once more returned to the subject of the horse. Feeling myself very angry, I told him that if he continued persecuting me in that manner, I should be obliged to quarrel with him; adding, that I believed his only motive for asking me to buy the animal was to insult my poverty. "Pretty poverty," said he, "with fifty pounds in your pocket; however, I have heard say that it is always the custom of your rich people to talk of their poverty, more especially when they wish to avoid laying out money."

Surprised at his saying that I had fifty pounds in my pocket, I asked him what he meant; whereupon he told me that he was very sure that I had fifty pounds in my pocket, offering to lay me five shillings to that effect. "Done!" said I; "I have scarcely more than the fifth part of what you say." "I know better, brother," said Mr. Petulengro; "if you only pull out what you have in the pocket of your slop, I am sure you will have lost your wager." Putting my hand into the pocket, I felt something which I had never felt there before, and pulling it out, perceived that it was a clumsy leathern purse, which I found on opening contained four ten-pound notes, and several pieces of gold. "Didn't I tell you so, brother?" said Mr. Petulengro. "Now, in the first place, please to pay me the five shillings you have lost." "This is only a foolish piece of pleasantry," said I; "you put it into my pocket whilst you were moving about me, making faces like a distracted person. Here, take your purse back." "I?" said Mr. Petulengro, "not I, indeed! don't think I am such a fool. I have won my wager, so pay me the five shillings, brother." "Do drop this folly," said I, "and take your purse"; and I flung it on the ground.

"Brother," said Mr. Petulengro, "you were talking of quarrelling with me just now. I tell you now one thing, which is, that if you do not take back the purse I will quarrel with you; and it shall be for good and all. I'll drop your acquaintance, no longer call you my pal, and not even say sarshan to you when I meet you by the roadside. Hir mi diblis I never will." I saw by Jasper's look and tone that he was in earnest, and, as I had really a regard for the strange being, I scarcely knew what to do. "Now, be persuaded, brother," said Mr. Petulengro, taking up the purse, and handing it to me; "be persuaded; put the purse into your pocket, and buy the horse." "Well," said I, "if I did so, would you acknowledge the horse to be yours, and receive the money again as soon as I should be able to repay you?"

"I would, brother, I would," said he; "return me the money as soon as you please, provided you buy the horse." "What motive have you for wishing me to buy that horse?" said I. "He's to be sold for fifty pounds," said Jasper, "and is worth four times that sum; though, like many a splendid bargain, he is now going a begging; buy him, and I'm confident that, in a little time, a grand gentleman of your appearance may have anything he asks for him, and found a fortune by his means. Moreover, brother, I want to dispose of this fifty pounds in a safe manner. If you don't take it, I shall fool it away in no time, perhaps at card-playing, for you saw how I was cheated by those blackguard jockeys the other day—we 'Gyptians don't know how to take care of money: our best plan when we have got a handful of guineas is to make buttons with them; but I have plenty of golden buttons, and don't wish to be troubled with more, so you can do me no greater favour than vesting the money in this speculation, by which my mind will be relieved of considerable care and trouble for some time at least."

Perceiving that I still hesitated, he said, "Perhaps, brother, you think I did not come honestly by the money: by the honestest manner in the world, for it is the money I earnt by fighting in the ring: I did not steal it, brother, nor did I get it by disposing of spavined donkeys, or glandered ponies—nor is it, brother, the profits of my wife's witchcraft and dukkerin."

"But," said I, "you had better employ it in your traffic." "I have plenty of money for my traffic, independent of this capital," said Mr. Petulengro; "ay, brother, and enough besides to back the husband of my wife's sister, Sylvester, against Slammocks of the Chong gav for twenty pounds, which I am thinking of doing."

"But," said I, "after all, the horse may have found another purchaser by this time." "Not he," said Mr. Petulengro, "there is nobody in this neighbourhood to purchase a horse like that, unless it be your lordship—so take the money, brother," and he thrust the purse into my hand. Allowing myself to be persuaded, I kept possession of the purse. "Are you satisfied now?" said I. "By no means, brother," said Mr. Petulengro, "you will please to pay me the five shillings which you lost to me." "Why," said I, "the fifty pounds which I found in my pocket were not mine, but put in by yourself." "That's nothing to do with the matter, brother," said Mr. Petulengro, "I betted you five shillings that you had fifty pounds in your pocket, which sum you had: I did not say that they were your own, but merely that you had fifty pounds; you will therefore pay me, brother, or I shall not consider you an honourable man." Not wishing to have any dispute about such a matter, I took five shillings out of my under pocket, and gave them to him. Mr. Petulengro took the money with great glee, observing—"These five shillings I will take to the public-house forthwith, and spend in drinking with four of my brethren, and doing so will give me an opportunity of telling the landlord that I have found a customer for his horse, and that you are the man. It will be as well to secure the horse as soon as possible; for though the dook tells me that the horse is intended for you, I have now and then found that the dook is, like myself, somewhat given to lying."

He then departed, and I remained alone in the dingle. I thought at first that I had committed a great piece of folly in consenting to purchase this horse; I might find no desirable purchaser for him, until the money in my possession should be totally exhausted, and then I might be compelled to sell him for half the price I had given for him, or be even glad to find a person who would receive him as a gift; I should then remain sans horse, and indebted to Mr. Petulengro. Nevertheless, it was possible that I might sell the horse very advantageously, and by so doing obtain a fund sufficient to enable me to execute some grand enterprise or other. My present way of life afforded no prospect of support, whereas the purchase of the horse did afford a possibility of bettering my condition, so, after all, had I not done right in consenting to purchase the horse? the purchase was to be made with another person's property, it is true, and I did not exactly like the idea of speculating with another person's property, but Mr. Petulengro had thrust his money upon me, and if I lost his money, he could have no one but himself to blame; so I persuaded myself that I had, upon the whole, done right, and having come to that persuasion, I soon began to enjoy the idea of finding myself on horseback again, and figured to myself all kinds of strange adventures which I should meet with on the roads before the horse and I should part company.

CHAPTER XLVI

I SAW nothing more of Mr. Petulengro that evening—on the morrow, however, he came and informed me that he had secured the horse for me, and that I was to go and pay for it at noon. At the hour appointed, therefore, I went with Mr. Petulengro and Tawno to the public, where, as before, there was a crowd of company. The landlord received us in the bar with marks of much satisfaction and esteem, made us sit down, and treated us with some excellent mild draught ale.

"So I suppose you are come for the horse; mercy upon us! who would have thought you would have become the purchaser? The horse, however, seemed to know it by his neighing. How did you ever come by the money? however, that's no matter of mine. I suppose you are strongly backed by certain friends you have."

I informed the landlord that he was right in supposing that I came for the horse, but that, before I paid for him, I should wish to prove his capabilities. "With all my heart," said the landlord. "You shall mount him this moment." Then going into the stable, he saddled and bridled the horse, and presently brought him out before the door. I mounted him, Mr. Petulengro putting a heavy whip into my hand, and saying a few words to me in his own mysterious language. "The horse wants no whip," said the landlord. "Hold your tongue, daddy," said Mr. Petulengro. "My pal knows quite well what to do with the whip, he's not going to beat the horse with it."

About four hundred yards from the house there was a hill, to the foot of which the road ran almost on a perfect level; towards the foot of this hill I trotted the horse, who set off at a long, swift pace, seemingly at the rate of about sixteen miles an hour. On reaching the foot of the hill, I wheeled the animal round, and trotted him towards the house—the horse sped faster than before. Ere he had advanced a hundred yards, I took off my hat, in obedience to the advice which Mr. Petulengro had given me, in his own language, and holding it over the horse's head commenced drumming on the crown with the knob of the whip; the horse gave a slight start, but instantly recovering himself, continued his trot till he arrived at the door of the public-house, amidst the acclamations of the company, who had all rushed out of the house to be spectators of what was going on.

"I see now what you wanted the whip for," said the landlord, "and sure enough, that drumming on your hat was no bad way of learning whether the horse was quiet or not. Well, did you ever see a more quiet horse, or a better trotter?" "My cob shall trot against him," said a fellow, dressed in velveteen, mounted on a low powerful-looking animal. "My cob shall trot against him to the hill and back again—come on!" We both started; the cob kept up gallantly against the horse for about half way to the hill, when he began to lose ground; at the foot of the hill he was about fifteen yards behind. Whereupon I turned slowly and waited for him. We then set off towards the house, but now the cob had no chance, being at least twenty yards behind when I reached the door. This running of the horse, the wild uncouth forms round me, and the ale and beer which were being guzzled from pots and flagons, put me wonderfully in mind of the ancient horse-races of the heathen north. I almost imagined myself Gunnar of Hlitharend at the race of——

"Are you satisfied?" said the landlord. "Didn't you tell me that he could leap?" I demanded. "I am told he can," said the landlord; "but I can't consent that he should be tried in that way, as he might be damaged." "That's right!" said Mr. Petulengro, "don't trust my pal to leap that horse, he'll merely fling him down, and break his neck and his own. There's a better man than he close by; let him get on his back and leap him." "You mean yourself, I suppose," said the landlord. "Well, I call that talking modestly, and nothing becomes a young man more than modesty." "It a'n't I, daddy," said Mr. Petulengro. "Here's the man," said he, pointing to Tawno. "Here's the horse-leaper of the world!"

"You mean the horse-back breaker," said the landlord. "That big fellow would break down my cousin's horse." "Why, he weighs only sixteen stone," said Mr. Petulengro. "And his sixteen stone, with his way of handling a horse, does not press so much as any other one's thirteen. Only let him get on the horse's back, and you'll see what he can do!" "No," said the landlord, "it won't do." Whereupon Mr. Petulengro became very much excited; and pulling out a handful of money, said, "I'll tell you what, I'll forfeit these guineas, if my black pal there does the horse any kind of damage; duck me in the horse-pond if I don't."

"Well," said the landlord, "for the sport of the thing I consent, so let your white pal get down, and your black pal mount as soon as he pleases."

I felt rather mortified at Mr. Petulengro's interference; and showed no disposition to quit my seat; whereupon he came up to me and said, "Now, brother, do get out of the saddle—you are no bad hand at trotting, I am willing to acknowledge that; but at leaping a horse there is no one like Tawno. Let every dog be praised for his own gift. You have been showing off in your line for the last half-hour; now do give Tawno a chance of exhibiting a little; poor fellow, he hasn't often a chance of exhibiting, as his wife keeps him so much out of sight."

Not wishing to appear desirous of engrossing the public attention, and feeling rather desirous to see how Tawno, of whose exploits in leaping horses I had frequently heard, would acquit himself in the affair, I at length dismounted, and Tawno, at a bound, leaped into the saddle, where he really looked like Gunnar of Hlitharend, save and except the complexion of Gunnar was florid, whereas that of Tawno was of nearly Mulatto darkness; and that all Tawno's features were cast in the Grecian model, whereas Gunnar had a snub nose. "There's a leaping-bar behind the house," said the landlord. "Leaping-bar!" said Mr. Petulengro, scornfully. "Do you think my black pal ever rides at a leaping-bar? No more than a windle-straw. Leap over that meadow-wall, Tawno."

Just past the house, in the direction in which I had been trotting, was a wall about four feet high, beyond which was a small meadow. Tawno rode the horse gently up to the wall, permitted him to look over, then backed him for about ten yards, and pressing his calves against the horse's sides, he loosed the rein, and the horse launching forward, took the leap in gallant style. "Well done, man and horse!" said Mr. Petulengro, "now come back, Tawno." The leap from the side of the meadow was, however, somewhat higher; and the horse, when pushed at it, at first turned away; whereupon Tawno backed him to a greater distance, pushed the horse to a full gallop, giving a wild cry; whereupon the horse again took the wall, slightly grazing one of his legs against it. "A near thing," said the landlord; "but a good leap. Now, no more leaping, so long as I have control over the animal." The horse was then led back to the stable; and the landlord, myself and companions going into the bar, I paid down the money for the horse.

Scarcely was the bargain concluded, when two or three of the company began to envy me the possession of the horse, and forcing their way into the bar, with much noise and clamour, said that the horse had been sold too cheap. One fellow, in particular, with a red waistcoat, the son of a wealthy farmer, said that if he had but known that the horse had been so good a one, he would have bought it at the first price asked for it, which he was now willing to pay, that is to-morrow, supposing—"supposing your father will let you have the money," said the landlord, "which, after all, might not be the case; but, however that may be, it is too late now. I think myself the horse has been sold for too little money, but if so all the better for the young man, who came forward when no other body did with his money in his hand. There, take yourselves out of my bar," he said to the fellows; "and a pretty scoundrel you," said he to the man of the red waistcoat, "to say the horse has been sold too cheap; why, it was only yesterday you said he was good for nothing, and were passing all kinds of jokes at him. Take yourself out of my bar, I say, you and all of you," and he turned the fellows out. I then asked the landlord whether he would permit the horse to remain in the stable for a short time, provided I paid for his entertainment; and on his willingly consenting, I treated my friends with ale, and then returned with them to the encampment.

That evening I informed Mr. Petulengro and his party that on the morrow I intended to mount my horse, and leave that part of the country in quest of adventures; inquiring of Jasper where, in the event of my selling the horse advantageously, I might meet with him, and repay the money I had borrowed of him; whereupon Mr. Petulengro informed me that in about ten weeks I might find him at a certain place at the Chong gav.

I then stated that as I could not well carry with me the property which I possessed in the dingle, which after all was of no considerable value, I had resolved to bestow the said property, namely, the pony, tent, tinker-tools, etc., on Ursula and her husband, partly because they were poor, and partly on account of the great kindness which I bore to Ursula, from whom I had, on various occasions, experienced all manner of civility, particularly in regard to crabbed words. On hearing this intelligence, Ursula returned many thanks to her gentle brother, as she called me, and Sylvester was so overjoyed that, casting aside his usual phlegm, he said I was the best friend he had ever had in the world, and in testimony of his gratitude swore that he would permit his wife to give me a choomer in the presence of the whole company, which offer, however, met with a very mortifying reception, the company frowning disapprobation, Ursula protesting against anything of the kind, and I myself showing no forwardness to avail myself of it, having inherited from nature a considerable fund of modesty, to which was added no slight store acquired in the course of my Irish education.

I passed that night alone in the dingle in a very melancholy manner, with little or no sleep, thinking of Isopel Berners; and in the morning when I quitted it I shed several tears, as I reflected that I should probably never again see the spot where I had passed so many hours in her company.

On reaching the plain above, I found my Romany friends breakfasting, and on being asked by Mr. Petulengro to join them, I accepted the invitation. No sooner was breakfast over than I informed Ursula and her husband that they would find the property which I had promised them in the dingle, commending the little pony Ambrol to their best care. I took leave of the whole company, which was itself about to break up camp and to depart in the direction of London, and made the best of my way to the public-house. I had a small bundle in my hand, and was dressed in the same manner as when I departed from London, having left my waggoner's slop with the other effects in the dingle.

On arriving at the public-house, I informed the landlord that I was come for my horse, inquiring, at the same time, whether he could not accommodate me with a bridle and saddle. He told me that the bridle and saddle, with which I had ridden the horse on the preceding day, were at my service for a trifle; that he had received them some time since in payment for a debt, and that he had himself no use for them. The leathers of the bridle were rather shabby, and the bit rusty, and the saddle was old fashioned; but I was happy to purchase them for seven shillings, more especially as the landlord added a small valise, which he said could be strapped to the saddle, and which I should find very convenient for carrying my things in. I then proceeded to the stable, told the horse we were bound on an expedition, and giving him a feed of corn, left him to discuss it, and returned to the bar-room to have a little farewell chat with the landlord, and at the same time to drink with him a farewell glass of ale. Whilst we were talking and drinking, the niece came and joined us: she was a decent, sensible young woman, who appeared to take a great interest in her uncle, whom she regarded with a singular mixture of pride and disapprobation—pride for the renown which he had acquired by his feats of old, and disapprobation for his late imprudences. She said that she hoped that his misfortunes would be a warning to him to turn more to his God than he had hitherto done, and to give up cock-fighting and other low-life practices. To which the landlord replied, that with respect to cock-fighting he intended to give it up entirely, being determined no longer to risk his capital upon birds, and with respect to his religious duties, he should attend the church of which he was churchwarden at least once a quarter, adding, however, that he did not intend to become either canter or driveller, neither of which characters would befit a publican surrounded by such customers as he was, and that to the last day of his life he hoped to be able to make use of his fists. After a stay of about two hours I settled accounts, and having bridled and saddled my horse, and strapped on my valise, I mounted, shook hands with the landlord and his niece, and departed, notwithstanding that they both entreated me to tarry until the evening, it being then the heat of the day.

CHAPTER XLVII

I BENT my course in the direction of the north, more induced by chance than any particular motive; all quarters of the world having about equal attractions for me. I was in high spirits at finding myself once more on horseback, and trotted gaily on, until the heat of the weather induced me to slacken my pace, more out of pity for my horse than because I felt any particular inconvenience from it—heat and cold being then, and still, matters of great indifference to me. What I thought of I scarcely know, save and except that I have a glimmering recollection that I felt some desire to meet with one of those adventures which upon the roads of England are generally as plentiful as blackberries in autumn; and Fortune, who has generally been ready to gratify my inclinations, provided it cost her very little by so doing, was not slow in furnishing me with an adventure, perhaps as a characteristic of the English roads as anything which could have happened.

I might have travelled about six miles amongst cross roads and lanes, when suddenly I found myself upon a broad and very dusty road which seemed to lead due north. As I wended along this I saw a man upon a donkey riding towards me. The man was commonly dressed, with a broad felt hat on his head, and a kind of satchel on his back; he seemed to be in a mighty hurry, and was every now and then belabouring the donkey with a cudgel. The donkey, however, which was a fine large creature of the silver-grey species, did not appear to sympathize at all with its rider in his desire to get on, but kept its head turned back as much as possible, moving from one side of the road to the other, and not making much forward way. As I passed, being naturally of a very polite disposition, I gave the man the sele of the day, asking him, at the same time, why he beat the donkey; whereupon the fellow eyeing me askance, told me to mind my own business, with the addition of something which I need not repeat. I had not proceeded a furlong before I saw seated on the dust by the wayside, close by a heap of stones, and with several flints before him, a respectable-looking old man, with a straw hat and a white smock, who was weeping bitterly.

"What are you crying for, father?" said I. "Have you come to any hurt?" "Hurt enough," sobbed the old man, "I have just been tricked out of the best ass in England by a villain, who gave me nothing but these trash in return," pointing to the stones before him. "I really scarcely understand you," said I, "I wish you would explain yourself more clearly." "I was riding on my ass from market," said the old man, "when I met here a fellow with a sack on his back, who, after staring at the ass and me a moment or two, asked me if I would sell her. I told him that I could not think of selling her, as she was very useful to me, and though an animal, my true companion, whom I loved as much as if she were my wife and daughter. I then attempted to pass on, but the fellow stood before me, begging me to sell her, saying that he would give me anything for her; well, seeing that he persisted, I said at last that if I sold her, I must have six pounds for her, and I said so to get rid of him, for I saw that he was a shabby fellow, who had probably not six shillings in the world; but I had better have held my tongue," said the old man, crying more bitterly than before, "for the words were scarcely out of my mouth, when he said he would give me what I asked, and taking the sack from his back, he pulled out a steelyard, and going to the heap of stones there, he took up several of them and weighed them, then flinging them down before me, he said, 'There are six pounds, neighbour; now, get off the ass, and hand her over to me.' Well, I sat like one dumbfoundered for a time, till at last I asked him what he meant? 'What do I mean?' said he, 'you old rascal, why, I mean to claim my purchase,' and then he swore so awfully, that scarcely knowing what I did I got down, and he jumped on the animal and rode off as fast as he could." "I suppose he was the fellow," said I, "whom I just now met upon a fine grey ass, which he was beating with a cudgel." "I dare say he was," said the old man, "I saw him beating her as he rode away, and I thought I should have died." "I never heard such a story," said I; "well, do you mean to submit to such a piece of roguery quietly?" "Oh, dear," said the old man, "what can I do? I am seventy-nine years of age; I am bad on my feet, and dar'n't go after him." "Shall I go?" said I; "the fellow is a thief, and any one has a right to stop him."

"Oh, if you could but bring her again to me," said the old man, "I would bless you till my dying day; but have a care; I don't know but after all the law may say that she is his lawful purchase. I asked six pounds for her, and he gave me six pounds." "Six flints, you mean," said I, "no, no, the law is not quite so bad as that either; I know something about her, and am sure that she will never sanction such a quibble. At all events, I'll ride after the fellow."

Thereupon turning my horse round, I put him to his very best trot; I rode nearly a mile without obtaining a glimpse of the fellow, and was becoming apprehensive that he had escaped me by turning down some by-path, two or three of which I had passed. Suddenly, however, on the road making a slight turning, I perceived him right before me, moving at a tolerably swift pace, having by this time probably overcome the resistance of the animal. Putting my horse to a full gallop, I shouted at the top of my voice, "Get off that donkey, you rascal, and give her up to me, or I'll ride you down."

The fellow hearing the thunder of the horse's hoofs behind him, drew up on one side of the road. "What do you want?" said he, as I stopped my charger, now almost covered with sweat and foam close beside him. "Do you want to rob me?" "To rob you?" said I. "No! but to take from you that ass, of which you have just robbed its owner." "I have robbed no man," said the fellow; "I just now purchased it fairly of its master, and the law will give it to me; he asked six pounds for it, and I gave him six pounds." "Six stones, you mean, you rascal," said I; "get down, or my horse shall be upon you in a moment"; then with a motion of my reins, I caused the horse to rear, pressing his sides with my heels as if I intended to make him leap. "Stop," said the man, "I'll get down, and then try if I can't serve you out." He then got down, and confronted me with his cudgel; he was a horrible-looking fellow, and seemed prepared for anything.

Scarcely, however, had he dismounted, when the donkey jerked the bridle out of his hand, and probably in revenge for the usage she had received, gave him a pair of tremendous kicks on the hip with her hinder legs, which overturned him, and then scampered down the road the way she had come. "Pretty treatment this," said the fellow, getting up without his cudgel, and holding his hand to his side, "I wish I may not be lamed for life." "And if you be," said I, "it will merely serve you right, you rascal, for trying to cheat a poor old man out of his property by quibbling at words." "Rascal!" said the fellow, "you lie, I am no rascal; and as for quibbling with words—suppose I did! What then? All the first people does it! The newspapers does it! the gentlefolks that calls themselves the guides of the popular mind does it! I'm no ignoramus. I read the newspapers, and knows what's what."

"You read them to some purpose," said I. "Well, if you are lamed for life, and unfitted for any active line—turn newspaper editor; I should say you are perfectly qualified, and this day's adventure may be the foundation of your fortune," thereupon I turned round and rode off. The fellow followed me with a torrent of abuse. "Confound you," said he—yet that was not the expression either—"I know you; you are one of the horse-patrol come down into the country on leave to see your relations. Confound you, you and the like of you have knocked my business on the head near Lunnon, and I suppose we shall have you shortly in the country." "To the newspaper office," said I, "and fabricate falsehoods out of flint stones"; then touching the horse with my heels, I trotted off, and coming to the place where I had seen the old man, I found him there, risen from the ground, and embracing his ass.

I told him that I was travelling down the road, and said, that if his way lay in the same direction as mine he could do no better than accompany me for some distance, lest the fellow who, for aught I knew, might be hovering nigh, might catch him alone, and again get his ass from him. After thanking me for my offer, which he said he would accept, he got upon his ass, and we proceeded together down the road. My new acquaintance said very little of his own accord; and when I asked him a question, answered rather incoherently. I heard him every now and then say, "Villain!" to himself, after which he would pat the donkey's neck, from which circumstance I concluded that his mind was occupied with his late adventure. After travelling about two miles, we reached a place where a drift-way on the right led from the great road; here my companion stopped, and on my asking him whether he was going any farther, he told me that the path to the right was the way to his home.

I was bidding him farewell, when he hemmed once or twice, and said, that as he did not live far off, he hoped that I would go with him and taste some of his mead. As I had never tasted mead, of which I had frequently read in the compositions of the Welsh bards, and, moreover, felt rather thirsty from the heat of the day, I told him that I should have great pleasure in attending him. Whereupon, turning off together, we proceeded about half a mile, sometimes between stone walls, and at other times hedges, till we reached a small hamlet, through which we passed, and presently came to a very pretty cottage, delightfully situated within a garden, surrounded by a hedge of woodbines. Opening a gate at one corner of the garden he led the way to a large shed, which stood partly behind the cottage, which he said was his stable; thereupon he dismounted and led his donkey into the shed, which was without stalls, but had a long rack and manger. On one side he tied his donkey, after taking off her caparisons, and I followed his example, tying my horse at the other side with a rope halter which he gave me; he then asked me to come in and taste his mead, but I told him that I must attend to the comfort of my horse first, and forthwith, taking a wisp of straw, rubbed him carefully down. Then taking a pailful of clear water which stood in the shed, I allowed the horse to drink about half a pint; and then turning to the old man, who all the time had stood by looking at my proceedings, I asked him whether he had any oats? "I have all kinds of grain," he replied; and, going out, he presently returned with two measures, one a large and the other a small one, both filled with oats, mixed with a few beans, and handing the large one to me for the horse, he emptied the other before the donkey, who, before she began to despatch it, turned her nose to her master's face, and fairly kissed him. Having given my horse his portion, I told the old man that I was ready to taste his mead as soon as he pleased, whereupon he ushered me into his cottage, where, making me sit down by a deal table in a neatly sanded kitchen, he produced from an old-fashioned closet a bottle, holding about a quart, and a couple of cups, which might each contain about half a pint, then opening the bottle and filling the cups with a brown-coloured liquor, he handed one to me, and taking a seat opposite to me, he lifted the other, nodded, and saying to me—"Health and welcome," placed it to his lips and drank.

"Health and thanks," I replied; and being very thirsty, emptied my cup at a draught; I had scarcely done so, however, when I half repented. The mead was deliciously sweet and mellow, but appeared strong as brandy; my eyes reeled in my head, and my brain became slightly dizzy. "Mead is a strong drink," said the old man, as he looked at me, with a half smile on his countenance. "This is at any rate," said I, "so strong, indeed, that I would not drink another cup for any consideration." "And I would not ask you," said the old man; "for, if you did, you would most probably be stupid all day, and wake the next morning with a headache. Mead is a good drink, but woundily strong, especially to those who be not used to it, as I suppose you are not." "Where do you get it?" said I. "I make it myself," said the old man, "from the honey which my bees make." "Have you many bees?" I inquired. "A great many," said the old man. "And do you keep them," said I, "for the sake of making mead with their honey?" "I keep them," he replied, "partly because I am fond of them, and partly for what they bring me in; they make me a great deal of honey, some of which I sell, and with a little I make some mead to warm my poor heart with, or occasionally to treat a friend with like yourself." "And do you support yourself entirely by means of your bees?" "No," said the old man; "I have a little bit of ground behind my house, which is my principal means of support." "And do you live alone?" "Yes," said he; "with the exception of the bees and the donkey, I live quite alone."

He led me behind his house, and showed me his little domain. It consisted of about two acres in admirable cultivation; a small portion of it formed a kitchen garden, while the rest was sown with four kinds of grain, wheat, barley, peas, and beans. The air was full of ambrosial sweets, resembling those proceeding from an orange grove; a place which though I had never seen at that time, I since have. In the garden was the habitation of the bees, a long box, supported upon three oaken stumps. It was full of small round glass windows, and appeared to be divided into a great many compartments, much resembling drawers placed sideways. He told me that, as one compartment was filled, the bees left it for another; so that, whenever he wanted honey, he could procure some without injury to the insects. Through the little round windows I could see several of the bees at work; hundreds were going in and out of the doors; hundreds were buzzing about on the flowers, the woodbines, and beans.

I was rather pleased with the old man, and much with all about him. As evening drew nigh, I told him that I must proceed on my journey; whereupon he invited me to tarry with him during the night, telling me that he had a nice room and bed above at my service. I, however, declined; and bidding him farewell, mounted my horse, and departed. Regaining the road, I proceeded once more in the direction of the north; and, after a few hours, coming to a comfortable public-house, I stopped, and put up for the night.

CHAPTER XLVIII

A FEW days after the circumstance which I have last commemorated, it chanced that, as I was standing at the door of the inn, one of the numerous stage-coaches which were in the habit of stopping there, drove up, and several passengers got down. I had assisted a woman with a couple of children to dismount, and had just delivered to her a band-box, which appeared to be her only property, which she had begged me to fetch down from the roof, when I felt a hand laid upon my shoulder, and heard a voice exclaim, "Is it possible, old fellow, that I find you in this place?" I turned round, and, wrapped in a large blue cloak, I beheld my good friend Francis Ardry. I shook him most warmly by the hand, and said, "If you are surprised to see me, I am no less so to see you; where are you bound to?"

"I am bound for L——; at any rate, I am booked for that sea-port," said my friend in reply.

"I am sorry for it," said I, "for in that case we shall have to part in a quarter of an hour, the coach by which you came stopping no longer."

"And whither are you bound?" demanded my friend.

"I am stopping at present in this house, quite undetermined as to what to do."

"Then come along with me," said Francis Ardry.

"That I can scarcely do," said I; "I have a horse in the stall which I cannot afford to ruin by racing to L—— by the side of your coach."

My friend mused for a moment: "I have no particular business at L——," said he; "I was merely going thither to pass a day or two, till an affair, in which I am deeply interested, at C—— shall come off. I think I shall stay with you for four-and-twenty hours at least; I have been rather melancholy of late, and cannot afford to part with a friend like you at the present moment; it is an unexpected piece of good fortune to have met you; and I have not been very fortunate of late," he added, sighing.

"Well," said I, "I am glad to see you once more, whether fortunate, or not; where is your baggage?"

"Yon trunk is mine," said Francis, pointing to a trunk of black Russian leather upon the coach.

"We will soon have it down," said I; and at a word which I gave to one of the hangers-on of the inn, the trunk was taken from the top of the coach.

It was now about one o'clock: Francis Ardry ordered dinner for two, to be ready at four, and a pint of sherry to be brought forthwith, which I requested my friend the waiter might be the very best, and which in effect turned out as I requested; we sat down, and when we had drunk to each other's health, Frank requested me to make known to him how I had contrived to free myself from my embarrassments in London, what I had been about since I quitted that city, and the present posture of my affairs.

I related to Francis Ardry how I had composed the Life of Joseph Sell, and how the sale of it to the bookseller had enabled me to quit London with money in my pocket, which had supported me during a long course of ramble in the country, into the particulars of which I, however, did not enter with any considerable degree of fulness.

"No very agreeable posture of affairs," said Francis Ardry, looking rather seriously at me.

"I make no complaints," said I, "my prospects are not very bright, it is true, but sometimes I have visions both waking and sleeping, which, though always strange, are invariably agreeable. Last night, in my chamber near the hayloft, I dreamt that I had passed over an almost interminable wilderness—an enormous wall rose before me, the wall, methought, was the great wall of China:—strange figures appeared to be beckoning to me from the top of the wall; such visions are not exactly to be sneered at. Not that such phantasmagoria," said I, raising my voice, "are to be compared for a moment with such desirable things as fashion, fine clothes, cheques from uncles, parliamentary interest, the love of splendid females. Ah! woman's love," said I, and sighed.

"What's the matter with the fellow?" said Francis Ardry.

"There is nothing like it," said I.

"Like what?"

"Love, divine love," said I.

"Confound love," said Francis Ardry, "I hate the very name; I have made myself a pretty fool by it, but trust me for ever being at such folly again. In an evil hour I abandoned my former pursuits and amusements for it; in one morning spent at Joey's there was more real pleasure than in——"

"Surely," said I, "you are not hankering after dog-fighting again, a sport which none but the gross and unrefined care anything for? No, one's thoughts should be occupied by something higher and more rational than dog-fighting; and what better than love—divine love? Oh, there's nothing like it!"

"Pray, don't talk nonsense," said Francis Ardry.

"Nonsense," said I; "why I was repeating, to the best of my recollection, what I heard you say on a former occasion."

"If ever I talked such stuff," said Francis Ardry, "I was a fool; and indeed I cannot deny that I have been one: no, there's no denying that I have been a fool. What do you think? that false Annette has cruelly abandoned me."

"Well," said I, "perhaps you have yourself to thank for her having done so; did you never treat her with coldness, and repay her marks of affectionate interest with strange fits of eccentric humour?"

"Lord! how little you know of women," said Francis Ardry; "had I done as you suppose, I should probably have possessed her at the present moment. I treated her in a manner diametrically opposite to that. I loaded her with presents, was always most assiduous to her, always at her feet, as I may say, yet she nevertheless abandoned me—and for whom? I am almost ashamed to say—for a fiddler."

I took a glass of wine, Francis Ardry followed my example, and then proceeded to detail to me the treatment which he had experienced from Annette, and from what he said, it appeared that her conduct to him had been in the highest degree reprehensible; notwithstanding he had indulged her in everything, she was never civil to him, but loaded him continually with taunts and insults, and had finally, on his being unable to supply her with a sum of money which she had demanded, decamped from the lodgings which he had taken for her, carrying with her all the presents which at various times he had bestowed upon her, and had put herself under the protection of a gentleman who played the bassoon at the Italian Opera, at which place it appeared that her sister had lately been engaged as a danseuse. My friend informed me that at first he had experienced great agony at the ingratitude of Annette, but at last had made up his mind to forget her, and, in order more effectually to do so, had left London with the intention of witnessing a fight, which was shortly coming off at a town in these parts, between some dogs and a lion; which combat, he informed me, had for some time past been looked forward to with intense eagerness by the gentlemen of the sporting world.

I commended him for his resolution, at the same time advising him not to give up his mind entirely to dog-fighting, as he had formerly done, but, when the present combat should be over, to return to his rhetorical studies, and above all to marry some rich and handsome lady on the first opportunity, as, with his person and expectations, he had only to sue for the hand of the daughter of a marquis to be successful, telling him, with a sigh, that all women were not Annettes, and that, upon the whole, there was nothing like them. To which advice he answered that he intended to return to rhetoric as soon as the lion fight should be over, but that he never intended to marry having had enough of women; adding that he was glad he had no sister, as, with the feelings which he entertained with respect to her sex, he should be unable to treat her with common affection, and concluded by repeating a proverb which he had learnt from an Arab whom he had met at Venice, to the effect that, "one who has been stung by a snake, shivers at the sight of a sting."

After a little more conversation, we strolled to the stable, where my horse was standing; my friend, who was a connoisseur in horseflesh, surveyed the animal with attention, and after inquiring where and how I had obtained him, asked what I intended to do with him; on my telling him that I was undetermined, and that I was afraid the horse was likely to prove a burden to me, he said, "It is a noble animal, and if you mind what you are about, you may make a small fortune by him. I do not want such an animal myself, nor do I know any one who does; but a great horse-fair will be held shortly at a place where, it is true, I have never been, but of which I have heard a great deal from my acquaintances, where it is said a first-rate horse is always sure to fetch its value; that place is Horncastle, in Lincolnshire, you should take him thither."

Francis Ardry and myself dined together, and after dinner partook of a bottle of the best port which the inn afforded. After a few glasses, we had a great deal of conversation; I again brought the subject of marriage and love, divine love, upon the carpet, but Francis almost immediately begged me to drop it; and on my having the delicacy to comply, he reverted to dog-fighting, on which he talked well and learnedly; amongst other things, he said it was a princely sport of great antiquity, and quoted from Quintus Curtius to prove that the princes of India must have been of the fancy, they having, according to that author, treated Alexander to a fight between certain dogs and a lion. Becoming, notwithstanding my friend's eloquence and learning, somewhat tired of the subject, I began to talk about Alexander. Francis Ardry said he was one of the two great men whom the world has produced, the other being Napoleon; I replied that I believed Tamerlane was a greater man than either; but Francis Ardry knew nothing of Tamerlane, save what he had gathered from the play of Timour the Tartar. "No," said he, "Alexander and Napoleon are the great men of the world, their names are known everywhere. Alexander has been dead upwards of two thousand years, but the very English bumpkins sometimes christen their boys by the name of Alexander—can there be a greater evidence of his greatness? As for Napoleon, there are some parts of India in which his bust is worshipped." Wishing to make up a triumvirate, I mentioned the name of Wellington, to which Francis Ardry merely said, "bah!" and resumed the subject of dog-fighting.

Francis Ardry remained at the inn during that day and the next, and then departed to the dog and lion fight; I never saw him afterwards. I too determined to mount my horse and leave the inn.

This horse had caused me for some time past no little perplexity; I had frequently repented of having purchased him, more especially as the purchase had been made with another person's money, and had more than once shown him to people who, I imagined, were likely to purchase him; but, though they were profuse in his praise, as people generally are in the praise of what they don't intend to purchase, they never made me an offer, and now that I had determined to mount on his back and ride away, what was

I to do with him in the sequel? I could not maintain him long. I bethought me of Horncastle, which Francis Ardry had mentioned as a place where the horse was likely to find a purchaser, and not having determined upon any particular place to which to repair, I thought that I could do no better than betake myself to Horncastle in the first instance, and there endeavour to dispose of my horse.

On making inquiries with respect to the situation of Horncastle, and the time when the fair would be held, I learned that the town was situated in Lincolnshire, about a hundred and fifty miles from the inn at which I was at present sojourning, and that the fair would be held nominally within about a month, but that it was always requisite to be on the spot some days before the nominal day of the fair, as all the best horses were generally sold before that time, and the people who came to purchase gone away with what they had bought.

On the following day at four o'clock I dined with the landlord, in company with a commercial traveller. The dinner was good, though plain, consisting of boiled mackerel—rather a rarity in those parts at that time—with fennel sauce, a prime baron of roast beef after the mackerel, then a tart and noble Cheshire cheese; we had prime sherry at dinner, and whilst eating the cheese prime porter, that of Barclay, the only good porter in the world. After the cloth was removed we had a bottle of very good port; and whilst partaking of the port I had an argument with the commercial traveller on the subject of the corn-laws.

The commercial traveller, having worsted me in the argument on the subject of the corn-laws, got up in great glee, saying that he must order his gig, as business must be attended to. Before leaving the room, however, he shook me patronizingly by the hand, and said something to the master of the house, but in so low a tone that it escaped my ear.

No sooner had he departed than the master of the house told me that his friend the traveller had just said that I was a confounded sensible young fellow, and not at all opinionated, a sentiment in which he himself perfectly agreed—then hemming once or twice, he said that as I was going on a journey he hoped I was tolerably well provided with money, adding that travelling was rather expensive, especially on horseback, the manner in which he supposed, as I had a horse in the stable, I intended to travel. I told him that though I was not particularly well supplied with money, I had sufficient for the expenses of my journey, at the end of which I hoped to procure more.

"I am going to take my horse to Horncastle, and when there I shall endeavour to obtain his full value—ay to the last penny."

"Horncastle!" said the landlord, "I have heard of that place; you mustn't be dreaming visions when you get there, or they'll steal the horse from under you. Come, friend, I drink to your success at Horncastle."

CHAPTER XLIX

I DEPARTED from the inn much in the same fashion as I had come to it, mounted on a splendid horse indifferently well caparisoned, with the small valise attached to my crupper, in which, besides the few things I had brought with me, was a small book of roads with a map, which had been presented to me by the landlord. I must not forget to state that I did not ride out of the yard, but that my horse was brought to me at the front door by old Bill, who insisted upon doing so, and who refused a five-shilling piece which I offered him; and it will be as well to let the reader know that the landlord shook me by the hand as I mounted, and that the people attached to the inn, male and female—my friend the postillion at the head—assembled before the house to see me off, and gave me three cheers as I rode away. Perhaps no person ever departed from an inn with more éclat or better wishes; nobody looked at me askance, except two stage-coachmen who were loitering about, one of whom said to his companion, "I say, Jim! twig his portmanteau! a regular Newmarket turn-out, by——!"

It was in the cool of the evening of a bright day—all the days of that summer were bright—that I departed. I felt at first rather melancholy at finding myself again launched into the wide world, and leaving the friends whom I had lately made behind me; but by occasionally trotting the horse, and occasionally singing a song of Romanvile, I had dispelled the feeling of melancholy by the time I had proceeded three miles down the main road. It was at the end of these three miles, just opposite a milestone, that I struck into a cross road. After riding about seven miles, threading what are called, in postillion parlance, cross-country roads, I reached another high road, tending to the east, along which I proceeded for a mile or two, when coming to a small inn, about nine o'clock, I halted and put up for the night.

Early on the following morning I proceeded on my journey, but fearing to gall the horse, I no longer rode him, but led him by the bridle, until I came to a town at the distance of about ten miles from the place where I had passed the night. Here I stayed during the heat of the day, more on the horse's account than my own, and towards evening resumed my journey, leading the animal by the bridle as before; and in this manner I proceeded for several days, travelling on an average from twenty to twenty-five miles a day, always leading the animal, except perhaps now and then of an evening, when, if I saw a good piece of road before me, I would mount and put the horse into a trot, which the creature seemed to enjoy as much as myself, showing his satisfaction by snorting and neighing, whilst I gave utterance to my own exhilaration by shouts, or by "the chi she is kaulo she soves pré lakie dumo," or by something else of the same kind in Romanvile.

On the whole, I journeyed along very pleasantly, certainly quite as pleasantly as I do at present, now that I am become a gentleman and weigh sixteen stone, though some people would say that my present manner of travelling is much the most preferable, riding as I now do, instead of leading my horse; receiving the homage of ostlers instead of their familiar nods; sitting down to dinner in the parlour of the best inn I can find, instead of passing the brightest part of the day in the kitchen of a village alehouse; carrying on my argument after dinner on the subject of the corn-laws, with the best commercial gentlemen on the road, instead of being glad, whilst sipping a pint of beer, to get into conversation with blind trampers, or maimed Abraham sailors, regaling themselves on half-pints at the said village hostelries.

On I went in my journey, traversing England from west to east—ascending and descending hills—crossing rivers by bridge and ferry—and passing over extensive plains. What a beautiful country is England! People run abroad to see beautiful countries, and leave their own behind unknown, unnoticed—their own the most beautiful! And then, again, what a country for adventures! especially to those who travel on foot, or on horseback. People run abroad in quest of adventures, and traverse Spain or Portugal on mule or on horseback; whereas there are ten times more adventures to be met with in England than in Spain, Portugal, or stupid Germany to boot. Witness the number of adventures narrated in the present book—a book entirely devoted to England. Why, there is not a chapter in the present book which is not full of adventures, with the exception of the present one, and this is not yet terminated.

After traversing two or three counties, I reached the confines of Lincolnshire. During one particularly hot day I put up at a public-house, to which, in the evening, came a party of harvesters to make merry, who, finding me wandering about the house a stranger, invited me to partake of their ale; so I drank with the harvesters, who sang me songs about rural life, such as—

> "Sitting in the swale; and listening to the swindle of the flail, as it sounds dub-a-dub on the corn, from the neighbouring barn."

In requital for which I treated them with a song, not of Romanvile, but the song of "Sivory and the horse Grayman." I remained with them till it was dark, having, after sunset, entered into deep discourse with a celebrated ratcatcher, who communicated to me the secrets of his trade, saying, amongst other things, "When you see the rats pouring out of their holes, and running up my hands and arms, it's not after me they comes, but after the oils I carries about me they comes"; and who subsequently spoke in the most enthusiastic manner of his trade, saying that it was the best trade in the world, and most diverting, and that it was likely to last for ever; for whereas all other kinds of vermin were fast disappearing from England, rats were every day becoming more abundant. I had quitted this good company, and having mounted my horse, was making my way towards a town at about six miles' distance, at a swinging trot, my thoughts deeply engaged on what I had gathered from the ratcatcher, when all of a sudden a light glared upon the horse's face, who purled round in great terror, and flung me out of the saddle, as from a sling, or with as much violence as the horse Grayman, in the ballad, flings Sivord the Snareswayne. I fell upon the ground—felt a kind of crashing about my neck—and forthwith became senseless.

How long I remained senseless I cannot say, for a considerable time, I believe; at length, opening my eyes, I found myself lying on a bed in a middle-sized chamber, lighted by a candle, which stood on a table—an elderly man stood near me, and a yet more elderly female was holding a phial of very pungent salts to my olfactory organ. I attempted to move, but felt very stiff—my right arm appeared nearly paralyzed, and there was a strange dull sensation in my head. "You had better remain still, young man," said the elderly individual, "the surgeon will be here presently; I have sent a message for him to the neighbouring village." "Where am I?" said I, "and what has happened?" "You are in my house," said the old man, "and you have been flung from a horse. I am sorry to say that I was the cause. As I was driving home, the lights in my gig frightened the animal." "Where is the horse?" said I. "Below, in my stable," said the elderly individual. "I saw you fall, but knowing that on account of my age I could be of little use to you, I instantly hurried home, the accident did not occur more than a furlong off, and procuring the assistance of my lad, and two or three neighbouring cottagers, I returned to the spot where you were lying senseless. We raised you up, and brought you here. My lad then went in quest of the horse, who had run away as we drew nigh. When we saw him first he was standing near you; he caught him with some difficulty, and brought him home. What are you about?" said the old man, as I strove to get off the bed. "I want to see the horse," said I. "I entreat you to be still," said the old man; "the horse is safe, I assure you." "I am thinking about his knees," said I. "Instead of thinking about your horse's knees," said the old man, "be thankful that you have not broke your own neck." "You do not talk wisely," said I; "when a man's neck is broke, he is provided for; but when his horse's knees are broke, he is a lost jockey, that is, if he has nothing but his horse to depend upon. A pretty figure I should cut at Horncastle, mounted on a horse blood-raw at the knees." "Oh, you are going to Horncastle," said the old man, seriously, "then I can sympathize with you in your anxiety about your horse, being a Lincolnshire man, and the son of one who bred horses. I will myself go down into the stable, and examine into the condition of your horse, so pray remain quiet till I return; it would certainly be a terrible thing to appear at Horncastle on a broken-kneed horse."

He left the room and returned in about ten minutes, followed by another person. "Your horse is safe," said he, "and his knees are unblemished; not a hair ruffled. He is a fine animal, and will do credit to Horncastle; but here is the surgeon come to examine into your own condition." The surgeon was a man about thirty-five, thin, and rather tall; his face was long and pale, and his hair, which was light, was carefully combed back as much as possible from his forehead. He was dressed very neatly, and spoke in a very precise tone. "Allow me to feel your pulse, friend?" said he, taking me by the right wrist. I uttered a cry, for at the motion which he caused a thrill of agony darted through my arm. "I hope your arm is not broke, my friend," said the surgeon, "allow me to see; first of all, we must divest you of this cumbrous frock."

The frock was removed with some difficulty, and then the upper vestments of my frame, with more difficulty still. The surgeon felt my arm, moving it up and down, causing me unspeakable pain. "There is no fracture," said he, at last, "but a contusion—a violent contusion. I am told you were going to Horncastle; I am afraid you will be hardly able to ride your horse thither in time to dispose of him; however, we shall see—your arm must be bandaged, friend; after which I shall bleed you, and administer a composing draught."

To be short, the surgeon did as he proposed, and when he had administered the composing draught, he said, "Be of good cheer; I should not be surprised if you are yet in time for Horncastle." He then departed with the master of the house, and the woman, leaving me to my repose. I soon began to feel drowsy, and was just composing myself to slumber, lying on my back, as the surgeon had advised me, when I heard steps ascending the stairs, and in a moment more the surgeon entered again, followed by the master of the house. "I hope I don't disturb you," said the former; "my reason for returning is to relieve your mind from any anxiety with respect to your horse. I am by no means sure that you will be able, owing to your accident, to reach Horncastle in time: to quiet you, however, I will buy your horse for any reasonable sum. I have been down to the stable, and approve of his figure. What do you ask for him?"

"This is a strange time of night," said I, "to come to me about purchasing my horse, and I am hardly in a fitting situation to be applied to about such a matter. What do you want him for?" "For my own use," said the surgeon; "I am a professional man, and am obliged to be continually driving about; I cover at least one hundred and fifty miles every week." "He will never answer your purpose," said I, "he is not a driving horse, and was never between shafts in his life; he is for riding, more especially for trotting, at which he has few equals." "It matters not to me whether he is for riding or driving," said the surgeon, "sometimes I ride, sometimes drive; so, if we can come to terms, I will buy him, though remember it is chiefly to remove any anxiety from your mind about him." "This is no time for bargaining," said I, "if you wish to have the horse for a hundred guineas, you may; if not——" "A hundred guineas!" said the surgeon, "my good friend, you must surely be light-headed; allow me to feel your pulse," and he attempted to feel my left wrist. "I am not light-headed," said I, "and I require no one to feel my pulse; but I should be light-headed if I were to sell my horse for less than I have demanded; but I have a curiosity to know what you would be willing to offer." "Thirty pounds," said the surgeon, "is all I can afford to give; and that is a great deal for a country surgeon to offer for a horse." "Thirty pounds!" said I, "why, he cost me nearly double that sum. To tell you the truth, I am afraid that you want to take advantage of my situation." "Not in the least, friend," said the surgeon, "not in the least; I only wished to set your mind at rest about your horse; but as you think he is worth more than I can afford to offer, take him to Horncastle by all means; I will do my best to cure you in time. Good night, I will see you again on the morrow."

I fell asleep; and in my sleep I had an ugly dream. I dreamt that I had died of the injuries I had received from my fall, and that no sooner had my soul departed from my body than it entered that of a quadruped, even my own horse in the stable—in a word, I was, to all intents and purposes, my own steed; and as I stood in the stable chewing hay (and I remember that the hay was exceedingly tough), the door opened, and the surgeon who had attended me came in. "My good animal," said he, "as your late master has scarcely left enough to pay for the expenses of his funeral, and nothing to remunerate me for my trouble, I shall make bold to take possession of you. If your paces are good, I shall keep you for my own riding; if not, I shall take you to Horncastle, your original destination." He then bridled and saddled me, and, leading me out, mounted, and then trotted me up and down before the house, at the door of which the old man, who now appeared to be dressed in regular jockey fashion, was standing. "I like his paces well," said the surgeon; "I think I shall take him for my own use." "And what am I to have for all the trouble his master caused me?" said my late entertainer, on whose countenance I now observed, for the first time, a diabolical squint. "The consciousness of having done your duty to a fellow-creature in succouring him in a time of distress, must be your reward," said the surgeon. "Pretty gammon, truly," said my late entertainer; "what would you say if I were to talk in that way to you? Come, unless you choose to behave jonnock, I shall take the bridle and lead the horse back into the stable." "Well," said the surgeon, "we are old friends, and I don't wish to dispute with you, so I'll tell you what I will do; I will ride the animal to Horncastle, and we will share what he fetches like brothers." "Good," said the old man, "but if you say that you have sold him for less than a hundred, I sha'n't consider you jonnock; remember what the young fellow said—that young fellow——" I heard no more, for the next moment I found myself on a broad road leading, as I supposed, in the direction of Horncastle, the surgeon still in the saddle, and my legs moving at a rapid trot. "Get on," said the surgeon, jerking my mouth with the bit; whereupon, full of rage, I instantly set off at a full gallop, determined, if possible, to dash my rider to the earth. The surgeon, however, kept his seat, and, so far from attempting to abate my speed, urged me on to greater efforts with a stout stick, which methought he held in his hand. In vain did I rear and kick, attempting to get rid of my foe.

At last, as I was still madly dashing on, panting and blowing, and had almost given up all hope, I saw at a distance before me a heap of stones by the side of the road, probably placed there for the purpose of repairing it; a thought appeared to strike me—I will shy at those stones, and, if I can't get rid of him so, resign myself to my fate. So I increased my speed, till arriving within about ten yards of the heap, I made a desperate start, turning half round with nearly the velocity of a mill-stone. Oh, the joy I experienced when I felt my enemy canted over my neck, and saw him lying senseless in the road. "I have you now in my power," I said, or rather neighed, as, going up to my prostrate foe, I stood over him. "Suppose I were to rear now, and let my fore feet fall upon you, what would your life be worth? that is, supposing you are not killed already; but lie there, I will do you no further harm, but trot to Horncastle without a rider, and when there——" and without further reflection off I trotted in the direction of Horncastle, but had not gone far before my bridle, falling from my neck, got entangled with my off fore foot. I felt myself falling, a thrill of agony shot through me—my knees would be broken, and what should I do at Horncastle with a pair of broken knees? I struggled, but I could not disengage my off fore foot, and downward I fell, but before I had reached the ground I awoke, and found myself half out of bed, my bandaged arm in considerable pain, and my left hand just touching the floor.

CHAPTER L

It might be about eight o'clock in the morning when I was awakened by the entrance of the old man. "How have you rested?" said he, coming up to the bedside, and looking me in the face. "Well," said I, "and I feel much better, but I am still very sore."

I surveyed him now for the first time with attention. He was dressed in a sober-coloured suit, and was apparently between sixty and seventy. In stature he was rather above the middle height, but with a slight stoop; his features were placid, and expressive of much benevolence, but, as it appeared to me, with rather a melancholy cast—as I gazed upon them, I felt ashamed that I should ever have conceived in my brain a vision like that of the preceding night, in which he appeared in so disadvantageous a light. At length he said, "It is now time for you to take some refreshment. I hear my old servant coming up with your breakfast." In a moment the elderly female entered with a tray, on which was some bread and butter, a teapot and cup. The cup was of common blue earthenware, but the pot was of china, curiously fashioned, and seemingly of great antiquity. The old man poured me out a cupful of tea, and then, with the assistance of the woman, raised me higher, and propped me up with the pillows. I ate and drank; when the pot was emptied of its liquid (it did not contain much), I raised it up with my left hand to inspect it. The sides were covered with curious characters, seemingly hieroglyphics. After surveying them for some time, I replaced it upon the tray. "You seem fond of china," said I, to the old man, after the servant had retired with the breakfast things, and I had returned to my former posture; "you have china on the mantelpiece, and that was a remarkable teapot out of which I have just been drinking."

The old man fixed his eyes intently on me, and methought the expression of his countenance became yet more melancholy. "Yes," said he, at last, "I am fond of china—I have reason to be fond of china—but for china I should——" and here he sighed again.

"You value it for the quaintness and singularity of its form," said I; "it appears to be less adapted for real use than our own pottery."

"I care little about its form," said the old man; "I care for it simply on account of——however, why talk to you on the subject which can have no possible interest to you? I expect the surgeon here presently."

"I do not like that surgeon at all," said I; "how strangely he behaved last night, coming back, when I was just falling asleep, to ask me if I would sell my horse."

The old man smiled. "He has but one failing," said he, "an itch for horse-dealing; but for that he might be a much richer man than he is; he is continually buying and exchanging horses, and generally finds himself a loser by his bargains: but he is a worthy creature, and skilful in his profession—it is well for you that you are under his care."

The old man visited me twice or thrice every day to inquire into my state. His words were few on these occasions, and he did not stay long. Yet his voice and his words were kind. What surprised me most in connection with this individual was the delicacy of conduct which he exhibited in not letting a word proceed from his lips which could testify curiosity respecting who I was, or whence I came.

On the evening of the fourth day, feeling tired of my confinement, I put my clothes on in the best manner I could, and left the chamber. Descending a flight of stairs, I reached a kind of quadrangle, from which branched two or three passages; one of these I entered, which had a door at the farther end, and one on each side; the one to the left standing partly open, I entered it, and found myself in a middle-sized room with a large window, or rather glass-door, which looked into a garden, and which stood open. There was nothing remarkable in this room, except a large quantity of china. There was china on the mantelpiece—china on two tables, and a small beaufet, which stood opposite the glass-door, was covered with china—there were cups, teapots, and vases of various forms, and on all of them I observed characters—not a teapot, not a teacup, not a vase of whatever form or size, but appeared to possess hieroglyphics on some part or other. After surveying these articles for some time with no little interest, I passed into the garden, in which there were small parterres of flowers, and two or three trees, and which, where the house did not abut, was bounded by a wall; turning to the right by a walk by the side of the house, I passed by a door –probably the one I had seen at the end of the passage–and arrived at another window similar to that through which I had come, and which also stood open; I was about to pass through it, when I heard the voice of my entertainer exclaiming, "Is that you? pray come in."

I entered the room, which seemed to be a counterpart of the one which I had just left. It was of the same size, had the same kind of furniture, and appeared to be equally well stocked with china; one prominent article it possessed, however, which the other room did not exhibit–namely, a clock, which, with its pendulum moving tick-a-tick, hung against the wall opposite to the door.

The old gentleman was seated in an easy chair a little way into the room, having the glass-door on his right hand. On a table before him lay a large open volume, in which I observed Roman letters as well as characters. A few inches beyond the book on the table, covered all over with hieroglyphics, stood a china vase. The eyes of the old man were fixed upon it.

"Sit down," said he, motioning me with his hand to a stool close by, but without taking his eyes from the vase.

"I can't make it out," said he, at last, removing his eyes from the vase, and leaning back on the chair, "I can't make it out."

"I wish I could assist you," said I.

"Assist me," said the old man, looking at me with a half smile.

"Yes," said I, "but I don't understand Chinese."

"I suppose not," said the old man, with another slight smile; "but–but——"

"Pray proceed," said I.

"I wished to ask you," said the old man, "how you knew that the characters on yon piece of crockery were Chinese; or, indeed, that there was such a language?"

"I knew the crockery was china," said I, "and naturally enough supposed what was written upon it to be Chinese; as for there being such a language –the English have a language, the French have a language, and why not the Chinese?"

"May I ask you a question?"

"As many as you like."

"Do you know any language besides English?"

"Yes," said I, "I know a little of two or three."

"May I ask their names?"

"Why not?" said I, "I know a little French."

"Anything else?"

"Yes, a little Welsh, and a little Haik."

"What is Haik?"

"Armenian."

"I am glad to see you in my house," said the old man, shaking me by the hand; "how singular that one coming as you did should know Armenian!"

"Not more singular," said I, "than that one living in such a place as this should know Chinese. How came you to acquire it?"

The old man looked at me, and sighed. "I beg pardon," said I, "for asking what is, perhaps, an impertinent question; I have not imitated your own delicacy; you have never asked me a question without first desiring permission, and here I have been days and nights in your house an intruder on your hospitality, and you have never so much as asked me who I am."

"In forbearing to do that," said the old man, "I merely obeyed the Chinese precept, 'Ask no questions of a guest'; it is written on both sides of the teapot out of which you have had your tea."

"I wish I knew Chinese," said I. "Is it a difficult language to acquire?"

"I have reason to think so," said the old man. "I have been occupied upon it five-and-thirty years, and I am still very imperfectly acquainted with it; at least, I frequently find upon my crockery sentences the meaning of which to me is very dark, though it is true these sentences are mostly verses, which are, of course, more difficult to understand than mere prose."

"Are your Chinese studies," said I, "confined to crockery literature?"

"Entirely," said the old man; "I read nothing else."

"I have heard," said I, "that the Chinese have no letters, but that for every word they have a separate character—is it so?"

"For every word they have a particular character," said the old man; "though, to prevent confusion, they have arranged their words under two hundred and fourteen what we should call radicals, but which they call keys. As we arrange all our words in a dictionary under twenty-four letters, so do they arrange all their words, or characters, under two hundred and fourteen radical signs; the simplest radicals being the first, and the more complex the last."

"Does the Chinese resemble any of the European languages in words?" said I.

"I am scarcely competent to inform you," said the old man; "but I believe not."

"What does that character represent?" said I, pointing to one on the vase.

"A knife," said the old man, "that character is one of the simplest radicals or keys."

"And what is the sound of it?" said I.

"Tau," said the old man.

"Tau!" said I; "tau!"

"A strange word for a knife! is it not?" said the old man.

"Tawse!" said I; "tawse!"

"What is tawse?" said the old man.

"You were never at school at Edinburgh, I suppose?"

"Never," said the old man.

"That accounts for your not knowing the meaning of tawse," said I; "had you received the rudiments of a classical education at the High School, you would have known the meaning of tawse full well. It is a leathern thong, with which refractory urchins are recalled to a sense of their duty by the dominie. Tau–tawse–how singular!"

"I cannot see what the two words have in common, except a slight agreement in sound."

"You will see the connection," said I, "when I inform you that the thong, from the middle to the bottom, is cut or slit into two or three parts, from which slits or cuts, unless I am very much mistaken, it derives its name–tawse, a thong with slits or cuts, used for chastising disorderly urchins at the High School, from the French tailler, to cut; evidently connected with the Chinese tau, a knife–how very extraordinary!"

CHAPTER LI

Two days–three days passed away–and I still remained at the house of my hospitable entertainer; my bruised limb rapidly recovering the power of performing its functions. I passed my time agreeably enough, sometimes in my chamber, communing with my own thoughts; sometimes in the stable, attending to, and not unfrequently conversing with, my horse; and at meal-time–for I seldom saw him at any other–discoursing with the old gentleman, sometimes on the Chinese vocabulary, sometimes on Chinese syntax, and once or twice on English horseflesh.

On the evening of the next day, the last which I spent with my kind entertainer, I sat at tea with him in a little summer-house in his garden, partially shaded by the boughs of a large fig-tree. The surgeon had shortly before paid me his farewell visit, and had brought me the letter of introduction to his friend at Horncastle, and also his bill, which I found anything but extravagant. After we had each respectively drank the contents of two cups–and it may not be amiss here to inform the reader that though I took cream with my tea, as I always do when I can procure that addition, the old man, like most people bred up in the country, drank his without it–he thus addressed me:–"I am, as I told you on the night of your accident, the son of a breeder of horses, a respectable and honest man. When I was about twenty he died, leaving me, his only child, a comfortable property, consisting of about two hundred acres of land and some fifteen hundred pounds in money. My mother had died about three years previously. I felt the death of my mother keenly, but that of my father less than was my duty; indeed, truth compels me to acknowledge that I scarcely regretted his death. The cause of this want of proper filial feeling was the opposition which I had experienced from him in an affair which deeply concerned me. I had formed an attachment for a young female in the neighbourhood, who, though poor, was of highly respectable birth, her father having been a curate of the Established Church. She was, at the time of which I am speaking, an orphan, having lost both her parents, and supported herself by keeping a small school. My attachment was returned, and we had pledged our vows, but my father, who could not reconcile himself to her lack of fortune, forbade our marriage in the most positive terms. He was wrong, for she was a fortune in herself—amiable and accomplished. Oh! I cannot tell you all she was—" and here the old man drew his hand across his eyes.

"By the death of my father, the only obstacle to our happiness appeared to be removed. We agreed, therefore, that our marriage should take place within the course of a year; and I forthwith commenced enlarging my house and getting my affairs in order. Amongst other property derived from my father were several horses, which I disposed of in this neighbourhood, with the exception of two remarkably fine ones, which I determined to take to the next fair at Horncastle, the only place where I expected to be able to obtain what I considered to be their full value. At length the time arrived for the commencement of the fair, which was within three months of the period which my beloved and myself had fixed upon for the celebration of our nuptials. To the fair I went, a couple of trusty men following me with the horses. I soon found a purchaser for the animals, a portly, plausible person, of about forty, dressed in a blue riding coat, brown top boots, and leather breeches. There was a strange-looking urchin with him, attired in nearly similar fashion, with a beam in one of his eyes, who called him father. The man paid me for the purchase in bank-notes—three fifty-pound notes for the two horses. As we were about to take leave of each other, he suddenly produced another fifty-pound note, inquiring whether I could change it, complaining, at the same time, of the difficulty of procuring change in the fair. As I happened to have plenty of small money in my possession, and as I felt obliged to him for having purchased my horses at what I considered to be a good price, I informed him that I should be very happy to accommodate him; so I changed him the note, and he, having taken possession of the horses, went his way, and I myself returned home.

"A month passed; during this time I paid away two of the notes which I had received at Horncastle from the dealer—one of them in my immediate neighbourhood, and the other at a town about fifteen miles distant, to which I had repaired for the purpose of purchasing some furniture. All things seemed to be going on most prosperously, and I felt quite happy, when one morning, as I was overlooking some workmen who were employed about my house, I was accosted by a constable, who informed me that he was sent to request my immediate appearance before a neighbouring bench of magistrates. Concluding that I was merely summoned on some unimportant business connected with the neighbourhood, I felt no surprise, and forthwith departed in company with the officer.

"On arriving at the place where the magistrates were sitting—an inn at a small town about two miles distant—I found a more than usual number of people assembled, who appeared to be conversing with considerable eagerness. At sight of me they became silent, but crowded after me as I followed the man into the magistrates' room. There I found the tradesman to whom I had paid the note for the furniture at the town fifteen miles off in attendance, accompanied by an agent of the Bank of England; the former, it seems, had paid the note into a provincial bank, the proprietors of which, discovering it to be a forgery, had forthwith written up to the Bank of England, who had sent down their agent to investigate the matter. A third individual stood beside them—the person in my own immediate neighbourhood to whom I had paid the second note; this, by some means or other, before the coming down of the agent, had found its way to the same provincial bank, and also being pronounced a forgery, it had speedily been traced to the person to whom I had paid it.

"In a few words the magistrates' clerk gave me to understand the state of the case. I was filled with surprise and consternation. I knew myself to be perfectly innocent of any fraudulent intention, but at the time of which I am speaking it was a matter fraught with the greatest danger to be mixed up, however innocently, with the passing of false money. The law with respect to forgery was terribly severe, and the innocent as well as the guilty occasionally suffered. Recovering myself a little, I stated that the notes in question were two of three notes which I had received at Horncastle, for a pair of horses, which it was well known I had carried thither.

"Thereupon, I produced from my pocket-book the third note, which was forthwith pronounced a forgery. I had scarcely produced the third note, when I remembered the one which I had changed for the Horncastle dealer, and with the remembrance came the almost certain conviction that it was also a forgery; I was tempted for a moment to produce it, and to explain the circumstance—would to God I had done so!—but shame at the idea of having been so wretchedly duped prevented me, and the opportunity was lost. I must confess that the agent of the bank behaved, upon the whole, in a very handsome manner; he said that as it was quite evident that I had disposed of certain horses at the fair, it was very probable that I might have received the notes in question in exchange for them, and that he was willing, as he had received a very excellent account of my general conduct, to press the matter no farther, that is, provided—— And here he stopped. Thereupon, one of the three magistrates, who were present, asked me whether I chanced to have any more of these spurious notes in my possession. He certainly had a right to ask the question; but there was something peculiar in his tone—insinuating suspicion. It is certainly difficult to judge of the motives which rule a person's conduct, but I cannot help imagining that he was somewhat influenced in his behaviour on that occasion, which was anything but friendly, by my having refused to sell him the horses at a price less than that which I expected to get at the fair; be this as it may, the question filled me with embarrassment, and I bitterly repented not having at first been more explicit. Thereupon the magistrate in the same kind of tone, demanded to see my pocket-book. I knew that to demur would be useless, and produced it, and therewith, amongst two or three small country notes, appeared the fourth which I had received from the Horncastle dealer. The agent took it up and examined it with attention. 'Well, is it a genuine note?' asked the magistrate. 'I am sorry to say that it is not,' said the agent; 'it is a forgery, like the other three.' The magistrate shrugged his shoulders, as indeed did several people in the room. 'A regular dealer in forged notes,' said a person close behind me; 'who would have thought it?'

"Seeing matters begin to look so serious, I aroused myself, and endeavoured to speak in my own behalf, giving a candid account of the manner in which I became possessed of the notes; but my explanation did not appear to meet much credit; the magistrate, to whom I have in particular alluded, asked why I had not at once stated the fact of my having received a fourth note; and the agent, though in a very quiet tone, observed that he could not help thinking it somewhat strange that I should have changed a note of so much value for a perfect stranger, even supposing that he had purchased my horses, and had paid me their value in hard cash; and I noticed that he laid particular emphasis on the last words. I might have observed that I was an inexperienced young man, who, meaning no harm myself, suspected none in others, but I was confused, stunned, and my tongue seemed to cleave to the roof of my mouth. The men who had taken my horses to Horncastle, and for whom I had sent, as they lived close at hand, now arrived, but the evidence which they could give was anything but conclusive in my favour; they had seen me in company with an individual at Horncastle, to whom, by my orders, they had delivered certain horses, but they had seen no part of the money transaction; the fellow, whether from design or not, having taken me aside into a retired place, where he had paid me the three spurious notes, and induced me to change the fourth, which throughout the affair was what bore most materially against me. How matters might have terminated I do not know, I might have gone to prison, and I might have been—— Just then a friend entered the room in the person of the surgeon of the neighbourhood, the father of him who has attended you. He spoke well and eloquently in my behalf —adding, that as he was fully convinced of my innocence, he was ready to enter into any surety with respect to my appearance at any time to answer anything which might be laid to my charge. Though my friend the magistrate—I call him so ironically—made two or three demurs, it was at last agreed between him and his brethren of the bench, that, for the present, I should be merely called upon to enter into my own recognizance for the sum of two hundred pounds, to appear whenever it should be deemed requisite to enter into any further investigation of the matter.

"So I was permitted to depart from the tribunal of petty justice without handcuffs, and uncollared by a constable; but people looked coldly and suspiciously upon me. The first thing I did was to hasten to the house of my beloved, in order to inform her of every circumstance attending the transaction. I found her, but how? A malicious female individual had hurried to her with a distorted tale, to the effect that I had been taken up as an utterer of forged notes; that an immense number had been found in my possession; that I was already committed, and that probably I should be executed. My affianced one tenderly loved me, and her constitution was delicate; fit succeeded fit; she broke a blood-vessel, and I found her deluged in blood; the surgeon had been sent for; he came and afforded her every possible relief. I was distracted; he bade me have hope, but I observed he looked very grave.

"By the skill of the surgeon, the poor girl was saved in the first instance from the arms of death, and for a few weeks she appeared to be rapidly recovering; by degrees, however, she became melancholy; a worm preyed upon her spirit; a slow fever took possession of her frame. I subsequently learned that the same malicious female who had first carried to her an exaggerated account of the affair, and who was a distant relative of her own, frequently visited her, and did all in her power to excite her fears with respect to its eventual termination. Time passed on in a very wretched manner. Our friend the surgeon showing to us both every mark of kindness and attention.

"It was owing to this excellent man that my innocence was eventually established. Having been called to a town on the borders of Yorkshire to a medical consultation, he chanced to be taking a glass of wine with the landlord of the inn at which he stopped, when the waiter brought in a note to be changed, saying 'That the Quaker gentleman, who had been for some days in the house, and was about to depart, had sent it to be changed, in order that he might pay his bill.' The landlord took the note, and looked at it. 'A fifty-pound bill,' said he; 'I don't like changing bills of that amount, lest they should prove bad ones; however, as it comes from a Quaker gentleman, I suppose it is all right.' The mention of a fifty-pound note aroused the attention of my friend, and he requested to be permitted to look at it; he had scarcely seen it, when he was convinced that it was one of the same description as those which had brought me into trouble, as it corresponded with them in two particular features, which the agent of the bank had pointed out to him and others as evidence of their spuriousness. My friend, without a moment's hesitation, informed the landlord that the note was a bad one, expressing at the same time a great wish to see the Quaker gentleman who wanted to have it changed. 'That you can easily do,' said the landlord, and forthwith conducted him into the common room, where he saw a respectable-looking man, dressed like a Quaker, and seemingly about sixty years of age.

"My friend, after a short apology, showed him the note which he held in his hand, stating that he had no doubt it was a spurious one, and begged to be informed where he had taken it, adding, that a particular friend of his was at present in trouble, owing to his having taken similar notes from a stranger at Horncastle; but that he hoped that he, the Quaker, could give information, by means of which the guilty party, or parties, could be arrested. At the mention of Horncastle, it appeared to my friend that the Quaker gave a slight start. At the conclusion of this speech, however, he answered, with great tranquillity, that he had received it in the way of business at —, naming one of the principal towns in Yorkshire, from a very respectable person, whose name he was perfectly willing to communicate, and likewise his own, which he said was James, and that he was a merchant residing at Liverpool; that he would write to his friend at —, requesting him to make inquiries on the subject; that just at that moment he was in a hurry to depart, having some particular business at a town about ten miles off, to go to which he had bespoken a post-chaise of the landlord; that with respect to the note, it was doubtless a very disagreeable thing to have a suspicious one in his possession, but that it would make little difference to him, as he had plenty of other money, and thereupon he pulled out a purse, containing various other notes, and some gold, observing, 'that his only motive for wishing to change the other note was a desire to be well provided with change'; and finally, that if they had any suspicion with respect to him, he was perfectly willing to leave the note in their possession till he should return, which he intended to do in about a fortnight. There was so much plausibility in the speech of the Quaker, and his appearance and behaviour were so perfectly respectable, that my friend felt almost ashamed of the suspicion which at first he had entertained of him, though, at the same time, he felt an unaccountable unwillingness to let the man depart without some further interrogation. The landlord, however, who did not wish to disoblige one who had been, and might probably be again, a profitable customer, declared that he was perfectly satisfied; and that he had no wish to detain the note, which he made no doubt the gentleman had received in the way of business, and that as the matter concerned him alone, he would leave it to him to make the necessary inquiries. 'Just as you please, friend,' said the Quaker, pocketing the suspicious note, 'I will now pay my bill.' Thereupon he discharged the bill with a five-pound note, which he begged the landlord to inspect carefully, and with two pieces of gold.

"The landlord had just taken the money, receipted the bill, and was bowing to his customer, when the door opened, and a lad, dressed in a kind of grey livery, appeared, and informed the Quaker that the chaise was ready. 'Is that boy your servant?' said the surgeon. 'He is, friend,' said the Quaker. 'Hast thou any reason for asking me that question?' 'And has he been long in your service?' 'Several years,' replied the Quaker, 'I took him into my house out of compassion, he being an orphan, but as the chaise is waiting, I will bid thee farewell.' 'I am afraid I must stop your journey for the present,' said the surgeon; 'that boy has exactly the same blemish in the eye which a boy had who was in company with the man at Horncastle, from whom my friend received the forged notes, and who there passed for his son.' 'I know nothing about that,' said the Quaker, 'but I am determined to be detained here no longer, after the satisfactory account which I have given as to the note's coming into my possession.' He then attempted to leave the room, but my friend detained him, a struggle ensued, during which a wig which the Quaker wore fell off, whereupon he instantly appeared to lose some twenty years of his age. 'Knock the fellow down, father,' said the boy, 'I'll help you.'

"And, forsooth, the pretended Quaker took the boy's advice, and knocked my friend down in a twinkling. The landlord, however, and waiter, seeing how matters stood, instantly laid hold of him; but there can be no doubt that he would have escaped from the whole three, had not certain guests who were in the house, hearing the noise, rushed in, and helped to secure him. The boy was true to his word, assisting him to the best of his ability, flinging himself between the legs of his father's assailants, causing several of them to stumble and fall. At length, the fellow was secured, and led before a magistrate; the boy, to whom he was heard to say something which nobody understood, and to whom, after the man's capture, no one paid much attention, was no more seen.

"The rest, as far as this man was concerned, may be told in a few words; nothing to criminate him was found on his person, but on his baggage being examined, a quantity of spurious notes were discovered. Much of his hardihood now forsook him, and in the hope of saving his life he made some very important disclosures; amongst other things, he confessed that it was he who had given me the notes in exchange for the horses, and also the note to be changed. He was subsequently tried on two indictments, in the second of which I appeared against him. He was condemned to die; but, in consideration of the disclosures he had made, his sentence was commuted to perpetual transportation.

"My innocence was thus perfectly established before the eyes of the world, and all my friends hastened to congratulate me. There was one who congratulated me more than all the rest—it was my beloved one, but—but—she was dying—"

Here the old man drew his hand before his eyes, and remained for some time without speaking; at length he removed his hand, and commenced again with a broken voice: "You will pardon me if I hurry over this part of my story, I am unable to dwell upon it. How dwell upon a period when I saw my only earthly treasure pine away gradually day by day, and knew that nothing could save her! She saw my agony, and did all she could to console me, saying that she was herself quite resigned. A little time before her death she expressed a wish that we should be united. I was happy to comply with her request. We were united, I brought her to this house, where, in less than a week, she expired in my arms."

After another pause the old man once more resumed his narration:—"If ever there was a man perfectly miserable it was myself, after the loss of that cherished woman. I sat solitary in the house, in which I had hoped in her company to realize the choicest earthly happiness, a prey to the bitterest reflections. My only amusement—and it was a sad one—was to look at the things which once belonged to my beloved, and which were now in my possession. Oh, how fondly would I dwell upon them!

"One day I sat at the breakfast-table. I heard myself saying, 'What odd marks!' I had fastened my eyes on the side of a teapot, and by keeping them fixed upon it, had become aware of a fact that had escaped my notice before—namely, that there were marks upon it. I observed that though they all bore a general resemblance to each other, they were all to a certain extent different. The smallest portion possible of curious interest had been awakened within me, and, at last, I asked myself, within my own mind, 'What motive could induce people to put such odd marks on their crockery? they were not pictures, they were not letters; what motive could people have for putting them there?' I turned the teapot round, and on the other side I observed marks of a similar kind, which I soon discovered were identical with the ones I had been observing. All the marks were something alike, but all somewhat different, and on comparing them with each other, I was struck with the frequent occurrence of a mark crossing an upright line, or projecting from it, now on the right, now on the left side; and I said to myself, 'Why does this mark sometimes cross the upright line, and sometimes project?'

"The things were at length removed, and I sat, as I had for some time past been wont to sit after my meals, silent and motionless; but in the present instance my mind was not entirely abandoned to the one mournful idea which had so long distressed it. It was, to a certain extent, occupied with the marks on the teapot; it is true that the mournful idea strove hard with the marks on the teapot for the mastery in my mind, and at last the painful idea drove the marks of the teapot out; they, however, would occasionally return and flit across my mind for a moment or two, and their coming was like a momentary relief from intense pain. I thought once or twice that I would have the teapot placed before me, that I might examine the marks at leisure, but I considered that it would be as well to defer the re-examination of the marks till the next morning; at that time I did not take tea of an evening. By deferring the examination thus, I had something to look forward to on the next morning. The day was a melancholy one, but it certainly was more tolerable to me than any of the others had been since the death of my beloved.

"One day, chancing to be at a neighbouring town, I was struck with the appearance of a shop recently established. It had an immense bow-window, and every part of it, to which a brush could be applied, was painted in a gaudy flaming style. Large bowls of green and black tea were placed upon certain chests, which stood at the window. I stopped to look at them, such a display, whatever it may be at the present time, being, at the period of which I am speaking, quite uncommon in a country town. The tea, whether black or green, was very shining and inviting, and the bowls, of which there were three, standing on as many chests, were very grand and foreign looking. Two of these were white, with figures and trees painted upon them in blue; the other, which was the middlemost, had neither trees nor figures upon it, but, as I looked through the window, appeared to have on its sides the very same kind of marks which I had observed on the teapot at home; there were also marks on the tea-chests, somewhat similar, but much larger, and, apparently, not executed with so much care. 'Best teas direct from China,' said a voice close to my side; and looking round I saw a youngish man, with a frizzled head, flat face, and an immensely wide mouth, standing in his shirt-sleeves by the door. 'Direct from China,' said he; 'perhaps you will do me the favour to walk in and scent them?' 'I do not want any tea,' said I; 'I was only standing at the window examining those marks on the bowl and the chests. I have observed similar ones on a teapot at home.' 'Pray walk in, sir,' said the young fellow, extending his mouth till it reached nearly from ear to ear; 'pray walk in, and I shall be happy to give you any information respecting the manners and customs of the Chinese in my power.' Thereupon I followed him into his shop, where he began to harangue on the manners, customs, and peculiarities of the Chinese, especially their manner of preparing tea, not forgetting to tell me that the only genuine Chinese tea ever imported into England was to be found in his shop. 'With respect to those marks,' said he, 'on the bowl and chests, they are nothing more nor less than Chinese writing expressing something, though what I can't exactly tell you. Allow me to sell you this pound of tea,' he added, showing me a paper parcel. 'On the envelope there is a printed account of the Chinese system of writing, extracted from authors of the most established reputation. These things I print, principally with the hope of, in some degree, removing the worse than Gothic ignorance prevalent amongst natives of these parts. I am from London myself. With respect to all that relates to the Chinese real imperial tea, I assure you sir, that—' Well, to make short of what you doubtless consider a very tiresome story, I purchased the tea and carried it home. The tea proved imperially bad, but the paper envelope really contained some information on the Chinese language and writing, amounting to about as much as you gained from me the other day. On learning that the marks on the teapot expressed words, I felt my interest with respect to them considerably increased, and returned to the task of inspecting them with greater zeal than before, hoping, by continually looking at them, to be able eventually to understand their meaning, in which hope you may easily believe I was disappointed, though my desire to understand what they represented continued on the increase. In this dilemma I determined to apply again to the shopkeeper from whom I bought the tea. I found him in rather low spirits, his shirt-sleeves were soiled, and his hair was out of curl. On my inquiring how he got on, he informed me that he intended speedily to leave, having received little or no encouragement, the people, in their Gothic ignorance, preferring to deal with an old-fashioned shopkeeper over the way, who, so far from possessing any acquaintance with the polity and institutions of the Chinese, did not, he believed, know that tea came from China. 'You are come for some more, I suppose?' said he. On receiving an answer in the negative he looked somewhat blank, but when I added that I came to consult with him as to the means which I must take in order to acquire the Chinese language he brightened up. 'You must get a grammar,' said he, rubbing his hands. 'Have you not one?' said I. 'No,' he replied, 'but any bookseller can procure you one.' As I was taking my departure, he told me that as he was about to leave the neighbourhood, the bowl at the window, which bore the inscription, besides some other pieces of porcelain of a similar description, were at my service, provided I chose to purchase them. I consented, and two or three days afterwards took from off his hands all the china in his possession which bore the inscriptions, paying what he demanded. Had I waited till the sale of his effects, which occurred within a few weeks, I could probably have procured it for a fifth part of the sum which I paid, the other pieces realizing very little. I did not, however, grudge the poor fellow what he got from me, as I considered myself to be somewhat in his debt for the information he had afforded me.

"As for the rest of my story, it may be briefly told. I followed the advice of the shopkeeper, and applied to a bookseller who wrote to his correspondent in London. After a long interval, I was informed that if I wished to learn Chinese, I must do so through the medium of French, there being neither Chinese grammar nor dictionary in our language. I was at first very much disheartened. I determined, however, at last to gratify my desire of learning Chinese, even at the expense of learning French. I procured the books, and in order to qualify myself to turn them to account, took lessons in French from a little Swiss, the usher of a neighbouring boarding-school. I was very stupid in acquiring French; perseverance, however, enabled me to acquire a knowledge sufficient for the object I had in view. In about two years I began to study Chinese by myself, through the medium of the French."

"Well," said I, "and how did you get on with the study of the Chinese?"

And then the old man proceeded to inform me how he got on with the study of Chinese, enumerated all the difficulties he had had to encounter; dilating upon his frequent despondency of mind, and occasionally his utter despair of ever mastering Chinese. He told me that more than once he had determined upon giving up the study, but to escape from the misery in his head he had as often resumed it. It appeared, however, that ten years elapsed before he was able to use ten of the two hundred and fourteen keys, which serve to undo the locks of Chinese writing.

"And are you able at present to use the entire number?" I demanded.

"Yes," said the old man; "I can at present use the whole number. I know the key for every particular lock, though I frequently find wards unwilling to give way."

"And in applying keys to the Chinese locks you employ your time?"

"Yes," said the old man, "in making out the inscriptions on the various pieces of porcelain, which I have at different times procured, I pass my time. The first inscription which I translated was that on the teapot of my beloved."

"And how many other pieces of porcelain may you have at present in your possession?"

"About fifteen hundred."

"And how did you obtain them?" I demanded.

"Without much labour," said the old man, "in the neighbouring towns and villages—chiefly at auctions—of which, about twenty years ago, there were many in these parts."

"And may I ask your reasons for confining your studies entirely to the crockery literature of China, when you have all the rest at your disposal?"

"The inscriptions enable me to pass my time," said the old man; "what more would the whole literature of China do?"

"And from these inscriptions," said I, "what a book it is in your power to make, whenever so disposed. 'Translations from the crockery literature of China.' Such a book would be sure to take; even glorious John himself would not disdain to publish it." The old man smiled. "I have no desire for literary distinction," said he; "no ambition. My original wish was to pass my life in easy, quiet obscurity, with her whom I loved. I was disappointed in my wish; she was removed, who constituted my only felicity in this life; desolation came to my heart, and misery to my head. To escape from the latter I had recourse to Chinese. By degrees the misery left my head, but the desolation of the heart yet remains."

"Be of good cheer," said I; "through the instrumentality of this affliction you have learnt Chinese, and, in so doing, learnt to practise the duties of hospitality. Who but a man who could read Runes on a teapot, would have received an unfortunate wayfarer as you have received me?"

"Well," said the old man, "let us hope that all is for the best. I am by nature indolent, and, but for this affliction, should, perhaps, have hardly taken the trouble to do my duty to my fellow-creatures. I am very, very indolent," said he, slightly glancing towards the clock; "therefore let us hope that all is for the best; but, oh! these trials, they are very hard to bear."

CHAPTER LII

The next morning, having breakfasted with my old friend, I went into the stable to make the necessary preparations for my departure; there, with the assistance of a stable lad, I cleaned and caparisoned my horse, and then, returning into the house, I made the old female attendant such a present as I deemed would be some compensation for the trouble I had caused. Hearing that the old gentleman was in his study, I repaired to him. "I am come to take leave of you," said I, "and to thank you for all the hospitality which I have received at your hands." The eyes of the old man were fixed steadfastly on the inscription which I had found him studying on a former occasion. "At length," he murmured to himself, "I have it—I think I have it"; and then, looking at me, he said, "So you are about to depart?"

"Yes," said I, "my horse will be at the front door in a few minutes; I am glad, however, before I go, to find that you have mastered the inscription."

"Yes," said the old man, "I believe I have mastered it; it seems to consist of some verses relating to the worship of the Spirit of the Hearth."

"What is the Spirit of the Hearth?" said I.

"One of the many demons which the Chinese worship," said the old man; "they do not worship one God, but many." And then the old man told me a great many highly-interesting particulars respecting the demon worship of the Chinese.

After the lapse of at least half an hour I said, "I must not linger here any longer, however willing. Horncastle is distant, and I wish to be there to-night. Pray can you inform me what's o'clock?"

The old man, rising, looked towards the clock which hung on the side of the room at his left hand, on the farther side of the table at which he was seated.

"I am rather short-sighted," said I, "and cannot distinguish the number, at that distance."

"It is ten o'clock," said the old man; "I believe somewhat past."

"A quarter, perhaps?"

"Yes," said the old man, "a quarter or——"

"Or?"

"Seven minutes, or ten minutes past ten."

"I do not understand you."

"Why, to tell you the truth," said the old man, with a smile, "there is one thing to the knowledge of which I could never exactly attain."

"Do you mean to say," said I, "that you do not know what's o'clock?"

"I can give a guess," said the old man, "to within a few minutes."

"But you cannot tell the exact moment?"

"No," said the old man.

"In the name of wonder," said I, "with that thing there on the wall continually ticking in your ear, how comes it that you do not know what's o'clock?"

"Why," said the old man, "I have contented myself with giving a tolerably good guess; to do more would have been too great trouble."

"But you have learnt Chinese," said I.

"Yes," said the old man, "I have learnt Chinese."

"Well," said I, "I really would counsel you to learn to know what's o'clock as soon as possible. Consider what a sad thing it would be to go out of the world not knowing what's o'clock. A millionth part of the trouble required to learn Chinese would, if employed, infallibly teach you to know what's o'clock."

"I had a motive for learning Chinese," said the old man, "the hope of appeasing the misery in my head. With respect to not knowing what's o'clock, I cannot see anything particularly sad in the matter. A man may get through the world very creditably without knowing what's o'clock. Yet, upon the whole, it is no bad thing to know what's o'clock—you, of course, do? It would be too good a joke if two people were to be together, one knowing Armenian and the other Chinese, and neither knowing what's o'clock. I'll now see you off."

Leaving the house of the old man who knew Chinese, but could not tell what was o'clock, I wended my way to Horncastle, which I reached in the evening of the same day, without having met any adventure on the way worthy of being marked down in this very remarkable history.

The town was a small one, seemingly ancient, and was crowded with people and horses. I proceeded, without delay, to the inn to which my friend the surgeon had directed me. "It is of no use coming here," said two or three ostlers, as I entered the yard—"all full—no room whatever"; whilst one added in an under tone, "That ere a'n't a bad-looking horse." "I want to see the master of this inn," said I, as I dismounted from the horse. "See the master," said an ostler—the same who had paid the negative kind of compliment to the horse—"a likely thing, truly; my master is drinking wine with some of the grand gentry, and can't be disturbed for the sake of the like of you." "I bring a letter to him," said I, pulling out the surgeon's epistle. "I wish you would deliver it to him," I added, offering a half-crown. "Oh, it's you, is it?" said the ostler, taking the letter and the half-crown; "my master will be right glad to see you; why, you han't been here for many a year; I'll carry the note to him at once." And with these words he hurried into the house. "That's a nice horse, young man," said another ostler, "what will you take for it?" to which interrogation I made no answer. "If you wish to sell him," said the ostler, coming up to me, and winking knowingly, "I think I and my partners might offer you a summut under seventy pounds"; to which kind and half-insinuated offer I made no reply, save by winking in the same kind of knowing manner in which I observed him wink. "Rather leary!" said a third ostler. "Well, young man, perhaps you will drink to-night with me and my partners, when we can talk the matter over." Before I had time to answer, the landlord, a well-dressed, good-looking man, made his appearance with the ostler; he bore the letter in his hand. Without glancing at me, he betook himself at once to consider the horse, going round him, and observing every point with the utmost minuteness. At last, having gone round the horse three times, he stopped beside me, and keeping his eyes on the horse, bent his head towards his right shoulder. "That horse is worth some money," said he, turning towards me suddenly, and slightly touching me on the arm with the letter which he held in his hand; to which observation I made no reply, save by bending my head towards the right shoulder as I had seen him do. "The young man is going to talk to me and my partners about it to-night," said the ostler who had expressed an opinion that he and his friends might offer me somewhat under seventy pounds for the animal. "Pooh!" said the landlord, "the young man knows what he is about; in the meantime lead the horse to the reserved stall, and see well after him. My friend," said he, taking me aside after the ostler had led the animal away, "recommends you to me in the strongest manner, on which account alone I take you and your horse in. I need not advise you not to be taken in, as I should say, by your look, that you are tolerably awake; but there are queer hands at Horncastle at this time, and those fellows of mine, you understand me—; but I have a great deal to do at present, so you must excuse me." And thereupon went into the house.

That same evening I was engaged at least two hours in the stable, in rubbing the horse down, and preparing him for the exhibition which I intended he should make in the fair on the following day. The ostler, to whom I had given the half-crown, occasionally assisted me, though he was too much occupied by the horses of other guests to devote any length of time to the service of mine; he more than once repeated to me his firm conviction that himself and partners could afford to offer me summut for the horse; and at a later hour when, in compliance with his invitation, I took a glass of summut with himself and partners, in a little room surrounded with corn-chests, on which we sat, both himself and partners endeavoured to impress upon me, chiefly by means of nods and winks, their conviction that they could afford to give me summut for the horse, provided I were disposed to sell him; in return for which intimation, with as many nods and winks as they had all collectively used, I endeavoured to impress upon them my conviction that I could get summut handsomer in the fair than they might be disposed to offer me, seeing as how—which how I followed by a wink and a nod, which they seemed perfectly to understand, one or two of them declaring that if the case was so, it made a great deal of difference, and that they did not wish to be any hindrance to me, more particularly as it was quite clear I had been an ostler like themselves.

It was late at night when I began to think of retiring to rest. On inquiring if there was any place in which I could sleep, I was informed that there was a bed at my service, provided I chose to sleep in a two-bedded room, one of the beds of which was engaged by another gentleman. I expressed my satisfaction at this arrangement, and was conducted by a maid-servant up many pairs of stairs to a garret, in which were two small beds, in one of which she gave me to understand another gentleman slept; he had, however, not yet retired to rest; I asked who he was, but the maid-servant could give me no information about him, save that he was a highly respectable gentleman, and a friend of her master's. Presently, bidding me good night, she left me with a candle; and I, having undressed myself and extinguished the light, went to bed. Notwithstanding the noises which sounded from every part of the house, I was not slow in falling asleep, being thoroughly tired. I know not how long I might have been in bed, perhaps two hours, when I was partially awakened by a light shining upon my face, whereupon, unclosing my eyes, I perceived the figure of a man, with a candle in one hand, staring at my face, whilst with the other hand, he held back the curtain of the bed. As I have said before, I was only partially awakened, my power of conception was consequently very confused; it appeared to me, however, that the man was dressed in a green coat; that he had curly brown or black hair, and that there was something peculiar in his look. Just as I was beginning to recollect myself, the curtain dropped, and I heard, or thought I heard, a voice say, "Don't know the cove." Then there was a rustling like a person undressing, whereupon being satisfied that it was my fellow-lodger, I dropped asleep, but was awakened again by a kind of heavy plunge upon the other bed, which caused it to rock and creak, when I observed that the light had been extinguished, probably blown out, if I might judge from a rather disagreeable smell of burnt wick which remained in the room, and which kept me awake till I heard my companion breathing hard, when, turning on the other side, I was again once more speedily in the arms of slumber.

It had been my intention to be up and doing early on the following morning, but my slumbers proved so profound, that I did not wake until about eight; on arising, I again found myself the sole occupant of the apartment, my more alert companion having probably risen at a much earlier hour. Having dressed myself, I descended, and going to the stable, found my horse under the hands of my friend the ostler, who was carefully rubbing him down. "There a'n't a better horse in the fair," said he to me, "and as you are one of us, and appear to be all right, I'll give you a piece of advice—don't take less than a hundred and fifty for him; if you mind your hits, you may get it, for I have known two hundred given in this fair for one no better, if so good." "Well," said I, "thank you for your advice, which I will take, and, if successful, will give you 'summut' handsome." "Thank you," said the ostler; "and now let me ask whether you are up to all the ways of this here place?" "I have never been here before," said I, "but I have a pair of tolerably sharp eyes in my head."

"That I see you have," said the ostler, "but many a body, with as sharp a pair of eyes as yourn, has lost his horse in this fair, for want of having been here before, therefore," said he, "I'll give you a caution or two." Thereupon the ostler proceeded to give me at least half a dozen cautions, only two of which I shall relate to the reader:—the first, not to stop to listen to what any chance customer might have to say; and the last—the one on which he appeared to lay most stress—by no manner of means to permit a Yorkshireman to get up into the saddle, "for," said he, "if you do, it is three to one that he rides off with the horse; he can't help it; trust a cat amongst cream, but never trust a Yorkshireman on the saddle of a good horse; by-the-by," he continued, "that saddle of yours is not a particularly good one, no more is the bridle. I tell you what, as you seem a decent kind of a young chap,

I'll lend you a saddle and bridle of my master's, almost brand new; he won't object, I know, as you are a friend of his, only you must not forget your promise to come down with summut handsome after you have sold the animal."

After a slight breakfast I mounted the horse, which, decked out in his borrowed finery, really looked better by a large sum of money than on any former occasion. Making my way out of the yard of the inn, I was instantly in the principal street of the town, up and down which an immense number of horses were being exhibited, some led, and others with riders. "A wonderful small quantity of good horses in the fair this time!" I heard a stout jockey-looking individual say, who was staring up the street with his side towards me. "Halloo, young fellow!" said he, a few moments after I had passed, "whose horse is that? Stop! I want to look at him!"

Though confident that he was addressing himself to me, I took no notice, remembering the advice of the ostler, and proceeded up the street. My horse possessed a good walking step; but walking, as the reader knows, was not his best pace, which was the long trot, at which I could not well exercise him in the street, on account of the crowd of men and animals; however, as he walked along, I could easily perceive that he attracted no slight attention amongst those who, by their jockey dress and general appearance, I imagined to be connoisseurs; I heard various calls to stop, to none of which I paid the slightest attention. In a few minutes I found myself out of the town, when, turning round for the purpose of returning, I found I had been followed by several of the connoisseur-looking individuals, whom I had observed in the fair. "Now would be the time for a display," thought I; and looking round me I observed two five-barred gates, one on each side of the road, and fronting each other. Turning my horse's head to one, I pressed my heels to his sides, loosened the reins, and gave an encouraging cry, whereupon the animal cleared the gate in a twinkling. Before he had advanced ten yards in the field to which the gate opened, I had turned him round, and again giving him cry and rein, I caused him to leap back again into the road, and still allowing him head, I made him leap the other gate; and forthwith turning him round, I caused him to leap once more into the road, where he stood proudly tossing his head, as much as to say, "What more?"

"A fine horse! a capital horse!" said several of the connoisseurs. "What do you ask for him?" "Too much for any of you to pay," said I. "A horse like this is intended for other kind of customers than any of you." "How do you know that?" said one; the very same person whom I had heard complaining in the street of the paucity of good horses in the fair. "Come, let us know what you ask for him?" "A hundred and fifty pounds!" said I; "neither more nor less." "Do you call that a great price?" said the man. "Why, I thought you would have asked double that amount! You do yourself injustice, young man." "Perhaps I do," said I, "but that's my affair; I do not choose to take more."

"I wish you would let me get into the saddle," said the man; "the horse knows you, and therefore shows to more advantage; but I should like to see how he would move under me, who am a stranger. Will you let me get into the saddle, young man?" "No," said I; "I will not let you get into the saddle." "Why not?" said the man. "Lest you should be a Yorkshireman," said I; "and should run away with the horse." "Yorkshire?" said the man; "I am from Suffolk; silly Suffolk—so you need not be afraid of my running away with the horse." "Oh! if that's the case," said I, "I should be afraid that the horse would run away with you; so I will by no means let you mount." "Will you let me look in his mouth?" said the man. "If you please," said I; "but I tell you, he's apt to bite." "He can scarcely be a worse bite than his master," said the man, looking into the horse's mouth; "he's four off. I say, young man, will you warrant this horse?" "No," said I; "I never warrant horses; the horses that I ride can always warrant themselves." "I wish you would let me speak a word to you," said he. "Just come aside. It's a nice horse," said he, in a half whisper, after I had ridden a few paces aside with him. "It's a nice horse," said he, placing his hand upon the pommel of the saddle, and looking up in my face, "and I think I can find you a customer. If you would take a hundred, I think my lord would purchase it, for he has sent me about the fair to look him up a horse, by which he could hope to make an honest penny." "Well," said I, "and could he not make an honest penny, and yet give me the price I ask?" "Why," said the go-between, "a hundred and fifty pounds is as much as the animal is worth, or nearly so; and my lord, do you see——"

"I see no reason at all," said I, "why I should sell the animal for less than he is worth, in order that his lordship may be benefited by him; so that if his lordship wants to make an honest penny, he must find some person who would consider the disadvantage of selling him a horse for less than it is worth, as counterbalanced by the honour of dealing with a lord, which I should never do; but I can't be wasting my time here. I am going back to the ——, where, if you, or any person, are desirous of purchasing the horse, you must come within the next half hour, or I shall probably not feel disposed to sell him at all."

"Another word. young man," said the jockey; but without staying to hear what he had to say, I put the horse to his best trot, and re-entering the town, and threading my way as well as I could through the press, I returned to the yard of the inn, where, dismounting, I stood still, holding the horse by the bridle.

I had been standing in this manner about five minutes, when I saw the jockey enter the yard, accompanied by another individual. They advanced directly towards me. "Here is my lord come to look at the horse, young man," said the jockey. My lord, as the jockey called him, was a tall figure, of about five-and-thirty. He had on his head a hat somewhat rusty, and on his back a surtout of blue rather the worse for wear. His forehead, if not high, was exceedingly narrow; his eyes were brown, with a rat-like glare in them; the nose was rather long, and the mouth very wide; the cheek-bones high, and the cheeks, as to hue and consistency, exhibiting very much the appearance of a withered red apple; there was a gaunt expression of hunger in the whole countenance. He had scarcely glanced at the horse, when drawing in his cheeks, he thrust out his lips very much after the manner of a baboon, when he sees a piece of sugar held out towards him.

"Is this horse yours?" said he, suddenly turning towards me, with a kind of smirk. "It's my horse," said I; "are you the person who wishes to make an honest penny by it?" "How!" said he, drawing up his head with a very consequential look, and speaking with a very haughty tone, "what do you mean?" We looked at each other full in the face; after a few moments, the muscles of the mouth of him of the hungry look began to move violently, the face was puckered into innumerable wrinkles, and the eyes became half closed. "Well," said I, "have you ever seen me before? I suppose you are asking yourself that question."

"Excuse me, sir," said he, dropping his lofty look, and speaking in a very subdued and civil tone, "I have never had the honour of seeing you before, that is"—said he, slightly glancing at me again, and again moving the muscles of his mouth, "no, I have never seen you before," he added, making me a bow. "I have never had that pleasure; my business with you, at present, is to inquire the lowest price you are willing to take for this horse. My agent here informs me that you ask one hundred and fifty pounds, which I cannot think of giving—the horse is a showy horse, but look, my dear sir, he has a defect here, and there in his near fore leg I observe something which looks very much like a splint—yes, upon my credit," said he, touching the animal, "he has a splint, or something which will end in one. A hundred and fifty pounds, sir! what could have induced you ever to ask anything like that for this animal? I protest that, in my time, I have frequently bought a better for —— Who are you, sir? I am in treaty for this horse," said he to a man who had come up whilst he was talking, and was now looking into the horse's mouth.

"Who am I?" said the man, still looking into the horse's mouth; "who am I? his lordship asks me. Ah, I see, close on five," said he, releasing the horse's jaws, and looking at me.

This new comer was a thin, wiry-made individual, with wiry curling brown hair; his face was dark, and wore an arch and somewhat roguish expression; upon one of his eyes was a kind of speck or beam; he might be about forty, wore a green jockey coat, and held in his hand a black riding whip, with a knob of silver wire. As I gazed upon his countenance, it brought powerfully to my mind the face which, by the light of the candle, I had seen staring over me on the preceding night, when lying in bed and half asleep.

Close beside him, and seemingly in his company, stood an exceedingly tall figure, that of a youth, seemingly about one-and-twenty, dressed in a handsome riding dress, and wearing on his head a singular hat, green in colour, and with a very high peak. "What do you ask for this horse?" said he of the green coat, winking at me with the eye which had a beam in it, whilst the other shone and sparkled like Mrs. Colonel W—'s Golconda diamond. "Who are you, sir, I demand once more?" said he of the hungry look. "Who am I? why, who should I be but Jack Dale, who buys horses for himself and other folk; I want one at present for this short young gentleman," said he, motioning with his finger to the gigantic youth.

"Well, sir," said the other, "and what business have you to interfere between me and any purchase I may be disposed to make?" "Well, then," said the other, "be quick and purchase the horse, or, perhaps, I may." "Do you think I am to be dictated to by a fellow of your description?" said his lordship, "begone, or—" "What do you ask for this horse?" said the other to me, very coolly. "A hundred and fifty," said I. "I shouldn't mind giving it to you," said he.

"You will do no such thing," said his lordship, speaking so fast that he almost stuttered. "Sir," said he to me, "I must give you what you ask; Symmonds, take possession of the animal for me," said he to the other jockey who attended him.

"You will please to do no such thing without my consent," said I, "I have not sold him."

"I have this moment told you that I will give you the price you demand," said his lordship; "is not that sufficient?" "No," said I, "there is a proper manner of doing everything—had you come forward in a manly and gentlemanly manner to purchase the horse, I should have been happy to sell him to you, but after all the fault you have found with him, I would not sell him to you at any price, so send your friend to find up another."

"You behave in this manner, I suppose," said his lordship, "because this fellow has expressed a willingness to come to your terms. I would advise you to be cautious how you trust the animal in his hands; I think I have seen him before, and could tell you—"

"What can you tell of me?" said the other, going up to him; "except that I have been a poor dicky-boy, and that now I am a dealer in horses, and that my father was lagged; that's all you could tell of me, and that I don't mind telling myself: but there are two things they can't say of me, they can't say that I am either a coward or a screw either, except so far as one who gets his bread by horses may be expected to be; and they can't say of me that I ever ate up an ice which a young woman was waiting for, or that I ever backed out of a fight. Horse!" said he, motioning with his finger tauntingly to the other; "what do you want with a horse, except to take the bread out of the mouth of a poor man—to-morrow is not the battle of Waterloo, so that you don't want to back out of danger, by pretending to have hurt yourself by falling from the creature's back, my lord of the white feather—come, none of your fierce looks—I am not afraid of you."

In fact, the other had assumed an expression of the deadliest malice, his teeth were clenched, his lips quivered, and were quite pale; the rat-like eyes sparkled, and he made a half spring, à la rat, towards his adversary, who only laughed. Restraining himself, however, he suddenly turned to his understrapper. saying, "Symmonds, will you see me thus insulted? go and trounce this scoundrel; you can, I know." "Symmonds trounce me!" said the other, going up to the person addressed, and drawing his hand contemptuously over his face; "why, I beat Symmonds in this very yard in one round three years ago; didn't I, Symmonds?" said he to the understrapper, who held down his head, muttering, in a surly tone, "I didn't come here to fight; let every one take his own part."

"That's right, Symmonds," said the other, "especially every one from whom there is nothing to be got. I would give you half-a-crown for all the trouble you have had, provided I were not afraid that my Lord Plume there would get it from you as soon as you leave the yard together. Come, take yourselves both off; there's nothing to be made here." Indeed, his lordship seemed to be of the same opinion, for after a further glance at the horse, a contemptuous look at me, and a scowl at the jockey, he turned on his heel muttering something which sounded like fellows, and stalked out of the yard, followed by Symmonds.

"And now, young man," said the jockey, or whatever he was, turning to me with an arch leer, "I suppose I may consider myself as the purchaser of this here animal, for the use and behoof of this young gentleman?" making a sign with his head to the tall young man by his side.

"By no means," said I, "I am utterly unacquainted with either of you, and before parting with the horse I must be satisfied as to the respectability of the purchaser." "Oh! as to that matter," said he, "I have plenty of vouchers for my respectability about me"; and thrusting his hand into his bosom below his waistcoat, he drew out a large bundle of notes. "These are the kind of things," said he, "which vouch best for a man's respectability." "Not always," said I; "indeed, sometimes these kind of things need vouchers for themselves." The man looked at me with a peculiar look. "Do you mean to say that these notes are not sufficient notes?" said he, "because if you do I shall take the liberty of thinking you are not over civil, and when I thinks a person is not over and above civil I sometimes takes off my coat; and when my coat is off——"

"You sometimes knock people down," I added; "well, whether you knock me down or not, I beg leave to tell you that I am a stranger in this fair, and that I shall part with the horse to nobody who has no better guarantee for his respectability than a roll of bank-notes, which may be good or not for what I know, who am not a judge of such things."

"Oh! if you are a stranger here," said the man, "as I believe you are, never having seen you here before except last night, when I think I saw you above stairs by the glimmer of a candle—I say, if you are a stranger, you are quite right to be cautious; queer things being done in this fair, as nobody knows better than myself," he added with a leer; "but I suppose if the landlord of the house vouches for me and my notes, you will have no objection to part with the horse to me?" "None whatever," said I, "and in the meantime the horse can return to the stable."

Thereupon I delivered the horse to my friend the ostler. The landlord of the house on being questioned by me as to the character and condition of my new acquaintance, informed me that he was a respectable horsedealer, and an intimate friend of his, whereupon the purchase was soon brought to a satisfactory conclusion.

CHAPTER LIII

It was evening: and myself and the two acquaintances I had made in the fair—namely, the jockey and the tall foreigner—sat in a large upstairs room, which looked into a court; we had dined with several people connected with the fair at a long *table d'hôte;* they had now departed, and we sat at a small side-table with wine and a candle before us; both my companions had pipes in their mouths—the jockey a common pipe, and the foreigner, one, the syphon of which, made of some kind of wood, was at least six feet long, and the bowl of which, made of a white kind of substance like porcelain, and capable of holding nearly an ounce of tobacco, rested on the ground. The jockey frequently emptied and replenished his glass; the foreigner sometimes raised his to his lips, for no other purpose seemingly than to moisten them, as he never drained his glass. As for myself, though I did not smoke, I had a glass before me, from which I sometimes took a sip.

The room, notwithstanding the window was flung open, was in general so filled with smoke, chiefly that which was drawn from the huge bowl of the foreigner, that my companions and I were frequently concealed from each other's eyes. The conversation, which related entirely to the events of the fair, was carried on by the jockey and myself, the foreigner, who appeared to understand the greater part of what we said, occasionally putting in a few observations in broken English. At length the jockey, after the other had made some ineffectual attempts to express something intelligibly which he wished to say, observed, "Isn't it a pity that so fine a fellow as meinheer, and so clever a fellow too, as I believe him to be, is not a better master of our language?"

"Is the gentleman a German?" said I; "if so, I can interpret for him anything he wishes to say."

"The deuce you can," said the jockey, taking his pipe out of his mouth, and staring at me through the smoke.

"Ha! you speak German," vociferated the foreigner in that language. "By Isten, I am glad of it! I wanted to say——" And here he said in German what he wished to say, and which was of no great importance, and which I translated into English.

"Well, if you don't put me out," said the jockey; "what language is that—Dutch?"

"High Dutch," said I.

"High Dutch, and you speak high Dutch,—why, I had booked you for as great an ignoramus as myself, who can't write—no, nor distinguish in a book a great A from a bull's foot."

"A person may be a very clever man," said I—"no, not a clever man, for clever signifies clerkly, and a clever man one who is able to read and write, and entitled to the benefit of his clergy or clerkship; but a person may be a very acute person without being able to read or write. I never saw a more acute countenance than your own."

"No soft soap," said the jockey, "for I never uses any. However, thank you for your information; I have hitherto thought myself a'nition clever fellow, but from henceforth shall consider myself just the contrary, and only—what's the word?—confounded 'cute."

"Just so," said I.

"Well," said the jockey, "as you say you can speak high Dutch, I should like to hear you and master six foot six fire away at each other."

"I cannot speak German," said I, "but I can understand tolerably well what others say in it."

"Come, no backing out," said the jockey, "let's hear you fire away for the glory of Old England."

"Then you are a German?" said I, in German to the foreigner.

"That will do," said the jockey, "keep it up."

"A German!" said the tall foreigner. "No, I thank God that I do not belong to the stupid sluggish Germanic race, but to a braver, taller, and handsomer people"; here taking the pipe out of his mouth, he stood up proudly erect, so that his head nearly touched the ceiling of the room, then reseating himself, and again putting the syphon to his lips, he added, "I am a Magyar."

"What is that?" said I.

The foreigner looked at me for a moment, somewhat contemptuously, through the smoke, then said, in a voice of thunder, "A Hungarian!"

"What a voice the chap has when he pleases!" interposed the jockey; "what is he saying?"

"Merely that he is a Hungarian," said I; but I added, "the conversation of this gentleman and myself in a language which you can't understand must be very tedious to you, we had better give it up."

"Keep on with it," said the jockey, "I shall go on listening very contentedly till I fall asleep, no bad thing to do at most times."

"Then you are a countryman of Tekeli, and of the queen who made the celebrated water," said I, speaking to the Hungarian in German, which I was able to do tolerably well, owing to my having translated the Publisher's philosophy into that language.

Hungarian. Ah! you have heard of Tekeli, and of L'eau de la Reine d'Hongrie. How is that?

Myself. I have seen a play acted, founded on the exploits of Tekeli, and have read Pigault Le Brun's beautiful romance, entitled the "Barons of Felsheim," in which he is mentioned. As for the water, I have heard a lady, the wife of a master of mine, speak of it.

Hungarian. Was she handsome?

Myself. Very.

Hungarian. Did she possess the water?

Myself. I should say not; for I have heard her express a great curiosity about it.

Hungarian. Was she growing old?

Myself. Of course not; but why do you put all these questions?

Hungarian. Because the water is said to make people handsome, and above all, to restore to the aged the beauty of their youth. Well! Tekeli was my countryman, and I have the honour of having some of the blood of the Tekelis in my veins, but with respect to the queen, pardon me if I tell you that she was not an Hungarian; she was a Pole—Ersebet by name, daughter of Wladislaus Locticus King of Poland; she was the fourth spouse of Caroly the Second, King of the Magyar country, who married her in 1320. She was a great woman and celebrated politician, though at present chiefly known by her water.

Myself. How came she to invent it?

Hungarian. If her account may be believed, she did not invent it. After her death, as I have read in Florentius of Buda, there was found a statement of the manner in which she came by it, written in her own hand, on a fly-leaf of her breviary, to the following effect:—Being afflicted with a grievous disorder at the age of seventy-two, she received the medicine which was called her water, from an old hermit whom she never saw before or afterwards; it not only cured her, but restored to her all her former beauty, so that the King of Poland fell in love with her, and made her an offer of marriage, which she refused for the glory of God, from whose holy angel she believed she had received the water. The receipt for making it and directions for using it, were also found on the fly-leaf. The principal component parts were burnt wine and rosemary, passed through an alembic; a drachm of it was to be taken once a week, "etelbenn vagy italbann," in the food or the drink, early in the morning, and the cheeks were to be moistened with it every day. The effects according to the statement, were wonderful—and perhaps they were upon the queen; but whether the water has been equally efficacious on other people, is a point which I cannot determine. I should wish to see some old woman who has been restored to youthful beauty by the use of L'eau de la Reine d'Hongrie.

Myself. Perhaps, if you did, the old gentlewoman would hardly be so ingenuous as the queen. But who are the Hungarians—descendants of Attila and his people?

The Hungarian shook his head, and gave me to understand that he did not believe that his nation were the descendants of Attila and his people, though he acknowledged that they were probably of the same race. Attila and his armies, he said, came and disappeared in a very mysterious manner, and that nothing could be said with positiveness about them; that the people now known as Magyars first made their appearance in Muscovy in the year 884.

Myself. Allow me to ask who you are?

Hungarian. Egy szegeny Magyar Nemes ember, a poor Hungarian nobleman, son of one yet poorer. I was born in Transylvania, not far to the west of good Coloscvar. I served some time in the Austrian army as a noble Hussar, but am now equerry to a great nobleman, to whom I am distantly related. In his service I have travelled far and wide, buying horses. I have been in Russia and in Turkey, and am now at Horncastle, where I have had the satisfaction to meet with you, and to buy your horse, which is, in truth, a noble brute.

Myself. For a soldier and equerry you seem to know a great deal of the history of your country.

Hungarian. All I know is derived from Florentius of Buda, whom we call Budai Ferentz. He was professor of Greek and Latin at the Reformed College of Debreczen, where I was educated; he wrote a work entitled "Magyar Polgari Lexicon," Lives of Great Hungarian Citizens. He was dead before I was born, but I found his book, when I was a child, in the solitary home of my father, which stood on the confines of a puszta, or wilderness, and that book I used to devour in winter nights when the winds were whistling round the house. Oh! how my blood used to glow at the descriptions of Magyar valour, and likewise of Turkish; for Florentius has always done justice to the Turk. Many a passage similar to this have I got by heart; it is connected with a battle on the plain of Rigo, which Hunyadi lost:—"The next day, which was Friday, as the two armies were drawn up in battle array, a Magyar hero riding forth, galloped up and down, challenging the Turks to single combat. Then came out to meet him the son of a renowned bashaw of Asia; rushing upon each other, both broke their lances, but the Magyar hero and his horse rolled over upon the ground, for the Turks had always the best horses."

Myself. I am glad that the Turk beat the Magyar. When I used to read the ballads of Spain I always sided with the Moor against the Christian.

Hungarian. The Turk is a noble fellow; I should wish to be a Turk, were I not a Magyar.

Myself. The Turk always keeps his word, I am told.

Hungarian. Which the Christian very seldom does, and even the Hungarian does not always. In 1444 Ulaszlo made, at Szeged, peace with Amurath for ten years, which he swore with an oath to keep, but at the instigation of the Pope Julian he broke it, and induced his great captain Hunyadi John, to share in the perjury. The consequence was the battle of Varna, of the 10th of November, in which Hunyadi was routed, and Ulaszlo slain. Did you ever hear his epitaph? it is both solemn and edifying:—

"Romulidæ Cannas ego Varnam clade notavi;
Discite mortales non temerare fidem:
Me nisi Pontifices jussissent rumpere fœdus
Non ferret Scythicum Pannonis ora jugum."

"Halloo!" said the jockey, starting up from a doze in which he had been indulging for the last hour, his head leaning upon his breast, "what is that? That's not high Dutch; I bargained for high Dutch, and I left you speaking high Dutch, as it sounded very much like the language of horses, as I have been told high Dutch does; but as for what you are speaking now, whatever you may call it, it sounds more like the language of another kind of animal. I suppose you want to insult me, because I was once a dicky-boy."

"Nothing of the kind," said I; "the gentleman was making a quotation in Latin."

"Well," said the jockey, taking a whiff, "make your conversation as short as possible, whether in Latin or Dutch, for, to tell you the truth, I am rather tired of merely playing listener."

"You were saying you had been in Russia," said I; "I believe the Russians are part of the Sclavonian race."

Hungarian. Yes, part of the great Sclavonian family; one of the most numerous races in the world. The Russians themselves are very numerous; would that the Magyars could boast of the fifth part of their number!

Myself. What is the number of the Magyars?

Hungarian. Barely four millions. We came a tribe of Tartars into Europe, and settled down amongst Sclavonians, whom we conquered, but who never coalesced with us. The Austrian at present plays in Pannonia the Sclavonian against us, and us against the Sclavonian; but the downfall of the Austrian is at hand; they, like us, are not a numerous people.

Myself. Who will bring about his downfall?

Hungarian. The Russians. The Rysckie Tsar will lead his people forth, all the Sclavonians will join him, he will conquer all before him.

Myself. Are the Russians good soldiers?

Hungarian. They are stubborn and unflinching to an astonishing degree, and their fidelity to their Tsar is quite admirable. See how the Russians behaved at Plescova, in Livonia, in the old time, against our great Batory Stephen; they defended the place till it was a heap of rubbish, and mark how they behaved after they had been made prisoners. Stephen offered them two alternatives:—to enter into his service, in which they would have good pay, clothing, and fair treatment; or to be allowed to return to Russia. Without the slightest hesitation they, to a man, chose the latter, though well aware that their beloved Tsar, the cruel Ivan Basilowits, would put them all to death, amidst tortures the most horrible, for not doing what was impossible—preserving the town.

Myself. You speak Russian?

Hungarian. A little. I was born in the vicinity of a Sclavonian tribe; the servants of our house were Sclavonians, and I early acquired something of their language, which differs not much from that of Russia; when in that country I quickly understood what was said.

Myself. Have the Russians any literature?

Hungarian. Doubtless; but I am not acquainted with it, as I do not read their language; but I know something of their popular tales, to which I used to listen in their izbushkas; a principal personage in these is a creation quite original—called Baba Yaga.

Myself. Who is the Baba Yaga?

Hungarian. A female phantom, who is described as hurrying along the puszta, or steppe, in a mortar, pounding with a pestle at a tremendous rate, and leaving a long trace on the ground behind her with her tongue, which is three yards long, and with which she seizes any men and horses coming in her way, swallowing them down into her capacious belly. She has several daughters, very handsome, and with plenty of money; happy the young Mujik who catches and marries one of them, for they make excellent wives.

"Many thanks," said I, "for the information you have afforded me: this is rather poor wine," I observed, as I poured out a glass—"I suppose you have better wine in Hungary?"

"Yes, we have better wine in Hungary. First of all there is Tokay, the most celebrated in the world, though I confess I prefer the wine of Eger—Tokay is too sweet."

"Have you ever been at Tokay?"

"I have," said the Hungarian.

"What kind of place is Tokay?"

"A small town situated on the Tyzza, a rapid river descending from the north; the Tokay Mountain is just behind the town, which stands on the right bank. The top of the mountain is called Kopacs Teto, or the bald tip; the hill is so steep that during thunder-storms pieces frequently fall down upon the roofs of the houses. It was planted with vines by King Lajos, who ascended the throne in 1342. The best wine called Tokay is, however, not made at Tokay, but at Kassau, two leagues farther into the Carpathians, of which Tokay is a spur. If you wish to drink the best Tokay, you must go to Vienna, to which place all the prime is sent. For the third time I ask you, O young man of Horncastle! why does your Government always send fools to represent it at Vienna?"

"And for the third time I tell you, O son of Almus! that I cannot say; perhaps, however, to drink the sweet Tokay wine; fools, you know, always like sweet things."

"Good," said the Hungarian; "it must be so, and when I return to Hungary, I will state to my countrymen your explanation of a circumstance which has frequently caused them great perplexity. Oh! the English are a clever people, and have a deep meaning in all they do. What a vision of deep policy opens itself to my view! they do not send their fool to Vienna in order to gape at processions, and to bow and scrape at a base Papist court, but to drink at the great dinners the celebrated Tokay of Hungary, which the Hungarians, though they do not drink it, are very proud of, and by doing so to intimate the sympathy which the English entertain for their fellow religionists of Hungary. Oh! the English are a deep people."

CHAPTER LIV

THE pipe of the Hungarian had, for some time past, exhibited considerable symptoms of exhaustion, little or no ruttling having been heard in the tube, and scarcely a particle of smoke, drawn through the syphon, having been emitted from the lips of the possessor. He now rose from his seat, and going to a corner of the room, placed his pipe against the wall, then striding up and down the room, he cracked his fingers several times, exclaiming, in a half-musing manner, "Oh, the deep nation, which, in order to display its sympathy for Hungary, sends its fool to Vienna, to drink the sweet wine of Tokay!"

The jockey, having looked for some time at the tall figure with evident approbation, winked at me with that brilliant eye of his on which there was no speck, saying, "Did you ever see a taller fellow?"

"Never," said I.

"Or a finer?"

"That's another question," said I, "which I am not so willing to answer; however, as I am fond of truth, and scorn to flatter, I will take the liberty of saying that I have seen a finer."

"A finer! where?" said the jockey; whilst the Hungarian, who appeared to understand what we said, stood still, and looked full at me.

"Amongst a strange set of people," said I, "whom, if I were to name, you would, I dare say, only laugh at me."

"Who be they?" said the jockey. "Come, don't be ashamed; I have occasionally kept queerish company myself."

"The people whom we call gypsies," said I; "whom the Germans call Zigeuner, and who call themselves Romany chals."

"Zigeuner!" said the Hungarian; "by Isten! I do know those people."

"Romany chals!" said the jockey; "whew! I begin to smell a rat."

"What do you mean by smelling a rat?" said I.

"I'll bet a crown," said the jockey, "that you be the young chap what certain folks call 'the Romany Rye.'"

"Ah!" said I, "how came you to know that name?"

"Be not you he?" said the jockey.

"Why, I certainly have been called by that name."

"I could have sworn it," said the jockey; then rising from his chair, he laid his pipe on the table, took a large hand-bell which stood on the side-board, and going to the door, opened it, and commenced ringing in a most tremendous manner on the staircase. The noise presently brought up a waiter, to whom the jockey vociferated, "Go to your master, and tell him to send immediately three bottles of champagne, of the pink kind, mind you, which is twelve guineas a dozen"; the waiter hurried away, and the jockey resumed his seat and his pipe.

I sat in silent astonishment until the waiter returned with a basket containing the wine, which, with three long glasses, he placed on the table. The jockey then got up, and going to a large bow-window at the end of the room, which looked into a court-yard, peeped out; then saying, "the coast is clear," he shut down the principal sash which was open for the sake of the air, and taking up a bottle of champagne, he placed another in the hands of the Hungarian, to whom he said something in private. The latter, who seemed to understand him, answered by a nod. The two then going to the end of the table fronting the window, and about eight paces from it, stood before it, holding the bottles by their necks; suddenly the jockey lifted up his arm. "Surely," said I, "you are not mad enough to fling that bottle through the window?" "Here's to the Romany Rye; here's to the sweet master," said the jockey, dashing the bottle through the pane in so neat a manner that scarcely a particle of glass fell into the room.

"Eljen edes csigany ur—eljen gul eray!" said the Hungarian, swinging round his bottle, and discharging it at the window; but, either not possessing the jockey's accuracy of aim, or reckless of the consequences, he flung his bottle so, that it struck against part of the wooden setting of the panes, breaking along with the wood and itself three or four panes to pieces. The crash was horrid, and wine and particles of glass flew back into the room, to the no small danger of its inmates. "What do you think of that?" said the jockey; "were you ever so honoured before?" "Honoured!" said I. "God preserve me in future from such honour"; and I put my finger to my cheek, which was slightly hurt by a particle of the glass. "That's the way we of the cofrady honour great men at Horncastle," said the jockey. "What, you are hurt! never mind; all the better; your scratch shows that you are the body the compliment was paid to." "And what are you going to do with the other bottle?" said I. "Do with it!" said the jockey, "why, drink it, cosily and comfortably, whilst holding a little quiet talk. The Romany Rye at Horncastle, what an idea!"

"And what will the master of the house say to all this damage which you have caused him!"

"What will your master say, William?" said the jockey to the waiter, who had witnessed the singular scene just described without exhibiting the slightest mark of surprise. William smiled, and slightly shrugging his shoulders, replied, "Very little, I dare say, sir; this a'n't the first time your honour has done a thing of this kind." "Nor will it be the first time that I shall have paid for it," said the jockey; "well, I shall never have paid for a certain item in the bill with more pleasure than I shall pay for it now. Come, William, draw the cork, and let us taste the pink champagne."

The waiter drew the cork, and filled the glasses with a pinky liquor, which bubbled, hissed, and foamed. "How do you like it?" said the jockey, after I had imitated the example of my companions, by despatching my portion at a draught.

"It is wonderful wine," said I; "I have never tasted champagne before, though I have frequently heard it praised; it more than answers my expectations; but, I confess, I should not wish to be obliged to drink it every day."

"Nor I," said the jockey, "for every-day drinking give me a glass of old port, or—"

"Of hard old ale," I interposed, "which, according to my mind, is better than all the wine in the world."

"Well said, Romany Rye," said the jockey, "just my own opinion; now, William, make yourself scarce."

The waiter withdrew, and I said to the jockey, "How did you become acquainted with the Romany chals?"

"I first became acquainted with them," said the jockey, "when I lived with old Fulcher the basketmaker, who took me up when I was adrift upon the world; I do not mean the present Fulcher, who is likewise called old Fulcher, but his father, who has been dead this many a year; while living with him in the caravan, I frequently met them in the green lanes, and of latter years I have had occasional dealings with them in the horse line."

"And the gypsies have mentioned me to you?" said I.

"Frequently," said the jockey, "and not only those of these parts; why, there's scarcely a part of England in which I have not heard the name of the Romany Rye mentioned by these people. The power you have over them is wonderful; that is, I should have thought it wonderful, had they not more than once told me the cause."

"And what is the cause?" said I, "for I am sure I do not know."

"The cause is this," said the jockey, "they never heard a bad word proceed from your mouth, and never knew you do a bad thing."

"They are a singular people," said I.

"And what a singular language they have got," said the jockey.

"Do you know it?" said I.

"Only a few words," said the jockey, "they were always chary in teaching me any."

"They were vary sherry to me too," said the Hungarian, speaking in broken English; "I only could learn from them half-a-dozen words, for example, gul eray, which, in the czigany of my country, means sweet gentleman; or edes ur in my own Magyar."

"Gudlo Rye, in the Romany of mine, means a sugar'd gentleman," said I; "then there are gypsies in your country?"

"Plenty," said the Hungarian, speaking German, "and in Russia and Turkey too; and wherever they are found, they are alike in their ways and language. Oh, they are a strange race, and how little known!"

"Come," said the jockey, "no more Dutch, whether high or low. I am tired of it; unless we can have some English, I am off to bed."

"I should be very glad to hear some English," said I; "especially from your mouth. Several things which you have mentioned, have awakened my curiosity. Suppose you give us your history?"

"My history?" said the jockey. "A rum idea! however, lest conversation should lag, I'll give it you. First of all, however, a glass of champagne to each."

After we had each taken a glass of champagne, the jockey commenced his history.

"My grandfather was a shorter, and my father was a smasher; the one was scragg'd, and the other lagg'd."

I here interrupted the jockey by observing that his discourse was, for the greater part, unintelligible to me.

"I do not understand much English," said the Hungarian, who, having replenished and resumed his mighty pipe, was now smoking away; "but, by Isten, I believe it is the gibberish which that great ignorant Valther Scott puts into the mouths of the folks he calls gypsies."

"Something like it, I confess," said I, "though this sounds more genuine than his dialect, which he picked up out of the canting vocabulary at the end of the 'English Rogue,' a book which, however despised, was written by a remarkable genius. What do you call the speech you were using?" said I, addressing myself to the jockey.

"Latin," said the jockey, very coolly, "that is, that dialect of it which is used by the light-fingered gentry."

"Pray continue your history," said I to the jockey, "only please to do so in a language which we can understand, and first of all interpret the sentence with which you began it."

"I told you that my grandfather was a shorter," said the jockey, "by which is meant a gentleman who shortens or reduces the current coin of these realms, for which practice he was scragged, that is, hung by the scrag of the neck. And when I said that my father was a smasher, I meant one who passes forged notes, thereby doing his best to smash the Bank of England; by being lagged, I meant he was laid fast, that is, had a chain put round his leg and then transported."

"Your explanations are quite satisfactory," said I; "the three first words are metaphorical, and the fourth, lagged, is the old genuine Norse term, lagda, which signifies laid, whether in durance, or in bed, has nothing to do with the matter. What you have told me confirms me in an opinion which I have long entertained, that thieves' Latin is a strange mysterious speech, formed of metaphorical terms, and words derived from the various ancient languages. Pray tell me, now, how the gentleman, your grandfather, contrived to shorten the coin of these realms?"

"You shall hear," said the jockey; "but I have one thing to beg of you, which is, that when I have once begun my history you will not interrupt me with questions, I don't like them, they stops one, and puts one out of one's tale, and are not wanted; for anything which I think can't be understood, I should myself explain, without being asked. My grandfather reduced or shortened the coin of this country by three processes. By aquafortis, by clipping, and by filing. Filing and clipping he employed in reducing all sorts of coin, whether gold or silver; but aquafortis he used merely in reducing gold coin, whether guineas, jacobuses, or Portugal pieces, otherwise called moidores, which were at one time as current as guineas. By laying a guinea in aquafortis for twelve hours, he could filch from it to the value of ninepence, and by letting it remain there for twenty-four to the value of eighteenpence, the aquafortis eating the gold away, and leaving it like a sediment in the vessel. He was generally satisfied with taking the value of ninepence from a guinea, of eighteenpence from a jacobus or moidore, or half-a-crown from a broad Spanish piece, whether he reduced them by aquafortis, filing, or clipping. From a five-shilling piece, which is called a bull in Latin, because it is round like a bull's head, he would file or clip to the value of fivepence, and from lesser coin in proportion. He was connected with a numerous gang, or set, of people, who had given up their minds and talents entirely to shortening."

Here I interrupted the jockey. "How singular," said I, "is the fall and debasement of words; you talk of a gang, or set, of shorters; you are, perhaps, not aware that gang and set were, a thousand years ago, only connected with the great and Divine; they are ancient Norse words, which may be found in the heroic poems of the north, and in the Edda, a collection of mythologic and heroic songs. In these poems we read that such and such a king invaded Norway with a gang of heroes; or so and so, for example, Erik Bloodaxe, was admitted to the set of gods; but at present gang and set are merely applied to the vilest of the vile, and the lowest of the low,—we say a gang of thieves and shorters, or a set of authors. How touching is this debasement of words in the course of time; it puts me in mind of the decay of old houses and names. I have known a Mortimer who was a hedger and ditcher, a Berners who was born in a workhouse, and a descendant of the De Burghs, who bore the falcon, mending old kettles, and making horse and pony shoes in a dingle."

"Odd enough," said the jockey; "but you were saying you knew one Berners—man or woman? I would ask."

"A woman," said I.

"What might her Christian name be?" said the jockey.

"It is not to be mentioned lightly," said I, with a sigh.

"I shouldn't wonder if it were Isopel," said the jockey with an arch glance of his one brilliant eye.

"It was Isopel," said I; "did you know Isopel Berners?"

"Ay, and have reason to know her," said the jockey, putting his hand into his left waistcoat pocket, as if to feel for something, "for she gave me what I believe few men could do—a most confounded whopping. But now, Mr. Romany Rye, I have again to tell you that I don't like to be interrupted when I'm speaking, and to add that if you break in upon me a third time, you and I shall quarrel."

"Pray proceed with your story," said I; "I will not interrupt you again."

"Good!" said the jockey. "Where was I? Oh, with a set of people who had given up their minds to shortening! Reducing the coin, though rather a lucrative, was a very dangerous trade. Coin filed felt rough to the touch; coin clipped could be easily detected by the eye; and as for coin reduced by aquafortis, it was generally so discoloured that, unless a great deal of pains was used to polish it, people were apt to stare at it in a strange manner, and to say, 'What have they been doing to this here gold?' My grandfather, as I have said before, was connected with a gang of shorters, and sometimes shortened money, and at other times passed off what had been shortened by other gentry.

"Passing off what had been shortened by others was his ruin; for once, in trying to pass off a broad piece which had been laid in aquafortis for four-and-twenty hours, and was very black, not having been properly rectified, he was stopped and searched and other reduced coins being found about him, and in his lodgings, he was committed to prison, tried, and executed. He was offered his life, provided he would betray his comrades; but he told the big-wigs, who wanted him to do so, that he would see them farther first, and died at Tyburn, amidst the cheers of the populace, leaving my grandmother and father, to whom he had always been a kind husband and parent—for, setting aside the crime for which he suffered, he was a moral man.

"I felt rather ashamed of my father's want of what I called spirit. He was not executed, for the chaplain induced my father to make some valuable disclosures with respect to the smashers' system. I confess that I would have been hanged before I would have done so, after having reaped the profit of it; that is, I think so now, seated comfortably in my inn, with my bottle of champagne before me. However, I am here with my bottle of champagne and the Romany Rye, and he was in his cell, with bread and water and the prison chaplain. He took an affectionate leave of me before he was sent away, giving me three out of five guineas, all the money he had left.

"I was quite determined upon an honest livelihood, and I soon found one. He is a great fool who is ever dishonest in England. Any person who has any natural gift, and everybody has some natural gift, is sure of finding encouragement in this noble country of ours, provided he will but exhibit it. I had not walked more than three miles before I came to a wonderfully high church steeple, which stood close by the road; I looked at the steeple, and going to a heap of smooth pebbles which lay by the roadside, I took up some, and then went into the churchyard, and placing myself just below the tower, my right foot resting on a ledge, about two foot from the ground, I, with my left hand—being a left-handed person, do you see—flung or chucked up a stone, which, lighting on the top of the steeple, which was at least a hundred and fifty feet high, did there remain. After repeating this feat two or three times, I 'hulled' up a stone, which went clean over the tower, and then one, my right foot still on the ledge, which rising at least five yards above the steeple, did fall down just at my feet.

"Without knowing it, I was showing off my gift to others besides myself, doing what, perhaps, not five men in England could do. Two men, who were passing by, stopped and looked at my proceedings, and when I had done flinging came into the churchyard, and, after paying me a compliment on what they had seen me do, proposed that I should join company with them; I asked them who they were, and they told me. The one was Hopping Ned, and the other Biting Giles. Both had their gifts, by which they got their livelihood; Ned could hop a hundred yards with any man in England, and Giles could lift up with his teeth any dresser or kitchen-table in the country, and, standing erect, hold it dangling in his jaws. There's many a big oak table and dresser in certain districts of England which bear the marks of Giles's teeth; and I make no doubt that, a hundred or two years hence, there'll be strange stories about those marks, and that people will point them out as a proof that there were giants in bygone time, and that many a dentist will moralize on the decays which human teeth have undergone.

"They wanted me to go about with them, and exhibit my gift occasionally, as they did theirs, promising that the money that was got by the exhibitions should be honestly divided. I consented, and we set off together. We lived honestly and comfortably, making no little money by our natural endowments, and were known over a great part of England as 'Hopping Ned,' 'Biting Giles,' and 'Hull over the Head Jack,' which was my name, it being the blackguard fashion of the English, do you see, to——"

Here I interrupted the jockey. "You may call it a blackguard fashion," said I, "and I dare say it is, or it would scarcely be English; but it is an immensely ancient one, and is handed down to us from our northern ancestry, especially the Danes, who were in the habit of giving people surnames, or rather nicknames, from some quality of body or mind, but generally from some disadvantageous peculiarity of feature; for there is no denying that the English, Norse, or whatever we may please to call them, are an envious, depreciatory set of people, who not only give their poor comrades contemptuous names, but their great people also. They didn't call you the matchless Hurler, because, by doing so, they would have paid you a compliment, but Hull over the Head Jack, as much as to say that after all you were a scrub; so, in ancient time."

But before I could say any more, the jockey, having laid down his pipe, rose, and having taken off his coat, exclaimed, in an angry tone, "This is the third time you have interrupted me in my tale, Mr. Rye; I passed over the two first times with a simple warning, but you will now please to get up and give me the satisfaction of a man."

"I am really sorry," said I, "if I have given you offence, but you were talking of our English habits of bestowing nicknames, and I could not refrain from giving a few examples tending to prove what a very ancient habit it is."

"But you interrupted me," said the jockey, "and put me out of my tale, which you had no right to do. Now stand up, and I'll make an example of you."

"Well," said I, "I confess it was wrong in me to interrupt you, and I ask your pardon."

"That won't do," said the jockey, "asking pardon won't do."

"Oh," said I, getting up, "if asking pardon does not satisfy you, you are a different man from what I considered you."

But here the Hungarian, also getting up, interposed his tall form and pipe between us, saying in English, scarcely intelligible, "Let there be no dispute! You ask a young man to drink champagne with you, you make him dronk, he interrupt you with very good sense; he ask your pardon, yet you not——"

"Well," said the jockey, "I am satisfied. I am rather a short-tempered person, but I bear no malice. He is, as you say, drinking my wine, and has perhaps taken a drop too much, not being used to such high liquor; but one doesn't like to be put out of one's tale, more especially when one was about to moralize, do you see, oneself, and to show off what little learning one has. However, I bears no malice. Here is a hand to each of you; we'll take another glass each, and think no more about it."

The jockey having shaken both of our hands, and filled our glasses and his own with what champagne remained in the bottle, put on his coat, sat down, and resumed his pipe and story.

"Where was I? Oh, roaming about the country with Hopping Ned and Biting Giles. Those were happy days, and a merry and prosperous life we led. However, nothing continues under the sun in the same state in which it begins, and our firm was soon destined to undergo a change. We came to a village where there was a very high church steeple, and in a little time my comrades induced a crowd of people to go and see me display my gift by flinging stones above the heads of Matthew, Mark, Luke and John, who stood at the four corners on the top, carved in stone. The parson, seeing the crowd, came waddling out of his rectory to see what was going on. After I had flung up the stones, letting them fall just where I liked—and one, I remember, fell on the head of Mark, where I dare say it remains to the present day—the parson, who was one of the description of people called philosophers, held up his hand, and asked me to let the next stone I flung up fall upon it. He wished, do you see, to know with what weight the stone would fall down, and talked something about gravitation—a word which I could never understand to the present day, save that it turned out a grave matter to me. I, like a silly fellow myself, must needs consent, and, flinging the stone up to a vast height, contrived so that it fell into the parson's hand, which it cut dreadfully.

"The parson flew into a great rage, more particularly as everybody laughed at him, and, being a magistrate, ordered his clerk, who was likewise constable, to conduct me to prison as a rogue and vagabond, telling my comrades that if they did not take themselves off, he would serve them in the same manner. So Ned hopped off, and Giles ran after him, without making any gathering, and I was led to Bridewell, my mittimus following at the end of a week, the parson's hand not permitting him to write before that time. In the Bridewell I remained a month, when, being dismissed, I went in quest of my companions, whom, after some time, I found up, but they refused to keep my company any longer; telling me that I was a dangerous character, likely to bring them more trouble than profit; they had, moreover, filled up my place. Going into a cottage to ask for a drink of water, they saw a country fellow making faces to amuse his children; the faces were so wonderful that Hopping Ned and Biting Giles at once proposed taking him into partnership, and the man—who was a fellow not very fond of work—after a little entreaty, went away with them.

"I will now shorten my history as much as I can, for we have talked as much as folks do during a whole night in the Commons' House, though, of course, not with so much learning, or so much to the purpose, because—why? They are in the House of Commons, and we in a public room of an inn at Horncastle.

"After being turned out of the firm, I got my living in two or three honest ways, which I shall not trouble you with describing. I might have got a very decent livelihood by throwing stones, but I much question whether I should ever have attained to the position in society which I now occupy, but for my knowledge of animals.

"I have thriven very well in business, and my name is up as being a person who can be depended on, when folks treats me handsomely. I always make a point when a gentleman comes to me, and says, 'Mr. Dale,' or 'John,' for I have no objection to be called John by a gentleman—'I wants a good horse, and am ready to pay a good price'—I always makes a point, I say, to furnish him with an animal worth the money; but when I sees a fellow, whether he calls himself gentleman or not, wishing to circumvent me, what does I do? I doesn't quarrel with him; not I; but, letting him imagine he is taking me in, I contrives to sell him a screw for thirty pounds, not worth thirty shillings. All honest respectable people have at present great confidence in me, and frequently commissions me to buy them horses at great fairs like this.

"This short young gentleman was recommended to me by a great landed proprietor, to whom he bore letters of recommendation from some great prince in his own country, who had a long time ago been entertained at the house of the landed proprietor, and the consequence is, that I brings young six foot six to Horncastle, and purchases for him the horse of the Romany Rye. I don't do these kind things for nothing, it is true; that can't be expected; for every one must live by his trade; but, as I said before, when I am treated handsomely, I treat folks so. Honesty, I have discovered, as perhaps some other people have, is by far the best policy; though, as I also said before, when I'm along with thieves, I can beat them at their own game. If I am obliged to do it, I can pass off the veriest screw as a flying drummedary, for even when I was a child I had found out by various means what may be done with animals. I wish now to ask a civil question, Mr. Romany Rye. Certain folks have told me that you are a horse witch; are you one, or are you not?"

"I, like yourself," said I, "know, to a certain extent, what may be done with animals."

"Then how would you, Mr. Romany Rye, pass off the veriest screw in the world for a flying drummedary?"

"By putting a small live eel down his throat; as long as the eel remained in his stomach, the horse would appear brisk and lively in a surprising degree."

"And how would you contrive to make a regular kicker and biter appear so tame and gentle, that any respectable fat old gentleman of sixty, who wanted an easy goer, would be glad to purchase him for fifty pounds?"

"By pouring down his throat four pints of generous old ale, which would make him so happy and comfortable, that he would not have the heart to kick or bite anybody, for a season at least."

"And where did you learn all this?" said the jockey.

"I have read about the eel in an old English book, and about the making drunk in a Spanish novel, and, singularly enough, I was told the same things by a wild blacksmith in Ireland. Now tell me, do you bewitch horses in this way?"

"I?" said the jockey; "mercy upon us! I wouldn't do such things for a hatful of money. No, no, preserve me from live eels and hocussing! And now let me ask you, how would you spirit a horse out of a field?"

"How would I spirit a horse out of a field?"

"Yes; supposing you were down in the world, and had determined on taking up the horse-stealing line of business."

"Why, I should— But I tell you what, friend, I see you are trying to pump me, and I tell you plainly that I will hear something from you with respect to your art, before I tell you anything more. Now how would you whisper a horse out of a field, provided you were down in the world, and so forth?"

"Ah, ah, I see you are up to a game, Mr. Romany. I whispers a horse out of a field in this way: I have a mare in my stable; well, in the early season of the year I goes into my stable — Well, I puts the sponge into a small bottle which I keeps corked. I takes my bottle in my hand, and goes into a field, suppose by night, where there is a very fine stag horse. I manage with great difficulty to get within ten yards of the horse, who stands staring at me just ready to run away. I then uncorks my bottle, presses my forefinger to the sponge, and holds it out to the horse, the horse gives a sniff, then a start, and comes nearer. I corks up my bottle and puts it into my pocket. My business is done, for the next two hours the horse would follow me anywhere—the difficulty, indeed, would be to get rid of him. Now is that your way of doing business?"

"My way of doing business? Mercy upon us! I wouldn't steal a horse in that way, or, indeed, in any way, for all the money in the world."

"There is nothing wonderful to be done," said the jockey, "without a good deal of preparation, as I know myself. Folks stare and wonder at certain things which they would only laugh at if they knew how they were done; and to prove what I say is true, I will give you one or two examples. Can either of you lend me a handkerchief? That won't do," said he, as I presented him with a silk one. "I wish for a delicate white handkerchief. That's just the kind of thing," said he, as the Hungarian offered him a fine white cambric handkerchief, beautifully worked with gold at the hems; "now you shall see me set this handkerchief on fire."

"Don't let him do so by any means," said the Hungarian, speaking to me in German, "it is the gift of a lady whom I highly admire, and I would not have it burnt for the world." "He has no occasion to be under any apprehension," said the jockey, after I had interpreted to him what the Hungarian had said, "I will restore it to him uninjured, or my name is not Jack Dale." Then sticking the handkerchief carelessly into the left side of his bosom, he took the candle, which by this time had burnt very low, and holding his head back, he applied the flame to the handkerchief, which instantly seemed to catch fire. "What do you think of that?" said he to the Hungarian. "Why, that you have ruined me," said the latter. "No harm done, I assure you," said the jockey, who presently, clapping his hand on his bosom, extinguished the fire, and returned the handkerchief to the Hungarian, asking him if it was burnt. "I see no burn upon it," said the Hungarian; "but in the name of Gott, how could you set it on fire without burning it?"

"I never set it on fire at all," said the jockey; "I set this on fire," showing us a piece of half-burnt calico. "I placed this calico above it, and lighted not the handkerchief, but the rag. Now I will show you something else. I have a magic shilling in my pocket, which I can make run up along my arm. But, first of all, I would gladly know whether either of you can do the like."

Thereupon the Hungarian and myself, putting our hands into our pockets, took out shillings, and endeavoured to make them run up our arms, but utterly failed; both shillings, after we had made two or three attempts, falling to the ground. "What noncomposses you both are," said the jockey; and placing a shilling on the end of the fingers of his right hand he made strange faces to it, drawing back his head, whereupon the shilling instantly began to run up his arm, occasionally hopping and jumping as if it were bewitched, always endeavouring to make towards the head of the jockey.

"How do I do that?" said he, addressing himself to me. "I really do not know," said I, "unless it is by the motion of your arm." "The motion of my nonsense," said the jockey, and, making a dreadful grimace, the shilling hopped upon his knee, and began to run up his thigh and to climb up his breast. "How is that done?" said he again. "By witchcraft, I suppose," said I.

"There you are right," said the jockey; "by the witchcraft of one of Miss Berners' hairs; the end of one of her long hairs is tied to that shilling by means of a hole in it, and the other end goes round my neck by means of a loop; so that, when I draw back my head, the shilling follows it. I suppose you wish to know how I got the hair," said he, grinning at me. "I will tell you. I once, in the course of my ridings, saw Miss Berners beneath a hedge, combing out her long hair, and, being rather a modest kind of person, what must I do but get off my horse, tie him to a gate, go up to her, and endeavour to enter into conversation with her. After giving her the sele of the day, and complimenting her on her hair, I asked her to give me one of the threads; whereupon she gave me such a look, and, calling me fellow, told me to take myself off. 'I must have a hair first,' said I, making a snatch at one. I believe I hurt her; but, whether I did or not, up she started, and, though her hair was unbound, gave me the only drubbing I ever had in my life. Lor! how, with her right hand, she fibbed me whilst she held me round the neck with her left arm; I was soon glad to beg her pardon on my knees, which she gave me in a moment, when she saw me in that condition, being the most placable creature in the world, and not only her pardon, but one of the hairs which I longed for, which I put through a shilling, with which I have on evenings after fairs, like this, frequently worked what seemed to those who looked on downright witchcraft, but which is nothing more than pleasant deception. And now, Mr. Romany Rye, to testify my regard for you, I give you the shilling and the hair. I think you have a kind of respect for Miss Berners; but whether you have or not, keep them as long as you can, and whenever you look at them think of the finest woman in England, and of John Dale, the jockey of Horncastle."

Leaving Horncastle I bent my steps in the direction of the east. I walked at a brisk rate, and late in the evening reached a large town, situate at the entrance of an extensive firth, or arm of the sea, which prevented my farther progress eastward. Sleeping that night in the suburbs of the town, I departed early next morning in the direction of the south. A walk of about twenty miles brought me to another large town, situated on a river, where I again turned towards the east. At the end of the town I was accosted by a fiery-faced individual, somewhat under the middle size, dressed as a recruiting sergeant.

"Young man," said the recruiting sergeant, "you are just the kind of person to serve the Honourable East India Company."

"I had rather the Honourable Company should serve me," said I.

"Of course, young man. Well, the Honourable East India Company shall serve you—that's reasonable. Here, take this shilling; 'tis service-money. The Honourable Company engages to serve you, and you the Honourable Company; both parties shall be thus served; that's just and reasonable."

"And what must I do for the Company?"

"Only go to India; that's all."

"And what should I do in India?"

"Fight, my brave boy! fight, my youthful hero!"

"What kind of country is India?"

"The finest country in the world! Rivers, bigger than the Ouse. Hills, higher than anything near Spalding! Trees—you never saw such trees! Fruits—you never saw such fruits!"

"And the people—what kind of folk are they?"

"Pah! Kauloes—blacks—a set of rascals not worth regarding."

"Kauloes!" said I; "blacks!"

"Yes," said the recruiting sergeant; "and they call us lolloes, which, in their beastly gibberish, means red."

"Lolloes!" said I; "reds!"

"Yes," said the recruiting sergeant, "kauloes and lolloes; and all the lolloes have to do is to kick and cut down the kauloes, and take from them their rupees, which means silver money. Why do you stare so?"

"Why," said I, "this is the very language of Mr. Petulengro."

"Mr. Pet——?"

"Yes," said I, "and Tawno Chikno."

"Tawno Chik——? I say, young fellow, I don't like your way of speaking; no, nor your way of looking. You are mad, sir; you are mad; and what's this? Why, your hair is grey! You won't do for the Honourable Company —they like red. I'm glad I didn't give you the shilling. Good day to you."

"I shouldn't wonder," said I, as I proceeded rapidly along a broad causeway, in the direction of the east, "if Mr. Petulengro and Tawno Chikno came originally from India. I think I'll go there."